U GOT TO HAVE U SOME FUN

A Literary Novel for the Everyman

Andrew Harkless

U GOT TO HAVE U SOME FUN

"If you're looking for a true literacy excursion, then hop aboard
U Got to Have U Some Fun and enjoy the ride!"

"Have you ever felt like life is passing you by and there are so many things left to
experience? Are you just working through the challenges life has thrown at you and
not really living? …you will be captivated to read the story about a group of people
who meet for a week trying to forget everyday challenges and have some fun."

"…remarkable voyage aboard a luxury cruise liner carrying a wonderful cast of characters."

"A heartfelt story that reminds us of the importance to live life to the fullest no matter what
challenges or sadness we may have to endure. Finding our inner dragon can help us fight our fears
and like the metamorphosis of a butterfly, change our lives forever."

"This is one cruise you don't want to set sail without you
on board. It's a ride you won't soon forget!"

"…a light and enjoyable read. It takes place on a cruise ship in the Caribbean. I felt like I
was actually on vacation with this eclectic group of characters all searching for happiness."

"…a delightful romp through the Caribbean with a diverse group of interesting characters."

"Overall it was a fun read…written by someone who worked for the cruise industry and you
learn little bits and pieces of insider information about the inner workings…had no idea how
hard the staff really works. With that said, it made me want to go on a cruise once I finished it."

"Keeps the reader on tenterhooks until the very end for the final
'revelation'. A compelling and entertaining read!"

Read more reviews on Amazon.com

DEDICATION

Without good parents, life is a difficult journey without a map. With great parents, the journey's destination eventually becomes clear as the light from the morning sunrise.

For Ron and Lynn—the greatest of parents.

TABLE OF CONTENTS

"However mean your life is, meet it and live it; do not shun it and call it hard names."

—Henry David Thoreau

THE TICKET

The Monarch butterfly makes its metamorphosis from caterpillar to butterfly
in as little as two weeks—quite a change in so brief a time....

JOHN SMITH PULLED INTO THE carport of his modest ranch home after a typical day at the factory. His five-year-old Prius sounded about the same with the ignition turned off as when it was switched on. Harvey-the-mailman had come and gone three hours earlier at 2:15 PM. John locked his car, walked back down the driveway—gravel crunching under his pleather wing-tips—opened his standard black mailbox, and removed a pile of rubber banded mail. He sighed, pulling the rubber band and letting it snap against the top envelope (one of two dozen credit card offers he received weekly).

He stood looking at the gray sky, which seemed as flat as the Kansas landscape. He meandered back, head hung down, to the carport. Entering the side door leading into his kitchen, he dropped the stack of mail on top of a slew of cruise brochures covering the Ikea dining table and headed for the fridge.

The kitchen, like the rest of the three bedroom ranch, hadn't been remodeled in the more than two decades since John and his ex-wife purchased it. In fact, it looked exactly the same as when it was built.

The old Kenmore fridge housed two cans of soda and a half gallon of milk. John grabbed the latter. No glasses sat in the neighboring cabinet. He stood over the sink and dug a glass out from under a spaghetti sauce encrusted plate. After a quick rinse, he poured some milk. Luckily, the smell of sour milk hit John's nose before the chunky liquid touched his lips. He emptied the glass and milk carton into the sink and returned to the fridge.

Sitting at the kitchen table, he cracked open the soda and stared at stacks of cruise literature. They had grown since John's son made him promise to do something for himself just a year ago. John's divorce two years earlier rendered him more lethargic than usual. The start of honoring his promise began by collecting information from the internet and Good Intent's local travel agency; the homework ceased over the course of the last six months.

John picked up one of the glossy brochures. The cover portrayed a young family perched high above the exposed gut of a modern cruise ship. A mother, father, and son stood on a catwalk as their daughter started her trip across a zip line. They cheered, all faces lit with Christmas-like smiles. Clearly displaying the company logo, the wall behind the happy family made the advertisement complete.

Chucking the magazine over his shoulder, John attended to the current day's mail. Credit card offer, bill, request for money for the Republican party, credit card offer, bill, request for money for the Democratic party, request for money to save abused animals, bill, request for money to save the children of some third-world country, and something different. He tossed the stack and looked at the envelope. A standard business envelope, but with no return address. He made out the word Afghanistan on the post mark.

Thumbing open the flap, he pulled out what appeared to be some sort of ticket and read aloud: "*The Princess of the Seas*…Miami?" Flipping the ticket over revealed a yellow post-it with two typed words: IT'S TIME.

Confused, John lifted his head and gazed out the kitchen's small window.

My son's way of not waiting any longer for me to honor a promise, he thought.

Procrastination had run its course; a decision had been made.

Someone that knew my son, knew he wanted this, must have arranged the ticket. Must have, John reasoned, *there isn't any other explanation.*

Carson Smith, John's only child, died six months ago.

DAY 1
(MIAMI)

WELCOME TO MIAMI

Miami—a city built on decadence and hedonism, steeped in a culture richly mixed with predominantly Latin American and Caribbean people, and known worldwide for its diverse population of immigrants and transplants rivaling New York City. A place that conjures images of palm trees, alabaster beaches, and non-stop parties; where, the average person, if lucky, might rub elbows with some of the most famous and beautiful people on earth. Miami, an ironically American oasis, that any Bob or Sue from small-town America can fly to and feel as though they've entered an exotic land. It is a place of hope and freedom, new beginnings, and escape; but, most importantly, it's a place to find *fun*.

So it was, on a delightfully mild, ninety degree November morning that John Smith found himself in line with hundreds of other passengers wearing Bermuda shorts and sunglasses, clenching boarding passes, and grumbling about their constant beads of perspiration. They were anyone and everyone. There were beauticians, construction workers, doctors, grandmothers, and business owners—all waiting as patiently as was humanly possible in the Florida heat to embark on the mega cruise ship towering fifteen stories at its peak.

John felt like a mouse in a maze. He kept looking forward and back, wondering when he would be free of the crowd and able to hide in the sanctuary of his economy cabin. He had never been on a cruise. All he knew about the impending journey came from the internet or his travel agent. It would be fair to say he was a cautious, sometimes nervous man. A forty-seven year old divorced guy who had never taken a proper vacation made him somewhat of an enigma to both those he knew and those he met. He was almost tall at five foot eleven inches, of average build, and had sandy brown hair. He had a face that caused almost everyone he met to say: "You look like someone else I know." His lips just naturally turned down at the corners. This personally annoying fact made people assume he was sad or upset even when he wasn't. He was more handsome when he smiled, but John hadn't had reason to smile in quite some time. He felt as depressed as he looked.

Sure, there were the annual trips to Kansas City to watch the Chiefs play a game. They were a perk from his employer, a token for his loyalty, now adding up to twenty-five years. Although not a huge sports fan, he did enjoy getting out of his small town and small office for a day and a night to see a place where hundreds of thousands of people lived seemingly on top of one another. He was both fascinated and petrified by the speed and sheer volume of a big city.

He graduated from his hometown college, aptly named Good Intent Community College, with a business degree. Shortly after, he married Page Bagly, his high school sweetheart. Page grew up in a house three doors down the same street as his own childhood home. She was always beautiful—too good for John and he knew it. As a kid, she'd been attractive in an awkward way, a flower which hadn't yet blossomed. If she knew, she would be flabbergasted to find her ex-husband waiting in line to board a cruise ship.

John's trepidation temporarily melted away when he noticed the passenger standing directly in front of him. She was tall, maybe five-foot-ten, even without her reptile patterned high-heels. She wore a plain white, short-sleeved, silk blouse tucked into a linen skirt. From the top of her heel to the bottom of her skirt were two of the most perfectly tanned and toned pillars he'd ever seen supporting a woman. Her thick, black hair fell just below her shoulder blades; he couldn't see if there was a bra beneath her blouse. On top of her head was a hat with a wide brim that extended to the edge of each shoulder. He found himself staring too long at her legs as she accidentally backed up just enough to stab his foot with her stiletto. Realizing her faux pas, she shifted her weight to the other foot, pirouetted to assess any damage, and in the act, raked John's eyes with the brim of her hat.

"Oh my *God*, I'm so sorry!" she said, with one hand on top of the hat and the other removing her designer sunglasses. "Are you all right? These damn shoes look great, but they can be deadly." She smiled just slightly.

John was balanced on one knee, rubbing his foot with one hand, and using the thumb and forefinger of the other to rub his eyes. After a few moments, he opened his eyes, wiped the tears away, and looked up at the woman. "Um, yes…I think so."

Still on one knee and clenching his foot, his eyes blinking and readjusting to the light, John finally saw her from the front. *Stunning,* he thought. She was of Latin descent, with sumptuous full lips, intense brown eyes, and curves that would make a roller coaster envious. He couldn't detect any make-up and noticed the only jewelry was a simple pair of silver earrings and two silver rings, one on either hand, but not the wedding finger. Her skin was naturally tan and taut, making her appear younger than she was. *Forty maybe?* She was elegant and classy, exotic and sexy. John had only seen women like her in movies, and only thought them beautiful thanks to the magic of Hollywood. She was a dime a dozen in Miami, but John had never been to Miami.

"My name's Rita," she said, removing her hand from her hat and extending it to John. "I hope I didn't hurt you too badly? Big hats are essential in the Caribbean sun. They also make great borders for a girl's personal space. You must have been too close." She laughed.

John hobbled to his feet, stretching his right hand to meet Rita's. "J-Jo-John…John Smith. Yes, you're right. I wasn't paying attention and must have been standing too close. I'm so sorry! Are you okay, Miss?" He finally let go of Rita's hand after it occurred to him he'd been holding it an uncomfortable length of time.

She let out a subtle laugh, realizing the effect her beauty was having on him, and exposed the full glory of her smile—perfect teeth and all. "Rita. Rita Hernandez," she said firmer and clearer this time so he would understand not to call her Miss. "Yes, John Smith. I'm just fine; better after we're finally boarded, checked into our rooms, make it past the lifeboat drill, and are set free to find a perfectly dry martini. Do you cruise much, John?"

"No, I've never been on a cruise ship before, or any kind of boat for that matter, unless, a two person canoe during summer camp counts?" His voice tapered off at the end, sounding of remorse.

Sympathetic, Rita said, "Well, you're going on one now and you're going to love it. Besides, how many boats do you expect to see in Kansas?"

"How did you—"

"Your hat, John. I'm a hat girl and yours says Kansas City Chiefs on it, almost as bright as a neon sign. I don't think the observation will win me any detective badges." She smiled, but not in a condescending way. "It was a toss-up between Kansas and Missouri, and you struck me as more of a Kansas guy?"

John had forgotten he was wearing the souvenir from one of the football games he had attended. It was the only hat he owned and had thought it wise to bring it along for such a sunny climate. After all, he didn't want to get skin cancer on his first vacation. He touched the top of his head to affirm the hat was there. "Yes. I'm from Kansas, born and raised."

"I always wanted to see Kansas, but I've never had the pleasure," she said.

"Why would you ever want to see Kansas?" he asked, with a puzzled look on his face. "People from other parts of the country make fun of Kansas, assuming there's nothing there. They usually think it's a vast, flat, lifeless state in the middle of nowhere."

Rita paused for a moment, looking up from underneath the hat, her lips tightly clenched. "Well, people often judge things based upon what little they know, instead of asking questions about what they don't know. I admit, I don't know much about Kansas, but that's what intrigues me. If I were able to spend some time there, maybe I would hate it. Then again, maybe I would fall in love and not ever want to leave. It's the possibility of new and different things that makes an adventure, John. So many people sit at home in front of the TV every night, judging people and the world from what that box tells them. It's like hypnotism, don't you think? But with a remote control instead of a swaying watch." She could see her words left him in deep thought.

The line of passengers in front of them had disappeared while the two were talking and the passengers behind John were becoming restless.

"Excuse me…excuse me!" said an impetuous woman. "We would like to board the ship before it returns seven days from now," she huffed.

Rita turned her eyes to the woman and transformed her dead-panned look into a full smile. "So sorry, dear. John Smith and I were just introducing ourselves. Since we're all going to be on this big yacht for seven days, we might as well make an effort to know something about one another. What if she sinks in the middle of the Caribbean Sea and we are the last people each other sees?" Rita watched the woman's jaw drop. There were also a few sighs from the line behind the woman.

Rita shouted, "Come on, gang, let's go have some fun!" She put her sunglasses back on, lifted her purse, spun around, and marched into the ship's lobby. The crowd behind her paused only a moment to contemplate about the ship sinking, then followed her in as if they were told to by the cruise director.

ALL ABOARD

CRUISE SHIPS USED TO BE called *luxury-liners*, vessels reserved almost exclusively for the well-to-do. In fact, the Titanic was not built to haul the common man around to touristy destinations at a bargain basement price. The ship John boarded was indicative of what the largest cruise lines were building the last several decades—massive. Called *The Princess of the Seas*, she was longer and wider than an aircraft carrier, fifteen stories tall, able to carry thirty-five-hundred passengers and twelve-hundred crew—representing sixty-eight different nationalities—more people than lived in John's home town.

The industry had come a long way since the era of ships like *Titanic* and Cunard's original *Queen Mary*. Virtually anyone could now afford to cruise, with fares starting at a few hundred dollars and escalating to the sky's the limit, depending on the line and length of the trip. Some cruises were just weekend excursions from Florida to the Bahamas and were geared for die-hard drinkers and gamblers. The casinos couldn't operate while in US port, but were legal just a few miles out. There were numerous lines offering more intimate ships with five star amenities, sailing for months to some of the most exotic and remote destinations. A guest could be in Fiji one day and wake up in the Soviet Union, docked in Saint Petersburg, a few days later. Cruising had turned into the best of all worlds when it came to travel. Unlike airplanes, trains, or cars, these modern day behemoths offered everything.

The Princess of the Seas was as grand as any hotel with her marble floors, ten story atrium, and grand pianos. Designed for every taste and occasion, there were burger joints and buffets and a variety of fine dining and poolside huts, clubs, and upscale lounges. There was a top-deck basketball court, rock climbing wall, miniature golf course, and an ice skating rink—yes, an ice skating rink. You could swim in one of the three pools, dry off before skeet shooting, and then have a facial or massage in the spa. In the evening, people gathered in the theatre, as elegant as any on Broadway, where singers, magicians, dancers, comedians, and actors entertained. *The Princess* was a never ending candy store, a haven of reprieve and opportunity for the weary masses beaten up by the grind of everyday life—and she moved. What little she couldn't offer was there waiting when she docked in foreign ports.

It was impossible to feel cramped aboard a form of transportation the size of *The Princess*, unlike any plane or train—regardless of their first class versus economy seating. John found *The Princess* formidable from the very first moment he walked into her lobby. Waiting his turn with the purser, taking in his new surroundings, John was overwhelmed. His hands became clammy and the Chiefs hat felt as though it was cutting into his brain. In that moment, John realized that he was out of his element, beyond the sanctuary of a content and mundane environment. The economy flight from Kansas City to Miami had not fazed him. Being strapped into a confined space and made to wait patiently until landing was like a day at the office for John.

This was something different. Here, he was not strapped in. Here, he was free to do whatever. Here, he thought it would be expected of him to leave his shell. *That* scared the shit out of John

Smith. But he reminded himself that he had made a promise to his son to do more adventurous things. So, when the purser addressed him, he stepped as confidently as he could fake, to her counter.

"Good morning, sir!" said the woman. "Welcome aboard *The Princess of the Seas*. May I see your boarding pass and ID?" Her voice sounded like a person who had too many cups of coffee and her smile looked almost painful.

"Yes, ma'am," John said, handing her the boarding pass while fumbling around in his pants to find his wallet.

"Regina! My name is Regina, Mr. Smith. Is this your first time cruising with us?"

"Actually, it's my first time on any kind of boat. Or a real vacation, for that matter." John couldn't help noticing the slight look of surprise on her face.

After accepting his ID, Regina began typing away. "We are so happy you chose us for your maiden voyage, Mr. Smith. You're going to have the time of your life! Your cabin is on our Mermaid Deck, number three-seventeen. Here's a map of the ship. You just go down this corridor to your right and take any of the elevators to the Mermaid Deck. You can unpack and get situated before the mandatory lifeboat drill. When you hear the alarm, take the life vest in your cabin to deck seven, where a crew member will brief you on what to do in case of an emergency. Your section number is stamped on your vest. Do you have any questions for me?"

John felt a faint tap on his left shoulder and when he turned there was no one there. "Good luck, John Smith. Come find me at the pool for a piña colada. They make the best piña coladas," Rita said on her way to the elevators.

John spun his head to the right upon hearing Rita's voice and watched her leave. Still walking, she turned back, beamed a smile, blew a kiss, and then she was gone—leaving John still staring.

"It seems you're making friends quickly, Mr. Smith!" said Regina. "We love to see that! Any questions?"

John slowly turned back to Regina. Only one question came to mind. "What if I get seasick?"

"This ship is state of the art. It has huge stabilizers in its hull, keeping us level as a car, even in twenty foot swells, Mr. Smith. But if you experience any problems, you can purchase some Dramamine in the ship's gift shop. Just use this card. Any purchases made on board require you to present this charge card. You don't ever really need to carry cash. The only time you'll need cash is when you're in port and for tipping your housekeeping and dining staff at the end of your cruise. Do you understand?" she asked, presenting him with a charge card embossed with his name and picture.

"Yes. Thank you, Regina." John turned toward the elevators, but Regina spoke again.

"Mr. Smith." Her voice softened, sounding more genuine than her routine greeting. "Have fun while you're here." John could see the sincerity in her eyes. He rewarded her with a smile.

After making his way into the elevator and pushing the button labeled Mermaid, he took a deep breath and watched the doors close. He was anxious while replaying the words Regina had last spoken. *Have fun.* He wondered how his dead son had engineered him into this strange and overwhelming place.

His single piece of luggage sat waiting outside his cabin door. The first thing he noticed upon entering the room was how small and efficient it was, reminding him of his college dormitory and work office, but more alive and festive. The bedding was awash with pastel blues and greens, the plush carpet patterned in beiges, and a vibrant painting hung in place of a porthole. Haitian by origin, it depicted several black-skinned women carrying baskets of fruit on their heads and their loose fitting clothes were a collage of bright colors against a Caribbean Sea background. John sat down on the queen bed with his suitcase at his feet. He scanned the cabin, acclimating himself, and stopped at the painting.

John appreciated art, although he didn't really own any. The few pieces he and Page owned went to her in the divorce. He could hear music and laughter from outside, passengers and luggage shuffling down the passageway, doors opening and closing, but John tuned it all out and focused on the vivid painting instead. After a few minutes, his anxiety dissipated and he found himself in a peaceful state—until the ship's alarm sounded.

He shot up from the bed and tripped face-forward over his suitcase. The alarm was shrill, a combination of flashing lights and two sirens; the first a pulsing deep sound like a child might make to force gas, and the second, a traditional fire-bell ring. Combined, they created enough commotion to wake the blind and the deaf. He jumped to his feet and sprinted out of the cabin where he noticed people casually strolling with life vests in hand, many holding cocktails and unconcerned by the alarms. He returned to the cabin to gather his life vest and his composure. John felt better prepared on his second exit, calmer and now wearing the life vest, though he had forgotten where Regina told him to go, so he followed the herd.

Over forty-five hundred crew and guests spilled out onto *The Princess's* port and starboard seventh deck containing her lifeboats. John thought how no participation or even attention is required during an airplane emergency drill. Passengers don't need to leave the comfort of—or lack of—their seats while the flight attendant delivers instruction. Now he found himself in the throes of a full dress, semi-attentive, semi-sober, mock emergency drill—mandatory for most crew and all passengers. John lined up with sixty-eight other people in front of lifeboat one-fifty-three. If an emergency ever forced an evacuation, he would come to know these fellow passengers well.

In their own little squadron, they all faced the officer charged to protect them. The officer began talking about their life vests and those not already wearing them put the neon orange vests over their heads.

"You will notice a light on the right side of the vest below your shoulder," he said, pointing at his. "The light becomes activated upon contact with water, able to be seen by a rescue plane or ship. It has an extensive battery life," he continued, while John panicked, unable to locate his light.

An older couple beside John noticed him fumbling around with his jacket. His chin was pressed into the vest causing a comically pronounced upside down smile.

"Sweetie, I think you're inside out," said the woman, smiling as if she were handing him freshly-baked cookies. John pulled the jacket over his head and flipped it around, revealing the light.

"Ah!" he said, his face flushed from embarrassment. "You're right. Thank you so much."

"It's difficult to be rescued if people don't know where you are," she said, still smiling.

Her words sent a profound sensation through John, as though he were being pinched. He had flashbacks of childhood, remembering how many times his mother, Nancy Smith, had unintentionally stilted or embarrassed him. She had protected him to the gates of stagnation. She forbid football for fear John would be hurt. He wasn't allowed to cross their cul-de-sac street in their residential neighborhood without an escort or an adult watching. When other students had their learner's permits as soon as they were sixteen, John's mother made him wait another whole year just so those kids had a year of experience and would be less of a threat to her son. She couldn't grasp the fact that the kids who were fifteen would be driving when John turned seventeen and that there would still be just as many sixteen-year-old drivers on the road, threatening her son—always.

My mother was neurotic, he thought. The woman spoke to him again.

"We're the Clawsons, dear. I'm Mary and this is my husband Richard. Is this your first cruise?" she asked, even though she already knew. Richard stood beside her, allowing her to dictate the conversation. They looked like a couple who worked well together, their years of marriage like a soft pair of old jeans. Mary looked like a comfortable, unmade bed. She had a plump, smooth face; naturally graying hair; and the most vivid, kindly blue eyes John had ever seen. Richard looked like a man who had been fit most of his life, but now was enjoying the good life a bit more. He was a big man and towered over John. His face was florid and his belt was inching toward the last notch although his height helped minimize a blossoming pot belly.

"As a matter a fact, it is. How did you guess?" John chuckled.

Laughing along, Richard said, "You'll get the hang of it, son. Sixty-seven!" he continued. John, thinking he looked older than that, wondered why Richard was telling him his age. "Mary and I have been on sixty-six cruises, this being the sixty-seventh. We've averaged about two a year for the past thirty years," he said proudly.

"That's wonderful!" John said, evoking glares from other passengers trying to listen to the officer explain lifeboat features. "Maybe I should be quiet and pay attention. After all, I don't want to be the one idiot who went down with the ship because I didn't pay attention during the emergency drill," he whispered.

Mary waved her hand toward the other passengers. "You certainly wouldn't be the only one," she whispered. "We've seen passengers and crew do some of the dumbest and funniest things you could ever imagine," she said, rolling her eyes and shaking her head.

"I bet you have," John said.

Mary turned to Richard and asked, "Remember Hilo?"

"Which time?"

"Missed the boat time."

"Oh, yeah," Richard said, holding his chin and laughing. "Listen to this one, John. Talk about going down with the boat. This doughnut must have been missing his cream center when he tried to stop the whole show. Tell him, Mary."

"So, we've taken a few cruises to Hawaii," she began. "Those were back in the days when there was actually an American owned, flagged, and staffed cruise line. It went bankrupt and is now being run by the Norwegians, but that's another story. Anyway, we were in the port of Hilo on the big island called Hawaii, and after a nice day of exploring the volcano and shopping, we rejoined the ship. Richard and I took quick showers so we could make it topside aft—that's the rear end of the ship, dear. We were going to have a drink and watch the sunset as we left the harbor. Most amazing sunsets in Hawaii," she pined, as Richard urged her to get to the good part. "So, it's no secret that many of the crew like to *tie one on* when they do get a little port time, no pun intended," she said, glancing back at Richard.

"Good one, honey," Richard chuckled.

Turning back, Mary continued, "The gates were all closed and the huge ropes tying the ship to dock were all released and being winched in by the crew as the ship slowly moved out to sea.

Everyone was aboard, or so we thought. Once the last horn blows, ships don't wait for anybody. Well, everyone on the back deck sees this guy, a crew member, on the dock, yelling, jumping up and down, and waving his arms like he's doing jumping jacks. It seemed obvious to everyone watching, he was supposed to be aboard. This stick of bubblegum takes a line that had been removed, but not drawn in yet, and re-attaches it to the mooring."

Mary put her head down for a moment and placed her hand over her eyes before looking back to John, whose mouth was wide open. "You gotta understand, John, those lines are as big-around as I am. You stretch them out far enough and they eventually snap like a rubber band. Many of the other passengers were laughing at this obviously drunk guy, not understanding how dangerous the situation was. The ship began moving and with every foot of ocean gained between her and the dock, that line got stretched out to the point where there was no slack left. If it snapped, it would've come back at the ship like a whip, removing heads and appendages from the crew who were working on the winches. It was an open deck where they had little protection."

Understanding the severity of what Mary was telling him, John gasped. "Oh my God, what happened?"

"Well, lucky for everyone, the word made it to the captain just in time. He cut the forward engines and slowly backed up the ship to where there was slack again."

"What happened to the drunk employee?" John asked.

Laughing, Mary said, "Richard and I asked the head of security about it later. He told us the company flew the guy back to Honolulu where he was given his personal belongings and his official termination. He told us there was no way he could ever step foot back on that ship, because the crew that was working would have killed him. And he meant it, literally. So the point is, John, we all miss the boat sometimes, don't try to hold on. Cut your losses and move on to the next port," she said, wisely shaking a finger.

By the time Mary finished her story, John noticed the other passengers returning inside the ship. He didn't feel remiss, rationalizing that in the case of an emergency, he would have the Clawsons to guide him. After all, they had now heard the drill sixty-seven times, and without them, he might not have ever discovered his light was on the inside.

Removing their life jackets, Richard helped with John's array of straps. "What are you doing for chow tonight, John?" Richard asked.

"I hadn't thought about it, sir."

"Rich, or Richard if you prefer to be formal about it. It's one of the best reasons to go on these things, you know," he said as his eyes lit up. "If you don't like to eat, then you booked the wrong vacation. You could've gone to India or one of them Chinese-type countries where you don't know what you're eating, or where it came from. Not here! This ship has six restaurants, plus an ice cream parlor, all-night pizza joint, bar hors d'oeuvres, midnight buffets, and of course, the main dining hall. But that's for penny-pinchers and suckers. Everything sits too long under a heat lamp, or on one of them little plate hats they use to keep it warm until they get around to serving you. We don't do the main dining room any more, not often anyway. Use to be that was about the only choice, but cruising has come a long way since those days. This younger generation wants everything they can imagine at their disposal at all times, and they don't want to have to go far to get it, either." Richard whispered into John's ear while placing an arm around John's shoulder. "In this case, their philosophy works for me."

"Leave the poor man alone," Mary said. "Maybe he doesn't want to build a big shed over his toolbox like you have. You know, John, this man used to be in shape before we started cruising." Mary affectionately touched her husband's cheek with one hand and his belly with the other. "If the ship goes down and you do miss the lifeboat, just stay close to Richard and use him as a raft." Mary absorbed Richard's frown with a loving smile. He knew she was simply poking fun for John's benefit. Richard leaned over to give her a small kiss while still holding on to John's shoulder.

Mary studied John, who was experiencing the comfort of acceptance a child feels when being chosen for adoption. "Besides, he probably has friends or family he's meeting for dinner?" she tactfully pried.

"No, actually, I'm on vacation by myself," he replied. "I'm divorced, two years now," he added, to let them know it wasn't recent, and therefore, not requiring a pity party.

"Ah, a bachelor!" Richard declared. "I can still remember my time as a rascal. Sometimes I would have three dates a week with different girls. We used to—" Feeling Mary's glare, Rich opted not to go any farther down memory lane. "Anyway, that was before I met the love of my life here in Mary. I put a ring on her as quickly as I could. Then I guarded her like a hawk 'til we got to the altar, for fear someone else might steal her away. But you're a lone ranger, John and this is a great place to be the Lone Ranger!"

"Although I believe my husband's imagination embellishes his pre-marital experiences, he's right about a couple things. He was right to guard me, because there were many attractive young men interested, and this is a great place to be a single person," Mary admitted. "So how 'bout it John, would you care to dine with a couple of old people your first night at sea?" Mary's eyebrows raised as her smile turned into a subtle frown; it was a trick she'd honed over the years to guilt people into doing what she wished.

The trick was wasted on John, who found the couple to be two of the most interesting people he'd ever met. Besides, they could show him the ropes, and he desperately needed someone to do just that.

"I'd love to!" he said.

Mary clapped her hands as Richard gave John a manly pat on the back. "Superb!" Richard said. "How about we all store our gear and then meet for cocktails—say six o'clock in the Lido Bar?" He looked at Mary. "That gives John plenty of time to acclimate himself and do a bit of recon. What do you think John? You can watch the ship leave Miami, which is beautiful at night, by the way, and Mary and I will make a reservation for the three of us at one of the restaurants. Sound good?"

"Sounds great, sir—I mean, Richard."

"Now you're getting it, son!" Richard winked. "We'll see you at six."

John noticed that the Clawsons walked off spryly for a couple their age. He fantasized about finding someone to experience life with like they had, to grow old with. That had always been the plan when he married Page, but as John became more content each year they were married, Page grew more restless. Although never excited, John was happy with his job and the modest life he and Page built in their small town, and when Page bore their only child he was complete. They were wonderful parents to their son, whom they named Carson.

It wasn't until their second year of marriage that Page was able to conceive. It was causing a strain on the relationship, right up to the moment when John returned home from work one Tuesday evening to find wine, flowers, the best china, and his beaming wife waiting for him. That was a defining moment for John Smith—the moment he discovered he was going to be a father.

Not fond of heights, and standing five feet from the ship's railing, John found himself in a pensive but peaceful state as he stared at the Miami skyline. He was still holding his life vest. He replayed recent events, beginning with last night's packing and everything else leading up to his present comfortable daydream. His reluctance for a first real vacation was now replaced with a hopefulness, and it was all because of the stimulation of meeting new people. He wondered where Page was at that moment and thought how great it would be if she could see him starting an adventure aboard such a splendid ship.

Surely, she would be both shocked and proud of me, he thought. He wondered again who sent his ticket and then the image of Rita's beautiful legs replaced everything else. John held onto the mental picture long enough to relay messages to his libido, leading it to believe it was *boarding time.* He quickly deleted the image, embarrassment washing over him as he felt the onset of erection. With a sense of urgency, John rotated his right hand bringing the life vest to the front of his tan cargo shorts. He turned, looked right and left, as if crossing the street, and then made his way inside the ship. Walking briskly down the corridor toward his cabin, he tried to act nonchalant by acknowledging the passing guests with a slight smile and head nod. Each person returned his gesture with a chuckle, leaving John perplexed. Little did he know how bright red his face was, or that his placement of the life vest allowed the circular cutout to showcase his effected area.

His bodily functions returned to normal by the time he made it to cabin three-seventeen. Pulling the electronic keycard from his left pocket, he slid it into the credit card-style device on the door, and promptly received a red light; the door was still locked. John tried several more times, turning the card forward and back, upside-down and face-forward, then dropped the life vest in frustration to give the task at hand his full attention. All the while he wondered how this technology was superior to a good old fashioned metal key. He was finally rewarded with a green light, and bulled his way into the room with his left shoulder.

He decided to unpack his lone suitcase, a stylish piece enviable to any seasoned traveler. The bag, made of rich dark leather, was a traditional shaped, large suitcase. Next to the handle was a rectangular, silver badge engraved with the words *A Bagly Bag.* It had been a college graduation gift from his father, Jack, who presented it to his son after the graduation ceremony. Jack worked for his good friend and John's father-in-law at the Bagly Bag Company. Inside, Jack had left a card for his son to discover later. The bag was more than twenty-five years old, but due to both quality craftsmanship and lack of use, it was timeless in style and looked as new as the day Jack gave it to John.

After removing the bag's contents and placing his clothing and toiletries in their appropriate places, John took a last look inside the bag to see if he had missed anything. Inside one of the compartments he found an envelope. Opening it, he read: "For all your future adventures."

He had forgotten storing the note there more than twenty-five years ago. John tenderly propped it up against the lamp on his bedside table. He lay down on the bunk, folded his hands across his chest, and closed his eyes. Drifting off to sleep he knew that for the first time, his father's gift was being used for its true intention.

HAPPY HOUR

THE GANGWAYS WERE ALL FOLDED away, fresh supplies were all aboard and being stowed or rushed to their destinations, the lines were all released from the dock's moorings, and *The Princess's* horn blew to let everyone know they were underway. The deep, long horn blasts weren't conducive to naps. John shot up from a sound sleep, wiped his eyes, and looked at his Timex—5:00. After throwing some cold water on his face and changing into a fresh shirt, he grabbed his copy of the ship's map and made his way topside to watch the departure.

Waiting for a free elevator, John turned to a tall man dressed in a white Navy uniform and asked, "Excuse me, will you tell me where the best place is to watch the ship leave Miami?"

"I'll do better than that," he replied in a Scandinavian accent. "Follow me." The two men squeezed into the first elevator that opened, along with as many passengers as it would hold. "It's really quite simple, whenever we leave a port, you take an elevator to the highest deck and turn aft—that's the rear of the ship. If we're heading into port you turn forward toward land."

The officer reminded John of his fifth grade teacher explaining geography. Welcoming the officer's candor, John asked, "If forward is called forward why can't the rear be named back instead of aft?" He asked, as both a way to learn and an attempt to be funny—a quality for which he wasn't generally known.

The officer smiled as laughter sounded from several people turning to hear the answer. "Good question, sir," said the officer. "It gets worse. The left side of the ship is called port and the right's called starboard, but *The Princess* could be in a port with the port side not facing port. And you can usually see stars off both the starboard and port sides, but not always!" Laughter filled the elevator.

When the doors opened, a couple appearing to be in their early thirties stood waiting and the wave of laughter inundated them. Exiting, John overheard the man say, "I told you everyone I talked to said this ship was a lot of fun."

Pausing to look both right and left, John realized he was still confused. The officer, who had turned right, glanced back, then returned.

"Just follow this corridor, sir," the officer pointed.

"Thank you," John said, offering a handshake. "This is my first cruise, if you couldn't already tell. I should be focusing more on what I'm doing and where I'm going."

"On the contrary, sir, just let yourself go and you'll find you're always exactly where you're supposed to be. Understand?"

"I think so."

The officer left John with a grin and a casual salute. John watched as the man's figure grew smaller, thinking surely a person so wise and in uniform had more important duties to attend to. Turning in the direction the officer had indicated, John began confidently walking. After what seemed like a half mile, he heard festive music coming from beyond the basketball court. Approaching the crowd, he could see the brilliant Miami skyline below a purple sky. After snaking through hundreds of bodies, John found himself as far as he could go without jumping. Aware of the height, he gripped the shiny wood rail with both hands, looked straight down into the ship's wake, and trembled.

The ship's diesel engines, producing sixty-eight thousand horse power, made for one hell of a washing machine. The ten mega cruise liners docked that day, looking like individual cities, joined with the Miami skyline for an awe inspiring view. No other city looked like Miami at twilight, with its bridges and buildings awash with purple and green neon lights, and South Beach sparkled in its own art deco way. He recalled watching an episode of "Miami Vice" back in the eighties and assumed it was an accurate portrayal of a seedy, violent, drug-infested Miami that was always a hundred degrees. He had enjoyed the music and exotic cars. Looking out at Miami now, he thought his first judgment might have been a bit hasty.

"How 'bout a cocktail, sir?"

John turned to find a young twenty-something woman wearing a Hawaiian shirt and holding a tray; her beautiful milk chocolate skin set off an ivory smile. *Janet, from Jamaica,* he read on her name tag.

"A piña colada or margarita?" she suggested with sensual salesmanship.

John appeared to be toying with the idea, when in fact, he was mesmerized with the girl's sexy demeanor. His awkwardness around attractive women couldn't be confused for coyness, and he knew they sensed it. His experience with women had been limited, with attractive women, almost non-existent. He hadn't dated much in high school until a happily monogamous relationship with Page, and other than a couple of blind dates his friends had sent him on after his divorce, he hadn't dated since.

What sort of woman would be interested in a late forties, divorced, average-looking man from Kansas, he asked himself.

"I would love one, but I'm supposed to be meeting some friends at six o'clock," John said, looking at his watch and realizing it was already 5:30.

"Mista, y' on holiday now. If y' haven't got time for a drink now, y' never got time for one," she said, head cocked to one side and eyes halfway closed. "D'ese friends o' y'ars, d'ey ever been on a cruise before?"

"Actually, this is their sixty-seventh."

"Well d'en, d'ey kickin' back right now jus' chillin' and don't expect y' d'ere when da clock strike six. Trust me. D'ey on holiday time now," she reassured. "How 'bout an ice cold Heineken, y' look like a beer man?"

Hesitating, John looked at his watch again, then asked himself what Carson would do. "You know, you're right, I am on holiday and I'd love a beer! Thanks. But only if you help me find the Lido Bar, so I'm not too late—deal?"

"No problem, I get y' d'ere." And she was off, firmly saying, "S'cuse me, comin' t'rough."

People cleared a path as she forged through the crowd like a lioness through a herd of gazelle. John hoped she wouldn't be too long. Holiday or not, he thought it was rude to keep people waiting, especially people he'd just met. Before he thought to examine his watch again the crowd parted, expelling Janet with a single Heineken balanced on her tray.

"I told y' I wouldn't make y' wait too long," she said, handing over the ice cold beer.

"Thanks for being so quick," he said, raising the green bottle in appreciation. "It's very busy. I hope I didn't keep you from bigger orders?"

"It's not a t'ing, we got plenty servers working right now and we all split tips," she assured. "Now, y' say y' got ta be at da Lido Bar—yes?"

"Yes."

"Easy d'en. Da Lido Bar on the Lido Deck, at mid-ship. Walk back to da elevators and it be marked next to da floor numbers. When y' exit, d'ere be a sign on da wall telling y' which way. It be round da corner from elevators. Any problem, just ask someone in uniform, d'ere be twelve-hundred of us around. Got it?"

"Got it! Thanks again, Janet."

"No problem!" she said, bouncing away.

Taking a large gulp and checking his watch again—5:45—he realized he didn't have to worry about driving or public open-container laws any more—roaming with alcohol was acceptable, even expected. He'd always followed the rules, telling himself, they were constructed for a reason and people who chose to bend or ignore them eventually paid a price. The freedom and laissez-faire attitude of the cruise ship mentality was something new to John. A scary and exciting reality.

Lifting his beer, taking stock of the remaining liquid, he said, "Half full," as if talking to the bottle. "Not half empty." He took another slug as he started back to the elevators, with little urgency.

Everywhere John looked people were enjoying themselves, leaving whatever problems they carried behind as if they had checked them into a storage locker in Miami or thrown them overboard. Couples, groups, and singles were dancing, talking, and laughing. Small children, seemingly unsupervised, chased each other around the basketball court. Lovers held each other close by the railing, staring out to sea, and in the pool a floating, bikini-clad woman was guided like a baby by her partner. Jimmy Buffet's "Margaritaville" helped sell many cocktails of the same name, while the salt air washed every other smell out to sea. Turning before the interior corridor, John gazed back at the fading Miami skyline and watched it be swallowed by the Atlantic Ocean. He inhaled as much of the salt air as one deep breath could hold, before slowly exhaling, and then it was time to join the Clawsons.

Janet's simple directions did the trick. The first thing John noticed upon entering the bar was how crowded it was, every table and bar seat occupied. The Lido Bar was an elegant watering hole, like one would find in a four or five star hotel. The bar itself was highly polished, dark hard-wood with shiny brass foot-rails, and slabs of Brazilian granite capping the top. A baby-grand piano sat in the middle of the room with a gallon sized brandy snifter on top for people who wanted to trade dollars for requests. Many guests hadn't changed clothes since the boat drill, still wearing t-shirts, shorts, and flip-flops, while the staff worked the room in jacket-less tuxedos. He spotted the Clawsons at a corner table, both wearing linen outfits; Mary in a skirt and Richard in a tie-less white shirt and blazer. Making his way, he saw Mary smile and raise her arm to wave him over.

"Hello again, dear!" Mary said. "Thanks for joining us. We just love spending time with new people on these trips."

"Welcome, John, great to see you again, please, have a seat," Richard said, standing up to shake hands. "I hope you're not carrying that empty bottle around to remind you of your limitations?" Richard took a seat next to Mary.

"I forgot I was still holding it. John looked at the empty bottle, then back to the couple. "It's wonderful to see you both again. Thank you for inviting me," he said, placing the bottle on the table, then sitting down. "You sure know where to find the hot spots, this place is packed."

After taking a sip of wine, Mary said, "They're all busy now, sweetie. If they're open, they're packed. It's the first night of the cruise and thirty-five hundred people, many with jet-lag, have all unpacked their bags, gone through lifeboat drill, and officially said goodbye to all, or most of, their troubles for the next seven days. It's officially happy-hour!"

"She's right, my boy, and you're dry. We need libations here!" Richard raised his hand, scouring the room with the neck and eye movement of an owl. He didn't have to wait long before a young woman darted in his direction.

"Good evening, sir, may I freshen you up?" she asked.

Richard looked into the girl's eyes and flirted. "If I weren't eighty and married, I might try to show you fresh, but I'll settle for some drinks." She humored the old man with a flirtatious smile, but Richard felt a shin kick, breaking the moment and causing him to wince and grunt. *"Right,"* Richard reached under the table and grabbed his shin, "well then, how about a real drink, John? Do you drink scotch?"

John tried not to laugh and said, "I don't often get the chance and don't know much about it, other than it comes from Scotland, but I've enjoyed what I've tried."

"You're in the teacher's hands, my boy. We'd like two Lagavulin's, light ice, and whatever this beautiful young lady desires." Richard motioned to Mary while still rubbing his leg.

"Your best glass of champagne, please. I'm going to celebrate my husband's continual, albeit infantile, growth spurts from caveman to adolescent." Smiling, the waitress left with their order.

"Did you get a chance to join the party on the sun deck and watch the departure?" Richard asked.

"I did. Although, I admit to taking a nap before going, but that ship horn made for a great alarm clock."

"After we've gone to a couple of ports, you'll get used to it, John," Mary said, settling back. "We don't know anything about you, except that you're here alone, divorced, and like to wear your life vest in a reversible fashion." Mary reached over and gave John's arm a mock pinch. "What part of the world are you from?"

The waitress arrived with their drinks before John could answer. Dropping beverage napkins, she quickly placed two scotches in front of the men, then to Mary, she said, "This is Veuve Clicquot, the finest champagne we offer by-the-glass." She winked at Mary, leaving without acknowledging either man.

"Where were we, John?" Mary asked, a satisfied grin on her face as she took a sip.

"Well…I'm from Good Intent, Kansas where I was born and raised. And I work for a company that makes rubber bands."

"What a charming name for a place," Mary said.

Raising his eyebrows, Richard asked, "Rubber bands?"

"Yes. Well, not just rubber bands, but paperclips and those clips the grocery stores sell to keep your snack food sealed tight. We also make several kinds of hair bands for women. The company's called Keep It Together, and we distribute our products internationally. We're actually very successful. Several foreign companies have looked into acquiring us. I'm kind of a jack-of-all, overseeing production, distribution, and sales operations. Basically, it's my job to foresee, address, listen to, and solve any problems our workers might encounter. It can be both stressful and boring, if you can imagine?"

"I bet!" Richard said, with a hint of sarcasm.

"I love rubber bands," Mary said. "And I used to use those hair ties all the time when I was younger. I had long hair back in the day, and needed them all the time—Richard always owned a convertible and the wind would knot long hair like sticking wet bubble-gum on your head. Genius invention, the rubber band!"

Simultaneously, all three took a sip of their drinks.

"How about you, Richard, what did you do for a living?"

Smiling at Mary, Richard answered while maintaining eye contact with his wife. "First and foremost, I was a loving husband and father to our five children—the *best* job there is." Mary lovingly touched her husband's hand. "But what you're really asking is how I paid the rent. And to answer your question, I did a number of different things, all stemming from interests I've had over the years. Luckily, I was always either too young or too old to volunteer or be drafted into one of these bloody wars the United States has been involved in over the course of my lifetime, or I may never have met my beautiful wife. Instead, I was fortunate enough to go to college and earn a degree in engineering."

"So you were an engineer?" John asked.

"We're all engineers, John. It's a prerequisite in life," Richard chuckled. "Every time we assemble a child's toy, fix a squeaky door, open a stubborn pickle lid, or juggle the many responsibilities in our lives, we become engineers."

"I never thought about it that way," John said, contemplating Richard's words.

Richard sat back, savoring another sip of scotch. "I look at it this way, my boy, life's full of daily challenges, some big, some small. The one commonality being they all require our constant attention, if for no other reason than to address them and prepare ourselves for the next batch, always waiting right around the corner. All of us engineer our way through or around these tasks in different ways, using the skills we were given, hopefully sharpening those skills through trial and error. And I believe in a reward system. Doesn't have to be a big reward, maybe chocolate or a nap, just something after each challenge to let us know we tried. Engineering plus reward builds character. Character helps prepare us for the next pain in the ass thing that we'll have to overcome. The reward could even be, considering yourself an engineer—even though no degree hangs on your wall."

"He likes to think his real degree is in philosophy," Mary said, grinning. Always acutely aware of other people's feelings, she didn't want John to feel uncomfortable.

"Is that what you are, Rich? An engineer *and* a philosopher?"

"All of us are a lot of things whether we realize it or not," Richard said. "Getting back to your original question, I worked as an engineer for a major oil company for almost ten years after college, before I realized there were other things I'd rather do with my time."

"What did you decide to do next?" John asked.

"Well, I always wanted to own a drive-in! You know, one of those joints where they used to drive up in those great old American cars and order burgers, fries, and malts through the loudspeaker. Attractive young ladies on roller skates would deliver the food to your car window. I always thought it would be a fun way to make a living and meet pretty girls." Richard's face lit up nostalgically.

"So, did you?" John asked.

"Sure did! I wasn't married at that time and I had saved a decent chunk of money from my years working for the oil company. All I needed was the right location. Found it too, in my hometown of Lynchburg, Virginia. I had enough to purchase most of it out right, and the bank loaned the rest. It was more work than I thought it'd be. Still, running that place was a hell of a lot of fun. It's where I met Mary. She was there on a date if you can believe it?" chuckling with Mary.

"Really? How'd you meet?" John asked, placing his elbows on the table and leaning forward.

"Actually, I didn't have to do much. The grease ball—it was the sixties you know and he had one of those James Dean kind of haircuts with all the grease in it, slicked back into what looked like a duck's ass, known simply as a DA back then. So, after their food came, Mr. Dean was trying to get fresh with Mary in the car and she wasn't having any of it—him or the food. I was emptying trash cans outside the restaurant when I noticed a bit of a tussle in this Mercury. Small fights and couples arguing weren't uncommon in those days, on a Friday or Saturday night after the kids had a couple of beers, but Mary caught my eye. She was *so* beautiful. When I saw how steamed she was at this punk, I just had to go to her rescue. She slapped him a good one in the face before I got to the car. She was trying to open the door, but he was holding her back."

"He tore my little pink sweater trying to grab onto my shoulder!" Mary angrily interjected. "That was my favorite sweater!"

"It *was* a pretty sweater, darling," Richard said softly.

"So how did you handle the guy?" John asked.

"Well, even back in those days I wasn't a small guy. Not too many people intimidated me. So I went up to the car window and said, 'I believe the lady would like to exit the vehicle.' The guy pulled a switch blade from his pocket, releasing the blade with his right hand as he held it up just inside the driver's window. He told me I should mind my own business and leave before I got hurt. We had aluminum food trays that attached to the side of the car door back then, and his was holding nothing more than a Cherry Coke. So I looked at him and said, 'I can't leave, because this *is* my *business*.' And then I grabbed his right wrist with my left hand, using my right hand to reach up under the tray and smash his face. He dropped the knife. I believe his nose was broken based on the amount of blood. He drove off after spitting a few bloody curse words. I went over to attend to Mary. She left the car when he pulled the knife. We didn't have to worry about getting sued for little incidents in those days. Men just handled things like men, without needing a lawyer in their pocket to try and square a discrepancy or get rich. Anyway, I told her who I was and she agreed to let me console her with a chocolate malt. The rest was, *the beginning*."

"He's very chivalrous…and used to make an excellent chocolate malt," Mary said, with a devilish smile.

John sat back enchanted. "That's a great story," he said. "Do you still have the drive-in?"

"No, no, no," Richard said. "Mary despised restaurant hours and wanted to start a family. I ended up selling the entire thing to McDonald's about four years after Mary and I started dating. Made a pretty penny too, I might add, at the risk of sounding gauche."

"Too many *distractions* around that place, and I couldn't risk him accidentally tripping over one of them. If you know what I mean?" Mary winked.

"I believe I do," John winked back. "What did you do after that, Rich?"

"I did a lot more, my boy, but I think those stories will have to wait, because we made a seven o'clock reservation and it's five 'til. You must be hungry by now?"

"Yes, I'm ready for some food, but I can't wait to hear what happened next."

"Next is something which continually happens, like breathing air, or the planet spinning around. It's happening whether we're aware of it or not. I'm talking to you right now and then I'm going to pay this check, slide the chair out for my wife, and walk towards the exit. Most people see these things as separate actions, each one a next, lined up in a row, marching one after the other. In reality, everything we do is one constant action, like a dance, sometimes tripping, while other times soaring. Problem is…people usually only care about the obvious parts of the dance, instead of watching the entire routine, start to finish." Richard sat back, reaching for his wallet as he scanned the room. He pulled out his ship charge card. Holding it above his shoulder, he noticed John studying his every move the way a child watches a father. "All I'm saying is, it's all one big next without beginning or end. I don't like to ever get too caught up with any part of it, except the ever present *now* of *next*. Every moment is equally important and people who focus on moments gone or not here yet, tend to lose their way in the ever present moment of right now. You know what I mean, John?"

"Oh stop it, Richard," Mary chided. "He thinks he's some Buddhist priest when he drinks, John. It's all those Deepak Chopra books I've given him for Christmas. Makes him think he's smarter than he is. Come on boys, I'm hungry. Please take me to dinner."

Finally noticing Richard's subtle gesture, the waitress rushed over with the check.

"Please, allow me to pay for the drinks, Richard." Fumbling through his pockets to locate his charge card, John was too slow; she snatched Richard's card and was on her way back to the bar.

"Not at all dear, it's our treat," Mary said.

"Thank you both very much, that's very generous of you," he said, annoyed with himself for not being quicker.

When the waitress returned, Richard quickly signed the check before standing up to pull back his wife's chair; something Mary didn't need help with, although she appreciated it and had grown accustomed to the gesture. Making their way towards the exit, John lagged behind, out of respect, and because he didn't have a clue where they were going for dinner. Richard escorted his wife and new friend into the nearest elevator and pushed six—Orca Deck.

"I don't know what kind of grub you like, John, but I made us a reservation at Café Milano," Richard said. "It's obviously Italian, but I'm sure they have a little bit of everything. Hope that's okay?"

"Sounds great! I hardly ever get to eat out, or try new things, so it's all a treat to me. Since my divorce, my meals have consisted of a lot of frozen dinners and spaghetti," John admitted.

The two men laughed while Mary wore an appalled look on her face. "Didn't you say you've been divorced for two years, John?" she asked.

"Yes, that's about right."

"If you don't mind me saying, sweetie, that's far too long to go without a home-cooked meal," Mary said. "I'm either going to find you a woman, or teach you how to cook—with your permission of course. I have tons of great recipes that I've mastered over the years with Richard and the kids as my guinea pigs. They're not difficult to make either. If you give me your email, I'll send them to you."

"Take her up on that, John, trust me, the woman can cook!"

"Thanks, Mary. That's really nice of you. My email's easy to remember. It's millions of john smiths at keep it together dot com."

A HAUNTING FIRST DINNER

THE ELEVATOR DOORS OPENED AND after exiting, the group paused to read the wall marker directing them to Café Milano. The ship's passageways were ornately decorated with tropical art work and the carpet was a bold mix of color in a swirling pattern. Walking the corridor and gazing at the carpet reminded John of a time when, as a child, he invented his own imaginative game. On hot, sunny afternoons the neighborhood children would gather in someone's front yard, playing games only children can invent. Sometimes he would look directly at the bright sun, briefly, before closing his eyes and rubbing them hard, igniting an internal kaleidoscope only he could see. The carpeting reminded him of why he had stopped playing the game. One day he had shared the game with his mother, telling her about all the beautiful colors when he rubbed his eyes hard, colors that reminded him of the Fourth of July. Her response was that he should stop doing it or else he could damage his eyes, even go blind. That was the last time he ever played the game.

Jolted from his reverie, he saw they were at Café Milano when Richard said, "John, John. This is it, my boy, we're here."

Raising his head, as if from a trance, John said, "Sorry, I must've been caught up in a bit of a daydream. Is our table ready?"

Looking at John as if they'd awakened him from a long sleep, Richard and Mary both appeared amused. "Yes," Richard said. "They're willing to seat us now—if you're ready?"

The maître d' waited at attention, three menus in his hand. "Absolutely," John said. "Let's eat!"

"Excellent!" Richard said. "I'm so hungry I could eat a vegan meal—but, I won't." Without skipping a beat, he turned to the maître d' and said, "I believe we're all ready!"

Mary led the way behind the maître d', observing various dishes placed in front of guests. Their host stopped at a corner table draped with a white tablecloth and four velvet armchairs.

"I hope this will be satisfactory?" asked the maître d', pulling out the chair with the best view of the restaurant for Mary.

"It's wonderful, young man," Mary said. "Thank you very much."

"Your waiter will be with you shortly. I hope you enjoy your meals," he said, handing each person a menu, placing a wine list between the men, and then whisking away the extra place setting.

Looking around the room, John marveled at how fancy everything seemed; certainly one of the nicest restaurants he'd ever been to. Not because he couldn't afford it; being frugal with his money over the years, only spending on his family and hardly ever on himself, enabled him to save a decent nest egg. No, not money—exposure was the issue. He'd just never traveled much. The one or two fine dining restaurants in Good Intent fell way short of Café Milano's ambiance.

"I hope everywhere I'm going to have a meal on this ship isn't as fancy as this, or I'll need to buy a new wardrobe to get me through this cruise."

"Not at all, John," Mary said, lowering her menu. "There's something for everyone here and the ship's crew doesn't give a fig how you're dressed, only that you're having a good time and spending as much money as they can milk out of you."

"She's right, John. We've experienced good to excellent service on most of our cruises, but the bottom line—as in any business—is money. You can wear a bathing suit, t-shirt, and flip-flops almost anywhere you go, and you won't get so much as a second look from the crew or other passengers. I'm not saying you should go to the swimming pool and then enter the theater without changing first, but as a rule of thumb, casual pants or shorts, and a simple short-sleeved collared shirt will suffice for the dressiest places on board."

"That's good to know, because I *did* bring a bathing suit!" John said, throwing in a sigh of relief.

Everyone laughed.

"Actually, our young bachelor, you can find places in many of the ports where you won't even need your bathing suit," Richard said, in a quieter voice. "And I'm not just talking about the beaches either. When some of these gals on board drink enough cheap tequila at Carlos 'n Charlie's, you'll see a few bikini tops start flying. How about it, Mary?"

"He speaks the truth, John. You have to keep in mind that every island isn't just an island, they're foreign countries. Many people treat their stay in port like a weekend in *Vegas*. The indigenous people don't seem to mind usually, because of the amount of money we all spend, but we've seen some people behave in a manner that I would never endorse, regardless of whether anyone I knew found out or not. But, to each his own as long as they're not infringing upon, or hurting anyone else. After all, we all came here to have a good time. That means something different to everyone. For me, that often means lying on a deck chair with a good book and a glass of wine." she said impishly. "But if I were twenty-five again, single, and drinking margaritas at Carlos 'n Charlie's—who knows?"

"Huh," Richard huffed. "I'd like to go back in a time machine and find out. Mary was always a looker, John. In her twenties and thirties the woman could stop traffic!"

"I could still make a few cars pause in my forties, Richard—if you remember?"

Before Richard could comment, their waitress arrived.

"Good evening!" said the girl, in a French accent. "Welcome to Café Milano. My name is Cinda and I will be your waitress this evening. Is everyone enjoying their cruise so far?"

The three guests simultaneously nodded and said, "*Yes.*"

John squinted to read Cinda's name tag while Richard asked, "Isn't it a conflict of interest for a lovely French girl to be working in an Italian restaurant?" Another witty attempt at flirtation.

"Tunisia," John said, surprised by his confidence.

Cinda faced John with an impressed smile. He wished he had the knowledge to back up his observation, or at least know what continent Tunisia was on. Instead, he had charged impetuously forward and now had to wait, hoping she would spare him. Cinda and John locked eyes; he blinked nervously.

"Yes!" she said. "That's correct. I'm from Tunisia. Has anyone visited there before?" making eye contact with each person, but merely brushing John's eyes.

Mary allowed Richard to answer, knowing how much he delighted in talking with beautiful, young women. She had never felt threatened, because she knew it was an innocent pleasure which had never in the past, nor would it in the future, be anything more than ego stroking.

"We have not!" Richard said, leaping at the chance to speak. "My wife and I have been to Morocco before, but never Tunisia. They're fairly close to one another, aren't they?"

"Yes," said Cinda. "Africa is a very large place, but both countries are on the north coast."

Africa, John thought. *Why didn't I know that?*

"You knew where she was from, John," Mary said, inadvertently putting him on the spot. "Have you visited Tunisia?"

Just when John thought he was given a pass, all eyes moved back to him. Since lying wasn't a quality he possessed, there was only one answer. "Uh…no, I uh, actually have never heard of it before. I've just gotten into the habit of reading name tags."

Cinda winked, careful to use her left eye so the gesture was hidden from the Clawsons. She proceeded to recite the dinner specials and then asked, "Would anyone care for a cocktail, or perhaps some wine?"

Richard said, "Yes! That's a wonderful idea. Do you care if I order wine for the table, John?"

"Not at all, Richard, I trust your expertise."

"We would like a bottle of red and a bottle of white, just so's everyone's happy," Richard joked. "How about bins sixty-three and thirty-one?"

"Excellent choice, sir. I will convey your order to the wine steward and give you a few minutes to look over your menus."

While Richard and Mary commented back and forth about appetizers and ingredients, John stared blankly at his menu. Haunted by memories, he half-heartedly perused the menu, wishing there was some magic water he could order from Cinda that would make him a new man who lived profoundly in the ever present moment, the way Richard had described.

John hadn't noticed missing the wine presentation until he heard Richard asking whether he preferred red or white.

"What do you think, my boy?" Richard repeated, holding a wine bottle in each hand. "I've never bought into that crap about having to drink white wine with white meat and red wine with red meat. Go with whatever your tongue tells you, I always say!"

"He would pour them together if that was the only way he was allowed to have a drink, John, so if you haven't decided yet, don't let him push you," Mary said.

"I would love a glass of white, thank you."

Richard poured everyone an equally healthy portion before raising his own glass. "Here's to new friends and grand adventures! May we never get Alzheimer's, so we can always remember both," he said, the second half softer to avoid offending any of the surrounding guests.

Touching glasses, they said "*cheers.*"

"I trust the wine is satisfactory?" Cinda asked, watching as the three swallowed their first sip.

Richard turned. "It's wonderful, Cinda, just wonderful! Where've you been? We missed you!"

"*Merci beaucoup!* I asked if I could just wait on you, but my manager said no."

"That's an outrage!" Richard said. "I say we make him walk the plank—at night!" After pounding his fist on the table, Richard sat straight-faced as everyone giggled.

When the joke ran its course, Cinda took appetizer and entree orders and then, to Richard's lament, she was gone again.

Comfortable in their high-back, emerald green armchairs sipping wine, Richard and Mary dictated most of the conversation, sharing stories about family and their travels. John mostly listened, absorbing the memories as if they were his own. He contributed when he could, but mostly he spoke in questions, strangely feeling both comfortable and inadequate.

John felt privileged being around two such weathered and worldly people, the way a person might feel around the Dalai Lama, or, heaven forbid, Madonna, or more appropriately, grandparents. He had always enjoyed talking with his own grandparents. They were more objective, with fewer expectations than his own parents. Maybe this was a universal merit badge bestowed on parents once they achieved the rank of grandparent. Finally able to relax after all the hard work they'd put into their own families, they'd earned the right to be listened to and admired for all their accomplishments and wisdom. Grandparents had nothing to lose since they were more often than not in the twilight of their years, rather than the middle.

"We've been monopolizing the conversation," Mary said. "I'm sorry. We tend to do that a lot."

"No reason to apologize, Mary," John said. "I'm enjoying every second of it."

"I'm delighted that you find two old people so interesting," she said. "Thank you for humoring us, but I'd like to hear more about you if you wouldn't mind sharing?"

"Not at all, Mary. What would you like to know?"

"You mentioned a son? What's his name and where's he during your maiden voyage?"

Instantly uneasy, John squirmed in his chair, reaching for his wine.

"Carson," he managed. "His name was Carson. He was the most beautiful person I've ever known." John felt the water rush in around his eyes, fearing it might be enough to drown him. Seeing the look of terror in Mary's eyes when he said the word "was" and not wanting his new friends to feel uncomfortable or responsible for his impending breakdown, John composed himself with a double gulp of wine.

Before anyone had the chance to say anything, Cinda arrived with an assortment of picture perfect starters. Noticing the mood had changed, she spent the bare minimum of time soliciting their table. Just enough to do her job properly.

"Would anyone care for anything else?" Cinda asked.

"No, thank you, Cinda," Richard said. "Everything looks wonderful."

No sooner than Cinda had left the table, Mary said, "I'm so sorry John. I feel horrible for bringing it up. Please forgive me."

"Not at all, Mary," John said, wiping his eyes. "You didn't know." John tried to assuage Mary's guilt with a tender gaze and reaching across the table for her hand. "I want to talk about him; I need to talk about him. Carson's the reason I'm on this ship. Somehow he got me here. I believe he's still with me. I won't disrespect him by pretending he doesn't, or never did, exist."

Mary's face lit up. Squeezing his hand, she said they would love to hear about his son. Richard—neither insensitive nor immune to loss—decided instead, to try levity.

"Would anyone care for mussels or some bruschetta?" Richard asked, serving himself.

"I'm light on one and ignorant about the other, so yes please, some of each," John said.

The three laughed as Richard served heaping portions and refilled wine glasses.

Tasting the bruschetta, John said, "That's delicious!"

"It's simple to make," Mary said. "All dishes vary slightly depending on who's making them, but the one commonality should be the freshest ingredients possible. Bruschetta is no different. All you need is bread, toasted or not, depending on your preference, fresh tomatoes, fresh mozzarella, some extra-virgin olive oil, and only fresh basil."

"Mary's always had an herb garden, no matter where we lived, so when she says fresh, she means thirty feet from the kitchen."

"I regret not being exposed to different cuisine," John said, forking a mussel. "Where I come from, most people are meat and potatoes people. Kansas, as I'm sure you both know, is made up of a lot of farmers, often working before the sun comes up and long after it goes down. We eat a lot of hearty meals which don't require tons of imagination, or hours of prep work. It would have been nice to expose Carson to different cuisines than we did. But, knowing him, I'm certain he did that on his own when he ventured out into the world."

"How long ago did you lose your son, John?" Mary asked.

"It's been seven months. He was an Army soldier. That's the risk soldiers and their parents take in order to keep other people safe."

Swallowing a scallop and dropping his fork onto his plate, Richard's disposition changed. He wiped his mouth and said, "And that's the true bitch of it which many people in this country still don't understand. Too many Americans take a free ride on other people's coattails, or do nothing at all while our government empowers them to do so with others' blood and taxes."

"Now don't start talking politics, Richard," Mary said. "It's not polite dinner conversation."

"Nonsense!" Richard said. "I'm agreeing with the man. And I'm going to tell him why, too. John, there are two really good books out there that I've read in the last couple years. The first one's called, *The World Is Flat*, and the second one's titled, *That Used to Be Us*. They're must reads for *every* American, and in my opinion, should be mandatory reading for all high school students. Both are factual, objective, and extremely well researched accounts of how America, and the world, arrived where we are today. They explain what we need to do to save our beloved country from going down the drain. Look at the troops we've sent to Afghanistan and Iraq over the last ten years. Their families make up less than one percent of the American population. So one percent of Americans make the ultimate sacrifice, while the rest make no, or little sacrifice at all. And lots of those people have the gall to live off the government and other peoples' hard work. That's what my generation used to call BS!"

"Honey!" Mary said, annoyed at Richard for being annoyed. "Remember your blood pressure!"

Richard flashed a childishly remorseless look at his wife. "Our youngest child, Oliver, is in the Navy," he said. "We have a great deal of empathy and admiration for families like yours who have paid such a price. It doesn't matter what I, or anyone else thinks about this war, or any past war. Shit! It's war. Sometimes war is blatantly necessary. Other times, governments venture into wars for more selfish and political reasons. In the long run, if you're a soldier and your government informs you that they're sending you to fight somewhere—you go fight. Soldiers don't get to pick and choose which battles they are going to fight based upon their politics or sense of right and wrong. They just fight! We can fault the powers that be for sending them there, but not the men charged to go—for going. That would be like having two boys, and telling the older one not to have any cookies before dinner. He not only has cookies, but he tells his younger sibling that it's okay to have cookies. Then you blame the younger one equally for the older brother's defiance."

John listened to every passionate word from Richard's mouth. Mary was trying to keep him calm and steer him away from the conversation at hand, fearing his blood pressure might escalate. Then, John's mind wandered to the meaning of the words sacrifice, courage, and belief. He wondered if he truly knew their core definitions.

Carson did, he thought.

That realization brought him back to Mary and Richard with the urgency of a rubber band being snapped. The two were still quibbling about the nature of the conversation when John interjected.

"Carson wanted to be a soldier from a very young age."

Silence.

"There was a boy named Felix who lived in our neighborhood. His family was originally from Mexico City. Our two boys played together. They had a penchant for anything that had to do with the military. The two of them just loved mock battles. They spent hours chasing anything from squirrels to each other, shooting everything from their fingers, to a number of toy guns the parents bought them over the years. Surely your boys were no different?"

Richard and Mary grinned.

"We had four boys," Richard said. "When they were growing up we lived in a house on a heavily wooded lot. The terrain created a natural playground for the imagination. Many fierce battles were fought there. We took more than a few trips to the hospital over the years to treat cuts, sprains, and breaks as a result of those imaginary battles." Mary shook her head remembering the anxiety those hospital trips caused.

"Carson's mother, Page, and I only had to experience one of those brutal trips to the hospital. Carson and Felix were about fourteen and lobbying for BB guns. Fourteen, after all, was much too old to still be playing with toy guns, they complained. Page wasn't going to allow her son to play with a loaded gun. Whether it was loaded with plastic pellets or tiny metal balls made no difference. I supported her decision because I knew I had no choice. I thought it would've been fine, as long as they were supervised. Page disagreed. She saw the BB gun one way—a threat to her son. Trying to convince her otherwise would have only caused a fight between us. Ironically, her fear became real."

Picking up another piece of bruschetta as the Clawsons were finishing off the oysters, John washed the mouthful down with a healthy share of the lovely white wine Richard had chosen.

"I don't see this story having a happy ending," Mary said.

"Well…Felix's parents decided to buy their son a BB gun. Page and I didn't feel it was our place to let them know we didn't think it was a good idea. Although, my wife certainly wanted to," John laughed.

"We told Carson that he couldn't play with Felix if Felix had the BB gun with him, but boys will be boys. One drizzling, gray afternoon—idealistic weather for mock battles—the two boys marched off to a wooded park in our neighborhood. One with a plastic machine gun, while the other proudly touted a brand new BB gun. Apparently, at some point there was a discussion about whether a BB could actually puncture human flesh. Carson told us they took turns testing their dilemma by shooting each other in their rear areas from twenty paces."

"Priceless!" Richard said.

"Oh my Lord!" Mary said, trying to contain laughter with her hand.

"Yes," John said. "A couple of real rocket scientists, huh? They were both wearing jeans. The most their stupid asses could feel was a slight sting, excuse the pun. So Felix at least, came to the conclusion that a BB could not break the skin. He suggested to Carson that they try it on their arms. All they had to do was flex their massive biceps, they reasoned. Carson told Felix that he didn't think it was a good idea. Or at least that's what he told us. He didn't want to be shot in the arm, and he didn't want to shoot Felix. Felix, not willing to concede the experiment, decided to take a shot at Carson when he wasn't looking. And, only having the gun a couple of days, Felix was not yet an experienced marksman. The BB struck Carson in the temple, just a quarter inch from his left eye."

"Oh my God!" Mary said. "Was he okay?"

"Well, yes and no. Although Carson said being shot wasn't that painful, the trauma of being shot, and the fact that he had to come home and tell his mother what had happened, *was* painful."

"For certain!" Richard said.

"After several trips to the hospital, the doctors concluded they didn't want to risk an operation to remove the BB. They said leaving it there would cause no harm, but if they tried surgically to remove it, there would be a risk that Carson could have permanent damage in the left eye. So… we left it there."

"He was lucky," Mary said.

"Yes," John said. "We all were—that time." John's head dropped slightly before lifting as the busboy came to remove empty appetizer plates. Cinda was right behind to ask if they were ready for their entrées or needed more wine.

"Did the two boys continue to play together?" Mary asked.

Giving Cinda the go-ahead for entrées, Richard handed over the empty bottle, winking while displaying a pointer finger. Understanding his request, Cinda silently departed with the empty.

"Oh yes," John said. "Those two were inseparable from the time they met. They weren't going to let something as small as a BB get in the way of their friendship. Before they were teenagers, they used to play with GI Joe's. Between the two of them they had hundreds of little toy soldiers, along with tanks, planes, and cannons. We used to have those old beanbag chairs in our house. The boys would mold them into mountains to house their soldiers and stage battles. Each boy made his own beanbag fortress. They used to watch old war films like *Patton* and *The Great Escape*. When they couldn't find something on cable, they'd rent whatever they could find from the video store. *Taps*, a movie about a bunch of children making a siege at their military prep school after they find out it is slated to be closed, made a huge impression on both boys. Page and I weren't excited about the idea of Carson joining the military, but by the time he was seventeen, he was far too headstrong and determined to allow his mother and father to influence him. At that time, both boys were receiving visits from military recruiters. They were hell-bent on joining the Army. They wanted to join together so they could at least go through basic training together."

"Did they get their wish?" Richard asked, refreshing glasses.

"Tragically, no. The Army recruiter came to Felix's house for a preliminary interview with his parents. They were astounded by his passion and credentials. He was an honor roll student, letterman in two sports, and dazzled the interviewers with his vast knowledge of the American armed forces and its history."

"What's wrong with all of that?" Mary asked.

"Nothing," John said. "The recruiters were practically salivating with the thought of getting a commitment letter from such an outstanding candidate, and without a sentence of sales pitch. At the end of the interview, they told Felix's parents he would make an excellent addition to the Army and they'd be lucky to have him. The recruiter said all they needed was a copy of Felix's birth certificate and Social Security number to start the ball rolling."

"Is everyone ready for dinner?" asked Cinda, holding plates of chicken piccata, chicken marsala, and shrimp scampi. The wine steward was in tow, vigorously working the cork of Richard's next bottle.

"Absolutely, my dear, thank you," Richard said. "They were illegals, weren't they?"

"I don't know what the parents' status was, but yes. As it turned out, I guess Felix had been born in Mexico and brought here when he was very young—illegally. His parents never made the necessary arrangements for his citizenship. The recruiters were dumbfounded. They told the parents that there was no way he could join the military without the proper paperwork, and they left. Felix was heartbroken. He couldn't understand what he'd done wrong. We only saw them one more time after the recruiters left. They packed up everything and left the city for fear the entire family was going to be deported. The country lost out on a productive addition to the military and society, while our son, lost his best friend. All because of negligence. It was a sad day. We never heard from them again."

"That's a shame," Mary said. "Carson must've been very upset?"

"Yes, he took it very badly for a while. It wasn't comprehensible to him why the Army couldn't make an exception. Page and I tried the best we could to explain it, but in the end, the best explanation we could offer was that what happened to his friend was the result of what happens when people don't follow the rules. He was reluctant, but I think he eventually accepted that explanation."

"I don't mean to suggest that the Army should have, or shouldn't have accepted this boy, but you do believe there's a time and place to at least *bend* the rules—don't you, John?" Richard asked.

John's fork, skewered with a jumbo shrimp, stopped short of his mouth, as if a conundrum was blocking its path.

"I…I don't know. I've just always followed the rules—all my life."

"And I'm sure you're better for it," Richard said. "Yes. I'm certain. And, the fact that you've chosen to follow all those rules certainly puts you in very elite company."

"I assume the Army accepted Carson?" Mary said, anxious to learn Carson's fate.

"Yes Mary. They did. Carson graduated high school with a three point eight average. After finishing basic training, he was stationed at Fort Meade, Maryland, home of the Army's intelligence division. Over the next few years, Carson traveled throughout the United States, at various bases and schools for special training. He wrote us every other month, although he never got into any specific details, due to his security clearance. He always raved about how much fun it all was, the Army, travel, the things he was doing."

"Real gung-ho!" Richard said.

"His mother and I used to joke that eventually, on a trip to the post office we would find an Army recruiting poster with Carson's face on it. We often needed an Army translator to decipher the acronyms in Carson's letters. The hum-v he rides in is an MRAP—mine resistant ambush protected. Orders don't come from headquarters, they come from TOC—tactical operations center, and unlike people drink energy drinks, Army soldiers gear up for missions with *Rip-It* drinks." John paused before feigning laughter. "Though, BBQ and WTF still stand for the same things as they do to us civilians."

Turning to Richard, Mary quietly asked, "What does WTF stand for?"

"Huh, it stands for…*why the face*, dear," Richard said, choosing to spare Mary the embarrassment of the true vulgarity.

"Did Carson have to go to the Middle East?" Richard asked.

"Yes. Yes, he did—three tours. He was the kind of soldier who volunteered for combat duty, the more dangerous the better. He proudly informed us he had been on night missions with elite black hawk teams, hanging out of a helicopter, landing into God knows where. He was one of the guys kicking in doors searching for the most wanted. It all scared the crap out of us every time we heard him mention something like that, but we suppressed our fear with Carson's devotion."

Imagining one of her own kids in the same scenario, Mary said, "The two of you must have shared many sleepless nights?"

"You just tell yourself that your child is doing a job—an important one. Just like I'm sure you both do with your Naval son, Oliver. Our job is to support them, and pray. That's what we did, until…one day we received word that Carson had been killed."

Richard and Mary stopped eating and sat back. Every sound in the restaurant deafened by John's last sentence. The couple froze, silently commiserating through dead-locked eyes.

"His support platoon received orders to make a run through a volatile sub-district in order to re-supply one of the Army's combat out posts—COP as Carson would call it, and I guess the Taliban preys on these areas. Carson was only going with the team this particular time, because he was going on his Mid-Tour leave. They thought they could drop him off at the forward operating base to catch his helicopter to Kandahar.

"Apparently, Carson was driving in the lead vehicle when the convoy encountered smoke close to a checkpoint. They stopped to assess the situation when his truck was rocked by an explosion. We were told the platoon engaged in a fight for about fifteen minutes. Our son's MRAP was the first hit, but we don't know exactly how, or when he died, just that all four passengers were found…still inside the burning truck. The doors were all damaged or combat locked.

"I hate the word *resistant*. My only son…was blown up, shot at, and burned…inside a *mine-resistant-ambush-protected*, Army truck."

John became acutely aware of surrounding smells. He deliberately took a deep breath, which might have been misconstrued for a sigh. He detected the essence of lilac from Mary's perfume, garlic from their cooling dinners, Italian espresso from the table behind, and something more sinister. He drew his eyes to the center of the table, where a clear glass sconce housed a white candle. Its humble flame danced before John's eyes. The flame was blue at its base, changing to oranges and reds, before becoming a white tip reeling off black string into the air—smoke. He clenched the cloth napkin on his lap as hard as he could, wondering for the millionth time if Carson died quickly, or was trapped, alive, with only fire and smoke to guide him to the next life.

Richard saw Mary starting to cry, and John seemed to be in a trance. Offering what he could, he took her hand in his.

"We are so sorry for your loss, John," Mary said. "We understand the hole that losing a child creates, and I can't imagine the magnitude of losing your only child. I…we, lost two children, a boy and a girl. I had miscarriages before our first successful pregnancy."

John pulled his eyes away from the flame and looked at Mary, who was languidly moving her head up and down.

"Nothing prepares you for it—does it?" John said. "It's your worst nightmare come true."

"That's absolutely true, John," Mary said. "I would give my own life for any of my children, without hesitation. The real pain of losing the people we love is—as far as any person on earth can prove—felt by those they leave behind. But…there's something else. Eventually we have to learn that there's a life worth living after those people are gone. We owe it to them to find that life, if for no other reason, than to honor them through a celebration of having been a part of their life while they were here. It's important to find hope, so we may finish our lives triumphantly. Hopefully, that earns us the privilege of being remembered by those we'll leave behind, and just maybe, the reward of meeting them again after death.

"Well put," Richard said. "She's a very smart woman, John. Can you see why I married her?"

"I sure can, Richard. You're a very lucky man."

"Let's have a toast!" Richard said, raising his glass while still clenching Mary's hand. John and Mary followed suit.

"To our friends both old and new! May we always be there to help one another weather this brilliant storm we call *life*, and to the ultimate gift—our children! No matter where you are or go, whether in this world or the next. Know we love you unconditionally for all eternity. Neither space, time, nor even death, can keep us apart."

Clink-clink-clink.

"Thank you, Richard," John said. "That was very eloquent."

"Very beautiful, honey," Mary said, kissing Richard's lips and then quickly on his cheek.

Cinda, in the process of serving herbal tea and brandy to another table had noticed Richard's toast, waiting until after, to ask if they cared for dessert.

"May I clear your plates?" she asked. Everyone nodded. "Would everyone care for coffee and dessert? In addition to the selections on the menu, we have a delicious chocolate cannoli made by a real Roman pastry chef. I had two before my shift and they're delicious!"

"You sold me, dear!" Richard said. "And two cups of decaf for my wife and I. Mary, John?"

"I'll just have a bite of his," Mary said.

John had immensely enjoyed the Clawson's company, but the wine, and overwhelming feelings from talking about Carson left him emotionally and physically drained. His right hand ached. Looking down, he realized he was still clenching the cloth napkin.

Slowly relinquishing his grip, John said, "I'm actually very tired. I think I should rest up for tomorrow. What port is Monday?"

"Tomorrow is a sea day," Cinda said. "We dock at Solace Point on Tuesday. You have all day and night tomorrow to enjoy the ship."

Feeling like he couldn't sit any longer and again feeling the need to escape, John reached into his pocket with his cramped hand. "I don't mean to be rude, but I think I'm probably a little jet lagged," he said. "I've enjoyed this so much, but I think I'll just take a walk and suck in some sea air before hitting the sack." Holding his charge card beneath the table's edge, John hoped it would catch Cinda's attention.

"We totally understand," Mary said. She could see in John's eyes that it wasn't the wine glazing them. "We're in Royal Suite number five if you want to talk, see a show, or share a meal again. Just call."

"I would absolutely love that," John assured.

"I'll be back shortly with your coffee and dessert!" Cinda said, leaving without John's card.

"John, will you do me two favors before you go?" Richard asked.

"Anything Richard, just name it."

"First: don't ever try to pay for anything when you're in our company. We're old, both of us just cracked double forty, but we have more than an ample amount of money. Old people have earned the right to spend their money however they choose. It's my honor to pay for the meal of a friend and proud father of a veteran."

"Deal," John said. "Thank you both. What's the second thing?"

"I hope you don't find this too audacious, but I often speak my mind, because of the reality of limited time and all," Richard said.

"Not at all, I find your candor refreshing."

"Good," Richard said. "We want you to have fun. I don't know much about your son, but he sounds like he was exceptional. More importantly, it's obvious that you loved him, and he loved you. He sounds like the kind of man who would want to see his father having fun. Besides, you paid for this cruise, you made it this far. You might as well enjoy it."

"You're more right than you know—he would have."

Pushing back his chair, John stood to shake Richard's hand. Mary walked around to see John off with a hug, leaving no space between them, she pressed her ear firmly into his chest—John, 5' 11", while Mary had shrunk a bit over the years to 5' 2". Afterward, the two men exchanged handshakes while Richard reached around to slap John's back a couple times—a modern sort-of *man hug*.

"Enjoy the salt air, my boy," Richard said. "It offers much perspective, especially at night, and don't hesitate to call if you need anything."

"I will. Thanks again for everything. You're wonderful people. Your kids are very lucky."

"As was Carson," Richard said.

"Goodnight, John!" Mary said.

"Goodnight," John said, turning back through the restaurant's maze of tables. He spotted Cinda at the computer and tried for eye contact while slowing his gait. Instinctually, she turned, smiled, and waved. John waved back, lip-synching, *thank you*. Exiting the restaurant, he meandered back to the sun deck, again wondering who sent his ticket.

THE LETTER

T HE AREA AROUND THE POOL was peaceful, but not vacant. Couples intermittently stopped by the ship's sides to witness the majesty of the ocean or to engage in a romantic moment. Therapeutic salt air dominated over the hint of chlorine evaporating from the pool and the occasional smell from a passenger's fragrance lifted by the breeze. Faint music wafted in the night air, a pleasant background noise to the sea breaking against the ship's hull. The sky's easel was painted black, punctuated only by thousands of incandescent stars pulsing in the shadow of a three-quarter moon's glow.

John lay below, staring up from a lounge chair where he'd collapsed, weary and half intoxicated. He thought about his ex-wife, Page, remembering how happy they once were and wondered when exactly that ceased.

To say that people are a product of their parents is often to assume they couldn't deviate or change from some inherited path—the contrary always being the reality. Page, like most children, was more similar in appearance and action to one parent than the other—Margret Bagly. Even from a pubescent age, Page resembled her mother. Both women were attractive in an unassuming way. Those close to them knew to look past the outdated frumpy clothes, un-styled hair, and reserved speech; these were not easily frightened or fragile women. They were both petite and well proportioned, but certainly not voluptuous. Both had eyes which reflected a kind of sadness from within.

Page's mother was a homemaker, a devoted wife who cooked and cleaned, and never swore or drank more than a glass of wine during dinner. She attended church with her husband, Fred Bagly, every Sunday morning before returning home to make a family brunch. Afterward, she usually fashioned some time to herself designated for reading—her favorite activity. Casual walks and bike rides around the neighborhood also topped her list.

Margret Bagly was not enterprising unless encouraged by her husband. They were both fairly social between church, school, and various charitable organizations. As a product, their only daughter was a well-functioning, polite, and happy girl from a young age. She fit in well enough, at least with others who shared her cautious but not popular personality.

John and Page grew up shy and awkward, small town kids. John always thought it was fate that they would be together, but was amazed either one of them had the courage to approach the other about the idea. In the end, it was Page who was responsible. The two knew each other for as long as they could remember, but had never dated each other—or really anyone for that matter. That all changed junior year when Page asked—passing him a note during science class—if he would take her to their prom. The two were inseparable after that magic evening. They relived it the following year at their senior prom before going off to college, just two miles away from their parents' homes where they stayed until after graduation.

Page's family could have afforded to send her to a more expensive school, but it would've been more difficult for John's. The couple agreed on two things: they loved each other and they wanted to have a family. Nothing else mattered. Good Intents' Community College seemed like the best way to get started.

John, being practical, got his degree in business while Page arbitrarily chose to study art history. Her decision was more of an easy choice to kill time until she and John could be married, but ironically, sparked a pilot light of love for the creative arts. The world of painting, music, and writing opened doors in her mind, briefly, before the roles of wife and motherhood took priority.

Rolling over on his side, John's arm laid limp with the back side of his hand almost touching the ground. He wondered why the life he and Page built turned out not to be enough for her, and why he never saw their marriage's approaching demise. He blamed himself for not paying closer attention to the now obvious warning signs, and not doing something, *anything* about them.

He recalled how cruelly, often maliciously, Page treated him towards the end of their marriage. She once told him during an argument—for which he could not remember the reason—when she became very emotional while he remained unruffled, "If a painting could feel and speak, it would say being painted by you is as arduous as watching paint dry." She told him on a separate occasion that she often cried in bed. When he wouldn't wake to comfort her she would place her fingers on his neck or wrist to check if indeed he had a pulse, or if possibly his veins were fueled by ice.

Their marriage limped along until one day John came home from work to find his wife in the living room, bags packed beside her. She said she wanted a divorce. She told him that Kansas was just Kansas and she wanted Oz. Page said that Carson didn't need her anymore and neither did John. She cited her son's passion and sense of adventure as an excuse to pursue her own—alone. That afternoon, Page moved to California to find herself, with no regard for the wake she left behind.

John's stroll down memory lane made him feel sick. Willing his listless body up, he walked to the ship's port railing. With both elbows stabilizing himself against the polished teak rail, he dangled his head towards the ocean. He wanted to throw up and then the idea of throwing himself overboard occurred. His decision was interrupted by the ship's PA system.

"Good evening, everyone. This is your Captain speaking. I hope all our guests are enjoying themselves on this lovely first night! I just wanted to inform you all that we have a pod of blue whales about to pass our port side. Anyone interested in viewing them will have about ten minutes to do so. It's quite a treat to see them, since they're an endangered species. We slowed a bit to monitor their progress and to be sure we don't get too close. Thank you, and enjoy your evening."

Putting self-pity aside, John lifted his limp head. The moon, low off the port side, sent a beam of light from the horizon to the ship's hull; a white carpet cast across the Atlantic. Five minutes passed as he was caught in its trance when he heard a series of methodical breaches, each one expelling what appeared to be smoke. Clenching his fists, he rubbed both eyes. After his vision adjusted, he realized he was witnessing the family of whales the captain spoke of, and the smoke was not smoke, but salt water spraying twenty feet high in exchange for a breath of fresh air. Somewhere in the brief moments before the whales passed, John found clarity and remembered why he'd come. He'd made a promise, and if nothing else, John was a man of integrity.

He took one last thoughtful breath, rubbed his hands on top of the lacquered wood rail, and began his way back, anxious for sleep. After three tries, the small light on his lock flashed green. Normally, John would have folded his clothes neatly before his bathroom routine of wash, brush, floss, and dress for bed, but he opted to just brush quickly before stripping down to his Wal-Mart boxers. Throwing his clothes on the corner chair, he moved the small chocolate from his pillow to the nightstand and pulled his bedding down. He opened a small compartment in his suitcase, pulled out an envelope, and returned to bed, slowly reading:

"Dad,

Greetings from the sandbox! I can't tell you exactly where I am or what we're doing. I can tell you this place is a suburb of nowhere, and it would probably make the temperature in hell feel like a Chicago winter. I love it though. We're always doing something or going somewhere, keeping us constantly on our toes. I have my good buddy, Sgt. Booty, to keep me company and watch my back.

Anyway, I'm not writing you this time to talk about stuff on my end. I want to talk about you. I know you've been all alone since Mom left. I'm worried about you. I love you both very much, but I'm not worried about mom. She made her choice and I know she's doing just fine out in California. She tells me she's sculpting and even opened a small working studio/gallery. I guess she has her own group of artsy friends who travel all around the west coast doing…well, whatever it is artists do; look at and talk about art, I guess.

I want you to know how much I appreciate all the things you've done for me over the years, and not done, like shelter me from myself. You always trusted me enough to give me the freedom to make and learn from my own mistakes (God knows I made a few). You gave me advice, shared your ideas and beliefs without ever pushing them on me. You instilled and nurtured all the qualities inside me today, attributes responsible for safeguarding me both mentally and physically—along with the lives I contact.

The Army teaches us about courage, honor, respect, and sacrifice. Many of these grunts are learning the definition of these things for the first time in their lives. I can understand why it's imperative that the Army pounds these qualities into soldiers. Armed without these tools in a combat zone is like passing out squirt guns and pacifiers. You (and mom) gift wrapped these tools for me long before the Army, along with something greater—the power of love—in all its many manifestations like trust and forgiveness. You taught me quitting for the right reason is okay, but running away is never acceptable. (My exception to that one is when you're out of bullets in a hot zone outnumbered two to one!) I blame Mom for not learning that lesson. Everything you did in life was done unselfishly for us. Thank you!

Now I'm going to ask you to do one more thing. It's been more than a year since your divorce. I'm deeply sorry for not being able to come home more in that time. I'm sure you needed me. It's clear Mom isn't coming back. It's time for you to find something for yourself. I don't want you to settle for who you think you are. I want you to find out who you can be. We test our potential on a daily basis here. I want you to do that too. And if you can't or won't do that for yourself, then I want you to promise you'll do it for me—your son!

The reality is that we can all bite the bullet at any time. My chances are greater, given my job. If something should happen to me, I want to know it wasn't for nothing and that my father didn't sit on the couch for the rest of his life questioning what went wrong, or what could have been. I want you to be happy and celebrate your life, and mine, even if I'm not here. I want you to…have fun!

I know it's not your forte, so I'm going to get you started. I'll leave the rest up to you. I want you to take a cruise on one of those big, fancy ships I see on TV. We have to get moved around over here from time to time and they often send us hitching a ride with the squids on one of their big aircraft carriers.

These guys live like kings compared to us! They have TV, games, good chow in a real mess hall, and they never have to dig a hole and engage in real combat. Hell, even the Marine pilots often pick up their mail and fly it to the ships after they've flown missions all day. These squids have the luxury of cozying up with the latest edition of Playboy in their racks. Anyway, I figure if life is that good on a Naval ship it must be like Vegas on a cruise ship. So that's what I want you to do, and I want your word. I know if you promise, you'll go. You've earned this. I love you very much, now, and forever.

Always, your son,

SGT. Carson Smith"

John neatly folded the letter, put it back into its envelope, and placed it on the nightstand beside the note from his father. He had answered his son's letter a couple weeks later, promising him that he would do what Carson asked. John regretted procrastinating on that promise when Carson was killed seven months later. But after that, John crawled into a bigger shell than normal, some days barely making it to work. After living that way for six months, he finally began yielding to his nagging conscience and then somebody anonymously sent his ticket. He took the gifted ticket to his travel agency where they helped him book a flight. Two weeks later, he drove to Kansas City and boarded a plane, his third flight ever.

Turning off the bedside lamp, John laid back in bed and spoke six words aloud before closing his eyes: *"I can do this—I promised."*

DAY 2
(SEA DAY)

WAKE UP

JOHN FOUND HIMSELF IN THE middle of the ship's theatre, sitting alone, when the lights suddenly dimmed. A movie began to play on the massive screen hanging from the rafters, previously hidden by a velvet curtain. He couldn't help watching, as the narrator began and the scene played out.

Last-minute FRAGO from the battalion came down at 0330, ordering the support platoon to make another run. Insurgent activity on the rise in a normally calm sub-district makes the mission more precarious.

The platoon sergeant is rallying the men and everyone is on task to accomplish this routine patrol. Sergeant Harmon—nicknamed Booty—is getting the vehicle prepared, having already stored the mandatory case of Rip-Its and a box of power bars.

It's a little past 0600 and already Route Slinky is starting to bustle. Route Slinky is the former Route Miller Lite. The politically correct crowd determined that naming routes after a hard-earned beverage was glorifying alcohol. The fuckards that never see combat, except from a big-screen TV in a tactical operations center, are determined that the hardened NCO's traveling them every day should not glorify the name. Slinky is more than a normal passage for resupply to the combat out-posts; it's the main thoroughfare for commerce to the sub-districts and a target for the Taliban.

The lead vehicle, driven by Booty and co-pilot and good friend Sergeant Smith, slowed as the market people started crossing the street. After morning prayer, the market picked up, and this morning was no different. More carts appeared and people came out of nowhere. The air, filled with the odor of fresh flatbread and unrecognizable slabs of meat, was pouring through the gunner's hatch prompting Booty, who had just chugged a third Rip-It, to open a power bar.

Smoke or fog on the road thickened as the caravan approached the first checkpoint. The lead truck slowed to a stop as the gunner reported seeing people running. The truck commander ordered everyone to shut the fuck up, as he listened to radio chatter in the back of the MRAP. Without warning, machine gun fire pelted the platoon and the truck's gunner started ripping off rounds from the ma-duce fifty caliber.

The vehicle lurched forward and a large IED explosion knocked them on their asses. Dust and smoke filled the cabin and Rip-Its and first aid supplies lay littered everywhere. Booty reached up, which turned out to be sideways because the MRAP lay on the driver's side. Booty's Oakleys were glazed with some sort of fluid. The stench of bad BBQ filled the air and there was pain radiating from Booty's chest and neck.

Booty cut free of the harness using an Army issued blade, fell forward, coughed, and called out to the other truck members. No reply. Seconds passed before reality set in. The doors were locked or damaged, the fluid on Booty's sunglasses was blood, incontinence had occurred, and the hideous smell was burning flesh. Booty's first inclination was to laugh, scream, and cry in unison.

Tac-tac-tac, dong, rattled the vehicle—small arms fire. Sucking deep breaths in order to calm down, Booty reached up for Carson, whose lifeless body was still strapped to the passenger's seat. Booty was helpless as the explosions continued. Smoke and the unbearable stench of burning flesh closed the noose on the last soldier. Booty died filled with regret for not being able to save Sergeant Smith and anger at the gratuitous death on a normal patrol intended to promote communications which could save lives.

John was frozen to the movie theatre chair as if someone had gagged and glued him to it. The credits were rolling when—*Rap-rap-rap.* "Housekeeping."

John shot up in bed, momentarily disoriented. He scurried to answer the door, after retrieving his pants from the corner chair. He got to the door knob at the same time someone was entering their key fob. Opening the door, he locked eyes with a young woman dressed in a housekeeper's uniform.

"Good morning, sir!" she said.

"Morning."

"I'm sorry if I woke you? My name's Silvia and I'll be in charge of keeping your cabin ship-shape while you're here! I came in earlier because the Do Not Disturb sign wasn't hanging on your door. I immediately left after I realized you were still here."

Silvia appeared to be in her early twenties, a bit heavy set, with a full, round face, and black shoulder length hair tied in a ponytail. Silvia turned to say hello to a passing guest and John noticed she had, what appeared to be, a hickey on the lower left side of her neck. She was cute and perky; her personality charged John as if she'd given him a shot of espresso.

"I'm sorry," John said. "I must've forgotten to hang it…what time is it?"

"Eight-thirty," she said, glancing at her watch. "You still have time to eat breakfast in the dining room, or you can enjoy the buffet in the Lido Restaurant until eleven. If you ever want to have breakfast in your room, there's a door tag along with the other ship information on your desk. You just need to hang it the night before—by midnight."

"I don't normally sleep this long. I think I'll just take a quick shower and head for the buffet, so I can clear out of your way, Silvia."

"You're not in my way…I'm sorry, I don't know your name."

"John. John Smith."

"Nice to meet you, John Smith! You do whatever your heart pleases. Let me know if I can help in any way. Just remember to use your door tag and you won't have me bothering you every morning—okay?"

"Thanks. It was nice to meet you, Silvia."

Silvia smiled and waved before returning to her cart. John couldn't detect the origin of her accent. He glanced at her name tag before closing the door—Romania. He had heard of the country before and thought it was in Europe, but probably couldn't find it on an unlabeled globe. Moving into the bathroom for a shower, images of vampires, cold stone castles, and gray, foggy skies above barren trees in a lifeless countryside flashed to mind. He asked himself how such an upbeat girl could come from such a dismal place. *Maybe that's why she came to work on the ship,* he thought. *Maybe she got fed up with gloomy days and obnoxious vampires.* Laughing out loud while shampooing his head, he realized the absurdity of his imagination.

Upon finishing his bathroom routine of shit, shave, shower, brush, floss, John inventoried his sparse, yet complete, wardrobe. The apparel he brought made up twenty-five percent of what he owned: one pair dress slacks, one sport coat, one pair khakis, two pair Khaki shorts, two short-sleeved polo shirts, two dress shirts, seven t-shirts, eight boxers, four pairs socks, a bathing suit, pair of sneakers, and loafers.

Figuring he'd wind up at the pool, he opted for the swim-suit, t-shirt displaying the words: *Kansas Loves Farmers*, and sneakers. He grabbed his ball-cap and Timex before remembering he left the two envelopes from his father and son on the nightstand. After looking at them for a moment, he decided to place them in the drawer. Not wanting to mentally replay his dream, he left the cabin with the hope of a fun day and hung the Please Service sign on the door handle.

GOT GAME?

THE LIDO RESTAURANT WAS BUSTLING like an ant hill pelted with a rock. There were dozens of tables, more than three quarters of which appeared occupied. Employees dressed in Hawaiian shirts were clearing and refilling chafing dishes from the unceasing buffet. Six full plates couldn't carry half the variations of eggs, fruit, and pastries. Separate island stations were manned with cooks in tall chef hats individually preparing omelets, as well as innumerable kinds of pancakes, crepes, and french toast.

John grabbed a plate and filed into the line, his brain struggling to process all the choices. He became confused about what his body needed nutritionally, versus the signals his eyes were sending his brain. Afraid to hold up the other passengers in line, only two sausage links rolled back and forth on his plate when he got to the end. Deciding to regroup, he returned to the beginning and focused on a typical breakfast at home. At the conclusion of his second pass, he was content with another pair of sausage links, two sunny side up eggs, cantaloupe, and wheat toast. He poured a large glass of orange juice and scoured the room for a table.

He chose an empty two-top pushed against the wall. Nearing the end of his first egg, sopping the yellow center with his toast, John sensed he was being watched. He noticed a boy sitting alone at the table just to his left. The two locked eyes as John flashed a friendly smile, before returning to his eggs.

"Can you play?" the boy asked.

"I'm sorry…were you talking to me?" John asked, with raised eyebrows and pointing to the center of his t-shirt.

"People your age don't wear Chuck Taylor's any more, unless they were ball players back in the day. They're making a comeback with my generation though. I don't see too many white ones—purple and orange are more popular," said the boy, staring at John's old Converse All-Stars.

"I used to play with my son when he was around your age—twelve?"

"I just turned thirteen last month," said the boy, proudly.

"My mistake. I should've known you were older. We had a basketball hoop above our garage, but I was never any good—not like my son. As for the shoes, it's nice to know I'm semi-fashionable! I used to wear them when I was a kid, but now-a-days I just like them 'cause you can throw 'em in the washer and dryer."

"Are you here with your *son* on vacation?"

John stopped cutting sausage links.

"No…he…unfortunately, he passed away in the war."

"The one they talk about on the news?"

"Probably. I mean, yes."

"That really sucks. I'm sorry…it must make you sad?"

John was taken aback at how frank and precocious the boy was.

"Sometimes it does, but then I just try to remember all the good times we had. I think about how much I still love him."

"So, did you come here with his mom?"

"No…we're not together any more."

"Divorced! My mom's divorced. That's why we came here, so she and her divorced friends and their kids could all be together. Did you come by yourself?"

Taking a bite of sausage, John looked around to see if anyone was paying attention to the interrogation from young Sherlock Holmes.

"Yes. I came by myself. How about you? Shouldn't you be with your mom, or be playing with her friends' kids?"

"Nah, they're all girls. My mom's with her girlfriends at the pool. She got these so we can stay in touch." He held up a yellow walkie-talkie his mother got from the ship to keep track of her son, while still allowing him freedom to explore. "Mom's friends both have daughters. One's seven, the other's five. They have my baby sister to play with, Jill, she's six. I'm too old to hang around them, plus, guys got to do guy things, especially when we're on vacation—you know. Who wants to hang around a bunch of women when you're on vacation?"

"I know what you mean about the guy thing, but you might find in a year or so that being around a bunch of women on vacation isn't necessarily a bad thing."

"Maybe. You can sit with me if you want? When we're done we can go shoot some hoops. They got a really cool outside court here."

Giving the boy a once over from head to toe, John thought he had a nice look about him, the boy-next-door type. His short blond hair had some kind of glue keeping it spiked up in the front. And the boy's white tee-shirt had a Nike swish with their catch phrase *JUST DO IT* stamped below. The boy seemed lanky for his age, based on his long fingers and how tall he sat above the table, almost looking straight down at his plate. A silver pole protruded from his right-side baggy cargo shorts and a brand new Reebok basketball shoe was fixed to the boys left foot.

High-tech prosthetic, like a miniature ski with a shock absorber, John thought. Not wanting to linger on the exotic stilt too long, he regained eye contact with the boy.

"Sure. Why not." John picked up his plate and moving to the boy's table, he extended his hand before sitting down. "What's your name, son?" he asked.

"Garrett. Garrett Green!"

"I'm John Smith, nice to meet you. That's a cool name. My dad told me once that he thought about naming me Garrett."

"Why didn't he?"

"Well…I guess my mom had more of a say in the matter."

As the two bachelors continued breakfast, John observed the pile on Garrett's plate. It looked as if he'd tried to sample everything. He had pancakes piled on chocolate covered strawberries, french toast on top a western omelet, bangers resting on hash browns, and whipped cream. He seemed oblivious to the mish-mash. John contemplated Garrett's miraculous age.

John finished up his old stand-by breakfast as Garrett cherry picked from his blob. John figured the congealed mess had solidified into one disgusting flavor when Garrett's face conveyed boredom and he stabbed his fork through the heart of what remained.

"You ready to play?" Garrett asked.

"Don't you need some time to digest?"

"Nah…basketball will do that for me. Let's go!" On the way to the door, Garrett stopped at the soda fountain for a last shot of Cherry Coke, guzzling it down quick enough for a fraternity entrance exam, then jogged past John to take the lead. "You from Kansas?"

"How'd you know?"

Glancing back and rolling his eyes, Garrett said, "Your t-shirt!"

"Oh. I forgot!"

"Kansas Jay Hawks rock! They have three national titles. Is that where you went to college?"

"No, I went to a smaller school," John said, trying to keep pace.

"I wanna go to Duke when I go!"

Garrett had to turn his head when he talked because youth and testosterone kept him two full steps in front. John was content to follow.

"You want to play ball there?"

"Who wouldn't? It's the best place in the world to play, even though, UNC produces more pro players than anyone else. I think I could play college ball with my NASA leg, but not at a big school like Duke. Nah, I want to go to Duke to learn nano-science."

"Nana what?"

"Nan-o! It's cutting edge shit that's going to change the world. I guess it would be like the internet was for you."

"What do you do with it?"

"Anything, everything…it's about organizing nano building blocks—anywhere from a few hundred to millions of atoms—into more complex, useful products and tools."

"Sounds above my pay grade."

They arrived at a hut allocating skeet guns, miniature golf equipment, and basketballs.

"Hello!" said the jolly attendant. "How're we doing today, my young friend?"

The chubby attendant's perfect teeth and spiked hair, combined with a pair of white sunglasses, reminded Garrett of a bad actor or cheesy cartoon character. Like most kids his age, he easily disregarded impostors, and this guy was as transparent as wet toilet paper.

"I'm *thirteen* and we would like a basketball!"

John stood with his hands in his pockets watching the basketball caretaker swallow any cute retort to Garrett's emphatic response. John assumed that Peter—from San Francisco, according to his name tag—assumed John was the boy's father and wouldn't risk a sarcastic comeback.

"Of course!" said Peter. "I was actually thinking you were closer to fourteen or fifteen. I shouldn't have called you a young man. Let me get you guys a ball!"

Peter bent down under a counter to retrieve a brand new Wilson basketball as John and Garrett knocked fists like two boxers confirming an impending battle.

"Here we go!" said Peter, handing the ball to Garrett. "Just remember, if it goes over the fence and happens to bounce overboard…don't try to go in after it!" Peter laughed wildly at his own joke.

Garrett glanced at John with a shit-ass grin before responding.

"It's a basketball, it floats. If you guys want it back, we can just pick it up on the way back. My dad's pretty tall. He could just hold you by the ankles while you scooped it up?"

Garrett's contempt caused Peter's pretty teeth to clench behind his artificial, lip-locked smile.

Ostentatiously dribbling, Garrett shifted his attention to John, who still had his hands buried in both bathing suit pockets. "You ready to play, Chuck Taylor?"

"Sure!"

Following Garrett to the blue-coated court—vacant except for a mother and her two daughters running around barefoot—John warmed the muscles of his forty-seven year-old body with toe touches, stretching, and stationary jogging while Garrett bounced around and practiced shooting.

Although John didn't consider himself out of shape, he certainly didn't think of himself as a finely tuned athlete either. It was years since he had really exerted himself, unless bowling counted. By the time Carson turned sixteen, he could beat his father at basketball and everything else they played. His main concern now was to not hurt or embarrass a thirteen year old with a handicap. Dare saying…he'd just take it easy and allow Garrett to have a good time.

"Okay!" John said. "I'm all warmed up. You wanna play horse or something?"

Garrett stopped dribbling and fired a look which implied he wouldn't be patronized. "One-on-one, old man," he said. "First one to ten, each bucket's a point, have to win by two—got it?" Bouncing the ball to John. "Shoot a free throw to see who takes it out."

"You asked for it," John said, frantically pounding the ball before taking aim and letting it fly. *Donk*, sounded the ball, coming up a good six inches short and bouncing back to John's feet from the front rim.

"My ball," Garrett said, stepping up to check the ball to John before taking it out.

Squatting down, Garrett began dribbling between his legs in a figure eight motion that required his feet to rapidly move two feet forward then backward, either foot moving in opposing directions. "You ready for this?" he asked, hypnotizing John with his speed and agility.

"Bring it, little man!" Before the words left John's mouth, Garrett was gone. He made a head fake to the right before slashing back to his left, sending the ball through John's legs with his right hand and retrieving it with his left on a dead run for an easy lay-up.

John never flinched. He was still squatting, face forward, palms up when he noticed the two little blond haired girls giggling and pointing in his direction from the other end of the court. By the time he was scratching his head, Garrett was back in front, dribbling.

"That's one!" Garrett said, standing upright, twirling the ball on his middle finger. "Ready?"

"*Yeah*. I just got caught looking into the sun that time," John said, jumping up and down and shaking his hands free of any tension. "Let's go!"

Garrett checked the ball for the second time.

"Okay…don't worry about the sun this time, 'cause I'm about to make it rain."

The ball never touched the ground. Taunting, Garrett moved the ball around John's face and feet. He planted his left foot while his makeshift foot stabbed six inches forward and back, before one rapid three foot forward thrust, in between John's legs, and back. As Garrett elevated for his shot, John's ass was half way to the ground. Simultaneously, John felt the bruising blow and heard the sound from a pure shot hitting nothing but net—*swish*.

"Not ready to quit yet…are you?" Garrett asked, extending his right hand to help John up.

"Thanks," John said, accepting the sportsmanship. "No, no! I'm just getting warmed up."

"Good. Two nothing, check," Garrett said, bouncing the ball to John.

Garrett high-stepped to his right side with a few dribbles before cutting back to his left. John stayed with him this time, watching the boy's hips instead of concentrating on the ball or Garrett's face. Back and forth, Garrett searched for a window to dart around his opponent, who was working feverishly to side step and block him. John kept his hands in a defensive position, but was afraid to make contact for fear he might hurt the boy. Impatiently, Garrett crossed the ball over to his right hand, lowered his left shoulder, and drove hard into John's left. Two dribbles and a hard upward push with his strong, teenage left leg, gave Garrett a hook shot and his third point.

"Nice shot!" John conceded.

"Thanks! You're moving better. The rubber on those old shoes must be getting warmed up?" Garrett cupped the ball in his right armpit while they took deep breaths and laughed. "Three zip, check."

"Check," John said, still trying to catch his breath.

It took Garrett the better part of a minute for his forth bucket, but only three seconds to register his fifth, after blowing by John, who was clearly still winded from point number four. John got his first chance to touch the ball—other than during the checks— on Garrett's sixth possession after a ten foot jump shot missed and ricocheted into his hands.

Stalling to suck some wind, John said, "You better watch out now. I'm much better on offense."

Standing in front of the foul line with his hands on his hips, Garrett recognized a stonewall when he saw one. "I can't imagine you could be any worse."

"Be careful!" John gasped. "You know what happens when you pull a tiger's tail?"

Shrugging. "You get to watch him run around in circles until he gets dizzy and passes out?"

As slow in a battle of wits as he was in basketball, John decided to focus on scoring a point. "Check!"

The ball hit the ground twice before Garrett's hand swatted it out of bounds.

John scratched his head while Garrett ran off to retrieve the ball.

"Check," John said, not giving Garrett too much time to settle in. He skipped the dribbling and went straight up for a jump shot. For a second he felt optimistic about his stroke, as it had a beautiful arc and path, until it fell short of the rim. Garrett was there to grab the lame duck. One bounce, one easy lay-up, and it was six nothing.

The Caribbean sun was nearing its apex for the day and, even with a constant breeze, the heat was causing both players to perspire. John noticed drips of sweat dropping from Garrett's right short opening, running down the shiny post, and it suddenly reminded John of Carson and the pain he must have endured. During play, John noticed the leg was missing below the knee and wondered if Garrett's shorts were cut so long—two inches below the knee—in order to help hide his prosthetic, or if it was just the latest fashion of shorts to not really be shorts, but just short pants.

"I thought that one was going in…the breeze must have got to it," Garrett said, thinking John could use a boost.

Appreciating the bone, John still felt border-line humiliation. "I thought so too, but the breeze doesn't seem to be hurting any of yours. It's more likely that it was just a weak shot. I think this game *belongs* to you, Garrett."

Garrett stopped bouncing and looked up at the rock climbing wall to his left. After a long pause, he placed the ball at his feet and took a seat.

"I wasn't always as good at basketball as I am now," he declared.

John sat down Indian-style in front. "When did you get so good?"

"After I lost my leg."

"Do you mind me asking how it happened?" John asked, his voice tapering off.

"My dad…he's a big sales guy. You know, like a broker for other people's money and shit. He picked me up from school one day about three years ago. He was talking on his phone the whole way home. He always talks on his phone. Anyway, he went through a pink light—one changing from yellow to red. He never saw the truck that was trying to time the green light—but I did."

"Was your father injured?"

"He had a broken collar bone and some cuts from all the broken glass. The truck—some kind of big work vehicle belonging to the city—struck my side square on."

"You're both lucky to be alive."

"Yes…but it took me a while to understand that."

"What do you mean?"

"My mom and dad got divorced about a year before the accident. Jill was only a baby, but I was nine. I understood what was happening. In some ways, their divorce was harder on me than losing my leg. I got to stay with my dad every other weekend after that, he would pick me up after school on Fridays. Then, after the wreck, when I was in the hospital, they told me I was going to lose my leg. I wished I'd been killed when they told me that. I don't know what it's like to be your age, and I'm sure it would be difficult for anyone to lose an arm or leg at any age, but I can speak for ten year old boys when I tell you—it really blows! I'd rather lose a leg when I'm forty, or sixty, than ten! Us kids use our legs more than older people. You don't need two legs to watch TV or work at a desk."

"You seem like a very confident young man to me. One who has accepted the loss of his limb, and not only making the adjustment, but excelling past the capabilities of other people with similar prosthetics."

"Sure," Garrett laughed, while adjusting the tongue and laces on his sneaker. "But you should've seen me during the six months after the doctors stole my leg. I hated everyone. I blamed the truck driver for jumping the light; I blamed my dad for being on his phone instead of paying attention to the road and me; I blamed my parents for being divorced, 'cause if they weren't, the accident would've never happened. I hated the doctors, because they sucked at operating, or they could've found a way to save my leg. The other kids at school looked and treated me different than they did when I had two good legs, and I hated them all for that. The person I hated the most…was me!"

"Why?" John asked, a perplexed look on his face. "You didn't do anything wrong." "Yeah. I know that now, but not then. I figured someone had it in for me. Made me broken, so I'd never be good enough for anything. I'm five-eight now and one of the tallest kids in my class, but I was one of the smallest before the accident and not very good at sports. When I had two good legs I always sat on the bench, now I'm a starter…funny, huh?"

"What changed?" John asked.

"Well, two things…first, we got a pile of money from the city. They didn't want the bad press from being sued by a family whose ten-year-old lost his leg because one of their employees was in a hurry. That's how I got my Terminator. That's what I call my titanium leg." Garrett rapped on the Terminator. "This is the same brand used by Special Olympic athletes!"

"It looks state-of-the-art," John said, feeling less awkward about staring. "What was the second thing?"

"I got pissed off."

"Excuse me?"

"Yeah, I got pissed! Even after I got the Terminator, I was feeling really sorry for myself. I went through tons of rehab to learn how to use it, which seemed harder than making the starting squad with two good legs. Mom kept telling me that none of it was my fault; not the accident, or the divorce, and although it wasn't fair, what's done, was done. She told me the only power I had was deciding how I was going to let it all affect me. That, she said, was totally up to me."

"Your mom sounds pretty smart."

"Yeah…I didn't think so when I was little, but I do now. She's always been there for me, but as much as I think it hurt her to watch, she never made it easy on me after I got the Terminator. She figured if she coddled me I would never fit in at all, and would just become lazy. I used to scream at her for not helping me more. I used to be really mean and call her terrible names. I regret that."

"I'm sure she forgave you."

"Thanks…I know she has."

"When did you stop being so…how did you finally…"

Garrett grinned, while John searched for the most non-offensive words he could think of. "When did I stop being such an asshole?"

"Okay. When did you stop being *that* guy and become the guy you are now?"

"Oh, I can still be *that* guy, but only when I find humor in it." Garrett admitted.

"Do you want me to throw the ball overboard so you can tell Mr. Smiles we're going to need him on the return trip?"

"I like the way you think, John! He's probably all right. I just hate people who're overly upbeat. They're usually either trained to be that way, or have just never seen any really bad shit go down. So they think they know what's going on based on TV or something. To answer your first question, it was a basketball game at school."

"You mean you found inspiration by watching other kids play ball?"

"No! Well, yeah, but…I guess it turned out that way, but not 'til it really pissed me off first. See, Mom got tired of watching me *veg* in front of the TV, so she tells me one day that she's taking me for ice cream. I love ice cream. Instead, she drives me to my school, parks, and tells me we have to go inside so she can sign some form. So I limp in with a crutch under my left arm, 'cause I can't walk on the Terminator yet without it."

"Your mom's nefarious."

"If that means sneaky as shit—you're right. So, she tells me I have to wait and I should sit in the gym until she's done. I tell her I don't want to be in the gym 'cause there was a game going on. We get to arguing about it, and before I know it, we're inside the gym and she sits me down. I'm feeling really scared and lonely at this point."

"You must've been petrified?"

"Not 'til after Mom takes my crutch and leaves me there."

"She didn't?"

"Yip. She said for me to wait there and she'd be back shortly. She said she was taking the crutch so nobody would steal it…now who the hell steals a ten-year-old, handicapped kid's crutch in the middle of a goddamn basketball game, was what I was thinking—then, she was gone."

"She didn't really leave you there?"

"As far as I knew. Mom told me later, she just hid by the door at the opposite end of the court and asked a teacher to stand by the one closest to me, just in case."

"What happened next?" John asked, sitting with his elbows on his knees, listening closer.

"Well, my first thought was to get up and leave, but that thought scared me more than staying—so I sat and watched the game. The longer I watched, the less scared I got and the more pissed off I got that she'd left me there. Then I got pissed 'cause I didn't have two legs. Then I looked at the kids on the bench. I remember thinking, I should be one of them. A couple more minutes passed before I changed my mind, thinking I shouldn't be on the bench. I should be starting, and playing. Before I knew it, all those thoughts and anger led me to make a decision."

"Which was?"

"I made a decision to leave, and not ever come back unless I was playing. It took some effort, but I propped myself up to a standing position, slowly turned towards the door, and hobbled out to the lobby—*pissed off* inspiring every step."

"Did you thank your mom?"

"Hell no! I was still big-time pissed off at her. She met me in the lobby and tried to apologize. She gave me back my crutch and I threw it against the wall. I told her I never wanted to see another fucking crutch! Afterward, she did take me for ice cream. We didn't talk much, but the ice cream was good. When we got home, I found my ball. I started to learn to walk and dribble again in our driveway that night, every night, until long after dark."

"Wow. That's a great story, Garrett," John said, moved by the boy's perseverance.

"It's my story, so far anyway. We all have one. I know you do." Putting his hands on both sides of the basketball, Garrett stood up with the ball behind his back. "My point is, nothing really *belongs* to us. We usually earn what we get and what we get—we only get to keep for a little while. So…how 'bout we finish this game?"

Pausing, thinking, John stood up and said, "I think we should. Your ball, six nothing?"

"Six zip, check."

As before, points seven and eight favored the young gazelle, but only after John had something to say about it; scrambling back and forth, face-guarding Garrett with his hand, even blocking him with forearms when Garrett tried to lower a shoulder to bully his way around.

"Someone's playing like he's still alive!" Garrett said. "How about it old man?"

"It's not over yet. Eight nothing. Check the ball smart-ass, talk less." John could hardly believe his own words.

"There it is!" Garrett said, again spinning the ball on the tip of his middle finger. "Yeah! The only way to beat the Terminator is to get pissed off! Are you pissed off, old man?"

"The irritating sound of your voice isn't exactly making me feel like laying in a hammock with a cold glass of lemonade…if that's what you're asking?"

"Good! Use that. Check."

Garrett dribbled one time through his legs, shifting to his left hand, then, driving hard to John's right, his young shoulder hit a concrete wall of a left forearm as John's right hand poked the ball from mid-dribble, sending it toward the sideline. After tripping over his own feet, John swam to save it as if he were a drowning man who saw shore. His left hand stopped the ball a foot short of out-of-bounds. Gaining control, he sprinted for an uncontested lay-up—his first point of the game. After the ball passed through the net, John saw Garrett laying on the court.

Rushing. "Garrett! Are you okay?"

Pointing a stern palm while brushing off a skinned knee, Garrett said, "I'm fine! Nice D, nice play."

"I didn't realize I fouled you."

"No foul. You had position and played good strong defense. Now we *both* have learned that motivation doesn't have to come from warm, fuzzy inspiration—*pissed-off* can work just as well!"

Reaching down, John helped Garrett to his feet. Garrett retrieved the ball, walked to the foul line, and handed over the ball in a sportsman-like manner.

"Your ball, eight one," Garrett said.

"What are my odds of scoring two in a row?"

"Slim."

Laughing. "Check."

Attempting a quick jump shot off a three step roll to his right, John served Garrett's next rebound—and ninth point. On this occasion, pissed-off wouldn't be any match for youth and talent. Garrett wasted no time, sinking a final bomb from three point range to end the contest—10-1.

"Wanna play again, John?"

"Sure!"

"Let's do it!"

"You've been reading your own shirt too much. You sure you don't work for Nike?" John smirked.

"I wish!"

The next half hour went by in a sweaty and bloody blur. Mostly Garrett's sweat and John's blood. Now familiar with each other's game, the competition and respect bars were raised; although, when said and done, the score didn't reflect it—10-2 Garrett.

"Thanks for the game," Garrett said.

"No, Garrett, thank you. This was truly my pleasure. You taught me a lot. Your mom made a heck of a gamble, and it really paid off. I wish my own mother was more like yours."

"Yeah, I guess so…thanks. And everyone always thinks someone else's mother is better than their own—everyone but me, that is."

"I would hate to see your mom pissed-off," John said, as they walked over to return the ball to fake Peter. Catching a pensive expression on Garrett's face, he asked, "What is it, Garrett? What's the matter?"

Placing the ball on the counter and slowly turning, Garrett said, "You know, you're right. I've never seen Mom pissed off." Garrett's mind raced, trying to recall a specific occasion. "When I was about five she caught me sneaking cookies before dinner. That made her pretty upset, but not pissed-off."

"What happened when she caught you?"

"That was about the time she taught me to dive. It was a crash course very different than how my friends were taught. Now that I think about it…I should've seen the crutch in the gym lesson coming. You're right, John, I *would* hate to see her pissed off!"

MEET THE GIRLS

ARRETT HAD PROMISED TO MEET his mother by the pool for lunch. On the way, the two new-found friends entertained themselves with a spitting contest off the starboard railing, a contest to see who could spot the most Hawaiian shirts, and they even stopped for a quick game of shuffleboard, which Garrett won. It was as though they had both subconsciously identified and accepted each other, regardless of any short-comings or age differences. John and Garrett shared a common interest. They both wanted and needed to feel like men, and be allowed to play like boys.

It was almost 1:00 when they finally arrived at the pool. The pool, actually a collection of pools and hot tubs, was a teeming oasis. A few of the younger guests, not wanting to be bothered with any clothing, managed to strip down to their birthday suits. Nobody seemed to mind, given their youth, nobody except their parents, who were trying to slather suntan lotion on the little creatures.

For the energetic, there were sliding boards and machine squirt-guns, and shallow wading pools and lounge chairs for those looking to relax with a book, sunbathe, or nap their first evening hangovers away. Those with more delicate skin sat on bar stools in the shade of the overhang on the outdoor bar, sipping ice cold coronas and frozen concoctions made by a team of bartenders at their beckon call. The head of the crew staff—the cruise director—was there organizing such activities as a belly-flop contest. Everyone was having a good time. Even the four man Reggae band, accustomed to playing in the heat, was enjoying the sea of bikinis.

John and Garrett were taking stock of everything when one voice rose above all others—even the band.

"Garrett! Garrett honey! Over here!"

Garrett located his mother's crew about twenty-five feet away. Mom was waving her arms in a conflicting windshield wiper motion. Garrett waved back, before smacking John's arm with the back of his hand.

"Come on," Garrett said.

"What? Nah…that's okay, Garrett. You go be with your family. I'm going for a dip and then maybe grab a fancy drink and relax."

"Bullshit. Come on…come meet the girls. You do like girls, don't you?"

Garrett's question left John ambiguous, not about his preference, but about the duration since he last indulged in the opposite sex.

"Yes, I like women!"

"Well then…sounds like a pretty good deal to have a guy who's no competition, introduce you to three single women—doesn't it?"

"I guess, when you put it that way."

"Good, then you'll come meet them?"

"Yes, but just for a minute or two."

"Whatever," Garrett said, and shook his head back and forth. Garrett had the gift of a wild animal's intuitive sense to smell the slightest amount of fear, and then use that fear before its prey escaped. "You don't have anyone else to share the cruise with. What's the big rush to run off and be alone?" Gently, he asked, "Alone won't bring your family back—will it?"

Garrett's words slapped John twice in the face. The first changed fear into anger; the second, anger into truth.

"I suppose I do have some time to spare," John said, his face melting from grimace to grin. "Just make sure your mother doesn't get pissed-off at me. I don't feel like taking ocean diving lessons, deal?"

"Deal!" Garrett said, punching knuckles to make it official.

Negotiating a jungle of chairs and beach bags, the two arrived at home base. The women had sequestered six lounge chairs in a horseshoe, designating the center two for supplies and a place for any of their girls—who were playing in the pool directly in front of their mothers—to reluctantly sit between romps in the pool. An attractive woman in her late 30's stood waiting to greet her son, while her two girlfriends lay face-up in their bikinis and huge sunglasses.

"There you are!" Garrett's mom opened her arms for a hug. "I was beginning to think you were going to make me eat lunch without you. Did you have fun?"

Quickly hugging his mother, Garrett said, "Yeah, I had one of everything at the buffet and then played ball with John. John, this is my mom, Dani."

"Nice to meet you, John!" Dani said, holding out her hand. "Thanks for entertaining my son! He gets pretty bored with nobody but us girls to hang around with. I hope he didn't drag you away from friends or family?"

Reciprocating the handshake, John said, "Not at all! He's an amazing young man, and I'm actually cruising by myself. I haven't played basketball in years. It was a lot of fun—playing, not the score," John laughed.

"He's pretty good, isn't he?" Dani asked, turning the compliment to Garrett.

"Very," John said. "And he also speaks highly of you."

"That's very nice to hear!" Dani jokingly placed her hand on the side of her mouth so Garrett wouldn't hear. "He doesn't always speak so highly."

"I heard that," Garrett said.

"I'm sorry…John?" Dani asked, flipping her palm over to the two women. "These are my friends, Elli and Buffy. We're all Jersey girls." Still lying back in their lounge chairs, John couldn't tell whether or not they were asleep.

Moving sunglasses to the top of their foreheads, fluttering eyes in the bright light, the two women raised to the introduction as if on stage.

"Hi ya…John? I'm Buffy," said the busty blond.

"Hi ya back," he said, reaching to shake. "Yes! John."

"Elli," the second woman said in a dismissive, *don't bother me*, way. Elli had beautiful, long brown hair and a perfectly tanned and proportioned body.

"It's my…it's very nice to…meet you, you both," John said, excited and nervous at the same time. They were women accustomed to being ogled. But, counter to Elli's stuck-up persona, Buffy stood for a casual hug.

"Did you say you're on vacation by yourself, John?" Dani asked.

"Yes, I'm…I'm divorced."

"Divorced!" Dani exclaimed. "Well hell then, you need to have a drink with us, John. We're all divorced! That's why we're here. All of our divorces are now final. You could say this cruise is a divorce party for us."

"Well…I wouldn't want to…" John turned to Garrett, who squinted back John's fear. "I wouldn't want to bring a *man* element into your divorce party."

"Ah, horse shit!" Dani said. "We don't hate men, John. We just hate our ex-husbands! Let me ask you a question, if you don't mind?"

"Sure."

"Was the reason for your divorce because you cheated or abused your wife?"

"No."

"That's all we need to know! You're more than welcome to be a part of our club then!" she said, firmly patting John's back.

"As long as there's no goofy initiation?"

The three women exchanged glances, then Buffy sat up with her pointer finger in the air.

"Ya half ta kiss a dolphin while wearing a bikini!" Buffy said.

Like so many men before him, John ignored Buffy's imperfections—including her stereotypical, high-pitched, *blonde* voice—because her large boobs more than made up for them.

"Okay," John said. "But, you may have to help me out, Buffy. I didn't bring either."

"What she really meant to say is," Elli interjected, "the price of membership is a round of frozen margaritas."

"Ooooh, with extra shots!" Buffy said.

"Yes!" Elli said. "I almost forgot—with an extra shot for all members of our club."

"I can do that," John said, slapping his hands together. "It sounds easier than the dolphin thing. I'll just go to the bar and be right back."

John didn't have much experience with being worked over by women, so it sounded like a great deal. All he heard from the two women was: *we want you to sit with us and have a drink*, not: *since our friend invited you to stay, buy us some drinks*. All in all, everyone still got what they wanted.

Dani monitored their three girls playing Marco Polo as Elli's eyes followed Garrett to the empty chair beside his mother.

"What's up, little man?" Elli asked.

Grabbing a towel from the supply chair to wipe his sweaty face, Garrett asked, "What do you mean?"

"You're a young stud!" Elli said, sparring with her big toes. "Couldn't you have asked a nice, hot, thirty-something year-old guy to play ball, instead of farmer John? You're like our mascot. You're in charge of screening the eligible, hot, rich men for your mom and her best friends."

Dani's head spun back across her shoulder. "That's enough of that," she said.

"What?" Elli asked, throwing her hands in the air.

"I won't stand for you using my son as your pimp."

"I was just joking with him, Dani, you don't have to get upset."

"If your ex-husband was here using Brie to meet women, you'd be upset. Right?"

"Knowing that prick, he probably would," Elli said, going back to playing with her toes.

"In a nerdy way, I think he's really nice," Buffy said. "And he *is* buying us drinks!"

"Garrett, what do you know about this guy?" Dani asked, placing her hand on Garrett's knee as the three women awaited his answer. "Is he okay or what?"

Looking his mom in the eyes, Garrett said, "He's from Kansas, he's divorced, and his son died in the war. He's not a great dresser or basketball player, but he seems honest. He listens and tries real hard." Glaring at Elli. "Isn't that what really matters?"

"Yes, it is…isn't it, Elli?" Dani asked.

"All I'm saying is, the guy looks a little suspect is all," Elli said.

"I think he sounds really nice," Buffy said.

"Oh shut-up, Buffy; you think anyone who buys you a drink is nice," Elli said, rolling eyes behind her sunglasses.

"That's not true!" Buffy said. Everyone, including Garrett, looked at her suspiciously. "Well… maybe it's true," she slowly conceded. "But a lot of nice guys have bought me drinks."

The laughter died down when Garrett pointed at John, who was giving the impression of walking a tightrope while carrying a cocktail tray filled with drinks. With eyes center-tray fixated, John still had twenty feet to cope with until returning safely to the nest.

Dani rushed to John's aid and said, "Let me help you, John. I'm sorry, I should've come with you!"

"No need, but thank you," he said. "I just didn't want to be the idiot who dropped a tray full of drinks on someone," he admitted, beads of sweat running down his forehead. Dani handed two frozen margaritas to Buffy and Elli. When she returned to the tray, John was sucking his straw to keep the melting booze from spilling over. "I got you a virgin strawberry daiquiri, Garrett. I hope that's all right?"

"Thanks!" Garrett said, as Dani handed him the drink.

"Why's there a plastic thingy in my drink?" Buffy asked.

"That's your extra shot of tequila, you cheesy-poof!" Elli said.

"Pretty cool, huh?" John said, pulling the plastic test tube full of *Cuervo* in and out of his drink. "The extra shot seeps in while you drink."

"Buffy, help Garrett clear our crap off that chair so John can sit down," Dani said.

Turning and lifting her sunglasses just above her eyes, Elli said, "Yeah Buffy, plow a place for him to sit."

"Huh?" Buffy asked.

Elli thought she'd spoken too softly for John to hear, although she didn't care one way or the other. Garrett finished clearing the chair while John stood sipping.

"My t-shirt, Buffy," John said, pointing to his chest. "I think she was making fun of me by using the word plow, because of my *Kansas Loves Farmers* shirt."

John's explanation caused the hamster in Buffy's cage to wake up and peddle. "Oh, I get it now!" she said. "You're a farmer?"

"No," John said, sitting down and leaning back like everyone else. "But, I can certainly understand why you'd think I *was* based on my t-shirt selection," he chuckled.

"What do you do, John?" Dani asked.

"I'm a production manager for a company that makes rubber bands, various types of paper clips, and those hairbands like Elli has in her hair," he said, double checking Elli's scrunchy. "It looks like one of ours."

"What an obscure job," Dani said. "Pretty cool!"

In one fast move, Elli removed the band from her hair, combed with her fingers, and retied. "This tie was twenty dollars," she said. "It's a Donna Karan."

John's test tube was empty and already he was down to his last couple ounces of margarita. Not what one would call a heavy drinker, he could feel the effects from the substitution of alcohol for water in an already dehydrated, over-exercised body.

"Are you friends with her?" John asked.

"Who?" Elli asked, assuming the slurping farmer was talking to her.

"That woman with two first names," he said.

"No, I'm not friends with Donna Karan. Why?"

"Well, it just seems odd that you would give someone whom you're not even friends with twenty dollars to stamp her initials on a product we sold her for seventy-five cents."

Infuriated, Elli said, "This hair band is not from Kansas. It's from New York!"

Taking another long sip, John said, "This Karen woman must have her logo somewhere on your hairband—right?"

"Of course," Elli huffed.

"Take a look and see if it says anything else."

Everyone waited anxiously as Elli removed the hairband. She carefully examined the band, making a point to show everyone where it said DKNY (Donna Karan, New York). "See."

"Very nice—big letters, very well printed," John stated, with no intentional sarcasm. "Are there any more letters anywhere—maybe really tiny?"

Lifting her sunglasses to the top of her head and holding the band close enough for an almost surgical examination, Elli said, "The only other thing I see is the word kit."

"Yip, one of ours!" John said, sucking wet air.

"Really?" Buffy asked. "Is that like Kit-Kat?"

"No, actually it stands for Keep It Together, Buffy. That's the name of the company I work for—a totally different company than the one that makes those delicious candy bars."

"They are yummy, aren't they?" Buffy relished. "My daughter, Kayla, loves them as much as I do."

Everyone, except Elli, shared a good chuckle at Buffy's innocent confession. Instead, Elli pulled her sunglasses down, shielding the bitter defeat in her eyes. Glancing over, John sensed a glare from behind her dark shades, but between the alcohol and a sense of pride in his company, he didn't care.

"My margarita seems to have disappeared in this heat," John said. "I'm going to get the D triple G's another round!"

"What are the D triple G's, John?" Dani asked.

"Divorced girls and guys group—our club," John said.

"I love clubs!" Buffy said. "So we can be the DG's? Oh my God, I just realized, my sunglasses have a D and a G on them! It's like already having the right uniform for our club. Elli, you have Dolce & Gabbana too! Isn't that awesome?"

Sliding her middle and forefingers under her sunglasses to rub, Elli said, "Yeah Buffy, that's fucking great."

Dani, more practical with her spending, pulled down her powder blue Oakley's and looked at Buffy. "I like the name, but I'm not wasting three-hundred-dollars on designer sunglasses, so you'll just have to make John and me t-shirts or something if you want uniforms. Right, John?"

"I'm with Dani," John squinted. "I forgot to even pack sunglasses, much less own a pair with a DG on them."

Elli, feeling like John had belittled her in front of her friends, said, "You mean you didn't get a free pair of goggles or a welder's mask with that t-shirt?"

"John…I think another round is a great idea, but it's my turn to buy," Dani said. "Why don't we go to the bar together? That way we won't need a tray this time."

"Sounds good," John said.

Dani popped straight up from her seat, while John's middle-aged body, relaxed from exercise and tequila, required extra seconds.

"Garrett, will you keep an eye on your sister and the girls for me?"

"Sure, Mom," Garrett said, unstrapping his Terminator. "I was getting in the pool anyway."

"Thank you, my love," Dani said, kissing her son's forehead.

John watched Garrett remove his Terminator, thinking the routine wasn't that different from any thirteen-year-old getting ready for a swim. Standing up on one leg, Garrett pulled his shorts down, revealing swim trunks underneath. Once the shorts hit the floor, he took one hop to free his foot, pulled his t-shirt overhead, and hopped to the pool's edge, where he sat, stirring his foot in the water, before thrusting his upper body into the pool. John thought Garrett was like a baby duck, a little ungainly on shore, but when he reached the water, he maneuvered with the same grace that he exuded on the basketball court.

"You ready, John?" Dani asked.

Snapping his head away from Garrett, John said, "Ready!"

After ten feet, Dani said, "Damn, John, I forgot my charge card…how about you get a head start on our order while I go back and grab it—okay?"

"Okay," John said. "Meet you at the bar."

Waiting a moment until John continued on, Dani turned back. "Listen," she said, standing over Elli. "I don't like the fact that you're being a total bitch to this guy."

Elli, squishing her back farther into the chair, played dumb and asked, "Farmer John?"

Dani, pulling her sunglasses off and using them to point, said, "Look! Just because your ex-husband was a dick to you doesn't mean all men are dicks!"

"Dani, this guy's a total geek. He didn't even bring sunglasses on a cruise to the Caribbean," Elli said.

"You might wanna be careful how you judge people, Elli," Dani said. "I didn't always look like this. Ten years ago, I had your sweet twenty-nine-year-old body," she said, panning a hand from Elli's head to feet.

"What are you talking about?" Elli asked. "You look great!"

"*Yeah*, well…I'm just saying—I don't look like I used to given my age and having two children. I would kill for Buffy's tits!"

Buffy had sat up, but remained quiet when Dani started her tirade with Elli.

"You don't need to kill anyone," Buffy said. "Just go see Dr. Robinson! They're five grand. He's awesome!"

"I'll pass," Dani said. "I don't need Dr. Robinson's magic scalpel to make me feel like I'm an attractive, confident woman. I'm just saying…all our husbands cheated on us, and maybe—and I cringe at the thought—some of the blame should fall on us?"

"Are you f-ing kidding me?" Elli asked.

"Well, we're the ones that chose to marry them, and maybe; and I'm just saying a maybe, we're partly to blame for their cheating? Or maybe, we were too blinded by their charms, money, or bodies to see that they never changed—maybe they were always cheaters?"

Dani's remark caused Buffy's brain gears to grind and smoke.

"I never did anything to cause Jake to cheat on me!" Elli said.

"And maybe that's true, but unless you want to sleep alone with your settlement money and the illusion that you're always going to look beautiful to twenty-year-old sexual robots...you might want to learn to give men a chance, not just those who look like Brad Pitt," Dani said.

"Whatever," Elli said, under her breath.

"You know...Garrett thinks this guy's all right, and that's enough for me to give the guy a chance. You have a daughter, Elli. You might want to consider what's good for her, not just yourself. Never mind; I spoke my peace. I'm going to get our drinks. All I ask is when we get back, you try to be nice...for our kid's sake, if nothing else, okay?"

Buffy nodded while Elli pulled out her plastic test tube and chugged.

SO YOU'RE AMERICAN?

D ANI ALWAYS TRIED TO APPEASE everyone, even though Garrett's love was enough for her. She believed that it was important for her to put forth effort with everyone she came in contact with—even if that effort turned around and bit her in the ass. Then she at least had the satisfaction of knowing she'd tried.

Somewhere over the course of her adult life and ten year marriage, Dani formulated a system—a sort of code to live by. Strangers received one strike before she stopped trying, friends and casual acquaintances got two—she felt Elli had just burned a half a strike—and husbands obviously got three strikes: one for a flight attendant, one for a member of the PTA, and one for neglect of a son and wife. After her divorce she mentally amended her husband rule to only two strikes for serious mistakes; abuse or infidelity, however, were now a one strike you're out rule.

Dani could see John hunched over the bar as she made her approach. All the seats were taken by serious drinkers trying to either avoid or find someone. John was squirmed into a small opening between the last seat and the wall, just enough space to rest his elbows on the bar top and be noticed.

Tapping John's shoulder, she waited for him to look back at her. "Hey there, stranger. Sorry I took so long."

"Hey!" he said. "Being a member of the DG's means never having to say you're sorry."

"Never?"

"Okay…almost never. It's a nice idea though."

Dani squeezed sideways between the guy sitting on the last bar stool and John, inadvertently pushing her small but shapely breasts against John's bicep. "Did you order yet? I got my card. This one's on me…and I'm really sorry for my rude friend."

John's first instinct was to move away from her personal parts, but the wall his back was now pressed against prohibited it; a logistic which he was happy to endure.

"Ah, I haven't ordered yet. The bartenders seem a little preoccupied with juggling bottles," he said, pointing at the bar staff without moving his arm away from the soft comfort of Dani's chest. "And, as far as your friend goes…don't worry about it. Although, I did wonder if I did something to upset her, or if she's just naturally—"

"A bitch?"

"I was going to say *snooty*. She doesn't seem as happy as you and Buffy, or your son for that matter, who's terrific by the way! You must be very proud of the way he handled his adversity and at such a young age. It's amazing."

"Thanks, John. He *is* a great kid, isn't he," she said, gazing down for a moment. "Garrett and I have learned—in our own ways—the certainty that adversity finds us all. There are only three unknowns about that fact: how many times, when, and what you do with it when it crashes your party. You know?"

Nodding. "Yes, I'm afraid I do."

Clenching her lips together. "The thing I don't think most people get is, *we* decide if adversity makes us better, or worse."

"You really think it's a choice?"

"Sure do. If you take something away from somebody, John, what does that leave them?"

Thinking a second about Carson. "Loss…a void, I guess."

"Loss, yes, a void in the interim, but every loss leaves behind a gift."

"What gift could loss possibly leave?"

"Opportunity! Garrett learned to use the loss of his leg as an opportunity to finally work hard enough to not only make the basketball team, but to be a damn fine starter. It's also made him more out-going with people than he ever was with two legs. He lost a proper dad in the divorce, and I lost a husband. We've learned to use that as an opportunity to be closer as mother and son, and I've learned to go after better things without settling, like I did when I was married to my ex. That's the problem with Elli…she allowed herself to be trapped in the bitterness of her loss when her husband cheated. She thinks all the money she got in the divorce will make her happy, which it obviously hasn't, instead of using the opportunity divorce gave her to find a way to replace her resentment with some sort of real confidence."

"I wish I had your courage," John sighed.

"If I were a betting woman, which I am—I won five hundred at the Kentucky derby last year—I would bet you have more courage than you know."

"You don't even know me. Why would you take that bet?"

"You're here aren't you? I don't think many guys from Kansas would ever be brave enough to take a cruise by themselves. Plus, I've never seen anyone put Elli in her place like you just did," Dani laughed.

"I think the tequila had something to do with that. And the fact that the way she spoke to me reminded me of how my wife used to treat me, before she asked for a divorce. Page used to say vanilla ice cream looked like rocky road compared to me."

"Fuck her, John! Let's drink to the opportunity she gave you." Dani's shoulders turned square to the bar, pushing John tighter to the wall, and squeezing the man to her left, half way off his bar stool.

"Excuse me," he muttered.

Realizing her discourtesy, Dani faced the man to apologize. "I'm sorry. I didn't mean to bump you. My friend and I are just trying to get some drinks and I think these bartenders are more concerned with performing bottle tricks than they are with serving us thirsty passengers," she said, thinking a little passenger camaraderie would alleviate any foul her bikini top couldn't.

Swiveling, the man glanced at Dani's face before rudely dropping his eyes to her purple bikini top. "That's okay, señorita! I love to be *bumped* by a beautiful woman. How about letting *me* buy *you* a drink?"

"Aw, that's really sweet of you, but we'll get our own," she said, jabbing her thumb backward. "Besides, we're getting a round for our whole group. They're waiting on us right now by the pool, but thanks," she said, patting him two times lightly on his shoulder before assuming her position at the bar top.

The man glanced at Dani's left hand, noticing the absence of any ring, then swiveled more to survey John. John threw the man a fake, close-lipped smile. He intentionally dismissed John with a pithy once over and a sharp *"huh."* Afterward, he got up from the bar stool and huffed off.

Watching as the man retreated, John noticed he was tall, taller than John by several inches. Shirtless, with board shorts, a Miami Heat cap, leather sandals, and a heavy silver watch hanging loosely from his wrist, he appeared to be in his early fifties. What really captured John's attention was a tattoo on the man's thick right bicep, actually three tattoo's dropping vertically; Chinese symbols that formed some kind of sentence, or possible warning.

Hopping up on the vacant bar stool, Dani liberated John from the corner. "That guy was a total player, but at least he was good for a seat," she said, happy about her prize.

"What's he play?" John asked.

"You know, a guy who hits on women just to get notches on his bed post. An egocentric troglodyte—player!"

"*Oh*," John said, feeling old and out-of-the-loop for not knowing the term. "I guess I've always been more of a watcher," he admitted.

Finding John's disclosure both refreshingly cute and empowering as a woman, she said, "That's a good thing, John. You know they say that good things come to those who watch."

"I thought that was wait?"

"No, wait implies doing nothing at all. Watching is better!"

"That's a relief," he said, wiping his forehead with the back of his hand. "It's nice to learn I've been doing something right."

The two laughed, followed by an awkward stare, as if an invisible force suddenly pulled their eyes together.

"Hey!" said an upbeat voice. "When did I get here?"

Turning, John and Dani saw the bartender waiting with his arms crossed, resting on the bar top like a little brother breaking up his older sibling's romantic moment.

"What?" Dani asked.

"Sorry," said the bartender. "It's a little phrase my friends and I use to amuse ourselves, usually when we're drunk. You know, you already know when you or your mates *got there*, but you still act surprised. Or, you can use it to welcome the arrival of your buzz. A few drinks, bang, when did I get here? Get it?" he beamed.

"Actually, I think I do," Dani said. "I like it!"

The bartender looked back and forth at them. "In this particular case, I used it sarcastically to try and make up for the fact that you both had to wait so long for a drink. It's a great little saying you can use in almost any situation," he said, as if teaching a class.

"How did you know we were waiting a long time for a drink?" John asked.

"There's only one person who knows more than a bartender," he replied, pausing to make the sign of the cross. "Do you know why God made bartenders?"

"Why?" Dani asked.

Staring at Dani. "Because he gave up trying to make a perfect woman. But you seem to be pretty damn lucky, my man, because this woman looks about as close as God could get."

Despite the bartender's plastic line, his flawless delivery caused Dani to blush. "Oh, I bet you get laid a lot," she said.

Smirking. "There've been occasions when I've had the pleasure of deeply knowing beautiful women."

"I bet!" she said.

"My name's Will, Will Catcher!" he said, extending his hand. "And you are?"

"I'm Dani and this is John."

"Nice to meet you both!"

"That's a pretty interesting name," John said.

"Thanks! Yeah, my parents had a sense of humor, all right. The deal is…anything thrown in my general area, I *will-catch-'er*," he said, holding up the palms of his hands. "That's kind of why you had to wait so long. Those women at the other end of the bar wanted to see if I could flip the bottles. I'm not a fan of it, since it wastes booze and time, but the guests like it. I've had enough dead time behind the bar over the years to learn how to do it for my own amusement, like Tiger Woods bouncing a golf ball off his putter-head while he waits to tee-off. Anyway, my bosses like it because everything's a show on the cruise lines." Will grabbed a bottle of liquor from the speed well. Throwing it end over end, and, true to his name, catching it with his opposite hand and finishing with a bow, earning applause from John and Dani.

"Most impressive, Mr. Catcher," Dani said, still clapping. "Your parents picked the right name for you."

"Thank you, dear! Now…what sort of refreshing libations will you be drinking today?"

"We would like four frozen margaritas," John said, holding up four fingers.

"With extra shots!" Dani demanded.

"Yes, with an extra shot for each," John agreed.

Snapping his fingers and pointing, Will said, "Excellent choice! It's perfect weather for drinking Alpine Mexicans with extra gas. I'll go downstairs to the freezer to whip-up a batch." Will turned to his right and pretended to walk downstairs, squatting down farther with each comical step, moving his head and arms in a pigeon motion. When he shrunk as low as he could go, he shot straight up in the air, arms raised. "There's a trampoline down there!"

Every guest at the bar howled at Will's animated absurdity. After taking another bow, Will walked over to the large igloo coolers where the bartenders had pre-made gallons of piña colada, strawberry daiquiri, and margarita mix. He poured a healthy shot of tequila into the bottom of four cups, scooping the slushy margarita mix on top. One-by-one he filled plastic test tubes with extra shots, stabbing them into the middle of each drink. They smoked like dry ice as the melting slush burned off into white mist. A wedge of lime and a straw completed the frozen concoction.

John and Dani studied Will as he made two trips to deliver their drinks. He looked to be six foot and built like a linebacker. John took Will for late 30s, early 40s. He was a man's-man, but a boyish face helped hide his devilish traits. He wore a thin goatee, looking more like manicured stubble. His dark hair was clean cut. A set of playful, almost baby-like eyes sealed the deal, making it nearly impossible for any female *not* to trust him. He was chewing gum, but trying to hide it by keeping it in his back tooth and only using enough chewing motion to make a mime proud. John detected a slight southern accent and a modest break or slowness in stringing complete sentences together. It was as though the words took a second to reach his mouth the way soda cans drop from a machine. John made a point to read his name tag: Will Catcher, United States.

Placing the second pair of drinks on the bar, Will said, "There you go kids, four brain slushies, guaranteed to keep the heat away—and anything else you don't want!"

"So, I see you're American?" John asked.

"Yezzir! Born and raised."

"What part?" John asked.

"Well…," Will said, chuckling and scratching his head. "The womb."

"Where?" Dani asked, looking confused.

"The womb," Will repeated, while making a crescent motion over his belly.

"Okay smart-ass, what state are you from?" she asked.

Chuckling again. "The state of inebriation."

"You have an answer for everything, don't you?" she asked.

"When you talk with dozens of people, day-in and day-out, who all ask similar questions about the W's—who, what, where, when, why—one learns to fabricate some creative answers to relieve some of the monotony."

"Fair enough," Dani conceded.

"The answer to John's question is that I was born in Kansas, but from the time I was ten on, we moved around a lot 'cause my dad was an Army colonel. So, I know most people want a straight-forward answer, but it's a little gray to me."

"I'm from Kansas!" John said, shooting up into perfect posture.

"Yeah…I figured," Will said.

"Why? Did I do something that you recognized from your time there? Something only someone from Kansas would do?"

"Yes and no," Will said, circling his chest. "I don't know too many people who would wear that t-shirt, unless they were actually from there. But you never know. I have a *Virginia is For Lovers* shirt, and I'm not from there."

Dani snorted in the midst of a long draw from her drink, patting John's back as he pulled his t-shirt out by his nipples and read the saying upside-down.

"I guess I should've put more thought into packing for this trip, 'cause I'm never going to hear the end of this t-shirt," he laughed.

"Not at all, my friend," Will consoled. "I love your shirt. And I love t-shirts! T-shirts represent who we are, where we've been, and what we believe in. They cut to the chase, saving others the time to read between the lines—pun intended. I would buy that shirt. I've been there. That phrase, *Kansas Loves Farmers,* is a statement of pride from the people who live there and do so much work for the rest of the country. We should be proud of every state in this country and what they all contribute collectively to make up the good old U S of A!"

"Well said, Catcher!" Dani said.

Turning to Dani, John said, "Okay, what would your t-shirt say, Dani? Give."

Still giggling, Dani took another long sip before answering. "We live in New Jersey, and I guess if I were to own a t-shirt about my state, it would say: *New Jersey, Too Proud to Want to Be New York, Not Proud Enough to Not Work There."*

Hunched over in laughter, Will and John slapped the bar top. After gathering some composure, Will helped the other two bartenders with the compounding drink orders. Five minutes later, when the staff was caught up, Will returned with an intent look.

"Hello again, my friends," he said. "How are the south of the border snowballs treating you?"

With only a quarter of their drinks remaining, John and Dani were nearing intoxication by the time Will returned. Anything he said would've triggered hysteria. Waiting for their cackles to subside. "Back to the t-shirt thing," Will said, pausing for another wave of laughter to subside. "My favorite t-shirt reads with a phrase I live by."

John and Dani looked up like dogs waiting for their owner to throw a tennis ball. "I can't wait to hear this," Dani said.

"What's the t-shirt say?" John asked, seriously interested.

Leaning over the bar as if he were about to give up a secret, Will said, "Pay very close attention to what I'm about to tell you, because it might save your lives. The one quintessential, life-saving, game changing, motivational, imperative; a nonnegotiable certainty in life, is this: *U Got to Have U Some Fun.*"

"Amen," Dani said.

John froze in utter dumbfounded silence. With his sermon complete, Will rapped his knuckles one time before walking down the bar to help the next passenger.

WHEN IT RAINS

DANI LISTENED TO HER SON'S voice. "Garrett to mom—over. Where's the drinks?—over. We're all hungry—over." Frantically rooting through her bag to find the walkie-talkie. "Mom to Garrett—over."

"What's taking you so long? Buffy and Elli are bitching about where their drinks are and everyone's hungry—over."

"I'm so sorry, honey. Tell everyone I'll be right there. The bar's really busy and it took us a long time to get our drinks—over."

"True that—over and out."

Returning the walkie-talkie to her bag and hopping off her bar stool. "We've got to get back, John. Everyone's—"

"Yes, I heard," John said. "These things make it easy to lose track of time," he said, biting his straw.

"Where's Will? I need my—" Will suddenly appeared with Dani's charge-card, receipt, and a pen. "Check. You must've been reading my mind," she said.

"It's my job," Will smiled. "And my pleasure."

"Thanks," Dani said. "We have to—"

"I recommend Motown Burger & Malt Shop, port side, just beyond the pool," Will pointed. "It's like an old drive-in, without being able to actually drive-in of course. Excellent burgers and shakes!"

Amazed, Dani stared a moment before turning to John. "John, would you like to come to lunch with us?"

"I'd love to, but you should be with your friends and family. Besides, I think it'll make Elli happy if I'm not there."

Sighing. "I have an idea!" Dani said. "How about I take the drinks back and go with them to lunch, and then I'll come back here for another drink? If you want to save my seat, that is?" She fluttered her eyelashes.

"Sounds great! I have my fellow Kansan to keep me company." Turning to Will as if to ask if that was okay.

Thumbs up. "I'll look after him and we'll make sure you have a place. Even if we have to throw somebody overboard!"

Laying his right arm over the bar and continuing to suck on his drink with his left, John felt Will gently place something under his hand as Dani spoke.

"John, can I bring you back a burger and fries from Motown's? You really shouldn't just eat margaritas all day."

"That would be lovely," he slurred.

Giggling at John, Dani said, "Great, that's settled. Now, if I can just get a…" Will closed John's right hand around the tray he'd placed underneath. John, raising his hand slightly, inadvertently offered the wobbling tray to Dani. "A tray," she finished, eyes racing back and forth between the two shit-grinning men. "I've never found *one* man who could read my mind, much less *two*," she blushed. "You boys are pretty good. You'd both do quite well trapped on a deserted island with a woman's volleyball team."

Winking at John, Will helped Dani place drinks on the tray. "Enjoy your lunch," Will said.

"Thank you, boys. See you soon!" As Dani walked away, John and Will watched as she balanced the tray easily with one palm. She sensed that the two men were following her with their gaze. She allowed her hips to sway more freely than normal.

Slapping John's hand again. "That's a beautiful woman, John."

"Yes, she is—very."

"Is she your girlfriend?" Will asked, playing dumb. His years behind the bar taught him to recognize the difference between real couples and people who'd just met.

"No, no. We just met. Actually, I met her son at breakfast—great kid—has a prosthetic leg. Anyway, he kicked my butt pretty good at basketball and then we came back here so he could join his mother for lunch. Dani's here with her son Garrett and her daughter, and two of Dani's girlfriends and *their* two daughters. The three women are celebrating their divorces together."

"How old is the son?"

"A mature thirteen."

"How old are the daughters?"

"Five, six, and seven."

"No wonder he asked you to play ball. I would hate to be thirteen again and be trapped with my baby sister, her friends, and their mothers!"

"Yeah, I guess when you put it that way...I wouldn't either."

"How about a glass of water, John? It's something people forget to do when they're in this heat and drinking alcohol. I've seen my share of people pass out from dehydration and wake up with nasty sunburns."

"Sounds like a great idea. Thanks, Will."

Pouring a cup of water from the soda gun. "Here you go, my friend."

John guzzled half the cup. "Will, I need to use the bathroom. I know it's busy, but is there any way to save my seats?"

"Sure, John. I got you! The bathroom's right around there." Pointing to the corner where John had been sitting.

After a much needed bathroom break, John rested against the starboard railing to watch the whitecaps from cresting waves. A flock of gulls dive-bombed into a school of fish not a hundred feet from the ship's hull. John looked up to the forward sky, admiring the purple and gray cloud bank awaiting *The Princess*. "How did Carson get me here?" he asked. "I miss you, son," he added, before returning to the bar.

Side-saddling onto his bar stool, John found a piña colada beside his cup of water. A coaster rested on top of the cup with the words: "Beware, don't sit here, Big John's seat," written in black marker. Flagging Will, John said, "Will. Will! Whose drink is this?"

Will's head was down, focused on the old fashioned he was muddling, but he still heard and saw everything. "That's yours, John," he said, never lifting his head. "It's from the lady."

"Lady? What lady?"

"This lady, Mr. Smith," a voice said from behind.

John whipped around. She wore a black one-piece bathing suit. Her curves stretched it in all the right places, putting every bikini at the pool to shame. Her beautiful hat provided enough shade for anyone within two feet, and even in the casual atmosphere of the pool, she wore a pair of deadly stilettos.

Removing her dark sunglasses, revealing her rich coffee colored eyes, Rita asked, "Is this seat taken?" A modest grin exposed a small dimple just to the left of her mouth.

Every nerve in John's body sprang to life, injecting an antidote that counteracted the remaining booze in his system. Hypnotically, John stared, his powers of speech stymied by a body on overload. And, when he tried to force speech, the sky suddenly ripped open and bled marble-sized rain.

Rita, unfazed by her obvious effect on him, deliberately walked forward to the protection of the bar's overhang, placed her drink on the bar, removed her hat, and sat her rear on the vacant bar stool to John's right. "That's quite a squall, eh, John?"

"It sure is," John replied, still in shock from seeing Rita. "How did you..."

"I was tanning over there," she pointed with her eyes. "I saw you sitting here, so I had the cocktail waitress send you one of these marvelous piña coladas. They're just heaven, John. Did you try yours yet?"

"No...no, not yet." John blindly reached for the drink, his eyes still locked on Rita, who was admiring the rain. Locating the cup, he pulled it under his chin. After poking himself a couple of times with the straw, he finally found the opening of his mouth.

"What do you think?" A perplexed look on her face.

"You were right...it's delicious."

"Are you sure it doesn't taste a bit watered down?"

The puzzled expression on Rita's face snapped John from his trance. Lifting the cup to eye level, he saw a blurred Rita through the clear liquid. "I didn't think it was as good as you'd bragged, but I was trying to be polite," he said, trying to act cool, exchanging his water for the piña colada.

"How's your cruise treating you, John?"

"It's been really good, so far. I met a bunch of nice people, including a kid I played basketball with this morning. The bartender here is a real character. Very entertaining, and he's also originally from Kansas—of all places! How's your cruise, Rita?"

A look of malaise came over Rita's face. "It's requiring more effort than I care to render on vacation," she said, gazing out into the rain.

John fidgeted in his seat, not knowing if she wanted him to dwell on the vague statement. Instead, he looked away, at the remaining passengers leaving the pool. Even the bar had emptied to just a half dozen guests. Out of the corner of his eye, he spotted a woman running towards the bar. She had a towel over her head and shoulders, protecting the tray of food she carried.

Dani ran the entire way to the bar, simultaneously hopping up on the empty stool to John's left, while slamming the tray on the bar top. Removing the towel, she began drying herself. "Whew!" she giggled, an invigorated look on her face. "Where did that come from? It was bright and sunny when I left."

"We sailed right into it," John said.

Dry enough, Dani placed the towel over her bare thighs. "That was quite refreshing, actually. Here's the burger I promised. I got cheese on it, hope that's okay?" she asked, sliding the tray in front of John.

"I love cheese. Thank you so much for braving the rain. You really shouldn't have," he said, picking up a fry and chewing.

Rita eyed Will who stood watching their little group like a cat who had just swallowed the family's prized parrot. When John continued facing forward, mulling his fries without introducing the two women, Rita subtly cleared her throat. But it took two more forceful attempts to get John's attention.

"I'm so sorry," John coughed. "Where are my manners? Dani, this is Rita. Rita, this is Dani," he introduced, then leaned back in his stool as the women exchanged handshakes across his lap.

"It's nice to meet you, Rita?" A look of confused amusement on Dani's face.

"The pleasure's all mine," Rita said.

John's eyes flailed through the empty back bar, desperately searching for a friend. Will's gaze latched on, as if saying, "It's okay, just breathe. I'm here to help."

"Are you…a friend of John's?" Dani asked.

"We met yesterday—at embarkation," Rita said. "I almost killed him with my shoe!" Both women consoled John with pats on his back.

"That's not so bad," Dani said. "My son kidnapped him from breakfast and then threw him in the middle of a group of bitter divorcees."

"Sounds like you've really earned a good cheese burger and piña colada today, how 'bout it, John?" Rita chuckled.

As if on cue, Will stopped cutting fruit and shot to center stage. "Good afternoon, everyone! And welcome to the shower bar. I see everyone's dressed appropriately. Nice to see you again, Dani, may I get you a beverage?"

"I would love a Coors Light! Rita, have you had the pleasure of meeting Will yet?"

"No, I haven't."

"Well…you need to. He's worth the price of the cruise."

"Ah shucks," Will said, placing his hands over his cheeks. "I'm Will. Will Catcher."

"Of course you are," Rita said. "But, it takes more than those baby-blues to *catch* me," she said, accustomed to pretty boy charms and maneuvers.

"Oh my!" Dani said. "We may have found your female counter part, Will."

Acknowledging Dani with a beer and a smile, Will turned to Rita. "Some women weren't made to be *caught*, just admired for their stormy provocation and raw grace," Will said, tossing a coaster on the bar and setting Rita's drink on top.

Rita remained silent, choosing to lubricate her robust lips with a tube of Chapstick. Enthralled, John and Dani hung on Rita's next words, as if she were about to announce the killer. After pursing her lips, she took a big inhale, and endorsed, "I like him!"

Laughing, the two women toasted over John's tray. Reaching for his burger, John realized they were still holding their drinks as a signal for him to grab his. He sipped hard after a second plastic *clank*, then returned to the sanctuary of his lunch.

"What does everyone have planned for this evening—post-dinner?" Will asked.

"I hadn't thought about it," Dani said. "What do you recommend?"

"Well, there's always the casino if you're trying to lose some money, but I recommend *that* towards the end of the week, when you're closer to deciding how much money you have left. The theatre puts on a great show, as professional as any on Broadway. When you're done there, the disco's always rocking on a sea day. I'm actually working there for a few hours tonight. And, if you get hungry, they have a great midnight buffet."

"That sounds like a plan," Dani said. "What do you guys think…wanna meet up in the disco later?"

Leaning back and coyly watching John finish his hamburger, Rita said, "Only if John promises to go. And he has to wear another snappy t-shirt, like the one he has on now."

"How about it, my man?" Will said. "You got something else in your t-shirt arsenal to rival that farmer slogan?"

All eyes on John, still trying to swallow the last bite of his burger. "I uh…" John stuttered, looking at Will, whose eyebrows were intently raised, his head slightly nodding. "I…I might have something else in my bag."

Will gave John an approving grin, like two athletes who had just helped each other score a basket.

"I'm going to hold you to that, John Smith," Rita said. "Women don't like to be disappointed, you know." Reinforcing her insistence.

Turning into Rita's steady gaze, John was interrupted just as he was about to speak.

"There you are!" said a man suddenly standing above John and Rita. Rita offered her cheek as he bent down to kiss.

"There you are," she replied.

"What've you been doing?" he asked. "I thought we were going to meet at the bar in the ice-rink?"

"After you left me, I came here to get-in out of the rain."

"What rain?"

The man's question caused John and Dani to pivot in their seats. Not only had it stopped raining, but the moisture was retreating on the deck; only a few raindrops remained on deck chairs.

"Meet my new friends, George," Rita said. "This is John, Dani, and the spicy one behind the bar is Will."

"That's the way it goes out here," Will said. "Rains like hell for five minutes and then you'd never know it happened," snapping a single wave at George.

"Yes, we know," George condescended, draping his arm over Rita's shoulder. "We've spent a lot of time in the Caribbean—seen almost every damn island with a coconut. Rita here was born in Cuba. I met her while on business. It was love at first sight! Now she's a part of the melting pot of the good old free world. Isn't that right, honey?" George massaged.

"Which part?" asked Rita. "That we've seen a lot of islands, we met while you were getting richer, or that *you* fell in love with me when we met?" she asked, tersely.

Dismissing Rita with a fake chortle and firm pinch of her shoulder, which she shrugged off, George officially introduced himself. "I'm George." Holding an open hand to John.

Hesitating. "John." Reluctantly shaking George's hand. George had put on a silk shirt covering his tattoos since John and Dani's last encounter with him at the bar, but he still wore the same silver Rolex.

"And you are…?" George asked.

"Same as I was earlier…with people," Dani said, opting to drink her beer instead of shaking hands.

"I see you've been busy making friends, as *usual*," Rita said, pleased with Dani's curtness.

"Huh?" George said. "No, we accidentally bumped into each other while you were sunning yourself. Remember, I left you for a drink and a bit of shade?"

"Yes, George, I remember. It certainly doesn't make a girl feel very special when all it takes to leave her is a drink and a bit of shade." Winking at Dani. "Then again, it shouldn't come as any surprise to me. I always knew you were a sucker for the shade, whereas I'm always hoping to find a nice bright spot," Rita said, gazing at John as she took another drink.

"One must be careful of too much sun, my love," George said, spotting the eye contact between Rita and John. "It could give you cancer if you're not cautious."

"George is so right," Rita said. "He's very wise of course. Still, I would rather risk cancer versus all the maladies hiding in the shade," she returned, glaring at George.

John felt the rum seeping into his bloodstream, where it aroused the remainder of tequila that survived his bathroom break. "This ship is so large you should both be able to find sun or shade," John deducted.

Dani choked on her beer, realizing John wasn't understanding the metaphor in the couple's banter. "John's so right!" Dani smirked. "There's something for everyone here."

Cracking his knuckles and then crossing his arms in a sign of male dominance, George inflated his massive biceps. John saw the bottom tattoo symbol sneak out from under his short sleeve. "You sound like an old salt, John," George said. "Spent a lot of time at sea, have you?"

"No. Actually, this is my first time on a ship, but I think it's pretty great so far. I can see why people cruise regularly."

"Yes," George squinted. "It's fun, isn't it?" Again sounding condescending. "You have to be careful though…you wouldn't believe how many passengers they lose out here."

"Lose?" John asked.

"Yes, *lose*. People have a little too much to drink and end up right over the ship's side. Especially at night…when there aren't as many people to notice," George glared.

Suddenly intimidated, John's stomach churned with acid, his hands became clammy and his throat restricted. Confused why George felt the need to threaten, he looked to Rita for help.

"Oh, don't pay any attention to him, John," Rita said, rolling her eyes. "George gets-off trying to sound like he knows everything. He figures the scarier the story, the more believable it sounds. I've never heard of anyone going overboard and not being saved."

"It happens, my dear, trust me…it happens. I'm merely telling John here about incidents the company doesn't want you to know about. We should all be aware that it happens. I was simply advising him to be careful," he said, with a grin and a wink at John.

Mustering some saliva, and forcing it down his throat, John said, "Thanks…I will."

George placed his hand back on Rita's shoulder. "If we're going to catch the last open skate before dinner, we should really get going," he said.

"Yes," Rita said. "I suppose you're right. After all, where else will I have the chance to ice skate on the ocean, unless I go to the North Pole?"

"Have fun," Dani said. "We'll see you later on I guess?"

"Yes!" Rita assured. "You will. And I look forward to reading John's next shirt."

A look of surprise came across George's face. "What do you all have planned?"

"We're all going to meet in the disco after the show tonight, even Will's going to be working there," Rita said. "It's going to be a hoot. And you'll get to show off all your first-rate dance moves," she joked.

"Sounds like fun," George said, making sure Dani was looking at him. "We'll see you later."

"It was a pleasure to meet you, Dani," Rita said. "Until the next time…John Smith."

"Thanks for the drink, Rita. It was really tasty." Holding up his near empty cocktail, John was beating himself up inside, thinking he just said something along the lines of, *gee, I think you're neat!*

Rita half smiled, her cute dimple filling John with enough pleasure to ignore George's sharp glare. John's eyes followed Rita and George as they wended their way through the lounge chairs that were beginning to fill back up with the sun's return. Rita's backless suit exposed taut, bronzed Cuban skin, and John permitted his gaze to fall on her full, round behind, fantasizing about what it would feel like to touch both supple cheeks.

"Quite the interesting couple, weren't they?" Dani asked.

Spinning around. "Yes, they sure are," John said.

"I guess they're married, but I didn't see a ring. Did you?"

"He had one, but not Rita. Why…why do you think they're married?"

"Come on, John. You were married. Only married people pick at each other the way they just did. There's a thin line separating loving jabs from bloody blows. That couple leaned toward the latter. I can see why too!"

"What do you mean?"

"That guy's a player, just like I said before. Didn't you see the creepy looks and innuendo he was throwing at me? And all that talk about shade!"

"What's wrong with shade?"

"John! The shade that guy's looking for is the shade of another woman's body lying naked on top of him."

As if a light bulb flashed on above John's head. "Now, I get why I felt like he wanted to throw me overboard. I'm not normally this slow Dani, or maybe I am and I'm just now realizing it." Chewing on the idea. "That's a scary thought at forty-seven."

Laughing. "There's nothing wrong with an old dog learning to read between the lines," Dani said, tapping John's glass. Her bag spoke.

"Garrett to mom—over!"

"Mom to son—over!"

"Elli and Buffy are going to the spa now for their appointment. You're supposed to meet them there—over."

"I forgot all about it, Garrett. Tell them I'll see them there. What are you going to do?—over."

"I'm taking the girls to the youth center to play until you guys tell me you're done—over."

"Okay. Thanks for watching them, honey. Have fun. I'll see you before we go to dinner—over."

"Is John still with you?—over."

"Sitting right beside me—over"

"Ask him if he wants to ride jet skis tomorrow—over."

Looking to John. "I told him at least one of us would go, but he'd probably prefer bonding with a male figure. It's totally up to you, John. Don't feel like you have to say yes if you don't want to."

Holding his hand out. "Which button?"

"This one to talk, then release it to listen," Dani demonstrated.

"I'd love to, Garrett—over."

"Roger that, Chuck Taylor! We can get you one with training skis if you're afraid of speed—over."

"You just worry about trying to keep up—over."

"Sounds like a dare! I'm in!—over and out."

"Thank you, John. That was really sweet. It must be…I mean, because you…"

"Garrett told you I lost my son?"

"*Yes*…I hope you're not mad?"

Hesitating. "Your son's outgoing and adventurous. He reminds me of my son."

"What was his name?"

"Carson."

"I don't know what it's like to lose a child, but I was scared that I might when Garrett and his father were in that car wreck," Dani said, delicately placing her hand on John's.

"Children are amazing," John sighed. "We spend our lives trying to protect and guide them, and then you wake up one day and realize they've taken our job." Sniffling. "I couldn't protect my son overseas, and he never had to deal with the demise of my aging body or failing mind. Even though I feel like we were robbed of our time, I feel him here, guiding and protecting—me."

Feeling tears starting to well-up in her eyes. "He sounds *very* special," she said, wiping her eyes and patting the top of John's hand. "Hey, would you like to have dinner with us tonight? We're just going to the dining room and I'm sure one more won't be an issue."

"I appreciate the offer, but I think all these drinks are going to force me to take a nap if I'm going to make it to the show and disco. I think I'll just grab something when I wake up. Plus, there's the midnight buffet that Will told us about. I don't think anyone's going to starve by taking a nap," he said, trying to lighten the mood.

"Okay. The offer stands though. We're in nine-five-seven if you change your mind before six thirty. Here's my email and cell number if you want to send a text instead of calling the room. Cell calls are expensive onboard, but texts are free, I think."

"I'll take them, but I didn't bring my phone."

"You can always use the business center. I guess Garrett's old enough now that I should buy him his own cell. He's always stealing mine to take pictures. I hate to, but he just loves taking pictures."

"Maybe he'll grow up to be a photographer?"

"As long as it's not for a dirty magazine, that would be just fine," she laughed.

Dani jotted her information down on a cocktail napkin, signed her tab, and gave John a full stand up hug. Her warm body seemed to fit perfectly in his arms. They both reluctantly let go. He watched as she walked away. Her gait was natural; no extra hip sway. John was filled with angst as he watched another beautiful woman leave, hoping his pain hadn't somehow added to hers.

NAP TIME

WHEN HE GOT BACK TO his cabin at 3:30, John felt more like it was 10:00. It took three swipes of his key-card before the tiny light flashed green. Silvia had clearly made up the room sometime after he left. Everything was spotless and organized. The sweet smell of tulips lingered in the air and John's bed floated a large swan made from the white Egyptian cotton of a fresh bath towel. Resting between its wings and back was a full supply of soaps and lotion.

Standing over the bed, looking at the swan, he experienced compassion for the symbolic creature. In a childhood flashback, he remembered an incident when he was about ten years old and neighborhood playmates stoned a large toad. Pity and anger sickened him as each throw opened another gaping wound on the helpless animal. The boys laughed as they maimed, only stopping when John enticed them away with a dip in a friend's pool. He returned hours later to find the frog still alive, bleeding, and unable to move. His mother found him wailing in his bedroom and had to call his father to come home from work to put the frog out of its misery. That day and those boys forever stripped a piece of innocence from John. They also taught him that pain and suffering were always going to be a part of life, and although he couldn't change that fact, he would never inflict them; not on an insect, animal, or person—never he thought.

Fully aware of how silly it was, John scooped up the towel swan, his left hand under its belly and his right protecting its graceful arching neck. He gently carried it into the bathroom, placing it on the vanity top. An appropriate place, he reasoned, next to the sink where it would be close to water. He looked at himself in the mirror, thinking he must be drunk or crazy. Maybe a nap would fix everything. He returned to the bedroom and moved the new chocolates from his pillow to the nightstand before collapsing spread-eagled on the bed like a dead man. The last thought he would remember before sleep set in was wondering if anyone else on board had protected their towel swan.

Surely, George and Elli destroyed theirs the first chance they got.

HIBACHI

THE PHONE RANG AT SIX o'clock. It wasn't until the third ring that John became lucid enough to roll over and answer. "Hell-o," he said, struggling to clear his throat.

"John, my boy! Rich Clawson here. How's *The Princess* treating you so far?"

"Hi, Richard. Not bad…it's certainly not been boring, that's for sure."

"Sounds like I may have caught you during siesta time?"

"You got me there, Richard. A teenage boy beat me up on the basketball court this morning. Then I met some ladies by the pool who introduced me to frozen drinks."

"Good for you!" Richard laughed. "Sounds like you're getting into the swing of what cruising is all about! Listen, if you don't already have plans with a super model, Mary and I wondered if you would like to join us for dinner again tonight—our treat!"

"That's very generous. Are you sure you want to take a chance on my melancholy spoiling a good meal?"

"Nonsense! We're going to The Wicked Dragon. A ten year-old girl who just had her puppy stolen couldn't be melancholy in this place. It's a Hibachi grill. Ever been?"

"Can't say that I have. Is it a Chinese restaurant?"

"Japanese!" Richard corrected. "Americans better start learning the differences between Filipino, Korean, Tai, Vietnamese, Japanese, and Chinese if we ever expect to compete with them."

"We don't have too many Asians living in my part of the world. I guess I've always been one of those ignorant Americans who always lumps them all together. It sounds like a good place to start my education though."

"You're going to love it, John! The chef prepares and cooks your meal right in front of you. He chops and flips and cracks wise with the guests the whole time. It's a blast!"

"Okay. Count me in, Richard. What time?"

"Reservation's for seven. That give you enough time to freshen up?"

"Plenty. Should I meet you there?"

"Deck eleven, aft. We'll have the sake waiting, my boy!"

After hanging-up, John wiped the sleep from the corner of his eyes. Sitting on the edge of the bed, he pulled the night stand drawer open. The two letters from his father and son lay safely inside. He placed them back inside the secret compartment of his Bagly Bag and picked out a pair of pants and dress shirt for dinner, draping them over his bed before showering.

The hot water felt marvelous on his shoulders and back, now aching from basketball. He caressed his upper arm, wondering what it would look like with a tattoo like George's.

Closing his eyes, he daydreamed about himself on an old black Harley, driving down Good Intent's main street, fresh off a road trip. Both his bike and body were covered with a sort of dirt and death familiar only to motorcycle riders; a paste of dust, dried sweat, and dead insect parts. His denim jeans and leather chaps protected his legs from the intense heat radiating from the manifold and exhaust pipes. No real bikers ever wore polyester—never. Towns-people made up of childhood school friends and their parents watched with cool adulation as he slowly rumbled back into town. He wore a sleeveless denim jacket; grown men stared at the tattoo burned into his upper arm. The onlookers all fearing—but also respecting—the rider and his engraved motto: a buxom female vampire with the words, *U Got to Have U Some Fun* written on her massive, bra-less chest.

In the fantasy, Page was drowning in a pool of paint, but John, trying to impress her, flexed his left arm. His elbow struck the tiled shower wall with significant force, ending the illusion.

Exiting the shower stall, his elbow still throbbing, he rubbed his injury while dripping on the bathroom floor and he thought about using the cotton swan. Instead he grabbed a towel from the reserve stack above the toilet and returned to the bedroom to dress.

After digging the ship's diagram out of a bundle of information on his dresser, he located The Wicked Dragon, and made his way to the elevators and his first Japanese dinner.

There was no confusion about being in the right place as he stood outside an open entryway, large enough to roll two grand pianos through without brushing the sides. The walls were constructed into a huge arch, a gateway to Chinatown—in this case, Japanese-town. Two elaborate golden dragon heads faced each other at the arch apex, separated by each one's breath of fire.

Inside, he was greeted by an extremely youthful girl, innocent and pretty enough to be an assassin in an old kung-fu movie. She brought him to a large rectangular bar, half counter and half grill. Mary and Richard were already seated at the corner so the three could better make eye contact. There were eighteen total seats. John claimed the last vacant one. Everyone seemed to be drinking something exotic out of real pineapples or coconut glasses; even the children's drinks had lit sparklers and crazy straws. Conversations blared as guests got ready, like pre-theatre, awaiting the opening act.

Richard, standing to greet. "John, my boy! Great to see you again."

"It's great to see you both," John said, bending over to kiss Mary's cheek.

"Please sit, John," Mary said. "It's sake time."

"Thank you, Mary," he said, looking around the room. Like everything John had seen onboard so far, The Wicked Dragon was as ornate and fabulous as anything offered in Disney's Epcot. The restaurant was a feast for the eyes, every statue and piece of artwork accentuated by hundreds of low-voltage lights. The mood was hauntingly mystical. There were life size samurai warriors guarding every doorway. A Japanese palace carved from Jade sat behind the main bar. John scanned every corner, thinking there might actually be a pet dragon, gorging on scraps, somewhere on a leash.

"Try this, John!" Richard said, passing a small ceramic shot glass and carafe to Mary.

"Do you like sake, John?" Mary asked.

"I haven't had any since a Chinese…I mean a girl of Asian descent, shared a bottle with a bunch of us in college. Her parents had given it to her after a trip somewhere."

"Well, there are all different kinds of sake," Mary said pouring. "People drink it chilled or heated. Richard and I prefer it heated. It seems more ritualistic somehow."

"Everyone does it a little differently, but we like to take a drink of ice water, chase that with sake, and then again with the water," Richard said, holding up both water and sake. "The cold-hot-cold slides right down the hatch without any burn."

"I'll follow your lead," John said, joining Richard. "You both seem to know what you're talking about."

"Banzai!" the couple said in unison.

"Smooth!" John said.

Richard refilled everyone's cup and said, "It's just rice wine, but it'll sneak up on you! I had my first sake with my father. He took me on a trip to California to visit his best friend and his son. We boys weren't old enough yet to drink, but we looked close enough, I guess. The Japanese waitress didn't think to card us, probably 'cause we were with our fathers. I remember having a hard time getting up the next morning to go see Shamu at Sea World," Richard snickered.

After the second "banzai," three men entered the center island wheeling carts filled with food and sauces. Each chef was clothed in traditional Japanese garb resembling black, silk pajamas. Embroidered on their chests were elaborate dragons, each one different. The three chefs split off, dividing the guests into sections of six. The men quickly inventoried their carts before greeting each other with loud, low growls and the high-pitched sound of steel knives being sharpened. The show had begun.

Richard's group was greeted with a sharp grunt and bow, the man's piercing eyes never lowered, careful to keep contact. After the acknowledgment, he dumped a heaping portion of vegetables and six jumbo shrimp onto the sizzling grill in front of the hypnotized guests. Wildly slicing and dicing, the chef's speed and precision was a match for any food processor.

Staring amiss at John, the chef asked, "You eat tonight?"

"Me…yes."

"Ooh…you come last after everyone else order and you still think *Kumo* honor you?"

"Kumo?" John whimpered.

Chopping ceased as the chef stood up straight. "Kumo!" he said, pointing at the dragon on his chest. "Kumo is name of my inner dragon. He mightiest of all wicked dragons. Kumo eat all other master's dragons as a snack," thumbing backward to the other chefs.

Relaxing a bit when he heard Mary chuckle, John apologized. "I didn't mean to dishonor *Kumo*. I should've been here a few minutes earlier…I'm so sorry."

"Kumo think maybe you *okay-dokay*. He might be able to kill something for you to eat. What you want?"

Quickly scanning the menu under his plate. "I uh…how about a number five?"

"Steak! Hi! Kumo impressed. Only true warriors eat steak! I tell Kumo make for you," he said, letting out the slightest and briefest of grins."

"Good recovery, John!" Richard said. "You don't want to piss off the man or his dragon responsible for cooking our meals."

Still laughing, Mary poured John another sake. "That's why people love these places, the food is good, but the entertainment…well, you never know what you're going to get," she said.

"I have to admit," John said. "I was a bit nervous for a minute. Sounds like you guys have been to your share of these places?"

"All the time…when we had the golf course," Mary said.

"You owned a golf course?"

"Yes, I guess Richard didn't get that far."

"After I sold the drive-in to McDonald's, we had enough money to spend more time with the family, but eventually, I needed another project. Mary agreed to pack everyone up and move to Scotland for two years while I earned a degree in golf course design."

"That must've been a culture shock for your kids?"

"Yes, a couple of the older ones weren't too keen on leaving their school and friends, but they all adjusted and learned to love it after we were there awhile," Mary said. "They all speak very romantically about the experience now. Every one of them loves to show off their best Scottish accent when they get together."

"Wow!" John said. "So you're a golf course designer, Rich?"

"I only ever built one. When we got back to the states I found some land and a couple investors in Virginia where we built Claw Creek. The other partners wanted a fancy country club type restaurant attached to it, but Mary and I wanted something less pretentious."

"We always liked these Hibachi grills and we thought it would help promote people staying for dinner after a round of golf instead of going home or somewhere else to eat," Mary said. "Plus, a lot of people golf with their children and we felt like the kids would love it. Ours did."

"What did you call it?"

"What else?" Richard asked, pouring another round. *"Banzai!"*

John joined the Clawsons in another shot then went back to watching their chef, marveling at how authentic it all seemed. In between bursts of flames from spices and oils that he somersaulted— even Will would be impressed—he read their chef's name tag: Hasamoto, Tokyo, Japan.

Hasamoto served his six guests appetizer bites of shrimp, allowing him to entertain each individual. Afterward, he served full meals, starting with Richard and working down the line, plating each order from the steaming piles before him. When it came time for the woman beside John to be served, Hasamoto tossed a knife in the air, catching it behind his back. He paused, grunted one time, and then leaned down to the woman, asking, "Do you have band-aid with you?" Expressing despair, she shook her head. After a lingering moment of suspense, Hasamoto revealed his uncut hand, assuring her it was okay. "Kumo already fixed it," he said.

John felt the dinner fly by. Sake flowed as the three talked and laughed, sharing stories about their children, work, and adventures. The restaurant's party atmosphere released John from his soup kitchen mentality. The dragons and Samurai warriors protected him, he imagined, from grief. He had become an active participant in the ever changing moment, not resisting the waves of laughter pushing him forward. By the time Richard paid the bill, John realized his feelings of satisfaction and enjoyment were reminders of something he'd been forgetting to do, something Carson had been trying to get him to remember—to live.

"Are you ready to see a brilliant show, John?" Mary asked.

"I'm looking forward to it. I haven't been to a play since college. It was a modest production of *The King and I*."

"That's a good one, but tonight isn't going to be a play," Richard said. "You're going to hear a broad range of show tunes performed by the ship's singers and dancers."

"It's all pretty top notch stuff, too," Mary said. "Richard and I have seen a lot of Broadway shows in New York, and the cruise line acts are usually comparable."

"I've never been to New York, so I wouldn't recognize the difference. I guess that's a good thing?"

"It's a great thing," Mary nodded. "Here…you don't have to deal with transportation, expensive hotel rooms, expensive tickets…"

"Or getting mugged!" added Richard.

"Yes," Mary said. "Our odds of witnessing any crimes are pretty slim here."

"I'm sold!" John said. "Sounds like I came to the right place."

"Well then…shall we break a leg as the theatre folks say and go a little early, so we can buy a drink and still grab a good seat?" Richard asked.

"Sounds like a plan," John said. As the three stood, John noticed Hasamoto still cleaning up and entertaining a couple of remaining diners. A question came to mind. He waited to make eye contact with Hasamoto, then asked, "Hasamoto, why is your inner dragon stronger than all the other dragons?"

Hasamoto grunted under his breath. His eyes squinted, and again, he shot John a small satisfied grin. "Because I believe it so," he said.

John registered the wisdom hidden in this concise philosophy, as if Hasamoto burned away what had hidden his confidence with one invisible breath of fire. "One more question?"

"Of course, Johnny-come-late."

"Good one," John chuckled. "How did Kumo get his name?"

"It's the name of a very mighty mountain in my native land."

"Oh…that makes sense."

Hasamoto added, "It's also the name of my cat."

"Your cat?"

Hasamoto's face hardened. "Kumo v-e-r-y fierce cat…he only eat dog food."

AS THE LIGHTS DIM

THE THEATRE WAS BUZZING WITH passengers when John and the Clawsons walked through the port entrance, joining the line of thirsty people waiting to be served from one of three bars inside the massive hall. John gawked in wonder at the twelve-hundred seat theatre and all its decadence. A burgundy velvet curtain hung from the rafters like a cape concealing the stage depth and wide enough to potentially house a small airplane. The grandeur and sheer volume of the room primed John with the anticipation of something magical.

"What do you think, John," Mary asked.

"It's amazing, like everyone at Keep It Together came to work early and decorated the plant for Christmas."

Mary enjoyed John as if he were one of her own children mesmerized by a new toy. "Yes, all the newer ships have pretty impressive theaters now-a-days," she said.

"What would everyone care to drink?" Richard asked, nearing the front of the line.

"White wine for me, honey."

"Perfect," John said.

"Three white wines coming up!" replied Richard.

"This one room is a small town inside a small city," John said, still rolling his head around the ceiling and high walls.

"What's the population of your home town, John," Richard asked.

"Around…five thousand."

"Well, I can see why you would feel that way, because that's about how many people are on board," Richard said. "Seems like more when you don't know anyone, and everyone is packed into less square footage than an entire town, don't you think?"

"Yes, it does," John said. "Plus, most of these people are here on vacation, so they're always out and about, not camped out in their rooms watching TV, I guess."

"That's why they make most of the cabins so small," Richard said. "Just enough space to sleep, bathe, and…you know." Winking as he placed his hand on Mary's back.

"Not really," John sighed. "I have to admit, it's been quite a while since *you know*."

"You might not have to wait much longer," Richard said, smiling over John's shoulder.

"Huh?"

"Somebody appears to be checking you out, my boy."

Turning, Rita stood five people away, waving. Her brilliant smile lit up the room, distracting John—but not Richard—from noticing that her little black cocktail dress exposed generous amounts of leg and cleavage. Not waiting for an invitation, she excused herself as she shimmied past two couples.

"Good evening, Mr. Smith," she said, kissing John's cheek. "What a surprise! I didn't think I'd get to see you again until after the show."

John's face instantly warmed like a sunburn. He hoped he wasn't as outwardly red as his internal temperature implied.

"Hello, Rita," he said. "These are my friends Mary and Richard Clawson."

"It's nice to meet you both!"

"John, you've been here one day and you already know the second most beautiful woman onboard," Richard said, taking Rita's hand and kissing it gently above the knuckles.

"Well…what a gentleman!" Rita said. "You have a real shark here, Mary."

"Yes," Mary laughed. "They're pretty easy to deal with once you remove the teeth. He's just for show now, like a big grouper in an aquarium—entertaining to watch."

"What splendid friends you have, John. How did you all meet?"

"We helped John with a little life vest adjustment during boat drill," Mary said. "It was love at first sight."

Gazing seductively at John, Rita said. "We all have a common bond then."

Unable to break-away from Rita's stare, except for brief dips into her cleavage, caused another involuntary appendage elevation. Without realizing it, Richard saved the day by handing him a glass of wine. John used the hand-off to insert his opposite hand into his pocket and adjust himself, hoping the maneuver wasn't obvious, especially to a mother figure like Mary. But Richard and Mary were too busy watching the man sneak up behind Rita, his index finger poised vertically over chin and nose.

Clear to everyone but George, squeezing Rita's hips and kissing her neck were two advances that he should've taken more time to consider, based on how her head snapped up and she stripped off his hands.

"Hello, George," Rita said.

"How did you know it was me?"

"Nobody else would act so vulgarly as to grab my ass while I was speaking with friends."

Glaring at John. "Well…you again…John is it?"

"Good evening, George. This is Mary and Richard Clawson."

Richard's elevated years couldn't negate his size and demeanor. Even the strongest of young bucks would be naive to cross him. George hesitated and then decided not to intimidate John after assessing Richard. Poising himself as if conducting business, George said, "Hello, pleasure to meet you both."

Richard had not only been around the block a few times; in some ways, he helped build the blocks. His years of experience gave him a tuning fork that sensed anything potentially dangerous or reeking of bullshit. As he extended his hand, his tuning fork rang loud. "Pleasure to meet you, George," the toothless grouper said, squeezing as hard as he could.

George winced in pain from the claw-like grasp. "And you…sir."

Thankfully for George, the lights dimmed on and off a series of times, signaling time for the guests to take their seats. Richard finally released his grip.

"There's our cue," Mary said. "We better go find some seats."

Turning quickly to move Rita along, George said, "She's right. Enjoy the show everyone. I guess we'll see you after, in the disco. Ready, Rita?"

"It was very nice meeting you both," Rita said. "Please, join us for drinks and dancing later in the disco. John's going."

"We just might," Richard said. "If you promise to save an old man a dance?"

"As long as it's okay with Mary," Rita said, looking for permission.

"If you don't mind getting your feet bruised, he's all yours."

"I think my feet are up to the challenge," she replied. "See you later, John. Enjoy the show. Oh…and remember our deal!"

"She's beautiful, John," Mary said after George swept Rita away. "And she's sweet on you."

Mary's comments both excited and embarrassed John. "What? No. She…we just met in line when we boarded. Plus, she's married."

"How do you know she's married?" Richard asked.

"She isn't," Mary quickly responded.

"How do you know that?" John asked.

"Call it…women's intuition."

"I think she's right, my boy. My men's intuition—which I call logic—didn't see a wedding ring. And she looked at you like you were a jewelry store giving away free diamonds. But that guy George; I didn't get a good vibe from him."

"He makes me nervous too," admitted John. "He's intimidating."

"I wouldn't worry too much about that," Richard said. "There are two kinds of intimidation: natural and insecure, and our guy George comes from the latter."

"What's the difference?" John shrugged.

Looking to the ceiling for the right words. "I'm a pretty big guy, John. And when pushed, even against someone much younger, I can hold my own. That said, do I intimidate you?"

"I wouldn't want to see you upset with me, but no, you're a very nice man and a peach to get along with."

"That's the point," Richard said. "To the average nice guy of any size, I don't appear to be a threat, unless they have some sort of confidence issue—then a big guy like me looks scarier than I really am. When those guys with the confidence problems get angry, they often try bullying other people. It's just an outlet for their own anxiety. This George dude is insecure about something, and although he may present himself as a Pit Bull, I would venture a bet that inside—he's a Chihuahua."

"Based on your definition, I'm a man lacking confidence and therefore should be trying to intimidate someone," John sighed.

"No!" Richard snapped. "You strike me as a man who's suffered great loss, and a guy with limited travel education. Don't confuse that with lack of self-reliance. Besides, you're changing those things as we speak. Women—especially gorgeous women, like Rita, can smell the difference."

"He's right, John, this time anyway," Mary smirked. "Intimidation is beneath your character. Without confidence, you wouldn't have booked this cruise. You may be scared—we all often feel that—but for reasons only you know, you've decided to stop letting that fear control you."

John felt instantly soothed, like they just helped him up, washed his face, looked him in the eyes, and told him to get back into the fight. He wanted to believe them. On the other hand, a voice inside said: *You didn't have the guts to book this trip—coward, liar. Someone else did it for you.* Telling the voice to keep quiet, John said, "You're both two of the sweetest people I've ever met."

"You get what you give, dear," Mary said, placing her hand on John's arm.

The lights dimmed and brightened again. "I think that's the final call," Richard said, glancing at his watch. "Everyone ready?"

"You bet!" John said.

The three walked down the port aisle until they found three seats together mid-way to the stage. Just as they sat, the lights dimmed and the cruise director entered from stage left. His bathing suit and floral shirt were replaced by a classic black tuxedo, but his perfect black hair and tanned face was still set off with a million dollar smile. Grasping the only tool required for cruise directors, a cordless microphone, he introduced himself as Bim Harris. Bim smoothly worked the entire room with a five minute monologue, pacing back and forth across the stage like a tiger. To John, his delivery and timing was impeccably effortless. Although the Clawsons recognized, from their dozens of cruises, the same scripted jokes and standard prods meant to get members of the audience involved, John had it better; it was all new. He settled comfortably in his chair, cackling at every joke.

When Bim finished welcoming everyone aboard with the same ten jokes he used every Monday, he introduced the ship's dancers; the velvet curtain split and parted. A stage full of beautiful young women and athletic men shot into action as the band keyed the opening note for their version of "You Give Me Fever." A rainbow of spotlights pulsed as the sultry girls snapped their fingers and contorted their bodies around the male dancers, using chairs as props. John watched in awe. His mouth dropped slightly ajar and his eyes were wide open. He hadn't seen anything so erotic since Page rented *Dirty Dancing*. Mary heard John softly singing when the chorus repeated:

You give me fever
When you kiss me
Fever when you hold me tight
Fever
In the morning
Fever all through the night

During the next hour, John was transcended beyond the mundane range of his usual and infrequent forms of entertainment. This sure beat drinking beer and eating hotdogs at a Chiefs game. Each song-and-dance rendition from famous shows like *Cats* and *Les Miserables* opened new doors, encouraging John's spirit to expand and his imagination to soar. And then the hour ended as quickly as it started, leaving John yearning for an encore that wouldn't come—not in the theatre, anyway.

Slowly exiting the show, waddling like penguins amidst waves of departing theatre-goers, Richard held Mary's shoulder in a protective manner as John followed. They paused in the lobby for some personal space and show critiques.

Mary could already see the pleasure on John's face. "What did you think, John?"

"I loved it! The music; the lights; the costumes…it was all well, quite extraordinary!"

Richard added, "You forgot to mention all the pretty girls!"

"I hardly noticed," John joked.

"You don't have to play dumb on my behalf," Mary said. "Even I couldn't help noticing all the lovely women with their perfect bodies shoe-horned into those sequined-clad bikinis they call costumes."

"I was really more caught up in the singing and dancing."

"Of course you were, my dear," Mary said, sporting a playful smile.

"Those girls sang?" Richard asked.

"Oh, hush up, you old pervert," Mary frowned. "You could take notes from John and learn to occasionally be a little more sly with your comments."

"I thought I was," Richard mumbled.

John said, "What do you say, will you both join me in the disco?"

"What do you think, honey?" Richard asked, using Mary's stock frown to sway her answer. "Should we go check out what the kids are doing to replace Motown and The Twist?"

"I believe we should, Mr. Clawson! Our kids will be delightfully shocked when we tell them we stayed out late at a nightclub."

"Great!" John said. "Oh, I…I just need to stop back at my cabin to change my shirt."

"You look fine to me," Mary said, eyeing his outfit.

"Thanks Mary, but I kinda promised the people I met today that I would wear a different shirt."

"You go ahead and put your party clothes on," Richard said. "That'll give us time for a stroll outside. Kind of a ritual of ours. We love the temperature and ocean breeze this time of night." Cupping his hands to his mouth and whispering. "Puts her in the mood. We'll meet you there around ten?"

People watching, Mary missed her husband's comment. "What did he say?"

Forcing a straight face. "He said we're going to meet at ten," John said.

"Perfect," Mary said. "That will give us time for a stroll. I do love to stroll this time of night."

SO YOU THINK YOU CAN'T DANCE

USING THE CLOSEST ELEVATOR, JOHN made his way back to his cabin and rooted through his suitcase until he found what he was looking for. He took the old shirt into the bathroom and acknowledged the towel swan. He stripped in front of the mirror exposing his red forearms and neck which contrasted dramatically with his pale chest. After a mental note to work on a more uniform coat in the next port, he rubbed a fresh glaze of Old Spice on his armpits, slipped on the fresh t-shirt, and located the disco on the ship diagram before shooting out the door like he was late for a hot date.

Nervousness and anticipation hastened his steps. His mind replayed the past day, lingering on the words and actions of each person he'd met. He thought back to lackadaisically packing for his trip, believing the only people he'd meet would be workers on the ship or shop owners selling him a souvenir trinket in one of the ports. Now he was walking briskly to join seven virtual strangers in a nightclub.

John stopped cold; panic set in. *I'm meeting women in a nightclub? Surely women will expect me to dance.*

Dawdling outside Pulse Nightclub, John checked his watch—9:50. He entertained a series of excuses allowing him to turn and leave: sickness, getting lost, falling asleep, or perhaps falling overboard. *George would appreciate that one,* he thought. He came to the conclusion that his inability to lie—especially about going overboard, which he could only pull-off by actually jumping or hiding for the rest of the cruise—gave him no choice but to enter and face the music, so-to-speak. So, tucking in his shirt and breathing deeply, he entered.

To his surprise, no other passengers had arrived yet. Motion lights flashed multi-colored lasers throughout the dark purple room. He made his way past the cocktail tables and cushy, leather love seats that occupied intimate niches in curved walls and stopped at the only bar in the room. He thought the ten foot long bar small for a room looking to hold a couple hundred people. The entire bar was built of glass and illuminated by lights under the counter and front wall. Sitting at one of six bar seats, wondering where the bartender could be, he found the club aptly named, as pounding bass shot into his chest like a defibrillator. Suddenly, from behind the bar a storage room door with a glass porthole window opened. The bartender was a welcome sight.

"John Smith!" cried Will. "Let the party start, the lady's man is here!"

Punching knuckles. "Hi, Will! It's good to see you again."

"Likewise, my friend. That was quite a display of man-cool you put on today at the pool. I enjoyed watching you work!"

"Huh? I assure you, I have the least amount of...*man-cool*...of anyone onboard—possibly the entire Caribbean."

"Are you kidding?" Will laughed. "You had beautiful women buying you drinks and bringing you lunch. Hell, you had them ignoring their friends and boyfriends! I even saw you put one of the hottest women at the pool in her place, while you just sat sipping your drink. Classic!"

"What?"

"The brunette with big sunglasses, perfect body, and the attitude of a movie star who didn't get a bidet in her hotel suite."

"Elli? How did you…"

"I told you, I catch it all. I'm a trained observer, my friend." Rubbing fingernails on his tuxedo shirt and then blowing on them.

"Thanks for the vote of confidence, but cool isn't a forte of mine. I'm here to meet everyone from today and I'm very nervous about it."

"What's to be nervous about? Options and opportunity are wonderful things. Not having them is something to be nervous about."

"It's not like that. We all just decided to meet for a drink—and probably dancing."

"R-i-g-h-t. If that's the case, what are you nervous about?"

"Well…I haven't danced since my wedding reception, and…they are…"

"A bunch of really hot women who you're afraid of embarrassing yourself in front of?"

"Nail on head! I haven't really been socially around a woman since my divorce. The only reason I'm here is because of my son. He was in the Army. He died in Afghanistan. *Carson*…he kind of made me promise that I would learn to be more adventurous, do more things for myself. I think I may be in over-my-head tonight."

Will was expressionless, thinking briefly about either slapping or hugging John. Instead, he flipped a bottle of Grey Goose and smacked a pint glass down on the bar. "Here's what you're going to do," he said, throwing ice into the glass with his left hand while pouring a triple shot with his right. "First, you're going to chug this." Cracking open a can of Red Bull and topping off the iced vodka to the rim.

"What's this called?"

"It's just Red Bull and vodka, but you can think of it as a drill instructor and a naked fireman armed with one glass of water inside a burning building—it's a beverage of motivating courage."

"Okay," John chugged. "That's pretty good—like a sweet tart."

"Yeah, just don't drink a lot of them unless you don't value sleep. There's about ten cups of coffee worth of caffeine in there. It'll help you summon your inner dragon."

"My what?"

Rubbing his chin. "My buddy's a Japanese chef. He swears we all have an inner dragon. It's a kind of attitude or ulterior personality for dealing with difficult situations. It's like Stallone in that arm wrestling movie. Every time he needed to focus, he turned his hat backwards like flipping a switch to wake his dragon."

"His name wouldn't be Hasamoto, would it?"

"You met Hazi?"

"He was our chef tonight."

"Great guy! I gotta meet Hazi's cat sometime. Anyway, you should understand what I'm talking about then."

"You're saying alcohol will give me courage?"

"No, not exactly. The drink will just temporarily block whatever it is that's blocking you from exercising your inner dragon. Think of it as clearing a path so you can go after what you want, instead of tripping over your own feet. Got it?"

"Yeah, I guess. But what if I don't know what I want?"

"You have to clear a path by getting out of your own way, by not making excuses; being open to new experiences; be honest; and what you want…will come to *you*."

"Okay, I guess I understand. What are you…some kind of philosopher?"

Laughing. "It's just part of the job. A bartender can't help but study human nature. Any more questions?"

Finishing his drink. "Yes. What do I do now?"

"Now you take your dragon, meet your friends, and dance. And remember, women aren't really watching if men can dance, they're watching to see if we can let go of our inhibitions."

"Okay…but, I don't want to dance with just you in the room. I think I should wait until they get here."

"John, this is the upstairs bar. Nobody comes up here unless they want a dark, private place to talk or make-out. The main area is downstairs. Your friends are waiting."

"Downstairs? They are? How do you know?"

Will pointed to the middle of the room where an oval balcony exposed the lower dance floor, beside it, a modern spiral staircase led to Pulse's main floor. "I watch everyone dance from that balcony when I work up here. There's not much else to do. Your group's down there now. I saw them before you walked in."

Standing up and turning toward where Will was pointing. "Right, I knew that. I guess I'll just go down stairs then," John said, adjusting his belt.

"If you need anything, I'll be up here. Remember, John, life's a game—sometimes serious, sometimes not so much—play the game with deliberateness, but have fun with it too. As you well know…it does end."

Sighing. "Thanks, Will. That sounds like good advice. You and Hazi have given me a lot to think about."

A prideful grin appeared on Will's face. "Another thing, John, when you find your dragon, it helps to name it. Gives it an identity when the master takes ownership."

Smiling back. "How about a beer for the road?"

Will popped the top off a Heineken and slid it across the bar. John picked it up, thanked Will again, and turned towards the stairs. When he got to the first step, he heard Will call. "John! One more thing…"

Turning back. "Yes?"

"I love the shirt!"

John descended the stairs thinking about what would be a good name for his inner dragon. The music thumped harder with each step and the caffeine and vodka shot to his head. The sound of multiple people yelling his name struck him at the bottom step. Everyone—even Richard and Mary—circled together on the flashing plexiglass dance floor, moving to the beat of "Good Feeling"—the latest dance hit by Flo Rida. Taking a deep breath, he willed his shoulders to gently sway and find the beat. Slowly, his hips and feet followed suit. Approaching the group, his drill instructor started screaming at the naked fireman holding nothing but a bottle of beer, *Get in there!*

Cheering, Dani and Buffy raised their arms as John made his landing in Bill Cosby style. Buffy shook her voluptuous ass on John's front side as Dani shadowed John from behind, rubbing her pert breasts on his back. Richard and Mary watched from a few feet away, bobbing up and down and clapping. Richard eyed Elli—dancing by herself, she moved with the grace of a ballerina turned exotic dancer—as unobtrusively as he thought Mary would permit. George shared Richard's enthusiasm for watching Elli, and tried masquerading his ogles by dancing behind Rita's body so she couldn't see his wandering eyes. Rita, shocked by John's lack of inhibition, danced indifferently to George's stares.

Richard and Mary bowed out when the song transitioned to the next. They headed to a table where they could be spectators and wish they were young again. The remaining six melted together in a tight jostling orgy, pushed closer and closer over the course of the next few songs by the growing number of people joining the club.

When George became more preoccupied with dancing closer to Buffy and Elli, Rita leaned into John's ear. "I would've never thought you would be such a good dancer!" she shouted.

John, still gyrating, put his mouth within reach of Rita's ear. "Me either! It's just my inner dragon!"

"Your what?" she asked, a perplexed look on her face.

"My inner dragon! I'm calling it *Carson*, after my son. It's what drives me to do things I would normally be too afraid to try!"

"Well…I like this inner-Carson-dragon side of you—it's hot! Is your dragon thirsty?"

"Parched," he said, dripping with sweat.

Nobody noticed as John and Rita left the group for the bar except the Clawsons, who had taken up a small table away from the thumping speakers, but could still see most of the action. The main bar had filled with passengers trying to grab the attention of the bar staff.

"It looks like we're in for a wait," Rita said, looking for an opening.

"Let's go upstairs," John suggested. "Will's working. He'll get us drinks faster than waiting here."

"I'll follow!"

John led Rita upstairs to the still nearly vacant lounge. Only a few tables were occupied by couples becoming more intimately acquainted. He escorted her to the bar where Will greeted them with a smile.

"Hello there, pretty lady…Rita, right?" Will asked.

"Good memory, Mr. Catcher! We thought we might receive quicker service up here? They're mobbed down stairs."

"You thought right. What can I pour you, dear?"

"Chardonnay for me," Rita said, shifting to John.

"Two, please," John agreed.

"So what's this dragon thing all about, John?" asked Rita.

Will's ears perked up, before reaching in the cooler for a wine bottle.

John noticed Will trying not to pay attention. "A wise man once told me to tackle fear by finding inner strength, or my dragon, and give it a name for the sake of identity. A name seems to make it more real, he told me."

"Interesting," she said, watching Will uncork a fresh bottle. "And you say you named your dragon Carson, after your son?"

"Yes. He was an Army sergeant and killed in the war. Six months before he died, he wrote me a letter asking me to go on this cruise, so I would learn to do more things for myself—adventurous things. I've always been kind of a bore. I've never been accused of being intrepid."

"Oh, I don't believe that. Maybe a late bloomer, but definitely not a bore."

"My ex-wife thought otherwise."

"Her loss," she said, holding up her glass to toast.

"Thank you. What about you, Rita? Do you mind me asking what the deal is with you and George?"

Searching for a starting point. "I was a naive Cuban girl, barely nineteen when I got married. He was four years older, a proud, but charming man who was very easy on the eyes. Diligence did him well at the bank where he worked. It didn't take long for him to rise through the ranks. Unfortunately, he had a proclivity for the casinos, and over time, his pride turned to hubris and denial. It reached a point where he gambled more than he made. We were married six years before I got smart and left."

"Okay. So not George?"

"No. *Juan*…the Latin John, don't you know?" Rita chuckled. "Debt, and the sickness of gambling eventually brought out his ugly side, previously hidden from me."

"Was he…abusive?"

Rita huffed. "What's abusive? Violent? Unfaithful? Verbally vehement? Yes, he dabbled in all those, but sometimes that stuff isn't as bad as the contempt of being dismissed and ignored. Anyway, after that I swore-off Latin men, thinking men from other places would be different. I wanted to go to the States for an education, so I could have a career. When I met George, who was in Cuba brokering a deal for video conferencing phone service, I got my chance. We fell in love and I moved with him to Miami, where we eventually got married and I earned a business degree from Miami University."

"Sounds like all your dreams came true?"

"No. Not motherhood."

"I'm sorry. That must be difficult."

"It doesn't get any easier at thirty-seven. The window's closing. Ironically, my first husband didn't want children until we were older. Isn't that funny…a Latin man who wanted to wait to have kids?"

"I wouldn't know, I'm from Kansas."

Half laughing and half crying. "And George, we learned, is unable to have children. That put a strain on our marriage…then I found out he was cheating. We booked this trip ten months ago. I discovered one of his affairs six months ago, although I'm sure there were others. We separated and the divorce is almost final."

"Wow. But why then are you on a cruise together?"

"He told me he would sign the papers if we made one last effort on this cruise. He had his attorney add a sweetener to the divorce papers. If I agreed to this trip, I get an extra hundred thousand. That's how I became a prisoner on a cruise ship," Rita laughed.

"That sounds more like bribery than an attempt to save a marriage."

"Yes, John, it is. I don't care about the money. I signed a prenup before we got married. It states I get a hundred-thousand upon divorce—now two-hundred after this trip. Unless I proved infidelity—which I can't. If I did, there's a clause in the contract that says I get ten-million. That was my contribution when he initially told me I'd have to sign a prenup if I wanted us to be married. But I just want him to sign the divorce papers…so I agreed to come. Look!" she said, pulling an envelope from her compact Coach handbag. "I carry them everywhere I go—two sets. One copy's the standard divorce and the other's the ten million draft. I've carried that one around since I caught him cheating, hoping I could catch him in the act, instead of lipstick marks, obscure calls, or soiled panties stuffed inside a suit jacket pocket. He's a very wealthy man, John. If I didn't come, he has the ability to make this divorce a very drawn-out and painful ordeal. It's a game. Wealthy men love games. I just want to be free."

"I wish…I wish there was something I could do."

"You already have, John," Rita sniffled. "You wore a new shirt!"

"You like it?" Pulling his t-shirt taunt. It depicted a basketball court carved out of a corn field, a slew of Kansas Jayhawks playing on the homemade arena. The top heading read: *2008 National Champions* and the bottom caption: *If You Build It, They Will Win.*

"I like it very much, almost as much as I enjoyed watching *Field of Dreams,* almost as much as having you all to myself while you truly listen to my pathetic problems. Thank you," she said, leaning in to hug.

John's head rested sideways on her shoulder, facing toward the staircase when George ascended to the top step. Quickly freeing himself from her grasp, he looked at Rita with a drawn, worried look. Confused, she wiped her eyes as George approached.

"What the hell's going on here?" George snapped.

Snapping back. "Nothing, George! We just came up here for a drink, because the bar downstairs was too busy."

Choosing to be invisible while polishing already spotless glassware, Will watched, without looking, from the end of the bar. Like a detective, he had eavesdropping down to a science.

"Don't kid yourself, darling, it appears to be busy up here too," George insinuated. "And why does it look like you've been crying?"

Rita's face tightened. With one convulsive grimace she turned into a female, Latin version of Hasamoto—not to be trifled with. "Not that it's any of your business, but John was telling me about his son, whom he tragically lost in the war!"

George, reining in his jealousy, turned to John. "I'm sorry about your son, but you really must be careful about touching another man's wife. A harmless gesture could easily be misconstrued as an attempt at theft—a dangerous venture."

"Stop it, George!" she said. "He didn't do anything wrong…and I'm not your wife!"

Laughing under his breath before suddenly changing his disposition. "Yes, well, I was hoping we still had a few days to discuss that. Don't we?" George asked, with puppy-dog eyes. "I was thinking we should check out the casino, see if we can break the bank like the old days. Maybe some roulette, like old times in Monaco…what do you say, honey?" Holding out his hand.

Rita used compromise to surrender, not wanting to embarrass John further with her domestic problems. "I'm going to say goodnight to John. I'll meet you *downstairs* in two minutes."

Raising palms to shoulder height. "Take your time, my love."

John used a jittering hand to lift his wine as Rita watched George, making sure he followed her direction. When the last sliver of George's head disappeared from the top step, she turned back. "I'm *so* sorry for that. I didn't mean to involve you in all this bullshit. Please forgive me?"

"There's nothing to forgive, you didn't do anything wrong," John said, trying to calm his fear and wondering where his inner dragon was. "You're just dealing with an unfortunate situation."

"Yes. The second time I've made a decision which propelled me into such an *unfortunate* place," she sighed. "Just like my first husband, George was good to me for a time. He has always been about power and control though. What is it about men that drives them to always want more? What tempts them to strive for what they can't have?"

"I don't think men have a monopoly on greed and narcissistic desire. I think when people have a hole inside, they often try to fill it with external things before searching for solutions internally."

"You're right, John. I think when George found out he couldn't have children, it emasculated him and he used that angst as an excuse to stick his dick wherever he wanted—pardon my French. He might have been compensating for something he had no control over—not that I care anymore."

"If it's any consolation, it sounds like you'll have a clean slate in six more days."

"Yes. Six more days," Rita beamed. "I better go, John. Will I see you in port tomorrow?"

"I'll be there. I have a date to ride jet skis first thing in the morning with Dani's son, Garrett. If I'm still alive, maybe I'll see you on the beach?"

Rita's eyes flickered when she heard John mention Dani and Garrett, envious of their chance to spend time with him without any restrictions or obligations. "That sounds like fun, but please be careful. I don't want to see you on the beach with a cast!" Sharing laughter. "Goodnight John. Please tell everyone else good night for me? And I regret being Cinderella."

"I will, Rita. Goodnight," he lamented.

Giving John a tender peck on the cheek, she dropped a twenty dollar tip on the bar, and pushed herself to go downstairs. John watched and then swiveled back to rest his arms on the bar, exhaustion from the day's events set in. The drill instructor and naked fireman had left the building sometime between John's dance routine and Rita's retreat. Dried sweat and intense longing were all that remained. Pulling the charge card from his pants pocket and motioning to Will, John yearned for escape.

Seeing and hearing everything, Will happily abandoned the redolent third-time cruisers in front of him for John's white-flag. "What's next my friend?" he asked, chewing on a straw.

"I'm pretty tired, Will. I think I'm going to pack it in for tonight."

"Sure? It's not even eleven-thirty, night's young. You could fuel up at the midnight buffet?"

"No. I'm not used to all this excitement. And if I eat again now, I'll probably have nightmares. I think I'll be better off resting up for port tomorrow."

"I hear you," Will said, running the card.

"Is there a chance I'll see you in port tomorrow?"

"Count on it! I have to get up at five to do stores."

"Stores?"

"That's what we call collecting booze and supplies. The hull of the ship is a huge warehouse. We use big carts to run all around locked cages to fill our inventories for the day. It all gets checked and signed, and checked again before we wheel everything off to our respective bars. Tomorrow we have to take a load over to Solace Point. It's really just a beach and marina with a few buildings and tiki huts. The company doesn't advertise it, but Solace Point is just an old Club Med that went under. Our company leases the land from the Haitian government."

"Huh…I didn't know that."

"The Haitians love it. They get six dollars a head every time a ship comes in. We employ five hundred locals to maintain the property and sell their wares. And, we've sunk over fifty million into improving the property, the bulk of it on the new pier. Before, we had to moor in the open harbor and ferry everyone and everything ashore. It was time consuming, not to mention a pain in the ass. Now, it's more like a self-contained resort than a third-world beach. We built a zip-line that stretches right over the water in front of the main beach. It's a good time. I don't think I have to work until sail away, maybe we can play some volleyball or something?"

"I'd like that. Maybe you'll have some fresh wisdom for me."

"Wisdom's like an Easter egg hunt. The eggs are all out there for us to discover. But I may be able to direct you to a few good hunting spots!"

Grinning. "I'm sure you can."

Making his way back downstairs, John thought he should say goodnight to everyone before leaving. Two hundred passengers had stormed the late-night spot since he first arrived. Scouring the crowd for anyone familiar came up empty and just when he thought of giving up and apologizing later, he felt a poke to his shoulder. Turning to find Dani, her glowing smile kissed his face like a gently smushed cream pie.

"And where have you been?" she asked in an escalating tone. "I thought I'd lost the best dancer here!"

"That's sweet of you to say, but I think Red Bull and vodka should open a dance studio together." Laughing. "Rita and I had a drink upstairs with Will. It was too crowded down here."

"It's packed! I was just getting ready to leave. Buffy's staying here. I think she's enjoying the attention," nodding to the dance floor where Buffy was grinding with two different partners.

"Where's Elli?"

"She went back to check on the kids. Garrett's watching them. He's an excellent babysitter. Oh…your friends, the older couple…"

"Richard and Mary."

"Yes! Sweet couple! Rita introduced us to them before you made your *Soul Train* entrance. They told me to tell you they were going to take a stroll before calling it a night. They said they hope to see you in port tomorrow."

"Thanks, I was wondering about them. I was also getting ready to leave and wanted to find everyone to say goodnight."

"You'll have to settle for little old me, John, I'm about all that's left," she giggled, swaying slightly from her buzz. "Would you mind walking me back to my cabin?"

"I would be honored."

Casually walking Dani to her cabin, the two made small talk about things they did during the course of the day. John shared what Will told him about their impending port-of-call, the early morning routine of the staff, and the definition of *stores*. The two talked with ease, like old friends. Before John knew it, they were standing outside Dani's cabin.

"Thank you for everything today, John. It was really nice what you did for Garrett, and I apologize again for Elli. I think she has terminal PMS sometimes."

"I should be thanking you. Today was a treat for me. What time should I plan to meet Garrett?"

"I'll make a reservation for ten. That work?"

"Sounds great."

John's boyish smile captivated Dani. The two shared a moment of silence; then Dani made a decision to make a move. Her single deliberate kiss touched John's lips briefly, but with velvety softness that would linger in his mind for a very long time. "I hope that was an acceptable way of saying goodnight?" Dani asked.

Perfectly frozen, searching his brain for the right answer, the door opened, saving him from inevitably mumbling. Elli frowned in disappointment at the couple. "Hello," Elli said. "I thought I heard voices out here. I hope I'm not interrupting anything?" she asked with polite sarcasm.

"No, honey," Dani said. "John walked me back and we were just saying goodnight. How are the kids?"

"They're all crashed, full of pizza and ice cream. I relieved Garrett about a half hour ago. Kayla and Brie are asleep next door in my room. I just brought Jill back here. Buffy still out?"

"Uh-huh. She had quite the fan club when we left."

"Shocker. Well, I'm going to the room for a glass of wine before bed. Why don't you join me after you check on Jill and Garrett?"

"I might. Thanks for putting Jill down."

Kissing Dani's cheek. "No problem. Night." Elli refused eye contact with John as she brushed by, but said, "Night farmer John…nice shirt," she scoffed, sliding her card into the lock and disappearing inside.

"Thanks," John said, after the door shut.

"Well…I better check on the kids. Thanks for walking me back, John."

Most of his composure returned since their kiss, although he still felt it; replaying it over and over in his head. "It was my pleasure, Dani. Goodnight."

John stayed long enough for Dani to enter her cabin. As the door closed, all the sweet smells of her washed over him. He breathed it all in, hoping to store them to memory: the smell of her perfume and body odor, her clothes, and the wonderful scent of children. The mixture intoxicated him more than anything he drank during the day. He'd never been prone to singing, but an overwhelming force coaxed him into repeating the chorus of the first song he'd danced to at Pulse: *"Oh, oh, oh, oh, sometimes I get a good feeling, yeah."* It didn't matter that he wasn't familiar with the group or song. All that mattered was he could relate. He whispered the words the whole way back to his cabin, where it only took one swipe of his keycard to gain entrance.

DAY 3
(SOLACE POINT)

FIRST FOOTSTEPS

WHEN JOHN WOKE AT 8:00 he fought the sudden onset of the conflicting feelings of joy and guilt. He could still feel Dani's kiss on his lips. It was as though he'd somehow cheated on Rita, or perhaps his ex-wife. *Nonsense,* he reasoned. Rita was married to another man, and he had only talked with her. Page divorced *him.* And Dani's kiss was simply a thank you goodnight gesture—or was it? After ten minutes of rolling back and forth in bed, his heavy conscience and full bladder urged him to the bathroom.

Jack and Nancy Smith had raised their son Catholic, although, John had never found answers to the ultimate questions in organized religion. Religion was full of rules—and loopholes for them—it all sounded too much like government to John. At home, when Carson was alive, the Smith's attended church for normality-sake and family stability, as much as to hear the choir music, sermons, and digest a soul-saving Eucharist. After the divorce, he stopped attending the local church, except on major holidays. Still…being raised Catholic had instilled in him an eternal sense of guilt. He woke feeling guilty about Dani's kiss.

John decided to rid himself of all his negativity by washing it down the drain. He stood in the shower as hot as he could make it for as long as he could stand it. But when he opened the glass shower door and stepped onto the bathmat, he was blind from the steam; he'd forgotten to turn the fan on. Stepping forward, he used his left hand to locate the counter and his right to wipe the foggy mirror. Apparently, the steamy shower hadn't absolved his guilt. The only reflection John made out was of his ex-wife, Page.

Agitated by the hallucination, he hastily turned into the door. Unfortunately—even blinded in a room full of steam—he knew exactly where the doorknob was. The sudden influx of pain sent him to his knees and rekindled a flashback of playing basketball in the driveway with Carson and two neighborhood kids. Page had come outside to ring the dinner-bell and when John turned toward her voice, Carson passed the ball. If John's knees had been bent in a ready position, the pass would've been at perfect chest level; instead, standing upright, the ball smacked him square in the teabags.

Laughing in pain, he slowly reached up to open the door and let out some steam. Still laughing, catching his breath, gingerly making his way to his feet, and still dripping on the tile floor, the pain in his groin trumped any normal tendencies towards compassion. He grabbed the cotton swan by the throat and whipped it against the floor. When he saw it as a towel again and nothing more, he dried himself.

His bathing suit was a given for a day at the beach, and the t-shirt of the day stated his company name, Keep It Together. His old Converse All-Stars didn't seem right for walking around in the sand. They were cumbersome at the pool, surely they would be like walking around on sheets of sandpaper after five minutes on the beach. He wondered if the shops were open on the Promenade. He'd forgotten to pack sandals, since he kept them in a rented locker at the YMCA. He and Page used the YMCA a lot when Carson was a child. He'd maintained the membership since the boy took his first swimming lessons there, but John used it more in the last six months to relive memories as both a comfort and a penance. To John, there was a thin line between a beautiful cathedral and a morbid prison.

Passengers on their way to breakfast or the disembarkation gates swarmed the halls. Everyone was dressed like they were on their way to a pool party. John did a double-take every time he passed a woman with a hat, thinking it might be Rita.

Arriving in the ship's main plaza, John gawked with an open mouth. The Promenade spanned three-fourths the length of the ship, with Italian marble flooring, and a fifty-foot ceiling over hundreds of cabins whose balconies opened over the shops and bars lining the busy street. Every inch of the ship offered something to do, but if there was a heart—it was the Promenade. John meandered by the liquor store and cigar club, passed an ice cream shop and a pizza counter, and just after the arcade and Champagne Bar, he found a fashion store.

"Good morning!" said a perky saleswoman, dressed South Beach casual—colorful, tasteful, and light; geared for outdoor heat or a cocktail party. She spoke with a British accent and smelled like freshly watered botanical gardens. "May I help you?"

"Huh…I hope so. I'm going ashore this morning and I think I may need something more suitable, and hopefully more fashionable, in the way of footwear."

"You might indeed," she smiled. "I don't think those will fare too well in all the sand. Let me show you our sandals."

Forgetting to read the woman's name tag, John asked, "Are you from England?"

"South Africa! The home of world class wine, great white sharks, and apartheid," she snickered. "Fortunately, we abandoned the latter, but we still have the sharks and wine. Have you been?"

"No. I'm from Kansas," he stated, for lack of a plausible reason for not having visited her country. "Gilda," John read, trying to amend his gaffe. "Pretty name."

"Thank you! I've met many fine people from Kansas while working here. Now…let's see if we can find you some beach shoes."

Gilda walked him to a wall holding dozens of sandals and boat shoes. After fitting himself for the correct size, he asked her to choose a pair of flip-flops that she found most appealing. Satisfied with Gilda's pick—assuring him everyone would be envious of the latest style—he paid, leaving with a plastic bag housing his old kicks.

Pleased with his purchase, he enjoyed a slight spring in his step on the way to breakfast. Like the theatre, the main entrance to the dining room splayed wide enough to drive a bus through. A husky, balding maître d' with dark circles around his deep set eyes—possibly from working long hours, or just too much alcohol the night before—greeted and sat John at a table for two.

He ordered eggs, toast, and fruit from one of the waiters flying around the room. Fascinated by the staff, John studied their efficiency. Their large trays towered with as many as twenty plates fitted with stainless warming tops. He thought the waiters must have one arm bigger than the other, unless they switched arms for lunch and dinner. The kitchen's double doors at the far end of the room opened and closed with such frequency that they never stopped shuttering. Above the room's center, the main chandelier hovered like a ten-carat diamond perched on top of a queen's finger. When it came time for John to be served, a tiny Asian girl—not more than 4' 9"—approached his table holding only one plate. "Fo u!" she said. After removing the warmer and setting the plate in front of him, she smiled, nodded, and scurried off.

John nibbled on his meal in a bubble of relative peace and quiet, the way a squirrel chewed on a nut in the middle of a busy park. He'd gotten used to, but hadn't fully accepted, eating alone after the divorce. The solitude wasn't selfish like a bachelor enjoyed. The ritual became as arduous, as that of a widower who feels the need to cook for no other reason than to go on. While eating, he was conscious of the other couples around him, conversing, laughing, and arguing. At home, he was immune. Here, he couldn't hide from the hole he had fallen into. Each person he saw reminded him that life was out there—waiting. If he didn't grab it, it wouldn't wait. Everywhere John looked, people were living. He yearned to be one of them. It didn't matter how Carson got him where he was; it mattered that he was there. *Now, what am I going to do?*

After finishing breakfast, he pushed his chair back, stood, looked down at his new purchase, and whispered, "Let's go get you dirty."

IT'S LIKE RIDING A BIKE

THE GANGWAY SPIT OUT PASSENGERS with the pace of a slot machine giving up. The bright sun and warm breeze smacked John in the face like a hairdryer armed with a spotlight. Why didn't he own sunglasses, or buy a pair before he came, or in the store where he just bought his flip-flops...*why*, he asked himself. He recalled the last pair he remembered owning. The kind you might see in an old Burt Reynolds movie. He never replaced them after setting them on his car seat, forgetting, and then smashing them the next time he got in.

At least he remembered to wear his Chiefs hat and bring suntan lotion. He pulled the brim of his hat as far down as vision would allow. The new concrete pier extended a couple hundred yards from ship to shore. It jutted right, like a left arm slightly bent. The water on either side was a milky turquoise from the wind and gentle waves stirring up the white powder bottom in the shallows. The walkway ended—or began, depending on one's starting point—at a sandy beach, a crescent smile of sand skirting the tranquil harbor. Dozens of boat and jet-ski slips fingered out from the next beach over. A large arch marked the entrance through the thick brush lining the beach's shoulders. Its sign read: Welcome to Solace Point.

John paused in the sand before following the other passengers through the open gate. The harbor was bigger than any lake he'd ever seen. *The Princess* stood firm like a child's toy boat in a calm bathtub. Haiti's small mountains—or large hills—hugged three quarters of the sound. Solace Point itself was mostly flat. A couple of modest hills marked the peninsula's two far ends. Only a few puffy, white, cartoon clouds floated by, low enough to cast brief shadows on the ship and water's skin. John had seen it all before—on postcards. In person, it all seemed surreal.

A group of women and children at the pier's elbow marched towards the beach. Many people were cruising with children, but something about this group was different. Even from a distance, John could see an air about Garrett, something rarely found in adolescent boys. He didn't wear it as a chip. He carried himself like a bodyguard holding a balloon. It was more than confidence. He was sarcastic—most kids his age were—but honest. Everything he did, he did with the transparency of someone who had nothing to hide. To say he was a thirteen-year-old, wise beyond his years, would be an understatement. Garrett had the ability to potentially hurt through action or speech, but not in malice. At the same time, he had a generosity of heart that even strangers recognized. John admired Garrett as he neared, thinking he had the gait of a leader. Surely, someone that in charge of their own life, could and would, someday help others do the same. John saw a lot of Carson in Garrett.

Jill and the other two girls stayed close to their mothers as Garrett led the pack. His keen teenage vision spied John fifty yards before making his first step from concrete to sand. But he made no gesture, no hyper waves or acceleration in pace, no yelling John's name. John couldn't tell through Garrett's dark tinted Oakley's that he'd been spotted. Not until he walked right up to him.

"Cool flops!" Garrett said, removing his glasses. "I've been trying to get Mom to buy me a pair of those."

Elevating the bill of his hat with his thumb. "Thanks, Garrett. How are you today?"

"Good! I'm ready to tear it up! Did you see all the jets down there?" Garrett asked, pointing to the rental slips around the bend of the beach. "There must be twenty of them. I'm going to get the fastest one they have!"

"I think you should," John said. "I'll get the slowest one, just 'cause I hate wasting gas."

"You know…I think they have bicycle boats for rent," Garrett said. "You could take my little sister out if you're afraid of speed? When you're done…I bet she'd show you her Barbie collection if you ask nicely."

"That's tempting, but I promised to go the *big boy* route. I'll hang with you. You know…I've got a reputation to keep."

Garrett laughed, kicked the sand, and reapplied his glasses. The girls approached from behind. Sighing, Dani dropped her heavy beach bag, Elli and Buffy following suit.

"Good morning, John!" Dani said, adjusting her bikini top. John took extra notice of the white floral top and matching bottom. All three women wore different suits than they did at the pool. He wondered why women always had to wear something new—even swim suits—where men could wear the same bathing trunks for more than a decade.

John said, "Hi, Dani! Good morning. Hi, Buffy—ladies," he said, bending down and fluttering his fingers at the three daughters. "Morning, Elli!"

"Hell-o, *John*," Elli forced in a condescending tone.

"Hi, John!" Buffy giggled. "That was fun last night, huh? I just love dancing!"

"Yes! It *was* fun," he replied.

"You and Garrett must be pretty anxious to get on the jet-skis?" Dani asked, raising a brow.

"You know it!" John said. "We're going to *spread!*" Extending his knuckles for Garrett to punch.

Pursing his lips and shaking his head, Garrett said, "I think you mean *shred.*"

"Right. That's what I meant to say. Let's get to some serious shredding!"

Garrett reluctantly touched knuckles. As John looked up, he saw Elli's head lowered and shaking.

"Whatever you're going to do, make sure you're careful," Dani said, glancing at her watch. "I made the reservation for two at ten o'clock, but I'm sure they won't mind you guys getting there fifteen minutes early."

"Do I need cash?" John asked.

"Our ship cards work for all the amenities here, but you don't need to worry about it. I already paid for you both. The reservation was just in case it was too busy. You guys just go *shred*—safely!"

"Thanks, Dani!" John said. "Let me help you with that." He grabbed the beach bag straps before Dani's hand reached them.

"Thanks, John. Come on everybody. Let's go find some chairs and mark our territory!"

The two men brought up the rear of the bikini brigade. Local Haitians playing acoustic guitar and steel drums welcomed them on the other side of the arch. Solace Point housed two main beaches separated by two hundred yards of sand, palm trees, and assorted buildings. A designated kid's water park sat on the ship side beach, in front of the jet-ski slips. Volleyball courts, horse shoe pits, and hammocks littered the park in sporadic fashion. Most of the buildings dispensed food and beverages. Other buildings housed the necessities of any community. There was a police station manned by Haitians working with the ship's security chief. The first aid hut dealt with mostly sunburns and alcohol poisoning. The strip of shops between the two beaches—providing indigenous entrepreneurs a place to sell their wares of colorful art, jewelry, and clothes—looked like a boom town in an old western movie except the dirt was bright white, not tan. Built in an idyllic spot, Solace Point was a water park oasis for kids *and* adults.

John followed the girls, beach bag hanging from his shoulder, through the island bazaar to the much larger ocean-facing beach. They claimed a string of chairs while John set the bag on Dani's chair and waited at attention in case she needed anything else, but she was busy attending to Jill. John swiveled his head to Garrett, who raised his hands to chest level, rounded his fingers like he was holding onto a bar, and rolled his wrists up and down. After a few faux revs, he jerked his head twice over his shoulder.

"Ah…I think Garrett's ready to head over to the rental place," John said. "Can I do anything for you before we go?"

Still fidgeting with Jill's clothes and lotion. "No. Thanks, John. You guys head over. I'll come over in a bit to watch you two Evel Knievels and take some pictures. You don't have my iPhone, do you?"

"Nah," Garrett said. "It's in your bag."

Garrett and John took a few jogging steps to the top of the beach, slowing to a brisk walk by the time they made the tree line. The main path steered them back through the resort's version of downtown. Pulling up, John spotted a stand selling sunglasses.

"Come on, dude!" Garrett said, noticing John fell behind. "You can shop later."

Trying a pair from the metal rack. "How much?" he asked the woman seated behind the counter. Deja vu, he sensed. She was beautifully dressed in the most vibrant colors he had ever seen anyone wear. Not even Americans during the 70s strange period, attempted to pull off a costume with so many bright colors. Her headdress was wrapped in similar color and pattern to her main outfit, an ensemble fit for a parrot.

Flashing her perfect ivory smile. "Normally? Ten dollars…but you have a kind face. Eight dollars and I'll throw in a leash."

The painting on his cabin wall, John remembered. She could have modeled for the piece.

"Sold! I love your outfit. It's very beautiful."

John couldn't tell through her charcoal skin, but she appeared to blush.

"Thank you! You'll love Haitian women. It's in our nature to embrace all of God's colors. They remind us even when life's dark, the gift of light always returns," she said, fastening a neon orange leash to the frame arms of the translucent blue glasses. "There. Now you too have color to remind you how special life is."

Slipping the chain over his head and thanking her, he hurried back to Garrett, who stood waiting, hands on hips with a sour look on his face.

"What do you think?" John asked, pushing the glasses between his ears and cap.

"Not bad. A little bright, but not bad. You finally ready?"

"Let's do it!"

The pair jogged along the quasi-trail, passing through dense brush and palms, before coming out into a clearing and the beach that housed the water craft docks. Anywhere else they might have looked out of place, John with his *Keep It Together* t-shirt and blue and orange sunglasses, and Garrett with his pirate leg. But on Solace Point, they fit in just fine, like every other tourist.

Arriving right on time, Garrett gave his name at the kiosk as the attendant handed them wet suits and life jackets and directed them to a storage bin for their personal items. A short black man addressed them as they sat stuffing themselves into the rubbery outfits.

"*Good*-morning, gentlemen!" said the man, looking and sounding as upbeat and cheery as the colors in the sunglass woman's dress. After his bare feet, the first thing John and Garrett noticed was the man's red and white striped bathing suit, more of a *banana hammock* than bathing suit. John couldn't help notice—his eyes being at waist level—his impressive…huh, flotation device. Men outside the US were obviously less modest with their attire. His yellow t-shirt read: *Solace Point Instructor.*

John and Garrett, feeling uncomfortable in their submissive position, stood up to finish dressing.

"My name's Barney!" said banana hammock. "Are we ready to have some fun today?"

"Yes we are!" John said, trying to erase the vision of Barney's candy cane.

"Excellent! Have either of you ridden wave runners before?"

"I have!" Garrett said.

"Superb! And how about you, sir?"

"No. This is my first time."

Barney belted out a deep throaty laugh. "No worries, man. It's very easy. Let's just fasten up your life vests and then I'll show you your rides."

"We want the fast ones!" Garrett said. "Not the ones you give little kids to ride with their parents." The last time he rode was when his mom and dad were still together. They used to vacation on the Jersey shore. Garrett was only six and had to be accompanied by a parent. He still remembered the instructor telling his father that they gave parents with small children a model with less horsepower.

Garrett was more of a timid kid before the accident, before Dani challenged him into independence. When he was young and she was still married, Dani, in normal first child mode, tended to be more protective. She always feared the worst instead of hoping for the best. The accident, and her son's withdrawn demeanor, changed that philosophy. After all, in her mind, the worst *had* happened and they were both still here. Some people fall hard when kicked, others stand up taller.

"*Ha-ha-ha!*" said Barney, hunched over slightly and pointing. "I might have something special."

Barney walked them over to an adjoining dock, separated from the slew of mono-colored wave runners. He held out his hand to two jets bobbing by themselves, as if they were bad children sent to a time out.

"I think this is what you're looking for!" said Barney.

Confused, Garrett replied, "They're pink! I said we want to go fast, not look like we're going to get our nails done!"

Another deep laugh. "Wolf in sheep clothing, young man!" said Barney. "Trust me."

Staring at each other. John, hoping for a more docile ride, said, "They look fine to me."

Exhaling a deep, reluctant sigh, Garrett surrendered. "*A-l-l right.*"

Barney walked them through the safety procedures, instructing them not to go beyond any of the orange buoys. He said one of the instructors was always out on the water and would tell them when their time expired and warned them to always look out for other riders. When he finished, they both crouched down and threw a leg over the hot pink seats.

"Just slip that bracelet on your wrist," said Barney, pointing to the rubber chain that looked like a smaller version of an old rotary dial phone cord. It attached to a black button just below the green starter button. "That's your lanyard. If you fall off, that'll engage the kill switch, so you won't have to swim far to rejoin your pink lady!"

Garrett pressed the green button. His pink lady came alive with a deep throaty purr, water churning behind his seat from the propeller forcing liquid though the jet. He glanced at John who was still trying to get situated.

"See ya!" Garrett shouted, rolling the throttle slightly and exiting the slip.

John watched as Garrett steered to his left and rolled harder on the throttle. In three seconds, he was gone. Touching his green button, John's pink lady squealed like a pig. A second try. Again, the starter spun, but didn't turn over.

Looking to Barney. "Maybe I don't know how?"

Smiling. "Sure you do! It's as easy as riding a bike. It hasn't run for a while. Try it again!"

"Okay," John said, pushing the button a third time, igniting a spark that brought his wave runner rumbling to life. A haze of white smoke rose from her rear.

"You might want to put those on," said Barney, waving his pointer finger up and down at John's glasses. "You might lose them if you don't."

Heeding Barney's warning, John slid the glasses on, although he found the request odd, since the glasses were harnessed to a strap around his neck. After one last glance at Barney, who had a nefarious look on his face and offered a thumbs up, John slowly rolled his right hand.

The pink lady purred a little louder as she moved from her slip and continued along Garrett's path. When he felt safely away from the dock, John rolled the throttle a bit farther, causing the rear end to sink deeper and the bow to lift. The smooth power and quick pace instantly made John smile from ear to ear; he was shooting through the harbor with tickled adrenaline, dancing on top of the blue green water like an ice skater. He could almost hear Mozart singing in his head.

For twenty minutes he glided through the harbor, literally footloose and carefree. The gulls above seemed to mimic his nonchalant riding technique, as if their flight bore no purpose other than the sheer joy of stretching their wings. The only time he was reminded there were other riders blasting through the harbor was when their wake crossed his path. Ironically, John's indifference to everything but the moment fueled deep emotions. He found himself laughing, crying, and screaming at any given moment for no reason other than he felt like it. Carson the Dragon was alive, exhaling a gentle flame.

Finally throttling down, John sat idly watching kids scream and dance, the way only youth can. Garrett carved doughnuts and figure eights out of a small patch of water, contorting his body and machine in a violent manner, testing both limitations. A couple of minutes passed before he took a break to talk with John.

"Hell yeah!" Garrett said, draping his forearms over the handle bars. "These things are a blast!"

"I have to admit, it's a lot more fun than I thought it would be," John said, a calm satisfied expression on his face.

"I passed you a couple times," Garrett jabbed. "You didn't look. You ride like a kite in a tame breeze."

"I didn't…I guess, I was just taking it all in. You know, enjoying the moment."

"Nothing wrong with that. I'm just giving you shit. Hey, you ready to throw down? See which one of these bitches has more balls."

"I don't know…mine's pretty fast."

"Are you kidding? I don't think yours is even warmed up. Did you even turn your throttle half way yet?"

"I used enough gas to get me going pretty good, I thought."

"Let's race to the other side of the bay."

"I don't know."

"Come on, John. It's just a straight line. We'll start from a dead stop and just let these bitches go!"

Thinking for a moment, concluding that as long as they were clear of other riders, there wouldn't be any harm. It wasn't like they were drag racing through town or anything. They were on water, in a giant open space. "Okay. But we go when I say it's safe. I don't want to see another boat or ski anywhere near us. K?"

"I'll say *go* when you say *ready*."

"Let's start from over there," John said, pointing to the non-beach side of the harbor, vacant of any activity. "We can go as far as the orange markers. That's a good ways and there's nobody over there."

"Sounds like a plan. Let's do it."

Riding over to the starting line with the preliminary pace of race horses being escorted to their gates, John made them separate by a good twenty yards and removed his sunglasses, allowing them to hang over his life vest to ensure unobstructed peripheral vision. Garrett reached inside his vest and dried his hands the best he could on his wetsuit. The pink ladies gurgled idly as John scanned the water for any potential dangers. When he felt it was safe he turned to Garrett.

"Okay. I think we're pretty good. If we see anyone headed our way, we stop, deal?"

Nodding.

"When I say *ready*.

Again nodding.

One last look around, and then… *"Ready!"*

"G-o-o-!"

Both riders rolled their throttles back as far as they would go.

John would later equate the next twenty seconds to what it must feel like for a baby to be ripped from his mother's womb, thrown down the birth canal, and shot through a half open door into a pool of saltwater—but at light speed.

The rear of John's machine dropped with so much force it was as if a great white was taking it down. The power, though strong and immediate, doubled every second. The kitty's purr instantly grew to a lion's roar. His Chiefs hat jumped off his head like it was caught on a fisherman's hook. He clenched the grips tighter and tighter, praying for a pinnacle of force. The ski's fuel injectors yawned wide, inhaling gas. The outside corners of his eyes flattened towards his ears and the incoming air pried his mouth wide open to his jaw bone limits, making his cheeks flap like clothesline laundry in a twenty-five mile an hour wind. He thought if any flying insect got caught in the suction, they would tear his tonsils through the back of his neck. If the concept of horizontal gravity existed, John was falling. This was the reason nobody tried parachuting from the side of a jet at Mach ten. His leash became a choker. The new sunglasses pulled their damnedest to free their arms from their sleeves. The power finally peaked, but John couldn't slow down, his throttle wrist locked in full backward position. Spray sheered off the bow and onto John's grips until, in a blink, the pink lady went on without him. It was as if he'd squatted, clenching a football with his ass, and someone came up from behind and kicked it through.

An instructor had been watching from a distance. Barney had earlier radioed him to keep an eye on the two riding the pink tampons—the moniker given by the instructors for the two souped up wave runners normally reserved for expert riders. He had witnessed John and Garret's take-off and was making his way to John's hat before the fall.

"Are you all right?" asked the instructor, wearing a more traditional length bathing suit.

"I think so," John spit.

"I see she buck you!"

"Probably a good thing. I think if I stayed on any longer, we'd have taken flight." John's lanyard had done its job. His pink lady rested thirty feet away, her throat choked by the shut-off switch. Chuckling, the instructor took John's hand and slowly towed him back to the ski.

"Here's your hat."

"Thanks...uh—"

"Fred!"

Really, John thought. *The instructors' names are Fred and Barney?* "That doesn't sound like a Haitian name?"

Laughing. "My dad's from Ohio. He met my mother here when he was in the Peace Corp."

Returning from the finish line, Garrett had his own struggles hanging on and never saw John fall. "Are you okay, John?"

"Yeah. I think the only thing hurt is my ego."

"I think we got our money's worth! These things look like tits on the outside, but they're all balls on the inside!"

"You got that right. I don't know if I can ride any more though, Garrett."

"You don't have to," said Fred, tapping his diver's watch. "Good news! Your time is up."

"Thank God!" John said, climbing aboard and driving at a snail's pace back to shore.

A GUIDE TO THE WIZARD

D ANI WAS STANDING BY THE kiosk, camera in toe, as John and Garrett dismounted.

"Hi!" she said. "Stay right there! I want the jet skis in the background."

They posed for the camera. Smiling, John looked a bit like the Joker with his wind-stretched face.

"That's a good one!" Dani said, continuing to snap away with her iPhone.

"We'll be here all day, if we don't do something," Garrett said. "She hates taking pictures, but when she does, she takes a shit-ton. I steal it every chance I get. That way we get more interesting pictures. When she isn't holding it, she forgets to take boring family photos."

"I hear you buddy," John said. "Hey Dani…how about I get a couple of you guys," he suggested, motioning for the camera.

Grumbling, Garrett said, "That's not what I had in mind."

"Too bad," John said, snapping away, thinking Dani looked even more beautiful, a prideful glow on her face as she hugged her son.

"Thank you, John. Did you guys have fun? You look a little…*spent.*"

Turning to Garrett and sighing, John said, "It was pretty fun, but it would have been better if they didn't give us the dogs."

"*Oh*…that sucks," Dani said, making a pouty face at Garrett. "That happened to you when you were little and you went with your dad."

Flashing teeth at John. "It's okay, mom. Next time we'll get *really* fast ones."

"I hear NASA has a couple!" John and Garrett cackled at their inside joke.

Shaking her head, Dani realized she'd missed something, but didn't feel the need to push her way into the boys' club. "Everyone wants to ride the zip line, honey. We've been watching everyone else. They fly right over the water where we're sitting. You in?"

"Sure!" Garrett said.

Raising her brows. "What do you say, John, you in?"

"You guys go ahead. I could use a beer and a rest first. And I'm sure it's five o'clock somewhere. I might try and find Will."

"Okay," Dani said. "Tell him I said hello if you see him. He seems like a really good guy."

"Yeah," John said. "I think he is."

Garrett stripped out of his outfit before John could even remove his life vest. The two pounded knuckles before Garrett and Dani made their way back to the beach.

John pried himself loose of the latex-like wetsuit and returned it the attendant. Retrieving his company shirt from the bin, he saw Barney walking towards him.

"Well, what did you think?" Barney asked, sporting a fiendish grin.

"I'll never look at the color pink the same way."

Barney's howl came out as if he'd been holding his breath for two minutes. "Get yourself a nice cold drink, mon!"

"As we speak, Barney. As we speak."

John made his way back along the path through town, pausing to admire the colorful Haitian paintings and jewelry. Tinny music from steel drums brought his pre-jet ski joy back. He stopped at the first thatch-roofed Tiki bar he saw.

"*Corona*, please," he said, handing over his charge card to a nappy-headed bartender. "Is Will Catcher working here today?"

"If volleyball's work, than he's doing a good job. He's over there," said the bartender, pointing with John's Corona.

"Thanks!"

Walking over to the pick-up game, he sat on a beach chair and took a satisfying gulp of beer. A dozen crew members were enjoying some much deserved R&R. The group was as diverse as a box of assorted chocolates. John couldn't speculate where they all hailed from without their name tags, but he could clearly tell they weren't all from the same neighborhood. Not even in New York or Miami would John find such a patchwork group, at least, not all playing and working together. The cruise lines hired everyone, throwing them together like the Olympic Games. It didn't matter where you were from, just that you could perform the job.

Will, true to his name, saw John before John saw him. He jogged over after spiking a point.

"Howdy, Mr. Smith! How goes it today?"

"Good, Will! Nice to see they give you some time off from dealing with us twenty-four-seven."

Laughing. "Here and there. How about joining us?"

"Aw, no. I don't want to interrupt your game, plus…I'm not any good."

"Life's not always about being good. It's about having fun! Don't you remember what I told you about that?"

"Fun just threw me on my ass over at the jet ski place."

"Let me guess. The pink tampon?"

"How'd you…never mind. Dumb question. Yeah."

"Fred and Barney love to fuck with people that ask for fast rides. Those two demons belong to them. They're race skis and the Flintstone boys are professional riders."

"It all makes sense now. I went with Dani's son, Garrett; he was on a speed mission. Oh! She said to say *hi*. I told her I was going to try to find you."

Perking up. "Nice woman! Pretty, too!"

"Yeah. I think her ex-husband really let a good one get away. I just met her though. I guess you never really know what goes on in other people's marriages. Her son's a really special kid, I know that."

"You *playin'?*" shouted one of the crew members.

"Go ahead. I'll be there in a minute." Will sat in the chair beside John and wiped his face with his shirt sleeve. "Sounds like you might be interested?"

"What do you mean?"

"Well…she's single. You're single. She's beautiful. And excuse me if I step over a line here, but…" Thinking pensively. "You lost your only son, and…I'm not suggesting anything could ever replace him…but, you seem to think a lot of her son. Maybe. Maybe it's something worth pursuing?"

"I'm not sure it works that way."

"It works however *we* decide it works, John. Free will—pun intended and all."

"Do you have kids, Will?"

"Summer kids."

"What?"

"Summer kids. You know, *some are* here *some are* there." Slapping John's knee. "That's an old bartender joke. No. I've never had any children."

Forcing a chuckle. "This may sound perverse to you, but I'm reminded too much of my son when I look at Garrett. It's not just that Carson was killed violently and Garrett lost his leg. Carson looked at, and handled life, the way I see Garrett living. The boys could be brothers in character and attitude—even personality wise. It's wonderfully too familiar to be around long term. I'm afraid I wouldn't be a proper role model for a boy like that, because I'd always be comparing him to a ghost. It wouldn't be fair to him or me. Even if for just a second, I saw him as anything else other than exactly who *he* is. Do you understand?"

Locked onto John's eyes. "I believe I do," Will pondered. "If you were to ever have a son of your own again, isn't there a possibility that the same thing could happen with him?"

"Sure. But I think it's different when it's your own child. The inherent love and responsibility is always stronger than it would be for someone else's children. Plus, I don't think I'll ever have another child."

"Why not?"

"Face the facts, Will. I'm forty-seven, average looking at best, divorced, and I work at a rubber band factory in the middle of nowhere—or at least a suburb of it."

"Bullshit! Sorry, but I think that's a copout. I think if you took the time to look, you'd find that most women care less about the wrapper and more about what's inside."

"You mean my dragon?" John smirked.

"Forget the dragon, John. I'm talking about character. That's the credit card that buys our dreams. You have a lot of credit in my book."

"Thanks, Will."

"Like my fellow Jamaican bartender brothers say: '*No Problem, it ain't a t'ing.*' You ready to play?"

"Okay, but I warned you. I'm not very good."

Facing the game. "Look out there, John. Everybody out there sucks at volleyball, yet they're still having a great time. Why do you think that is?"

Examining the players, John could plainly see Will was right. No great digs, blocks, or spikes, just everyone laughing and jumping around. The free-for-all contest seemed more about catchy epigrams and playful sarcasm than scoring.

"Because they're in paradise?" John asked.

Sighing. "Because they're *drunk*, John! Look…half of them can barely see the ball. We're *F and B* people. If you're a proctologist, you enjoy sticking your finger up people's asses. Food and beverage people enjoy food and beverage—a lot. We got four hot girls to play this week. What's better than drinking three cases of beer and a bottle of rum for breakfast and then coming out here to watch those pretty girls jump up and down in bikinis? I thought you were more perceptive—really, paradise?" Will scoffed.

"I guess I'm still learning."

"Stick with me, John. I'm going to make you an honorary crew member for the rest of the week. Show you the *wizard* behind the curtain. It's a great education. It's a great education. You up for it?"

"Sounds dangerous."

"Very," Will said, folding his hands across his legs. "Are you trustworthy?"

Thinking. "I can't remember the last time I lied. I never cheated on my wife. I've never fudged my taxes, and I've never given-up a secret."

"Sounds a little suspect," Will frowned playfully. "But it'll have to do. Come on!"

Will stood up and held out his hand to lift John. The two shook hands before breaking out into laughter. John was flattered that a cool guy like Will would take the time to befriend a passenger and take him into his inner circle. John had never been the *cool kid* before, but for the first time, walking onto the volleyball court, he knew what it felt like— great.

With his best Vanna White impression, Will said, "Everybody! This is John Smith. John, this is everybody!"

"Johnny! Yeah! Mr. Smith! Smith and Wesson! Woo! Jon Jon!" said everybody.

John spent the next ninety minutes jumping and diving in a blissful blur, occasionally admiring the four bouncy women frolic for shots; their tanned, sand-peppered skin glistening in the sun, erased any memory of banana hammock. He played as well, if not better than, anyone else—except for Will, who lettered in volleyball in high school—scoring several points for his team in each game.

On the last point of John's final game, he dove after a ball that veered for the sideline. He hit the sand chest and face first, while balling his right fist and flicking the ball backhanded with enough force to send it eight feet high to his teammates. Will finished the save by cracking it at its apex. The heavy topspin strike cleared the net with ease, and then dropped like a rock at the feet of a bear-like guy guarding the back corner.

"Shit, Will!" the bear cried. "Next time *you* rotate for both sides. It's not fair having one side loaded up. And then you rub salt in the wound by pulling John Smith the ringer out'a nowhere."

"Hey Garth, can I get you some cheese to go with that *wine* of yours?" Will asked, slapping high-fives with John and their fellow teammates.

Garth ducked under the net, stomping over to Will, who saw him coming and spun into a lowered wrestler pose. Garth arrived just in time to snag the back of Will's lower thighs, squeezing Will's legs together with locked wrists. And with one deep grunt and hoist, Will landed on Garth's shoulder like a sack of potatoes.

"Na," Garth said. "That's okay, Will. I think I found the *cheese* I'm looking for."

"I'm warning you doughboy! You're about a second from getting deported back to Africa, via my foot!" Will squirmed.

"You impotent American! Stop with the sweet talk. If I wanted someone to tongue my ear, I'd call your girlfriend."

Will, despite being in excellent shape and weighing around two hundred pounds, couldn't free himself from Garth's grip. Garth went six-three and weighed close to three hundred, much of it looking like flab. Underneath Garth's thick façade though, was plenty of muscle; he was not to be underestimated.

"Why don't we just call yours?" Will twisted. "She's waiting naked in my cabin right now!"

Everyone steered clear of Will and Garth, for fear they might be trapped underneath if they fell. The girls clapped and whistled. The other crew members egged-on their favorite or spewed sarcasm for the sake of adding fuel to the fire. Everyone laughed, except John, who couldn't tell if the fight was real or show.

"That's it!" Garth said, hammering elephant-size footsteps towards the water. "Pretty boy needs a bath!"

"You sure you want to do this?" Will giggled. "You're going to get your tampon wet!"

"It'll be worth it to shut you up with a mouth full of ocean. Everyone will finally find out whether you spit or swallow!"

Garth walked into the water—gaining attention from many guests sunning themselves by the water's edge—until it reached the top of his knees. He squatted into a power lifter's position, drew a deep breath, and leaped up and forward; driving his shoulder, and Will, through the water. After twenty seconds of what looked like a shark feeding frenzy, the two re-emerged, free of Garth's bear hug. They embraced each other with loud cackles and hard slaps on the back. Garth draped one forearm around Will's neck and raised the other in a boxer's fist as they exited the water to an ovation of claps and cheers. John finally realized the two were friends and their performance was just a grab-ass show, for the amusement of the rest of the crew and passengers.

"Next week I'll give you Roxy and Sugena for Abby and Tara," Will offered.

"Deal! That should be perfect. I may still lose, but at least the *assets* and *pairs* will be in their correct places for my visual enjoyment."

"Amen, brother. Amen!"

John sauntered over.

"*Ah,*" Garth said, "the ace in the hole—Mr. Smith!" Offering a hand. "Garth Rubino, South Africa, at your service!"

John's hand disappeared inside Garth's mitt. "Nice to meet you, Garth. South Africa, huh? The home of world class wine, great white sharks, and the lingering stigma from the times of apartheid," John said, quite matter-of-factly.

Rolling his eyes at Will. "Somebody met Gilda."

"Definitely!" Will agreed.

"She sold me my new shoes this morning!" John said, holding up his flip-flops. "Nice woman."

"That she is, John," Garth said. "Too bad she's married to the first mate."

"Nice!" Will said. "I wondered if you were going to wear those old sneakers the whole trip."

"Yeah," John chuckling. "I guess I was due. Kansas isn't a big shopping mecca, you know. You guys made me nervous for a second, 'til I realized you were just friends horsing around."

"Garth and I go way back," Will said, punching Garth's thigh-thick bicep.

Returning the favor with more vigor. "Yeah, I met Willy here over thirteen years ago when we were both back on Carnival."

"Wow! You guys have worked on cruise lines for a long time."

Snickering. "Sort of," Garth said. "My mom works in Carnival's administration office in Miami. She helped me get hired as a bartender. I worked there 'til nine-eleven happened. All the cruise lines took a big hit after that mess. I went back to South Africa and worked on our ranch. But Willy and I raised some hell back when we first met in 99-2000. He quickly outgrew us, though, and took his American ass to Hawaiian Cruise Lines. Those dumb assholes went bankrupt eight months after he stepped onboard. Americans! They always think they can do everything better than the rest of the world—*just* because they're Americans. No offense, boys."

"A lot of times we can," John defended.

"I agree with you, but in this case Garth's right. HCL was this little company with one ship built in the early 1900s. *The Constitution*—a good American name. They operated for decades, teetering between red and black ink, with just one boat. This small steamer catered to mostly older people who loved the nostalgia of the classic ship and Hawaiian culture. You know: wood, brass, formal seating, Don Ho, girls in grass skirts, a lot of Hawaiian staff, Pearl Harbor, the works."

John added, "Elvis Presley in *Blue Hawaii!*"

"Jesus," Garth said. "Are you that old?"

"Saw it once when I was a kid."

"Well, anyway, you get the picture," Will said, snapping his fingers as if he just remembered something. "Where's the water?"

Garth's eyes widened. "I *am* thirsty. I left the bottles under the chair."

"Can I buy you guys a cold beer?" John asked.

"No," Will said. "Crew aren't permitted to consume alcoholic beverages on the Solace Point property. And, we're never permitted to drink with guests, or in guest areas, while onboard the ship," he said, like reading a warning sign.

"Why do they care, if you're not on duty?"

"For all intents and purposes, the company's the law here," Will said. "There's a gate at the beginning of the peninsula. No one who doesn't work here is allowed in. And no passengers are allowed to exit that gate. We lease this place from Haiti, but it really belongs to our company by default of how much money they've sunk into it. So it's like, when we're here, we're still on the ship—most of the rules still apply. Now *tomorrow's* a different story. Once we walk off the ship, we're on Mexican soil and can do whatever we want. The company doesn't lease or own anything there, so they can't tell us what to do!" Will and Garth performed a *Top Gun* windmill high-five.

"I'll grab the water," Garth said running off.

"I guess I can see the liability side of it, and the practical side," John said.

"Yes," Will said, gesturing for them to sit. "It wouldn't be practical to allow twelve hundred employee's to join the party. Can you imagine the problems? I can! But, like Garth said, we Americans often view the world through judgmental, sympathetic, and sometimes arrogant eyes—thinking we know how to do everything better. That's what happened when I went to HCL."

Pulling up a chair Garth said, "Here you go, brother."

"Thanks!" Will said as he took a big swig from the water bottle. "Where was I? Oh! *The Princess* here, and every other mega cruise-ship on the planet, is foreign-flagged. They're registered in countries where they can receive the best tax breaks. Panama, Bahamas, etcetera. Because they're not American owned and registered, they don't abide by US labor laws. That was a part of HCL's demise. When they were bought out by another American company, they became a publicly traded company, right there in black and white in the *Wall Street Journal*. The Miami office bought a used second ship and hired Americans from all over the country instead of just Hawaii. Those employees had to join the Seafarer's union and attend coast guard school. HCL and its employees had to pay US taxes like everyone else. Every dollar of every tip went on a paycheck and the ship was taxed at a much higher rate than if it were registered in say…Costa Rica."

"Those arrogant bastards didn't plan for that!" Garth said.

"Yeah, but that was just a small part of their fuck-up," Will slurped. "From the employee standpoint it was a pretty good deal, although most of them didn't realize it. Most had never worked for a foreign line—not the regular crew, anyway. We worked sometimes half as long for twice the money."

"And I bet you still bitched about it?" Garth said.

"I made a few waves, but not about money," Will laughed. "That's another story. Anyway, HCL couldn't afford to operate, paying union wages, dumping money into two broken ships, and incurring all the expenses involved with being American instead of a foreign country, not without raising the cost of the cruise. Raising the cruise price would've meant fewer passengers. They had to match their competition. On top of that, the home office on Oahu now had to take orders from Miami. They didn't like that and I didn't blame them much. They'd been operating this company—poorly, but alive—for over fifty years and now someone four thousand miles away was telling them how to do their job. The executives in Miami were all ex-bigwigs from other cruise lines hired to bring HCL back to profitability. I sat in on some of those early meetings—I was originally hired as a manager and then changed my mind before I flew to the ship—and, like Garth said, these guys were arrogant! They all thought the way they had run their respective companies: Costa, RCCL, Carnival, was the way HCL should be run. Instead of coming up with one common, fresh policy for Hawaiian, they swamped her with their own egos and foreign line practices that weren't relevant to an American cruise line. There are lots of other reasons why they went bankrupt, but those are the main reasons and the day's too short to keep talking about the past."

"Why after all that did you come back to work for a foreign line, Will?" John asked.

Garth, making a puppy-dog face. "He missed us."

"You wish!" Will huffed. "I swore I never would. I went back to bartending. An old buddy got me into buying real estate. I made a killing flipping properties in the Washington D.C. area after nine-eleven. Luckily, I cashed in just as the whole housing fiasco started to hit in 08. I'm not married, don't have any kids, and I missed traveling, so I figured I'd see if I could get back on one of these big party boats until the economic smoke cleared. It's been four years…the smoke keeps building. Glad I got out when I did; I know plenty of people who weren't so lucky."

"And you missed us," Garth added.

"Okay," Will gave in. "Maybe a little. What can I say? I have issues."

Will and Garth knocked water bottles.

"Enough stories for now. I'll tell you guys another one at bedtime. Let's get our zip line on!" Will said.

"You *know* that's just for the passengers," Garth said.

Will shook his head. "Not today! Today we're as good to go as our friend John here."

"Says who?" Garth asked.

"Yoda himself!"

"You talked to him?"

"Had the purser call when we made the flip Sunday."

"Who is Yoda?" John asked.

"He's a little green Jedi master, of course," Garth said looking annoyed. "Haven't you seen Star Wars?"

"He's my mentor, John. His name's Tony. He's the second American bartender to ever finish a six month contract for Carnival. I'm the third. He was our bar manager when we started. He's a hotel director now, the head dude for F and B on the ships. Only the captain has more power."

"The cruise directors think *they* do," Garth said. "I didn't tell you I put in for assistant cruise director training."

"They're nothing more than talking, washed-out, Vegas PEZ dispensers, with giant egos— you'll be perfect!" Will said.

"Thanks, Will," Garth grinned.

"Cruise directors aside, Yoda has real power and he says we can zip today."

Garth sipped more water. "What ship is he on now?"

"*Clarity*, I think."

"Willy's the man," Garth said. "He gets things done the rest of us can't. I think the company's afraid of him. Afraid he might give them bad press, 'cause he's American and all. We used to have to eat in the crew mess. Nothing but rice, leftovers from the dining room, and mystery meat. The Filipino guys love it, but it ain't great food. Will went straight to the top. Told the Captain he was American and couldn't eat rice every day while the officers and crew-staff—the entertainers, shop keepers, and casino people— ate like kings. Captain gave him and another three of us permission to eat the officers' food, as long as we took it somewhere else. Now we eat carved turkey, fish, fresh fruit, and veggies every day!"

"He's a good guy to have on your side," John said.

Shaking his head, Garth said, "The best!"

"Stop it," Will said. "I don't want the girls to see both of your lips on my ass. Here, John," offering his water bottle. "You better stay hydrated. The salt air will knock the water right out of you."

"Thanks," John said, gulping as Will and Garth anxiously watched. "*Holy shit!*" John choked. "That's vodka!"

"Welcome to Solace Point, John!" Will said, as Garth thumped John's back. "To the zip!" Will said.

"To the zip!" Garth returned.

Still coughing, John managed, "*Ta-da-sip!*"

A DIFFERENT VANTAGE POINT

T HE MOTLEY TRIO HEADED DOWN the beach, following a path cut through the thick brush at the sand's end. The path snaked back and forth, gently increasing in elevation, until finally opening to a kind of tall fort rising in a small clearing. Garth and Will hurried up the platform's center staircase while John hesitantly stood at the base, hands on hips, looking up. He counted four stories worth of stairs beside a thick steel column which supported the actual zip lines.

Noticing John hadn't followed, Will paused at the railing, calling. "Come on, John! There's no elevator. Those stairs aren't going to climb themselves!"

"I'm coming. Just catching my breath!"

Carson had no fear of heights when he was alive. He thought paratrooper training was like getting free skydiving lessons, and loved every second of it. He wrote home every time he made a training jump, explaining in detail how great the *rush* was.

John, on the other hand, had never shared his son's joy of heights. He might not have minded them so much if it weren't for a childhood incident. Jack and Nancy Smith had never been wealthy and they instilled in John, at a young age, the value of earning an honest buck for a hard day's work. When he was twelve, other kids in his neighborhood were all getting BMX bikes; all of them, purchased by their parents. When John approached his parents for a bike, they told him they were too expensive and he would have to earn the money himself.

So he worked in the neighborhood for the next two months raking leaves, cutting grass, and other odd jobs. When he came within thirty dollars of the two-hundred and fifty dollar bike of his choice, Jack Smith, feeling very proud of his son, offered John one last task for the remaining sum. All he had to do was clean the leaves and loose debris from his father's gutters.

In Jack's defense, they lived in—and still do—a modest one story house. The two gutters—one spanning the front; the other the back of the rectangular box—were not more than nine feet off the ground. Jack thought there would be no danger in his twelve-year-old son climbing a ladder to reach the grimy muck. It turned out, his assumption was incorrect.

John fell from the ladder reaching for the last three feet of the back gutter. Instead of climbing down and moving the ladder over a couple feet, he stretched his arm and fingers beyond their limitations, sliding with the ladder to the point of no return. Although the ladder fared fine, John broke his left wrist and forearm. The memory of hitting the ground was always in the back of his mind. Even at the ship's sturdy railing, John had been a bit uneasy for a minute. Still, he had learned to be more leery than petrified of heights, a minor phobia requiring him to *gear up*, rather than abandon them.

Using both railings and the middle of each step, he cautiously climbed. Annoyance and motivation set in after he was passed by several youngsters, and a few others who appeared a couple of decades older than forty-seven. Five minutes after Garth and Will, he finally appeared on the zip's top deck. The massive steel column he had seen from the ground, broke through the floor and peaked five feet over his head. It housed three thick cables which stretched across the water in front of the beach, connecting to an identical contraption on the opposite end, but at ground level. Gravity, literally would be the driving force.

"Hey man," Garth said, "what took you so long?"

"It takes me a minute to get comfortable with heights," John admitted, standing like a sailor who'd just stepped onto land after six months at sea.

Sensing his uneasiness, Will offered reassurance. "Don't worry, this thing's perfectly safe. I stake our lives on it! They say gravity kills, but in this case, it just makes for a nice ride with a great view. Take your time to get acclimated."

"Here," Garth said. "Drink some water."

Trying to regain his bearings and parched from the climb, he took a larger drink than normal. "M-y gawd!" John gagged. "For-got 'bout da wa-ter."

Two Haitians stopped fitting people with harnesses and looked over at John. "Are you okay, sir?" one of them asked.

"He's just really excited to do this," Will offered.

"I think he swallowed a mosquito," Garth said.

Using his fist to pound his chest. "*Fine! Just had…some water…go down the wrong pipe.*"

Grabbing hold of the platform railing, John tried to regain his composure by gazing out over the blue-green water lapping the beach. Out past the pure blues of the deeper ocean, his eyes found the horizon as a firm sea breeze massaged his face. Sucking in a deep, vodka-free breath, he slowly released his grip and raised his palms as if to stop the wind, allowing it to dry his sweaty hands.

Will approached. "Hey, buddy. You know, if you're uncomfortable up here, we can take you down."

Will's words sat on John's shoulder like a sparrow resting its wings. A tiny smile came to him as he turned. "I'm just fine. Thanks, Will. Ready?"

"That a boy!" Will said, pinching John's shoulder. "He's ready!"

"To the Zip!" Garth said, raising his water bottle.

The two Haitians fitted the group with a kind of diaper and straps made from thick nylon, then hooked them to the cables and checked everything.

"Last one across buys the first round at Carlos 'n Charlie's tomorrow!" Will challenged.

"You're on!" Garth accepted.

"I'm game," John joined, grabbing hold of the triangular bar.

"One!" Will started. "Two!"

"Three!" John finished, jumping from the deck.

Garth's size quickly used gravity to make up for John's head start. Will, having zipped many times, used excellent aerodynamic technique to make up *his* ground. John watched the two sail by. Admitting defeat long before the half way point, he decided to enjoy the view.

The world looked different from above. People on the beach became ant size, void of any asset or flaw. They were just small, alive, and insignificant compared to the bigger picture laid out above and below John. He admired a flock of birds crossing above. *All men dream of flying,* John thought. John remembered an old interview with Michael Jordan. The journalist asked Mike if he could really fly. Michael returned the question with a joyful grin and the words: "For a little while."

John's body became so limp and relaxed, his momentum stopped just short of the landing point. A worker reached up and dragged him home as Will and Garth greeted him.

"Guess I'm buying," John said, a content expression on his face.

"We thought maybe you were stopping for lunch up there," Garth ribbed.

Will laughed. "Told you, nothing to it…right?"

"That was a lot of fun," John said. "It all looks different from up there."

"You wanted wisdom," Will said, patting John's cheek. "Enlightenment is a first step."

Pulling the harness off, John said, "I think it's more like…perspective."

Garth rubbed his stomach. "My perspective's hungry!"

"You guys wanna grab some burgers?" John asked.

Will shook his head. "Can't, John. Food policy with guests is the same as the alcohol policy. We have to go back to the ship and eat the officers' food. After that, it's nap time. Got to sober up before our shift starts tonight. Where you working, Garth?"

"They still got me in the casino. You?"

"Both shows in the ice rink."

"We doing *Cinco de Mayo* tonight?"

"Yip. And we're bringing John. How about it, John? You wanna party with a bunch of lowly crew tonight?"

"Sure. But…I thought that's off limits?"

"Don't worry about that," Will said. "You *can't* get in trouble."

Thinking, Garth asked, "What do you got in mind, Will…a *Halloween*?"

Scratching his thin goatee. "No. It might look too suspicious dressing up an ordinary-looking American. No offense, John."

"None taken."

"I was thinking about a *business as usual*," Will decided.

"You giving him a *treasure map* or *escort?*" Garth asked.

"I'm going to *scout* him myself."

"You want to *train* him? I'll run *caboose*."

"That's a good idea!"

Lost in translation, John said, "Ah…what?"

"Sorry, John. Garth and me watch the *Ocean Eleven* movies repeatedly. We try to perfect our Clooney/Pitt routine of snappy sayings and finishing each other's lines— it's a hobby. Do you know where the pizza stand is on the Grand Promenade?"

"Yeah. I passed it today on my way to buy my shoes."

"Good," Will said. "Be there at eleven-thirty. There's a door beside the pizza stand. I'll knock on that door at exactly eleven-thirty. If nobody in a white uniform is standing around you, knock back. Got it?"

"Yeah, but I don't want to get you guys in trouble."

"We won't get in trouble," Will grinned. "Remember John, life's an adventure and you got-to have you some fun!"

Thinking about Carson's wishes and the uninhibited feeling he just felt on the zip, John said, "Okay, Will. I'll be there. But…just one more question?"

"Shoot!"

"I thought Cinco de Mayo was in May?"

"We have Cinco de Mayo every Tuesday night before we dock in Cozumel," Will said. "It's too good a holiday to just celebrate once a year."

"I guess there's no arguing that," John said.

TWO CARS

S OLACE POINT WAS OVERRUN, AS the bulk of passengers had decided to come ashore for the day. Only the hard core gamblers and those who traded crowds and sand for the pool or spa stayed on-board. John zigzagged his way through the crowd like the only human amidst a seal colony, and spotted a circle of people huddled around a fire pit. The smell of BBQ wafted with the wood burned smoke, enticing anyone within a hundred feet. His stomach told his head to follow the titillating scent.

He found an opening in the ring of hungry guests who were patiently waiting to be served. The chef meticulously studied a bevy of shrimp and chicken kabobs, burgers, chicken breasts, and rib racks; rapidly turning and plating them as they achieved seared perfection.

"Looks and smells great, doesn't it?" a man standing beside John asked.

"Sure does."

"You gotta try the chicken kabobs," the man said. "They rub them with some kind of local jerk spices. If you like a little *kick*, they're out of this world. I wish my wife could cook this good." The man lurched toward John as his wife threw a sharp elbow.

"I think she heard you."

"Ya think?" said the man, rubbing his arm.

"What'll you have, sir," the chef asked John.

"I think I'll try the chicken kabobs!"

The chef plated two kabobs and a spoonful of rice from a large steamer pot. "Here you go, sir. Utensils are over there," pointing to an open pavilion.

John took the steaming kabobs, ordered an ice tea from the bar, picked up a fork and napkin, and sat down at one of the picnic tables inside the pavilion. Just after stripping his first prong, a couple sat opposite.

"Okay if we join you?" a short, husky man asked.

"Go right ahead," John said.

"Thanks!" the woman said. "We're the Weavers! This is my husband, Carl, and I'm Carol! Our friends call us the Carcars!"

"John. John Smith."

Carol's pasty complexion and peppy personality reminded John of Casper the Friendly Ghost. Carl wore a floral shirt, tuffs of hair sprouting out from its top button. He looked how John thought a lumberjack should look. His arms and face were over-run with hair and John couldn't tell where Carl's lips began, unless he opened them to speak. The chia pet commercials John had seen around Christmas time came to mind. He found Carl's dirty John Deere hat ironic, looking like he was in need of a good mowing.

"Where you hail from, John Smith?" Carol asked.

"Kansas. How about you guys?"

"We drop our home anchor in Anchorage, Alaska!" Carol chortled.

"I've never been, but I hear it's beautiful."

"*Oh*…it is, John," she said. Meanwhile, Carl gnawed on a rib, his beard mopping up sauce.

"It's a great place to cruise," Carol said. "The air's so clean and crisp and the glaciers drop icebergs into the ocean! Sounds like thunder when they shear off!"

"That would be something to watch. I've only seen that happen on TV."

Carol picked up an ear of buttered corn. "It's not the same, John. You have to be there and see it from the ship to get the visceral experience!"

"I'll have to keep that in mind if I ever take another cruise."

Trying to wipe his face without much success, Carl said, "Do you cruise much, John?"

"First time."

"I remember our first time," Carol said. "You must be loving it?"

"It's been pretty great, so far."

Carol spoke with a mouth full of corn, butter dripping from the corners of her mouth. "We try to go once a year. We took this exact cruise thirteen years ago. Carl works for BP and we won the trip in his company's Christmas raffle. It was our first cruise and we thought this year it would be nice to relive it."

John gulped a healthy swig of tea, his mouth tingling from the jerk spices. "You must've had a good time to want to do it again?"

A partially chewed kernel flew out of Carol's mouth as she burst out, "On the contrary! Carl got seasick. He slept the whole time with a Dramamine patch glued to his neck, and I got *so* sunburned I spent the cruise plastered with aloe vera."

"That sounds horrible. I'm surprised you wanted to take another cruise after that."

"Carl never had another problem after that first cruise, and I learned to wear sunblock. The sun down here is so intense it's enough to burn the hide off an elephant's behind!"

"This place has changed," Carl said, his face looking like a wet paintbrush.

"I heard they added the dock," John said.

Carl mashed his face into an unfolded napkin. "Yeah. That's the biggest addition. They used to have to tender everyone over from the ship. It took time. The poor staff had to get up at five am to load all the ice, booze, and food onto the barge before they started shuttling the passengers. Then they had to serve everyone for ten hours. Some of them we talked to had to pull a couple of hours back on the ship after working here all day. And at the end of the day, when the staff packed everything up, they had to keep a close watch on the locals. Haitian's would steal anything they could. It wasn't gated back then. Most of them don't have ice and they would hover around until the staff gave them what was left. But I don't know where they took it, or what they did with it once they got it there."

"That's hard work," John said. "For the employee's and the ice thieves."

"All work is hard work, unless you love it," Carl said. "I work hard and I love my job. Other guys I know, work hard just for the money. Most of the regular crew on the big cruise lines work their asses off for very little money. It's a couple of rungs up from slave labor. The cocktail waiters at the pool make fifty dollars a month, plus tips, meals, and room and board. The bartender's salary is three-hundred-fifty dollars per month."

"They must make a lot in tips?" John asked.

"You would think," huffed Carl. "Most of them won't talk to guests about this stuff, even if you ask. They're scared of losing their job because the company tells them *not* to discuss it. Carol and I have seen *60 Minutes* do a couple of shows over the years on big cruise line incidents and practices. We learn a little bit more from the crew's perspective every trip we take. Over the years, a few of the waiters, housekeepers, and bartenders have shared stories with us. One bartender told us the most he ever made in tips was three hundred dollars."

John perked up. "That sounds like good money where I come from. Most people I know would be happy to make three hundred dollars a day."

"That's three hundred dollars for the week," Carl said. "He made that much on the millennium cruise of 2000. Bill Gates headlined the celebrity list. This bartender told us he never worked harder while on his tour. He opened champagne bottles—two hundred he said—until his hands bled. He told us the average tip runs two hundred twenty five dollars for the week. Thirteen-hundred dollars for a two-hundred-eighty hour work month isn't very good. That's less than five dollars an hour, and those guys still have to pay for a home wherever it is they're from. They work six months on and six weeks off. They must have a place to keep their stuff and live when they're not working. That's pretty tough on five dollars an hour. On top of that, their weekly tip is given to them in cash, stuffed into an envelope. But the company wants us to feel like we don't need to carry cash or credit cards while we're on-board."

"Yeah, I like that," John said holding up his card. "These charge cards are a lot easier and safer than carrying a purse or wallet everywhere."

"We agree," Carol said. "If you lose it, they just issue you another one. No harm, no foul. Whatever you charged is in the ship's computer."

"It's a good tool," Carl said, eyeing where to start on a new rib. "You don't even have to worry about tipping. They automatically add eighteen percent to all the drinks you order—seems like a fair amount. What you may not know is that the entire gratuity for the week is divided evenly among all the bartenders. So someone going over and above gets the same amount as someone who just does the bare minimum. Most people won't tip more if the tip is already included, especially if they're encouraged not to carry cash. Plus, when the company pays them in cash, there's no accountability. The crew doesn't get to see paperwork that shows them what the total bar tip was for the week. They don't get a pay stub for their tips, just their salary. Any number of fingers in the counting room could skim from the kitty. Nobody would be the wiser. I like to know how my boss came to the figure I get every week. It's all right there on my pay stub."

"You've both really done your homework."

"Nah," Carl said. "I'm an engineer. I like to know how things work. I also like to know what I'm getting for my dollar, and where it's going after I spend it. Too many Americans got away from frugal, prudent financial practices in my opinion. That's why our country—along with those who followed our lead—is so screwed up. And our government wants to throw its weight around even more than it already does to fix things. Most of the so-called leaders we have in there now couldn't manage a toilet paper dispenser in a men's room—unless it was in their own bathroom, of course."

"I don't disagree," John said. "I've always been cautious, too cautious really, with money. This cruise represents one of the few things I've done for myself in a long time. I'm an operations manager for a small company, so I'm always looking for more effective, cost-cutting ways to perform—without sacrificing quality of course."

"For sure, you have to," Carl said, licking the BBQ sauce from his fingers. "The internet changed everything. We all have to change and adapt, change and adapt. Get too comfortable, and you'll find you missed the boat, so-to-speak."

Carol had been waiting for an opening to comment, shooting erect. "I love the internet!" she said. "You just push a button and the whole world's at your disposal!"

Carl glanced at his wife without turning his head. "You would know, hun'. She's a librarian back home. Spends the whole day on the net, John. When she gets home, she goes back on-line. Music, books, cooking, weather, bills, you name it; she's online doing it. Unless you're really into being outdoors all the time, Alaska isn't the most happening place, but I can't sit in front of a computer all day. I think she's cheating on me with some guy on-line, but I don't know what to do about it. Think about it, John. What am I supposed to do…kick the computer's ass?"

Carol snorted at her husband's remark; John leaned back, anticipating more corn spittle.

"He's such a kidder!" she said. "Carl knows he's the only *hard-drive* I'm interested in!"

Waving the ravaged bone, Carl said, "Sorry, John. Like I said, we don't get out much."

"Not at all," John said meekly.

"What time is it, hun?" Carol asked.

Carl paused in mid typewriter bite to rotate his left wrist. His watch was sunk down in his thick arm fur like a yardage marker in the middle of a fairway. "One forty-five."

"We better finish up," Carol said. "I told the kids we'd meet them at two thirty. We have our two teenage daughters with us, John. The ship's dancers are giving salsa lessons at three. We told the girls we would join them. He might not look it, but Carl here, is very excited about learning some sultry Latin moves!"

Carl lifted his eyes from rib to John. "What red-blooded American man couldn't contain his excitement for the chance to learn a stupid foreign dance?"

John chuckled. "You never know, you might enjoy it."

"It's like kissing a moose," Carl said. "I might like that, but it's highly unlikely."

"But you never know?" John returned.

"True," Carl smiled, "you never do."

Stretching her arm across the table. "It sure was nice meeting you, John Smith. If we don't see you again, look us up if you're ever in Anchorage. We're in the book! Swing by the library if nobody answers!"

Shaking Carol's hand, despite the two chunks of corn clinging to her flat palm. "I will. Thank you."

Carl, reluctant to abandon his last rib, stood to shake John's hand. "Nice meeting you, John. I hope you enjoy the rest of your trip. Talk to the staff, they have some great stories."

Again, John didn't hesitate to shake Carl's greasy BBQ hand. "Good advice. Thank you for sharing all your inside information. And break a leg!"

Peering with one eye, Carl said, "If that's all it would take to get out'a this dance stuff, I would."

John had never been accused of being anal retentive, but prior to losing his wife and son he enjoyed a certain amount of order and cleanliness. He made certain the Keep It Together factory was always spotless. But not ever wanting to hurt people's feelings, he waited until the Weavers were out of sight before heading to the bathroom to wash his hands. The timing was perfect, his body was letting him know he had ventured off the path of gastric routine. Page had never been one to experiment with cooking spicy food. He felt the local jerk seasonings jerk through his bowels. "I should have had the burger," he muttered to himself, scurrying to the bathroom.

!!WARNING!!

JOHN EXITED THE BATHROOM FEELING like a new man, however, he thought a nap was duly earned. After picking up a bottle of water from the bar and a towel from a bin located on the beach, he found an empty hammock chained between two palm trees. He spread half the towel over the hammock and rolled the remainder into a sort of pillow, and then placed his flip-flops under the netted bed and lay down. Crossing his legs, lowering the still wet brim of his hat over his eyes, and resting his hands across his belly, he sighed deeply; allowing the events of the morning to replay in his mind. The hot Caribbean breeze fanned him and steel drums muffled the noise of children crying in the background. Rustling palm fronds above his bed, lulled him like wind-chimes. Sleep…soon arrived.

"Would you mind lending a girl a hand?" a voice whispered.

At first, John thought the voice was a dream, but when his eyes fluttered open, the smile, gleaming under an awning hat, was unmistakable.

"Good afternoon," Rita said. "I'm sorry to wake you, but I was just passing by and the temptation was too great."

Not flinching. "Hello, Rita." No alarm clock, or ship's horn, no screaming kids, or anxious thought for the impending day; just the sweet sound of a beautiful woman. *What a perfect way to wake,* he thought.

"Nice to see you're wearing another snappy t-shirt. Keep it *Together*, huh? Is that to remind yourself to stay calm?"

"Unfortunately, I've never needed help in that area. Actually, it's the name of the company I work for. It's a rubber band manufacturer."

Trying to contain her laughter, Rita said, "I never did ask you what you did for a living."

"Not very glamorous, is it?"

"On the contrary, John, it's…adorable. Now…Mr. Latex, would you mind?" Rita smiled holding up a bottle of lotion.

Pivoting his legs and slowly propping himself up. "No, of course not."

Rita turned and sunk her knees into the sand. "I just can't reach the middle of my back and I don't want George touching me."

Squirting lotion onto his hand, the bottle made a fart noise. Rita giggled. He rubbed his hands to warm the lotion. "Huh…where *is* George?"

"He said he was going to grab us drinks. After waiting twenty minutes, I went to get my own," she said, sipping on a rum and coke. "I saw him at the horseshoe pit playing with your friends—the ones from last night."

"Dani?" John snapped.

"Yeah, and the buxom blond and the striking brunette—pretty women," Rita snarled.

John took his time with Rita's back. She wore a bright red bikini instead of her one piece. He tried to control his slightly trembling hands on her exotic skin. "He didn't ask you to play?"

"*No*, he didn't. He sure has a funny way of working on a marriage—don't you think?"

"It wouldn't be the way I'd go."

"No. I'm certain it wouldn't. I'm beginning to believe he made me come along to punish me."

"My ex did a bit of that with me."

"Silly, isn't it?"

"Waste of time, if you ask me."

"Yes, John. Life's too short," Rita moaned.

"I think you're covered."

"Make sure you get under the straps, John. *Please*."

Like a school boy being waved through to second base, John did as he was told, caressing every inch of skin hiding below her bright restraints. The innocent act stirred his libido and dispelled any memory of Dani's kiss. Not wanting to stop, but neither did he want to linger. "All done."

"Thanks, John. What would I do without you?"

Still trembling, he answered, "I guess you might have tan lines?"

Rita stood and turned. "I take it off when I lie on my front," she smiled. "I saw you and Will on the zip line. He's a lot faster than you."

"Yeah, well…he's done it a gazillion times."

"It wasn't a derogatory observation. You seemed to be taking it all in. Looked like you were enjoying yourself up there?"

"I did. I was."

"When you go too fast, you miss things. When you wait too long, you miss everything. I like your pace, John. It's very attentive. Attentive people get the most out of life." Rita glanced at her watch and sighed. "I better get back to our chairs. If he's there and waits too long, he'll make a thing of it."

"He did it to you."

"Don't get me wrong. I don't give a shit. I just want this to be as painless as possible." Rita lowered her head and used her toes to play in the sand.

John wanted to tell her how beautiful she was, how wonderful her presence was to him, but the words stuck in his throat.

Rita looked around without seeing anything. "Well…thanks for the suntan lotion, John. I guess I'll see you later." She began to turn.

"Rita!" John blurted louder than he wanted.

"Yes…" she paused.

"I…I…really love your bathing suit," he sputtered.

Flashing a dimple. "Thanks, John. Find me later," she said over her shoulder.

After she walked away, John spanked his forehead with the palm of his hand. "I love your bathing suit," he repeated. "What am I, thirteen? No. Not even Garrett would've said something that weak."

When he finished beating himself up with his self-inflicting vocal assault, he wrestled back into the hammock and covered his face with the damp Chiefs hat. The smell of saltwater filled his nose. "Dumb ass!" he shouted into the brim.

He never saw George, who had witnessed everything from the time under the bra straps. George—with Elli as his teammate—had won his game of horseshoes and John's hammock caught his eye on the way back from getting drinks. He'd spied from under a palm tree. The sight of Rita with another man infuriated him. Not wanting to agitate Rita, he waited, chugged his beer, mashed the can, and threw it into the sand. Then, he marched back to the bar for another.

Warm rum cascaded off John's hat, ran under the brim, and down onto his face. Forgetting he wasn't in a normal chair, he shot up trying to plant his feet. His left foot dove through the hammock, spinning him into a forward, sandy face plant, but the foot remained entangled as if he'd been hogtied.

"What the…" John spit.

"Sorry, John," George said casually. "I just wanted to buy you a shot."

John flipped over and tried to clean the sticky sand from his face. "Why did you do that?"

George bent his knees and dropped his ass into the sand. "You don't like rum? I should've known. You're from Kansas! I should've gotten you something with grain…or corn, perhaps? Whiskey! Sorry, John. Maybe next round."

Still spitting. "What did I do to you?"

George slugged his beer. "Me? Nothing, John. But see…I get upset when I see another man rubbing my wife."

John worked at freeing his foot. "She just asked me to put some suntan lotion on her back!"

"Here! Let me help you with that." George grabbed the top of John's ankle, yanking it down.

"Ow!" John screamed.

"Sorry, John. Looks like it's still tangled." George spun the hammock.

"It was just suntan lotion," he winced.

Flexing his arm. "You see these tattoos, John? You know what they mean? Do they have tattoos in Kansas? Never mind, I'll tell you. I got them in China. In English they roughly translate to *only the strong survive*. I like that. Simple, to the point, and quite true!"

"What's your point?" John asked, rubbing his leg.

George's tone darkened. "My point, asshole, is stay away from Rita!" Repeatedly stabbing his finger into John's chest. "Take a lesson from your shirt…*Keep It Together* and mind your own fucking business. I don't want to hurt you. After all…I'm on vacation!"

George headed back to the bar to finally get Rita's drink.

Even as a kid John had never been in a fight. The mere thought of gratuitous violence seemed futile. When Billy Everett bullied him out of his second grade milk money, John found it easier to submit. Eventually, Billy became bored with the lack of confrontation and found somebody else to extort. John understood that war was often necessary to ensure people's freedoms and he respected Carson, but not so much for serving his country, as for knowing exactly who he was and following his own path. Still, the fact that his son's job was to embroil himself in potentially violent situations, weighed heavily. Truly, soldiers like Carson fought so people like his father didn't have to.

John poured the rest of the water bottle over his face. After shaking his towel, he wiped his sandy body and laid back in a fetal position on the hammock, covering himself with the towel. Closing his eyes, he replayed the scene with George over and over in his mind. Feeling impotent, he manipulated the events, coming up with snappy comebacks to George's bullying.

In one scenario, he actually broke George's nose. When George said "Sorry, John. I think it's still tangled," John responded with, "That's okay, George. I got it," and then *bam*…a knee to the nose.

John struggled with a sick satisfaction over the thought of George's bloody face and chose instead, to replace it with the memory of touching Rita's supple skin.

For the second time…sleep arrived.

THEY'RE NOT CARIBBEAN LOBSTER

T HE FIRST HORN SOUNDED AT 6:00. John shuddered. Not wanting another spill, he braced himself by sprawling his limbs out in spider fashion. Sitting up and collecting himself, his ankle seemed fine, but the right side of his face hurt. He touched the waffle triangles left behind from sleeping face down on the Hammocks' coarse rope. As a result, on the way back to the ship, he received several odd glances from fellow passengers.

Back in his cabin, anxious to wash off the day's salt and sand, he took a warm shower. Silvia had the room squared away with fresh chocolate on his pillow. Dismantling the new towel swan, he folded it into squares and added it to the stack in the bathroom. As he was contemplating what to do for dinner he saw the blinking light. The voicemail said: "John! Rich, here. Mary and I are hitting the dining room for chow tonight. We'd love for you to join us if you haven't already made plans with one of your harem. Seven o'clock. It's lobster night! No need to call, we'll save you a chair."

Richard's voice made John happy. Excited to join his new friends, he checked his watch—6:40—and dressed quickly.

The same maître d' from breakfast greeted John in the dining room, but he looked totally different. Still husky and balding of course, but the circles around his eyes weren't as dark, and he wore a classic tuxedo, right down to the black cummerbund.

"Good evening, sir," he said. "May I help you?"

"I'm joining a couple for dinner."

"Last name?"

"Clawson."

"Yes. They just arrived. Please follow me," he smiled.

The dining room looked much different than at breakfast—more sophisticated and relaxed. John found that the candle-lit tables, dim lighting, and a string quartet all added style and grace to a space that felt more like a banquet hall during the breakfast service.

"Here you are, sir," said the maître d', pulling out a chair. The Clawsons stood.

"John, my boy!" Richard said. "Great to see you!"

"Hello, John!" Mary said.

John accepted the chair after handshakes and kisses. Seeing them both filled him with satisfaction. "So, I hear it's lobster night!"

Rubbing her hands together. "Yes it is! They always pick one night to feature lobster."

"You can get them any night in the other restaurants, but then you're paying extra for it," Richard said. "We usually only eat in the dining room on lobster nights. *Maybe* one other night."

"Do you like lobster?" Mary asked.

Touching his lips with his index finger. "I've had shrimp a bunch of times, but I don't ever recall trying lobster."

"If you like shrimp, you'll like lobster," Mary said. "Just think of it as a jumbo, jumbo shrimp!"

"Sounds great. I can't wait."

Richard lifted a bottle of white wine from the ice bucket. "Care for wine, John?"

"Love some. I think I earned it today."

"Sounds like you found some of that adventure Carson wanted you to have?" Mary asked.

"Thanks, Rich," John said, tasting the wine. "Delicious! Yeah Mary, you could say that."

"Couldn't have been that bad," she said. "You still seem to be in one piece."

Laughing. "Barely! Garrett and I—he's Dani's son, you met her last night at the disco."

"Yes!" Richard beamed. "Pretty girl."

"They *all* were," Mary said. "We looked, but couldn't find you to say goodnight. We asked her to let you know."

"Yes, she told me. I felt bad that I missed you. I was upstairs talking with Rita. I walked Dani back to her cabin after everyone left, all but her friend Buffy, who was having too much fun to leave."

Richard's face lit up. "So you were with *one* upstairs and then walked *another one* home. *That* sounds like an adventure I'd like to hear about!"

"Not much to tell, Richard. It was all pretty innocent." Guilt set in. Recalling Dani's kiss made him feel like he'd just lied. Not really, he rationalized, he did say *pretty* innocent.

Richard didn't say a word, but registered a look of disbelief. Thankfully, he chose not to pursue the subject and John returned to sharing his day.

"So, her son and I rode jet skis that made NASCAR seem like VW bugs. Mine left me behind after I gave it too much gas. Then I played volleyball with the drunk crew. Two of the bartenders and I rode the zip line thing after that. Then I had a jerk chicken lunch—which tasted great, but didn't agree with me. I ate with a strange looking couple from Alaska."

"That *is* an adventurous day!" Mary said.

"I didn't hear him say anything about a woman," Richard said. "An adventure isn't complete without it. They always seem to wiggle their way into our enterprises—for better or worse," he added.

"It worked out pretty well for you," Mary reminded.

Lovingly gazing. "Yes…it did, my dear."

Raising his hand in guilt, John said, "Richard's right."

"I knew it!" Richard said.

"Will and Garth—my bartender friends—went back to the ship. So did the couple I met at lunch. I was a little worn out, so I thought I'd take a little snooze in a hammock."

"You wasted port time on sleeping?" Richard asked.

Smirking. "Don't listen to him. Richard slept the whole day in his beach chair—when he wasn't ogling young women, that is."

"I was merely resting my eyes in both cases."

"He tends to snore like a jackhammer when he's *resting his eyes.*"

"I can relate, Rich. I was out like a light until Rita came along and asked me to put some suntan lotion on her back."

"Now it's getting interesting," Richard said.

"So I did. She left, and I tried to go back to sleep."

"Something tells me that wasn't the end of it," Mary said.

"Yeah. Her soon-to-be ex-husband apparently witnessed everything and got upset. So he poured a shot of rum over my head and proceeded to threaten me to stay away from his wife."

"I'm confused," Mary said.

"I'm not," Richard said.

"Why is she on vacation with her *soon-to-be* ex-husband?"

"That's what I learned last night at the disco. He bullied her into taking this cruise, which they booked before separating. He'll sign the divorce papers only after giving marriage one last shot over the course of this trip."

"Sounds like blackmail," Richard said, buttering a piece of bread.

"That's what I said."

"I knew there was something about him I didn't like," Mary said. "I had my suspicions when we met in the theatre. And, when we were in the disco, he was more interested in Dani's two friends than Rita. John, you and Rita left, but we sat at a table and watched everyone dance. You should've seen the way he danced with Dani's friend…"

"Elli?" John helped.

"Yes!" she said. "It looked more like sex, than dancing. People don't work up to it any more. I don't want to be around to see the end of romance and courting. Sex and violence have been around as long as human beings. That doesn't mean we need to be so explicit about them in our music, movies, games, and the darn internet."

"I agree, Mary," John said. "I think that's what I like most about where I live. It kinda still works like it always did. I hope we don't belittle the traditions that built the country by calling them outdated or old-fashioned."

"You might not have a choice once all that money from windmills and new technologies starts luring people in droves to places like Kansas," Richard warned. "A gold rush makes for one hell of a melting pot of people, and *money* can change people and places."

"You might be right," John said. "We *are* starting to see some of that. Especially the wind technology. It's hard to miss them. Seems like they're building more every day."

A young waiter approached the table, refilled the water glasses, then hustled off to the next table. Another waiter came a minute later; using silver tongs, he dropped hot rolls onto everyone's B&B plates. Two minutes more and a third waiter pulled the wine from the chiller. After topping everyone off, he asked Richard if he would care for another bottle. Richard answered with a simple "please." Two more minutes passed and a fourth waiter brought calamari, tomatoes stuffed with blue cheese, and baked zucchini cakes.

"We sure do have a lot of waiters," John said.

"You haven't seen our waiter yet," Richard said. "We ordered lobster from him before you sat down. We figured if you didn't want lobster, it would be easy enough to change."

With a puzzled look, John asked, "None of those people were our waiter?"

Mary took the time to explain the hierarchy by pointing out examples from other tables. "You have food runners, assistant waiters, back waiters, wine stewards, busboys…the number of positions seems endless," she said.

"Back in Kansas we have a local restaurant called Joe's. A bunch of us from the factory frequent the place for breakfast or lunch. It's owned by a guy named…well, *Joe*. In addition to proprietor, Joe's the cook, cashier, waiter, and constantly on-call maintenance person. He's just open for breakfast and lunch—seven days a week. He employs one assistant who also shares all duties."

"Now that's old-school!" Richard said, helping himself to each appetizer.

"Sounds charming," Mary said.

John scooped a zucchini cake for Mary, along with one for himself. "The couple today told me about the poor wages these people make."

"It's true, but relative," Richard said.

"They said the bartenders make three-hundred-fifty dollars in wage for a seventy-hour work week? They told me tips amount to another thousand a month."

"Sounds about right," Richard said.

"I don't know how they live on that," John said.

"Over the years Mary and I have had the chance to talk to a few of them about wage and living conditions."

"A lot of them won't talk to you about it," Mary said.

"That's true," Richard said. "This is still a good job for most of them, at least 'til the *US* dollar tanks, and they don't want to jeopardize that. And the cruise lines don't want them talking about it. Makes for bad press—especially American press."

"But how can it be a good job if they only make thirteen-hundred a month?"

Richard swallowed. "Like I said, it's relative. I'll explain it this way: if you take three head waiters from three different countries: the US, England, and Turkey…okay?"

"Yeah."

"They make about a grand a week in cash tips. That's why they put those envelopes in your cabin. The housekeepers and dining room staff get tipped by the passengers at the end of the cruise. You don't have to, but it's how they make the majority of their wage. As you learned, the company pays them next to nothing, like in the states. The minimum federal wage for tipped restaurant workers is less than three dollars an hour. That doesn't even cover the taxes on their tips."

"I didn't know that," John said. "I thought the minimum wage was the same for everyone. What is it now…seven or eight bucks an hour?"

Scraping some calamari onto Mary's plate. "Something like that. Anyway, you know what a thousand-dollars a week buys you. *Not bad.* Especially for a young waiter. Then you do the math. These guys work breakfast, lunch, and dinner every day for six months straight. They get some morning and/or lunch shifts off by rotating or swapping, so they get some port time. But they all work dinner. *Now* a thousand dollars doesn't look as good. Plenty of waiters in the US can make a grand in three or four nights. The English waiter takes a thousand dollars back to England and loses about twenty-five percent in currency exchange. But, the Turkish waiter takes the same money back to Istanbul and lives like a king. It's literally enough money to buy a couple homes and a brand new BMW. A thousand American dollars goes a long way in a country like Turkey. Ergo, you'll see a lot of Turkish dining room staff. On the flip, not too many Americans. That's why you hardly ever see Americans in places like the dining room or bar departments. The bar department is even worse for Americans. They make a quarter what the head waiters are making for the same amount of work."

"There's an American bartender on this ship," John said.

Mary perked up. "Yes, we met him. He's very nice—funny too! We gathered, through our conversation with him, that he's financially stable. He's not here for the money."

Nodding in agreement. "He told me that too."

"Exactly," Richard said. "You would have to have been fired from every bar and restaurant in the United States to think being a bartender on a big cruise line is a good job—money wise anyway. This guy… *Will*, I think he said?"

"Yes," John said. "Will Catcher."

"Right!" Richard laughed. "He didn't miss much, I'll give him that. Will's the exception to the rule. The point is, it's not exactly where you work, but where you're from that determines your station on the ship. Filipino's make up forty percent of ship employees. They do most of the nut and bolt jobs deep in the bowels. They're from mostly poor islands and have been in the boat business as long as they've inhabited those islands. There are over seven-thousand islands in the Philippines with seventy-six million people. Much of the housekeeping department is made up of Latin, Russian, and poorer European countries like Hungary and Romania. The money they make here can support their entire family back home. You'll find refined service-oriented people from Europe, Latin America, and India in the dining rooms. The indigenous people from the Caribbean—predominately big islands like Jamaica and the Dominican Republic—make up the bar departments. The money they make here is much better than they could find on most of these poor islands. And the guests love them—makes it more authentic to the Bob Marley cruise mentality. The Americans are concentrated in the entertainment departments; theatre, games, child care, and ice rink, for examples. They're called *crew staff*. They can socialize with guests, and make better wages, and have much nicer living quarters."

"What about the officers?" John asked.

"Europe," Richard said. "Mostly Scandinavian countries. Many of them paid their dues on tankers, hauling containers around the world for decades. They bring their expertise here, where they make great money and live very well."

"You sure know what you're talking about," John said.

"You would too after sixty-seven cruises!" Richard said.

The team of waiters returned, clearing plates, topping-off wine and water, bringing fresh bread and silverware. Not a minute later than the pit crew finished, Mary received the first crustacean. She looked like an eighty year-old child receiving her first Christmas present. Richard didn't mirror his wife's expression.

Acutely aware of his frown, John asked, "What's wrong, Rich?"

Recovering his smile. "Nothing, my boy. Not a thing."

"He prefers Caribbean lobster," Mary said. "He thinks they're sweeter. *Ironically*, he doesn't like the New England claws much."

"What's the difference?" John asked, trying to figure out how to assault his meal.

"These lobsters are from New England. They're reddish in color and have claws. Caribbean lobsters are brownish gold and don't have claws, and in my opinion, taste sweeter. What the cruise lines serve depends on the time of the year."

"I'm amazed we still have things like lobster," John said. "I mean, this ship has over three-thousand people. That means there's at least that many lobsters on-board. They'll need another three-thousand next week. If you multiply that times however many cruise ships are running at one time, plus everyone back home eating them, that's *a lot* of lobster. They must breed fast?" John sawed a piece of tail meat from the blossoming incision in his lobster's armor.

"Indeed!" Richard said, feeling a bit petty. "I guess I've learned to take things for granted over the years. Remember when we used to catch our own?" Looking at Mary.

"I miss that chapter of our life," Mary reminisced, staring at the meat on her fork.

"Don't tell me you had a lobster tank at *Banzai?*"

Shifting his eyes. "No, John. But we did serve lobster at the restaurant. We sold our share of *Claw Creek* to my partners and became homebodies, caring for the kids, working on the house, and reading a lot of books; until restlessness set in. Eventually, all five of the kids were in college and Mary and I started thinking; we loved the ocean and always wanted to learn how to scuba dive. So we assembled the family for a meeting. We told them we wanted to move to the Florida Keys and open a dive shop. They loved the idea," Richard chuckled. "Most of them figured they would have a free place to stay during spring break."

"It was a fond period of our life," Mary said. "We sold the house in Virginia and moved to Knight's Key, Florida, a part of the city of Marathon, in the Middle Keys. We bought a two story house right on a powder white beach and earned our PADI diver's certification from a dive shop in Marathon. Shortly after, we earned the rank of dive masters and kept going until we were certified instructors. We lived upstairs in one of the tiny three bedrooms and turned the first floor into our dive shop."

"Sounds wonderful," John said. "What did you call the place?"

Cracking into his lobster claw with a pliers-like tool. "We love seafood. In crab season we used to fly to Miami for long romantic weekends. We had a regular room in our favorite hotel on Miami Beach—The Clevelander Hotel."

"The staff got to know us by name," Mary said.

Richard continued. "Miami Beach is the home of our Joe's. Joe was a Hungarian immigrant who lived in New York. He discovered what they now call South Beach in 1913 after his doctor advised him to move to a climate more conducive to his asthma. He opened a small lunch counter in the backwater town of Miami Beach, and served fish sandwiches and fries. In 1918 he opened *Joe's*. A few years later he discovered that the harbor was filled with edible stone crabs. I think back then he used to sell four or five of them with hash browns and coleslaw for a buck and a half. Everyone loved them! Joe's Stone Crab Restaurant was born, and the rest is history. He passed away, but his family still runs the place. Every night we would go to Joe's for our fill of those beautiful, sweet crabs. So, when we were trying to come up with a name for the shop, Mary says to me, 'How about incorporating stone crabs into the name.' That's how we came to name The Stone Crab Claw Diving Shop."

For the next hour, The Clawsons continued to regale John with stories from the dive shop. They talked about several Hollywood stars—who preferred the off-the-beaten-track anonymity of the place—who came to be dive certified. There were fish tales and shark stories. They compared the hurricanes they weathered to scenes in Key Largo and talked about their moonlight skinny dips in the effervescence created by schools of bait fish. Mary spoke highly of their pet turtle, Shelton. "He washed up one morning with a bloodied flipper—probably the result of a shark bite," she said. They nursed him back to health, after which he chose to never leave the sanctuary of the shop's beach and gentle waters.

John savored each story like the last bite of lobster on earth. Something else needled the back of his mind. The reality of his own mundane job yawned in the background. His career seemed so unfulfilling and pointless with no family to support. His entire work history paled next to one day at Richard and Mary's dive shop. He contemplated the currency of time. He always considered himself to be prudent with his expenditures—both monetarily and with general risks. He now wondered if what he'd considered prudence was actually apprehension or worse, procrastination. A fear of what *might* happen if he gave everything, like a gambler going all-in, or someone who sacrificed a career for love or family.

John's family had been his joy, but he had come by them almost as easily as they had been taken away. If you take a great parcel of land away from a cautious man and give him a tiny island in return, he tends to be even more cautious, for now his less is more to lose. John was living on an island, but between whoever sent his ticket, and the people he was meeting, there was now a seed of an idea planted inside him that he could build a boat and leave his island for a bigger and greener home.

When the last dessert plate had been cleared, he was still trying to decipher from Mary's tutelage, who his waiter was. He looked at Richard to ask a question when—Richard began coughing violently. His face turned blood red. He loosened the Windsor knot on his tie and began pounding his chest.

"Honey!" cried Mary. "Where's your pills?"

Barely able to speak, Richard forced the words, "M-y po-ck-et!"

Mary sprang to her feet like a teenager and calmly frisked Richard's pockets as he guided her hand. Locating a plastic vial, she twisted the top off and fed her husband one small white pill. Within seconds, he relaxed and waved her away like she was a nagging mother.

Watching helplessly, John said, "Rich, should I get a doctor?"

Richard wiped his mouth with a napkin. *"No. I'm fine,"* he grimaced. "I just get a little excited sometimes. Once you get to be eighty, your body sends more reminders that you're not going to live forever."

Mary reluctantly returned to her seat, a concerned look on her face. "I think we should check in with the ship doctor—just in case."

Richard's color returned to normal. "I just need some fresh air. Why don't we go play some putt-putt? What'a you say, John. Do you like golf?"

"You know, Mary's right. It probably wouldn't hurt to just check in with the doctor. Better safe than sorry, right?"

Mary used her stock puppy dog look. She knew the trick melted Richard like ice cream in July. "We'll just go have him check your blood pressure. *Please.*"

Tapping his fingers on the table and sipping water, Richard gave in. "I guess I better introduce myself to the doctor." Tilting towards John. "It's the only way she'll let me do what I want the rest of the trip."

"Would you like me to go along?"

"Thank you, John, but that's not necessary," Richard said.

"Mary, will you do me a favor?" John asked.

"Anything, dear."

"I have plans later and I'm going to relax in my room until then. Would you mind calling when you're done with the doctor, so I know everything's all right?"

"Certainly."

"Thank you."

Richard looked mischievous. "Hot date?"

"Hardly," John laughed. "Just meeting my bartender buddies."

"Stop interrogating the man," Mary said, standing up. "Come on. Let's go get you a clean bill of health."

"Yes, dear."

IN HONOR OF AN ADOPTED HOLIDAY

RICHARD'S HEALTH TROUBLED JOHN THE whole way back to his cabin. Not accustomed to being a night owl, the only way he figured he was going to make his 11:30 rendezvous with Will and Garth was to rest up. Using the TV for light, he grabbed a bottle of water from the mini-fridge, sat down on his only chair, and started flicking through channels. Serendipitously, he stopped on TCM (Turner Classic Movies). John had always been fond of old movies. He remembered being a child and watching *The Wizard of Oz* for the first time. It affected him more, being from Kansas. Not more than six or seven years old at the time, the line between reality and make-believe was thin at best. Tonight, he joined the station just in time for the hurricane landing in *Key Largo*.

There was something pure about watching a movie in black and white. People seemed to either love or hate it. Early in their marriage, Page loved curling up with her husband on rainy nights to watch old black and whites. She would open a bottle of wine, pop some Jiffy-Pop, and wrap her and John up in an old quilt her grandmother had stitched. But those joyous times were long gone.

The hurricane seemed to spin right through the TV into John's windowless cabin. The villains stranded in the *Key Largo* hotel ordered Will to make drinks. One villain threatened a woman looking just like Rita. John saw himself in a suit, smoking a cigarette, and talking in a Humphrey Bogart voice. His back was against the wall, but somehow, he knew he was still in charge. His calm, practical, borderline cocky demeanor would triumph over any villain's pistol. Bullies always feared those with real confidence. They hated and envied what they didn't have. The hurricane winds blew open the lobby doors and…the phone rang.

Answering. "Hello."

"Hello, John. It's Mary."

"How is he?"

"Just fine! The doctor said it was probably a case of heartburn. He gave Richard some antacid and told him to watch what he eats."

"That's great news!"

"Yes. Unless you're the one who has to monitor his food and drink habits," Mary sighed.

"Let me know if there's anything I can do."

"Will do, thanks. Have fun tonight. I'm going to try and coax him to bed now. Hopefully we'll see you tomorrow?"

"I look forward to it. Tell him I'm watching *Key Largo*."

Mary laughed. "He'll get a kick out of that. Goodnight, John. Thanks for joining us for dinner."

"It was my pleasure. Goodnight, Mary."

Feeling relieved, John propped his feet up on the ottoman and returned to the movie. The next thing he knew, Sam was playing *As Time Goes By*. Bewildered, he tried to recall the name of the black pianist in *Key Largo*. He checked his watch: 11:05. He'd slept through *Key Largo* and woken up in Morocco's *Casablanca*.

After splashing water on his face he figured he could use a pick-me-up, and decided to go to the promenade for a coffee before meeting Will and Garth.

Like Times Square, the promenade bubbled with energy, its street packed with passengers winding in and out of shops. A five piece Dixieland band played on a small center stage; children kited balloons filled by a clown manning a CO_2 tank; the sweet stench of cigars wafted out into the street from the cigar bar and mixed with the smell of fresh baked pizza and hot coffee. Pausing like he was casing a bank John made a note of the door Will told him about in front of the pizza station. Feeling confident with his reconnaissance work, he walked across the street to Kona Bean, ordered a black coffee, and sat down at the outside cafe.

Not having put much thought into it until now, he didn't know what to expect from Will and Garth and the caffeine was mixing with anxiety. Was this a good idea? What if he got in trouble for being somewhere he wasn't allowed? What if he got Will and Garth in trouble? What if they took his cruise away? What if he chickened-out? What if following this yellow brick road actually led to some sort of epiphany? He sat, sipping, stirring, and jittering his leg for fifteen minutes.

The moment of truth arrived at 11:25. He left the table and made his way back across the street, feeling his palms moisten. Standing beside the vacant pizza cart with his back against the door, he paced lightly while scanning the street for white uniforms. Suddenly, two officers with a string of gold bars on their shoulder boards passed John and then turned around. John flashed an awkward smile.

"Good'a evening," one of them said with an Italian accent.

"Hi," John squeaked.

"Is' it a any good tonight?"

"I'm sorry?"

"The pie," the second officer said pointing at the cart.

"Honestly," John said. "I've had better. I think it's been sitting a while. I'm waiting for them to bring fresh."

The first officer shook his head in disappointment. "That'a always happens. Thanks for letting us know. I'a hate stale pie! I'm a from Italy," he smiled pridefully. "Pie has to be fresh!"

"I'll radio the food and beverage manager," the second officer said.

As the man pulled a walkie-talkie from his hip, John heard a faint rap from behind. The first officer looked up as if something grabbed his attention.

"Did'a you hear that?" he asked, looking at John.

John shrugged. "Hear what?"

"I thought'a I heard birds. Sometimes they get trapped in here when we are in port. I'a like birds. What'a I don't like is a bird crap."

"They say it's good luck if you're hit," John said hearing a second faint knock.

"Not'a in Italy," said the officer, waving a finger.

"F and B is sending up fresh pizza," the second officer said.

"Excellent!" the first officer rejoiced. "You should'a have fresh pie in a few minutes, sir."

"Thanks." Rubbing his belly. "I can hardly wait!"

"Enjoy!" Officer number two said. "And have a pleasant evening, sir." Walking away, the Italian officer checked the rafters for incoming bird shit.

John backed up closer to the door and lightly tapped his knuckles against the metal. The door cracked open. Moving out of the way and turning around, he saw the top of a sombrero breach the opening, but couldn't see who was under the hat. An index finger appeared below, pulling back and forth like coochy-cooing a baby's chin. Glancing around one last time and thinking the coast looked clear, John slipped inside, into the unknown.

Will's sombrero was big enough to be a bird bath. Its strings, drawn tight at the chin, dangled below his goatee, and his t-shirt read *El Presidente*. Garth rattled a wooden maraca with one hand while chugging a corona with the other.

"Welcome, Señor Smith!" Will said. "Here." Will pulled the leash toggle down and lifted the sombrero onto John's head. "Perfect! Here's what we're going to do. I'm going to go first. When I wave my hand, you follow, but stay ten feet behind. Garth will be ten feet behind you, watching for any unfriendlies sneaking up from the rear. There'll be a lot of stairs, but it should be a smooth mission."

"What if someone stops me?" John asked.

"The crew doesn't know, or care, who you are," Will said.

"Especially with that hat on," Garth said. "Just keep it pulled down a little in the front, like you are a resting drunk Mexican."

"Right!" Will said. "The only danger would be an officer, particularly one of our bar managers. But it's a huge ship. We have the same odds of being stopped by one of them as we do of being eaten by a shark tomorrow. Okay?"

"That's less than comforting," John said. "What do I say if I *do* get stopped?"

Will thought. "Well…we'll wing it!"

John's face filled with dread. "That's not my strong suit. I already had to lie—a couple times I think—to two officers who stopped to talk to me at the pizza stand."

"How'd that turn out, John?" Garth asked.

Reflecting. "Pretty well, actually."

"Did that lie hurt anyone, John?" Will asked.

"I might have gotten a pizza cook scolded for stale pie."

"I think he'll survive," Garth said.

"Listen," Will said. "Here's what you say if you ever get questioned: you're drunk and got lost. The only thing that'll happen is the person who stopped you will escort you back to a passenger area. Okay?"

"I trust you, Will."

"My brother!" Will said, slapping John's shoulder. "Now, let's commence operation *business as usual.*"

Will put his armpits over the narrow stairwell railing, lifted his legs like a gymnast on parallel bars, and slid to the landing without touching a step. He scanned the second staircase, saw nobody coming, and waved John on before descending another flight. Garth, waiting until he couldn't see John, hummed the theme from *Mission Impossible*. The big man couldn't fake stealth; instead, he tread with brazen ownership. The loose train continued descending deep into the bowels of the ship. When they reached the main corridor running the length of the ship, Will stopped and waved John to his side and said, "Through this door is I-95. It's a very wide corridor connecting all the crew areas. It'll be very busy, but don't worry. All we're doing is crossing it and we'll be almost home. I'm going out there now. If I don't see any officers, I'll knock on the door. You open it and walk quickly to the stairway on the other side. Okay?"

Adrenaline pumped through John's veins. He remembered feeling equally invigorated at nineteen. He and Page had snuck into a neighbor's barn to make love. Mr. Wilford had a surly disposition and didn't like people much. He used a pitchfork to scare off anyone bold enough to enter his farm. John could still almost feel the dry straw stabbing his back as Page rode on top, all the while, praying old Wilford didn't catch them.

Reading the wall in front of him: *WARNING! NO PASSENGERS ALLOWED IN THIS AREA* painted in bold black letters, John swallowed and heard a whistle. Turning to his left, he saw Garth leaning against a bulkhead, giving a thumbs-up. Two minutes passed and John hadn't heard a knock. He listened closer, for fear he'd missed it. Another minute passed, sweat now running down his cheeks. Suddenly, the door flew open, narrowly missing him. A man entered, brushing John, but paying no attention to him or his silly hat. John's eyes followed from under the sombrero as the man walked away in haste. Garth shot another thumbs up. Another minute passed, and the door had opened two more times, and two more crew had dashed by without regarding him.

Finally, Will knocked. Looking back at Garth, who snapped another firm thumbs up, John pulled the door latch down and stepped onto I-95. Glancing right and left, the corridor was so long he couldn't see an end on either side. Crew in various uniforms darted by like cars on a freeway. Will waited on the other side, frantically motioning John to cross. Acting his best parody of a mouse who had just stolen cheese, John made his move. Will was already at the bottom of the next stairwell when he reached the other side. They descended two more sets of stairs, made a U-turn through a water tight door, climbed one staircase, through another water tight, and down a fifty yard corridor, where all three were visible to passersby, yet inconspicuously spaced twenty feet apart. Extending his arms like airplane wings, Will banked left into their final destination: a short hall leading into the bartenders' neighborhood.

The ship grouped departments together, and the bartenders' quarters were made up of twenty or so cabins wrapping around a rectangle. This was their own segregated block of the small city comprised of twelve-hundred people from dozens of countries. The bar staffs' particular neighborhood resembled a sort of Greenwich Village, bohemian section of the city—although the entertainers' hood was a close rival.

Able to now walk together, Will led them to his and Garth's cabin. Along the way, half the doors were propped open and John peered in as they passed. Various genres of music fought for top billing and each cabin looked like a jail cell. But they all shared a common theme; everyone appeared to be engaged in some sort of fun. There were card games and drinking contests; book readers and movie watchers; sleepers and video game players. Some sat on the corridor floor outside their rooms, smoking, talking, and drinking. *This is the college experience I missed by living at home and attending a small school*, John thought.

Will unlocked their door and extended his arm for John to enter. "Welcome, John!" he said. *"Mi casa es su casa!"* John and Garth entered as Will wedged a rubber stopper under the door.

"What do you think?" Garth asked, pulling three coronas out of a small fridge.

"I thought *my* cabin was small."

Will offered their only chair while Garth sat on his lower bunk. "This is the Ritz compared to most ships," Will said. "When I worked for HCL we had four guys to a cabin instead of two. We had two sets of bunk beds, four wall lockers, and a TV, which we had to buy ourselves."

Jamming a pre-cut lime wedge into his beer, John said, "Thanks, Garth. What about a bathroom?"

"Unlike our little piece of heaven here…" Will said, pointing to what appeared to be a small closet, "we all shared a community bathroom. Two guys is one thing, but you put four guys who all work different shifts together in a barely ventilated box, and make them shower together, then you have a recipe for fights."

"How do you guys do it? I mean, you must never be able to sleep with all the distractions?"

Sitting next to Garth. "I guess it helps to have a little natural Navy mentality," Will said. "I imagine we deal with it the same way they do. Unless you're a *battyman* as the Jamaicans say." Will slipped his arm around Garth's shoulders.

"Which I definitely am not!" Garth responded, reaching up with his left hand and crunching Will's fingers into his vice grip.

Will lurched forward in pain before Garth released. "Point taken," Will grunted.

"We look forward to meals, drinking, women, and port time was what Will's trying to say," Garth said. "With ten hour work days, life boat drills, random drug tests, constant safety classes, department meetings, and countless time walking everywhere on this behemoth; we sleep two ways. We either nap or drink ourselves into a light coma."

"Sounds unhealthy," John laughed.

Staring stoically at John. "Man's got a point, Will. What do think we should do?"

"*Well*…that he does. I don't like to make any rash life changing decisions in mid-cruise. Maybe we should seal our honest intentions to turn over a new leaf with a shot of Patron, before reflecting upon our wayward lifestyles on say…a Sunday disembarkation?"

"You're wise beyond your years," Garth said. "At this rate, we'll be calling you Yoda in no time." Garth opened a desk drawer and pulled out a bottle of silver tequila, three shot glasses, and a salt shaker. "Pass the limes, John."

Still chuckling, John retrieved the cup of lime wedges from under his chair. "Getting down here was pretty scary, but exciting."

"Yeah," Will said accepting a shot from Garth. "The first time in the gauntlet can be a little overwhelming. Remember when you snuck that fat girl down here, Garth?"

"She wasn't fat, just big-boned."

Making quotation marks with his fingers. "Garth smuggled a *big-boned* girl through the maze one night when we were back at Carnival. I thought the whole top bunk was going to come crashing down and kill me."

"I thought we were respectfully quiet."

"You were. Like two elephants during mating season."

"As you can tell, John, crew romance can be a bit primitive with virtually no personal space or time," Garth said.

"I believe I'm getting the picture," John grinned.

Will motioned for the salt. "See what you did now! Your sexual escapades have left John with a scarring mental picture. I thought you were a better host than that?"

John squinted. "I believe you were the one who brought it up, Will."

Will licked the top of his hand and sprinkled salt on the saliva. "Point taken! Pardon my uncouth story on the eve of this proud and glorious holiday. Here, John." Offering a shot and salt. "A toast! To John Smith, a friend and excellent example of our newest honorary crew brethren!"

Garth added, "And to *Cinco de Mayo!* The finest of adopted holidays!"

John licked and salted. "Here, here!"

No sooner had the three downed their shots and Garth started another round. The Merengue music from next door merged with the Reggae music from the opposite side, converging into a sort of hybrid hysteria in Will and Garth's room.

"Garth, why don't you go inform the Rastas that we aren't celebrating their homeland until tomorrow night. I know they account for two-thirds of our bar staff, but they're interfering with our south-of-the-border brothers' turn."

"I'm on it!"

"Won't they get pissed if you guys tell them what to do?" John asked.

"They'll turn it down," Will said confidently. "Most of them are really cool. They know it's Latin night. You should be around here for Christmas. Nat King Cole takes a back seat to Bob Marley. 'Sides, Garth has a way with words. Arguments don't last long when you weigh three-hundred pounds."

"I see your point."

Not more than two minutes passed before the reggae music bowed out and Garth returned. He clapped his hands together in an all-taken-care-of motion.

"How was the rest of your day, John?" Will asked, passing the second round.

"Pretty interesting. I met a couple who gave me the inside scoop on Oz. You know, what ship life's like for people like you guys. I've also been spending time around this wonderful couple— The Clawsons. I believe they said they met you, Will."

Perking up. "Richard and Mary? Exceptional couple! That Richard sure loves the ladies."

"I met them at the casino!" Garth said. "They are special people. They have more stories than any bartender I know."

"Yip, that's them," John said. "We had dinner tonight. They confirmed everything the couple I met earlier told me."

"Hold that thought, John," Will said, starting another lick and salt session. "To our beloved guests! Richard and Mary Clawson!"

After choking down his second shot, John told Will and Garth all about the two couple's synopsis of crew life. Both bartenders listened intently, often showing awe at John's extensive knowledge. It took another round of shots before John finished.

"What do you guys think? Is all that stuff fairly accurate?" John asked.

"Wow, John," Garth said, "you really did your homework today. You want us to get you an application, or an interview, maybe?"

"Not unless I have a shot at captain or lose my job back home," John snickered.

"I hear they're looking for one on Costa," Will said. "You just have to know how to steer clear of the coastal rocks in Italy."

"No shit," Garth said. "That asshole cost people's lives. He must have learned to sail on the *Exxon Valdez.*"

"I saw that on the news," John snapped. "That was horrible! How does something like that happen? I can understand a plane going down in bad weather or due to a malfunction, but how does a cruise ship sink that close to shore?"

"Arrogance," Will said seriously. "There's a lot of it associated with these big companies, especially in the higher ranks. Some people get too wrapped up with their titles instead of concentrating on *doing* the right things. That couple you talked to today…did they tell you about this company not informing passengers about being in Haiti?"

"No," John said.

"This was a long time ago, but I remember reading the article somewhere. Before the zip line, security gates, and fancy dock, Solace Point was just a strip of beach that the company leased. They covered up the fact that people had purchased a cruise with a port in Haiti. Most people knew Haiti was, and is, a third world country. Many people have heard about the high disease rates, including AIDS. The company certainly didn't want to advertise a port in an AIDS stricken third-world country. Passengers stepped onto Solace Point and that's all they needed to know. A reporter, vacationing on one of the cruises, caught wind of the thing and wrote an article about the company not informing passengers they were actually in Haiti. As a result, the company dumped a lot of money into the place, including hiring a bunch of locals, hoping to clean up the company's image after that story broke. Solace Point is advertised as being in Haiti now, but it started out with arrogance and deceit."

"All these big lines do what they want, until they get caught," Garth added. "Once somebody calls them on their shit, they apologize, throw a bunch of money at the problem, and sweep it under the hull, so-to-speak. Remember the whole thing with ships dumping all their trash and human waste at sea? Now we recycle everything. Most of the lines got *green* before the public understood what the word meant, but they wouldn't have done shit unless someone wrote an article about it."

"They had to change that big stuff or they would've lost business," Will said. "Maybe even gone bankrupt. But why are we talking about all this work shit? It's a holiday!"

"I'm curious, Will," John said. "I've never really done anything or been anywhere. This is all a revelation to me. I feel naive and selfish for not making more of an effort to understand how things work in other places and for other people. We all have an obligation to ask questions, especially when it comes to major institutions, companies, and government. After all, our country was built on checks and balances. Things certainly don't always balance, but that doesn't mean we should stop checking. So, is all the stuff they told me true?"

"Down to the exact penny," Will said. "You were not misinformed about anything."

"Plus, now you know first-hand what a crew cabin looks like," Garth joked. "They don't put pictures of that on the company website. And they certainly don't offer a brochure on crew interviews."

"Stick with us, John!" said Will, setting up more tequila shots. "Between what you get up top and what you get down here, you should have one hell of a cruise!"

John held up his shot. "Let's skip the training wheels on this one."

"Look out!" Garth said, joining John's raised glass. "I think *El Nino* just showed up."

"To the best damn bartenders anywhere!" John said. "*And*…to my cruise!"

"Cheers!" Will gulped.

The trio chased their third shot with a series of animated Neanderthal grunts. Fanning himself with Garth's maraca, John turned when he noticed Will and Garth gazing over his shoulder. A pretty Latin American girl was leaning against the door frame.

"Hola boys!" she grinned. "Is anyone up for poquito merengue tonight?"

"Hey, Roxy," Garth greeted.

"Roxanne, you remember John, don't you?" Will asked.

"Yes!" she smiled. "From volleyball today. Welcome! Do you work here?"

"Huh…"

Will jumped in. "He's my…*uncle*. He's an assistant cruise director on one of our *other* ships."

Roxy took Will's emphasis as code for passenger. "I *see*. Well Mr. Assistant Cruise Director, do you know how to merengue?"

"No. I'm afraid not."

Sauntering in and placing her hand on top of John's sombrero, Roxy tilted the hat upward until his face was fully exposed. "Well then. It's about time someone taught you. Pour us all some tequila, Will. It helps the hips."

Garth pulled another shot glass from the drawer and began pouring a round.

"Roxy and the other girls are great teachers," Will said. "She'll have you moving like Travolta when she's done."

Roxy raised her palms at John and started baby stepping forward and back as her wide hips rocked side to side.

Entranced by the movement, John asked, "Where you from?"

"The Dominican Republic. The country opposite of where we docked today."

"Sounds *lovely*," John melted.

Will and Garth laughed as they passed shots. The quartet licked and salted. Still dancing, Roxy held her hand down for John to lick.

"Oh yeah!" Garth shouted.

Looking at Will for direction. "Lick her, John!" Will said. "A toast! To the wonderful language of merengue!"

John licked Roxy's hand, and in turn, she bent down to lick his. Everyone gulped their shot and sucked limes. Afterward, the gang rose and danced out into the hallway where Roxy took John by the hips and patiently taught him the sexy moves of merengue. He thought about Carl Weaver as he studied the lovely girl, allowing her to move him in ways he had never moved before. John thought Carl must have been crazy to dread his dance lessons.

Before long, a dozen couples packed the co-ed hall. Some danced while others clapped and sang words John couldn't translate. Will and Garth found themselves two Jamaican cocktail waitresses and danced in a way that would've made Mary Clawson cover her eyes.

The bartenders' stash of coronas and tequila dwindled down to nothing over the next hour. Once the alcohol ran out, people started disappearing to their cabins and by 1:15 Will, Garth, and a couple of stragglers were all that was left. Will noticed John slouched down on the floor in the hall corner, an empty corona resting in his open hand. He snapped for Garth and the two moved over to their wounded amigo and examined him.

"John!" cried Will.

"Yeeeaa," John mumbled, without opening his eyes.

"John!" Garth tried. "Can you hear me?"

John smiled lightly as if he were enjoying a pleasant dream. "Mmm-haa."

"What do you think?" Will asked, still staring at John.

"Too drunk to get back through the gauntlet," Garth said, matching Will's stare. "What do you want to do?"

"*Pig in a blanket.*"

"You sure?"

"There aren't any cabin inspections tomorrow. Roxy's solo until she gets her replacement on the flip."

"I'll go set it up." Garth started to turn when he remembered something. "We diving?"

"First thing." An idea brought a wicked smile to Will's face. "When we wrap the pig, let's leave him with an indelible. I think he should join us."

"I don't know a better cure!" Garth waddled off.

DAY 4
(COZUMEL)

INTO THE SHALLOW DEEP

T HE SHIP'S HORN BLEW AT 8 a.m., signaling the onset of disembarkation. The sound woke John—sort of. Every dehydrated cell in his body pleaded to ignore the alarm. His eyes cracked open to blackness. Breathing required effort. He opened his mouth to get more of the thick, stale air; he was sweating profusely, wrapped up in some kind of comforter. Clawing his arms free and stretching them upward, his fingers smacked against an un-budging partition. All he could think was that someone thought he had died and placed him in a coffin. Panic set in. Rolling hard to his right, he fell two feet. He heard a curtain rip open above him and saw the light from one dim bulb.

"You okay?"

John recognized the girl's voice from eight hours earlier. "Roxy?" he gagged.

"Morning, my little dance student," she yawned.

John rubbed hard to clear the crusty deposits gluing his eyes together. "Where am I?"

"My room. You got pretty drunk last night. The boys thought it would be better to let you sleep it off here than try to get you back to your own cabin."

John wrested himself free of the blanket, to find himself still fully dressed. "What about your roommate?"

Roxy swiveled her legs from the top bunk and used her arms to brace herself while inching her butt forward. "Heads up!" Clearing John by six inches. "My roommate went on vacation last week. I have the cabin all to myself until the flip on Sunday. Coffee?" she asked, flicking on the main light.

Sitting up and leaning against the bottom bunk. "Sure. And water?"

Roxy handed John a plastic cup. "The sink in the bathroom. It's filtered."

Struggling to his feet, joints cracking in the process, he glanced at Roxy's sleep attire as she fired up the coffee maker. *Cute*, he thought, *in her men's PJ's.* They were long sleeve white cotton, stamped with green marijuana leaves. He opened the bathroom door and was instantly confronted with three choices: one step left for a shower, one step forward for the head, or a half step right for the sink. Opting for the latter, he set the cup on the sink, turned on both nozzles, and with eyes closed, began massaging his face with the soothing water. After scrubbing away all eye nuggets, he opened his bloodshot eyes to discover a forehead painted with black graffiti. Gaping into the mirror, he read:

*Congratulations! If you're reading this, you're not dead yet. Bathing
suit—credit card—room key—hat—dock by 8:30, diving*

John sighed deeply. *Diving, what did that mean?* After a solid two minutes of surgical scrubbing, the writing barely faded. Two more minutes passed before he gave up, dried, chugged a glass of water, pee-d, and returned to Roxy.

"They sure don't give you guys a lot of space," John said, scratching his head.

Handing a cup of coffee. "Claustrophobia makes a great incentive to return to work."

"I suppose it does. Thanks for the coffee."

"You look like you're going to need it."

"What does that mean?"

"Didn't you read your face?"

"Were you in on that?"

"I'm just the innkeeper, John. They put you to bed and wrote your note. There's no way they could've gotten you back to your cabin without getting caught. You were wasted."

"I *did* drink too much. I guess I should go next door and thank them for looking out for me—and you."

"They're gone, John. You're supposed to meet them in twenty minutes."

"You mean they're serious about that?"

Roxy looked at her watch and smiled. "Those two, no matter how drunk they get the night before, are waiting at the gate every Wednesday to go into town. The horn blows, the gate opens, Will and Garth are the first people to leave the ship. You can set your watch by it."

"I'll have to be honest, Roxy, I had fun last night, but I don't know if I'm feeling up to more adventure today. What do you think I should do?"

Roxy wriggled her lips and lifted her ass onto the tiny desk top. "I'll tell you what I tell *all* men. If you want to dance, use your feet. If you want to love, use your heart. If you want to have sex, use your...well, I hope you use all your body parts. But for most anything else, use your head." Staring at John's forehead. "What's your head telling you?"

"It's split between going back to bed and going to the pier."

Sipping coffee. "Our heads, by design, are there to make decisions about choices. When your hangover's gone, and you think back about this day, which choice will you realize was the right one for you?"

Pausing to think about Carson's wishes and whoever sent his ticket, John handed his cup to Roxy and kissed her on the cheek. "You're a wonderful dance instructor. Thank you for your hospitality." Turning to the door.

"Hey, where're you going?"

Turning back. "I only have fifteen minutes to fetch my bathing suit."

Roxanne saluted by raising her coffee mug.

Disorientation set in after his third step. "Huh, Roxy..."

Already pulling a piece of paper from the desk drawer. "This is the way back, John."

"You drew that quick."

"I keep it for...," smirking, "times when *my* uncles come here. You shouldn't have any problems. Just start at the door and follow the right, lefts, ups, and downs."

"Should I worry about anyone stopping me?"

"Just walk quickly, act like you belong, and you'll be fine. Now get going or you'll be late!"

"Thanks, Roxy."

She was right. The directions were precise, basic enough for a six year old to follow. John weaved his way back up the stairs, across I-95, twelve steps, left at door. His head was pounding every step of the way and his stomach was churning like someone turned on a blender. Finally reaching the landing that opened into the pizza stand, he took a deep breath, firmly opened the door latch and stepped out from enemy lines into the friendly and familiar Promenade.

Already 8:20, John hurried into an elevator; an old woman inside shot him a curious look. Conscious of his rumpled clothes and the BO emanating from alcohol soaked pores he kept his embarrassed eyes forward, counting floors. Outside his cabin, exercising consideration, he slowly and deliberately slid the door card in the proper direction, entered, stripped naked, and threw on his suit and a clean t-shirt. After locating his sunglasses, hat, sandals, and credit card he darted back out the door.

By the time John cleared security, it was 8:35; he walked out onto the dock in the already sticky heat. A throbbing headache let him know how pissed his body was about leaving the air conditioned ship and the beautiful water made him even thirstier. He searched the crowd filling the pier, but no sign of Will or Garth. Shielding his eyes with the new sunglasses, he sat down on the edge of the concrete dock. Five minutes passed, during which, he seriously considered returning to his cabin, but a voice let him know he'd waited too long.

"Come here often, sailor?" Will asked.

John turned painfully.

"Morning sunshine!" Garth barked.

"Hi guys." John managed. "Sorry I'm late."

"On the contrary," Will said. "We're proud you made it at all. Now let's commence operation clean-up! Garth, you want to get that shit off his face."

John sighed. "I forgot about that. No wonder people were staring at me."

Garth said remorsefully, "Sorry about that, John. You were really drunk. We wanted you to join us today, but we didn't think we could get you up this morning. Will thought if we gave you a note you couldn't ignore, you'd make your own decision." Holding up a rag and brown plastic bottle. "This is rubbing alcohol."

Stepping back. "I can't drink anymore!"

"Relax, John," Garth laughed. "It's to clean the ink off your face."

"Oh. Okay."

Garth gently wiped all the ink away, then handed John a tube of aloe vera to rehydrate the skin.

"Here, John." Will said, handing John a sausage, egg, and cheese burrito from his book-bag. "And here's a bottle of water and a guava-mango juice. Drink it all. They'll help."

"Thanks, Will. When you say water…you don't mean vodka do you?"

"It's really H2O today," Garth said.

The three sat on the dock while John ate a bite of his salty burrito and then killed the bottle of water. Will pulled out three waters and a jar of aspirin, shelling out two each, and Garth shared three granola bars from his own sack.

"Yes!" Will said, a pleased look on his face. "It's a beautiful day! We're going to suck some marrow from the bone of life today!"

"Who said that?" John asked.

"I don't know," Will said. "I just remember Robin Williams saying it in *Dead Poets Society*. Seems like an appropriate quote for today."

"About today," John said. "What's this diving stuff all about?"

"You ever been snorkeling, John?" Will asked.

"In a swimming pool."

"Well...today you're swimming in one of the best pools on the planet. Cozumel has the third largest coral reef in the world. You're going to love it!"

John contemplated while rolling the cold water bottle over his temples. "I suppose the water might be good for my hangover."

"Oh, I guarantee!" Will said, sharing a coy look with Garth. "What do you say, John. You feeling refreshed enough to get going?"

Cramming the last burrito bite into his mouth. "The food and water's definitely helping. Thanks, guys."

"Good!" Will jumped up. "Let's stick our spurs in and *get-t-up*!"

The three crossed the wave of passengers—who were speed walking towards Cozumel's endless jewelry stores. When they reached shore, John noticed a large group of short men peeling off in the opposite direction from that of the passengers.

Pointing, John asked, "Where are all those guys going?"

"The love shack," Garth said, pointing down the road to a free-standing building painted bright yellow.

"That a bar?"

Laughing, Will said, "Of sorts. All the Filipino guys go there every week to find a date. Its real name translates to *Island Dolls.*"

"So it's a singles bar?"

"Of an *extreme* nature," Garth said.

"It's a whorehouse," Will said, "built almost exclusively for cruise ship employees. They have forty Mexican girls making a living almost exclusively from horny, overworked, lonely ship guys. Between our boat and that NCL ship next to us, those girls will make a lot of money today—even by American standards. We can always tell who went there by the red scorpion stamps. You can go just to drink, but if you want a girl, you pay the doorman, who in return, stamps the top of your hand with a red scorpion—lets the girls know who's serious and who's broke or scared. Anyway, after you do the deed, the girl uses a black marker to x-out the scorpion. If you want to go again, you have to get a new stamp. They must not wash off easily, 'cause I always see stamped employees back on the ship—and some passengers.

"Huh," John huffed. He always considered sex to be a sacred thing between a husband and wife, but didn't make a habit of throwing around his personal code of morality. "What ever happened to love?"

"Trust me," Garth said, "everyone who goes to Isla Munecas falls in love."

"I think our definitions vary," John said.

Aborting the discussion, Will ran ahead, turning left onto the beach. "Eduardo! My brother from a Latin mother," he cried.

"Who's that?" John asked.

"That's our ride," Garth said. "Come on!"

John followed down to the sand where Will waded out into the water to a flat-bottomed boat. The three jumped on board as Will helped Eduardo pull in the anchor.

"Eddie, this is John," Will said, "the guy I told you about."

Eddie was tanned through his deepest skin layer and his dark hair and bright teeth were indicative of Mexican men. Shirtless, he wore a summer wet suit rolled down around his hips. His perpetual, trustworthy smile immediately put John at ease.

"Welcome, Juan!" Eddie said. "Welcome to my boat—*The Dirty Mermaid*."

"Thanks, Eddie," John said, struggling for balance. "That's the same name as my deck on the cruise ship—minus the *dirty*." The boat's rocking reminded John of his post-tequila condition and he quickly sat on *The Mermaid's* bench seat.

"Looks like somebody's fighting the agave nectar," Eduardo said.

"He'll be all right when we get him in the water," Will said.

Eduardo fired up the Big Johnson outboard. After motoring past the no wake zone he opened up the throttle, and soon they were skipping off the calm, jewel-colored waters on their way around the north end of Cozumel. John studied the BC vests fitted to scuba tanks chained opposite him.

"Are you a scuba instructor, Eddie?" John asked.

Glancing back from the helm. "Si! Dive master. Are you certified, Mr. Juan?"

"No. But I always thought it would be fun to learn."

"Si! I might be able to help."

"Thanks, but I'm not feeling great. I think the snorkeling will be plenty."

The boat slowed. Will dropped the anchor while Garth pulled a wet suit from his pack. Eduardo threw a bright orange dive buoy over the side. Opening a hatch in the front of the boat, Will started throwing flippers, masks, and snorkels onto the deck.

Watching, while rubbing his sick stomach, John asked, "Can I help with anything?"

"Yeah, John," Will said, tossing a wet suit, "you can put this on."

"Is the water cold?" John wondered. "I thought we could just swim in our bathing suits?"

"You want to put it on," Eddie smiled. "It will prevent chafing."

John slipped his feet into the suit. "Chafing?" he said aloud.

Everyone else zipped up their suits and sat on the bench across from John, and began fishing fins and assorted gear from the stack Will had piled on the deck.

"Great!" said Eduardo, seeing John was almost suited. "Juan, why don't you sit over here now, so I can show you how to operate your BC."

Eddie's playful voice made it easy to follow.

"Sure," John said, starting to stand. "Wait a minute…BC?" Sitting back down. "What's a *BC*? And why do I need one to snorkel?"

"It's a buoyancy compensator," Eddie instructed. "It allows you to float on top and underneath the water."

"*Oh*, okay…wait a minute…underneath!" John cried. "You're talking about scuba diving? I don't know how to scuba dive. I'm not certified! Will, you said we were snorkeling!"

"No. I asked you if you'd ever been snorkeling. I *said*, we're going to swim in one of the best swimming pools on the planet. You assumed we were snorkeling."

"*Yeah, but…*" John gazed at the smiling trio. "It's too dangerous without going through school. I could get that *bends* stuff."

Will stood. "John, meet Eddie again. Eddie's the *Harvard* equivalent of scuba diving instructors! He's going to show you everything you need to know in five minutes and he's even going in with you. He'll be on your hip every second!"

Eddie shot John a reassuring look. "You're going to be fine, Juan. I picked this spot because it's calm and shallow. There's almost no current and the deepest we can go is twenty feet. *No bends.* My eight-year-old daughter can dive that deep without a tank!"

"Yeah, but..."

"Will told me you came on this trip to try new things," Garth said.

"Yeah, but..."

Will clapped his hands one time. "Times a wasting! Let's get to it. We have a lot to do today."

The three helped their dazed, ill-looking student to the opposite bench, where they began fitting him with a BC. Garth slipped a pair of fins on John's feet, Will snapped a mask over his forehead, and Eddie zipped up the wetsuit and tightened the straps on his vest.

"There!" Will said, staring at their handy work. "You look just like a certified diver now."

*"Yeah, but...*I don't feel so great." John's face looked a little green.

"You'll be a brand new man as soon as you hit the water," Eddie said, slapping the back of John's tank. "It's eighty-two degrees! Very refreshing!"

Everyone suited up quickly so John had little time to think about what he was about to do.

"Okay!" Eddie said, hoisting John up by his BC's shoulder straps. "Now let's have a little chat on the side of my mermaid. Juan, I want you to pinch your nose, close your mouth, and blow."

John did as he was told.

"Did your ears pop?"

"Yes."

"Excellent, you can dive then," said Eddie, looking very pleased. "Any time you feel pressure in the water, do that, and the pressure will go away. Got it?"

"Yeah, but..."

"Now!" Eddie continued. "This is your mouth piece. You breathe through it." Demonstrating on his own vest. "Next. These buttons inflate and deflate your BC. Inflate takes you up. Deflate takes you down. You have weights in your BC to make you sink and air from your tank to make you rise."

"Yeah, but..."

"This gauge shows you how much air you have left," Eddie speeded on. "Red is bad. Time to swim back up. And last but not least, when you get water inside your face mask, you can get rid of it under water." Eddie pulled his mask down over his eyes. "You just lift the bottom like so, and blow air through your nose. The water will leave. You can take your mask totally off under water, put it back on, use this technique, and no mas water! Any questions?"

"No but..." shaking his jaundiced face.

"He looks a little green around the gills," Garth noticed.

"He's just psyching himself up!" Will said. "You ready to get in and practice a little, John?"

"Um...do I have a choice?"

"Always, John!" Will said. "And you made the right one by not staying in bed!"

"Everyone ready to see the fishies?" Eddie asked, jumping up on the side of the boat.

Will and Garth followed. "Hey, Eddie," Will said. "Did you turn his tank on?"

Releasing an infectious laugh, Eddie said, "I knew I forgot something! Maybe he doesn't need it? He might be part fish. We won't know until he gets in. You want to try, Juan?"

"No—air please," John requested, wondering what kind of instructor forgets to turn on the oxygen tank. Regret began filling his split skull.

"Okay, air it is," said Eddie, turning the tank valve and testing the mouthpiece before sticking it in John's mouth. "Can you breathe, Juan?"

"Yes," John mumbled.

"Thumbs up for yes; thumbs down for no," Eddie signaled. "We can't talk in the water. Got it?"

John lifted a half bent thumbs up.

"Now," said Eddie. "Inflate your BC and fall back into the water. You should float!"

"Should?"

Will and Garth splashed backward over the side as soon as Eddie said *float*. Shortly after, Eddie followed. The three emerged, lifted their masks, and waited for John. Hesitating, visions of sharks ran through John's head and his stomach churned with acid.

"Come on, John," Will said.

"You can do it, Juan," Eddie said. "We'll be right beside you!"

John replaced the shark images with a vision of Carson cheering his father into the unknown. He pulled his mask down and faithfully tipped backward. The inverted plunge simultaneously rinsed away a layer of hangover sweat, while also purging John's stomach contents. To his chagrin, he surfaced in a pool of bubbles churning with burrito, granola, and guava-mango juice.

"Goddamn, John!" Garth said, swimming backward.

John spewed and coughed salt water, along with the remaining bits of breakfast. Eddie, not shy of diver's vomit, swam to his aid.

"Nice job, Juan!" Eddie said. "We'll see more fishies now. They love a free meal!"

"I'm here to help," John sarcastically choked, rinsing his mouth with saltwater.

"How do you feel now, John?" Will asked.

Spitting. "Actually...*better.*"

"I thought you might," Will said. "Trust me, John, we've all been there. I threw up at a hundred feet one time."

"How do you breathe when that happens?"

Eddie pushed the button on John's mouthpiece, expelling oxygen and any lingering debris. "It's designed to allow continuous airflow," he reassured, "you can puke all you want and it won't block your oxygen."

"That's comforting," John said.

Eddie helped John practice inflating and deflating his BC. Surprised, he quickly got the hang of it, rising up and sinking below the water surface. Next, Eddie had him clear his face mask just below the water line and again John was proud of himself for mastering the trick after a few tries. Will and Garth patiently checked their gauges and spit into their masks to help reduce any fog.

"I think he's ready," said Eduardo. "When we get low on air and start to ascend, swim slowly. Stay parallel with me and pop your ears. You ready, Juan?"

John, still nervous, gave Eddie a thumbs up.

"If anything should go wrong with your air, I'll be right beside you," Eddie comforted. "Our BC's have an extra mouthpiece for emergency situations. Understand?" Displaying his extra respirator.

"I understand."

"Good! Last, try not to touch the coral. The oils on your skin kill them. And all the fishies are protected, so they grow very big and are used to divers. If we see any sharks, don't worry. You taste like doggy shit to them."

"Again, very comforting," John said.

"Just don't try to play dentist with them, John," Garth teased. "They don't like that."

"I think they're safe," John said. "I work at a rubber band factory."

"They don't like being rubber bands, either," Garth said.

"Let's *get-er-done*," Will said, pulling down his mask.

"Let's go visit the fishies," said Eddie.

The four men raised their BC hoses and pressed the deflate button. The last thing that went through John's mind before his head disappeared below the surface was one of Carson's first swimming lessons at the YMCA. He remembered how it took a half hour of parental encouragement before Carson dove off the diving board for the first time. The pride they both felt was no different than if he had just landed on the moon. Two months after that first dive, he performed back and front flips with ease. John had never learned to flip, but watching Carson seemed just as fulfilling.

John slid down through the crystal water, instantaneously realizing the world around him was meant for visiting only. Dozens of brightly colored fish were still jockeying for burrito chunks. The world below his feet lay fully exposed, a feast for the eyes. No amount of imagination or speculation could do it justice just staring through the surface from a boat. Snorkeling was the equivalent of window shopping compared to the wonders of scuba. John's breathing relaxed and his heart slowed, as the eerie bubbles mixing with the current lulled him. The usual cautionary voices inside his head quieted. He wondered if the voices in his head were being calmed by these sea sounds, or if the sounds were thoughts trapped inside his head or perhaps, they were simply reminiscent music all humans listen to for nine months in the womb. Regardless, John found this first experience scary but peaceful, and surreal.

The group inflated their BC's near the twenty foot bottom; they were suspended just above white sand littered with brilliant corals. John struggled to match his partner's depth, but after several inflates and deflates, he hovered like a spider on a single strand of silk.

The next twenty minutes passed orgasmically. Everywhere John looked Eduardo pointed out some new mysterious sea creature. There was a moray eel hiding by the entrance to its den. Its ominous spike teeth lined mouth opening and closing, a trap waiting for any fishies rounding his coral home. A black grouper, weighing as much as John, sat stoically siphoning saltwater through its gills. It paid the divers little attention, barely moving as they passed by within a foot of its personal space. John delighted at all the Caribbean lobster, wishing he could bring one back for Richard. Eddie was right; each grew big enough to provide a healthy meal for two people.

Lobster took a back seat when a barracuda cruised into John's peripheral vision, the predator's eye jumping and rolling over the terrified diver. Its menacing teeth looked like strings of barbed wire, capable of ripping through flesh and bone. John remained wide-eyed and still as the barracuda shifted in an instant, going from cruise to warp—almost too fast to see. Mesmerized, John witnessed its strike decapitate an unsuspecting red snapper. Eddie's eyes opened round as saucers as he shot John a thumbs up in honor of the silver reaper's victory.

Schools of tropical fish, each one more colorful than the next, chased one another through Crayola reefs. Everywhere John turned another vivid marine drama was unfolding. He pretended he was a giant flying over a vast underwater city. Eddie suddenly rotated a hundred-eighty degrees, swimming upside down and parallel, waving his hand in front of John's mask and pointing above. John turned and kicked himself into the backstroke position with the use of some extra flailing. A huge loggerhead turtle swam just below the water's surface. Its shell listed back and forth as if steered by a drunken soldier struggling to drive a tank over sand dunes.

Checking both his and John's pressure gauge—the needle getting close to the red zone—Eddie tapped his submariner watch and flashed five fingers. John returned a thumbs up as they both rolled back into tank-on-top position. Will and Garth were stopped about fifteen feet in front, frantically waving the stragglers ahead. When John and Eddie caught up, they saw the reason for the excitement. The bottom dropped off five feet in front of the coral heads; everyone but John stopped. A seven-foot, white tip, reef shark was trolling a large sandy area barren of coral. It slowly patrolled the clearing's borders like a guard dog around an athletic field.

The last to join the scene, John experienced difficulty stopping forward momentum. Gazing admiration suddenly shifted to terror as he continued to drift directly into the shark's path. He tried back peddling with his arms, but found it to be counterproductive. He and the shark locked eyes from six feet, and then John was too close. With one powerfully incisive snap of its tail, the majestic creature relinquished its territory, swimming out of the divers' sight in two seconds flat.

John could feel his heart pounding through his wetsuit and BC vest when Eddie swam up and congratulated the top of his head. Facing each other, they grinned like children with huge straws in their mouths. John looked back. Will and Garth were clapping with both hands and flippers. Eddie checked their gauges before stabbing his finger upward. Pinching their noses, filling their BC's with air, and fanning their flippers, the group methodically made their way to the surface.

One by one everyone breached. Eddie immediately started swimming the fifty yards that separated him from *The Dirty Mermaid*.

"Goddamn, John!" Garth said with a new found look of respect. "I thought I told you not to play dentist with the sharks."

In awe, John dusted off some rarely used sarcasm. "I thought he needed a check-up."

Laughing, Will asked, "What were you thinking?"

"Thinking? Other than trying to figure out how to stop drifting, *Oh shit* came to mind."

"I bet! Will said. "We dive with Eddie every week and hardly ever see a shark, not one that big anyway."

"It was beautiful," John said. "So graceful. We looked into each other's eyes, and in that moment, amazingly, fear seemed to disappear. Somehow...I felt like we were one."

"Any closer and you might have been *one* inside its stomach," Garth said.

While the three laughed, Eddie idled up in *The Mermaid* and lowered a ladder from her stern. Will climbed up first so he could help Eddie with Garth's massive wet body. Garth removed his BC in the water to help reduce the load while John continued scanning for signs of life with his face-mask.

"Dude, you got to lose some weight or else we need to start diving off the beach so you can walk to land," Will said.

"I told you. I'm just like some of the women I date—big-boned."

"*Right*," Will replied.

When Garth was loaded, Eddie extended a hand to John. "Hand me your flippers, Juan."

Will and Eddie pulled John up the ladder with ease.

"Thanks, guys."

Helping unclip John's BC straps, Eddie said, "Hell of a first dive, Juan! You seem to like the big fishies!"

"Hell of a dive," John repeated. "I thought you were going to be right beside me the whole time?"

Eddie laughed. "We had your back."

"It wasn't my back I was worried about."

Passing out bottles of water, Will said, "You look like you're feeling better?"

"Like a brand new man," John beamed. "What's next?"

"I'm glad you asked!" Will said, checking his watch. "Eddie's going to run us back into San Miguel so we can catch the next ferry over to Playa del Carmen."

"What's in Playa del Carmen?"

Will looked at Garth who mimed spooning food into his mouth.

"Huh…we know a great local place for lunch," Will said "After that, we thought we'd run up the coast to Cancun. We thought you might enjoy that rather than spending the whole day here. This way you get to visit three different cities. You know, a little taste of everything."

"Sounds good!" John said. "But I thought you wanted to hit Carlos 'n Charlie's?"

"Oh, we're going to," Will said. "We don't have to be back on the ship 'til seven. If Eddie's Big Johnson is working correctly today, he can get us to the ten o'clock ferry. We should be done in time to catch the two or three o'clock back here to San Miguel."

"The perfect time to hit the bars!" Garth said.

Eddie's teeth sparkled like pearls in the sun. "Lots of drunk tourist boobies, Juan! You like boobies?"

Laughing. "Yeah, Eddie. Almost as much as all those fishies you just showed me."

"You know we have a bird named the Booby in parts of Mexico and South America?" Eddie looked up when he heard Will clearing his throat and tapping his watch. "I'm on it," Eddie said. "You store the gear, Will, and I'll warm up the boat."

"Roger that, Captain!"

Working frantically, Will and Garth stripped out of their wetsuits, stored gear, and secured tanks, while Eddie hauled in the dive buoy and anchor.

"What can I do?" John asked.

"Get dressed," Will said. "There's a towel in my bag. Your stuff's in there too." Will did a double-take. "By the way, pretty generic shirt selection today, John. Solid blue—no witty Kansas saying? A little boring wouldn't you say?"

"Some days you just feel *blue*. Know what I mean?"

Will frowned and nodded. "Fair enough. Given your state this morning, I accept that."

"You should've worn a *green* one," Garth jabbed.

"I'm saving that in case you guys have a Saint Patrick's night."

Garth chuckled. "Not a lot of Irish in the Caribbean, John. We got to work with what we got."

Will stopped throwing gear into the hatch. "We had one working for us a while back…Sean something."

"O'Brien," Garth said. "What ever happened to him?"

"He melted," Will said without hesitation.

"That's *right*," Garth expanded, "the company had to ship him back to Dublin in a big glass vase. His family thought it was a joke. The poor bastard looked like a giant green candle."

Sounds of laughter filled the air as Eddie fired up the Big Johnson V6 outboard.

"We clear?" Eddie shouted.

"Clear!" Will said.

Eddie wasted no time throttling through the shallow turquoise waters. John sat in a Zen-like state during the ten minute ride, elbows resting on top of his knees, the wind drying salt into his short brown hair. Everything suddenly felt true and honest as he thought about Garrett and Dani, and then he exchanged that thought for the memory of rubbing lotion underneath Rita's bright red bikini straps.

It was 9:52 and the last stragglers were making their way aboard the ferry. Eddie banked *The Mermaid* against the rubber tires fixed to the bulkhead just in front of the shuttle.

"Do we need to buy tickets?" John asked.

Will pulled three tickets from his bag. "Did it when we were waiting to see if you'd show up today."

"Oh. How much do I owe you?"

"It's on me. You only had to pay me back if you *didn't* show."

"Good thing I showed," John laughed. "How about the diving?"

"Taken care of," Will said.

"Listen, Will," John said. "I'm not rich, but I'm not poor. I really appreciate you guys setting all this up. And I had a great time. The least I can do is help pay."

Will pulled a wad of cash from his bag, while Eddie stabilized *The Dirty Mermaid* with a boat hook. "It's not that," Will said. "This wasn't something you picked to do. It's our treat. 'Sides, Eddie isn't set up for credit cards."

"His company doesn't accept credit cards? How do they stay in business?"

"Well, see…the thing is," Will peeled off four one-hundred-dollar bills and stuffed the rest into his bag. "Eduardo doesn't really work for a dive company *per se*. He's more of an independent contractor."

"I thought you said he was a certified instructor?"

"Oh, he is," Will assured. "It's cheaper for us to go through his old PADI shop, but Eddie saves us time with curbside service. We've developed a rapport with him. It's not legal for a company to take you scuba diving without your certification, but our friend Eddie makes exceptions—for a fee, of course. No paper work. You just need to know how to blow through your ears and clear your mask. Cool, huh?"

Becoming suspicious, John asked, "Why doesn't he work for the dive shop any more?"

Will avoided eye contact. "They had kind of a falling-out."

John grimaced. "You mean he got fired?"

"Let's just say the relationship wore out its symbiotic nature."

"What happened?"

Will patted John's arm. "We have three minutes to be on that ferry. I don't want to wait for the next one. I'll tell you about it when we get back," Will whispered. "Deal?"

"All right, but I'm holding you to that explanation," John capitulated.

Will winked at John before turning to give Eddie a half hug with his left arm, using his right hand to transfer the money. John couldn't help but think the exchange looked more like a drug deal than a business transaction. Garth had already climbed onto the dock, waiting with an extended hand.

"Thanks, Eddie!" Garth said. "See you next week."

With Will's transaction complete, John approached Eddie in a courteous, almost Asian manner. "I want to thank you very much for teaching me how to scuba dive. The whole experience was very sublime."

Scrunching his eyes. *"Sa-lime?"*

"It means excellent," John translated.

"Excellent! Oh, good. I'm very happy you liked the fishies and didn't get bitten by the big one!"

"Me too, Eddie. Take care!"

As John climbed out of the boat Will and Garth were already trotting towards the ferry.

"Sublime, huh?" Garth said. "I wonder what word he'll pick a couple of hours from now."

Will huffed. "I don't know, but I can think of a few he might use before it's over."

"You think we'll have any problems getting the monkey in the tree?"

Huffing again. "I think we might have a bigger problem getting it down."

"It won't be in our hands at that point, Will."

"We're still responsible—sort of."

Stopping at the ferry's ramp, Garth said, "Hurry, John! They're holding the gate."

Quickening his steps. "Coming!"

"Look at him, Garth. The guy's a walking epiphany. I wish I could do it all over again," Will sighed.

"You are, Will. Remember your own credo, every day's a new day."

Finally catching up, John read the ferry's side. "Hey! Check out the name. *The Mako*. That's a kind of shark, isn't it?"

"Sure is," Will said. "Now let's get aboard, *Ahab*. We got things to do."

"I'm ready!" John said, having found aspirations from some previously locked interior place.

THE FERRY TO PEPE'S CAFE

EVERYONE ON *THE MAKO* WAS in good spirits, their only concern, bartering a memorable price on souvenirs. The crowd checked their maps, lathered up with suntan lotion, or hit the bar for a morning happy hour that would be frowned upon at home. The cliché *all's fair in love and war* could be amended to include vacation.

"John, why don't you see if you can wrangle us up some Mexican sodas," Will suggested. "Me and Garth are going to grab three topside seats."

"I'm on it," John said. "Ah…I'm assuming you're talking about beer?"

Will shot a terse look, which John took for a *yes*.

Hiking up to *The Mako's* highest seating deck and pleased to find the chairs were only a quarter occupied, Will and Garth commandeered four seats—Garth requiring two—against the port side. The two men were in their element, unlike the tourists who were curiously gawking at everything. The bartenders were void of any trepidation and open to any and all possibilities.

Will spotted John when he reached the top step, his back arched to help balance six cans of beer cradled in his arms. Will was quick to help.

"Is that all you got?" Will grinned.

"I figured one wouldn't be enough for a half hour ride," John said.

"Good thinking." Will grabbed three cans, tossing two to Garth.

Choosing a seat across from his friends, John put on his new shades. "It's not very full," he said, cracking a beer.

"They have two shuttles," Will said. "They fill up more in the early morning and late afternoon when all the locals are coming and going. Only about five percent of the island is developed. Most of the workers live on the mainland—too expensive here."

"I guess they have to go where the jobs are," John sipped.

"They have a lot of jobs in Cancun," Garth said. "That place is filled with hotels, bars, and shops."

"That's true," Will said. "Not enough, though. Almost half this country lives at, or below, the poverty line. Tons of these people walk, bus, hitch, or whatever they can to get to a five-and-a-half-dollar an hour job every day. It amazes me how the US subsidizes millions of people to do next to nothing. People back home on welfare have it better than a lot of our crew working ten hour shifts, and certainly better than these Mexicans who are busting their asses every day at one of these menial jobs. Between all our unions driving up the cost to do business and our government giving handouts, I'm shocked the United States is still a world power at all."

"We still produce millions of hard-working people," John said.

"Sure we do!" Will said. "But fewer than we used to, if you ask me. In general, Americans work very hard, but much of the rest of the world is working harder, longer, for less—in many countries, a lot less."

"Agreed, but, how do we change that?"

"I don't have all the answers, John, but I do know regular hand-outs without incentives usually does not increase productivity. You put a check in someone's mailbox every month without them working for it, and I'll show you someone who weighs three-hundred pounds. No offense, Garth."

Finishing his Corona. "None taken. I'm just big-boned. It's your country."

Will continued. "I'd take the candy out of the baby's hands. You put it on the other side of the room and watch how fast that baby will learn to crawl. When the baby becomes dissatisfied with how long it takes to crawl there, he'll learn to walk, then run. Incentive, John. That's what brought you here, isn't it? Would you have taken a cruise without promising Carson?" he asked delicately.

John lingered. Will's questions made him think about his marriage. It occurred to him that his stagnant personality eventually gave Page the incentive to leave. "No, Will, you're right. I wouldn't be here without the incentive of a promise to Carson. God bless him."

Having been briefed by Will, Garth lowered his head out of respect.

Will held up his can. "A toast," he said solemnly. "To John's son, Carson Smith, thank you for all you sacrificed in order to help keep the rest of us *safe* and *able* to share epic days like this. You have a great father."

Everyone touched cans.

"Thanks, guys," John said. "I do hear and believe what you're saying, Will. I think our country goes into these places sometimes trying to give them our same kind of democracy and then we sit back and wait for them to thank us."

"Exactly!" Will said. "Often in the past, the common Joe in these countries didn't understand what we were selling. Now, everyone has the internet. The majority can push a button and see how everyone else lives—anywhere. That tool gives them the incentive to obtain whatever the next guy has. Instead of thanking us, it's more likely they're working their asses off to cut into our big piece of pie. And why wouldn't they? For decades our government and pop culture have been throwing American pie out there for the world to envy. Life's full of choices. People back home need to decide on whether they want to work harder and adapt, or give up some of what we've always believed is indisputably ours."

Garth chuckled. "I take it you're not an advocate of socialism?"

"Hell, no!" Will frowned. "I don't believe people are storming the US borders because they're in love with mediocrity. I won't speak for my fellow countrymen here, but I prefer the opportunity to climb the ladder as high as I can. If everyone gives the bulk of their paycheck to the government, they might get education and healthcare given in return, but at what cost? We sacrifice the power to run the government. It runs the people, for better or worse. Utopia isn't everyone being financially equal; not in my book. People in those Scandinavian countries pay over half their wage to taxes. A cheeseburger costs like fifteen bucks. I don't care if that tax goes to healthcare and education. No matter how clean and beautiful the countries are, or how hot the women look, I don't want to give all my money to the government to live there."

"But how do you really feel, Will?" Garth joked.

"Look, all I'm saying is, incentive plus hard work takes people to better places than not. If someone is happy where they are…*fine*. I just don't want to listen to a healthy guy living off welfare badmouth those who have more, when those people worked harder. Take the Champagne Lounge for example. Have you been, John?"

"The fancy bar on the promenade?"

"Exactly," Will said. "There are only two bars on this ship that don't rotate bartenders. We have two Brits who only work the English Pub and Ajay only works the Champagne Lounge. Ajay is a great guy from India, and he's very well-traveled. He speaks four languages fluently. He doesn't split tips with the rest of the bartenders and he makes in a week what we make in a month, because he gets all the high rollers who spend two to five-hundred dollars on a bottle of wine. A lot of guys resent him, but I don't—he worked very hard for years to get that job and he's the right man for it."

Garth scoffed. "We could do his job."

"You really think so, Garth? It's not about making drinks or even making the guest laugh."

"What's it about then?" Garth asked.

"It's about fitting in with the kinds of people who hang out there. Lots of the people who go there now are the sort who throw their shirt away after a button falls off. Rich people aren't buying exorbitantly priced booze. They're buying an experience, something that makes them feel elite. You don't get that from smart-asses like us, or some bartender from Guatemala with a gold tooth and heavy accent."

Garth nodded. "I get your point. I could still do his job though. I know how to be fucking fancy!" Garth crossed his legs like a lady and lifted the can to his mouth, extending his pinky finger outward.

"I think Garth would be an excellent candidate for the Champagne Lounge," John said, crossing his legs in support.

"See, Will! A passenger thinks I'd be a fabulous addition to our posh bar."

"You'll have my vote too, when the clientele starts going there to order a bowl of chili and a can of beer."

John raised a finger. "Careful…I thought you were pro-rich?"

"I don't care how rich somebody is—as long as they earned it, and don't squander it all on themselves. I'm against rich people who were handed everything without giving back; lottery winners who don't start a charity; athletes who make millions a year for playing with a ball and then parade around like they're God's gift to the rest of us. If you have it, have fun with it, but respect it. Give back to those who have little chance for success in life. Behave like grown-ups instead of spoiled brats hogging all the marbles—you know? Nothing should get nothing, not a free ride!"

"Will's right," Garth said. "Some of the people we see come deliberately to con the company. They're all about themselves. That's why some of our rules are so strict when it comes to what the crew can do. We have a great bartender named Felipe—nicest guy. One day he was walking with another bartender in a public corridor on their way to work. A woman with some sort of handicap, which I don't recall, was walking towards them. Felipe laughed at something the other bartender said and when he did, he happened to glance at the woman; not because the remark had anything to do with her or her handicap, his eyes were just roving at the oncoming traffic, like you do in a mall. She goes to the hotel director claiming Felipe laughed at her because of her disability! Felipe gets demoted to working in the crew bar while this bitch gets a cabin upgrade and a free cruise."

John's face tightened. "Really, just for laughing in her general direction? She should've confronted Felipe if she thought that was the case."

"It happens," Will said. "Sometimes it's a con and sometimes it's just a misunderstanding. We see it all. There was a guy who brought a passenger down to his cabin one night—that's not permitted," Will winked. "This guy has consenting sex with the woman, and in the morning she goes to the Captain, claiming one of his crew raped her in his cabin. The Captain is suspicious since the crew areas are a maze and are clearly marked that passengers aren't permitted. She says she was drunk and he lured her down to his cabin on a dare. The Captain asks her to show him the exact cabin. She takes the Captain back to the cabin where she willingly had a great time and, end of game. The poor shit-head was terminated on the spot and flown to Miami three hours later by a Coast Guard helicopter. We never really know the real outcomes, but the company usually settles with the con artist for an undisclosed amount of money—exactly what they were looking for in the first place. As a rule of thumb, if it doesn't make the papers or go to court, it was a con, swept under the carpet with cash and signed disclosure papers."

Staring at the deck, John mulled the thought of someone lying maliciously for personal gain.

"You okay, John?" Garth asked.

Slowly raising his head. "Yeah. I just don't understand people sometimes. I mean…at the end of the day, we have to live with ourselves. Lying and cheating seem to blind us to that fact. Sanding our conscience doesn't seem to be worth what you get in return. I know you guys might think I'm naive—a small town guy who's never really done anything—but I…" John pulled his glasses away, letting them drop to his chest and scanned the ocean past them.

"I think when people wear dark glasses long enough, they convince themselves the world is better with less light. The light might hurt sometimes…but it's real. If we're constantly trying to manipulate the light, how will we ever know what things actually look like? Change the *colors* and we change the truths." John downed the remainder of his beer, set the empty can on the deck, closed his eyes, and leaned back. His neck drooped over the back of the chair and he smiled as the sun warmed his face.

Garth removed his sunglasses and turned to look over Will's shoulder at the sea. "I like this guy…he's a diamond," Garth said.

Still gazing at John, the corners of Will's mouth curled up. "Yeah," Will whispered, "even his flaws are flawless."

Will stood, turned to the ocean, removed his sunglasses, and stared out beyond the horizon. His profound gaze was broken as Playa del Carmen appeared on the horizon.

"Land ho!" Will cried. "Everyone ready for an early lunch at Pepe's?"

John and Garth stood and stretched.

John asked, "What's Pepe's?"

"He's a local cafe owner," Garth said.

Will bent over for a couple of toe touches. "Playa del Carmen is filled with great restaurants, but Garth and I like the off-the-beaten-track joints. The less refined places offer more bang for your buck, are often *as* good if not better, and have way more personality. Much like people…you know what I mean, John?" Squeezing John's shoulder.

"We found Pepe's cafe about a year ago," Garth said. "Pepe's a sweetheart—full of energy. He's excellent at service—treats everyone the same, whether it's a hot chic or raging asshole."

"The only difference," Will said, "is how he talks about people once they're gone. That's when you get the truth about what he really thought. And he doesn't hold back."

"It's interesting too, how he was born in Costa Rica, lived in the states for ten years, and then moved to Mexico," Garth said.

"Why did he move to Mexico?" John asked.

"He married a Miss Mexico," Will said. "They met at a bar in Vegas after she lost some sort of contest—Miss Galaxy or some shit. He says they traded shots of tequila and made jokes about each other's country until the sun came up. Eventually they got married and moved here. She's originally from this area and wanted to come back, since her family's all still here."

"Sounds like a character worth meeting," John said.

The ferry's engines powered down as she jockeyed into the pier. The boys shouldered their packs, trashed the empty cans, and marched down the stairs. A Pavlovian gurgle came from John's now empty stomach as he smelled tacos and hot coffee at the concession stand.

Once clear of the dock, Will led the way north along Playa del Carmen's main shopping street. John, expecting Mexico to be made of dirt towns with chickens roaming in the streets, was shocked to see how cosmopolitan it was. He had pictured outhouses and men dressed in ponchos. Instead, he saw white tablecloth restaurants, fine galleries, jewelry stores, mature trees strung with white lights, and locals wearing the latest fashions. Good Intent was more rural than Playa del Carmen.

The scenery and architecture started to decline when Will veered off the main drag. Two side streets and an alley later, the group arrived at their destination. A small mangy dog, whose coat appeared to have barely survived an electrocution, lay panting in the street underneath a weathered sign that read: Pepe's Cafe. Two empty tables guarded the open entrance. The three men entered, each one giving Mangy a token pat as they passed.

The cafe was small. John counted eight tables—all empty. A large cactus—a miniature version of the kind drawn in cartoons—potted in terra-cotta, was the cafe's only vegetation. John noticed that the floor's ornate mosaic tiles were free of dust and debris as he wandered over to a wall littered with cheaply framed photographs, mostly of the same man or woman holding a fish. The woman, in her teeny-weenie bikini, distracted from each trophy fish. Will walked up to the vacant bar and repeatedly slapped a rusty bell.

"I'm coming! I'm coming!" shouted a man charging out from the kitchen. "Son-of-a-bitch! Is it Wednesday already?" he asked.

"Damn right it is, Pepe," Will said. "We just recovered from last week's food poisoning, so we thought we'd see how you're serving this week's salmonella."

The man came around the bar to give Will and Garth each a man-hug. He was good-looking, salt and pepper hair, dark bronze skin, and wore Armani glasses. A full white apron covered his black tee-shirt. The words Chef and Owner were embroidered on the left breast pocket. His blood and fish parts speckled apron had a slogan in big black letters: *INSTEAD OF COMPLAINING—LEAVE*.

"You fuckers are in luck today," Pepe said, literally giggling like a school girl. "I just got some fresh fish heads in!"

"Maybe you should think about serving the tails, Pepe," Garth said. "You're not exactly packing them in."

Feigning a punch to Garth's belly. "It's ten forty-five," Pepe giggled, "you know *spicks* eat late lunches! We work hard in the morning, eat, then it's siesta time."

Will asked, "Do they still let you into Costa Rica now that you've abandoned your beloved country to be a wet-back?"

Still giggling. "I can go wherever I want. Still got my *US* passport. You guys don't need to get jealous just because Latin women are much more beautiful than anything you both could ever get."

"Speaking of which…where's your better half?" Garth asked.

"She's doing what every trophy wife does best. She's shopping and then headed to the beach!" Pepe continued giggling. "Who you got with you today, Will? I hope he isn't a food critic, since we've all been slamming my restaurante."

"Pepe, meet our new friend John Smith."

"Hey, John! Welcome. You work on the ship?"

Grinning from all the good-natured ribbing. "No. I'm a passenger."

"A passenger! And you couldn't find anyone better to spend your vacation with than these two assholes?"

"Actually, Pepe, they've been really great. This is my first cruise and they've been nice enough to take me under their wings. We just came from some illegal scuba diving."

More giggling. "Be careful around these guys, John. If you're not…you could find yourself in one of two places—jail or a body-bag!"

"We're going to grab a quick bite here with you, Pepe, before we head up to Cancun. So odds are in favor of the body-bag," Will said. "What are you burning us today?"

"You in a hurry?" Pepe asked.

"Kind of," Will said. "We're cramming a lot in today."

"Why Cancun? You guys can have just as much fun here, or on the island."

Leaning in, Will whispered, "We're on a little *grande banda de goma* mission."

Pepe snuck a peak over Will's shoulder. John had gone back to perusing Pepe's pictures. "This a cherry run?"

Will nodded. "We wanted to go way up, but couldn't 'cause of the forty-eight hour rule."

"Gotcha buddy," Pepe winked. "I just got some snapper an hour ago. Want me to whip up something special for you guys?"

"Thanks, Pepe," Will agreed.

"Why don't you grab the beers, so I can get started."

"You want one?"

"When I'm done cooking."

"Sounds good!"

Following Pepe behind the counter, Will pulled three frosted mugs from a cooler, filling each one from the Dos Equis tap sprouting from the bar top. He confiscated one of the vacant tables as Pepe ducked out from the kitchen to turn on a stereo. Finding the upbeat salsa music comfortably reminiscent of the previous night, John sat. The jolly group sipped on cold beers while recapping the adventures from their dive. John basked in the camaraderie forgotten since his college days, when he and Page gathered with friends at the local pizza pub.

Waiting for lunch, John considered the experience of fun. Where had it been in his life? How and when did he lose his desire to seek it out? Fun, he was learning, is an attitude. With the right attitude and a touch of incentive—certainly two compelling bartenders and a free cruise ticket qualified—fun is everywhere; even in the most mundane tasks. Fun isn't something to do, it's a continual action, a transportation of a state of mind. A man without the right attitude would always be searching in the dark. If this is true, he reflected, is it possible to find happiness even in death? Clearly, his son would advocate so. Carson wanted John to be happy badly enough to find a way to send a ticket, even after death took him. A prideful grin snuck onto John's face at the realization that his son's attitude was exceptional.

Noticing John's pensive face, Will asked, "You okay, John?"

"I'm great, Will. I'm also starving...guess I shouldn't have given my breakfast to the fishies."

Garth chimed in. "Forget all that crap we said about bad food. Pepe's a hell-of-a chef. Despite the rustic look of this place, all the food is local and fresh. The only way to get fresher seafood is to eat it off the hook."

"He's right, John. Pepe used to work at the Four Seasons in Washington D.C. He saves a lot of money by being off the beaten path and serves food just as good as any fine dining restaurant in Playa del Carmen, but at half the price."

On cue, Pepe appeared from the back with three steaming plates balanced on his left arm, stopping at the taps to pour a beer. After serving each man, he sat beside Will.

"Dig in while it's hot, gentlemen," Pepe said, sipping his beer.

"This looks wonderful," John said.

"Fresh snapper, caught about an hour ago. I grill them head and all, but it's just for effect. They're filleted so you don't have to worry about the bones. I used some lemongrass, pineapple, and mango salsa for flavor. It balances the heat in the spicy rice."

"Looks great," Will said.

"Thanks," Pepe beamed. "I gave big-boy the largest one."

Garth's snapper was so large its head and tail draped onto the table. "You the man, Pepe!" Garth salivated.

Giggling. "I know it's hard work keeping up those big-bones of yours."

"See!" Garth said. "Finally someone understands the difference between fat and big-boned. In my opinion you're the best damn American, Costa Rican, Mexican, spick in the world, Pepe."

Still giggling. "And I've never met a finer South African reject in all my life, Garth."

"A toast!" Will said. "To Pepe's! Where the only two vulgar words are: politically correct. And the only way to get your feelings hurt is to show up on a Monday, when Pepe and his beautiful wife close so they can make love in the tranquil waters of the Mexican Rivera!"

Everyone clanked glasses and shouted, "Here, here!"

"Mondays *are* the best day of the week," Pepe giggled once more.

EL GRANDE BANDA DE GOMA

THEY SAVORED EACH BITE OF Pepe's cuisine, licking every fish bone clean, and leaving not one grain of rice or bit of pineapple salsa on their plates. Will paid the humble twenty-dollar bill with a fifty, insisting Pepe should use the change to launder his apron.

The well fed trio returned to the main street to hail a cab. Not more than two minutes passed before an anxious blue and yellow Astro van snapped a U-turn, horn blaring—barely missing several tourists oblivious to their surroundings. The van's brakes brought the driver to a high-pitched halt in front of the group. Merengue music poured out of the open windows loud enough to make the rear view's pink fuzzy dice sway and bounce.

"Hola!" the young cabbie welcomed.

"Hello, my friend," Will said. "Cancun?"

"Si! Cancun. I take you."

"Hop in boys…this is our horse."

John and Garth pulled the sliding door and jumped in the back as Will lingered at the driver's window, negotiating a price and volume control. Satisfied, he joined his partners in the back. After beeping at some lazy tourists crossing his path, the cabbie sped north out of town.

"Where in Cancun I take you?" the cabbie asked.

Will removed from his bag three of the six beers Pepe had contributed. "Playa Tortugas," he said.

"Si! You go to el grande banda de goma?"

Quickly squirming between the two front seats, Will leaned into the cabbie as close as he could without kissing him. "Si, señor…secreto."

"Si," whispered the cabbie. "I understand."

"What's banda de goma?" John asked.

"It's a nice spot on the beach where people go to swim and enjoy outdoor activities," Garth grinned.

"Oh…good," John said. "I guess that's why you guys told me to wear my bathing suit? All this water stuff feels great and it's so beautiful—clear as the pool at the YMCA back home."

"It's funny you say that," Garth said. "I saw this woman one time when I was walking on the beach here. She had one of those glass jars with the screw lid that old women use to save food."

"A mason jar?" John helped.

"Yeah! She filled it with ocean water. I saw her looking at it real close, so I went up and asked her what she caught. She tells me she collects different colored water from all the beaches she goes to."

Spewing beer over the back of the front seat, Will asked, "What did *you* say?"

"I was kind of speechless at first. Then I asked her if all her jars looked the same when she put them together. That made her think. She finally says, 'Yes, now that you mention it, they do.'"

"Did you straighten her out?" John asked.

"I almost didn't have the heart, but, yes, I did. I told her the color she saw at the beach came from sunlight and sand color."

"How'd she take the news?" John asked.

"She just stood there for a minute, staring at me with a glassy look on her face. Then she says, 'Thanks' and proceeds to dump out the water and replace it with sand. She smiled at me like she'd done something bad and walked off without saying a word."

With all three laughing, Garth sprawled out on the rear bench seat, leaned his head against the window, and watched the Mexican landscape whip by.

"Classic," Will said.

John got comfortable in the corner of his bench seat. "What did you do before real estate and the cruise lines, Will? Did you go to college?"

"Yeah, I did a little stint at The University of Tennessee."

"How long?"

"Three and a half years."

"Jeez, Will, why didn't you just finish?" John asked.

"Ah…I came to the realization that college was just another big business. Its main concern is to take your money. Every time you switch majors it's like starting over. Besides, they really didn't offer the curriculum I was interested in."

"A school that size must offer every major in the book?" John wondered.

"Not bull riding," Will smiled.

"Bull riding! You serious?"

"Serious as a steer has horns. I did my schooling in your neck of the woods—Sankey Rodeo School in Wichita, Kansas."

"Wow, that's pretty cool," John imagined. "I always thought you guys were crazy."

"It helps," Will chuckled.

"How did you get started and what's it like?"

"After I quit college, I started bartending for Fuddruckers. I went around to country bars when I wasn't working to talk to people about how to get started. After I finished school in Kansas, I started entering events. Fuddruckers actually sponsored me. I loved it. It's pure adrenaline."

"Did you ever get hurt?"

Breaking into laughter. "All the time! I broke my collar bone, half a dozen ribs, a compound foot…I broke my cheek bone and eye socket when the back of the bull's head slammed into my face. Oh…I also got my pinky mangled when it got caught up in the bull rope—that's what you hang on to."

"Holy shit, Will," John gasped, "I hope you at least made a lot of money."

"Na…people don't do it for the money. Depending on the size of the event, you pay a fifty to two hundred fifty dollar entrance fee, and you can win anywhere from fifty to five thousand dollars. You do it for the rush. From the time you step up to the gate and straddle two thousand pounds of pissed off animal, every part of your body's on full alert. You can be injured before the gate even opens. That bull has a flank rope around it to make it kick more and it ain't happy being trapped in a cage. Once you set a rider wearing spurs on his back—look out! Kevlar vest and chaps give you little protection against something ten times your size. Once you wrap that bull rope around your hand and give the thumbs up, there's no turning back. Coming out of the chute is like stepping into a tornado."

"I bet!" John imagined. "What's the strangest thing you ever saw?"

"I traveled around to events in a dozen states and saw a lot of guys get messed up, but the most brutal thing I ever witnessed was in Missouri where a guy got trampled. The poor SOB got both legs and his skull crushed by the bull's hooves. I had a lot of my own injuries by then and knew it was about time to get out. Shortly after, I got hired at Carnival."

"That must have been a change of pace?"

"We had a pool going whether he would make it to the end of his six month contract," Garth said. "Nobody had ever seen an American in the bar department—other than Yoda."

"I guess you enjoyed it," John said.

"Most of the time I hated it! I completed that contract out of spite."

"I don't understand…why didn't you just quit?"

"I started calling the company's home office in Miami when I was phasing myself out of rodeo competition. I spoke with this guy in charge of HR—Nash Amani—and checked in with him every few weeks until eventually, one time I called and he asked me if I could be in Miami the next day. So…I packed a bag and flew to Miami where I spent a bizarre night in a company sponsored cheap hotel room. Guys kept coming and going, in and out of my room all night. I learned later they were employees who were either coming back or leaving for vacation and got assigned to my spare bed."

"*That* must have freaked you out," Garth cackled.

"I didn't sleep much. They never said a word, just came in and went right to sleep, then they got up a few hours later and walked back out. Nash neglected to brief me on that policy. The next day I met Nash, the first and last time I ever saw him, signed some paper work, walked across the street for a physical, and then boarded the ship. We sailed away a couple hours later. When I checked in with the purser, he told me he needed eight hundred dollars before he would issue my crew charge card—like the passengers, we use it for everything we buy. When I asked him why he needed a deposit he told me it was to secure a flight back to my country of origin in case I quit or got fired. I shot him a smart-ass look and told him that I was American and if either of those things happened, they could just drop me off in Miami on Sunday."

"I bet that put a snag in his panties," Garth said.

"Oh, he didn't know how to respond. They're so used to pushing a bunch of third world people around."

"Did he make you give the money?" John asked.

"I made him call the home office and talk to Nash. It took two days before I got word my request had been denied. They did allow me to pay it from my wages over the next few weeks. You only get the money back if you complete the six month contract. So…that's what I mean when I say I stayed out of spite—had to fight to get my money back on the day I left for vacation, too. I was there for an extra four hours 'til they cut me a check. They wanted to mail it! I knew I wasn't coming back, and didn't trust them to mail me my money. But, eventually I got it."

John sighed, "I sure am jealous of you guys."

"Why do you say that, John," Garth asked.

"You guys have done so much with your lives—so many great experiences. I feel like I've wasted *my* life."

"Every new day you're alive is a chance to do something different," Will said. "There's millions of people who do the same thing over and over until the day they die. I think that's great…*if* they love what they do. All those people who never take a chance to change their unhappy lives leave more opportunities on the table for those of us who overcome our fear of change." Will's voice softened. "I don't know how you can say what you've done so far has been wasted. You got married and had a child. So many people take those responsibilities too lightly. You're not one of them, John. So it didn't work out the way you planned…that's how life works sometimes. You can't blame yourself for what happened to Carson. And you shouldn't fault yourself too much for your marriage either. It's my understanding you're not the one who left. I've never had the privilege of a wife or children. Do you think you'd be better off never having them?"

"No. I don't regret either and I'd do it all again."

Will smiled. "Then you didn't waste anything. You just have a new opportunity to figure out what you're going to do next. This trip's a good start…don't you think?"

Returning Will's smile, John turned to the window. The rural, often barren landscape, reminded John of Kansas with cactus. A single tear slipped from his left eye, and rinsed away a little more pain. Maybe life hadn't left him; it was knocking on his door. Will's words reminded John that his hand was on the doorknob…all that remained was the decision to pull.

The three men sat quietly for fifteen minutes drinking their second beer. The cabbie's heavy foot got them into Cancun in forty minutes. There was nothing rural about Cancun. It was as if someone picked up Miami's South Beach and moved it to Mexico. The towering hotels and condos blocked the view of Cancun's gorgeous beaches. Stunning women, showing off as much of their bodies as their string bikinis would allow, filled the sidewalks. The cabbie stopped in front of the famous watering hole: Fat Tuesdays.

"We here," the cabbie said. "Playa Tortugas!"

Will inched forward, handing the cabbie the seventy dollars he had counted out. "Thank you, my friend."

"*Gracias!*" said the cabbie. "Have fun!"

"Okay boys, let's get to it," Will said.

"Get to what?" John asked. "We going for drinks?"

"After," Garth said, leading the way through a tunnel that cut between bars and shops. "We told you…we're diving today."

Jogging to catch up, John asked, "What are you talking about? You mean we're scuba diving again?"

Garth weaved around the sandy outdoor seating areas without answering, only stopping when he reached the crowded beach. Before them was a pier that held a tall wooden fort. His mates joined him; John followed Garth's gaze. A long steel plank extended from the top of the sixty-six foot wooden tower. The beach crowd cheered from the water below as an instructor dressed in a red polo shirt and shorts counted off: *uno! dos! tres!* A pretty woman in a bikini, her feet lashed to a long red cord, dove face-first from the gangplank. Her head broke the shallow water just before the rope jerked her back into the sky. She oscillated above the emerald waters until another man dressed in an identical red uniform passed her a rope from the end of a long boat-hook. Once she slowed enough to grab it, they pulled her safely onto an air mat at the fort's base.

Both men turned to John. "What do you say, John," Will asked, "ready to get your feet…I mean head, wet?"

Staring upward, John's Adam's apple rose and sank like a fishing bobber. "That's diving, all right, but…not exactly what I thought you guys had in mind."

"There's nothing to it," Garth said. "We've done it twenty times."

"This bungee jump's only a year old," Will said. "Still lots of life left in the cord."

"Yeah," Garth agreed, "it probably won't kill anyone 'til next year."

Not laughing, John continued to stare at the device, remembering when he fell off his father's ladder. He tried summoning his inner dragon by clenching both fists at his sides. Taking a step forward and then turning to face the two men, John said, "Well…if it's not due to break until next year…I guess there's only one question: what are we waiting for?" Without waiting for a reply, John turned away and proceeded towards the pier.

Garth's brows raised. "It would appear we underestimated somebody."

"Indeed," Will said. "I would've lost my ass on that bet."

Garth extended his hand with a half curtsey motion. "Shall we, bull-rider?"

Will copied. "Big-boned before beauty."

"Why thank you, kind sir!"

When Will and Garth caught up, John was seated at a table signing a waiver. He turned over his credit card and informed the instructor to run it for three jumps. "Poor choice of color for uniforms don't you think?" John asked.

"Don't think of red as a symbol of blood," Will said. "Think of it as the color of adrenaline."

"Oh…okay." John said, rolling his eyes. "I guess a waiver is pretty standard for something labeled *Extreme Games*." Jabbing his pen at the sign fixed to the fort emphasized his point.

"It's a misprint," Garth said. "It should read *Extremely Fun Games*."

"How do you get the rope to stop before breaking people's necks?" John asked the instructor.

"It's set every jump according to the person's weight," he answered.

Accepting his answer, John read over the forms with the instructor before starting his ascent. The narrow staircase seemed safer than the one at the zip; still, he clenched both railings. When he reached the top, an upbeat Mexican instructor sat him in a chair, fit his ankles with two thick Velcro harnesses, and clipped a safety rope to the anklets. By the time John was primed, and the plank instructor was busy resetting the rope, Will and Garth arrived.

The ankle fitter, beaming with encouragement, held up two fingers. "Two minutes, sir!"

"Still feeling bold?" Garth asked.

"Like Superman holding kryptonite," John said, forcing a chuckle. The next two minutes passed like a caning. Perspiration and anxiety increased with each passing second.

"You should be happy we took you scuba diving first," Will said.

"Why's that?"

"We normally go skydiving, but we can't scuba and skydive in the same forty-eight hour period. Your blood could boil!"

"Oh, good, this is a much better idea than boiling blood," John said shaking his head, wondering what he'd gotten himself into.

"You up!" cried the instructor. "Just walk the catwalk to the other instructor."

John stood. "Well…if I don't see you guys again…thanks for all the *fun*."

"Just think how good the beer's going to taste," Garth said smiling from ear to ear.

"How about we go get one now? My treat!" John asked.

Will shooed John forward. "You have to earn it!" he said.

Focusing on the instructor at the ramp's end, John understood why the team wore bright red uniforms. The color acted like a bull's-eye keeping him moving forward without glancing down. He baby stepped to the spot *bull's-eye* pointed to before the instructor exchanged John's safety rope for the bungee harness. Then holding John by the shoulders, he scooted him to an opening in the platform's railing that was secured only with a single hooked rope. When in place, the man unchained the rope, explained how to jump, and told John he should go on the count of three.

Raising his arms as he was instructed, John's body was screaming with warning signals—*this could kill you!* His mouth felt like if he coughed, ashes would fly out; his knees buckled and swayed and the palms of his hands dripped sweat. The salt from the gentle breeze filled his overloaded, olfactory senses. Scared too stiff to move, he heard Will and Garth shout, "You can do it!" over top of the screaming beach crowd and then, "*uno...dos*" from his shadow. And then..."*tres!*"

Looking down for the first time as his torso fell forward, the light green water rushed towards his face like a big league fastball. Death was a certainty in the two seconds right before John's head pierced the ocean. What went down, in this case, had to go back up, and he shot out of the water as if *God* had him by the feet. John's lunch, which had slammed against the bottom of his esophagus, now smacked the top of his colon hard enough to move whatever waste lie inside a few more feet through his intestines. He bounced more softly two more times before a pendulum motion took over, and, like he saw earlier, the base instructor extended a boat hook with a rope wrapped at the end. John clawed the air dizzily until the rope found his hand. Then the instructor hauled John to the side, placing him on an air mat, gentle as a baby in a crib. The instructor proceeded to unclip and un-velcro John, who just lay on the mat with spent relief and elation. The worker pulled him upright with a strong tug. Glowing, John followed the man back to the Extreme Games sign, where he received a Diploma Al Valor and a photograph.

Rejoicing to be alive, John made his way back to the beach to watch the boys' turns, receiving high-fives along the way. Two minutes later Will Catcher wasted no time leaping sideways off the platform before the instructor said "*dos*." Roaring laughter exploded from his mouth; Will looked and sounded like a deranged spider-man. This man who had been repeatedly kicked by bulls had zero fear of jumping sixty feet off a gangplank with a rope attached to his ankles. Will refused to take the rope from the instructor's stick until his ride came to a full stop.

Five minutes later, with Will joining John, Garth looked like a grizzly bear on a tightrope waddling down the platform.

"Are you sure it'll hold him?" John joked.

"He's been here before," Will said. "I worry more about the gangplank than the bungee cord!" Will cupped his hands over his mouth. "Hey *big-boned!* Jump before the ramp collapses!"

A sack of potatoes would've had more style points as Garth dropped feet first. The cord appeared to strain twice as hard with Garth's barrel-like girth.

"Now that rope knows how it feels to reel in a fifteen hundred pound marlin!" Will ridiculed. "Let's go get him, John. It's beer thirty!" Tapping his watch.

Posing for a group photo, their facial expressions told the whole story—pure joy. When the men had fully congratulated themselves with slaps and high-fives, they retired to Fat Tuesdays' outdoor bar and ordered three beers and a round of tequila to toast John's virgin jump.

"Based on your dive, Will, if you ever committed suicide from a tall building, I believe you'd be the only jumper in history to enjoy yourself on the way down," John said.

Will laughed. "Bungee jumping's nothing! When I was in Hawaii we would cliff jump. Now *that* is a rush. There's hundreds of beautiful waterfalls scattered over the islands that make for great jumps. That one from the TV show *Fantasy Island* is there. We went to this one on the big island—Hawaii—and all these tough native guys watched as I climbed way up a sheer cliff. This thing was so tall, when I jumped, I screamed until I was out of breath and then I let out another full scream before I hit the water. All the locals, who usually aren't overly friendly to outsiders, congratulated me. They told me in all their years of diving, they had never seen anyone jump from where I jumped."

"You're lucky you survived," Garth said.

"Oh, my entire left leg was purple from landing crooked—hurt like hell!" Will hopped off his stool. "Save the shots. I'm going to hit the head."

Garth propped his foot up on the rail of John's stool and said, "I got to hand it to you, we thought we might have to carry you up and push you in order for you to go through with jumping today. Instead, you jumped like a pro—and without any prompting!"

Pondering, John said, "I think I've been carrying guilt around for a long time. Today, for some reason, I guess I just figured my fear of jumping wasn't as bad as adding to my guilt by *not* jumping. I picked the lesser of two evils. That make any sense?"

Nodding. "Yeah, John, it does. But did you enjoy it?"

"I absolutely loved it! But with that said…I don't feel the need to make bungee jumping a habit. It's like giving a football player smelling salts after he loses consciousness. In a lot of ways, I'm realizing I've been unconscious for a long time. Things like this bungee jump are just the smelling salts I needed, I guess, but that doesn't mean I want to have to rely on them to live. I think I could get used to scuba diving though. I definitely want to get certified now, but more life-threatening things like bungee jumping are probably best to try once or twice—for me anyway."

Garth ruminated. "Makes sense. Kind of a Clint Eastwood thing."

"Sorry?"

"You know…'A man's got to know his limitations.'"

Laughing. "Yeah, exactly."

Will came back to the table toting a plastic bag.

"They selling souvenirs in the bathroom now?" Garth asked.

"Yeah, second stall on the left," Will said, picking up his tequila shot. "I've only known you for three days, John, but I think you're a damn good guy."

"Are you proposing?" Garth asked.

John clucked. "I'm divorced, Will, but you're not my type."

"Oh, you guys are funny," Will said. "May I continue?"

"By all means," John said.

"It's your show," Garth said.

"Thanks! Anyway, you strike me as a guy busting out of his cocoon." Will paused and scratched his chin. "I think I just found a good moniker for you. Everyone needs a call-sign. From now on, John, you're to be known as *Butterfly* to us."

"I like it," Garth said.

"Me too," John said.

"Good!" Will said pleased. "A toast! To a fine day with good friends! And to Butterfly's first flight!"

Having grown accustomed to the bartender's rituals, John clicked plastic shot cups and downed the agave juice.

"In honor of this special occasion we got you a gift, John," Will said.

"We did?" Garth asked.

"Yeah, *we* did. Don't worry 'bout it, my real estate money's paying for it."

"I got the round and the cab back," Garth agreed.

"Sold!" Will reached into the bag. "I think we can ditch the blue t-shirt, John. It's too fine a day, so we got you one more fitting." Handing over a red t-shirt.

"Thanks, guys!" John opened the shirt and read: "*If at first you don't succeed—bungee jumping is not for you*. I'm glad this really doesn't apply to me!" John ripped the tag off, and his blue shirt, and slipped the gift over his hairy chest.

"The picture of the busted cord and the little dead guy really makes the shirt," Garth joked.

"I thought so," Will said checking his watch. "We should probably catch a cab if we're going to make the three o'clock boat."

"Check!" Garth said, flagging a waitress.

"I have a question for you guys," John said.

"Shoot," Will said.

"I don't see any signs for el grande banda de goma anywhere. I thought you guys said that was the name of this place. What does it really mean?"

Garth threw some money on the bill and Will stood and shouldered his bag. Then they looked at each other and laughed.

"You, of all people, should know, John," Will teased.

"Why's that?"

"It's what you do for a living," Garth said.

"I don't get it."

"El grande banda de goma, John, is Spanish for the big rubber band," Will illustrated.

"Son-of-a-farmer! You guys got me again."

Laughing, Will and Garth both shouldered an arm around John as the three friends marched back to the street.

WHEN DID I GET HERE?

THE GANG USED THE FORTY-FIVE minute trip back to Playa del Carmen to regenerate, and their cabbie employed his iPod to drown out the cacophony of snoring from his back seats. At 2:45 the taxi dropped the three groggy passengers off where they had started. They stretched and yawned in the heart of Playa del Carmen's main shopping street. John stood out like a flashing traffic signal with his bright red shirt and neon sunglasses leash.

"Well…I guess we should get to the ferry," Will said, just as John heard a familiar voice calling his name. He scanned a hundred-eighty degrees and back before pinpointing the caller. A woman stood on the corner waving her arm from across the street. Her face was shaded by a tasteful grass hat and the tail of a black silk ribbon tied around its crown, lay across the brim. Even from a distance, John could tell it was Rita…..she was gorgeous.

"Rita!" John said, quickly squaring his ball-cap. "I'll be back in a minute, guys!"

"You've got five minutes," Will said.

John, trying to act casual crossing the street, made a car halt and beep, causing him to spring back and then jog forward again.

"Hi, Rita!"

"Hello, Mr. Smith! You having some fun with our bartender friend?"

"Actually, they've shown me a great time. We went scuba diving this morning and we just got back from bungee jumping in Cancun."

Surprised. "I didn't realize you were such an Indiana Jones?"

Rolling his head. "I'm not really. It was my first time for both."

"Good for you, John. I'm sure Carson's smiling wherever he is."

"I hope so." John glanced around. "Not that I care…but where's George?"

"We shopped in Cozumel and then had lunch. I wanted to come here and he wanted to play golf at the country club, so we did what any semi-divorced couple does…we separated and I took the one o'clock over here! How about you, John? What do you have planned for the rest of the day?"

"Will and Garth are taking me to a place called Carlos 'n Charlie's. Have you been?"

Laughing. "Not for about ten years. It's sort of Mexico's version of a TGI Friday's—but much rowdier."

"Maybe I should skip it?"

"No! You should go. Everyone should experience it at least once. It's fun but you have to be in the mood, you know what I mean?"

"I guess I will after I see for myself."

"Afterward, we can compare notes," Rita grinned.

Will shouted from across the street. "John!"

Turning to see Will tapping his watch, John bought another few moments holding up a pointer finger.

"You know, there's another ferry that leaves twenty minutes after the three o'clock," Rita said. "If you wanted…we could grab a coffee and you could meet them after?"

Grinning. "I would love a coffee. Let me go tell them real quick, okay?"

"I'll be right here!" Rita dropped two shopping bags onto the sidewalk, sat down on a bench, and crossed her legs.

Sprinting back to Will and Garth. "It's Rita, Will!" John gasped.

"I *see*," Will said.

"We're going to have a coffee. She says there's another ferry twenty minutes after this one."

"Go for it, John!" Garth said. "She looks hot from here, and I can barely see that far."

Will studied John's barely contained delight. "I think that's a great idea, my friend. You guys should *definitely* have a coffee. Come join us when you're done."

"Thanks, Will. Is the bar hard to find?"

"Nah. Just hang a left off the ferry dock and start walking. You can't miss it." Will slapped John's shoulder. "Go get her, John, it's not polite to keep a lady waiting—especially one that classy."

"I'm off!" John said, glancing both ways before jogging back.

"Lucky guy!" Garth said.

Will studied John. "I don't think *luck* has anything to do with it."

Will and Garth boarded the ferry while John made it across the busy street without incident this time.

John carried Rita's bags as they walked to a small cafe four shops down. Inside, the tiny black and white tiled floor and old-fashioned display counter gave the cafe an Old World feel. Antique mahogany-bladed ceiling fans whirred, their chains rattling against the motor's base. The smell of freshly ground beans and warm sweets permeated the air. They ordered at the counter before sitting at a small marble-topped corner table.

John shared his prior night's adventure in the restricted crew area, including his head-splitting hangover and magical dive—complete with shark encounter. Rita patiently sat, a genuine smile playing on her flawless face the entire time. He knew twenty minutes would pass in a flash and by the time their coffee arrived, Rita had been briefed about the most exciting fifteen hour period in John Smith's life.

Now, aware he'd been talking like an excited schoolboy, John said, "I'm sorry, Rita, I didn't mean for the conversation to be all about me."

"You're sharing it with me so it can't *all* be about you," she assured with a dimple flash. "I like today's t-shirt. It looks new?"

"The boys got it for me after our jump. How 'bout you…looks like you found yourself some good buys?"

"I *did!* It's not a problem for most women to find things they like to buy," she said shyly. "It's more like research for me though."

"How do you mean?"

"I told you I graduated from Miami University?"

"Yes, you did."

"My major was in business, with a minor in fashion. I own a little boutique in Coconut Grove. We sell men's clothes too—in case you're ever interested?"

"I could use some help, as you can tell. I don't know much about fashion. These flip-flops and sunglasses are the first new things I've bought in years—other than socks and underwear."

Rita chuckled. "As long as you keep up with those, you're doing all right." Rita sipped her espresso. "I'm glad George wanted to play golf. This city has some wonderful shops. I usually don't like any company when I'm shopping—especially with somebody I don't want to be with in the first place."

John had been toying with the idea of asking if she'd like his company the rest of the day, until her declaration quashed the idea. Although his time wasn't up, he rushed to think of a new way to see her again.

"Do you…do you have to see him later?" he asked, wishing to reel in the words as soon as they left his mouth. *Of course she has to see him later.*

Rita pursed her lips. "I don't have to see him until nine o'clock—we each get our hour."

"Your hour?"

"Yeah. We share a cabin, but not a bed. Besides two beds, another stipulation I made him agree to before we came on this trip was that we each got an hour to ourselves to shower and dress. We board at seven, that's when I get my hour. That leaves an hour before I have to meet him in the jazz bar. Would you like to meet at eight?"

Battling both fear and desire, John forced the words, "Sure. Where?"

Thinking. "How about your cabin?"

If John was watching his old box TV—before he'd thrown it away—and the nightly news called off one of his occasionally purchased lottery ticket numbers as the winner, he couldn't have been more excited and shocked.

Coughing with a swallow of bitter coffee, he managed, "Okay."

Even though Rita understood the effect of her request, she asked, "Are you comfortable with that, John?"

Still clearing his throat. "Sure! I mean it's not like…you're almost…"

"Relax, John, you're not doing anything wrong. It's the safest place for us to meet. Not that I care, but George will never find us and I don't want him starting something for no reason. Okay?"

"I'm fine with it," John said, still sounding nervous.

"You better get going if you're going to catch the ferry."

John didn't want to go, but she was right, he had five minutes.

Standing. "Eight then?"

"I'll be there!"

"I hope you enjoy the rest of your shopping," he smiled. Slowly turning towards the door, his hand reached the doorknob when Rita spoke.

"John," she said in a seductive voice.

Snapping around. "Yes?"

"I'll need the room number."

"That would probably help, wouldn't it?" Rita just grinned. "Three-seventeen, Mermaid deck."

"See you at eight, Mr. Smith."

"I look forward to it," John said, fidgeting with the antique doorknob. Their eyes locked in a way he'd never experienced—not with Dani or even Page. Unable to handle the intensity, he forced the knob and fled.

Hustling back to the dock, he scampered up the ramp with two minutes to spare and returned to the top deck. Soon after, the ferry's rumbling engines vibrated every seat as they churned up the water. It had been years since John had been fortunate enough to have so many positive events to replay, and he toyed with the day's amusements the way a cat played with a ball of twine—the thirty minutes passed in an instant.

When the boat docked he disembarked without urgency, dawdling down the pier with a child's lightness. Per Will's instructions, he hung a left at the main street, a newfound confidence guiding him as though he was walking in his own neighborhood. Festive music, mixed with drunken cheers two blocks down, made Carlos 'n Charlie's easy to find. Upon entering, an almost immediate call sounded, reminding John of a Norm from "Cheers" opening.

"John!" shouted a group from a four top in the center of the crowded restaurant. He heard the cry, but was unable to locate its origin until seeing Garth standing, arms out like King Kong atop a building. Garth bummed a bright green chair from the next table. Surprised by all the familiar faces, John made the rounds before sitting.

"Hi everybody!" he said. "This place collects all the finest people."

Dani stood to hug. "I'm glad you made it," she said. "We can commence the dancing now!"

"Hi, Dani!" he hugged. "We may just have to do that."

Buffy stood, waiting next in line. "Hi, rubber band man!"

John didn't hesitate to accept a boob-pressed hug from the blond Barbie. "Hi, Buffy! You having a good time?"

"A blast!" she squealed. "Check-out my awesome peach margarita! It comes in this cool Genie glass!" John glanced at the plastic half-yard stamped with the bar's logo. "If you want…the waitress blows a whistle and juggles your boobs when she delivers it!"

"Lucky her," John muttered.

"They only rub your shoulders and twist your head if you're a guy," Buffy pouted.

"That sounds good too," John said.

Next, choosing to stay seated, Garrett picked through a pile of nachos as John held out his fist. Garrett punched with his right while shoveling bean dip and sour cream into his mouth with his left. "Want some?" he asked.

Plucking a loaded chip. "Thanks, buddy!"

"Here you go, Butterfly," Will said, patting Garth's borrowed chair.

"Thanks, bull-rider!" John said, swigging from the bottle of Corona Will had waiting for him. "It's still cold!"

"To Garth's surprise," Will said. "We had a bet on whether or not you'd make it."

"Who won?"

"Drink all you want," Will smirked. "Beers are on Garth."

"So we heard you were having some *coffee*, John," Dani accused playfully and waited for a response, a curious grin on her face.

John half glared at Will. "She saw us when we walked in," Will defended, "and asked about our day."

Still intoxicated from his Folgers moment with Rita, John sighed. "I did. Have some coffee that is," he back peddled.

Clapping her hands, Dani said, "I knew it! Look at him…he's smitten with Rita."

"I'm not *smitten,*" he said out of guilty obligation.

"I've seen smitten before," Will said, "and it's definitely found a home on your face."

"I don't know what you're talking about," John lied.

"Go with it, John," Garth said. "If she looks half as good up close as she did from across the street you have my blessing!"

"You ever find out what the deal is with that guy George?" Dani asked.

Not one to talk about other people's business, John hesitated. "They are...in the process of divorcing."

Pulling her face out of her margarita, Buffy asked, "Why are they on vacation if they're getting a divorce?"

Shocked by her friends astuteness, Dani said, "That's a good question."

"Thanks, Dani!" Buffy giggled.

Squirming. "Well, he...they booked this trip before she discovered he hadn't been faithful. And...a condition of the divorce is that she was still required to come on this cruise," he said reluctantly.

"That's blackmail!" Dani said. "Did she sign a prenup?"

"Yes."

"Stupid!" Dani said. "Doesn't the infidelity negate it?"

"If she could show proof."

"And I'm assuming she doesn't have any?" Garth wondered.

"Nope."

"That's *very* interesting," Dani said.

Trying to change the subject, John asked, "Is Elli babysitting?"

"Our three sweethearts are playing at the Youth Club," Buffy said.

Not that he much cared but he tried again, "So, what's Elli doing?"

Dani pointed to the bar. John's lower jaw dropped when he witnessed Elli leaning against the counter stroking the Chinese proverb on George's arm.

"Looks like she's making a new friend," Garth said.

Stunned, John asked, "How...how long have they been here?"

"She spotted him at the bar about an hour ago," Dani answered. "She hasn't been back to our table since. Why?"

"Just wondered," John drank. "What's he thinking?" he mumbled.

Overhearing the rhetorical mutter, Will said, "It would appear he's thinking about coffee."

Buffy joined. "It's too hot to drink coffee!"

"You're very right, dear," Dani said, "it certainly is."

"I thought so. It's like a hundred degrees!"

"How do you guys all know each other?" Garth asked.

"I own a beauty salon in New Jersey," Dani said. "Buffy's my number one stylist and friend, and Elli—the tattoo connoisseur at the bar—is a casual friend and regular customer."

Nachos weren't enough to contain Garrett. "She's a bitch."

"Garrett, we don't say mean things about people!" Dani reprimanded.

"Sorry, mom." Going back to his nachos.

"Anyway, we all share the bond of divorce, and divorcees and beauty salons go together like abused women at a psychologist's convention—similar situations create needy friendships. Elli's usually all right but she can be a bit...abrasive, as my son tried so tactfully to express."

"Like steel sandpaper," John muttered at Garrett, earning a quick grin and knuckle touch.

Will rubbed his head. "I could use a cut!"

"I brought my scissors," Dani said eagerly. "I could take care of you tomorrow, in Jamaica, if you're not busy? I know we're not allowed to socialize together on the ship."

"I'll take you up on that, Dani. But only if I can show you guys this great non-touristy spot. It has a great little cliff jump, if Garrett's interested?"

Garrett shot up. "Cool! Can we?"

"I guess you got your answer," Dani said. "Are you coming, Garth?"

"I'd love to, but Jamaica's my morning to sleep. There's too many Rastas hounding you for money or to buy drugs…besides, I have to work at the pool at one."

"You'll be missed," Dani said. "How about you, John?"

Again looking to Will for direction. "He'll be there like a fat kid at a doughnut factory!" Will said.

"Can I go?" Buffy asked.

"It wouldn't be a party without you, Buffy," Will said. "I know a great place for authentic Jamaican cuisine when we're ready for lunch."

"That sounds great," Dani said.

"Let me buy a round to seal the deal," Will said.

Buffy clapping. "Oh! Shots!"

Will signaled a waitress. "Shots it is!"

Preoccupied with the less than casual body language between George and Elli, John continually wrenched his head back to the bar. A shrill whistle finally forced his attention back to the table.

A chubby Mexican waitress had Buffy's head tilted backward as she repeatedly trumpeted the whistle and free poured a stream of booze down Buffy's throat. After swallowing the steady stream without coughing up a drop, Buffy raised her arms and began whooping as the waitress proceeded to grope, juggle, and squeeze Buffy's large breasts.

Dani leered at her friend. "Nice example you're setting!"

Pouting. "They're just boobies."

Garrett had just touched his first set six weeks earlier when, at a birthday party, Abby Stewart allowed his nervous hands under her tank-top. Shooting his mother a terse look, he said, "I think I can handle it…I'm *thirteen*!"

Dani turned to Will. "They grow up so quick."

Grinning. "We have to in order to give ourselves a fighting chance to understand you all," Will returned.

The whistling waitress moved behind Dani. "I'll do the shot, but if you want to keep your hands, please don't touch my chest," Dani warned. "The only person who gets to publicly touch my breasts is me."

Next up, Will and Garth's turns complimented Dani's PG-13 version with innocent head-pats and quick shoulder rubs. John, not wishing to be drunk for his eight o'clock encounter, tried to think of an excuse valid enough for the group to let him slide. Unable, he bent his head back as the gang cheered. The waitress finished with Garrett. Not a person to ever exclude anybody, Will had requested a non-alcoholic version.

Dani cheered and clapped when the DJ announced a limbo contest, but had to straighten

Buffy out, who thought the DJ had said *Bimbo* contest. Everyone, including Garrett, moved to the dance floor to test their flexibility.

Over the next half hour the string of contestants waddling under the broom stick dwindled. Garth failed to make it past the first round. Buffy thrilled the crowd, but lost out in the third round when her silicone became the proverbial straw that broke the camel's back. John lasted one round longer. Will, whose strength couldn't compensate for his lack of flexibility, fell the round after John.

In the final rounds, Dani and Garrett joined two twenty-something girls, along with a very limber-looking fellow with pink shorts and a mint polo. The lowered bar immediately claimed the two girls as its first victims. Garrett didn't fare any better. However, Dani managed, with help from her vivacious friends, to finish without any part of her body brushing the underside of the bar. In an odd pre-limbo warm-up, Pink Shorts guy psyched himself up with slaps to his cheeks as he danced around like a ballerina.

Garth turned to Will. "This should be interesting."

Will turned to John. "Estrogen's going to power him under!"

John gave a cursory smile and nod before his thoughts drifted back to George and Elli. After scanning the crowd he glanced back towards the bar where the couple remained flirting. From a distance it looked like they could already be lovers. John huffed.

The last man standing slowly arched his back as he eyed his landing. Somehow, he had the ability to manipulate his body into an *L* that someone had pushed over. Inch by inch his baby steps pulled him under. His pastel shirt scraped, but didn't dislodge the stick from its rack as the crowd went crazy.

While an employee lowered the stick one impossible rung lower and the DJ segued into the next song, Dani showed her age by singing and dancing along to Gloria Estefan's infectious beat:

"Come on, shake your body baby, do the conga
I know you can't control yourself any longer
Come on, shake your body baby, do the conga
I know you can't control yourself any longer

Feel the rhythm of the music getting stronger
Don't you fight it 'til you tried it, do that conga beat..."

She continued singing through her approach. With her knees and stomach safely under, the tips of her small breasts vibrated the bar. She paused, breathed deeply, allowed her head to hang, and crept her U-shaped body under the obstacle; once through, she collapsed to her back clapping. Will helped her to her feet and the two shared a congratulatory hug before joining the gang to watch Pink Shorts' attempt.

The freaky contortionist started with his obnoxious warm-up routine. Once out of his system, he started his descent. The bar raised and shuddered at the middle of his torso when he too tried a deep breath and head drop, but the strain was too great. Mr. Pink-Shorts collapsed.

Dani celebrated her victory with hugs and high-fives as a waitress came over to present her trophy—a free shot of tequila. Trophy consumed, the group returned to their seats, except Garth, who changed the seating arrangement by sitting next to Buffy.

Will ordered another round without the vulgar gropes and loud whistles. "That was amazing!" Will said. "How did you do that?"

"She does yoga four days a week," Garrett said.

"Yeah," Dani bragged, "limbo's nothing compared to some of my yoga positions."

"You should see our house, Will," Garrett said. "Everything looks like it came from a Zen-monastery catalogue."

Tilting her head. "It promotes tranquility."

A minute later, the waitress dropped a fresh round of beers and shots on the table. Dani was enjoying Will's company when she noticed John's chaperoning gaze towards George and Elli. "You all right, John?" she asked.

John whipped around. "Me? Yeah! We doing this shot?"

"To Dani!" cried Will. "The best damn limbo-er in Mexico!"

John drank his shot, chased with beer, and felt nature call. "I have to use the restroom."

"It's back there, Butterfly!" Will pointed.

"Thanks." As he stood, John heard Dani ask why Will called him Butterfly and knew Will would explain but couldn't wait to listen.

Making his way around packed tables, gravity was squeezing his bladder harder. Normally he might have paused to examine the restaurant's myriad tacky signs and Mexican knickknacks; instead, he danced into the bathroom, feeling like he was about to burst. The smell of strong urine and faint vomit hit hard as the door closed behind; his zipper was barely open before a steady stream blasted into the urinal.

Doors opened and closed while John, eyes closed, sighed in relief and swayed a bit from the day's alcohol. A voice broke his stream—and certainly his relief.

"Well, if it isn't Mr. Smith," said the voice.

Opening his eyes and turning to the left urinal. "*George.*"

"Sorry about yesterday, John. I just get a little protective when it comes to my wife. I hope you can forgive me?"

George's condescending tone sent chills down John's spine. Looking down, he had to give his penis permission to proceed. Reluctantly, the stream slowly sputtered back on. John's eyes shifted as George braced himself by slapping his right palm against the wall. A red scorpion stamp—marked out with a black x—on the back of his hand, infuriated John.

George flushed and moved to the sink. "Am I to take your silence as a lack of forgiveness, John?"

The last drill instructor shot of tequila mustered enough inner dragon for John to respond, albeit, sarcasm had never worked well for him before. "How was golf today, George? What did you shoot?"

The crafty demeanor surprised George as he shut off the faucet. "What are you... you talked to my wife?"

"We ran into her shopping in Playa del Carmen and she mentioned that you were playing golf after lunch."

Calming his blood pressure by lying. "*Yeah.* Yeah I did…only played nine though, too fucking hot." Turning the faucet back on.

Feeling vulnerable, John forced his seemingly everlasting piss. "I guess the country club gives you a hand stamp when you pay…and an X when you finish?"

Happily zipping up and starting to turn, John heard the thud of George's knuckles smack against his eye socket. Stunned, John tried grasping for something to hold onto with his right hand, finding the inside of the urinal offered nothing but wet porcelain. George's second punch—a straight jab—popped John's nose like a chocolate covered cherry, dropping him to his knees. Blood streamed down his face and the back of his throat.

"Pay attention, John. I'm willing to forgive you for your feeble attempt at courage and sarcasm, but if you mention any of this, or so much as say another word to Rita, I'll beat you so hard the coastguard will have to fly you home. You understand, mother-fucker?"

Holding his nose with cupped hands and choking on his own blood, all remains of an inspirational drill instructor and an inner dragon fled in a downpour of bright red. Blood ran down his throat and over his body; the vital solution sickened him as it streamed through the cracks between his fingers and onto his knees and the cheap linoleum tile floor. George was menacingly awaiting a response when the door opened. A stocky Mexican employee wearing a Carlos 'n Charlie's shirt entered and studied the scene. "What's going on?" he asked.

Changing his attitude and body language like a chameleon. "He slipped and hit his face on the toilet…I'm going to get him some ice," George said. "Will you stay with him?"

"*Si.* Yes."

"You hang in there, dude," George feigned concern. "I'll be right back with some ice, my friend." George sauntered out as the employee helped John to his feet. Surprised his face didn't hurt more, he hobbled to the sink and stared in the mirror.

"Is it possible for you to find me a rag and some ice?"

"*Si!* The other man went to get."

Turning. "No, he didn't. I didn't fall…he hit me."

The workers eyes widened. "Oh! Son of a bitch! I get you ice!"

John turned on the cold water and began rinsing his tender face. "Nice going, smart-ass."

Two minutes passed before the employee rushed back in. "You going to be okay?"

Accepting the bar rag and cup of ice. "Yes. Thank you. You don't have to stay."

"You sure?"

"Positive. I'll live. Thanks again."

John cleaned himself the best he could. The blood on his new shirt dried darker than the vivid red. He filled the rag with ice, folded the corners over into a handle, and managed his way back to the table, carefully scanning the bar for any sign of George—thankfully, he had gone.

"What the hell happened?" Garth shot up.

John stood at the table watching everyone's face turn to shock. "I had a little *accident* in the bathroom."

Dani stood to play nurse. "Are you okay, John?"

"Yeah. I'm fine. But I'm going to head back to the ship."

"Did you fall?" Dani asked.

"Not exactly. I really don't want to talk about it right now. I don't mean to be rude, but I just want to go back to my cabin."

"I'll take you back," Will stood. "Stay here Garth. I'll come back when I know he's all right."

"You got it," Garth said.

Having initially taken notice, Garrett chose not to stare; rather, he scanned the room with his mother's phone for his third photograph of the illusive booby flash.

Outside, Will took a minute before saying anything. "Does this have something to do with Rita's husband?"

John pressed the compress to his eye. "He told her he was golfing this afternoon. He was in the bathroom with a red scorpion stamp on his hand—X'ed out. Plus, he was all over Dani's friend at the bar."

"That fucking prick! Garth and I will take care of this."

"No! It's got nothing to do with you guys. I got myself into this."

"No offense, John, but the guy's pretty big."

"Not to stay away from, he isn't," John chuckled, then turned quiet for a minute. "Hey! You owe me a story."

"What?"

"Eddie! You said you'd tell me what the deal was when we got to the bar."

Will laughed. "Eddie *is* a dive master, but he's banned from working at any of the dive shops around here."

"I sense a fuck-up." John hardly ever used the word, but blood and pain seemed to make it more appropriate.

"Yeah," Will chuckled, "you could say that. It was before Labor Day—a slow time for the dive shops. Eddie had seniority at his place. He could basically pick and choose who he wanted to take out. So one day this Playboy model comes in by herself—Eddie says she was on vacation with her boyfriend, but they had been fighting. Of course Eddie jumps at the opportunity for the charter—says her tits were as big as dive buoys. Normally, he would've waited for a whole group, but, like I said, it was slow. So she fills out the paperwork and Eddie takes her out—just the two of them."

"Sounds like a good time," John spit, another habit he'd never acquired, always opting for a sink or tissue.

"Too good! So Eddie takes her down to see the fishies and everything goes business as usual. They get back on the boat and start stripping out of their wet suits. She had such a good time, she suggests they have a drink. Eddie tells her he can't—he's working. She pulls a bottle of silver Patron out of her bag, insisting that one shot won't hurt. Eddie pleads with her, saying he'll meet her when he's off. She tells him the time to celebrate is right then, the moment wouldn't be the same at a bar."

"I'm thinking he gave in?"

"You and a glistening wet Playboy bunny alone in a boat, beautiful water all around, begging you to drink with her? Yeah, he gave in. I don't know if the bottle was full to start, but it was bone dry by the time Eddie's boss came looking for him an hour later. They never saw or heard the boat coming. Apparently, Eddie had the music turned up while he engaged in some extracurricular diving. Bunny was bent so far over the starboard side, her hair touched the water. It was quite a surprise for everyone when Eddie learned he wasn't the only one...*boarding*."

"What happened?"

"Well...when the happy couple realized they were caught, they were so smashed, all they could do was laugh. This pissed off Eddie's boss real bad, fired him on the spot…told him no dive shop would ever hire him again. Eddie didn't much care at the time. Now Bunny's boyfriend, who came along when he didn't find her back at the shop, wasn't used to boats. He swung so hard at Eddie that he missed and fell over the side. After they pull him out, Eddie's boss takes the unhappy couple back on his boat. He took the keys to the other boat and told Eddie to wait for another instructor to pick him up."

"What did Eddie do?"

"He waits 'til they're gone and then proceeds to suit up with a fresh tank, swimming to shore, drunk as a sailor in port. After that, he hangs low for a while. One day he gets a check in the mail. I guess Bunny felt real bad about Eddie getting fired. She asked around and found out where he lived. She sent him enough money to buy his own boat. That's the story of *The Dirty Mermaid*. He says she comes back once a year. The two spend the weekend together diving with the fishies and rocking the boat."

It pained John to laugh, but he did anyway. "That's a great story, Will."

The two stopped in front of the ship's boarding gate. "Are you going to be all right, John?"

"I'll be fine. Thanks for walking me back."

Will dug into his bag and pulled out an iPod. "Take this, John. It's loaded with every Bob Marley song ever. Use it to get ready for Jamaica. Nothing lifts the spirits like a little Marley. Remember John…tomorrow's a new day. *You* get to decide how to spend it."

Accepting the iPod. "Thanks, Will. I hope I can figure out how to use it."

"No problem, it's easy." Will started to turn.

"Hey, Will?"

Turning back. "Yeah?"

"When did I get here?"

Smiling. "It doesn't matter *when* you got here, or *how*, the important thing is you showed up."

AN UNSANCTIONED DATE

BACK AT HIS CABIN, JOHN showered and was dressed casually by 5:50. Afterward, he filled the bathroom sink with cold water and a bag of ice he bummed from the Schooner Bar. The sharp cold soothed his bruised face. When numbness set in, he retreated to his bunk with a cold compress made from a hand towel, ice, and a company rubber band. He inserted the iPod's earphones, laid down, pushed play, and placed the icepack on his face.

The first song called "It Hurts to Be Alone" evoked memories and tears, painful reminders of his past life. But the smooth rhythms and hypnotic beats alive in every song—combined with Bob's consoling voice—made for a timeless lullaby that eventually eased despair better than any counted sheep. He drifted off into peaceful sleep thinking about Carson, Page, and who sent his ticket sometime during the fifth soothing song.

He woke to Marley's "Coming in From the Cold," but it took a minute to register the faint rapping on his door. He removed the earphones, checked his watch—7:55—and answered the door. The sight of Rita energized John like a warm spring breeze.

She glowed, holding up a 95' Meursault. "I brought wine! Oh my God! What happened, John?"

"Please, come in, Rita."

"You look like you were in a fight?"

John offered his only chair before sitting on the bed. "I think two people have to throw punches for it to technically be a fight."

"So I'm right?"

"I ran into George in the bathroom of Carlos 'n Charlie's while I was…while I was there."

"What? He went to that dive after golf!"

"Excuse me for saying, but the only holes George got in today had nothing to do with golf."

"What are you talking about? I think I need a drink for this."

John snatched a couple of glasses from the bathroom. "I don't have a corkscrew."

"I opened it before I came so it could breathe."

John filled Rita in on every detail since he left her at the coffee shop; her lovely face morphed from Jekyll to Hyde. Her jaw fell open when he related the bathroom scene and her eyes started to water when he admitted his passive response.

"That bastard!" Rita sniffled. "I'm so sorry, John. I hope you can forgive me?"

"For what? You didn't hit me," John grinned.

"For getting you involved in this mess. You don't deserve this."

"I think it's the exact opposite…I like to think I deserve it all—in more ways than one."

She saw he meant it affectionately. "You don't deserve to be hit. Honestly, John, this is a side of George I never knew existed. He was always overly protective, but I thought he was all bark and no bite…and going to a Mexican whorehouse…that just makes me sick."

"I think most people have an alter-ego. This trip is certainly teaching me that I have one."

Smiling. "I like both of yours."

"You mean that?"

"I wish I could have met you a long time ago," she said softly.

"A very smart bartender I know reminded me today that the past is the past…the only thing that matters is what we do with today."

"Even if your hands are tied?"

"Everyone's armed with excuses—many of them valid—that doesn't mean we have to use them."

"You're right. I'm not going to stand for any more of George's torture. He's going to witness the wrath of a pissed-off Latina woman first-hand tonight!"

Raising his hands. "I don't think that's the right way to go."

"Why not?"

"First of all, it might get me killed. Second, you only have to play along for three more days. Third, you still have to share a cabin."

Raising her brows. "Unless I found another cabin…"

Her suggestive words caused John to quiver and he tactfully crossed his legs. "I think it's safer for both of us if we just forget about today…at least 'til the cruise is over and you get your divorce."

Sighing. "You're right, John. I wish I would have hired a private investigator to come on this trip to tail the SOB. If I wasn't so blind and naive I would already be divorced—and rich!"

John lifted the cold glass to his nose when he heard "The Girl from Ipanema" play from Rita's iPhone. As she fiddled with the touch screen, he said, "I can go outside if you would like some privacy?"

"No honey, it's just a text from work. Sorry…I have to reply."

"What's the name of your store?"

"*Chic Linen!* You like it?"

"Very classy. You must have a good staff to be able to leave for a week without worry?"

"The best! Her name's mom. I was able to bring her from Cuba after I got married. Before that she'd only been to the states one time. My grandparents wanted their first born to see the world beyond Cuba, for her sake and the sake of their future grandchildren, so they saved some money, helped her get a temporary travel visa, and sent her to New York the summer between her junior and senior year of high school. Oh, how she still loves to talk about that time. She used the summer to travel the whole way from New York to Los Angeles; hitchhiking the entire way with nothing more than an old laundry bag filled with clothes, a toothbrush, and a bar of soap—very strong lady!"

"Wow, I'll say. That takes courage. Where did she keep her money? Wasn't she worried about being robbed?"

"She kept it where all buxom women kept their money back then. She's tough. I wouldn't want to be the thief who tried getting down her shirt. Besides, times were different then—simpler. Everyone hitched. Probably not many women though."

"Kansas is still kinda that way. It's nice. But I feel the world's changing so quickly now-days, like somewhere it just passed me by. I wouldn't be surprised if pretty soon these fancy phones were able to just beam people wherever they want to go."

"Don't you have an iPhone or something?"

"I have a basic phone from Walmart; it doesn't even have a camera. I didn't bring it 'cause the travel agency told me it probably wouldn't work on the ship. Which reminds me, I've been meaning to stop at the business center to check my email. Not that I really get any, but I like to know everything's okay at work."

"Hell, John, we can do that right now," she said, moving to the bed, close enough for John's swollen nose to touch her hair. "What's your address?"

Desperately trying to inhale the scent of her shampoo, his swollen nose just gurgled as if he had a sinus infection. "Ah…millions of john smiths at keep it together dot com."

Laughing. "Aren't you the clever one!" Rita's thumbs flicked back and forth before handing over the phone. "Here you go. Just enter your password."

John typed the word Carson into the tiny window. His junk box was teeming, but there was only one new message in his inbox from harmony23@gmail.com. He clicked on the unfamiliar address, thinking it was junk mail that made it through the filter, and silently read:

John: You're doing great!

"I left the woods for as good a reason as I went there. Perhaps it seemed to me that I had several more lives to live, and could not spare any more time for that one."

Quote by: Henry David Thoreau

P.S. Keep it up!

"That's strange," John said, typing "*Who is this?*" into a reply message.

Reaching for her glass. "Everything all right?"

John wore a half perplexed, half scornful look, like someone had just played a cruel joke. "I… it's just…" As he struggled for words, his phone rang.

After the third ring, Rita said, "Are you going to get that? It may be important."

"Huh? Yeah, sorry," he said, reaching for the phone. "Hello."

"Hello, John! It's Mary. I hope I'm not disturbing you?"

"Not at all, Mary, what's up?"

"Well…Richard had another little episode today when we were in town."

"Is he okay?"

"Oh, you know him, if he isn't he'd never let on. But, yes, he seems fine. He's relaxing in the living room. I took him to see the ship's doctor again and he said it might have been the heat and told Richard to take it easy for the rest of the day."

"Is there anything I can do?"

"Now that you ask…he was afraid of bothering you but had no problem with me doing so."

"It's no bother, Mary, I was just relaxing after a hectic day."

"Good. Well, I think he's tired of having me baby him and is aching for some boys company. Maybe you'd like to come to our cabin for a little male bonding?"

"Sure, Mary, that sounds great."

"You're a saint, John. I just worry about him. We're nearing the end of our lives and he's already had one heart attack a couple of years ago. He has high blood pressure and still eats and drinks like a teenager. I'm scared he won't live through another one. But don't tell him I told you that."

"My lips are sealed. What time would you like me?"

"Whenever you're ready. In case you forgot, it's Royal Suite five on deck thirteen."

"Got it. I'll be there as soon as I can. Can I bring anything?"

"Just yourself, John. Bless you. Anything you guys need you can just call for when you get here."

"Perfect! See you soon."

"Thanks, John!"

"Was that the sweet couple from the disco?" Rita asked.

"Yeah. Mary and Richard Clawson. We've had dinner together every night—exceptional people."

"I could tell from the start, in the theatre."

"Rich has a bad heart and had a little scare today, but Mary says he's fine, just wants me to come over and hang out."

Moving closer and looking deep into his eyes, she was overwhelmed by his loyalty to people he barely knew. "Well…you shouldn't make them wait. I have to meet George in twenty minutes anyway."

Sadness washed over John's battered face. "Rita…"

"Yes, John?"

"Would you…would you mind…just for a few…"

Gently taking his hand, Rita slowly leaned in as he trembled with anticipation. Their mouths hovered within a feather's distance before she was first to cross the invisible barrier. Her full lips touched John's as if she were kissing a newborn's forehead. The pain and sadness in his face vanished like the last sliver of sun at sunset. They melted back onto the bed, where, for fifteen minutes, they lay holding each other, tenderly kissing and caressing. The world around them faded away…vanquished by the unstoppable force of new love.

WANNA WATCH A MOVIE?

JOHN SOAKED HIS FACE IN ice water one last time in preparation for meeting the Clawsons. It had been much more painful to close the door behind Rita than any throbbing from his face. They made a promise to avoid confronting George and shared one last gentle kiss prior to saying their goodbyes.

Outside Royal Suite number five's impressive wooden door, John discerned the contrast between Economy and Royal. He pressed the doorbell to the sound of wind chimes and twenty seconds later, Mary opened.

"Good evening, John! Come in, come in!"

Stepping into the marble foyer. "Hello, Mary!" John hugged.

Mary studied. "My God, John…what happened to your face?"

"Oh, a little accident in the bathroom today. I'm fine."

Mary's mouth hung open. "You don't look fine. You look like you were in a fight!"

Richard's voice sounded from some hidden room. "Is that John?"

"Come on, John, the bear's growling." Following Mary into a decent sized living room, he took stock of the very tasteful sofa, coffee table, end tables, and two muted gold, velvet club chairs with matching ottomans.

Richard propped himself up into a seated position as John made his way to the sofa. "Hello, my boy! Thanks for joining my house arrest party! Please, sit!"

John sank into one of the supple lounge chairs. "Thanks, Rich. What's this I hear about you not feeling well again?"

Richard hit the mute button on TCM's screening of an old Abbott and Costello movie. "Oh, that was nothing!" John caught Mary shaking her head. "I just had a little sunstroke is all…it felt more like the inside of a steel factory than an island fanned by trade winds today."

"It *was* hot," John said agreeably.

Richard squinted. "What's wrong with your face?"

John touched his upper cheek bone, which was beginning to transition from red to brown. "I had an accident in the bathroom of Carlos 'n Charlie's today."

"I *see*," Richard said, turning to Mary. "My darling wife…why don't you bring that 99 Petrus. John looks like he's earned it." Mary scurried off without saying a word.

Mary came back carrying a bottle of red wine in one hand, a single glass and corkscrew in the other. "If you don't mind…I'm not very good," Mary said, handing the wine tool to John.

"I'm not great either, but I think I can manage. Thank you, Mary."

"Where'd you go for chow tonight?" Richard asked.

John stripped the foil off into shreds over the coffee table. "I had some nachos at the bar."

"Nachos!" Richard scowled. "You can have nachos in Kansas!" He looked at Mary, who wavered between her husband's impending request and supervising John's sommelier skills. Like any long married wife, she interpreted Richard's hand gesture, a mock phone call, and off she went. Cringing at John's mutilation of the cork, Richard asked, "You need some help?"

"Nope, I think I got it," he said, pulling at the chewed-up cork instead of allowing the double-hinge to do its job. The bottle spat its cork with a champagne *pop*.

"Pour a glass, but wait a few minutes before you try it," Richard said. "That sucker needs to breathe a while."

"Okay," John poured. "I feel guilty…I mean…I guess you're not allowed to have any?"

Stabbing his left index finger into his right palm. "Not until the smoke clears," he whispered.

John grinned. "Your cabin's very…palatial."

Scanning his surroundings. "The way I figure, we all come into this world after spending nine months cramped up in a small room and we leave the same way. Honestly, I would like to know which is worse…nine months in the womb, or an eternity in a coffin. I'm going to enjoy a little elbow room before experiencing the latter."

John crossed his legs. "If you're cremated you can have your ashes spread in an infinite number of places that would allow ample room."

"Indeed! And as my will dictates, I'll wind up back at the beach in front of our old dive shop. Our daughter and her husband run it now. If I'm lucky, I'll be able to swim with the ghost of our old pal, Shelton the turtle."

"I hope you do, Richard, but how about waiting a few years…okay?"

"Oh, it's going to be what it's going to be. Sure, we might be able to get an extension, the way a criminal gets early parole for good behavior. I can eat one less cheeseburger hoping it buys me another day. That's the great thing about life's choices. We don't have any say about coming into this world, and as far as anyone really knows, we don't get any say about what happens when we leave. But, in the middle lies this kind of recess…a time to play, if you will. It's here in this fleeting middle where we get the say.

"Nothing can totally kill free-will except death. It doesn't matter whether you get lemons or cherries, there's still plenty of choices flowing through the slot machine of our lives. We get to pick them up and make decisions. Prisoners get to make decisions on how they spend their time within the parameters of jail. People in the gravest situations we can fathom have the gift of decision, and as far as anyone can prove, even the worst choices are better than not being here to make decisions about them. Worst case scenario…if you're being tortured you can still exercise free-will with decisions: resist, abate, scream, cry, spit, or laugh.

"A person's choices may be as grim as drowning versus hanging or as tame as liver versus broccoli—you make a choice, and if the choice is made for you, you make a decision how you're going to handle it. Hell, on some occasions, not making a decision can be appropriate.

"You ever see that Mel Gibson movie, *Braveheart*?"

"I did. With Carson."

"Even though that's just a movie…when they're killing him in the closing scene he screams *freedom!* And my point is, we all possess that power to scream for our freedom—even in the most horrific times of decision. People now days wallow in self-pity, saying they didn't have a choice. That's bullshit! Choices are perpetually there for everyone from the moment you're aware you're here, to the moment you're not. Even people in comas may have a say on whether they stay in that state or recover, but nobody knows. In a way…what we each scream here, echoes for generations."

Waving a limp hand. "Sorry, John, I'm opinionated and have a tendency to go off on rants. I didn't invite you here to subject you to an old man's philosophies and tirades."

"You asked me to never try to pay for anything in your presence."

"I did."

"I'm going to ask you for something now…if I may?"

"Name it!"

"Don't apologize for sharing who you are and what you think. I relish whatever you choose to rant about. I'm a better person for meeting you and Mary, and in my opinion, you both have earned the right to be opinionated."

Smiling and patting his hand on the shoulder of the sofa. "Is your father still living, John?"

"Yes. He and Mom still live in Good Intent."

"If you wouldn't mind, tell me about them."

"Well…my dad's name is Jack. One of his biggest objections in life was his name, believing the only way it could've been more bland was if his last name were *Doe*." Laughing. "Can you imagine the jokes? John Doe—I would've been compelled to take a job at a funeral home. He told me he wanted to give me a name with more pizzazz, but Mom won that battle. John was *her* father's name."

"John is still a good sturdy name."

"It'll have to do at this point," John shrugged. "He met my mom, Nancy, at Kansas State. Story goes, they met at a mixer between their respective fraternity and sorority. I think they were a popular couple, from the old stories they tell from time to time, and life was full of new ideas and adventures during that period."

"College is a great experience."

"Yes. It was." They paused for a moment of nostalgia. "I believe motherhood often brings permanent changes to women's bodies *and* behavior—Mom wasn't the exception to that rule. Dad says she was both diligent and balanced when they met. Says she would sit in the sorority house as people gathered for a party with an open finance book in her lap and an un-opened bottle of rum at her feet. Even with music blaring and the onset of binge-drinking and debauchery all around, he says she wouldn't flinch until the lesson was absorbed. When it had been, she'd close the book, untie her hair, and drink Bacardi.

"Dad says she used to love rum and cokes back then—I've never seen her have one. Apparently after a few she often skipped the coke. But they swear no matter how late she stayed up, she always met her obligations on time. Mom was—is—very prioritized, a balanced machine of yin and yang, and Dad loved her from the moment they met."

Mary appeared from the bedroom—unbeknownst to her convalescents—when the sound of wind chimes interrupted her guilty pleasure, reading a Nicholas Sparks novel. She opened the door for the bellman, who rolled his buffet cart into the living room and stood patiently waiting for Mary's signature. The steward laughed along at an Abbott & Costello skit. She added a twenty-five percent tip for his reaction to a classic made long before his birth.

Mary spoke into John's ear after dismissing the bellman. "Thank you for coming," she whispered. "He can eat what he wants. I ordered pretty healthy food. There's shrimp, hummus, and a veggie platter—the dip's low-fat. The popcorn without parsley has butter and salt…that's for you. I know he's going to drink some wine with you. See that it's not too much, will you dear?"

"I'll do the rationing," he assured. "Thank you for your kindness."

Mary kissed John's cheek. "There should be a chocolate soufflé for *you* under the skirting. I'll be reading in the bedroom if you need anything. Stay as long as you'd like, John. There's a spare bedroom in the back if you don't want to go back to your cabin."

He reciprocated the peck, and said, "Thank you, again."

As Mary shuffled off to the bedroom John dug into the buffet, offering Richard a plate, but having eaten earlier, he refused. He did, however, charge John with the mission of sneaking into the kitchenette for an extra wine glass.

Pouring a quarter glass. "Here you go, Rich. If Mary catches you, I didn't give it to you."

"Mum's the word, my boy—my decision," Richard winked.

Picking up his own glass. "Has this breathed enough?"

"Help it out, John, it's hyperventilating." Richard swirled, rolled, and sniffed. "So what happened to Jack and Nancy after college?"

John set his plate down and wiped his mouth. "They got pregnant with me their last semester at K State and quickly and quietly married after graduation. They moved back to Good Intent where Dad found a job with his childhood acquaintance, Fred Bagly, my then future father-in-law. And Mom wriggled into the nest of motherhood."

Richard swirled and sipped. "Shot-gun weddings were fairly common back then."

"I guess," John said, mimicking Richard's wine procedure. "I think by the time I was about six or seven Dad realized that something had replaced his college sweetheart with someone who resembled a drill instructor."

Richard laughed. "Boys often aspire to one day be a better version of their fathers, wanting to excel past them to express their appreciation and to make their fathers proud. Women, on the other hand, have a tendency to wake up one morning, look at themselves long in the mirror and say: 'Oh my *God*, I've become my *mother*.' And for some people—discovering they've become something they didn't anticipate or even admire—is akin to finding one's own shadow walking in front, instead of behind—the revelation can be unnerving."

"When you're an only child in a small house, you pretty much hear everything. I think from what I remember over-hearing, Dad saw Mom's shadow make the transition long before she would ever admit it—even now."

"How did Jack respond to Nancy's metamorphosis?"

John took a moment to think, comfortable silence enveloping them both. "In retrospect, I believe mom's dominance weakened Dad and caused him to retreat. It didn't happen overnight and I wouldn't call Dad spineless, but I can't recall them ever fighting. Her overbearing views wouldn't tolerate the effort, and that definitely sanded away some manhood bone."

"That's good, John…*manhood bone*," Richard repeated and sipped. "I like that!"

"Thanks. I'm not known for being clever. Anyway, without the stimulation of an occasional argument, Dad got numb and their marriage grew stale. His inability to be assertive may have started when she refused to name me something more original like Toby or Alex. *John* was a prelude of more traditional and unimaginative things to come—the promise of Dad's college days ended abruptly with graduation, parenthood, and a less than thrilling career. I think he felt a malaise towards marriage and some of his choices. When we made them grandparents they both seemed to re-spark like two musicians with creative differences that had parted and gotten back together. Dad especially, was different with Carson than he was with me, more playful and encouraging—less afraid."

"It's not personal, John. It's just easier with grandchildren. We've already made our mistakes, and grandchildren are gifts of absolution. They're an almost free ticket. Grandchildren are gifts without rules…we aren't worried about breaking them. And spoiling them is a grandparent's prerogative, a way to say we're sorry for any mistakes we made on the first go-around."

"Did you say *free ticket?*"

"Yes. As in limited responsibility or chance of regret; a joyful, effortless reward; or a second-chance. Why?"

"*A second-chance,*" John murmured, while staring at Richard inquisitively.

"John? John, you okay?"

"Yeah, sorry, just thinking about what you said. I guess I'll never know what it's like to be a grandparent."

"You don't know what's waiting around the next bend." Not wanting to give John time to stew, Richard asked, "What did your old man do for a living?"

"Dad and Fred Bagly—my ex-wife's father—both work for the same company. Dad's the accountant and Fred owns the place. It's a boutique luggage company passed down to Fred Jr. when Fred Sr. passed away about fifteen years ago. It's called Bagly's Bags. 'Everyone has to go somewhere, sometime. When they do, they're going to need a bag,' Fred always says, like his father before him."

"Smart guys! With a good internal tool-box and a quality piece of luggage, a man can go anywhere."

"It's good equipment. I still use the bag my dad gave me when I graduated from school—although not often. I think when he gave me that bag it was his way of telling me he wanted something better for me—something he didn't know how to provide. It was his way of saying 'don't make the same mistakes I did,' although I didn't know it at the time."

"Huh." Richard pondered. "You said they're childhood friends?"

"They were both raised in Good Intent and knew each other, but they didn't become friends until Dad joined the company after college. Both share a penchant for hard work, but, I think for Dad, work is more habit and escape. On the other hand, Fred inherited the passion for work that comes with ownership. He's a natural leader who constantly listens to and acknowledges his employees and customers. As a result, he's well respected and liked. Despite a small stature, Fred possesses grand character."

"He's a little guy?"

John smiled. "They call him Little Claus around town. He's short, not a hair over five-one, portly, and has always sported a full, pre-maturely almost white beard. It's 'cause of Dad that Fred volunteers to dress up as Santa every year at the local mall."

"He lose a bet to your old-man?"

"Nah. Dad jokingly made the suggestion at a BBQ he was hosting one August. He'd had a beer more than usual and said he regretted the remark as soon as it spilled out of his mouth. He thought Fred might take offense at the observed resemblance. Instead, Fred belted out a loud, low-pitched *Ho-ho-ho.* He told Dad it was a splendid idea, and then ran off to pitch the idea to Page's mom. Dad told me—when Mom wasn't around of course—that when Fred dashed off he stood there holding a beer, dumbfounded, wondering why it wasn't as easy to get Mom to listen to suggestions. Rather than torture himself, he got another beer."

"That's great, John! Fred sounds like a good father-in-law."

"He's the best! We're still close. I think he feels empathy for Page and sympathy for me. I don't blame him…or her. I've probably been…*bewildered* for a long time. Not Fred, he's salt of the earth and knows exactly who he is. After all these years, he's still the first one into the office every day and the last to leave. And not because the baggage biz in Good Intent has a line of customers waiting every morning. Fred learned from his father to lead by example, which means showing the team the boss is working just as much, if not more."

"Very true!"

"He greets each of his five employees by saying: 'Good morning, *so and so*, you okay?' At that point, *so and so* will either share their concerns or return the question with 'I'm okay if you're okay?' Fred will then either express his concerns or return the phrase 'As long as you're okay, I'm okay. Thanks for asking.'"

"I like it! Straight forward, opens the door for communication, and boosts morale!"

John sipped the velvety Merlot, appreciatively. "Yeah, like I said…he's a good guy. Dad always considered himself fortunate to work for Fred and to say the two families were friends. And he always loved Page. When we started dating in high school he acted like a teenager every time she came around; probably prayed at night that I wouldn't do anything to screw it up. Now that I think about it…he always sort of envied the Baglys. He might have wondered why he didn't have the same connection with his own family."

"What sort of connection is that?"

"Well…Fred and Margaret complement each other but with fundamental differences in personalities. Fred's an out-going, confident people-person who welcomes new ideas and actions. Margaret's a loving and empathetic wife and mother, satisfied with dual roles. She doesn't yearn for much else. Although their personalities differ, their core beliefs don't. When it comes to politics, religion, morals, and ethics the two follow the same program—rarely butting heads. Their centers are solid so their spirits can play, whether that means curled up on the couch with a good book for Margaret, or a day of shooting paintball with friends from work for Fred. One thing's obvious at the end of the day, when they get together as a family they love and respect one another. Dad always knew that."

Richard scooped a bit of hummus. "And you too envy and miss that?"

"Yeah, but you can't live through someone else's relationships. I don't know…I suppose I absorbed some of the indifference that crept into my marriage by watching my parents. It's no excuse, I allowed it to happen. Shit, I was stupid enough to believe things would always be fine."

"Marriage is a two way street."

"I know you're right, Rich, but it doesn't make it any easier to re-do."

"Don't." Richard stared into his glass. "That bag of yours won't take you back in time. In my opinion, you have one hell of an internal toolbox. You take that, point your bag in the right direction, and you can go anywhere. And if you ever need help fixing or building anything along the way…you can call me. If you're ever short a wrench, I might have one to spare."

John reached over to touch Richard's glass. "You're the first one I'd call."

Richard radiated pleasure. "Mary said you caught *Key Largo* the other night?"

"And I woke up in *Casablanca*!"

Laughing. "Old movies are the best way to fall asleep. I love TCM not only for the old gems, but for their commercial free airing and Robert Osborne's impeccable narration. It's like going to the theatre, but in the comfort of your own home. What do you say, John, wanna watch a movie?"

"Love to." John pulled the dessert from under the cart.

"What do you got there?" Richard quizzed like a hungry child.

"This? This is for me."

"Feel like sharing?"

"Maybe. If you tell me where I can buy more of this delicious wine."

"It's hard to find and a little pricey. But I can send you some?"

"Nah, that's okay Richard. I don't want you to go out of your way. Is it more than twenty a bottle?"

Richard smiled. "It starts around twelve-hundred—if you can find it."

John's eyes widened. "I ah…think I'll stick with grocery store box wine."

Richard laughed and grabbed the remote from the far end of the couch. Jack Lemon, Tony Curtis, and Marilyn Monroe had replaced Abbott & Costello with "Some Like It Hot." John put a good dent in the buffet and the two had no problems draining the last drop of Petrus. When the credits rolled at midnight, John glanced over at Richard sprawled out on the couch, hands cupped on his chest and seemingly asleep. He used a blanket draped over the back of the couch to tuck Richard in, turned off the TV, and tip-toed to the door. Richard stopped John in his tracks as his voice pierced the night.

"John?"

"Yes." John froze with his hand on the doorknob.

Not moving or opening his eyes, Richard said, "Three things. First: thanks for the company. Second: life's a board-game and sometimes we get sent back to Go. That doesn't mean we made the wrong decisions or took the wrong path, just means there's another road waiting to be explored. Third: I know why people have…*accidents*—it's how I got Mary. There are only two choices when it pertains to the heart…grab hold and don't ever let go…or turn and run, never looking back. Ice your face, son…goodnight."

John sighed deeply and left without responding. He mulled over Richard's advice the entire way back to his cabin, where Bob Marley again lulled him to sleep.

DAY 5
(JAMAICA)

STRIKE ONE

D ANI WENT NEXT DOOR TO Elli's cabin at 7:45 Thursday morning to meet her gang. The three women planned on taking the kids to breakfast before heading into Jamaica.

She hadn't laid eyes on Elli since she made a quick exit with George, right before John hauled his battered self from Carlos 'n Charlie's bathroom. Elli had stopped at the Youth Center sometime after and told her daughter, Brie, that Dani and Buffy would pick them all up in a little bit for dinner.

Dani had learned to be more patient over the years; a lesson honed with the experiences of dealing with a distant husband and the often vague language used by Garrett's doctors. Still, when she and Buffy picked up the kids after leaving Cozumel, she wasn't happy with Elli's lack of communication. It was one thing to leave the bar without informing her friends, but quite another to leave a note through Brie. By Dani's scorecard, Elli's MIA behavior had earned her another half strike.

The girls had left a note on Elli's door saying that they took the kids to the Wicked Dragon for dinner, stating that if Elli didn't join them, they would all be at the Aqua Theatre for an acrobatic show after and would bring the kids back to the rooms by 10:30. The only time Elli showed her face was at 10:40, when she came to pick Brie up from Buffy's room. Buffy, of course, thought nothing of it. The two women stayed up until midnight drinking wine while their two daughters played together. Dani put Jill to bed in her own cabin when she and Garrett returned from the show. She stayed up until 12:30, talking with Garrett about their trip.

Dani, Garrett, and Jill knocked on Buffy's door. "Hi guys!" Buffy shouted. "Come on in!"

Elli knelt with her back to the door, retying Brie's pink designer sneakers while Buffy's daughter, Kayla, blew bubbles with a plastic wand. The smell of strawberries filled the room from the scented bubble soap.

"Hi, Elli," Dani said. "Long time no see."

Elli half turned. "Hi, Dani. We're having a little shoe problem. Her magic poke-a-dot laces are just too long. For what I paid, you'd think they could tie themselves."

Dani scoffed. "That would certainly make it easier on *you*."

Elli finished and stood. "What's the matter, Dani…do you need to borrow a tampon?"

Buffy's face lit up. "I have a whole box if you do! They were on sale at Walgreens."

"Thank you, Buffy, but that won't be necessary," Dani said, looking at Garrett. "I forgot something in our room. You guys stay here while I go look for it, okay honey?"

Garrett already knew the deal. He could hear the silent kneading of his mother's claws. "Got it."

"Elli, would you mind helping me?"

"It takes two?" Elli asked coyly.

Dani squinted. "Yes, it usually does. Be a doll and lend a hand."

"Sure!"

Elli followed inside Dani's cabin. When Dani reached the far end she turned and placed her hands on her hips. "Now…what the hell is going on with you?"

Elli crossed her arms and casually leaned against the bathroom door. "What are you talking about?"

"Don't play dumb! Where do you get off leaving Brie with Buffy and me without checking first?"

Elli's head cowered. "Sorry about that. But I had plans. I talked with Brie first."

"You *didn't* talk to me! You didn't even tell us you were leaving Carlos 'n Charlie's yesterday."

"Well…something came up. Besides…what's the big deal? We all agreed to watch each other's kids before we took this trip."

"We agreed to take turns and if an exception arose, we would all discuss it. You circumvented that last detail all by yourself!"

"Well…something came up. Don't worry, I won't do it again without checking with you guys first."

"You're damn right you won't…or I'll page you from the purser's desk!"

"What is it, Dani? What's really got your panties in a wad?"

Dani huffed and sat down on the bed. "You do know this guy George *is* still married?"

"So was Jake when he cheated on me."

"What…so that makes it okay?"

"It means I don't really give a shit. Besides, George is signing his divorce papers as soon as we get back to Miami. It's just a technicality that he's still married."

"Then why did he drag Rita on this trip? And why did he beat up John in the bathroom of Carlos 'n Charlie's? Shit, Elli, John and I met the self-indulgent prick at the pool-bar. I didn't like him from the start. He hit on me while Rita lay by the pool."

Elli's face lit up. "*That's* why you're pissed off! You're upset farmer John got his nose popped for sticking it in where it didn't belong."

"So you knew? That's why you left so quickly?"

"Yeah. George said he saw him in the bathroom. He said John threatened to tell Rita about blowing off golf to hang out with me…so he hit him. I'm glad. It's none of that asshole's business."

"It's none of my business who you spend your time with, or how you spend it, but it is when I get stuck babysitting your kid and the asshole you're seeing starts hurting people I like."

Elli smirked. "You have quite the crush on Mr. Rubber band, don't you?"

"We're just friends. He's a great guy, but you wouldn't know that…you never gave him a chance."

"Just friends, huh? It looked like more than that outside your cabin post-disco," Elli glared.

Dani snapped to her feet. "What? You were spying on me?"

"Take it e-a-s-y. I heard voices, so I looked through your peep hole. Looked like more than a friendship kiss?"

Dani wavered. "It was just…I had a lot to drink…I just felt like kissing him! It doesn't matter anyway…he's fallen for Rita."

"Oh! Isn't she still married?"

"It's different!"

"How?"

"Well…from what John tells me, the reason for their divorce in the first place was George's extra-curricular activities."

"And here I thought you were above those kind of rationalizations?"

"Look, Elli! The fact is that I think John and Rita are nice people. If you want to screw around with that guy, nobody's stopping you, but you make sure you take care of Brie and keep that asshole away from John."

"Or what?"

"You've already burned one strike with me, Elli. A half strike by being mean to a really decent guy who's been through a lot. You used the other half by abandoning us and your daughter, without a word to us and for an asshole that is as bad as all our ex's combined! You only get two strikes with me, and I don't see any more *half* strikes in your future the way you're acting."

Elli stopped leaning and raised her right hand. "I'll have to be on my best behavior then," she feigned sincerity.

"I'd settle for civility." Dani started towards the door. "Come on, we better go get the kids before they start eating the furniture."

"What's the plan for after breakfast?"

Dani stopped and turned. "Buffy, me, and the kids are meeting Will at ten—the bartender from the pool."

"The hot American guy?"

"Yes. That's the one."

"Great! A private tour from a hot bartender—now you're talking! Where's he taking us? We going to smoke some Jamaican herb?" Elli laughed.

"No…I don't think that's anything our kids should be around. He's taking us to a private local's beach and then somewhere for lunch. And Elli…John's coming with us."

Elli sucked her teeth. "I'm sorry, Dani, but I don't think I can stand to spend the day with someone that annoying. I love Buffy, but I don't think I'd last around her, farmer John, *and* the kids. This was supposed to be a fun girl's trip!"

"The only one complaining is you."

"Sorry, but I think I'll be better off by myself today."

"That's your choice, but what about Brie? You know she's going to miss playing with Jill and Kayla. Jamaica isn't a great place to be dragging around a five-year-old."

"Can we just compromise today, so we can all get what we want?"

"You want us to take Brie?"

"It's the best thing for everyone."

Dani frowned. "Especially you."

"Give me a break, this is a vacation. She isn't going to miss me. She sees me every day."

Dani thought about the quandary. Her contempt for Elli's lack of maternal skills was trumped by her concern for Brie's well-being and what her own daughter would want. "We'll take her," Dani sighed. "But only because I know she won't want to be without Jill and Kayla."

"You're a saint! If you have any problems just call me. You have international calling on your cell…don't you?"

"Yes. What are you going to do by yourself?"

"I'm a big girl, Dani. I'm hot, single, and in Jamaica! I'm sure I can find something to occupy an afternoon."

"Fine. But don't call me if you wind up stoned in some filthy jail. I'll just take Brie back home with us. I'm sure your ex would love that?" Dani opened the door.

"I wish I could learn to be as good a mother as you are, Dani," Elli jabbed.

"You have a long way to go. And by the way…you might want to ask your new boyfriend why he visited a whorehouse before he met *you* yesterday."

"What?"

"Did you see a red scorpion stamp on his hand?"

"Yeah, so? He told me he stopped for a drink after dropping Rita off at the ferry."

"That means he was there. Will told us all about the place. The black X means he went through with the act."

"I think you're just making shit up because you don't like the guy."

Dani knocked on Buffy's door. "Whatever, Elli. I just thought you should know."

JUST ANOTHER DAY AT THE BEACH

OHN AWOKE TO THROBBING FACIAL pain and a sharp piercing sensation in his ear. Will's iPod had run out of juice hours ago and one earphone remained lodged in John's left ear. He eased the pain with the memory of holding Rita eleven hours earlier, her scent still lingering on his pillow.

He decided to rally himself after ten minutes of basking in his sweet daydream. He stumbled towards the bathroom wearing only cheap boxer-shorts. A piece of paper underneath the cabin door caught John's eye. The note read:

Dani will pick you up in your cabin at nine.

Don't worry about breakfast. Your attire for

the day is taped to the outside of your door.

Get ready!

Will

John scratched his head while opening the door. A clear plastic bag containing a new t-shirt dangled by a single piece of duct tape. Silvia watched the half-naked man from her cleaning cart parked outside the next cabin.

"You know it's going to be a good day when it starts with gifts," Silvia smiled.

John snapped around, covering his genitals with the plastic bag. "Hi, Silvia. I didn't see you there."

Her smiling face changed to horror. "Oh my! Mr. Smith—your face!"

John stood frozen. "Yeah…I…had a little too much fun in Mexico."

"I will bring you some ice right away!"

"Thanks, Silvia. That would be great! I'm just going to put some clothes on. I'll leave the door cracked."

"Okay. I'll be right back!"

John ripped open the bag the instant Silvia dashed off, threw on the shirt, and ducked back inside. Staring at himself in the bathroom mirror, his black eye contrasting with the white t-shirt, he couldn't help but laugh when he read the slogan: *NO PROBLEM MON!* John said to himself, "Today's a new day! Better get ready."

Silvia peered through the open door. "Mr. Smith?"

"Yes, Silvia, come on in."

Trying not to laugh. "I'm sorry…but you look…"

"Maybe I can buy an eye patch in town," John joked. "Do you think that would complete this ensemble?"

"They sell dreadlock wigs. If you got both, you would look like a Jamaican pirate." Both burst into laughter.

"Thanks, Silvia! Is that my ice?"

"Yes, Mr. Smith."

John continued to laugh. "I think that'll be all for now. I have to take a shower, but I'll be out of your way at nine."

"Take your time, *Captain High.*" Silvia clenched her lips together; her cheeks looked as if they were about to burst. John popped them with his own loud burst of laughter.

"Get out of here! All this laughter is making my face hurt more."

"I'm going now," she giggled. "Have fun today, Mr. Smith!" They continued their tennis match of giggles through the wall that separated the bathroom from the hall.

John showered, iced his face, and dressed in his bathing suit and new shirt. He sat in the corner chair waiting for Dani while re-playing his evening with Richard. *The Clawson kids sure won the lottery,* he thought. *To be raised by such positive and outgoing parents must have been a treat.* Feeling guilty, he reminded himself how much he loved his own parents and knew they had done the best they knew how. Like Richard said, where Jack and Nancy fell short with John, they compensated by being wonderful grandparents.

Still…although he knew he was raised by parents who truly loved him, that love was cloaked in routine and discipline, instead of the other way around. Imagination got washed through the cracks of structure in the Smith household. Where Jack learned to ignore and accept, John was oblivious. As a result, he grew into his adult life with the appearance of success—at least on paper. He'd turned into a man with no apparent vices, a college degree, a stable job which supported a wife, and eventually a son, but he had often sensed something was amiss.

One's personal resume doesn't present the whole truth of a man's life. It can't tell people if he's happy and truly fulfilled. John now found himself emerging from a one-way street, into an intersection of highways that he could take anywhere.

A knocking at the door propelled John from daydreams.

Dani jumped back as if a jack-in-the-box had opened the door. Her shock quickly subsided into good natured laughter. "Good morning…Jamaican Rocky."

"Very funny. And good morning to you, Dani."

"That looks like it really hurts."

"Looks worse than it is. Where's everyone else?"

"Waiting on the dock. We just finished breakfast."

The two gave each other a cursory hug before starting down the corridor.

"How did you know where my cabin was?"

"Will called the purser. He said I should get you at nine, that you would know to be ready 'cause he had a security guard slip a note under your door last night. I take it you got it?"

"Along with this shiny new t-shirt that's going to ensure I stand out today like a tourist from Kansas."

Examining the shirt. "I think it looks very…*en vogue.*"

"I hope so. The last thing I need is for some local to take offense and blacken my good eye. I don't want to look like a raccoon for the remainder of the trip—I'm content with the pirate look."

Dani giggled. "It makes you look tough, John. No one's going to mess with you now for fear of what the other guy might look like."

"That's a relief, since all I did was beat-up his knuckles."

"Will told us everything. That George is a real asshole. I wish there was some way we could get him back."

"Do me a favor and keep it between us. I don't need that gorilla coming after me again." John pushed the elevator button for the gangway level.

"About that…"

John looked with fear. "You didn't?"

"I had a little discussion with Elli before breakfast—she's not coming with us, by the way. I'm not happy with her at all…for a lot of reasons."

"You told her about the fight?"

"She knew. That's why she ducked out of Carlos 'n Charlie's with George."

"And the whorehouse stuff?"

"Yeah…Will told us about that. I thought Elli should know. Why…is that bad?"

"You could say that! I doubt George is going to take it kindly that everyone knows. After all, that's why he hit me."

"Oh, shit! I wasn't thinking."

John struggled to summon his inner dragon. "It's okay, you did what you thought you should. It's my fault anyway. But, if Elli knows everything, George is going to know I told someone."

"She's in denial that he paid for a hooker. Don't worry…none of us are going to let that son-of-a-bitch touch you again, John."

"Like Richard told me, it's going to be what it's going to be." The couple disembarked onto Ocho Rios' dock. "Where are we going?"

"Will said just to follow the crowd into town. We're meeting up at Burger King."

"His note told me not to worry about breakfast. I hope fast food isn't what he had in mind. I had time to grab something on the ship."

"He told me the same thing, but we couldn't wait 'til ten to feed the kids. I just had some eggs and juice." Dani started waving. "There's the kids! Come on." John followed as she ran ahead.

Buffy and kids frolicked through a school of Kayla's soap bubbles. Too old for their silly games, Garrett used his mother's iPhone to take pictures of the colorful Jamaicans hustling tourists. Dani jumped in to stab and slap bubbles while John greeted Garrett.

"Morning, Garrett!"

Garrett lowered the camera and turned. "Hey, John! Damn, your face is twisted!"

"I'll live. I see you're putting your mom's phone to good use."

"Yeah. Look at all these guys…everyone looks like Bob Marley. My friends back home will love these shots."

"Maybe there's a career in photography in your future instead of that nano stuff?"

"I don't know…I just like taking pictures of cool shit."

"That's what being a photographer is all about. Let me see what you got."

Garrett held the phone as he scrolled through his work. John quickly noticed his eye for improvisation. The half dozen shots were all captured without the subject knowing; as a result, each one told a story. John could see real-time emotion on the faces of tourists, confronted by ragged, imposing Rastafarians trying to sell tours, cab rides, or drugs. He wished someone had taken similar pictures of his first four days. He imagined the pictures as a cartoon storyboard, full of comedy and bewilderment, fear and revelation, and wondered what his face looked like as Rita first leaned in for a kiss.

"I wondered where my phone was," Dani said, leaning over the two men's shoulders.

"He's got talent," John said.

"Yes he does. I always steal the credit after I see all his wonderful pictures," Dani chuckled. "You guys ready? Will said walking into town would be a bit of a patience-tester with all the local beggars."

"Whenever you are," John said. "I'm hungry."

Dani clapped her hands in motivating fashion. "Let's go everyone! And you girls take an adult's hand. I don't want to worry about something happening to any of you."

Kayla took her mother's hand, Jill took Garrett's, and surprising both Dani and John, Brie looked bashfully up at John, offering her hand. The gesture made John's heart literally skip a beat.

"O-o-o-h," Dani yearned. Brie's little girl sweetness filled Dani with indignation towards Elli's request to not join the group.

John accepted the soft, tiny hand with a loving squeeze and full smile. "I'm John."

"I'm Brie," she giggled.

Garrett led the way through the customs gate while Dani took Jill's other hand. Once through, mother and brother humored the six-year-old with heaving swing-set rides.

The street leading into Ocho Rios was a lot like the football drill where the running back has to carry the ball through two parallel lines of teammates hitting him with blocking pads. Jamaica's Chamber of Commerce clearly needed to work on their hospitality skills. The group's joviality quickly became first humbled, then saddened, and finally annoyed.

John's paternal instincts kicked in when an aged Rastafarian man with one arm began following behind at an uncomfortable distance. His pungent smell and barking tone caused John to squeeze Brie's hand tighter.

"Nice shirt, mon! Whatch'a need? Smoke? Sniff? Guide? Come on, mon…I get you anyt'ing you want!"

John focused forward trying his best to ignore the man's intrusive barrage. If he had been alone he might have been too afraid to say anything, as it turned out—he wasn't either. One too many pokes finally woke the Dragon. "Listen!" John said, looking over while continuing a brisk walk. "We are with children! You should be ashamed of yourself! Now allow us to pass without bothering us!"

The man's crystal green eyes stared into John's with dark intensity and his evil, weathered face studied John's very soul for seven footsteps. Two days earlier John would have blinked—not today. The man grinned, exposing rotten brown teeth before slowly drifting away.

Dani's head had been turned watching the entire exchange. "Nice job, John! I told you that black eye made you look tough."

"Ew! Did you see his teeth?" Buffy asked.

John looked down at Brie. The fire inside him subsided at the sight of her tender face. He loosened his grip, smiled, and used his finger to tickle the inside of her palm. Brie giggled wildly.

Up ahead, another motley man sat on an old crate playing a guitar and singing—sounding just like Bob Marley. Like Garrett, he too was minus a leg, but with no prosthetic to fill the void. A cardboard sign leaned against his seat and Garrett stopped to listen and read:

A SHARK TOOK MY LEG
PLEASE HELP

Looking to Dani. "Can we?"

"Do you really think a shark ate his leg?" she asked.

"Does it really matter?" Garrett's lips turned flat and straight.

Dani smiled. "No…I guess it doesn't." She reached into her bag, dug out a five-dollar bill, and handed it to Garrett.

He dropped the bill into a plastic gallon sized milk carton with its top cut off.

The man stopped singing, but continued strumming. "Bless you, little mon! What happened to yours?"

"Car accident," Garrett said.

"You got a new one now," he gleamed. "Everything *irie* for you now…no worries." The man began singing where he left off.

John pulled a dollar from his bathing suit pocket, handed it to Brie, and flashed his eyes towards the milk carton. Tentative at first, she walked with John to deposit the money.

"Bless you, little girl," the musician said.

The group finally arrived in the heart of town; the harassment, cackles, and solicitation still hounded them at every corner. There were more tourists to feed off of in the open city than on the single entry road. Buffy was especially targeted, her blond hair and large breasts were very exotic to the black-skinned local men—as well as to some married tourists dragging their wives' bags around. The gang trudged through, trusting that Dani knew where they were heading.

Taking in the carnival atmosphere, John said, "It's the same as Mexico…but different."

"How so?" Dani asked.

"It's alive. Smell the smoke from cooking meat. There's music coming from everywhere. These people are like busy bees, obviously proud of their heritage."

Dani asked, "How's that different from Mexico?"

"It feels more…primal…real, in a harsh way," John said.

"They say this island has one of the highest murder rates in the world," Dani said.

"That's a shame," John lamented. "The people are *so* colorful and animated. I guess it's like Will said…when you're not given everything like a lot of Americans, you have to work—or fight—harder."

Dani scoured the street for a Burger King. "He's pretty smart, isn't he, John?"

"Intelligence is relative," John said. "But I think Will could do anything he put his mind to. I like him a lot."

Dani turned and smiled. "Me too."

"He's got my vote," Garrett said.

"Vote for what?" Dani asked.

"There it is," Garrett avoided, pointing to the Burger King sign towering above the shop lined street.

"Yeah!" Dani skipped, quickening her pace into the fast food parking lot. The place was teeming with locals more interested in loitering for hand-outs than buying food. She spotted Will on an outdoor bench sitting next to a large garbage bag.

"Hey, Will!" Garrett cried and ran up.

John envied the clearly cooler Will Catcher, but then was immediately ashamed of his twinge of jealousy.

"Howdy!" Will said, standing to throw the bag over his shoulder as the sound of shuffling ice echoed through the plastic.

Offering knuckles, John said, "Morning, Will!"

"Morning, Butterfly! Hi, Buffy…girls."

"I hope this isn't your big secret lunch spot," Dani joked.

"You mean they have these in Jersey?" Will asked.

Jabbing Will's chest. "Very funny. What's in the bag?"

Before Will could answer, the restaurant door flew open, banging against the door stop meant to protect the glass.

"Hey, when did you get here?" Garth asked, standing outside the entrance as the door recoiled and smacked against the large trash bag over his left shoulder. An order of super-sized fries seemed like a small inside his right paw.

"Hey, Garth!" Buffy smiled.

"Morning, big man," John said looking surprised.

"I thought this was your morning to sleep?" Dani asked.

"Willy talked me out of it by finding someone to cover my shift. I think he just wanted me to carry the heavy bag."

"I gave you the light one! Mine has the ice…you want to switch, you big baby?"

"Nah…I'm good." Garth stuck his mouth into the cardboard fry pocket like an angry badger going into a rodent's burrow.

"This is great!" Dani clapped. "The more the merrier!"

A beat-up, late eighties Jeep Wrangler beeping its horn and a white minivan cab whipped into the parking lot. The Jeep's driver shouted from the exposed roll cage. "Will!"

Hustling over. "Lloyd!" Will dropped his bag and shook hands. "Everybody…this is Lloyd. Say hi."

Everybody shouted "hi!"

"Welcome everyone," Lloyd said. "I can take four, the rest go in the cab."

Will took charge. "Garrett…why don't you, your mom, Jill, and John jump in with Lloyd. The rest of us will be right behind in the cab. Okay?"

"Cool," Garrett said. "I always wanted to ride in a Jeep!"

"Help your sister," Dani said.

John held the door before joining Lloyd in the front. "John Smith!"

"Nice to meet you, John," Lloyd said.

"This is Garrett, his sister Jill, and their mother Dani."

"Welcome everyone and use your seat belts. You ready to see one of Jamaica's hidden paradises?"

Everyone anxiously nodded. "And we can cliff jump?" Garrett asked.

"Yes you can, my friend."

The cab beeped to give Lloyd the go ahead.

"How do you and Will know each other, Lloyd?" John asked.

"I'm a chef. For years I've traveled around the states working seasonal jobs at resorts. We met a few years back when I was working at a resort in Telluride, Colorado. Will was on a ski vacation and stayed at the hotel. He said he wanted to meet the man who made his coconut shrimp. We hit it right off; the next day he took me skiing for the first time. Despite having a bob sled team, we don't get snow here. Anyway, we stayed in touch and I see him at least every other week now that his ship makes a weekly run to Jamaica."

Dani leaned forward. "Are you a good skier now?"

"The *worst!* But I love it. The fresh air, beautiful colors at sunset reflecting off the white snow, and the chairlift; I love riding the chairlift. What I don't like is cold. Jamaicans don't do well with cold."

"How's Will?" Garrett asked.

"He skis like he does everything—like he's done it forever."

"I ski," Garrett said. "I have special poles with little skis."

"I bet you're pretty good, too," Lloyd said.

"I just started last year, but I'm getting better. You ever ski, John?"

Turning sideways. "I never have, but I think I'd like to. This trip is making me want to do a lot of things I never thought I would."

"That's good," Dani said. "I hope that means falling in love again?"

John's facial expression said it all. "Maybe…"

Dani and John shared a silent smile. "How about you Lloyd, you married?" Dani asked.

"Twenty-two wonderful years. Her name is Susan."

"Any kids?" Dani continued.

"Two girls…both in school here at Northern Caribbean University."

"What do they want to do?" John asked.

"They both want to stay here and work in wildlife conservation."

"That's great," Dani said.

"Uh…" John pointed out the windshield at an oncoming truck taking up three-quarters of the road. Lloyd swerved to the left embankment, tilting the Jeep to a forty-five degree angle and making the pass within an inch of John's side mirror.

Lloyd glanced over with a sinister smile. "First time driving on an island?"

Clenching the dash so hard his finger joints turned white, John said, "Yeah. And first time driving on the left side of the…*road?*"

"The worst roads in your country are similar to our best," Lloyd said. "Jamaicans don't slow down around corners."

"*Y-o-u d-on't say,*" John clattered as they bumped along the pock-marked blacktop.

"This is better than a roller-coaster!" Garrett laughed.

Dani turned to wave at the cab driving not six feet behind. "These roads sure put a beating on cars," she said.

"Island car!" Lloyd said. "We don't buy cars for their looks, but for their reliability. My daughter has an old Suzuki Samurai with three-hundred-thousand miles on it. Most of the floorboards and body panels are rusted away, but it runs like a bull."

"I guess they're pretty lax with inspections down here?" John asked.

"What inspection?" Lloyd grinned. "If it runs…it's inspected."

The mountainous terrain continued to punish the Jeep, causing it's passengers to shuck and jive like lottery balls. The suspension continually dove and rose as Lloyd drove around the steep decline at a speed less comfortable than John thought safe. His face contorted into a series of grimaces one would equate with having a colonoscopy. A steep elevation change in Kansas was considered to be twenty feet.

Finally, the road leveled off as Lloyd made a sharp left onto a dirt road that looked more like a path almost concealed by jungle. He slowed, following the twisty sand trail as thick palms brushed the Jeep's exterior. Without warning, the vehicle halted at the end of the tree line. A beautiful lagoon lay before them as if God had built His own swimming pool. Pulling the emergency break. "We're here!"

Garrett and Jill stood in the back. "Wow!" they shouted in unison.

"That's amazing," John said.

"The locals call it Nancy's Dream, after one of our most famous Reggae artists—Sister Nancy."

"Is it ocean?" Dani asked.

"It's natural spring water, over two-hundred feet deep. Water runs down the falls there and also up from the ground. The run-off mixes with the ocean…there," Lloyd pointed to the stream running through a break in the forest. The group stared over the cut of fresh water bleeding out to the open ocean. "There's towels in the back, Garrett," Lloyd said exiting the Jeep.

"Pretty sweet, huh?" Will asked.

"It's beautiful," Dani said.

"Nice place to get a haircut," Will suggested.

"I brought my scissors!"

The group gathered their things and walked onto the white sand surrounding the water's edge; a half dozen Jamaican children were taking turns jumping from the falls. Will and Garth laid out a large blanket and dropped their trash bags in the middle.

"Who's hungry?" Will asked.

"I am!" John said rubbing his belly. "What'd you bring?"

Will fished through Garth's bag. "I got us a local's breakfast. When in Rome…" He began placing items on the blanket. "I have bananas, mangos, oranges, passion fruits, cherries, and June plums—they're like apples. These are fried breads called Johnny Cakes."

"What's in these Styrofoam containers?" John asked.

"That's ackee and salt fish, a Jamaican breakfast staple," Will said. "The fleshy yellow section of the seed pod from the ackee fruit is cooked with cod. The fruit looks and tastes like scrambled eggs. Try it, John. Here's some plastic forks."

"Can I try?" Jill asked.

"You sure can, sweetie!" Will said. "Everyone help yourselves."

"What are these?" Buffy asked.

"*Gizzada,*" Garth said. "It's a pastry made with coconut, sugar, nutmeg, and vanilla. They help keep my figure!"

Buffy took a healthy bite. "Mmmm…yummy! Here Kayla, try some."

"Lloyd, did you hook us up?" Will asked.

"Yeah!" Lloyd remembered and jogged back to the Jeep.

Garth rummaged through the other bag. "There are drinks on ice in this bag if anyone gets thirsty. We have coconut milk, Red Stripe, water, and Ting."

Looking strangely at Garth, Garrett asked, "What's Ting?"

"It's grapefruit juice soda," Garth said, displaying an ice cold bottle. "Want one?"

"Sure!"

"What's this, Will?" Dani asked.

"That's cooked breadfruit…comes from trees transplanted here by the British. It's okay. Tastes like potatoes."

John handed Brie a piece of sweet Gizzada. "This was really nice of you guys to take the time to bring all this stuff," he said. "Thanks, both of you."

"No problem!" Garth said.

Lloyd returned with a large stainless steel thermos and stack of Styrofoam cups. "Here you go, Will. Pour me a cup while you're at it."

"Thanks for remembering," Will said. "If anyone likes coffee, Lloyd was kind enough to bring us some freshly made Blue Mountain."

Dani raised her arm. "Me, me, me!"

"Here you go," Will said, pouring cups. "John?"

"Please."

Not willing to wait for the adults to finish breakfast, the girls waded into the lagoon.

"Mom, can I jump with those other kids?" Garrett asked.

Dani looked to Will. "Is it safe?"

"Oh yeah," Will said. "It's about fifteen feet high, no rocks in the water, and there's stone steps leading up there. He'll be fine."

"I'll take him," Garth stood.

"Go ahead, honey," Dani said. "But I don't want him jumping with his Terminator."

Examining Garrett's leg while slugging a beer, Garth said, "We can walk around the lagoon and he can take it off when we get to the top. I'll bring it back down to him when he's ready for another jump. That work?"

"Works for me," Garrett said.

"There's a rope swing up there," Will pointed. "He can either jump from the edge or use the rope."

"Just be careful," Dani said, but they were already on their way. Garrett responded with a half-hearted, back-handed wave.

John watched enviously. Nancy Smith would never have allowed her own son to do something so daring. If he were in Garrett's position he'd surely be restricted to the beach.

"What did you call these things, Will?" Buffy asked.

"That's a Johnny Cake."

Lloyd picked up one of the fried breads. "Sometimes we call them *Journey* Cakes 'cause you can take them wherever you go. They can save your life!" Lloyd offered the cake to John.

Studying the cake. "I wish I had this in the bathroom yesterday," John chuckled.

"In the *bathroom?*" Lloyd questioned.

"Nothing," John said, taking a bite.

"I notice you don't have much of a Jamaican accent," Dani inquired.

"I spent a lot of time in the United States. I still have one, it just depends on who I'm talking to—*mon,*" Lloyd laughed.

Sampling a June Plum, John asked, "You don't work there any more?"

"No. I'm tired of being away from my family. I'm fifty-two…too old to be chasing jobs all over the world. I cook here now, for one of the big resorts."

Lloyd's eyes widened as Buffy removed the t-shirt covering her bikini top. "I'm going to join the kids," she said. "Is there anything in there that will bite me?"

"Not unless we get in," Lloyd said.

Buffy giggled. "You're funny!"

Dani shook her head at the three men ogling Buffy's backside as she arched into the water like a supermodel on a photo shoot. "You ready for a haircut, Will?"

Shaking off his gaze. "Ready! Where you want me?"

Looking around. "How about you sit on that log over there? I can stand up and cut while still keeping an eye on Garrett."

Will looked at the dead tree lying twenty feet away on the border between beach and jungle. "Perfect!"

"Go dip your head," Dani pointed.

Lloyd used two fingers to scoop some breadfruit. "I couldn't help noticing your eight ball, John."

"What?"

Sticking his fingers in his mouth, Lloyd poked his eye with his opposite hand.

"Oh…yeah," John said. "It's a long story. I kinda got into a fight with another passenger."

Lloyd picked up his coffee cup from the sand. "What's the other guy look like?"

"Like brand new."

"Huh…sounds like a real *blood clot.*"

"Sorry?"

Lloyd sipped. "It's Jamaican for calling someone a dirty tampon. Based on what you said, that's the sort of guy I imagine."

"How would you know…I mean…all I said was that I got into a fight?"

Lloyd gazed over the water. "There is more truth in what people don't say and how they say what they do, than what they actually say. Too many people waste words, overcompensate. Women are usually more guilty then men. Besides, I'm a good judge of character." Lloyd faced John. "So is Will."

John smiled before turning around to the sound of giggling. Dani was intermittently combing and snipping Will's hair, using her teeth to alternate tools. Taking note of the way she gathered Will's locks, John recognized a tender, almost sensuous manner in her work. Will just sat contentedly, the way some dogs enjoy being bathed.

"Everything look *irie* between those two," Lloyd said.

"They're great people," John said.

"Will tells me you also met a nice woman?"

"When did he say that?"

"He calls from Cozumel to see if I'm working on Thursdays."

"Did he say anything else?"

"What he needed. He doesn't waste words," Lloyd smiled.

John leaned back against his elbows. "Her name is Rita," he sighed joyfully.

"You jus' say a lot," Lloyd grinned.

"I can see why you and Will get along."

"Look!" Dani shouted and pointed towards the rope swing. "He's going to jump!" On the jump platform one cross-armed Jamaican boy stood ten feet from the edge next to the Terminator while five others observed from the water. Garrett lifted his single leg so Garth could pull him farther and farther back by his hips before rumbling forward and releasing him five feet before the rock's edge. John heard Dani gasp as her son let go from the height of his swing, falling like a stone into the jade water. Anxiously holding her breath, she waited for him to emerge from the bubble wash. Four seconds passed and Garrett shot through the water's surface letting out a loud *"yeah!"* Everyone, even the Jamaican boys, clapped and whistled.

"Do you want me to bring your leg down?" Garth yelled.

"Hell yes! I want to do that again!"

Garth walked over to where they had placed Garrett's leg as the Jamaican boy bent over to study the oddity. "Excuse me," Garth said, snatching the leg and starting down the rock steps.

"That's my boy!" Dani said, returning to her cut.

"He's a natural," Will said.

"Brave little man," Lloyd said.

"He could be a General someday," John agreed.

Rooting out a bottle of coconut milk, Lloyd said, "I understand you're having a fine vacation so far?"

"Yes, Lloyd, I am. Learning a lot about myself—and other people. It's kind of strange though…the way…" John situated himself. "I take it Will told you about my son?"

"Yes."

"Well…I didn't tell Will, but my cruise ticket was bought and sent to me by someone else—anonymously. And that's not all. Yesterday I received an email from the person responsible—I think."

"What did it say?"

"It said I was doing great and then there was a quote from a famous American author."

"Which one?"

"Thoreau."

Lloyd swished coconut milk in his mouth. "Him I don't know."

"He's been dead a long time, but he wrote a famous book about leaving society to live alone in the woods for a couple years. Now that I think about it…Will used one of *his* lines the other day." Glancing back to the haircut.

"You think he sent the ticket and the email?"

Thinking. "He couldn't have. I mean…he didn't know me or my son, and I never gave him my email address."

"You could ask?"

Peeking back again. "Nah. I think I'll wait to see if I get anymore emails."

"Smart."

"How do you mean?"

Lloyd stood, and lifting his shirt over the greying nappy stubble on his head, flashed a smile filled with ivory teeth. "We are only supposed to know what we know when we're supposed to know it."

John considered. "Yes…I think I'm learning that."

"The sun's getting hot, think I'll join the ladies. Care to join us?"

"Thanks, Lloyd, but I think I'll wait a bit. I'm going to let the sun burn off a layer of pastiness. I'll never hear the end of it from the guys at work if I go home looking like this."

"Mind yourself, she burns quick for people like you." Lloyd smiled again then strolled away like he was in his own back yard.

John grabbed a Johnny Cake and Ting from the bags and watched everyone doing their own thing. Garrett had made his way back up the cliff where he and two of the Jamaican boys jumped simultaneously from the edge while Garth guarded the Terminator and chaperoned closely in case Garrett needed bracing. Dani and Will laughed and poked each other like two horny teens who couldn't stop touching each other. And Lloyd and Buffy took turns throwing the tireless girls in the water. In the midst of contentment, John missed Rita. He removed his new t-shirt and lay back.

Climbing high in the sky, the sun sucked fluid from his sweating pores.

"Ah…I think you're getting red," Dani examined.

John stirred. "What? I was—"

"I think you dozed off, Butterfly," Will snickered.

Sitting up. "How long was I out?"

Droplets from Dani's body fell to John's like rain on burning hot blacktop. "Maybe…forty-five minutes? We've all been swimming. You should get in. There's no salt residue to dry your skin. It's wonderful!"

"Give him some sunscreen before he blisters," Will said.

"Nice cut," John noticed.

"Damn right," Will said. "Almost worth going to Jersey for."

Dani hid her smile as she rooted for lotion. "I'll do your back," she said.

"Thanks. How's Garrett doing?"

"Jumping like a frog," she said. "He even got Jill, Kayla, and Buffy to jump with him, but Brie was too scared."

Cracking open a Red Stripe. "We're going up now, you coming?" Will asked.

"Let me use this lotion to finish up what Dani started and then I'll meet you up there."

"Roger that!" Will said.

Before their gait broke the bond, John thought he saw them briefly holding hands as they scampered down the beach. *Lucky guy*, he thought, squeezing a palm-full of lotion—too much he assessed. He did his best to use the whole glob by massaging it into his entire front from toe to neck and the remainder on his bruised face. After two minutes of rubbing, his face had its fill, and without a mirror, John couldn't have known his face now looked as though someone had burnt a pancake, placed it on his eye, and then pushed his face in wet flour.

Everyone had taken a turn by the time he reached the platform, all but Garth, who stood on the edge looking down as everyone scurried to clear a hole.

Reaching the top, John said, "Leave some water in the lagoon, *big-bone*."

Garth turned. "Holy shit!" he lurched back. "You scared the piss out of me! What the fuck, John…are you going on the warpath?"

"What?"

"Your face! You look like Michael Myers!"

Sweat on John's face was starting to make the lotion run. He didn't care for horror films but *was* familiar with the main character reference from the *Halloween* movies. "Oh…I used a little too much sunscreen…sorry." John started to slowly walk towards Garth.

"Stay back, dude, you're freaking me out!"

"Little old me?" John crept forward thrusting a raised clenched fist in a stabbing motion.

"I'm serious dude, back up!" John continued until Garth turned and jumped. Taking Garth's place at the top of the dive he stared down at the swimmers. Everyone gasped. Five of the Jamaican kids swam for shore as if they'd seen a fin periscope from the water. John laughed wildly, making the image more menacing.

"Behind you!" Garrett shouted and pointed.

"No. Behind *you*," John shouted and pointed back.

"Da leg," shouted the last Jamaican boy in the water. "Da leg!"

"Duhleg," John repeated. "What's duhleg?"

Will and Garth frantically swam to shore. "There's a man stealing Garrett's leg!" Dani screamed.

John twisted around in time to see a black man with long dreads sneaking away with Garrett's Terminator. Having jumped, Garth forgot it wasn't guarded. At the edge of the jungle the man—gripping the Terminator in his right hand—looked back just in time to make eye contact with John. Horrified by John's face, the man screamed out before ducking into the trees.

Looking back to the water. "What do I do?!"

"Get him!" everyone cried.

After a moment of hesitation, the image of Garrett having to finish his vacation on crutches flashed into John's mind—Carson the inner dragon exhaled fire. He reacted without thinking. Like a football team storming a paper banner, John shot into the trees and didn't let up when the fallen debris began stabbing his bare feet. The pitch of the land escalated slightly and branches slapped and scratched his shirtless chest. John plunged on—over and around each obstacle. He could hear the man somewhere in front; the sounds from his reckless retreat were becoming louder. When the thief paused to listen for any demon pursuers just before the ground made a steep dive toward the ocean, John leapt and caught a right calf. Chained together, the strange-looking couple tumbled down the hill.

Will and Garth entered the jungle at the beginning of the path leading up to the jump zone. Will yelled, "John! John! Which way?"

The leg teif's—Jamaican for thief—back slammed against a mahogany tree, ending their downward tussle. John held on to the man's lower leg with all his strength.

"Bumboclot!" the man screamed, pulling back his left leg and releasing it on John's face, the blow splitting John's lower lip. "Mek it stay!" *Let it be!*

John held on. Using the sloping terrain, he clawed his feet into the embankment to gain leverage as he rolled his back around onto the dread's lap, inching his way up the leg and deeper into the scissor position to block any further kicks.

"Get away from mi buddy, you battyman!" *Get away from my genitals, you fag!*

Now up to thigh, John screamed into the man's leg. "Will! Over here!"

The cuss-cuss—shouting fight with bad words—continued. "Bloodclot! Get off mi baldhead! Yu wanna romp wit me? Naa mess wit no raggamuffin!" *Get off me you white non dreadlock person! Do you want to mess with me? Don't mess with a ghetto person!*

"Will...over here!"

Rude bwoy—gangster—unleashed the Terminator with both hands, striking John's back and hip. In turn, John sank his teeth into the soft flesh of the man's inner thigh.

"Ahhhh! Bumboclot! A fuckery dat!" *Fuck! That was a messed up thing!*

"Over here!" John snarled.

"Naa mek mi vex, mon!" *Don't make me mad, man!*

John strangled the man's leg between his left bicep and forearm while blindly reaching around for something—anything. His right hand found a fist-full of spongy dreadlocks and he yanked as hard as he could. "Will! Will!"

"Ahhh! Ya obeah! Gweh!" *You are evil! Go away!*

"Drop the boy's leg and I'll let go of your mop!"

Leg teif grabbed John's wrist with his left hand while continuing to beat him with the Terminator. "Bumboclot!"

"You're a bumboclot! Damn it, Will, where are you!?" John loosened his leg grip enough to thrust his left elbow as hard as he could into the bottom of the V between the teif's legs.

"Mi wood!" *My penis!* The man's scream rang loud enough for people back on the ship to pinpoint his where-a-bouts. He raised the Terminator in preparation for a blow to John's head, but luckily for John, the backswing found a hand.

"Naa touch wi t'ings!" *Don't touch our things!*

The thief angled his head—with John still clenching his dirty locks and gripping his thigh like a Pit bull—to look up at Will. The exposed profile made a perfect target. Garth dropped all three-hundred pounds and the bottom of his fist like a hammer onto leg teif's jaw. And dat, as dey say, was the end of that.

John released his grip when the hapless thief went limp and Will and Garth quickly helped him to his feet.

"You okay?" Garth asked.

John spit blood from his split lip—a familiar taste. Adrenaline blocked out most of the pain from the lotion stinging his eyes, and his bruised hip and back, cut feet, and scraped chest. He released a half sigh, half laugh. "No problem, mon."

Will and Garth broke into triumphant laughter. "Nothing like looking the shark square in the eye, right John?" Will asked, patting John's back.

"I think I earned a swim in that beautiful lagoon," John said.

"And a whole lot more," Garth said.

"Lean on us," Will said. "There's a boy back there waiting to walk."

"Well, let's get going then," John said, throwing his arms over each man's shoulders and allowing them to lift him slightly so his feet wouldn't have to take all his weight. The three men limped back through the woods to the point of entry—John carrying their prize in his right hand.

The trio emerged from the dense vegetation to find Lloyd standing guard over the flock of women and children sitting on the beach.

Rushing to his aid, Dani said, "Oh my *God*…you're all hurt! John—"

"I'm fine, just a little banged up."

"You're bleeding!" she said.

"I'm growing accustomed to it," John grinned. "Just another day in the office."

"How hurt are you all?" she asked, continuing the investigation. "What happened?"

Will and Garth slowly lowered John next to Garrett at the water's edge. "I believe this is yours," John offered, cradling the Terminator in cupped hands.

Unlike in Cozumel, the sight of John's physical pain caused Garrett to tear up. He accepted the prosthetic and rewarded John with a hug. Choked-up, Garrett whispered, "Thank you."

"What happened to that horrible man?" Buffy asked.

Rinsing their feet by the water's edge. "He wanted a leg, but settled for Garth's hand," Will said.

"I call that one the *hammer*, John," Garth said. "It's more effective than pulling out hair and chewing off thighs."

Everyone chuckled.

"What kind of person steals a boy's leg?" Dani asked.

"As you know, they're very expensive," Lloyd said. "We have a lot of amputee's who can't afford them. He surely would have found a buyer on the black market."

Dani knelt in the sand beside the four men as Garrett fixed his leg and the rest examined their feet. "Are you sure you're all right? All your feet are bleeding. Should we find a doctor?"

"We're fine," Will said. "Just cuts and bruises—nothing a few beers can't fix."

"We might want to get going in case rude bwoy comes back with friends," Lloyd suggested.

"He'll be sleeping for a while," Will said. "I think John scared the shit out of him—looking like he does. A lot of these Rastafarians are pretty superstitious, John, and you look like a shit-bag full of evil with that face. But, you're probably right, Lloyd...we should pack it up."

"I'll call the taxi back," Lloyd said.

Everyone started walking around the level side of the lagoon.

"You want us to carry you, John?" Garth asked.

Washing his feet and chest. "Nah, I can walk." He slowly stood, turned, and looked up at the rock platform. "I'll meet you over there."

"What do you mean?" Garth asked.

"I haven't taken my swim yet and I owe someone something." John started gingerly up the steps.

"What's that mean?" Garth asked.

Staring at John's ascent, Will said, "Man's on a mission. Sounds like an old debt to me."

John finished his climb and took a deep breath ten feet back of the rock's edge. Like the stoned, battered frog from his youth he teetered with exhaustion, his face still white, bruised, and bloody. From the depth of his bowels he released the pent-up anger that had been suffocating him into a painful, indifferent coma through a cry for *freedom*. Shouting, "This is for you Carson!"

Everyone stopped and turned at hearing the roaring declaration. With all the speed John's feet could muster he raced ahead with reckless abandonment, hurling himself off the rock in a forward somersault. He moaned and contorted as his feet rotated around where his head began. His virgin flip wouldn't have earned any points for style, but nobody could deny 10's for courage. His over rotation stopped a quarter short of a one-and-a-half, causing John's scratched chest and face to smack the water.

After cringing groans from the gallery, Garth started into the water for fear John might be unconscious.

Stopping him with a hand to the chest, Will said, "Wait."

Longer than Garrett had been under, John finally popped up on his back, and lackadaisically wind-milled for shore as everyone clapped and cheered. He enjoyed a few minutes of peaceful floating under the hot Jamaican sun before making his exit. Dani greeted him with a towel and Will offered a cold Red Stripe.

"Nice jump," Will said. "But we have to work on your form."

"Stung like hell," John chuckled and sipped.

"Washed off half your sunscreen," Garth joined. "Now you can audition for the *Phantom of the Opera*."

"That was awesome!" Garrett approved.

Gazing up into the blue sky. "I never had to teach Carson how to do a flip. As it turns out... he taught me."

THE BEST CHICKEN

JOHN REFLECTED—LITERALLY AND FIGURATIVELY—IN THE side view. Rubbing his chin, he read: *Objects in mirror are closer than they appear.* He tried reaching out to touch his face in the dusty glass, but the racing Jeep jostled his arm. Out of frustration, he tried leaning forward, only to be stopped a few inches short by the seat belt. "Not close enough," he muttered. "Maybe it's not time?" he wondered.

"Will said he was taking us to a great place for lunch," Dani said.

"He is," Lloyd said, battling the steering wheel.

"Have you eaten there?" Dani asked.

Laughing. "Many times!"

John smiled through the mirror at Dani, but with all the movement he couldn't tell if she saw him. With only two seat-belts in the back, Jill sat strapped into her mother's lap—asleep. "Amazing how kids can sleep anywhere, regardless of distractions," John said.

Checking the rear view, Lloyd returned, "When your only worry is sleep...you sleep."

"How true," John said. "I used to sleep very well when I was married—out by ten thirty, up at six thirty."

"And your wife?"

Bracing for the oncoming turn. "Apparently...she had *many* worries."

"And now?"

"My wife?"

"Yes."

"She's fine...I guess."

Lloyd laughed. "What?" John asked.

"That's the difference between Jamaican women and American women. Jamaican women are never just fine. Either they're happy or they are...*in a state*. When it's the latter, we *gweh* 'til it changes or stay and make *dem* happy again."

"Jamaican men are smart," Dani said.

Holding onto the outside of his door, John stared into the side mirror again. "I never had much practice," he said. "She's the only woman I've ever really been with. For whatever reasons, I guess I never understood that she was ever *in a state*—until her bags were packed."

Dani and Lloyd restrained from commenting. John noticed Garrett holding onto the roll cage, watching the Jamaican landscape wiz by, an entertaining expression on his face. He was in the moment, taking it all in—so reminiscent of Carson. John remembered Carson often having a similar satisfied look about him, like a kid who saw everything despite where his eyes focused. In retrospect, John realized his own upbringing had been too pedestrian to hone the introspective tendencies predominantly equated with *only* children. There were no trips to Jamaica; no organized sporting accomplishments to celebrate or console, only quasi-games with neighborhood kids; no heartbreaks; no family feuds; no groundings or spankings—only stifling routine.

The Jeep passed a small field on John's side, surrounded with a rusted barb-wire fence and a lone goat lazily chewing a mouthful of grass and hardly flinching at the passing vehicle. The goat struck John metaphorically. He did a double-take out the window, rationalizing that being raised an only child without the fuel of any drama or real passion in small town Kansas was like making a pretzel without salt.

A moment of anger—perhaps a leftover from leg teif—towards the static and overly protective environment for which his parents had veiled him enveloped John. A question popped to mind: *How can a child ever grow into a well-rounded adult without building confidence and appreciation from a multitude of challenges and struggles? I am no goat,* he told himself. *Certainly there was nothing wrong with chewing grass, but there must be more to life than the safety of the pasture?*

Alternating his seat belt strap to his left shoulder, John leaned in with his right and extended a rigid arm out the open window; his knuckles wavered two inches before the side view. Like a switchblade, he released his middle finger. The nail returned a stinging pain from striking the mirror. Sensing a strange look from Lloyd, he stifled wincing, returned his belt, and sat back. A minute later the taxi beeped a short tune. Lloyd slowed and pulled over into a patch of high grass. Watching through his mirror, John sucked his middle finger as Buffy hopped out and made her way to Dani's side.

"What's wrong?" Dani asked.

"The girls wanna go back to the ship," Buffy said, adjusting her bikini top through her t-shirt. "I'm going to take them back to play in the youth center. Garth said he would go with us."

"You want us to go too?" Dani asked.

"Not unless your kids want to."

Dani turned to Garrett. "I want to stay," he said.

Jill fidgeted in her mother's lap. "Buffy's taking Brie and Kayla back to play on the ship. Do you want to stay with me and your brother or go back with them?"

"Them," she said sleepily.

Carrying Jill to the taxi, Dani passed Will. "You staying or going back with the kids?" he asked.

Dani flashed a smile before buckling the seat belt, whispering into her daughter's ear, and handing Jill's boarding pass to Buffy. "Text me when you get back on board," Dani said.

"Okay," Buffy replied.

"You promised me a great lunch," Dani said, touching Will's cheek on her way back to the Jeep.

Will leapt into the small utility area in the Jeep's rear.

"You good?" Lloyd asked from the rear view.

"Hit it!" Will said.

After snaking through the lush mountains for twenty minutes, Lloyd turned off on an unmarked dirt road meant only for four-wheel drives. The half-mile stretch of fish bowl potholes opened up to a well-manicured, upward sloping farm of fruit trees and palms. John marveled at the segregated communities on either side of the drive. Pigs, chickens, and goats were each given their own allotted acreage. At the top of the hill, a small white stucco house looked down over Mother Nature's grocery store. Prison bar windows and a blue tin roof gave the home some character, along with a spattering of palm stumps sitting on a concrete slab patio. Each palm stool was painted a different color and peppered with vibrant circles.

"Welcome everyone!" Lloyd said.

"Is this your home?" Dani asked.

"And *yours* today," Lloyd said.

Everyone piled out and followed Lloyd onto the patio where a well-rounded black woman sat on one of the palm stools ripping feathers from a dead chicken. Lloyd kissed the woman's protruding cheek and asked, "Everyt'ing irie?"

"If not, you be the first to know," she smiled. "Hello, Will! I see you're in fine company today."

Will rushed up to hug the big woman—his hands barely meeting around her far side. "Afternoon, Mommy!" he said, kissing her cheek and shaking her like a parent meeting their child after a prolonged absence.

"Stop it, you crazy white mon!" she said. "I got to clean the bird." The decapitated chicken lay across an unpainted palm stool with a bloody cleaver stuck in the top and two buckets bookended the butcher block. "Who your friends?"

Letting go. "Dani, her son Garrett, and my new best friend, John Smith," Will pointed. "This is Lloyd's wife, Susan."

Susan continued to pluck, throwing the feathers into one of the buckets. "Welcome! Make yourselves at home. There's Red Stripe and Ting in the cooler there," she said, pointing to an igloo sitting beside a lime green picnic table. Lloyd and Will rushed over. Still plucking, Susan stared down her nose over the tortoise readers leashed around her neck. "Wa happened to you?" she asked John.

"Ah…" The lingering effects of triumph and bravery shaped his answer, but the words that found their way out of John's mouth were laced with guilt. "I got into a fight…*two*, actually."

Sizing him up. "You don't look the type," she said and went back to plucking.

"Can I go check out the animals?" Garrett asked.

"Of course you can," Susan said. "And you can take this to the pigs." She picked up one of the tin pails.

Garrett took the handle and looked inside. A bloody head lay on top of gutted chicken parts. He imagined the open beak screaming for its life before the cleaver came down. "Pigs eat this?"

Susan teased the boy with a wild smile. "Pigs eat anything! Just dump it over their fence."

John peered into the bucket with a disgusted look. "I'll never look at a ham and cheese the same way again," he said.

Susan chuckled.

"Come on, honey," Dani said, "I'll go with you." She grabbed a beer and a soda before they headed off down the hill.

John accepted a beer from Will on his way to a steel oil drum smoking in the corner. "That smells great!" John said.

"Pimento wood," Lloyd said. "What we use to cook the jerk chicken."

"Mommy makes the island's best jerk chicken!" Will bragged. "I think she might be a better chef than you, Lloyd?"

"There be no doubt about it," Lloyd answered.

"No offense, but if she ever leaves you…she's all mine," Will said.

Lloyd laughed.

Susan feigned seriousness. "I'm too much woman for any white man to handle, even you, Will! Maybe that cute friend of yours…what's his name?"

"Garth?" Will asked.

"Yes! Now that boy have a nice shape about him." Susan laughed into the dead bird. "He say he big-boned! The more you feed the bird the bigger the breast grow…da bone stay the same size!"

The three men laughed through the sweet, citrusy smoke streaming from the oil drum.

"I'll have to remember to remind him of that when I get back to the ship," Will said. "What other delights are you cooking for us today, Mommy?"

Susan struggled a bit to stand. The naked bird dangled from her hand by its chopped wing. "Everything ready inside. The chicken is marinating, the rice and peas on the kitchen counter, homemade rum raisin ice cream in the freezer. I clean dis one to take to the girls," she said, shaking the bird at Lloyd. "I would love to stay, but I go to visit my babies today. They doing some water experiment at Dunn River falls today and invite me." Her face changed to that of an excited schoolgirl. "I going to be a college student today!"

"That's great, Mommy!" Will said. "But we'll miss you."

Now shaking the bird at Will. "You come by again next week and we talk 'bout what to do with you! Time for you to find a nice woman to take care of you and settle down!"

"There's nobody as good as you!" Will said. "But it's a date. That's my last week before vacation."

"Where you go be evil this time?" Susan asked.

"Not sure just yet," Will said, looking sly. "I have an idea though. We can talk about it next week."

"Dat we will! I go get ready now. Lloyd, come get the chicken. These people be hungry."

"Yes, wife!" Lloyd said, following Susan into the house.

Will and John stared out over the property.

"What do you think, John?"

"I think I'm in Oz. Thanks for sharing all this with us. I thought I'd have to take tours to see anything worthwhile, but I can't imagine any tour as wonderful as what you've shown me."

Bottles clicking. "Looks like they're enjoying themselves," Will said, gesturing to the chicken enclosure.

John watched Dani throwing feed from a bucket while Garrett ran back and forth antagonizing the scampering birds.

"Time to cook," Lloyd said, carrying a foil tub full of chicken. "You boys hungry?"

"Hell yes!" Will said.

"Very," John said.

"Good," Lloyd said, placing the tub on the table. "Will, go inside and get a bowl of water."

"I'm on it."

"That looks great," John said. "I have to admit though…I had some jerk chicken kabobs in Haiti and as good as they were, they did a number on my digestion."

Lloyd scoffed. "*Jerk* is Jamaican! Nowhere else makes chicken like we do—especially Haiti." Lloyd picked up a handful of pimento leaves and sticks from a pile laying next to the grill. "Pimento is from the allspice tree. It gives the meat a sweet, smoky flavor. Smell," he said, holding a handful under John's nose.

"Delicious!"

"Here's the water," Will returned.

Lloyd dunked some twigs in the bowl. "We wet them before putting it on the grill. The fire is nice and low now—lots of coals," he said, placing the wet leaves on the grate. "The chicken will cook slowly on top of this bed and the water keeps the leaves from burning. The fire smokes the wood, leaves, and berries into the meat. We cook it nice and slow to keep the meat tender and moist."

"Damn, that smell is like an aphrodisiac!" Will said.

John filled his lungs. "I've never smelled anything like that. It's very complex."

Lloyd smiled. "The chicken is rubbed and marinated with sage, ginger, thyme, nutmeg, cinnamon, lime, soy, scallions—along with other things. But the most important ingredient is Jamaica's very special scotch bonnet pepper. It makes a Jalapeño taste like baby food."

"That's what I'm afraid of," John said.

"Just try it," Lloyd said. "Susan's rum raisin will heal any injustice."

"I'll trust you," John said, "It's like what you were saying at the lagoon—maybe it wasn't time for me to know what real jerk chicken tastes like when I first tried it?"

Lloyd flashed an impressed smile.

Susan exited the house dressed in a colorful sundress doing its best to compliment her figure. She carried a straw bag in one hand, big enough to hold more than one dead chicken, and a metal box in the other. She set the white box—its lid marked with a red cross—on the table. Glaring over her glasses at the three men, she said, "Since Lloyd looks to be in one piece, I wait to hear why dat man all banged up and Will is walking funny. I gweh now." Susan kissed Lloyd and hugged Will. Pausing in front of John and again looking over her glasses, she said, "You look like a mon living contradictory to his shirt, but something in that black eye tell me you on your way to being *irie*. Good luck on your journey, John Smith." Susan smiled and hugged John; a strong familiar hug, leaving him with a *positive vibe*—as the locals say.

John never said a word. He sensed a tear rising behind his bruised eye; a strong warmth filled his heart for having met her, along with sadness for not having more time together. He watched as she climbed into the Jeep and sped down the drive, beeping a farewell to Garrett and Dani as she passed the chicken compound.

After Lloyd finished bedding the chicken, he said, "We have some time to rest ourselves and let the Red Stripes work."

Will grabbed the first aid kit and sat on a stool; he opened a cotton pad, soaked it in peroxide, and started swabbing his feet. "Mommy's a hell-of-a woman," he said. "I think she catches more than I do."

Following Will's lead, John sat and swabbed. "This property's beautiful," he said. "How much do you have?"

Lloyd grabbed another beer and sat. "About seven acres. It was Susan's parents'—we moved in after they passed." Lloyd looked out over the property as if they were still there. "Almost everything we need is here. All the ingredients in the chicken can be found out there."

John blotted his busted lip. "Must be nice to not have to run to the grocery store all the time?"

Will wrapped his feet in gauze and passed the roll to John.

"Sometimes you have to go far away to find what you need," Lloyd said. "Sometimes it's right in front of you. One way is not better than the other."

"Unless it's another beer," Will said.

The three men laughed.

"True dat," Lloyd said.

Will faced John with a look of admiration. "So tell us, Butterfly…what's it like being a hero?"

"I wouldn't say that," John said shyly.

"You don't need to be modest," Will returned. "You put yourself in harm's way to save a crippled kid's leg. If that doesn't merit using the word, I don't know what does."

John looked to Lloyd, who seemed to be patiently awaiting a response. "Well…after I got over the shock of what was happening, I just acted. I really didn't think about *what* I was doing."

"It made you mad," Lloyd stated.

"Yeah. *Yeah*, it did!" John said. "More so after, though."

"Why?" Will asked.

John drank. "When I was chasing him, and even when I was just holding on for dear life, it seemed like the thing to do. But when it was all over, I felt…rage, I guess is the best word to describe it. I've never experienced rage before, not when my wife left me, not even when I learned Carson was dead. It may sound strange, but after Garth gave him *the hammer* and I could concentrate on all the pain in my body, I felt…liberated. It's like being sick for a long time and then feeling healthy again, or maybe all the things that hurt me were being forced to the surface and burned away in my anger.

"Now that I think about it…all those scars are just bullies really. When we cower to them, they grow stronger; when we find a way to confront them, they lose some of their power. I guess that's why sympathy really has no benefit—as good as it might feel, it can also enable, or justify more wallowing. Everyone eventually tires of a person yielding to their pain. Strength sells movie tickets, not weakness. No one is ever immune to pain—although some get more than others—we all have to face it sooner or later. What we do with that pain is what sets an example for others." He laughed at his own insight. "I'm realizing I've been a poor *example* the last couple years. With that said—I honestly hope both of you never have to experience the pain of losing a child." John stared through the brown beer bottle clenched in his hands.

Will spoke lightly. "So…sometimes a fight can be beneficial?"

John pulled himself away from his worst memory. "I'm not a violent man, always hated the idea, even in movies. Never even been around anyone who was really, unless witnessing a couple of grade school fights count. But yes, Will, I believe, like most things, there is a time for it—especially in the figurative sense."

Lloyd stood to check the chicken. "There is a time to fight and a time to resist the temptation. Men do too much of both, usually on the wrong occasions."

"I've ridden a few bulls I later wished I hadn't fought," Will said.

"I never understood that," Lloyd said.

"What?" Will asked.

"Why you chose to chew your steak before it was cooked," Lloyd smirked.

"Someone's got to tenderize it," Will laughed.

John felt a wet nose nuzzling his naked back skin between his shirt and bathing shorts. He straightened up so fast it sent Red Stripe shooting up through the bottle neck and onto his face. Lloyd and Will laughed like they had surprised John from an alcove.

"That's Cotton," Lloyd said, bending down to feed the Maltese a piece of chicken skin.

Using his shirt to wipe his face, John said, "Hi, Cotton! Thought you were a snake." Still chewing some skin, the loving dog walked around in front of him for a more human hello. "Her hair feels like cotton candy."

"That's what Susan thought when she named her," Will said.

"She's second queen of the palace," Lloyd said. "We see her at meal times or when the goats need some exercise." Returning to study the smoking birds. "Susan already precooked these, Will. You can call your friends."

Will tussled a moment with Cotton before standing to put his right thumb and fore-finger between his lips and blow. The shriek caused Cotton to bark and John covered his left ear. "Come and get it!" he said. After seeing two heads turn from the goat pen, he sat back down.

To John's surprise, Cotton chose his company instead of a spot close to the grill.

"She likes you," Will said. "Do you have a dog?"

"Used to. *Bones*. Page and I rescued him from the shelter—a chocolate Lab pup someone had neglected to feed." John gazed fondly at Cotton, who enjoyed a thorough ear massage from her guest. "He was a present for Carson's sixth birthday. Poor kid could barely hold the sad creature. The dog hadn't an ounce of fat between rib cage and skin—cried if you squeezed too tight—until we fattened him up."

Dani and Garrett raced up the hill and reached the patio in a tie.

"If my mouth is as happy as my nose is right now, I may have to buy property beside you and Susan just to get invited for an occasional meal," Dani said, patting Cotton on her way to the grill. "What can we do?"

Lloyd grinned at her compliment. "Big help if you can find supper utilities, wax paper, and a big knife in the kitchen," Lloyd said. "When I go to work I'm really in someone else's kitchen, and the same's true here—nothing is arranged for a man's mind. Perhaps you'll have better luck."

Dani rubbed Lloyd's back in a consoling manner. "You poor man," she pouted. "Come on Garrett…help me find some things." She winked at Will on her way to the kitchen.

"And the rice and peas," Lloyd said.

"Is Bones still alive?" Will asked.

John sighed. "He died when Carson was overseas. He had been hit in the hind parts when he was ten. Someone left the backyard gate open—maybe me—and he wandered out into the street one night. When Bones got older he could hardly lift himself and we had to put him down."

"That's a tough thing," Lloyd said, guarding the chicken.

"Yes, it was," John mourned. "The news wasn't as hurtful to Carson since Bones had been more my companion than his. I think parents, especially young ones, have this idyllic belief that children need pets and don't always insist that they take the responsibility. The irony is that parents often become more attached to their kid's animals—and wouldn't we…after years of caring for them like they were children? Don't get me wrong…I think pets, especially dogs, are a good thing for kids. Dogs are more loyal friends than most people and kids and dogs look at the world the same way: hungry and excited. That's hard for parents to compete with twenty-four hours a day. But most children don't, not on a regular basis anyway, take on the burden of feeding, walking, and bathing their dogs. Not when they know Mom and Dad will. And they know. We teach them. It's easier when you have a nice big place like this for them to run around in—Cotton doesn't need humans as much. We—I have a nice yard at home. I could never understand why people keep dogs in cities? Needy I guess, the owners that is. Why else would someone keep an animal, born to run, in the confinement of a city apartment with no lawn or squirrels to chase? I think half of those people keep dogs as status symbols."

Dani and Garrett returned to the patio with all the tools for the meal. "Here we go!" Dani said. "*Everything* was exactly where I would have put it."

Lloyd chuckled under his breath. "Woman's kitchen."

"What are you boys talking about?" Dani asked.

"John was just telling us about his love for big cities and dogs," Will laughed.

"Which do you want, Hoboken, NJ, or *Bear*?" Dani asked. "You can have both if you like. Saint Bernards make great rugs if nothing else. Garrett never plays with him."

"I do too!" Garrett defended.

John turned to Will with raised eyes. "See what I mean?"

"What do you want me to do with the wax paper?" Dani asked.

"Spread a big piece out on the table there," Lloyd said.

Will studied John who was still rubbing Cotton's neck. As if stating a rhetorical question, Will asked, "So people shouldn't bring anything into their lives that they're not prepared to take care of properly?"

"I believe fish are fine for career oriented people," John said. "Maybe turtles too."

Will thought for a moment. "You know, John, even abused and ignored dogs often still return love. It's quite rare in life—unconditional love—a fine thing to be around. I see another dog in your future and I don't think Bones would mind. What do you think?"

Smiling at Cotton. "Perhaps."

Lloyd transferred the meat from grill to plate to wax paper and then using the largest blade Dani could find, he hacked into each breast several times. "Dig in!" he said, like a man who had just slaughtered his prize pig for some great occasion.

Everyone claimed a palm stool. John took his first bite apprehensively, but after the sweet smoky spice kneaded his taste buds, a junkie was born. *Why couldn't this have replaced Page's salt and peppered frozen chicken and potatoes?* Like a nipple pinch in foreplay, the scotch bonnet teased his tongue with just enough pain to want more. Time passed with little conversation—just *umm's* and *ah's*.

"Can we trade Bear in for a goat?" Garrett asked.

"If you find one that keeps my carpets clean and makes its own cheese, we can talk," Dani said. "This is exceptional, Lloyd. Thank you so much and please thank Susan. Are all Jamaicans so gracious?"

Lloyd licked his fingers as if they contained the last drop of water on earth. "Like people anywhere, we are mostly good. Americans often get the wrong impression from your media."

Will added, "Tom Cruise mentality."

"Yes," Lloyd said. "Jamaica isn't so different from most Caribbean islands—or any place. It's true that we have much crime and poverty, but we offer so much more. Too many come here just to smoke ganja and party at places like Hedonism. They could stay home and do that in your Key West or New Orleans. It's the *idea* of Jamaica that draws people. Your states are legalizing ganja, but so many still come here just for that. Ironically, they have a much greater chance of being arrested here, and our jails aren't as nice."

John thought twice before asking, "Do you smoke ganja?"

"No!" Lloyd said shaking his head vigorously. Preferring his fingers to a fork, he picked some chicken as a wry smile appeared. "But…like your president Clinton said: 'when I was in college!' Except for me it was grade school."

Lloyd's confession triggered laughter from his guests, even Garrett, whose mother humorously placed her hands over his ears.

John quietly finished his meal and enjoyed the anecdotes from what now felt like a surrogate family. He was mildly shocked though, when Lloyd was able to give names to the birds that comprised their lunch. When Will asked what John thought "Maggie" tasted like, only one answer came to mind: "Like chicken, of course." By dessert time the inside of John's mouth felt like the end of a jawbreaker.

Susan's rum raisin not only doused the flames, it added even more complexity to the lingering flavors. Her home-made ice cream—Lloyd admitted only the raisins were store bought—tasted like no other John had ever had. The extra creamy goat's milk, combined with coconut milk and natural sugar cane—a half-acre growing behind the house—served as another reminder of what could be if one chose not to settle for the high fructose versions in life.

By lunch's end not even a scoop of rice and peas remained. Everyone pitched in to wash Susan's colorfully glazed dishes before the sun hardened the ice cream residue. John found the kitchen as outdated as his own. The difference was in its cleanliness and organization. He had no idea what Lloyd meant by a *woman's* kitchen—thinking he'd made the comment to help Dani feel useful. John *had* loaded his own piled high sink into the dishwasher before leaving for his flight in Kansas City, but as he dried plates being passed to him in assembly-line fashion, it occurred to him that he might not have pushed *start*.

He enjoyed the teamwork in Lloyd's kitchen; taking him back bitter-sweetly to times with his own family. John and Carson had always helped Page straighten the kitchen after dinner and Carson never let his gender restrict him from helping out with the weekly tasks of vacuuming and laundry. Conversely, he helped his father with mowing, raking, and shoveling in winter. Even in his teenage years, Carson squared away his bed every morning without being told. That's when John knew his son's intentions to join the military were dead set. John had asked the neighbors, and parents at the factory, if their kids made their beds every day without being asked. The answer was always a resounding "Are you kidding?"

Melancholy mixed with nostalgia inside John, as if remembering some great passion he was forced into abandoning. Garrett rambled on about pigs and goats while Lloyd and Will reminisced about old times as they shelved plates. Dani asked John at one point: "Penny for your thoughts?" He responded with a gentle smile. "Just thinking about the past," he said without giving any specifics.

After the kitchen was spotless, Lloyd and Cotton took their guests on a mini-tour of the grounds. The tour was as good as any the ship offered. Lloyd stopped to explain every nut and piece of fruit, most of which the group had only seen in grocery stores at best. There were jackfruit and pomegranates, nutmeg and cinnamon trees. Everyone appreciated their breakfast and lunch so much more when Lloyd pointed out the thirty foot tall pimento and ackee trees. The flowering dogwoods acted as natural insecticides against fleas and lice. Lloyd put on a show by removing his sandals and climbing a fourteen-foot banana tree to the fruit. After, Garrett attempted an envious try, but only made it a few feet before he gave out.

Lloyd moved on to his grand finale when the ginger plants and cashew trees didn't stir much excitement. Everyone loved seeing the cocoa trees, even though they were disappointed that the red fruit containing the delectable beans wasn't mature and couldn't simply be eaten like a candy bar. For some reason the sight of a tree bearing raw chocolate aroused the kid in everyone. John remembered a similar feeling about wrapped boxes under the Christmas tree at his local mall. As a child he knew they were empty, but still wanted to tear them open.

Four o'clock came quickly and another shore adventure was coming to a close. Lloyd wrapped up the tour by chasing frantic chickens inside their pen. John's feet hurt too much to join in the game. He watched and cheered as Dani and Garrett came close, but Lloyd and Will were the only ones able to scoop up the birds from behind. Inside, John briefly mourned the death of Maggie who he imagined running just as freely earlier that morning. He dismissed the foolishness by speaking to the inside of his cupped hand, "The towel swan was just a towel."

The destruction of beauty, the loss of joy, the senseless murder of life, even a defenseless frog; these haunting memories bored a pit in John's stomach. Ironically, thanks to a dose of rage, the birth of a new feeling was growing. The buds of hope blossoming on his inner tree were helping to elevate John from that bottomless pit. As if a switch were flicked, he ceased mourning his afternoon meal and decided instead to think of Maggie for exactly what she was...*the best chicken ever*.

A DOG LICKS HIS WOUNDS

JOHN STEPPED INTO HIS CABIN with the comfort of finally being home after a long trip. The room smelled fresh from cleaning. Something in the air reminded him of morning. He flicked on the main light and followed his nose to a wicker basket resting on the dresser top. A hand written note leaned against two bags of coffee beans and purple flower blossoms filled out the dead space. He recognized Jamaica's national flower from touring Lloyd's property earlier. The note's elegant script looked feminine, but read masculine. He immediately took it for a dictation as he read the note out loud—the beginning of what would be a one-sided conversation with himself:

"John, my boy, a little something from Blue Mountain.

We didn't know if you liked decaf or full strength, so there's one of each. Mary and I toured the factory today. We're going to *Tuna Roll* for chow at 7:00 (doc says sushi is good for the ticker) and the ice show at 9:00. No need to respond; we'll see you if we see you. Here's another bottle of medicinal grapes…enjoy!

Richard and Mary"

Rummaging under the flowers, he discovered a bottle. "Chateau Mar-gaw-x," he tried. Two classes of college Spanish was the extent of John's foreign language skill, and pronouncing Margaux correctly was too much to ask. "Sounds French. And a corkscrew. That was nice. I wonder if they're looking to adopt?" John chuckled. "Let's let you breathe while I go see how pretty I've become."

After uncorking the French wine, John stripped out of his clothes and headed to the bathroom for a self-examination. Standing naked in front of the mirror, his pink skin was a testament to his pre-lotion nap, but it *had* solved the farmer tan. With each stretch and prodding flick of his tongue to his swollen split lip, blood seeped through the tear. His eye had darkened to full black, his nose was still swollen, and the collection of small cuts and scrapes on his chest looked painful, but were nothing more than superficial marks that would quickly fade. Some aching pulsed from the middle of his back where leg teif had drummed with Garrett's leg. He stretched to reach the exact spot. "Nothing like kicking a man when he's down." Laughing at his own joke. "Maybe a warm bath will wash this all away?"

John's bathroom was tiny but still twice the size of Will and Garth's. The Clawson's guest bathroom was larger, even without a shower. The abbreviated tub, at least for John's purposes, was better than having just a shower. Having retrieved the wine, John sat bare-assed on the toilet seat and drank straight from the bottle as he watched the tub fill, rationalizing that anyone who decided to drink in the bathroom was either an alcoholic, or else they really had a tough day—either way, a glass seemed like an unnecessary formality.

Lloyd had returned his guests to the ship dock promptly in time for the 5:00 horn. When Dani and Garrett started towards the ramp and Will towards the separate employee gate, John was still thanking his host. Lloyd left John with a question, prefacing it with a smile, "I am far too seasoned to believe I actually know anything but good questions. Could your ex-wife have been the one who sent your ticket?" After unwrapping his bandaged feet and stepping into the bath, John started looking for answers to not only Lloyd's question, but some of his own.

John emptied a shampoo miniature into the rushing water and waited until the white foam was six inches above the water line before shutting off the faucet. "Maybe she regrets leaving me? She had a year and a half before Carson died to figure *that* out. No...*regret* is a word I think she reserves for too much time spent *with* me. How many high school sweethearts actually make it *'til death do us part* anyway?

"Maybe she sympathizes with my pain and sent the ticket out of mercy—or pity? She didn't express either when she left me—not even at the funeral. She barely acknowledged me, much less allowed us to share our misery. I never saw her so cold. Maybe I was just too painful a reminder of Carson? It was like she became a different person somewhere in our marriage, and another after Carson died." John slid his ass towards the drain, causing his knees to fold and his head to float just above the snapping bubble-line. He took the Margaux from the tub ledge and swallowed a healthy portion.

"My parents could have arranged the ticket? Highly unlikely knowing my mother." He slowly closed his hands on a pile of soap bubbles, a faint resistance coming just before the vice closed and his hands touched. "Christ, she didn't even let me trick-or-treat without her until two years after the other kids were going by themselves! That was a long time ago, but I haven't seen any signs that she's changed. The woman still calls once a week just to ask if I'm okay...like she thinks the sound of her voice will wash my troubles away! Dad should take *her* on a real vacation. Perhaps Silvia knows a good hotel in Transylvania?" He chuckled.

"Maybe if she had encouraged me to try new things when I was young instead of protecting me from everything I'd still be married? I *should have* fought to do new things—playing football would've been nice. And what's the danger in tennis!? I guess she thought the disappointment of losing would have harmed me more than not trying at all?

"I wish I could have known you in college when Dad said you were fun. Dad could have arranged it on his own? But he would eventually have to explain to Mom why he did—a losing battle." He laughed and blew at the crackling bubbles. "She would make him feel stupid for thinking a vacation could solve my problems.

"*Maybe* Page's parents sent the ticket? Nice people.

"This is stupid! How would any of them know how I was doing on the ship? That's what the email said. 'You're doing great.' I need to check for more emails."

Gulping more wine. "This stuff is good. I wonder if French people drink while they bathe. I bet they do! French people are so decadent—in movies anyway." Sticking his big toe in the spigot. "Cotton sure was a nice dog. I miss Bones."

By 6:30 the air conditioning had joined forces with the Margaux to lower both the water and John's body temperature; he had nodded off. The cold forced his cramped knees to unfold abruptly. His bruised back smashed against the tub's rear wall, he flinched and then shot upright in shivering waves. He released the drain and opened the hot water full bore, prematurely pulling the bypass to the shower head when the water seemed warm enough. The transition from soothing heat to scalding hell happened in a split second. The steaming water hit John's pink skin like shards of glass as he danced to turn the cold nozzle. When finally achieving a happy medium he breathed out a deep sigh.

A few minutes later, after gingerly patting his body dry, he phoned.

"Hello."

"Yes, housekeeping, this is Mr. Smith in room…"

"Yes sir…your room shows on my phone," said a Hispanic woman's voice. "How may I help you?"

"Would it be possible for somebody to deliver some aloe vera?"

"*Wallo Wera?*"

"Aloe Vera, the green cactus gel…for sunburns."

"Oh! *Si*…sunburn! Yes, sir. I will send for you!"

"Thank you."

John stayed in his towel, choosing to drape an unbuttoned dress shirt over his shoulders while he waited for housekeeping. Not even five minutes passed when a knock sounded.

"Oh my God!" Silvia's expression of shock doubled from morning. "Mr. Smith…you look…"

"Pretty?" John smiled, causing a red bead to bubble from his lip.

Silvia split the difference between laughter and shock. "Maybe you shouldn't leave your cabin anymore?"

"I wouldn't want you to have to discover the body."

Silvia seemed embarrassed with her giggling. "Here is your cream, Mr. Smith."

"Thanks, Silvia. God willing, I'll see you tomorrow."

Silvia scrunched her face in amusement and made the sign of the cross. "Good evening, Mr. Smith. Call if you need anything else."

Some force triggered by the door closing caused John's towel to give way. An insignificant event as far as he was concerned. The adrenaline from saving Garrett's leg, along with any pats on the back from John's ego, wore off at some point during bathing. His normal reaction, regardless of any onlookers, would have been to immediately exercise modesty, but he simply shrugged and walked to the cabin's sole chair to apply aloe. Unlike the bottom rung feeling of depression which more recently had caused him to skip normal formalities at home, his current step was more respectable and higher up the emotional ladder. Humility, after all, is like turpentine to paint; it strips away any useless forms of pride.

John grabbed the remote with one slimy hand while using the other to cake his body with aloe just as liberally as he had earlier with suntan lotion. "Let's find something appropriate to my day in whatever movie TCM is showing," he said out loud.

The station was right on cue. "Perfect!" he chuckled. "I haven't seen *The Good, the Bad and the Ugly* for years. And I don't need to look any further than the title to find the symbolism. I *have* done good today; I *have* met bad today—unfortunately I don't think I'll ever forget the taste of his thigh. I don't know about ugly, but I'm definitely no candidate for a fashion shoot."

Clint Eastwood's anti-hero character roles in the trilogy of spaghetti-westerns that transformed him into a movie star always had one scene where he *got* as good as he *gave*—John tuned in during the got scene. Tuco—the ugly—was making Clint—the good—walk through the scorching desert while taunting him from horseback with water and the shade from an old-fashioned parasol. Collapsing from sunburn and dehydration, Clint finally rolls down a sand dune, seemingly about dead, only to take Tuco by surprise minutes later when an out of control stagecoach full of dead soldiers comes to a halt. When Tuco learns there is a graveyard where stolen gold was buried by the only soldier still alive on the stagecoach, he runs off to find water for the man. While Tuco is fetching water Clint learns the name of the graveyard as the soldier dies. Tuco now has no option but to nurse Clint back to health. John found himself suddenly hungry and rooting for the persecuted main character.

"Now you got 'em Clint." John dialed. "Yes…room-service, this is Mr. Smith in room number—"

"Yes sir, I have your room number," said a man with what John thought was an unrefined European accent. The phlegmy tone side-tracked John into thinking about what Kansas would be like if people spoke with as many accents as he had experienced on vacation. "May I help?"

"Huh? Yes…I would like…is it possible to get a cheeseburger and fries?"

"Of course! How would you like cooked?"

"Medium please."

"Would you be needing any condiments?"

"Mayo and ketchup on the side, please."

"Anything else?"

"Do you have malts?"

"Malz?"

"Milkshakes?"

"Yes, yes, of course! What flavor do you like?"

"Vanilla?"

"Certainly! Anything else?"

"No thank you."

"Very well! I send right away, sir."

"Thanks."

A few minutes later John's skin had sucked in enough aloe for him to put on underwear, shorts, an unbuttoned dress shirt, and two pairs of socks to provide his cut feet extra cushion. When he returned to the chair, Clint and Tuco were blowing up a bridge that separated the warring Northern and Confederate armies. Neutral about the civil war they destroyed the bridge to eliminate the obstacle, end the battle, and be on their way to the hidden gold.

Room service delivered John's food during the closing scene. He left twenty percent and hurried back in time to discover the name on the grave site—not remembering from the first time he saw the movie. Angel Eyes—the bad—also found the graveyard and the three formed a triangular standoff around a rock where Clint had written the name on the grave. Clint of course, wins out by shooting Angel Eyes and sabotaging Tuco's gun, but reveals the blank underside of the rock.

"That's right," John remembered. "The Unknown Soldier! That's something Will would've done. Nice move Clint…well done!"

John placed the burger and shake on the ottoman and imagined himself parked at Richard and Mary's drive-in. After his brush with leg teif he felt like he could relate more to Richard's story about smashing a tray into the face of Mary's presumptuous date. But he realized he had never done anything to earn Page. They lived in the same neighborhood all their lives. She asked *him* to their prom. His time with her had been a gift—taken away as easily as it had been given.

In the closing scene, Clint leaves Tuco in a noose, his feet wobbling on top of the unknown soldier's wooden grave sign, half the gold laying in front of him while Clint rides off with the other half. The story ends similarly to how it began. From a dramatic distance, Clint turns back to shoot the rope and free Tuco. With his hands still tied, Tuco screams after an indifferent but merciful hero as he rides away.

Slouched in his chair, he said, "I should have saved Page. I should have rescued her from *something* instead of boring her into leaving. It wasn't hard to fight for the right thing today. I want to be the hero for a change. I left her there to hang—she shot her own way down."

LIFE'S A CIRCUS

JOHN FOUND HIMSELF WATCHING MORE TV than usual after Page left. Living alone for the first time in his life taught him two things: there was more to laundry and cooking than just deciding to do it, and television had turned into an insidious evil, like some sort of 40s secret government experiment that had discovered a way to hypnotize its citizens. Most shows used as much of their allotted time for commercials as for the actual program. For the life of him, John couldn't understand why two or three commercials shown one time during a thirty minute sit-com—or a total of four shown on two different occasions—wasn't ample payment to the networks for his entertainment. His realization of and reaction to this frustration happened in stages, like waking from a deep sleep and slowly going through his morning routine until he was free enough from the nights slumber to go to work.

The initial motivating spark came one night at the end of an hour long show when he couldn't remember the title. All that came to mind was that he had just watched an hour's worth of GEICO ads. The conundrum both infuriated and baffled John since he found his own insurance company quite amicable and charged two thirds the fees. He thought about writing a letter to GEICO suggesting that if they limited their costly ads the company might be able to save enough in fees to lower their rates, which would attract more customers who would then also be able to actually remember the shows they watched. The next day, thinking a letter would just be thrown away by some minimum wage employee, he lost his will to follow through. Commercials had done their job by this time and filed away his remaining sensibilities. After that day, like people tend to do, John exercised arrogance, instead of the power of a pen.

At first he tried using the mute button during commercials. This was soothing to his ears, but the visual aspect was still offensive. Next, he tried bringing in a book to join forces with the mute button, but he found himself reading too long or looking up too much during the commercials, so he either missed parts of the program, or couldn't focus long enough to get any real reading done. A fellow employee suggested John purchase a TIVO to record his programs so he could fast forward over commercials. He tried the recording device but thought it too arduous to plan out and follow up with his picks, feeling the relaxation and entertainment value of TV should be spontaneous, not something that required more effort than planning a road trip.

John considered sporting events, especially football, particularly vulgar for their numerous and frequent commercials. The death of his twelve-year-old RCA TV happened during a Super Bowl. Like all the forgotten TV shows laden with cancerous commercials, he forgot who was playing. He had been reduced to finding new ways to kill time between ads, so when the third commercial in ten minutes for feminine products cut to the screen, he ended his nail clipping long enough to snip through the TV cord with the tenacity of a rat gnawing through a cardboard box. Still optimistic about Page's return, he taped his favorite picture of her—from prom—on the convex glass. Satisfied that the old TV made a better picture frame than source of entertainment; he returned to man-scaping.

He replaced Page's picture after Carson died. It was one of Carson on his sixth birthday, holding Bones. After two weeks, the anguish from seeing the picture every day when he returned home from work was the final straw. The picture went into a box and the old TV went to the curb. He canceled his basic cable, and from that day on, used the internet on his work computer to check daily news. Other than indifferent glances at the bowling alley or in restaurant bars, it had been six months since John watched TV.

On the cruise, John was enjoying TCM, since the channel hadn't been included in his basic cable. TCM had an ingenious way to hold its viewers; they only played commercials between movies, and even then they were only self-promotional. The five to ten minute break between movies created an opportune intermission for John to use the bathroom or grab a snack and return in time for the start of the next movie. If he had been watching a station that bombarded him with ads for chain-restaurants and the latest pill from some pharmaceutical company he might have given in to his urge to check email at the business center. Instead, he nestled himself back into the chair, finding enjoyment again from the square box that had once served as a symbol for so much pain and frustration.

John checked his old Timex when the ice skating scene from *The Bishops Wife* prompted him to consider the Clawson's invitation. "It's eight thirty-three. If I leave now I can check my email and still meet Rich and Mary at the rink." He stitched up his shirt buttons, pulled on a pair of khaki's, and gingerly slipped on his loafers after removing one pair of socks. Reluctant to push the power button, he spoke to the TV. "I wonder if the cable company will let me just have TCM if I buy a new TV? Probably not—makes too much sense to just be able to pick the channels you want," he scoffed before checking the ship diagram for the business center and ice rink.

An anxious tension that comes from something one wants to know charged John by the time he entered the business center. The vast modern lounge, with two of its four main walls made of glass, looked void of people. Contemporary furniture arranged in living room style sat vacant in front of book-filled shelves. Padded chairs were neatly tucked under the half dozen desks that housed brand new Apple computers. John sat, typed in his log-in information, and waited. "Nothing," he said in a disappointed tone.

He returned his chair and glanced at the time. Still in the mode of conversing with himself, John spoke openly as he headed to the show. "I can't believe I'm on my way to watch people ice-skate on a ship—in the Caribbean! And I thought the new bowling alley back home was a big deal."

Entering The Crystal Pond, he had the feeling of entering an event in Disney's Magic Kingdom. Even before the show, the lights and multi-colored furnishings were a sight for John's eyes. Blue-chaired bleacher seats lined two sides of the ice which was being prepped like intermission at a hockey game. Two bars, standing sentry on either side of the entrance, were mostly being ignored by passengers, still full and buzzed from dinner. John glanced right and left for signs of Will or Garth before Mary's arm caught his gaze.

"John!" Mary, watching for him from a reversed bar stool, waved vigorously.

The couple's facial expressions changed dramatically as John approached. "Hi, you two!" John said, initiating hugs and handshakes.

"Maybe you should start pissing over the side of the ship?" Richard suggested.

"Huh?" John squinted. "Oh…my face! No. I did fine in the bathroom today, except for scalding my sunburn after falling asleep in the tub. I think drinking your wine while I watched the bath fill was the culprit. Thanks so much, by the way. Your gift was very kind!"

"I'm not sure the French intended for that vintage to be savored in the Loo," Richard smirked.

"Stop it, Richard," Mary said. "The boy's obviously had a hard enough day without you jabbing him."

"It was a great day!" John suddenly replayed how all his words must have sounded. "Sorry. Maybe if I back up and explain my day, it'll all make more sense?"

"It couldn't hurt," Richard said. "I have a suspicion this is going to call for a drink. John?"

"Maybe just a light beer, thanks."

Richard swiveled to the bar, ordered a light beer, and despite Mary's frown—which he could feel without looking—two glasses of chardonnay.

John recounted the details of his day starting with receiving Will's t-shirt. The Clawsons registered a roller-coaster of animated expressions—particularly from Mary—as he recapped his adventures. By the time he finished, the lights were blinking the start of the show and Richard and Mary wore wide-eyed looks of incredibility.

Richard laughed. "Quite a day, my boy. Quite a day!"

"Yes it was," John said. "I guess we should find some seats?"

"May I hug you first?" Mary asked.

"As long as it doesn't make Richard jealous."

Mary delivered a compassionate hug reminiscent of their first night's dinner when John told them about losing Carson. "That was a wonderful and brave thing you did for that mother and her son today," she said. "I hate to sound like a mother, but I'm very proud of you." She held back a tear while taking John's arm and allowed him to escort her to a seat. Richard chugged and signaled the bartender to quickly refill his glass before catching up.

John combed the other seats for Rita like a pubescent boy searching to locate his crush at a high school pep rally. Someone, perhaps, with a large hat? *No,* he thought. *She wouldn't be rude enough to obstruct other people's view.* His hope died when the main lights cut off and a moving rainbow started the show.

Bim skated onto the ice with cocky, cruise director flare. John imagined Bim's pajamas were probably like one of those t-shirts made to look like a bikini, except Bim's surely had a black tuxedo façade. He used his cordless microphone to excite the crowd with a deep ring-announcer voice. Afterward, the spotlight, loyal as a seeing-eye dog, escorted him off center stage. The lights briefly fell to black before their full glory lit up the ice for the start of the first act.

John quickly fell under the spell of a dozen skaters dancing around to the beat of the famous disco anthem from *Saturday Night Fever.* The skaters' costumes took John back to his childhood and family trips to see the circus—a rare treat his mother saw no danger in. He was always permitted one souvenir and each year his pick was the same: a plastic sword with an ornate handle. In his backyard between the strings of maples guarding the property-line, John pretended he was a Persian prince; he played with the swords long after the bright cloth frayed loose on the handles, and the blades bent or cracked from his vicious attacks on unforgiving hardwoods. The circus provided teeming cups from magic waters, when, once a year, John's imagination could drink its fill.

Double axels and toe spins resurrected his childish delight in going to the circus. All John needed was cotton candy and the smell of sweat and animal dung. He loved every second like a kid depositing quarters in an old arcade game. Separately, each act differed greatly from the next. The performances shifted between fast songs and ballads, couple's skates and solo acts. Collectively, John considered the entire show as one symphonic piece that ebbed and flowed the way classical music does.

Where John deemed the men's costumes as distractions from their skating abilities, the women struck him as being beautiful ballerinas spinning around inside a glass snow-globe. The laser-beam lights bounced off the girls' sequined mini dresses and danced on John's face like fireflies.

The crowd let out a long sigh during the featured woman's solo skate when her attempt at a two-and-a-half ended with her ass kissing the ice.

"Ouch!" Mary flinched.

John leaned in. "I can relate."

Mary chuckled and patted his knee.

Cupping his mouth, Richard leaned in over Mary's opposite side and said, "Looks like she has enough padding to recover."

"You're terrible!" Mary whispered loudly.

The finale featured every skater arm-locked and high-kicking to "One" from the Broadway hit *A Chorus Line*. They slowly circled like a lawnmower blade's last two spins in order to reach every guest. Once the crowd finished their applause the athletes skated off behind a curtain and the lights returned to mostly white as John and the Clawsons remained seated, letting the crowd empty.

John's delight contradicted his bruised, swollen, and cracked face, like a mask illustrating both joy and sorrow. "Great show!" he said. "I think that was even better than the show in the theatre?"

"Yes," Mary agreed. "I always enjoy the ice shows more. They remind me of the Winter Olympics. Skating is just lovely—so graceful and elegant!"

"I like the short skirts," Richard confessed.

"And they say puberty only lasts a few years," Mary shook.

"You wouldn't change him," John said.

"No," she whispered. "No, I wouldn't."

After winking, John said, "Thanks again for the coffee. Was Blue Mountain worth seeing, Richard?"

Mary leaned back to create a speaking lane.

"It was! We both drink the stuff, and The Mavis Bank factory gives a damn fine tour. We've been to Jamaica several times, but today was our first trip up the mountain to see the beans and all. Mavis does everything from tree to bag."

"Just being in those lush mountains with the mist and the sounds from all the birds and animals was a treat," Mary said. "The coffee's good too…very mild, not bitter."

"Nothing worse than bitter coffee," Richard grimaced.

"I'll put that first on my list if I ever get back here."

"You should," Richard said, coveting his last gulp of wine. "The only bitch of it is getting there. A couple of hours on those roads treats the organs like popcorn, but I guess you got a taste of that yourself today, eh, John?"

"It was very different than driving in Kansas."

"I'm too old for rough roads," Richard added. "Or vibrating beds."

"How about water beds?" John joked.

"Only if it's a raft in our pool."

"Looks like we're about the last ones here," John observed.

"How 'bout a nightcap?" Richard suggested. "It's only ten-fifteen."

"You've had enough for one day, unless you want to spend tomorrow's allowance?" Mary scowled before raising an inquisitive brow.

"No, no, no!" Richard said. "It's a sea day…too much idle time to relinquish consumption! What would I do? The rock wall? Basketball? Even reading a good book is thirsty work!"

Enjoying Richard react to Mary's ultimatum, John said, "I've had a long day and think an early night would do my body good. I've been up way past my bedtime every night so far."

"Might we have the pleasure of seeing you tomorrow?" Mary asked.

"You can't hide. I know where you live," John teased.

"Good," Mary said as the three stood and stretched their stiff joints.

Richard asked delicately, "How about that other thing? Any updates?"

John played dumb. "What?"

"The hot tamale!"

"What my graceless husband means to ask is: How is Rita, dear?"

"I haven't heard from her today. I think it's wise to wait until Sunday to try and see her. I'm running out of body parts to injure."

"Yes…the head knows better than the heart," Mary said.

The two men followed Mary down the bleachers and out the lobby doors where the foyer outside buzzed with energy. People were coming and going from a dozen spots still teeming with activities. John witnessed one couple jubilantly kissing with their arms wrapped around one another and casino chips filling their hands.

"Are you still feeling fine, Rich?" John asked.

"Fine as cashmere, but thanks for asking. I plan on sending out invitations the day I decide to die."

"Which means he's going to make me do it," Mary said.

John laughed. "That's a piece of mail I don't want to see for a long time."

"I'll see what I can do," Richard said. "Rest up for a big sea day, my boy."

"I will," John said finishing hugs and handshakes. "I'll see you both tomorrow,"

"One more thing," Mary pointed upward. "Not to be perverse, but just because the head knows better, doesn't mean it's right." She parted with a little-girl wave.

Brows raised, Richard got the last words in. "Goodnight, my boy! See you tomorrow."

John took Mary's words for a long methodical walk around the ship's outside promenade as the warm breeze helped sooth chills from his sunburn. The moon shone like a night-light hung on a black wall. No one inside would know from movement that the sea waves were being pulled high. The salt air worked at prying John's constricted sinus passages open and the moon's light combined with the deck height to provide depth and dimension to an otherwise seemingly flat landscape.

John recognized the picture; he had seen it before. In his adolescent years he discovered it wasn't a long walk from Good Intent to the suburbs' sea of wheat. Whenever a farmer left one of their grand harvesting machines sitting unattended in a field, John would climb—until falling from his father's ladder—to its roof, where he sat as a spectator watching the baton of light being exchanged from sunset to twilight. On those rare, precious evenings before curfew, he imagined the world was made of boxes, and only rich or brave men built their homes on the top. During his stroll he recalled having brought a toy circus sword along to one of those tractor visits, where, on top of a John Deere, John Smith played king of the box.

The promenade wrapped around the bow below the ship's bridge and continued aft. Wind direction marked the only change until he passed the pools. He stopped in a rounded corner between port and stern, resting his forearms on the teak rail. To his left, rows of lounge chairs faced the churning wake of the ship's engines. He turned to study the vacant chairs, trying to imagine their past and future occupants and the reasons for their trip.

The faint sound of sexual groans broke his train of thought. A couple in the opposite corner, their chair wedged between two rows behind them and the front stern railing, sat facing each other. John could see from the couple's silhouette, and the rhythmic bob of a woman's head cast against the horizon glow, that some lucky guy was receiving an extreme lap-dance. The wind bent the woman's cries like flack from a shotgun blast—sometimes hitting John's ears. When she arched her back the moon's reflected beam illuminated a triangle between the woman's hairline and lower back. Her pelvic thrusts sent moon-silvered waves through her long hair, causing it to toss and flail. He could barely see the dark profile of her partner beneath her.

The shock of John's first voyeuristic experience prompted him first to flee, but then instead, to freeze. He was amazed at the audacity or freedom that drove the couple to have sex where any wandering passenger might see them. He remembered on several occasions, when they were young, making love to Page outdoors, but never in a place where there were high odds of being caught. Minutes passed as he stared, heart pounding, thinking he was wrong to watch. Suddenly, John thought of Rita, mentally imagining their faces on the anonymous couple, turning the public obscenity into a more appealing romantic bonding.

A flash of light ended John's fantasy. He couldn't tell where it came from, thinking maybe the couple were teenagers, newlyweds, or even porn stars on vacation snapping self-portraits. He ceased caring. The flash broke the spell, sending him back to earth. He turned away and sauntered back to his cabin. On the way, he continued his atypical lopsided conversation. "Were my own parents ever that passionate? They're like robots. Dad told me *work* was the best way to deal with Carson's death…Mom stops by once a week just to keep my dishes from piling up and to make sure I have enough toilet-paper…Lloyd talked about not wasting words…If he met my folks, he'd need to buy more than a vowel to get a sentence!"

Back in his cabin John threw his clothes on the ottoman, brushed his teeth, applied a light coat of aloe, and slipped into his freshly made bed. The soft sheets and black room almost compensated for his aching body. One last memory kept John from the day's finish line of sleep.

The inside of his eyelids provided the backdrop for a movie forgotten—until now. John saw an eleven-year-old boy entering his house on the eve of the circus' return to his hometown. While expediting homework in his room, the boy's jubilation was abruptly interrupted by his mother's screaming. The sounds were foreign and scary. He understood the meanings of *cheat*, *slut*, and even *asshole*. The boy turned on his radio and pulled a beat up toy sword from his closet and began playing by himself to stifle the noise of the fight coming from the kitchen. The house returned to its normality by dinnertime. When the boy asked, over mac and cheese, which day his family would visit the circus, his mother told him, "We aren't going this year. You're getting too old for the circus, anyway." He never heard his parents fight again, and they never saw another circus together as a family. That same evening just before bed, the boy placed the broken sword in the trash can beside his desk.

John finished his conversation with himself before falling into a deep sleep. "Why do the children always pay the price?"

DAY 6
(SEA DAY #2)

LET THE GAMES BEGIN

T HE PHONE CALL INTERRUPTED A sleep that John would have preferred to prolong, but his callers had other ideas.

"*Hello,*" John answered.

"Surf's up, dude!"

"Garrett?"

"Yeah! Mom said I should call before you left your cabin for the day."

John cracked an eye in the direction of the nightstand clock—7:32. "You still had time," John groaned. "What can I do for you, Garrett?"

"I'm going to hit the wave-rider pool after breakfast…thought you might want to join me for some boogie-boarding?"

"Wouldn't you rather find some kids your own age to do that stuff with?"

"Nah. Kids my age are annoying. They talk too much. I like hanging with old, I mean… *older* people. They listen better to kids, although I'm still not sure how much they actually hear." Garrett's voice tapered off as he thought about his father. "Young people don't have much luck changing older people's minds. Mom says it's because older people have more experience, but I think it's because they have more habits. So…you in, or what?"

"How about nine?"

"See ya there!"

The cabin's lack of light—the only breaches were a digital clock and the dying hallway light bleeding from under the door—helped John fall back asleep until the telephone rang like a snooze button.

"*Hello,*" John answered.

"Good morning, dear! I hope I'm not waking you?"

"Mary?"

"Yes. I thought if I waited 'til eight you would be up, but not out yet."

John cracked his eye again—7:58. "You thought right. I just got out of the shower." He was pleasantly surprised his lie caused no guilty feelings. It seemed justified and appropriate, like the prior day's fight.

"Good! How do you feel about bingo?"

"I've never been a lucky man."

"Perhaps you're due?"

"I would like to believe *long past,*" he laughed.

"Well…Richard and I are playing at five-thirty in the Sky Lounge. There will be tea, treats, and hopefully, a glorious sunset. It's not bingo for the whole ship, just an intimate game offered for passengers who booked suites."

"My cabin's far from a suite."

"We are permitted a guest and immediately thought of you." Mary paused before continuing. "I believe the environment will be safe—unless you forget to blow on your tea," she giggled.

"Sounds perfect…if I don't win, the conversation will be worth the agony of defeat."

"Great! I'll tell Richard. Just give our name if anyone questions you."

"Will do. Thanks for the invite, Mary."

"See you then. Have a great day, John!"

"You too."

John blindly hung up the phone and toyed with the idea of fifteen more minutes of sleep, but decided against it, thinking the phone would again punish him, or Sylvia would break into his room—he couldn't remember if he hung the Do Not Disturb sign the night before.

Standing in front of the bathroom mirror, John thought the aloe had done its job, as his skin looked worse than it felt. His eye had softened to a milk chocolate brown and a good starter scab sealed his lip. A minor pain from somewhere behind reminded him of his bruised back. He twisted to investigate, but the mirror didn't reveal any strong bruising. Oxygen flowed freely through his nostrils, telling him the swelling had subsided.

"Everything considered…I feel pretty good!" he said smiling at his reflection and then brushing his teeth.

Five minutes later—foregoing a shower for the chlorinated wave machine—John was fully dressed and ready for breakfast. "I could get used to wearing this uniform every day," he said, while collecting his glasses, room card, and watch. "Maybe I should get a job as a lifeguard at the YMCA when I get home? I would have a better chance of being a hero there than working at a rubber band factory," he laughed. "This change stuff isn't so bad…at least when it comes to small things—like wearing my bathing suit every day." He flipped over the door tag to Please Service and headed to breakfast.

At the buffet, he did a full lap looking over people's shoulders, mentally filling his plate the same way he would have on any other day, but suddenly that seemed too safe and boring. Inside, a boy standing atop a tractor was screaming for something new. The satellite stations offered the new and unknown, so he stopped at one with the shortest line.

When it came his turn he asked the chef, "What are those?"

"These are crepes, sir, a thin pancake if you will, filled with just about anything you can imagine," said the chef, a crescent grin accentuating an overly rounded head. "Would you care for one?"

"Yes! Yes, I would…raspberries?"

"Certainly! Fresh made whip cream?"

"Yes. That sounds good. Thank you!"

Ricky from Columbia poured batter onto a round hotplate that had no sides or handles. In a matter of seconds he used his spatula to fold the berries and cream inside the crepe, giving it the look of a loosely rolled cigar; he handed the plated crepe to John. "It's good with powdered sugar, but we have many options," Ricky said, extending an open palm to an array of syrups and toppings.

"Thank you, Ricky. I'll trust your recommendation," John said with an assured, pleasing voice.

John completed his break in routine by choosing soy sausage patties over the meat version and tomato juice instead of orange. A sense of satisfaction won out over the nagging voice that must have been hiding behind his eyes, whispering to return to line for scrambled eggs and real sausage as John found a seat and eyed the unconventional breakfast.

By the end of his meal the nagging voice—an invisible gatekeeper of sorts, probably a cousin of conscience, its sole purpose to protect and warn against mutations—let down its guard and welcomed the most recent anomaly into John's traditional mind. Soy patties, tomato juice, and especially sweet crepes were now allowed to come and go without argument whenever future cravings arose. His routine's gatekeeper was obviously growing tired from the week's assault.

To kill time before meeting Garrett, John took his new predilections for a walk around the top deck. He started towards the bow, figuring a three-quarter lap would help the digestion. Numerous diehard runners, dressed like they were in a televised marathon and taking advantage of the early hour, whizzed by John, leaving drops of sweat in their wake. The sound of encroaching feet smacking the deck made John question his lane. Like any good driver, he moved as far to the right as the railing permitted. A soft wind fluttered over the ship as if two people were slowly shaking a giant blanket and the salt air streamed through John's sinuses. His body was rebuilding itself.

He rounded the starboard side and stopped near a small group of passengers looking intently out to sea. The sinister sound of churning rotor blades reached John's ears before he located the black mark splitting the seam between blue sky and water. Everyone anxiously watched the speck grow and take form.

"Coast Guard," a man said, not five feet away, built short and square with no extra length in his limbs or neck.

"How can you tell?" John asked.

The man turned and read John's t-shirt with a blank expression before replying. "Sound mostly—Sikorsky. Nobody else would be flying a helicopter this far out to sea." He went back to watching the bird's approach.

"Were you in?"

The man turned back. "Marines—sixty-eight thru seventy-two," he said curtly and went back to studying the flight path.

Within minutes, the black speck evolved into a massive billboard advertising American might and rescue; the helicopter was orange and white with a black nose and US COAST GUARD on her sides. John noticed the helicopter pad railings were collapsed and the mast had been lowered to make room for landing. The crowd thickened on the observation deck above the bridge and John listened to speculation and wise-cracks from the assembly of passengers. One man said, "They heard there was free food!" A woman's voice said, "Somebody must be sick." And another said, "One of the crew or passengers probably did something wrong."

The sea was calm and the winds gentle; still, the ship slowed but did not stop. The pilot put on a flawless show by keeping pace and landing the hulking craft on the green circle marked with a bulls-eye H.

John checked his watch—9:01. He gave up his railing spot to the next person crowding him from behind and squeezed through the crowd towards the port side. *Will or Garth will know why the Coast Guard is here. I'll ask them after I meet Garrett.*

Upon reaching the wave pool, John found the design much like the scoop of a giant blue snow shovel, flat to the ground at the blade and tilted up about 30 degrees in the back, where riders entered into a wading area. He studied the three thousand gallons per minute pumped back up the slope in a thin sheet, like a continuous retreat of ocean water from a beach. The undertow rushed over the crest, collected in the wading area, and was then funneled back down to continue its cycle.

Two teens, separated by a divider, their bellies pressed firmly against foam boards, were twisting and shredding like acrobatic salmon. Nervousness set in, but not from performance anxiety; there were dozens of spectators gathered around all four sides. Unlike natural performers who live for an audience, John had found even the smallest tasks were harder for him with people watching. He thought back to early high school while the boys rode the current.

Nancy Smith, along with a hip priest at the church the Smith's attended, talked John into becoming an altar-boy during his tenth grade year. When spiritual fulfillment—his mother's selling point—didn't work, she asked him to go to the church rectory and just meet with Father Pauli.

John recalled the anxiety he felt knocking on Father Pauli's door. It instantly subsided when the priest opened the door and spoke his first words: "I love those guys! Saw them live last year." John had forgotten about his t-shirt. The Police were in their prime long before Sting ever went solo. John's parents didn't allow him to go to concerts—citing drugs, fights, and harmfully high decibel levels as the reasons for their decision—but, as long as the group wasn't too offensive in appearance, sound, or lyrics, John could listen to their music and wear a non-authentic concert version of their t-shirts. That day John Smith and Father Pauli formed a friendship that started with their love of a British rock group. Although their friendship lasted for many years, John's stint as an altar boy lasted only nine masses.

He couldn't stand being watched by the entire congregation—about 125 souls on a good Sunday. Each mass his eyes got dry and he sweat so profusely that his hands got slick and clammy. He dropped so many hosts and spilled so much wine that St. Matthew's Church had to order larger quantities and steam clean the altar carpet after every-other mass that John worked. He missed his cues, fell face forward twice tripping on his robe, and once sent a thurible containing smoking incense into the front row—luckily hanging onto the chain, he barely missed hitting an elderly woman.

The final straw occurred at his ninth mass when John fainted while assisting Father Pauli with communion. His only job was to hold a paten at breast level for each person receiving communion. Patti Higgins happened to be in line that day—she was two years older, attended John's school, and was considered by most to be the largest breasted girl in school. John spied her approaching in line. She wore a dress conservatively cut at the neckline with buttons running down to waist level. Her hands were folded, but hardly noticeable under what looked like small watermelons stuffed into her dress. His face flushed. Sacrilegious thoughts flamed amorous feelings. As Father Pauli raised the Eucharist and said, "The body of Christ," John extended the paten by its wooden handle. The body tends to follow the direction of the eyes, and John's eyes never stood a chance. His hand had turned over a few degrees in its weakness, so when he extended the paten it was vertical instead of horizontal. Unfortunately, the dress buttons were too few and spaced too far apart. The paten slid right between, popping the top button free from the material. John didn't help matters by wrenching his wrist, turning the plate to its intended horizontal position. The bottom button, and John, hit the floor in unison.

He woke to the faces of his parents, Father Pauli, and a wide-faced smile from his fellow altar-boy. Nancy Smith, a horrified look on her face, was fanning her son with a mass card while the two men looked more sympathetic—almost amused. Father Pauli dismissed the congregation after ensuring the crowd their sins were forgiven up to date. Father Pauli helped John to the dressing room and told him not to worry, that it could have happened to anyone. "She was quite blessed," he said. The two mutually agreed that morning that John's service would be recognized by God and no fault would be bestowed upon him if he chose to quit the altar service. "Surely you will have greater callings," Father Pauli assured. Fortunately for John, the episode happened in April and Patti Higgins graduated the following month and went off to study medicine at Johns Hopkins University. Years later, he heard through the grapevine she was working as a technician to help develop new drugs to treat breast cancer. John smiled, remembering the buxom girl he never even spoke one word to.

"You're late!" Garrett said, punching John gently in the arm.

John turned. "Morning, son!" Using the word *son* came unexpectedly and made him feel a bit unfaithful to his own son. "I got caught up at the bow. There must have been some kind of medical emergency, 'cause a Coast Guard helicopter landed on the ship."

"No shit! Is it still there?"

The loud music used to pump up both crowd and riders around the wave pool made it impossible for John to know if the chopper had taken off. He gazed forward and scanned the sky. "I think it's gone, Garrett, see that black speck?" John asked, pointing to the sky.

"Maybe somebody died?"

"Possibly," John shrugged. "You going to show me how to ride this thing without the Captain having to call a medivac for me?"

Garrett laughed. "It's just like boogie boarding in the ocean, but easier. This thing's controlled—not like real waves."

"I've only been to the ocean three times and never used anything except my own body to surf."

Garrett looked perplexed. "*Really?* Not even when you were a kid?"

"My parents never took me to the ocean. My dad was always too busy with work and my mom said it was too far and a waste of money. We used to go to a local recreational area to swim in the summer. My ex-wife and I took Carson three times when he was young."

"Where'd you go?"

"Galveston, Texas."

Garrett squinted his face.

"What?" John said.

"Nothing. I guess I don't think of beaches when I think of Texas."

John grinned. "You're an east coast kid. I bet California kids feel the same way. If you were raised in a place like Kansas it would make more sense."

"I guess." Garrett seemed full of energy, even standing still. "You ready? We should be up soon and I want to put the Terminator in my bag."

"Lead the way!"

They entered the short foam walls that comprised the wave pool perimeter. Garrett unstrapped his leg, stowed it in his bag, and sat down in a pre-arranged chair; Dani had already signed her son's waiver. John sat with his feet dangling in the backwash of the pool's collection area thinking the crest of the wave looked higher from behind than it did below.

"Two minutes 'til your turn," an instructor told John.

John jokingly asked, "What are the odds of getting hurt?" The instructor paused, his eyes rolling up and down over John. The damage to John's face was obvious. Only a couple of scratches on his legs were visible and his t-shirt covered the rest. Realizing his question had opened a window for a multitude of snappy comebacks, he added, "For a klutzy person that is?"

The instructor smiled. "It's all rubber coated...pretty hard to get hurt. It gets easier to pull a muscle or bruise something the more vertical you try to get. You body boarding or using one of our wave-boards to try and stand-up surf?"

"The lay down method should be plenty," John laughed. "As I'm sure you can tell, I'm not doing too great with pushing my luck."

"You'll be fine!"

"Any advice?"

"Just go with it and have fun. It's a blast!"

"Let's hear it for Dan and Kerri!" another instructor yelled into his microphone as the crowd cheered. "Next up, we have Garrett and John. Let's make some noise!"

Dan and Kerri handed their boards off to the instructors. The crowd made John feel like he was back in church. He didn't know which was worse: facing a subdued church congregation or fifty half-naked, half-drunk, screaming cruise passengers about to critique his every move. Seeing the instructors help Garrett to a place where he could drop-in, brought perspective to John. Garrett fell face forward down the rushing slope as soon as the instructors let go of his armpits. Like everything else John saw him do, his disability didn't hinder Garrett in the least. He used his arms to shred the face of the wave in typewriter rhythm. His single leg acted like a rudder, helping him change direction and yo-yo up and down the slope. Barrel rolls and figure-eights were executed with ease.

"You going?" the instructor asked. "You only get so much time."

John stood watching Garrett with the gaze of a prideful father. "Huh? Oh, yeah! I just wanted to watch him for a minute." Pounding his chest two times, John summoned his inner dragon while recalling his Jamaican flip and leapt over the crest. The bodyboard smacked down and water began spraying John's face like a 3-D movie come to life.

"Everybody give it up for John, who decided to join the party!" the instructor teased. In turn, the crowd raised their drinks and hollered.

Modern, fast paced, California-style music machine-gunned through the air. John's substitute shower provided all the water pressure a bather could hope for. His attempt at a barrel roll, like his lagoon flip, had too much rotation. The current shot him up and over the slope back into the wading area. Not allowing the feeling of being regurgitated fish food faze him, John dove back over.

Frolicking, gliding, spinning, the thing John found most enjoyable was his inability to not smile. His smile felt different, unlike the smiles he put on for work with no more thought than putting on his underwear in the morning. This smile radiated unrelentingly while he swished back and forth. Real smiles aren't courtesies or costumes, they can't be forced, faked, planned, or controlled by any means—babies don't try. The smile John wore was a product of pure joy and he could no better hold it back than he could the water streaming over him. Real smiles are reactions to humor, ecstasy, beauty, and kindnesses. Real smiles are signals that joy is near, and where there is joy, love isn't far off. Zip lines and bungee jumping, scuba diving and water sports brought flashes of joy back to John—the joy of genuine smiles. In the midst of his perma-grin, just before his time ended, the noise from the cheering crowd reminded him that joy could only turn into love if it was shared with someone.

I wish Rita was here.

"Time's up!" the microphone instructor announced. "Everyone give it up for John and Garrett!"

Garrett rotated 180 degrees and let the water push him back into the wading area where an instructor helped him back to the chair. "Nice job, kid! Really…nice job! You're an inspiration."

Garrett looked him in the eyes. "'Cause I'm good or 'cause I have one leg?"

The instructor let out a small burst of air through his nose and grinned. "Because you're *damn* good *and* because you don't allow the other to stand in your way…so to speak," he winked.

"Next time I'll use the stand-up board."

"I bet you will!"

Garrett reattached the Terminator while John accepted a towel from Garrett's instructor. "Hell of a kid you got there," the instructor said.

"Oh, he's not…yes. He sure is!" John said, smiling from ear to ear.

"If you want to come back later we can help you with your barrel rolls," the instructor jabbed.

"Thanks for the offer but I think, at least for me, my satisfaction comes from the attempt—not from perfection."

The instructor smiled and patted John's shoulder. "I can tell that about you. Enjoy the rest of your day, sir."

Garrett and John dried off in the increasingly hot sun while playing eighteen holes of miniature golf. It came as no shock to John's competitive ego when Garrett led by ten strokes after seventeen holes, including four holes-in-one to John's one lucky ricochet.

"What time is it?" Garrett asked.

"Eleven-fifteen," John said. "Why? You got a date?"

"Yeah. We both do. With the rock-wall."

"Somehow I knew you were going to say that sooner or later. Haven't you shown me up enough?"

Garrett laughed. "It's there. We should use it. What's the good of paying for things you don't use?"

"You've got a point." John thought back to throwing his TV away. "But no racing against each other. You can climb like a monkey if you want, but I'm going to spider my way up—deal?"

"That's cool. Mom and Will are coming. I'll race Will."

"I thought the staff couldn't use the passenger amenities?"

"I don't know," Garrett said, lining up his starting putt on the eighteenth hole. "I asked Mom last night if he could go and she said she'd check. This morning she told me they would meet us at eleven." Garrett brushed his putter. They both watched in anticipation as the ball rose, fell, and turned over a series of small mounds. The ball's final roll, as if electronically programed, dove over the cup lip. "Yes! That's five holes-in-one!"

John offered knuckles. "Nice putt!" Mentally replaying the boy's line, John lined up and swung. The orange Titleist rolled three inches left of the hole, careened against the back wall, and bounced two feet in front of the cup.

"Nice putt," Garrett said, twirling his putter. "Ready for the wall?"

"Ready as I'll ever be." John cleaned up the last two feet and looked at Garrett. "It'll be a nice change of pace to go up instead of down."

"That reminds me, it sure would be cool to see the bridge…don't ya think?"

"They probably do tours."

"Mom checked. We needed to sign up a couple of days ago," Garrett sighed.

"I don't think I can help you much there, my friend."

"It's okay. I can take a cyber-tour on-line."

The two kids—at least that was how John felt about himself around Garrett—signed in with the rock wall attendant. By the time they suited up with harnesses, helmets, and shoes, Will and Dani had arrived and signed in. The four rock-mates greeted each other inside the railing that separated spectators from participants.

"There's my two hot surfer dudes!" Dani said. "Catch any tubes?" she asked, shaking her hand with an outstretched thumb and pinky.

Rolling his eyes, Garrett said, "It doesn't make *tubes,* it makes current."

"My bad," she said, slapping Garrett's helmet and kissing his cheek. "Morning, John! You taking Will's advice and having some fun?"

John straightened to attention. "I am!"

Will gazed at John's shirt. "Not worried about pissing off any ex-Naval officers on the ship, I see—or Marines who may be vacationing?"

"Huh?" John remembered his shirt. "Oh…I didn't think about that. It was my son's." He held the front of the shirt as if Carson was still inside. It depicted a civilian's back, above him were four men sitting at four desks, each representing the four major branches of the military. A line of young men waited in front of the Army desk while the other desks remained empty. The caption read: *Real Recruits Choose the Army.* "He got it from a recruiter when he was a teenager." John paused. "No wonder that guy gave me the cold shoulder."

"What's that?" Will asked.

"Oh, nothing," John dismissed him with a single downward hand gesture, "just a guy beside me watching the helicopter."

Dani walked up very close to Will and said, "We're going to go first, okay?"

"Sure. John and me will watch from *behind* while we catch up," Will said with a smitten expression. Dani walked away with a little extra hip sway like she had the first day the three met. "You talking about the Coast Guard chopper this morning, John?"

"Yeah. You see it?"

"Heard it. I'm working at the pool."

"How did you get time to do this? Thought you guys weren't allowed to join the passenger activities?"

"They make exceptions if you ask nice enough. I got about forty-five minutes." Will pinched his plain white t-shirt. "I had to run to the cabin to change clothes so I blend in like a passenger, and I have to run back before returning to the pool. Management is more likely to okay stuff when they know you're close to the end of your rotation, like I am."

"You must be looking forward to vacation…six weeks?"

"Yeah." Will's voice trailed off as he watched Dani and Garrett start their climb. "Maybe a little longer this time." He quickly changed the subject when he saw John wanting to ask a question. "Pretty cool watching those choppers land on the ship, huh?"

"Very! Do you know why they were here?"

Will smirked. "Of course I do!"

"I figured…*Mr. Catcher*."

"Coast Guard visits aren't that rare—usually for medical emergencies that the ship can't handle. Today was a two-fer."

"A what?"

"They came to collect two employees."

"Why?"

"Because they didn't like their jobs. My dad told me once, if you don't like your job or agree with your boss, one of two things are destined to happen: either you'll quit or be fired." Will looked quizzically. "Do you like your job, John?"

"I never thought about it when I had a family, but now…it just seems like something to fill the time and pay the bills."

The two stood with their backs against the railing watching the neck-and-neck race between mother and son.

"Seems strange sending the Coast Guard for two workers who quit or got fired," John said.

Will huffed. "One intentionally cut off his pinky in a water tight door last night and the other was a gofer-golfer."

"Is that another one of your esoteric sayings?"

"He got busted for drugs."

"Don't you guys get tested?"

"At the beginning of your contract, after that, chances are slim. They do random screenings once or twice a tour, but they only test a small percentage of the twelve hundred employees. They called me once; fucking pissed me off too. I worked all afternoon at the pool and finished with six hours in the disco. I hit my rack at three-thirty in the morning, only to be woken up an hour later by my boss informing me I had won the random lottery. When I got to the infirmary there were almost fifty people wearing PJ's waiting to see one doctor and one nurse. I lost it. I raised my voice and demanded to see who was in charge of making us all wait—I had to be back at work in four hours! Everyone in line was shocked by my audacity—*crazy American*, they probably thought. Head of security guy escorted me to the front so I could get back to bed as soon as possible. They don't like Americans influencing the rest of the crew or doing anything to cause bad press."

"So you got right through?"

"After thirty minutes drinking water," Will laughed. "My dumb ass did what everyone does when they first wake up—I took a piss. It took three bottles of water 'til I could fill that damn plastic cup. *But*, they never picked my name for another one. Dumb-ass management with zero common sense!"

"Is that how they caught this guy?"

"No. I mean I doubt it. This guy was a cocktail waiter. He played golf every week in Jamaica before he had to work his shift. His caddie always runs off at the second hole and returns like clockwork when the guy is on the sixth. Well, the caddie isn't leaving 'cause the guy needs more balls. He goes somewhere, nobody knows where, to pick up cocaine. The employee tapes it under the arches of his feet so even when security makes us take off our sandals they don't see it. He was bringing it aboard mostly for the entertainers who need something to maintain their already wacky personalities. Word is, every run made four times what he made in a month working for the ship. The quantities kept getting bigger and eventually everyone knew he was doing it. It was only a matter of time before security caught him or somebody snitched."

"Huh. I guess the Coast Guard *would* be interested in that. What about the other guy? Why would anyone intentionally cut off their finger?"

"Same reasons: money and job dissatisfaction. He was a Filipino engine room worker—shit job, low man on the totem-pole stuff. It's an unadvertised fact that the company pays five grand for the loss of a finger. Some guys get drunk and wait until the middle of the night when most people are asleep. They hold up their finger—pinkies are most expendable and easiest to hold against the door frame—and hit the button to close the steel water tight. The anticipation must suck—they take a long time to fully shut!"

"But, don't they get fired?"

"Yeah. Hence the helicopter, but five grand goes a long way back in the Philippines. He can buy a new house and take care of his family for a long time with that much."

Dani joined the men. "He wants to race you, Will," she said, removing her blue helmet. "Do you mind skipping your turn, John?"

Holding his chin, John tried looking like a veteran climber. "Not at all. It'll give me more time to plan my route."

Will put his helmet on. "It should be easy for you, Butterfly. Just flap your wings, they'll take you anywhere."

Dani assumed Will's spot. "Thanks for entertaining Garrett again. He likes the teen center, but he doesn't like to spend all day there like the girls."

"Where's Jill?" John asked.

"Everyone's at the pool. Buffy's in charge. She might be an airhead, but she's good with hair and kids—and a good friend...unlike Elli."

"I take it you two aren't getting along?"

Dani's face turned sour. "You know what she traded her daughter in for yesterday?" John stayed quiet, knowing an answer was on its way. "She paid fifty bucks to gain access to one of those hedonistic resorts where everyone runs around naked. She spent the day on the beach, topless, smoking marijuana with complete strangers. Then, they took turns in a mechanical bull contest—naked! You fucking believe that?"

"She told you this?"

"She wouldn't dare! She told Buffy. Buffy told me. I don't want to argue with her any more until we get back home. All it would do is spoil our last two days. I did ask if she had seen George yesterday."

John perked up. "What did she say?"

"She said she ran into him last night but I didn't ask where."

"And...did you ask about the brothel in Cozumel?"

"I *did*. She said she confronted George about it and he said he followed the ship workers, thinking it was an unadvertised local's bar. She said he had a couple beers and figured out it was a whorehouse after the girls kept approaching him. She said he learned the truth from the bartender and tipped him five bucks to put a black X on his stamp so the girls would leave him in peace, thinking he had already bought a girl and was *spent*."

"And you believe that?"

"No. But Elli does. I told her she was an idiot. She said *whatever* and that I should mind my own business. And then I said, 'Ignorance is bliss.'"

John tried steering the conversation away from Elli, who had been nothing but mean to him. In two days he would never have to witness or hear about her narcissistic tendencies again. "Looks like Will picked the most difficult path," John pointed.

Dani cracked an understanding grin. "He's leveling the playing field without making Garrett feel inferior. A real keeper that Catcher, can't believe he's not married. There something wrong with him I should know about?"

"Not that I'm aware of."

"Oh! Pictures! I always forget to take pictures." Dani started rummaging through her bag. "It's never here!" She walked closer to the wall and cupped her mouth. "Garrett! Do you have my phone?"

Garrett turned his neck as much as he could. "In my bag!"

Dani found the iPhone wrapped inside a towel. "That kid loves to take pictures and his mother hates to," she chuckled.

"I can snap some if you want to stand over there underneath them."

"Thanks, John. That would be great!"

Garrett's Terminator worked surprisingly well, propelling him three quarters up the rock face. He compensated with his good leg and strong arms.

Will's path had him stuck underneath a ledge, his back angling more to the ground than out to sea. Garrett's wiry frame and long fingers were better suited for keeping him connected than Will's solid build. Gravity eventually won out over great strength and John's third picture captured Will's surrender.

"We have a winner!" John said.

Dani laughed and clapped. "Nice try, Will! You won, honey! But don't stop until you reach the top!"

"Let's see how far I can get before he reaches the top," John said, handing off the camera.

"You can do it, John." She turned her fingers into a V and pointed at her eyes.

"Eye of the tiger!"

John turned back before making his first foothold just in time to see Will and Dani sneaking a small, but fully pressed kiss. Their affection made him feel both happy and jealous. He used the idea that if he made it to the top, Rita would be there to reward him with a similar kiss. Methodically, he began to climb.

Five minutes later, Garrett had not only rung the bell, signaling his conquest, but he was down, unhooked, and drinking water next to Will and Dani while John, shakily clung one step below his triumph.

"You're almost there!" Dani yelled.

"Come on, Butterfly!" Will said. "I have to go back to work! Use your wings!"

"He's got it," Garrett said confidently.

Exhausted, fingers aching, John turned his head. He felt a trembling three quarters up, and a warning from his cautionary voice; it was sending waves through his body signaling danger. Inside, he screamed at the voice, reassuring it that the ropes would save him. The voice gave way to the demands of his burning limbs. With deep breaths, just two feet away from something he honestly wanted, he stared out to sea. "It won't come to you by staring at it," he whispered. "Even if it does…it will blow right by you. You have to earn it. Take it. Cherish it." He looked up, took another deep breath, and pushed with every tired fiber in his body, until—*ring*. He imagined Rita and Carson congratulating him with hugs and kisses. John let out a deep sigh, released his trembling muscles and allowed himself to drift back down like a fallen angel, arms limp and sprawled out. Cheers from the ground crew brought John back to life. They greeted him as if he had just scored the winning touchdown.

"Great climb," Will said. "I didn't know if I was going to last to see it. I got to get back," he said looking at his watch.

"What time is it," Dani asked.

"Eleven-forty," Will returned.

Dani looked at Garrett. "Did you tell John about his appointment?"

"Oops," Garrett frowned. "I forgot. You were coming here anyway."

"Yes, but the reason for you calling him so early was to tell him before he made plans!" Dani said, giving her son the evil eye. "John, did you make any plans for this afternoon?"

Still trying to catch his breath. "I have to meet Richard and Mary at five-thirty for bingo, but nothing else. Why?"

Dani perked up. "Good! You better go grab some lunch then. You need to be at the spa by twelve forty-five."

"Why?" John gasped.

Shaking her finger, Dani said, "Didn't your mother teach you to never ask *why* when a woman tells you to do something?"

"All the time, 'til I got married, then my wife took over the job," he feigned a laugh.

"Good," she said. "Spa, twelve forty-five. *You*, I'll see at the bar," she said to Will. "Garrett, are you coming with me?"

"I'm going to stay for a couple more turns."

"Have fun!" Will said, winking at John like he knew something John didn't, before jogging to his cabin. "Later everyone!"

"I'm going back to the estrogen crowd," Dani said. "*You*…climb great. I love you. *You*…go eat. Spa, twelve forty-five!"

In unison, John and Garrett answered, "Yes, ma'am."

UTOPIA

Lunch was an opportunity for more experimenting, this time with selections of lobster salad, figs, asparagus and goat cheese quiche rolls, and pumpkin bread. John picked a dark German beer—which he couldn't pronounce even after the bartender made the recommendation—to wash down the exotic flavors. His cautionary voice was now ironically busy opening doors instead of guarding them. *Change* poured into its new home, enticing John to sample new and endless choices. Prior to the cruise, he thought of the word *adventure* as something to describe a *Star Wars* movie, not a realistic way to live.

Having spent more time than usual enjoying lunch, he was kept from checking emails before his appointment; John had to hurry to get to the spa by 12:45.

The spa lobby had the feel and smell of a botanical garden—or a Beverly Hills plastic surgeon's office. Instrumental music flowed with the soothing sounds from a water feature. Exotic orchids served as knick-knacks on the side tables between each of the four ergonomically designed Swedish chairs and rainforest granite reception desk. The air was fresh, crisp, and clean like January air in a ski resort.

Helen, from England, greeted John with a warm smile. She looked to be in her twenties with pale skin and bobbed, ash-blonde hair. "Good afternoon," she said. "May I help you?"

"Ah…I was told to come here at twelve forty-five." The atmosphere seemed almost sacred to John. Out of respect, he removed his ball-cap on approaching the counter.

Helen exposed a lopsided grin, much like Rita had when John met her. "You wouldn't happen to be Mr. Smith, would you?"

Trying harder to sound witty and comfortable with a new experience, John replied, "I didn't know I had become famous?"

"Fame is not nearly as rewarding as having real friends…Ms. Green called yesterday and made your appointment. She said we should take excellent care of you!"

"She shouldn't have," he said, looking a bit embarrassed. "But, how did you know I was Mr. Smith?"

"She said you would look very kind and…" Choosing her words carefully, "Slightly wounded."

"Thank you. And *beat-up* are probably better words."

"Not at all, Mr. Smith."

"John. Please. Call me John."

"Are you ready to feel like a new man, John?"

"If you only knew," he laughed.

"We have all your treatments lined up. All you need to do is relax and enjoy."

Feeling it was an important detail, he declared, "I've never been to a spa before, just the steam room in the YMCA back home."

She wanted to laugh, but kept a professional demeanor. "I think you will find us to be much nicer than your YMCA. The only con against becoming addicted to spa treatments is: like any habit, it can get expensive. Fortunately for you, everything has been taken care of by Ms. Green. I promise you will enjoy your time with us. Please. Follow me and I'll show you to your villa where you can store your things and change into one of our comfy robes."

Helen informed a second receptionist to watch the front before leading John down a hall, along the way, pointing out the salon where he was to have his first treatment. Around the corner, they arrived at a formidable door resembling the one guarding the Clawson's suite. Helen tapped four numbers into the digital door lock and entered. John gazed stupidly at the palace before him. *"Holy cow!"*

"What do you think?"

"Are you sure you didn't mix up the reservations?"

Helen laughed. "No. It's in the name of John Smith until five."

Suspiciously, John said, "A name as common as portholes on a cruise ship…sure there's not more than one onboard?"

"I think Ms. Green got the right one." John stayed put while Helen began showing the vast open room in realtor style—minus the eagerness for a commission. "Everything you need should be here: dry sauna, hydro-therapy pool with rain shower, private water closet next to your massage tables, heated lounge chairs, four variable temperature showers with mood lighting and aroma infusion, and over here," she motioned to John to follow. "This room offers a place for you to relax between or after treatments. As you can see, we have prepared fresh fruit and champagne. The cooler is stocked with juice and water—all complimentary of course. What do you think of the view?"

John looked out at the sea through the giant picture window bookended with two couches. "I guess it'll do."

Helen couldn't tell if he was being facetious or not. She had learned not to judge people based upon looks or things they said. She had seen millionaires dressed as casually as John and vice versa; she had dealings with well-spoken, smartly dressed guests who fought over every dollar or treatment minute.

"Your first appointment is a manicure, pedicure. Go ahead and take a shower and then use the robe and slippers on either of the massage tables to dress. There is a small closet beside the bathroom where you can store your clothes. When you're ready, just go back to the salon I pointed out on the way here. I'll let them know you're coming. You have two treatments after that—both in this room—so come back here when you finish your nail treatment. The code to get in is 1-2-3-4. Simple enough?"

"I can remember that."

"Do you have any questions for me, John?"

"Yeah. Ah…so, other than the robe, I'll be…naked?"

Helen kept a straight face. "Correct. The masseuse will announce herself before entering. Ms. Green assumed you would prefer a female?"

"Yes. I think my first time should be with a woman," he said, thinking he was getting better at sounding cute.

"Good!" Helen grinned. "She will direct you. I assure you it's all done very discreetly. They're trained to protect modesty. Anything else?"

"I guess not. But…is it common for men to get their nails done?"

"It *is*," said Helen, still grinning at John's reticence. "Just think of it as a massage for your hands and feet."

"Okay. I'm getting used to trying new things," he said. "I had figs and quiche for lunch!"

Helen laughed. "That's a commendable attitude, John. If you have any more questions, there is a phone in your sitting area. Just press nine to reach me."

"Thank you, Helen!"

"Enjoy your afternoon, John." Helen paused at the door before leaving. "Oh…the volume controls for the music are right here," she said, turning up the sensuous instrumental music.

John was too busy looking around. By the time the increase in volume registered, the door closed behind Helen.

He showered in a glass and marble tiled area, exposed to the majority of the twelve-hundred square foot villa that was more appropriately designed for Aquaman than a rubber band factory manager from Kansas. Luxury took some getting used to as he washed with herbal shampoo versus the more medicinally scented miniatures Sylvia left behind each day in John's towel swan. Part of him felt like a king, while another part felt like he had just broken into a king's home and was now showering in his living room. Still, he quickly rationalized that this sort of change was something to which he could gladly grow accustomed.

Helen had not embellished a bit about the robe being comfy. The plush, white cotton robe stamped with the spa's insignia—Pamper Me Spa & Health Club—rubbed his naked body like a million cotton balls. He ripped open the plastic bag containing new flip-flops and headed for the nail salon.

Not knowing what to expect, John paused outside the entrance and tightened his cotton belt, so as not to accidentally expose himself to a bunch of strange women. Once secured, he opened the glass door. An attractive Asian woman without a visible pore on her face immediately greeted him by his first name, a familiarity he assumed she received from Helen. She escorted him to an elaborate and more comfortable kind of barber's chair, where two more Asian women stood ready to begin sanding, soaking, buffing, and massaging his hands and feet. If only Page could see him now; she'd think he must have gone mad, looking like a polar bear at the Playboy mansion.

Submissive discomfort set in as he waited for direction from the two women. He skipped "Hello" and went straight to: "I've never done this before," choking nervously at the two smiling faces. "You're not going to…paint my nails are you?"

Latishar, from Thailand, surprised John by speaking with very little accent. "Are you sure? I think midnight blue would *really* look good on you."

Before John could respond, Maelynn, from China, said, "How about a simple high-gloss clear coat?"

The two women let John squirm in the chair as he tried to figure out if they were serious. If he walked out of the spa with blue nails, surely people would make judgments. Black eye, split lip, and colored nails. No man should wear color, he thought, unless it was from the sun or his clothes. "I, uh,—"

The two women laughed and started pinching John's shoulders. "Don't worry, John," said Latishar. "We are going to take good care of you. Your nails will look the same, but better, when we are finished."

"Okay." John thought saying something cute again might ease his nervousness. "I'm in your hands! I have to warn you though, my feet are a little delicate due to…recent events."

"Let me see," said Latishar, kneeling down to examine John's feet. "Ah-huh. Not too bad. Just surface cuts. I'll be extra careful!"

"Thank you," John said, trying to be inconspicuous about tucking some robe into his crotch.

Awkwardness turned to guilty anticipation. But in moments, guilt surrendered to relaxation as the soothing melodies of Kenny G lulled John into blissful rest while the two women rubbed muscles, tendons, and bones that were decades past simple neglect. Thumbs pressed into and circling his oiled feet and hands sent his eyeballs into the back of his head. The girls went to work with emery-boards, sanding and buffing rugged nails that were normally trimmed with a rusted clipper. They soaked and removed cuticles and exfoliated dry skin. Tension from the morning activities faded away.

He thought back to rubbing Cotton's head. Will was right; dogs give love without ever demanding anything in return. Bones had been that way. Sometimes he went hours or even days without his family paying him any real attention. It didn't matter. He found ways to kill time until his family, or a stranger even, came to scratch his ears or play a game of fetch. Reduced to taking long naps, chasing squirrels and birds in the backyard, or sessions of self-gratification, the poor dog never failed to love his owners enthusiastically when they finally made time for him. His love and affection for them was reliable and unconditional; for that, he, and every dog like him, deserved every belly rub and ear scratch they got—and more. John found himself in a very relaxed state, feeling what Cotton must have felt while receiving his affections. He wished he'd paid more attention to Bones, and everything else in his life. It's much harder, although still possible, he thought, to do things for people once they are gone. Carson found a way to teach that to his dad.

Latishar and Maelynn gently brought John back from a placid state by squeezing his toes and fingers; it was time for his next appointment. He was happy to see that no midnight blue made its way to his polished, sculpted nails.

"That wasn't so bad, was it?" Maelynn asked.

"I'm sorry," John said, sounding groggy. "Is this heaven?"

"It is," Latishar giggled. "And we are angels."

"*So*, what do you think?" Maelynn asked.

John raised his hands and feet and inspected. "Nice! I didn't realize how bad they were until now. And no paint or white tips like I see on all the women around the pool. I appreciate that," he said, fluttering his fingers and toes. Both girls swiveled John around and helped him into his shoes. Once upright, and his full weight made its way down to his feet, his knees buckled before springing back tight. "Whoops! I think my feet are on strike now. They feel more like feathers than paperweights." The two technicians escorted him to the reception desk.

"You look very relaxed," the receptionist noticed. "Let me see your hands."

John splayed his fingers over the counter. "They feel brand new!"

"Very nice," she said. "Any woman would be happy to let those hands touch them."

Given John's relaxed state and the receptionist's Asian accent, he took her comment more sexually than it was intended, but didn't dare attempt innuendo. "Good to know. Ah...am I supposed to leave a tip?" he whispered. "I never know about when, who, or how much."

"Normally, yes, it is customary, but I understand that gratuities for all your treatments have been pre-arranged. All you need to do is protect your hands and return to your villa for the next treatment, which is," glancing at her watch, "in five minutes."

John smiled and held his hands up like a surgeon waiting on gloves. "If I didn't know better,

I'd think it was Christmas." Using his elbow to push the door open, he made his exit. Female laughter followed him down the hall and he was happy to have humored them.

Once inside the villa, John did a little disco celebratory dance comprised of a single spin, fake split, and finished with one arm in a teacup handle, the other fully extended and pointing to the ceiling. Standing frozen, he became aware the environment had changed. The lights were dimmed, candles were burning around the entire room, and the music had been adjusted to the perfect volume for listening *and* talking.

"I don't think that move was designed for Trance music," said a voice.

John collapsed to attention. "Rita?!"

"In the flesh—literally," she replied, fluttering her fingers from the face down position on one of the massage tables.

John stood with his mouth—and robe—open when a knock sounded on the door. "Who's that?" he jumped.

"That would be our masseuse, John. Be a doll and let her in. My lumbar is killing me."

Still in shock, John said, "Okay."

"But, John!"

"Yes?"

"Masseuses are far from being prudes, but you might want to tighten up a bit," she said, flashing a finger towards his waist. "If you answer the door like that, I don't think your pedicure will be the first thing the poor girl is going to notice."

John looked down. Something in his disco move had loosened the robe's belt causing a... *dislodgment.* He quickly adjusted himself and retied the belt. Fully embarrassed, he answered the door.

"Hi," he said, feigning a smile.

"Hello," a stunning blonde returned. "I'm Anika." She wheeled a cart past John and started setting up between the two tables. "Hello. I'm Anika."

"Hello, dear. I'm Rita and the nervous looking fellow is John. Come lay down sweetie. We don't bite."

Rita came into clear view in the dim candlelight as John walked to the second table. Having thrown her towel onto the floor before he arrived, a single sheet lay across her, leaving her upper back and the skin below her buttocks exposed. John quivered inside.

"If you will please disrobe and lay face down for me," Anika directed, holding up the sheet, shielding her and Rita. John dropped his robe and laid down as Anika covered his backside and tucked the excess material, leaving only his butt cheeks covered.

"I will be performing two treatments for you both today. The first will be a couple's Swedish massage. I'm going to alternate between you both for a one hour session. The second treatment will be a botanical facial."

"Are you from Sweden?" Rita asked.

"Norway, actually."

"Close enough," Rita said. "Doesn't that sound heavenly, John, a Swedish massage from a real live Scandinavian beauty?"

"Su-sure!" John yelled through the face pillow.

"Do either of you have any questions, problem areas, or requests?"

"My lumbar area is feeling tight," Rita said.

"Certainly," Anika said. "And you, John? Any requests before I begin?"

"Please, don't hurt me."

Rita broke out in laughter, kicking her feet wildly against the table. Anika covered her mouth with the back of her hand to contain herself from Rita's reaction.

"Relax, John," Rita said. "She's here to help. When is the last time a woman made you feel physically satisfied?"

John thought. "Wednesday night."

"Oh…you are so sweet," Rita said. "If I didn't have my face planted in this doughnut I'd kiss you!" She smacked her lips through the horseshoe pillow.

Anika warmed some oil. "If you feel any discomfort, let me know."

"Oh, you'll know!" John said.

Anika spent the first five minutes working John's right leg. He winced every time she slid her hands up his inner thigh. Rita chuckled after each gasp, sigh, and squeak. She'd had dozens of massages since living in the states. Her muscles were accustomed to all types and intensities of massage.

"How's it feel, John?" Rita asked.

"G-o-o-d," he moaned, provoking more laughter.

When Anika shifted to Rita's leg, John rotated his cheek into the pillow hole, wanting to ask one of a dozen questions running through his head, but feeling uncomfortable about asking around a third party stranger—a beautiful one at that.

"Rita?"

"Yes, dear?"

"Why are you…I mean…how did you…?"

"It's all Dani's doing. She was going to call me, but I was in the British pub last night and I spotted her and her kids walking by. George was off gambling, or whatever, so I thought I'd enjoy a beer and some people watching. She told me all about your Jamaican adventures and said she wanted to do something nice for you for saving Garrett's leg. You're quite a hero, by the way. I never would have thought that first day at embarkation that you were so dangerous. Women love a hero, don't they, Anika?"

"*Yes*. Very much so," Anika sighed romantically.

"I don't know about hero, but this is certainly a hero's reward," John said.

"She's definitely good people. And her son is precious. A real pistol too, doesn't seem to miss anything. Reminds me of a young Will Catcher."

"Yes. That's a good comparison. That the first time you met Garrett?"

"Yip. Her daughter too. She looks just like Dani. A little shy, probably just her age."

Anika shifted to John's left leg, stifling further questions with kneading waves of bliss from her silky palms. He felt contently guilty about having such a beautiful creature touch him so intimately while the woman he had feelings for lay beside. Not even his dreams had ever been so erotic. A longing for more set in when five minutes passed in a blink, and Anika moved on to Rita's left leg.

"Did you know she booked a manicure for me?"

"Yes. We conspired together. She wanted us to have some alone time. I think she feels bad about her friend and George. I told her it didn't matter. She knows the deal. Anyway, we thought it would be more comfortable for you to start with one treatment by yourself, to loosen you up a bit."

"And what better than a nail treatment?"

"Just us girls having a little fun with you. You know you enjoyed it. Don't forget I saw your little dance."

"Ah, let's try to forget about that. But I have to admit, the nail treatment was very relaxing. Not to spoil the mood, but where does George think you are?"

"Here. He wanted to come, but I said it wasn't a part of the deal to do everything together."

Trying not to sound jealous, John asked, "Did you spend the day together, yesterday?"

"We spent the day at Dunn River falls, even though we've been there before. I think he believes the romantic nostalgia of doing things we once enjoyed will woo me into giving him another chance."

John didn't want to ask, but did. "Could it?"

Rita rolled onto her cheek to face John. She shot an intense look right into his eyes and mouthed the word *no*.

Her answer set John's mind at ease and any further questions could wait. His body followed suit when Anika returned for ten minutes on his back and neck. She purged anger, pain, and tightness from his muscles—a pain that John hadn't even realized was there. Even the agony she bullied from a rock-hard knot in his shoulder felt like a soulful release. She finished with five minutes on each arm; the entire time, nothing disturbed the air but the aroma of linen candles and ambient meditation melodies.

"I have finished with your massages." Anika's voice sounded as tranquil as the music, almost like a voice in a dream. "Would you both prefer me to leave the room for fifteen minutes in order for you to use the restroom or have something to drink?"

John remained quiet, hoping Rita would answer.

"Just keep going," Rita said. "We can do that other stuff when you're done. That work for you, hun?"

"Mm-hum."

Anika untucked both their sheets and asked them to turn over. For the next hour she shuffled back and forth like a multi-tasking chef working over several dishes. She introduced herself by warming up both faces with a gentle massage, followed by foaming botanicals and skin toner. She worked back and forth between them wiping their faces clean with steam towels between rounds. After exfoliating both faces with an electric scrubbing brush and using more steamed towels, they each got their obligatory cucumber slices and Anika began applying a Dead Sea clay mask.

"It's finally happened," John mumbled.

"What's that?" Rita asked.

"I got away with it in the nail salon, but these girls found a way to paint me with something."

"I don't think it's permanent, you big wussy."

"This is a special clay," Anika explained, still painting around John's vegetable slices. "It's known for its high concentration of minerals. It helps increase circulation, rebuilds collagen and elastin, draws out impurities, exfoliates, and nourishes the skin."

"Wow," John said. "Can it fix a rusty bicycle chain? 'Cause I have one of those at home."

"I don't think so," Anika chuckled, flicking the top of John's nose with clay. "But it will help your bruises heal faster."

"I don't see you for more than a day and all of a sudden you have jokes," Rita said. "You're just full of surprises."

"I'm a really late bloomer."

"They say timing is everything—lucky me."

Rita's words eased John into a peaceful trance for the next twenty minutes while the clay worked its magic. Anika rubbed their hands until it came time for more steamed towels and the last layer of moisturizer. John touched his face when she finished, thinking it felt as soft as his son's skin on the day he was born. Like most fathers, he considered that day to be the proudest one in his life.

"I'm all finished," Anika said, organizing her cart. "Feel free to enjoy the room until five. You still have most of an hour. I would allow the moisturizer to settle into your pores before you expose your face to water or any cleansers, in case you use the hydro-therapy pool or showers."

Rita turned her head towards the opposite table. "That spoils my plans for his next *treatment*," she said, gazing at John like a hawk studying a mouse. He received the gaze, bashfully inching his sheet farther up his chest.

Anika blushed. "Well then, I hope you both enjoyed everything and I'll leave you now," she said, hastily pushing her cart towards the door.

"Thank you, Anika," John said, feeling a bit nervous about being left alone with Rita, like a young man with an older, wiser, more experienced seductress.

"You're welcome," John heard faintly before the click of the door closing.

"Should we have a bite and some champagne?" Rita asked.

"That sounds nice," John said, sitting up, trying to figure out how to retrieve his robe from the wall hook hanging a few feet from the table. Grasping the sheet with his left hand behind his back, he swiveled his legs off the table. The weight of the robe proved too heavy for John's big toe to hook and pull. Surely if he stood, his ass would have to be exposed briefly in the transition. He tried using two big toes. No help. Leaning back perpendicularly across the table, he attempted to extend his feet farther. Light from the low voltage ceiling cut out as Rita tossed the robe across his face.

"Not feeling so *disco,* now?" Rita asked, standing over him with her hands resting in her own robe pockets. "I'll meet you in there."

His voice chased after her. "Be there in sec!"

John dressed, found his slippers, and used the bathroom.

A *pop* sounded just before he entered the sitting area where Rita was filling two glasses. She turned, offering one to John. "Not a bad way to spend an afternoon, is it, John?"

"Oh, I do this kind of stuff all the time back in Kansas," he sipped.

Rita plucked a strawberry from the platter on the coffee table. She teased John's mouth before allowing him to take a bite. "Just a typical day, huh?"

"Yip," he chewed.

She picked a blackberry for herself. "How decadent. Now I'm even more intrigued to see this homeland of yours."

She sat against the sofa arm and propped her feet up on the table. John used the opposite arm, squirming to find an uncontrived position.

"Yeah. People overlook the YMCA. It might not be glamorous, but you can get in a good workout and a hot steam."

Rita gently nibbled on the rim of her glass. "That important to you, is it? A good *workout* before you get *hot*."

"I ah…try to use the exercise bike and swim some laps a couple times a week."

"Good for the heart," she said, splitting her robe at the top and rubbing her chest.

John tried not to stare at Rita's perfect cleavage which was exposed enough to reveal tan lines. He swallowed some champagne. It went down like hard candy. "The heart runs everything else in the body, slightly more important than the other organs—even the lungs have a backup," he said.

"Yes. It is important to give it a good *pump*—for the sake of endurance and purging." Rita watched John's forehead perspire in the air-conditioned room. "It's really not fair that such a vital organ is vulnerable on two fronts…is it?"

John brushed his forehead. "Two fronts?"

Rita removed her hand. "Our poor hearts are responsible for running the rest of the body and our mental happiness. People can't hurt our spleen with words or indifference. Infidelity doesn't cause our kidneys to feel like they are going to explode. But the heart…the heart feels it all. Malnutrition, lack of exercise, and cruelty from others. It's just too much to ask one little muscle to overcome."

"Maybe its defense is to become numb?"

"Is your heart numb, John?"

John stared out the window at the rolling sea. "After my wife left it was. Numbness turned bitter when my son died, after that…it felt like stone."

Rita leaned forward, offering her hand. John reluctantly accepted before gazing back out the window.

"Please," she said. "Continue. I'm listening."

John sighed, finished his wine, and held the glass tightly against his chest. "I learned something last night, or maybe *remembered* is a better word since I think I blocked it out in my childhood. The only fight I can ever recall my parents having came when I was a little younger than Garrett. It came around the time the circus was in town. I thought we would be going, but without knowing it the night of their fight, I had already gone to my last circus with my mother and father. The cause for the argument was apparently an affair—or single indiscretion—I don't know which."

"It doesn't matter to women. They're lying when they say otherwise. It's all or nothing with my kind."

"Makes sense. It was different for my parents, though. They got through it—endured it maybe. They are still together, I mean. I think for some people it's more important to not fail than it is to actually, succeed. That's where I went wrong. Page and I did a pretty good job with Carson. We tried giving him things I never had. But, I at least, allowed mediocrity into my marriage—not intentionally of course. I probably learned it from watching my parents. They never really talked, especially after Dad cheated.

"In my own marriage, I never asked for, or wanted, anything more than we already had. Not from myself or from my wife. And I never asked her what she needed or wanted. I think when you're married you need to continually ask those things, and realize the answers are constantly changing. When those questions aren't asked, you wake up one day and find guilt, anger, and resentment have crept into your bed, creating a whole new set of questions. If they aren't dealt with, those questions can make a person numb. She never really tried and I never really noticed… until it was too late."

Removing the champagne from the ice bucket, Rita refilled John's glass. "Marriage is a two way street. It always comes down to communication. You learn and move forward—sometimes that means with someone else."

"I know you're right," John sipped. "I just feel bad about letting someone down I loved for so long."

"Don't think of it as a failure. The important thing is for you both to be happy again—even if it's not together. Is she happy?"

"We hardly ever talk. I know a piece of her will always be broken from losing Carson. But, I see her parents from time to time and they say she is much happier than she ever was in Kansas."

"And you?"

John paused. "This trip has made me realize that Carson still lives inside me, as long as I allow it. All the new people I've met and the things I've tried this week—which I never would have dreamed of trying before—are making me better understand who my son was and why he wanted me to take this trip. He loved life. And he wanted *me* to love life—not just live it. I owe it to him, and myself, to be happy. I believe I will see him again someday and I don't want him to be disappointed. So, to answer your question, I think I'm getting there."

Rita lifted a lone tear from her cheek. "I'm sure he *is* and will be, very proud of you, John. I've known you for six days—and I am."

John smiled. "I don't know. I don't think getting manicures and pedicures is exactly what my Army son had in mind for me."

Lifting her feet onto John's lap, Rita said, "I should've gone with you. My little piggies are jealous."

"They look perfect to me," he said, yearning to touch them.

"Aw! Thank you," she said, wiggling her toes. "Did you enjoy your massage and facial?"

"Are you kidding, they were great! I feel like I have a new body. And my face feels super clean. The oak and peppermint smells very manly."

"Next time we'll get oxygen facials."

"Oxygen? What's that mean?"

"They use a special tool to blow pure oxygen and vitamins into your pores. It plumps up the skin and fixes everything. It's heavenly, John. You'll love it!"

"Huh. And all this time I thought my face was getting enough oxygen just by walking around. Who would've thought?"

Tickling John's stomach with her toes, Rita said, "You silly Smith!"

John clenched her feet, something he found quite intimate and erotic. "Rita? You said *next time*. This thing. Us. Is this…just casual? Some kind of vacation fling or rebound from your divorce, or…something more?"

Rita retracted her feet. "When was the last time you took control of your destiny, John?"

He pondered. "A long time. Maybe, never," he sighed.

Rita stood. "Don't you think it's time?" She walked to the opening leading out to the main villa.

Her words *it's time* echoed through John's head. "Where are you going?"

"We have a little time left. I think we should take advantage of all the amenities. After all,

Dani paid for them. We haven't used the pool yet." Rita turned her back to John and dropped her robe. "Leave the fruit, bring the champagne," she said, slowly walking towards the kiddy-pool sized Jacuzzi. It was fizzing with bubbles from the jets and a cascading rain shower flowed from the ceiling.

Dumbfounded, aroused, John stared at Rita's posterior. For a woman on the wrong side of thirty-five, no man would know based on her lean, unblemished back and apple-like buttocks. Like a south pacific goddess wading into the sea, she gracefully eased into the water. For some strange reason, baseball entered John's mind. Although he had never played on an organized team, the moment had the feel of the bottom of the ninth, bases loaded, two outs, game on the line scenario, and the coach was calling him off the bench. Quivering with anticipation, he pulled the bottle from its chiller and slowly made his way into the main villa. Rita leaned against the far side of the pool, her arms floating at shoulder level, the top of her breasts breaching the water. He stood at the edge across from her, silently requesting direction.

"*Well?*" Rita toyed.

"My suit is in the closet," he said, feeling stupid for uttering the words.

"I won't mind if you don't get it," she said, squirting water through her fist. "Your birthday suit was good enough to get you into this world, it should be good enough for this bath. Besides, I've already seen your peek-a-boo dance. What do you say let's try out some of that newfound confidence?"

Her words and irresistible smile were all the encouragement he needed. He placed the champagne on the floor and disrobed. Instead of using the steps for a model's descent, he used a quick squat and drop entry.

"That a boy!" she clapped. "Isn't this wonderful?"

"It is. Like dessert after dessert!"

"You're kinda far away. How about we meet in the middle under that alluring rain shower?"

"Okay." John stopped on his way over. "What about Anika telling us not to get our faces wet?"

Rita pursed her lips and looked up. "I have an idea! We'll stop just before that happens and see if we can still make each other out through the steam and water."

"I suppose that couldn't hurt my oaky makeover."

They moved slowly to their respective sides of the two foot diameter waterfall that glistened like thick strands of poured silk dripping from a treetop spiderweb. With knees fully bent, the base of their necks touched the effervescent water line. They stopped and gazed through the translucent liquid.

"I can barely make you out," Rita said, her eyes fighting to see through the blur. "You're like a twinkling abstract painting."

"First time anyone's ever called me that. You know I always wondered why such gifted painters can't make a legible signature at the bottom of their painting?"

"Forget about artists handwriting and take my hands, John. We'll make a bucket and pretend we are in a desert collecting water in a tiny utopia."

John made a half circle on top of the water with his arms. Rita completed the circle, her pull causing their knees to join and brace.

"What do we do now?" John asked.

"It's all a façade, you know."

"What is?"

"This barrier between us. It can't stop us from truly living any more. None of it...your pain; my marriage; our pasts; it's all a river, condensed into a thin sheet of water blocking our faces. All we have to do is pull through."

Rita squeezed John's trembling hands. In turn, he closed his legs and as if they were forklifts raising fragile cargo, he brought her closer. She tilted her head back as it slipped through the shower, rinsing her black hair away from her face. She came to rest on his lap, exchanging her grasp for the back of his neck, her lower legs dangling below his thighs. John placed his hands above her hips. She could feel his fully erect penis fluttering against her belly. His champagne breath came fast and uneven. The lightning John felt for Rita their first day by the pool was back and striking every cell of his body.

"I guess we made it through," John muttered.

"I don't think so." Rita planted her feet and turned John. "Your turn!"

He closed his eyes and leaned back into the shower. When he emerged, blinking profusely, he said, "I guess I'm going to be late meeting the Clawsons for bingo."

Rita laughed. "I say with confidence, it's been a long time for both of us. I don't think it's going to take very long to get to *bingo*. Do you think they'll mind if you're a few minutes late?"

Before John could respond, Rita lifted her feet, making John support them again. With one swift, but deliberately tender motion, she released her right hand into the water and cupped his penis. After a loving hello, she set the desired angle, arched her back, and slid into John's lap as snuggly as if she were fastening a seat belt. Her legs wrapped around his waist and locked at the ankles. The rest of their concerns ceased to exist with each slow, short, and then deep pulse from their hips. Frustrated, their tongues could not penetrate deep enough. John grabbed the back of Rita's head and back, and pressed the right side of his face between her ample breasts. Water lapped against his chin with every rhythmic compression. He continued unselfishly after climaxing; Rita didn't require much longer, biting his ear with the utmost delicacy and joining John's deep exhales moments after she felt him throbbing inside.

BINGO

JOHN REACHED THE ENTRANCE TO the Sky Lounge at 5:32. The MC, still welcoming the players and briefing them on the format, hadn't called the first number yet. Although not overly concerned, because he was still on a high from his tryst with Rita, he was happy to arrive before the first game started.

It had taken two phone calls from the reception desk to finally encourage Rita and John to vacate the villa at 5:15. John hung back an extra couple of minutes on the outside chance George was waiting to meet her. Helen recognized the post whoopee air in John's body language when he thanked her and sauntered out of the lobby. He stopped at his cabin to change into a polo and pants and everyone he passed on the way to meet the Clawsons smiled at his jovial whistling.

A well-dressed man standing behind a podium was guarding the Sky Lounge entrance. He greeted John. "Good afternoon, sir. Are you here for bingo?"

John giggled. "Yes. I love bingo—great activity!"

The man smiled vacantly for a moment before asking, "Do you have your invitation, sir?"

"Ah. I'm a guest of Richard and Mary Clawson—John Smith."

"Mr. Smith," the man repeated, checking a guest list. "Yes! I have your name right here. Go ahead in, sir. And good luck!"

"Thank you. I am feeling rather lucky today!"

The lounge opened like a ballroom in a semi-circle shape. The curved sides were built of large glass panels and they provided panoramic views from one of the highest passenger permitted areas. A small stage set against the straight rear wall gave the MC with his ball churning machine a place to coordinate the games. John weaved his way through the room; it was filled with contemporary patterned, low-backed arm chairs huddled around tables in groups of two's and four's. Aromas from the hot and cold buffet laid out on the lounge's bar were over-powered by the strong perfumes and cologne wafting from the blue-haired crowd who sat, nibbling on finger food, nursing bourbon and gimlets, and guarding their cards. The average player age seemed relative to the total number assembled, between seventy and a hundred, making it harder for John to locate Richard and Mary. Instead, they saw him first, since he stood out like a baby in a sea of teenagers. Richard stood, while Mary sat and waved. Richard's hulking stature caught John's attention.

"Good afternoon, my boy!" Richard said, offering a handshake.

Firmly, exuberantly, John shook. "Hello, Rich! And do I get a hug from the second sweetest woman onboard?" John held out his arms.

Mary stood. "*Second* sweetest? When was I demoted?"

"I regret lowering your rank, but after Dani just treated me to an entire afternoon in the spa, I feel I have to—at least for the day!"

The three sat.

"That hardly seems fair, John," Mary said, sternly crossing her arms. "The day isn't over, you know? I don't think you gave me a fair chance at maintaining my title."

"You're absolutely right," John said, raising an index finger. "I hear-by dismiss the jury until bedtime. Fair?"

"Deal," Mary said.

"Don't take this the wrong way," Richard said, shoveling some fat-free dip with a piece of celery. "But, did you have an extra bowl of Wheaties this morning? You seem especially chipper."

John laughed. "No, I incorporated this change stuff into my meals today—like sushi for your heart. I had crepes and tomato juice for breakfast, followed by quiche and figs at lunch—wonderful things figs—I've only ever tried the cookie version."

"Good to hear, my boy! You gotta try new things—give a fig, get a fig." Richard frowned at his celery.

"Every day is a new day and they just seem to be getting better! Garrett and I rode the wave machine, played eighteen holes of miniature golf, Will and Dani joined us to conquer the rock wall, then I had a manicure, massage, and facial! I understand now why Gumby was always smiling. I tell you…my body feels like a team of mechanics restored it to brand new—minus a spot of rust on my eye and lip of course."

"B-34," the MC announced.

"Louder!" cried a man fidgeting with his hearing aid.

"Here we go!" Mary said. "We bought two cards for each of us. These two are yours, John. Use the gold coins to mark your numbers. There, see, you have a B-34."

John picked up one of the souvenirs from the middle of the table. Stamped on both sides was the company name and a picture of the ship. After covering his number, he asked, "What are we playing for?"

"Money, honey," Mary said.

"All righty then!" John said, leaning forward to pay closer attention to his cards. "Do I owe you some kind of entrance fee?"

"We talked about that," Richard glared. "You're our guest!"

"G-76!"

"Say again?" a woman said, cupping her ear.

"Okay," John said. "But if I win…I pay for the six cards—deal?"

"I'll concede that," Richard said. "It'll give us something else to root for."

"I-6! I-6!"

"You better catch up," Mary said. "There are only five rounds and you're already falling behind from the looks of your card."

"Not a problem, Mary. I'm feeling very lucky today!"

"I guess Dani wanted to thank you for saving Garrett's leg yesterday," Mary said. "Did she join you at the spa?"

"No. I think she wanted to stay as close to the pool bar this afternoon as she could. She and Will seem to have really taken a liking to each other. But yes, you're right about the reason for her treating me. At least that's what Rita told me."

"0-45! 0-45!"

"Dang!" John said. "I still only have one number." Looking up from his card, he was surprised to see Richard and Mary staring at him with raised brows and small smiles. "What? Did I miss a number?"

"No, dear," Mary said. "We just thought you two were trying to keep your distance until after the cruise. I guess you bumped into her today?"

"N-2! N-2!"

"Ah…" John dunked a smile onto his card. "She joined me for a couple of the treatments today."

"B-12! B-12!"

"Well take me to the prom," Richard said. "Somebody has afterglow!"

Radiating, John looked up. "What? What was that last number?"

Richard howled out loud, causing rickety turns from the neighboring tables.

"Richard!" Mary slapped her husband's arm.

"What? The boy is obviously experiencing post-nookie-i-tis."

Mary tried covering her laugh. "That's none of our business."

"G-61! G-61!"

"*Bingo!*" a woman cried from the far side of the room.

"We have a winner," the MC declared.

"Oh, fizzle-sticks," Mary said. "I only needed one more number. And I apologize for Richard's crudeness. I hope we didn't make you feel uncomfortable?"

John removed his sole coin and leaned back. "Not at all." Leaning forward again. "Can I tell you a little secret, Mary?"

She joined him center table. "I can be trusted."

"I don't know exactly what it means, but he's right, I do have post-nookie-i-tis."

"I knew it!" Richard bellowed.

"Sssshhhh," Mary sputtered. "Good for you, John, good for you! She seems like a lovely woman."

"Are you kidding?" Richard asked. "She's finer than the teeth on a sea-horse's mustache comb! That 55 Thunderbird we used to have wasn't as pretty."

"I think so too," John said.

Richard slapped the table. "This calls for a drink!"

"I'm game," John said.

Richard turned to Mary with a look that signified asking permission.

"Yes," she said. "I believe this does call for a toast. We have a few minutes before the next round. Why don't you two virile men grab a bottle of wine from the bar."

"Yes, ma'am!" Richard said, pushing back his chair. "Come on, son. I'm sure you don't kiss and tell, but I'm here if you want to."

"You leave the man's intimacies to himself," Mary said. "And hurry back! I don't want to be in charge of six cards."

Three more games passed without a winner at the Clawson table. John talked about the two crew members flown away by the Coast Guard, how talented Garrett was at everything he did, the feeling of accomplishment he felt by reaching the top of the rock wall, Dani and Will's stolen kiss, and the uninvited memory of his parents' only fight. He did manage to avoid, with Mary's help, Richard's sly quizzes, noting only that he found the hydro-therapy pool to be the most invigorating water experience he had ever had. The bottle of wine was long gone at the break before the last game. Richard, successful at convincing his wife that a second bottle was in order, refilled their glasses as the first number was called.

"Here we go," the MC geared up. "G-5! G-5!" The crowd fiddled with prosthetic earlobes, anxious and agitated, in a hurry to yell Bingo.

"Have you given any thought to what you and Rita might do after Sunday?" Mary asked. "I mean, do you think you'll see each other again? You both live very far away from each other."

Mary's words jolted John like a bucket of ice water on a sound sleep. "Geez, Mary. All of this stuff happened so fast, I haven't thought about that. What do I do?"

"O-15! O-15!"

"I don't know, John," Mary sighed. "In my experience, older people don't have much luck in advising younger people what to do. Our children are a living testament to that. They might listen, but it sometimes takes years until they hear. I hate giving advice. I've learned, for better or worse, it's better to listen and support. Younger people often have too much to prove to themselves to take the advice of us dinosaurs."

"N-11! N-11!"

"That's funny," John said. "Garrett said something similar this morning, except he was referring to older people not listening to younger people."

"I think it works both ways," Richard said.

"I'm finally listening to Carson. It took years to hear what he was trying to say to me, so I guess you're right, Rich."

"O-60! O-60!"

"Sometimes we don't know what to do until it's time to know it," Richard said. "Maybe it's not time for you, yet."

"Wow. This is getting spooky," John said.

"G-13! G-13!"

"Come again?" Richard said.

"Lloyd, the friend of Will's I met in Jamaica, told me the same thing before the whole leg-thief incident."

"He sounds like a smart man," Richard laughed.

"B-18! B-18!"

"He is," John agreed. "All this doesn't help me much though. I have a flight back to Kansas in less than two days. I believe I really…love this woman. I don't want to lose her. Another part of me is telling me love doesn't happen this fast. Maybe I should take some time to get to know her better? Maybe we could meet each other after her divorce is finished?"

"I-44! I-44!"

"*What?*" a man questioned right in front of the stage.

"I-I-I-44-44-44!"

"That guy must have one foot in the grave if he can't hear the numbers from where he's sitting," Richard said. "Goddam old people."

"I will say this, John," Mary started, "I believe couples in their twenties and thirties, and especially their teens, God forbid, should spend a lot of time before jumping into a serious commitment."

"N-55! N-55!"

"But once you're in your forties and up, people should trust their instincts. If the heart tells you to dive in when you're that old, what's the worst that can happen? We only get so many chances before we die. But this is just my opinion. To quote one of the greats 'to influence a person is to give him one's own soul. He does not think his natural thoughts, or burn with his natural passions. He becomes an echo of someone else's music, an actor of a part that has not been written for him. The aim of life is self-development. To realize one's nature perfectly—that is what each of us is here for.'"

"O-12! O-12!"

John thought pensively. "I like that a lot, Mary. It wouldn't happen to be Thoreau, would it?"

"No," Mary said, studying her cards. "Those words of self-independence belong to Oscar Wilde."

"She studies all the classics," Richard said. "Voracious reader. Had the kids reading *Moby Dick* before they could ride a bike. Neighborhood kids the same age were still reading comic books."

"I-1! I-1!"

"I won," John said.

"Yes," Richard said. "*I-1*. Good to know you're still too young to need a hearing aid."

John checked his numbers. "No! You don't understand—*I won!*"

Mary glanced at John's cards. Five gold coins slashed diagonally through the center free space. "Hurry John, yell *Bingo!*" she urged.

John scrambled to his feet, slamming his knee underneath the table in the process. "Ouch! I mean…*Bingo!*"

"We seem to have our final winner," the MC said as deep sighs and moans sounded from the crowd. "Come on up and let's check your numbers!"

"I told you I was feeling lucky! If there's enough money left over after I reimburse you for the cards, I'm buying their best champagne!"

Richard and Mary watched John fumble through the crowd, rubbing his knee along the way. The not so sporting losers weren't going out of their way to ease his path. Being as young as he was didn't help matters. John noticed several grumbly faces that would have been more gracious with a peer.

"This should be interesting," Richard said, gulping some wine.

A couple of minutes passed. John found his return to the Clawsons much less impeding, since most of the crowd was fleeing or scavenging the remainder of the buffet.

"Here he comes, Richard. He looks a little dazed." Mary greeted John with an anxious smile. "How did you make out, dear?"

John slumped to his chair, his fingers sifting through a thick stack of cash. "There must be some mistake. They gave me over nine-thousand dollars."

"Sounds about right," Richard said, looking satisfied. "The cards were five-hundred a piece and there must be seventy-five to a hundred people here. I don't think many people bought more than one card."

John stared at the money like a kid who thought he'd won a bike and it turned out to be a motorcycle. "This is a lot of money! It takes me months to make this much. This isn't right. I can't accept this."

"You damn well can," Richard barked. "You have just as much right to it as any of the rest of these rich mummies. They aren't going to miss it and you bet the family dog they wouldn't think twice about keeping yours! They didn't all buy suites because they are hard-up for cash."

"It's all yours," Mary said, reaching across and rubbing his forearm.

"Not all of it," Richard said. "I believe you owe us three grand and some primo bubbly. A deal's, a deal—right?"

"Yes it is, Rich." John licked his thumb and started counting hundred dollar bills in front of Richard. "I never thought I would be this happy to give someone else three thousand dollars."

"Just don't skimp on the wine!" Richard said, winking at Mary. "Remember, Mary and I have discerning palates. We'll know if you try to pull a fast one."

"That's why you're coming with me. I won't get past the fancy French pronunciation without you."

With the card reimbursement complete, John and Richard waited at the bar while the bartender called a sommelier to deliver a 1995 Louis Roederer Cristal. Richard dismissed the wine expert as soon as he showed up carrying the six-hundred dollar vintage nestled in a silver champagne bucket. To the sommelier's dismay, Richard was just as knowledgeable and didn't care for a frivolous presentation or dissertation on the particular year's especially pear and toasted nut tones. However, the wine master did insist on carrying his precious cargo as far as their table before he removed his white gloves and retreated the room. Richard did the honors, popping the cork with one swift turn of his baseball glove sized hand. John held three flutes as Richard poured.

"What are you going to do with all your loot?" Mary asked.

"I don't know," John said, tilting his glass for Richard. "I've never had this much disposable income at one time. Maybe I can buy all the people I work with something nice in St. Thomas tomorrow? Or I could host a reunion for all the wonderful people I've met on this cruise? Carson would like that. I don't think everyone would want to come to Kansas though."

"We would!" Mary insisted.

Richard raised his glass. "Here's to whatever you decide, John. May it buy something you find satisfying and enjoyable! You deserve it."

"Hear, hear!" Mary said as the three toasted, sipped, and sat.

"Thank you both for inviting me. And thank you for being the people you are. You've made this trip very special for me. I can't put it into words." John used a finger to catch the onset of a tear.

"Give credit where credit is due," Mary said. "People, like places and activities, provide the paint, but you're the canvas that gives them a home and makes them a picture. They live inside you in memory, action, and speech. Memory of your experiences gives them life and meaning. Hopefully you will pass them on to others so they can continue to live on. In short, the reason your trip is so special—is because of you."

"And a pocket full of cash doesn't hurt either, does it, John?" Richard asked, raising his glass.

"No it doesn't," John laughed. "Hey! I wonder if I can bribe an officer into giving a bridge tour for Garrett?"

"The ship does bridge tours for passengers," Mary said.

"He told me this morning they missed the window to sign up. I don't think they are doing any more tomorrow."

"Hell, John, the kid doesn't need to wait 'til tomorrow," Richard said. "Let me have the cell, Mary."

While Mary rummaged through her bag, John asked, "What are you going to do, Richard, call the Captain?"

Mary handed over the phone. "That's exactly what I'm going to do," Richard said, pressing numbers. "Captain Bill! Rich Clawson here." … "Yes, yes, everything is top notch as usual." … "Hope you're enjoying the wine." … "No, the ticker is fine, just a little gas I think, probably from all the damn broccoli your mess serves." … "Yes, yes, I'll do that." … "Hey, I hate to disturb you while you're driving and all, or whatever you guys do up there, but I have a few people who were told they can't get a bridge tour. You got any time to show your bells and whistles to a thirteen-year old?" … "Ah-uh, yes, that should be fine." … "Thanks Bill." … "I will. You can see him Sunday." … "Yes, he's coming to pick us up." … "Okay." … "The same to you, sailor." … " Bye."

Astonished, John asked, "You *know* the Captain?"

"Of course I do," Richard said, shrugging his shoulders. "Who do you think you're dealing with?"

"He's a friend of our son—Oliver—the one that's in the Navy," Mary said. "Years ago, Bill was in the Navy too. Used to be Oliver's CO at one point. He retired and took a job with this cruise line. It's a pretty good life, from what we understand."

"Sure is," Richard said. "Bikini's, Caribbean islands, and champagne sure beats the Persian Gulf and guns. Still a lot of responsibility, but not the same kind."

"You guys have done more interesting things and know more interesting people than *Forrest Gump*," John said.

Richard laughed. "Bill's a good guy. And I like this company more than the others because of him. He looks out for us. How do you think I got all my wine onboard?"

"You mean you can't just bring it in your bag?" John asked.

"Na," Richard scowled. "Everything changed after nine-eleven. The ships tightened their belts like everyone else. This company allows one bottle per passenger as a carry-on. It's not that I mind paying for my booze, it's just that a lot of the wine we prefer isn't available on the ship. I know that sounds odd, as big a stock as they carry, but we have found many boutique vineyards that we support. Plus, many of the famous bottles, like that Petrus that you and I shared, would cost three times what I can buy it for. That's a big difference when you're talking about fifteen-hundred versus forty-five-hundred. We have money, but there's no reason to just throw it away."

"I see your point," John said, savoring his champagne. "How many do you bring?"

"Twelve," Richard said.

"We give some to Bill and his officers," Mary said.

"You of all people can appreciate this," Richard said. "I have a custom made suitcase designed just for holding twelve wine bottles. We phone ahead and either Bill or one of his guys comes down to check it before we board, then they deliver it to our cabin with the rest of our luggage. 'A man's got to go somewhere, sometime. When he does, he's going to need the right bag.' Right, John?"

John sat with a pleasant grin, wishing his father and Fred Bagly could have heard Richard recite the slogan, complete with substituting *the right* for *a*. "That's absolutely correct!"

"I thought you'd get a kick out of that," Richard said. "Anyway, Bill said for whoever wants to see the bridge to be in the main lobby at eight. An officer will be looking for you. You should go too, John. It's worth seeing."

"Are you both going?"

"We've seen several," Mary said. "Once you've seen one…well you know the rest."

"We can't anyway," Richard said. "We have to meet someone for dinner."

"You have friends onboard?"

"Not exactly," Richard said. "It's more of a business thing. I'll tell you about it later."

"And we should get going," Mary said, glancing at her watch. "It's almost seven. That give you enough time to find Dani?"

"Yes," John said. "I'm going to check my email now and she gave me her address. I'll send an email to her phone, she should get that. If that doesn't work, I'll have the purser page them."

"Splendid!" Richard said. "Hey, there's a party at the pool bar at ten tonight. Supposed to be a great band playing. What do you say we all meet up there later?"

"That sounds like a plan," John said, pouring the remainder of the champagne into their glasses. "We can't leave this."

"No we can't, my boy," Richard said. "The wine gods would strike us down."

"You mentioned Thoreau earlier," Mary said. "Is he a favorite of yours?"

"No. Not really. I mean…I read Walden in college."

"Do you read much now?" Mary asked.

"A fair amount, mostly before bed, popular stuff, you know, Grisham, DeMille, Clancy—that kind of stuff. I find myself reading more since Carson passed and I threw away my TV. Reading helps me sleep. I bowl on Saturdays with some of the guys from work. And I go into town or to my parents for dinner most nights. Other than odds and ends around the house, the occasional movie, swimming at the YMCA, and walks in our local park, I don't do much besides work. I'm going to try to change that routine when I get back though. I think I'm even going to buy another TV. At the very least, I can watch commercial free movies on TCM." Smiling at Richard.

"They don't make 'em like they used to," Richard said.

"I advocate reading more than watching TV," Mary said, "but I do enjoy the old black and whites. Since you brought up Thoreau and we were talking about giving advice and the difficulties of exchanging that advice between young and old, I'll leave you with one more quote—from Mr. Thoreau this time—if you like?"

"Certainly," John said.

"'Age is no better, hardly so well, qualified for an instructor as youth, for it has not profited so much as it has lost.' Take what you will from that, John, and then any further questions you may wish to ask; start by asking yourself what *you* need and want and then find a way to make it so." ⌣

John paused to absorb Mary's words before saying, "I suppose the point…the answer…is that we each hold the answers to our own questions inside us?"

Richard stared blankly. Mary tilted her head slightly from side to side while subtly lifting and lowering her hands from the table.

The edges of John's lips curled upward a tad. He raised his glass, offering his last mouthful for a toast. "To the best advice! Which sometimes, ironically, is no advice at all!"

Glasses touching. "Hear, hear," the Clawsons returned.

"And Mary," John said.

"Yes, dear?"

"I'm sorry I ever suggested demoting you. You truly are the sweetest woman."

Mary peered through one eye. "Like all women, I'm a sucker for compliments, but let's keep that one between us. After all," pausing to plump her hair, "I don't want to make Rita jealous."

****ING CHINA

RAFFIC THROUGH THE HALLS AND in the elevators was light. The early dinner seating helped drain the otherwise bustling streams of people shuffling from the pools, bars, shops, and shows on a full sea day. The dinner bell didn't ring yet for John. He was still content from consuming several Tai peanut chicken skewers and some artichoke dip during bingo. He kept checking the outside bulge of his left pants pocket en route to the business center. The folded wad of hundred dollar bills was crammed so tightly in his pocket, he thought even the most talented pick-pocket couldn't wrestle it out. The wine and champagne left him with a friendly tingle, magnified by the lingering memory of Rita's mouth, kissing, licking, delicately biting, while her wet naked body writhed away on his lap. The top of the world, it seemed, was less than a hundred feet above sea level.

As on his last visit, the room was vacant. Most people, John was learning, had internet access on their phones. Fixed computers were falling by the wayside, used only by thrifty, stubborn people hell bent on resisting change until their final days. The concept wasn't new. Since the beginning of mankind there were those who jumped on the band wagon and those who walked behind. The idea of having to go somewhere to use a large machine for mail or to surf the world's invisible information cloud seemed archaic to the current generation. John made mental notes, taking a seat at the same terminal he had used before: *buy TV, buy touch screen internet phone, buy Wi-Fi; time to make more changes when I return.*

He logged on to his @keepittogether.com account, by-passing his inbox to compose Dani a quick note saying: "The Clawsons arranged a bridge tour for us. We need to meet by 8:00 in the main lobby. Is Garrett still interested? Email back if you are receiving this, John. P.S. Spa was wonderful, thank you so much!"

John sat back, staring at the screen, waiting. His eyes latched onto ten unread messages stacked on top of old mail. There was an obvious uniformity to each one. All were from different senders, but from the same place—*@keepittogether.com.* The first message was instantly reduced before his eyes to number two as Dani responded. He clicked: "Super! We'll meet you at 8:00!"

The second message immediately opened upon deleting Dani's response. John recognized the sender, Terry Underwood, in charge of the Banbury mixer where the rubber is combined with sulfur for vulcanizing. Terry was a regular companion of John's. They met for lunch a couple times a week at Joe's and he occasionally joined John for laps at the YMCA. John's face drew long by the end of the second paragraph.

Sara Wilson, in charge of the mandrels—long aluminum poles coated with talcum powder, used for holding the milled rubber before cutting it into individual bands—sent message number three. She brought food and pies once a week for three months after John lost Carson and had also consoled him after his divorce from Page. Although less loquacious than Terry's, her email said the same things. And on it went. Ten emails from ten employees—most he considered friends—under John's supervision. Each message stung like a fresh lashing. By the time John finished reading the last lines of Gary Learner's email—number nine, "Sorry to ruin your vacation. Thought you would want to know as soon as possible. Gary," he couldn't take any more. Phyllis Anderson, the company's switchboard operator and a regular bowling companion sent email number ten. It found the trash bin without John ever reading it. His luck it seemed, had taken a U-turn.

John checked his watch—7:50.

Punctured, deflated, he moped towards the lobby, leaking hard earned confidence from deep within. The vibrant colors from the busy corridor carpet taunted John, as if to say he wasn't bright or ornate enough to walk on them. The voices in his head returned, working static triage that blocked external sounds. Cowardly comforts screaming between John's ears pleaded for him to run, hide, or collapse. His jaw clenched at the thought of the word *change*. Change, as a decision, he found exhilarating; change as an unwelcome consequence, like infidelity, provoked anger and despair—John grappled with both.

The air was thin, as if from altitude. A great warmth pushed against the inside of his skull. His nostrils flared, sucking in offensive odors from the wakes of those he passed. Cheap perfume, BO, and remnants of meals: hot wings, beer, blue cheese, and cigarettes all flew up John's sinuses like crows to corn.

Irritated and becoming nauseated, dizziness caused John to duck into a communal restroom off the conveyer belt hallway. He dashed into the far stall, crouched to his knees, unraveled two turns of toilet paper, which he used to lift the seat just in time to create a larger opening for a very expensive spew. John barked into the receptacle, purging six-hundred dollar champagne soaked artichoke and peanut chicken chucks through his mouth and nose. His internal voices were clearly reversing the valves on change.

John realized he wasn't alone when a sputtering release of gas trumpeted inside the commode to his left.

"Feelin' buggard?" a voice asked.

John turned his head. From the missing bottom section of the partition he could see a calf, overgrown with thick black hair, one leg of plaid shorts crumpled around a purple penny loafer at the base. "I've been better," John said, turning back to the seat opening to blow the remaining bits from his nose.

With an accent John found similar to Garth's, the man continued dialogue asking, "Do you think it's food poisoning?"

Disinclined, John returned, "Could be."

"Oysters maybe? I had a batch last night and have been in the *loo* ever since."

Feeling certain the last dry heave signaled the total vacancy of his stomach, John wanted to free himself from any further conversation. "No. No oysters, but I'll keep that in mind. I'm feeling better," he said, flushing before the man could respond.

"Good on ya then. Fight on, mate."

John hurried to clean himself in the sink before the man flushed. The embarrassment of throwing up was one thing, having to converse with a stranger who was taking a crap while doing it was another. He didn't want to put a face with the voice. This experience was not one he wished to perpetuate in memory. He finished dousing his face and gargling when the flush sounded. He grabbed a fist full of paper towels and scurried to the door before the latch clicked.

The corridor opened to the main lobby not far from the restroom. Unable to find a trashcan, John crammed the wet towels into his *poor* pants pocket. It contained only his ship-card and

Will's iPod, which he'd retrieved when changing clothes for bingo. He was afraid he'd forget it was in his bathing suit pocket while swimming somewhere, so he waited for a better occasion, one calling for pants, where he might see Will.

Dani, Jill, and Garrett were standing by the reception desk with the same officer who had shown John the best place to watch the sail-away in Miami. Feigning a smile, John joined them from a slightly unreceptive distance, not wanting to offend anyone with his breath.

Dani spoiled John's courtesy with a bear hug. "There you are!"

"Here I am," John said, holding his breath.

"Wow! Are those tennis balls in your pockets or did I send the wrong girl to the spa?" Dani giggled, winked, and trifled with flirting pokes.

"Ah, hey, easy now! No, no, I won some money at bingo."

"You did? That's great! Let me take a look at my little professional gambler after all his pampering!" Dani grabbed John's shoulders and pushed him back. Her face turned to disappointment. "Geez John, you don't look so hot. Why is your shirt all wet? Your hair is going in strange directions," she said, using her stylist hands to fix the unruly tufts.

"To tell you the truth, I'm not feeling so good."

"Aw…was it something you ate?"

"No, I don't think so. Maybe just too much excitement today. I…I think it may be better if I don't go on the tour."

Dani pouted. "But we want you to go! It's 'cause of you Garrett gets his wish. Besides," she said, glancing back at the smiling officer before whispering, "How exciting can a bridge tour be? It's not like having a private massage with someone you have the hots for," she mischievously winked.

"And trust me…I'm beyond thrilled about that. I owe you big-time for acting as cupid, but I—"

Garrett walked closer. "Did you say you don't want to go?"

"No, Garrett. It's not that. I'm just not feeling so good."

"You smell like barf," Garrett said pinching his nose.

Dani sniffed then stared into John's eyes. "What happened, John? Something happened. I can see it. You look pale and hollow. You can trust me. Something with George?"

John watched Garrett retreat back to his sister, then shifted to the patient officer, wondering if he remembered giving him directions or their jokes about forward and aft, starboard and port.

"Good evening, sir!" the officer greeted, escalating his voice to compensate for the added distance. "I trust you found a good spot to watch the Miami skyline?"

"Oh, yes. Yes, I did. Thank you for helping."

"Don't mention it. Have you learned letting yourself go brings you to the place you're supposed to be?"

"Ah…yes and no…I mean…sort of."

"Sounds like you're close," the officer grinned. "Maybe you haven't let go quite enough yet? We still have thirty-six hours before docking in Miami—perhaps by then?"

"I hope so. There's not much left to hold."

"Ah…I don't mean to hold up the tour, but would you mind if John and I step away for a moment to talk?" Dani asked.

"Go right ahead," the officer said. "I'll watch the kids."

"Thank you," Dani said, taking John by the hand and leading him away from the traffic to a seating area in the lobby corner.

"Okay," she said with sympathy on her face, "now tell me what's wrong."

"Well…I had the best day I've had in years. One of the best ever, thanks in big part to you and Garrett."

"Sounds good so far."

"The spa treatments were exceptional, but not half as good as seeing Rita. We…we made love and I believe we have mutual feelings for each other that could turn into something very special."

"Oh, John, I think that's wonderful!"

"I had a great time with Richard and Mary at bingo and I even won close to ten grand."

"That's fan-freaking-tastic!"

"Yeah, it was. And it turns out the Captain is a friend of one of the Clawson kids. That's how Richard could arrange this tour. Everything was going great. After I went to the business lounge to tell you about it, I checked my email."

"I'm guessing your inbox wasn't full of Christmas cards or winning lottery notices?"

John sighed. "I lost my job."

"What? How do you lose a job when you're on vacation?"

"Like I told Richard one night, our company has been courted by several larger rubber companies from China. I guess I thought if something like this ever happened we would all keep our jobs—many families have been there for two or even three generations. But I guess it all comes down to money."

"So you're being bought out?"

"I got ten emails from people at work saying it was all done very hush-hush. The paperwork was signed yesterday. They made the announcement to everyone this morning—everyone but me. New management is coming in at the end of the month and everyone is to be phased out by years end."

"Leave it to fucking China to ruin Christmas!"

"Yeah…well, I don't think the Chinese celebrate Christmas. I guess our accounts are what sealed the deal. They all signed contracts promising to stick with the new ownership. We distribute to the US post office and a bunch of international florists."

"Florists?"

"They use rubber bands for the stems and gift boxes. I guess the good news is that everyone is getting a severance and at least a partial pension. But that won't be enough for the people who haven't put enough time in. Probably not enough for those of us who have—not if we live long enough." John dropped his head. "I don't know what happens with our medical benefits."

"I'm so sorry, John. Why does it always seem like bad things happen only to good people?"

"I think because bad people don't know the difference." He looked over at the officer, who appeared to be getting anxious. "You should go. I'm sure they have more important things to do than just give tours."

"I feel horrible, John. You shouldn't be alone."

"I need the time to think. Will you do me another favor though?"

"Anything."

"Richard and Mary want everyone to meet at ten for the pool party. I'm not going to make it tonight. You can tell them why if you like. I don't lie and I don't want anyone else lying on my behalf. Just tell them I needed some time to myself. Okay?"

Dani wanted to cry, but she knew that wouldn't help. She wished she could hug John's pain away, but instead, she touched his cheek lightly and said, "I will. I know you don't have a phone, but you know how to reach me and any of us can be paged by the purser. If you need anything: company, a sounding board, or just someone to get drunk with; you let us know and we'll come running. Promise?"

"I promise. Now take your kids to see the bridge. You don't want to miss out on a chance to learn something new. Oh. I almost forgot." John reached into the pocket with the wet towels and pulled out Will's iPod. "Give this back to Will for me—I won't be using it any more."

Dani didn't like the glazed look in John's eyes as she accepted the music box with a limp hand. "Are you sure you're going to be all right?"

With his body faintly wobbling and his face looking haggard and pale, John said, "No problem." Then he flicked his eyes and head upward for Dani to get going. She hesitated, but left.

Not wanting to give Garrett or the ship officer a chance to convince him to tag along, John disappeared back down the corridor. It was 8:10. He descended to the lowest passenger deck and started walking without urgency until he made a complete circle. Back where he started, he went one flight up and repeated the routine. And again, and again. He kept his head angled at the deck to avoid any eye contact; he had no desire to respond to other passengers' cursory hellos. By 10:35 he had circled every deck. He skipped only the second half of the Lido Deck where the pool party was in full swing.

Perhaps out of familiarity, the only place John stopped was the forward section where the previous night he witnessed a couple making love. The sky above should have been black, but the ship cast a dispersion of artificial light. Once when Carson was very young, he and John lay in the back yard on a particularly humid summer evening. Waiting for darkness to provide the perfect backdrop for an impending meteor shower, they debated the instant when one color turned to another. The line separating blue from black and black from blue was the most anticipated—like a grand finale or new beginning. As John leaned against the ship railing staring upward, the sky had the look of a blue, black transition, a mirage created by the ship's light. The ship was a shelter, a man-made refuge built for escaping from how things really are; without it and its crown of light the sky would be as black as John felt inside.

Everything turned black when John closed his eyes, providing the perfect backdrop for a barrage of tiny glorious snapshots whizzing by, sacred memories of times as real as the short-lived light from any ancient meteor.

Cravings urged John away from the top forward deck. He descended without laps to the promenade shops, buying Tylenol from the gift shop and a bottle of Lagavulin—Richard's favorite scotch—from the liquor store. On the way back to his cabin, he made a final stop at the pizza cart. He stacked a half pie's worth of triangles one on top of another, sandwiching them between two paper plates.

Once back in the solitude of his cabin, the only light John turned on was from the television. He set the pizza and pills on the chair ottoman, dumped his bingo winnings onto the floor, and cracked the cork seal on the sixteen-year old bottle. It was 11:02 and Robert Osborne (TCM's host) had just finished introducing the late Paul Newman's classic performance in *Cool Hand Luke*; a story about a war vet sent to a Florida prison camp for cutting off the heads of a small town's parking meters. John sucked the smoky liquor from the bottle-neck before dropping into his chair. He had seen the movie twice in his lifetime and nestled in for his third. After taking another healthy swig, he recited the line for which the movie was named: "Sometimes nothing can be a real cool hand."

MEANWHILE THE PARTY GOES ON

B Y 10:30 THE POOL PARTY was gearing up. A rock band played classics under strings of
white lights cast across the pools. People danced in quirky motions. A smoke machine, puffing
sporadically, helped lower inhibitions by concealing awkward dance maneuvers. Sweat and
perfume evaporated into the sea air. Based upon the occasional bird swooping in for a look, the
ship must not have been far away from the next port. Dani, having left her kids with Buffy, was
the last to join the group at Will's corner of the bar. After exchanging a round of hugs, thanking
Richard and Mary for an educational tour, and whispering some private girl-talk into Rita's ear,
Dani batted her eyes at Will and ordered a double rum and coke.

"Where's John?" Mary asked. "Didn't he go with you on the bridge tour?"

"Yeah, where is our boy?" Richard asked. "You gals didn't wear him out too badly today, did
you?" Smiling at the two women in a suggestive manner.

Still tingling from her spa treatment, Rita said, "Not any more than he could handle." She
grinned and lowered her mouth onto a margarita straw.

"Be good!" Mary glared at Richard. "Just tell him to buzz off. He's always sticking his nose
into other people's business."

"I think he's…what's the phrase?" Rita asked, tapping her nose. "The cat's meow! Don't you
think, Dani?"

"Maybe we should ask Mary if she'd mind us two girls taking you dancing?" Dani teased. "Do
you think you could handle the both of us?" Dani salaciously rubbed the middle of her chest just
above the small cleavage line peeking out from her sundress.

It wasn't often Richard found himself tongue-tied. He wiped his forehead to buy time while
searching for a comeback.

"The two of you are going to give him another heart attack," Mary said. "He can barely
handle me much less the two of you."

"You going to take that, Rich?" Will asked, leaning over the bar.

"I'm afraid, young buck, my wife is correct," Richard admitted, raising his wine glass. "But
it's still fun to dream."

Everyone laughed.

"You still didn't answer the question," Will said. "Where is John? You were the last one to see
him, weren't you, Dani?"

Dani took a long drink and sighed. "John got an email after he left you guys at bingo that said
Keep It Together was bought out and he'll be out of a job soon."

Everyone gasped and rolled their heads.

"Where's the company from?" Richard asked.

"China, I think," Dani said.

"Fucking China," Richard shook. "Worse than locusts."

"That was pretty much my response," Dani said.

"How did he take the news?" Rita asked nervously. "I mean…how did he look?"

Dani thought hard. "I'm not sure. He said he wanted to be alone for a while to think. He told me to let you all know he wasn't coming to the pool party. And when I asked if he was all right he said 'no problem' and grinned. But…"

"What is it?" Mary asked.

"I don't know," Dani hesitated. "The guy's been through a lot. Even though he seemed to take it well—encouraged us to go on the bridge tour without him—there was something I didn't like about his eyes."

"Vacant?" Richard asked.

"Yeah. But scary too. Like someone just knocked the wind out of him and he'd recuperated enough to be thinking about responding in kind. He smelled and his shirt was wet. I think he got sick before I talked with him." She retrieved Will's iPod from her bag. "He gave me this and said to return it to you, Will. Said he wouldn't be using it any more."

"I don't like the sound of that," Rita said. "I'm going to his cabin."

"You don't think he would…do something…do you?" Mary asked.

"I don't want to wait to find out," Rita said.

"I think we should give the man some time," Richard said, trying to calm the panic. "We've all been through difficult ordeals. Let's give the man a chance to come to grips with what's happened before we go rushing in to cut some self-imagined noose. The boy's wife left him and his son died and he's gotten through those things thus far without physically hurting himself. Let's give him 'til morning to lick his wounds, is my suggestion."

"Richard makes a point," Dani said. "Maybe I'm just overreacting?"

"I don't know," Rita said. "I don't see the harm in checking on him."

"What are you going to do?" Richard asked. "Stay there all night and watch him? Dani said the man wanted some time to think. Let's give him 'til morning."

"But what if you're wrong, dear?" Mary asked.

Richard sighed. "I know most women don't understand this, but men need to be men. We need to take charge. We have to fumble through directions to assemble our kids' toys; we need to drive over the speed limit occasionally to feel more alive; we need to spit, fart, and drink with our own kind from time to time; and when we get knocked down, we want to pick ourselves back up on our own accord, not have our mothers run to our aid with cookies and tissues. We've known the man for less than a week. Mr. Smith has character and great strength—more than we think. I also believe he's discovering that about himself. Give the man a chance to pick himself up."

Rita looked at Will who had been quietly listening while his co-workers made all the drinks. With elbows resting on the bar, Will gnawed away on a plastic drink stir as if it were a blade of grass. "You've been pretty quiet, oh great wise one," Rita said. "Do you throw anything back or just catch everything? I'm feeling pretty apprehensive here! You have any input? And comforting advice? Isn't that what you guys are known for?"

Everyone's attention focused on Will.

"Sure," he said calmly. "There is no place in an economy cabin that will support a noose. Most suicides jump over the side, in which case there's not much we can do. When a body hits the water at twenty knots from ten stories, that's all she wrote. The man's come a long way, but he's still not fond of heights."

"That's hardly what I was looking for," Rita said with hostility.

Will shifted the straw into his opposite hand. "Wanna hear a joke?"

"*Will,*" Dani frowned.

"Just listen," Will said. "It's good. See, there's this hypocrite who walks into a bar one night and sits down next to an Amish fellow. The hypocrite says to the bartender, 'I'll have what he's having.' The Amish man looks over at the hypocrite and says, 'I'm drinking cranberry juice.' The hypocrite says to the bartender, 'That's perfect.' Then he asks the Amish man, 'Why are you drinking cranberry juice in a bar?' The Amish man says, 'I'm Amish. We aren't allowed to drink alcohol. I shouldn't even be in here, but I'm trying to change. You know…something different than just work and church.' The bartender brings the hypocrite a cranberry juice. He takes a sip and turns back to the Amish man and says, 'I used to drink a lot but I got some bad news from my doctor recently. I'm trying to live healthy now.' The Amish guy says, 'Well, you're off to a good start, cranberry juice is very healthy.' The hypocrite replies, 'Yeah. I know what you mean though about change being difficult. I had to drink a half bottle of vodka in my car just to work up the nerve to come in here and not drink.'"

Mild laughter from the three women was muffled by Richard's bellow.

"Good one," Richard said.

"I thought you might appreciate that one, Rich," Will grinned. "Fact is, John Smith is tunneling out of a deep hole. He's learning that change will get him to where he wants to be. He may resort back to his old ways after the recent news, he may not. Let's give him tonight to decide for himself. However, the morning is different; we only have one day left."

"Sounds like Mr. Catcher might have a plan?" Richard asked.

Will huffed and shrugged. "Of course I do. It's already in motion. Losing his job is nothing but a wrinkle. If someone spills wine you don't stop the party. Is everyone in?"

Everyone nodded. "We're listening," Rita said.

"Good," Will said. "Now…I can't tell you everything, but lean in and I'll tell you what we're going to do…"

DAY 7
(THE VIRGIN ISLANDS)

INTERVENTIONS AND REVELATIONS PART 1

T HE *PRINCESS* DOCKED IN ST. Thomas' Charlotte Amalie harbor before the first blink of sunlight peeked over the horizon. St. Thomas is the epitome of everything American—commercial. Her harbor can hold more ships than most places in the world. During the winter months, its more than fifty-thousand residents are bombarded with sometimes almost half their population. Ship passengers storm the beaches, historic landmarks, and seemingly endless duty free shops. From its steep mountain tops, the main towns are as picturesque as any Caribbean postcard. But once within the confines of the road bustle and heavy foot traffic, the island can feel as familiar and overwhelming as any big American city.

The ship grunts hastily worked at mooring the goliath while the first passengers readied themselves for breakfast, eager to cram in a hectic day of sightseeing. By 8:15 a select group gathered outside John Smith's cabin, anxious as five siblings awaiting the go-ahead from their parents to start opening Christmas presents.

Rita pressed her ear against the door. "I don't hear anything," she said.

"He's probably still sleeping," Mary said. "Maybe we should wait 'til nine?"

"We can't," Dani said, biting her finger nails. "Will wants us all outside by then. He must be up. The letter is gone."

"What letter?" Richard asked.

"Will wrote John a letter last night after he was done cleaning up the pool bar. He made me wait so I could deliver it." She looked to the bottom of the door. "I slid it half way under around two in the morning. It's not there now."

"Are you sure?" Garrett asked, bending down to look through the slim crack. "I don't see anything."

"How about we just—"

Rita finished Richard's sentence by rapping her knuckles against the metal door. Everyone straightened up, trying to look natural. Thirty seconds passed and she knocked harder, followed by, "John. John, it's Rita. John, are you awake? The Clawsons are with me—Dani and Garrett too. We're all going ashore. John! Are you in there?" She pounded harder when a woman's voice sounded from behind.

"Are you looking for Mr. Smith?" she asked.

"Are you in charge of cleaning this room?" Mary asked.

"Yes. My name is Sylvia. Mr. Smith is a very nice man. He likes when I turn his towels into swans. I can make other animals, but he prefers the swans. He puts them on the sink so they can be close to the water."

"Have you made a swan inside Mr. Smith's cabin this morning?" Rita asked.

"Not yet. I didn't know if he wanted the room made up. He forgot to hang the door tag." Sylvia's expression changed as if some great worry struck her. "Is everything okay with Mr. Smith?"

"We're sure it is," Mary said. "Have you seen him this morning—or perhaps heard any noises from inside?"

"No. Quiet as a mouse. Sometimes he sleeps longer than he wants to."

"Ah…Sylvia was it?" Richard asked, taking a step forward.

"Yes. Sylvia."

"That's a lovely name for a beautiful girl. If I was single and a few decades younger…well, I might try to steal you away before anyone knew you were missing."

Blushing, Sylvia dropped her head in embarrassment. "Thank you."

"Maybe you can help us, Sylvia?" Richard suggested. "We are friends of Mr. Smith and we're all supposed to go ashore together this morning, but he isn't answering the door. Like you said, the lazy bum is probably over-sleeping again. Would it be possible for you to go in and check? We're on a tight schedule, you see." Richard flashed one of his favorite looks—equal amounts of charm and flirtation, an old stand-by he used like waving a magic wand. He loved to watch the results.

"Of course!" Sylvia said, making eye contact with Garrett's smiling face. "I'm sure he would want me to wake him if he knew his friends were waiting. Right?"

"Thank you, sweetie," Dani said, gently pushing the housekeeper forward.

Sylvia knocked and waited a polite amount of time before using her card. She stepped inside, everyone creeping in behind her. The room was dark. She called again for John and when he didn't answer, she flicked the light switch.

"Oh my!" she gasped, pinching her nose.

"What is it?" Rita asked pushing in beside her.

"It's a little…stinky," Sylvia declared. "Normally, I hardly need to clean."

Everyone scampered in and scanned the room.

John's bed, crisp from Sylvia's previous morning change, appeared as though it had not been slept in. John's outfit from Friday lay crumpled on the chair while the floor in front was littered with dozens of white pills intermingled with hundred dollar bills.

Garrett's eyes widened as he said, "Damn! Did John win the lottery?"

"Those are bingo winnings," Richard said.

Placing her hands over her face, Rita cried, "He ate a bunch of pills!"

"Oh my God," Dani said, hugging her own stomach. "I knew I should have checked on him."

Mary walked over to comfort the two women. Frozen, Sylvia stood staring at the floor. Richard scratched his head as Garrett moved to sit on the ottoman. He picked up one of the pills, turning it over in his fingers.

"It's just Tylenol," Garrett said, reaching down to sift through the bills. "Here's the bottle. It's still half full." He pivoted on the stool, sweeping his hand through more money. "Here's another bottle. It's half full too."

"Maybe he didn't go through with it?" Rita said.

"Here's a half bottle of La-gav-u…" Garrett stammered.

"Lagavulin," Richard helped. "The boy simply went on a bender last night. Exactly what I would have done." Richard chuckled. "Seems I've helped the man develop an expensive palate. Bad timing with the loss of a job."

"I don't think this is a time for jokes!" Rita barked.

"What is that smell?" Dani asked, waving a hand in front of her face.

Garrett picked up a trash can sitting next to the chair and stuck his nose inside. "Pizza!" he said. "A whole bunch of half-eaten pieces. Looks like pepperoni, onion, and green peppers." Sniffing, Garrett chased the bitter air, leading his nose towards the chair. He picked up John's pants. "Yuck. They're all wet!" Pulling them closer, he took a whiff before dropping them in disgust. "Smells like piss! I gotta wash my hands." Garrett frowned and scurried to the bathroom.

"It happens," Richard shrugged in the direction of the four women.

"Is Mr. Smith all right?" Sylvia asked.

"That's what we are trying to figure out," Mary said. "But I'm sure he's just fine."

"So what are we supposed to make of all this?" Dani asked.

Richard sat on the ottoman and faced the women. "I'd say our boy was feeling depressed about losing his job. He had some pizza and scotch to fuel the self-pity while he…" Richard stopped in mid-sentence to find the remote. After retrieving it from the bills, he clicked. "Yip. Just as I thought. Watched old movies on Turner. Pretty harmless, typical behavior for a crap ending to what was a great day. Damn shame! You just can't trust China. Something about their faces—stretched too tight—hard to get a read on what they're thinking. Good for the complexion, I guess." Richard noticed all four women's faces turning disconcertingly.

"That's enough!" Mary scolded. "Can't you see we are all concerned about John—not what the Chinese are thinking?"

"And your theory doesn't explain the pills," Rita said. "Tylenol is highly toxic to the liver. What if he chased a bunch of them with a bottle of scotch and decided to jump overboard?"

Richard scanned the floor. "By the looks of it, I don't think many made it to his mouth."

Growing angry, Rita snapped back, "You're so damn sure, are you? I find your cavalier attitude irritating!"

Like a beagle, Richard rolled his eyes up from the bottom of their drooping eyelids. "I don't mean to upset you. I just think we should stay positive and realize there are possibilities other than your worst fears. Why don't we call the purser to page him to his room?"

"That's a good idea," Dani said. "Let's do that!"

"I'm sorry, Richard," Rita said. "That *is* a good idea. I'm just so—"

"No need to explain." Richard stood to console Rita with a hug.

Dani picked up the phone when she heard Garrett say, "Hey, John! Forget to use the toilet last night?"

After furrowing a brow towards the bathroom, John said, "I think you're holding the wrong girl, Rich?"

Next thing John knew, a stampede of women flocked to kiss his cheeks and ruffle his hair.

Even Sylvia rubbed his arm briskly enough to start a fire. She said, "I'm happy you are alive! I will come back later to clean your room. I'll make two swans today!"

"Ah…okay," he said. "Thanks. I guess. I'm really sorry about the mess. I was going to clean it up after breakfast. I didn't want you to see it."

"Don't worry yourself," Sylvia beamed. "I'll have it shipshape in no time! Enjoy the day with your friends." She waved to everyone and went back to her other rooms.

John shifted a bagel into his opposite hand in order to accept Richard's firm shake. "I told them everything was fine," Richard said.

John sat in the chair as the three women rested their behinds against the edge of his bed.

"So…I take it this little intervention is because you all know about my job?"

"We were *concerned*," Rita said.

"That what? I might try to kill myself?"

Everyone dismissively shook their heads.

"You didn't look too good last night," Dani said.

"We missed you at the party," Mary said.

"They all thought you took a bunch of Tylenol and jumped over the side," Garrett said, standing outside the bathroom smelling his hands.

Examining each face. "Why would you think that?"

Sweeping her eyes around the ottoman, Rita said, "Look at the floor, John. What would *you* think if you came in here and saw this mess? What's with all the pills and money?"

"Well." John slipped in a bite of bagel before continuing. "After I left Dani…by the way, how was the bridge tour?"

"Cool as shit," Garrett said.

"Language," Dani said. "There are ladies present."

"It's okay," Mary said. "I have boys."

"You can thank Richard and Mary," John said. "I just told them you wanted to go. Turns out our Captain is a friend of theirs. Rich made the whole thing happen."

"Thanks, sir," Garrett said.

"Glad you enjoyed it son," Richard said pulling up the ottoman to sit. "After you left Dani?"

"Yeah. After I left Dani I walked around for hours. This ship is huge! Anyway, I was feeling really down so I thought a walk would help. I couldn't shake off feeling sorry for myself. It's an unwelcome feeling I've grown to know quite well over the last couple of years. It just seems to show up like an estranged relative at the worst time. You don't want to deal with it, but you kind of have to. I guess there's never a good time for either.

"I kept asking myself what am I going to do now without my job? It's not just the paycheck. I should have enough money—for a while anyway. The people at work are basically the only friends I've ever had. I knew most of them in college, and high school, and grade school before that. Say what you want about small towns, but there is something to be said for the routine and stability they provide. Good Intent has always been like a warm blanket for me. And like the name suggests, it means well. All the memories, the friends, my family, places, and people that serve as strong reminders of who I am. Then I thought: what if it's not me? Not all of me, I mean. Maybe the rest of me—the things I've never ventured to find—is out there waiting. Like Mary said, we are a canvas. Colorful collections of the people we meet, places we go, and the experiences we have. We should use our time to allow as many colors to touch us as we can. Memory is the real home—not a place. And we can build on and share that home wherever, with whomever. I know this now. When these big things are gone, no matter what the reason, we want to physically return to them in order to have something tangible to touch, smell, see, or taste. There comes a time for all of us when we can't.

"I thought, especially last night, I'd lost the last thing I had left to care about. When I was up on deck, I remembered a time with Carson when he was little and we lay in the yard, staring at the sky, talking about the instant when one color becomes another. I looked for one of those colors last night, but the ship's lights got in the way. Something always gets in the way. I closed my eyes and there it was—so was Carson. They'll both be right there as long as I am, and if we are really lucky—maybe longer."

Garrett disappeared into the bathroom and returned seconds later offering a box of tissues to Dani. She thanked him and passed it down the line. Sniffling, each woman took one.

"After that, I walked the promenade. I kept thinking about the ship's employees and how hard they work while having to endure drills, training, cramped living quarters, mediocre food, as well as grinning and bearing some less than ideal guests—we know a couple," he said smiling at Rita and Dani. "All the while, most of their families wait to see them again in some distant country. I suppose most of them cope for the money, but some of them I believe, the ones that last a long time, do it for all the colors they get to collect. Each week brings new passengers, every revolving contract constantly brings new co-workers, or even a new ship. Some of the stories I've heard made me feel almost sorry for the crew. But now, after all the wonderful things I've experienced this week, along with the sting of losing my job, I'm quite envious. What an adventurous way to live. Depression steered me into the duty free liquor store where I found a bottle of the wonderful scotch Richard turned me onto during our first happy hour. I suppose memories of things we enjoy take a back seat when the real thing is at our disposal. They don't make a store where I can go to buy my son, marriage, or job back, so I settled for the scotch and some pizza.

"On the way back to my cabin, I still kept hearing a voice in my head telling me that without my job, I don't have anything left. The same negative voice that taunted me when Page left me and when Carson died. The same voice I've probably listened to all my life, keeping me from asking what I really wanted, keeping me from going anywhere or trying anything new. I rationalized that damn voice wasn't all bad. Like a small town, it tries to protect me, keeping me in a safe and stable routine. But it's no good at promoting imagination or bringing color to my life, and it certainly doesn't care much for change.

"I believe my parents listen to the same voice—especially my mother. They are not imaginative people—not that I've ever seen in my lifetime. Maybe in college, or before that when they didn't know each other. Maybe my father's affair ruined their imagination and sense of adventure? For Christ's sake, my mother uses a recipe book to make plain lemonade and my dad has been an accountant most of his life for a small luggage company. Adventure to them is a weekly card game when they get together with neighborhood friends to play Spades. The only vacations they take are once a year to Nashville, TN to hear the Grand Ole Opry for the weekend. It doesn't matter. It's their life. But this is mine and I don't want to live like them any more.

"I heard another voice last night and many times this week. The voice sounded faint but strong as if it was screaming, but from a distance—from behind a door or the deepest parts of my brain. It was reminding me about some pretty great people and all the things they've overcome and accomplished. People like you, Garrett, and your Terminator. I can't imagine what it's like at such an impressionable age to watch your parents divorce, lose your leg, and come out so strong in spite of it all. I'm sure your mother has a lot to do with it. She's generous, spirited, and loves you very much. And, Richard and Mary…you exceptional people! You both could write a book on change. You've done so many wonderful things in your lifetime and raised a family while doing them. And, Rita…you educated yourself and started a business. After suffering two men who are crazy for not treating you the way you deserve, you remain as passionate, caring, and lovely a woman as I've ever met."

Richard added, "Don't forget beautiful!"

Rita blotted her eyes.

"And *very* beautiful," John said.

"What about the pills?" Garrett asked.

"The pills? Oh, I had a headache so I picked them up before I bought the scotch."

"Why are they all over the floor?" Dani asked.

John laughed. "I got into watching *Cool Hand Luke* when I got back to the cabin. Great movie about perseverance, bucking the system, and keeping a sense of humor. Any-hoo, by the time I tried opening them, I guess I'd had too much scotch. Spilled the darn things on the floor trying to get the cotton out."

"Why two bottles?" Mary asked.

"They were on special, two for one! I obviously didn't have any better luck opening the second bottle."

The explanation dispelled any remaining fears the group may have had about the chance of a suicide attempt. An odd tune of mixed laughter sang out, finally giving John time for another bagel bite.

"The rooster must have crowed early for you to go to breakfast before we got here?" Richard asked.

Swallowing. "If the rooster is a metaphor for dehydration, you're right. I'm ashamed to say I didn't even make it to the bathroom last night. I showered early this morning when I discovered that, instead of aspirin, I should have bought diapers. Once I was up and clean again, I thought I'd get some breakfast and still have enough time to get back here and tidy the room before Sylvia arrived. I was going to hang the Do Not Disturb sign when I saw an envelope under the door." Retrieving the envelope from his back shorts pocket. "I forgot about the sign and read this letter from Will on my way to breakfast. Anyone here have any idea how it found its way under my door?"

Dani slowly raised her hand.

"Thanks for playing postwoman, Ms. Green!" Pulling the letter from the envelope. "I'll read it for everyone. Before I start, has anyone ever had a honey-walnut, cream cheese bagel?"

Everyone except Mary shook their heads.

"I make cream cheese at home with almonds and vanilla," Mary said.

"That sounds good also!" John said, studying his last bite. "I've had a bagel before, but never with flavored cream cheese, or normal cream cheese for that matter— only butter. Back home, I usually go to breakfast at Joe's before work. Sometimes I meet up with some of the people from the factory. Sometimes I eat by myself. Regardless, I always order the same thing: scrambled eggs, sausage or bacon, black coffee, and for dessert, always a powdered-sugar doughnut. I love those things. This morning, I wondered how many more of Joe's doughnuts I would ever have now that I've been let go. I told the voice in my head that was craving a powdered-sugar doughnut '*not today*. Today we're going to have a bagel! And you better get used to it,' I said. I thought about Lloyd and all the wonderfully exotic foods he had growing on his property. And all the local Jamaican goodies Will and Garth brought to our lagoon picnic. And how the Jamaican kids were so excited when we gave them the leftovers. It occurred to me that I might want to start a garden when I get home. Sort of, feed my inner dragon something better than powdered doughnuts so it can help slay voices that impede change. So…I had a bagel." John popped the last bite into his mouth, joyfully grinning at everyone.

"I've never seen anyone so delighted by a bagel," Richard said. "Maybe you can get a job at a Jewish delicatessen?"

"I'm entertaining all ideas at this juncture," John said. "Will made me really think about whether I actually enjoy my job."

"What did you come up with?" Rita asked.

"I don't. I mean it's okay. I deal with customers from all over the world and trouble-shoot problems on the line, but it's basically a lot of phone and computer work—nothing blows my kilt up, so to speak. I guess that's the residual scotch talking. Can you imagine the stimulating conversation my wife was reduced to listening to after I came home from working in a rubber band factory every day? In retrospect, I'm relieved she just left me instead of strangling me with a W-8—the technical name for our strongest band."

Everyone laughed.

"I can see the headline," Dani said. "*Rubber Man Choked By Wife with Band.*"

"It would definitely sell some papers around Good Intent," John laughed. "Will was telling me the reason for the Coast Guard's visit yesterday was to pick up two employees who were fired, one for selling drugs, the other for intentionally cutting off his finger in a water tight door to get a five-thousand dollar settlement from the company. I believe people should enjoy their work—like all of you. I don't want my next job to drive me to cut off my finger."

"I guess we can rule out a job in a cutlery factory?" Mary joked.

"Yes," John said. "Well…back to Will's letter." He leaned back and began reading.

"Dear Butterfly,

"Word through the grapevine is that the company you've devoted over twenty years of your life to, sold out and shit-canned everyone. I'm sure, not the gold watch you were expecting. Like Dani and Richard said, fucking China! But, what's done is done. This too shall pass and the rest of those clichés that are supposed to make us feel better.

"If you made it through the night—I told them you would—you'll find, like we talked about in Mexico, a new day to spend how you like. It belongs to you, but I think we should celebrate. And you know me. I've made a few arrangements. Skip the beaten path stuff and join the gang for a Catcher tour.

"Now. I want to tell you a story about getting fired from Hawaiian Cruise Lines. Yes, they fired me, then hired me right back. And all because of a little facial hair! My neatly trimmed goatee to be exact. As I told you before, HCL, like your company, was bought by another company. The only difference was that all our employees maintained their jobs. Even the executives at the home office in Hawaii kept their positions, but instead of answering to themselves, they now had to answer to Miami headquarters, and ultimately, to the shareholders. Me and my goatee worked in the Miami office for six weeks prior to teaming up with the company's lone ship. They'd bought a second, used ship, but it was in a Portland dry-dock getting refurbished.

"When I finally got to Hawaii, I briefly met one of my bosses while boarding—a closed-minded food and beverage manager, career cruise ship employee, and genuine Austrian SOB named Hans. Hans gave me a weird look, but said nothing. Later that evening a bar manager friend of mine, Louis, whom I had worked with in Miami, came to my cabin to inform me that Hans told him the company didn't allow its employees to wear facial hair and that Louis was to tell me to shave. Louis and I laughed it off since we had worked alongside the president of the company in Miami and nobody there had a problem with facial hair.

"So I went to work the next day without shaving. I met some of the other bartenders, all clean shaven, but envious of my dirty lip and chin. That night, Louis delivered another warning from

Hans. And the next day I showed up again without shaving. This went on for three more days, starting an uprising, not purposely mind you. A silent mutiny of prickly-faced bartenders who also wanted goatees. Eventually, the others gave in to their razors. I received one final warning and when I showed up unshaven the next day, Louis, laughing, came to collect me for dismissal.

"He brought me to the hotel director's office where a semi-circle of my peers sat waiting for the head honcho's arrival. My union representative, Louis, the Hawaiian office secretary, and even Hans, finally joined the group for the lynching. Joe, the director, entered the room and sat at his desk. Puzzled, he stared at me and said, 'This is why we're here? I thought you would have spiked pink hair or some metal rod pierced through your nose.' Everyone laughed. He asked me why I wouldn't just shave. I told him I've always worn it, nobody in the Miami office told me it was an issue, and besides, I like the way I look. He leaned back and thought for minute, then he said, 'I know what you mean. I had to have my chest shaved one time when I was in the hospital and it really bothered me. I like my chest hair,' he said. Then, returning from memory lane, he said he understood, but he didn't make the rules. He asked me again if I would shave. I said no. He signed my termination papers and they gave me a ticket to fly back to Oahu.

"The secretary hooked me up with a cheap room at a fancy hotel reserved for ship employees. She forged the paperwork so it looked like I was still employed. I think she felt bad. It didn't matter to me. I was still turning in all my expenses to Miami and they promptly reimbursed my account. I called the guy who hired me in Miami and he was pissed that they'd fired me—told me to hang tight and he'd get me to Oregon to join the other dry-docked ship. I lived it up in Honolulu for a week—all on the company's dime.

"When I got to Portland, the guy from the office up there wasn't too happy to see me. I guess the news of the rebellious bartender had spread through the company by then. He was a big guy, but seemed almost afraid of me. Delicately, before permitting a photograph for my employee ID card, he escorted me outside and asked me nicely to shave. Six-hundred employees were showing up the following week and he didn't want them to think they could have facial hair. So I did. He thanked me and took my picture and I never shaved again.

"A few days passed, I had ample new growth, and a new Hans to give me shit. I just ignored him. Then the new employees all showed up. By this time, everyone had heard and I developed an infamous reputation. Everyone liked me, like I was some kind of Charles Bronson vigilante. It was kind of fun.

"Then, I get pulled into new Hans' office and he tells me they are going to start training and procedure meetings for all the workers and insists I shave. I asked him why they even had the rule. He said anyone who handles food or beverages has to be clean shaven so no hair gets into the product. John, you've seen my goatee. There is a far greater chance that an eyelash could fall into a drink before a two millimeter chin hair. 'Policy,' he says. 'No facial hair around food and drinks.' I say to him: 'What food? What drinks? What passengers? We are in dry-dock.' I think that pissed him off, but he couldn't argue with the logic. So…we determined that I didn't have to shave until we took on passengers.

"It was funny. I sat in on meetings, listening to the powers that be spout on about ship policies, including, no facial hair. People would turn to look at me, giggling and giving me thumbs-up. It all didn't make our bosses look good. I'm sure they were pissed about not looking like they were in charge. I didn't care. The boat had too many other problems to be concerned about some whiskers—big problems, like the idiots that bought the boat didn't do an inventory before they took her over. The former employees stole everything, sabotaged all the heads with anything they could flush, and left every key that unlocked anything on the ship unlabeled, in one big box. They had to change thousands of locks. It was a mess and there were signs of bigger problems to come.

"Well, eventually we pulled out of Portland to pick up our first batch of passengers in California. It took two tries. A few fires and dropping one rusted anchor into the Pacific set us back a couple of weeks. We do *finally* get there and collect our eight hundred guinea pigs for the maiden voyage of the *S.S Rusty Turd*.

"A couple of days go by and I'm slinging drinks in the theatre bar when this short, stumpy guy with a full Grizzly Adams beard is watching me with shifty eyes. I ask him if I can help. He tells me his name and says he's the head Seafarer union rep. I say, 'nice to meet you' and he chuckles through this bee hive of hair surrounding his mouth and says, 'You really got 'em by the balls now.' I ask him what he means and he says, 'They can't fire you twice for the same thing. You have single-handedly changed the policy for the entire company. All employees are now allowed to have facial hair.' I bought him a drink and we had a good laugh about it all.

"So why tell you all that, you might ask? Besides being a pretty good story, I thought you might like to hear about someone else losing a job—sort of. That whole misery loves company thing. But if you want a point, John, consider this…

"Sometimes we are forced into horrific change. Other times we get to decide what changes are right for us, even if that means not changing. And sometimes, the decision to not change turns out okay too, and can even help others to change—even a big cruise line.

"That said…they did go out of business eight months later, but I don't believe facial hair had anything to do with it. Fact is, Miami and Hawaii couldn't change or compromise. It was their way or no way, just like the assholes in Washington. Miami wanted everything their way—which in itself was a microcosm of different ideas and beliefs—and Hawaii wanted it to be the way it always was, even if that meant little or no profit. In the end…something breaks.

"Losing your job was a forced change, but it opens all kinds of doors for you to make changes of your own choosing. Seize the opportunity. Besides, I got the impression that wasn't your dream job anyway. You're too good for that place. Don't let 'em snap you around! Ha Ha.

"Now. Get your suit. Throw on a good t-shirt, and let's have some fun!

"Your friend, Will Catcher."

"Hell of a good story!" Richard roared.

John repacked Will's letter and said, "That was really nice of him to take the time. Pretty good advice too, don't you think?"

"As you know," Mary said, "I'm not in the business of giving advice, but Will is a bartender so I guess that qualifies him. If he got a degree, sounds like he would make a darn good psychologist."

"I think you've made a pretty good friend," Rita said.

John looked at Garrett before turning to Dani. "He's a keeper—don't you think?"

Dani returned John's gaze with an agreeable smile.

"It's eight-fifty," Garrett said. "Aren't we supposed to be outside soon?"

The women hopped up from the bed. Rita, still feeling bad for barking, offered a hand to help Richard off the ottoman.

"Anyone know what Mr. Catcher has in store for us?" John asked.

"We've been briefed," Richard said. "I think you're on a need-to-know."

"Well then, you must feel special?" John said with hands on hips. "I guess I'd better throw on my suit."

"Don't forget a funny t-shirt," Dani said. "He'll give you shit if you don't have another one."

"I think I might have packed something that will work." John dug into his suitcase before hustling into the bathroom to change out of his shorts and polo. Two minutes later he held the front door open and said, "I'm ready! Let's get this show on the road."

Chuckling, each person passed by piling into the corridor. Last in line, Rita stopped, smiled, and planted a single but passionate kiss on John's lips. She flicked the brim of his Chiefs ball-cap before examining his t-shirt. "Good Intent Community College—Not Big, But Smart," she read. "That's a hell of a sales pitch. Will should get a kick out of that."

"It must be true," John said. "I graduated from there and I wound up here with you." Flattery earned him another kiss.

"You guys coming, or you just going to stand there all morning making out?" Dani asked.

"Shall we?" Rita asked.

"I'm ready. By the way, where's George?"

"He's meeting us at Magens Bay. I told him I was going into town early to buy some souvenirs and would take a cab to meet him."

"What? Us? What are you talking about? Are you trying to get me beat-up again?"

"It's going to be fine—I think."

"You think?"

"Will told me to make sure George meets us at the beach. Specifically, by the boat dock. He said it's crucial that George joins us."

"He must be crazy!"

"Will said to trust him and nobody is going to let anything happen to you. I trust Will's plan is going to somehow be beneficial. I don't know how, but I trust him. Do you?"

"I suppose so. He's not making it easy though! Maybe I should plan ahead and take some of those Tylenol now?"

"Not a good idea since I'm sure we're going to be drinking today."

"I'm ready right now! Where's my scotch?"

"Let's go!" Garrett cried impatiently.

"Come on, John," Rita said taking his hand. "It's you and me. Let's go do this."

"Okay. But if I don't come back from port, tell my parents they can have my house and Prius."

INTERVENTIONS AND REVELATIONS PART 2

L IKE HUNKS OF RAW COTTON, puffy white clouds hovered in the bluest of blue skies above the lush green mountains. Passengers spilled onto Havensight Pier where they poured into shops or were scooped-up by safari buses shuttling them to the island's hotspots: Water Island, Coral World at Coki Beach, Fort Christian, Mountain Top, the duty-free shopping mecca in Charlotte Amalie, or the world famous three-quarter mile strand of gypsum white beach in Magens Bay.

The six compadres—on one hand looking like an odd duck group, and on the other, looking like any extended family—met up with Buffy, Elli, and their three girls. The kids were dressed for a day at the beach and fidgeting with youthful impatience. After two minutes of formalities, including a curt brush-off from Elli to John, Will suddenly materialized from the pier crowd. He spoke only four exuberant words: "Good morning! Follow me!" before marching ahead. His pace suggested urgency, but he did turn every dozen or so strides to make sure he hadn't lost any of his flock.

Halfway down the pier, Will slowed his gait as he called and waved Garrett to his side. John watched the two exchange dialogue as if they were hatching a plan. Will's intermittent glances to check on the group made whatever the two were discussing seem more like a conspiracy than chit-chat.

An empty sort of Mr. Rogers or San Francisco style open-air trolley on wheels waited at the end of the pier. Will greeted the driver of the electric blue vehicle as if they were friends, helped Garrett up the first step, and turned like a good host to usher everyone else aboard.

"Good morning again, everyone, and thank you for coming! I've rented Dave here and his comfortable trolley to shuttle us around for the day. We have it all to ourselves! I've already taken care of Dave, but he's not shy about accepting tips, so if anyone wants to kick in a few bucks at the end of the day, he won't be offended. There is an icy tub of adult beverages in the back along with juice and water. Everyone help yourselves. The drive to Magens takes close to a half-hour. It'll be a lot of steep ups and downs and twisty turns over the mountain on the way to the north side. So be aware, you've been warned, and you'll want to keep an eye on the kids. It makes Dave look bad when someone flies out—just kidding," he said, extending his palm to help everyone climb aboard.

Buffy and Elli helped their daughters, followed by Jill and Dani. Dani kissed Will's cheek before safety-guarding Jill's waist up the steps.

"Aw shucks," Will said. "Morning, Mary!"

Rubbing Will's arm, Mary said, "And good morning to you! Thank you for arranging private transportation. And nice letter. Sound advice," she snapped and pointed.

"I try," Will said.

"Morning, son!" Richard said, shaking hands harder than usual in response to Will's equally firm grip.

"Sir!"

Next in line, Rita sent him a relieved smile from beneath her broad hat and said, "You were right."

"Told you so," Will said, clicking his tongue against his tooth.

"Don't rub it in," she shot back from the top step.

"And last but not least!" Will said. "Rough night, Butterfly?"

Grinning. "Every rubber band has to break sometime."

"I hear you're good at bingo—ever think about opening a parlor?"

"The same day you shave that peach fuzz off your face."

"Don't hold your breath!"

"Seriously. Thanks for the letter, Will. It meant a lot."

Striking John's back with the flat of his hand, Will said, "Love the t-shirt! *Not big, but smart,* that cracks me up. Now let's get going," he said, pushing John towards the steps. "I have a feeling it's going to be a big day for you!"

"You know something I don't?"

"Tons of stuff, John, but you're *catching* up…pun intended, of course!"

Dave opened a trunk behind the driver's seat normally reserved for his personal belongings and helped the women store their beach bags. After firing up some obligatory Bob Marley tunes, he steered into the thick traffic and rubbernecked out of town towards the abruptly steep countryside.

Will played bartender as if he were still on *The Princess*, opening bottles of wine and beer and mixing juice concoctions for the kids. Everyone's mood turned light and jovial, everyone but Elli, who kept glaring at John and Rita. Oblivious to Elli's sharp glances, the couple talked and laughed out the trolley's windowless side while admiring the soaring view. Elli's daughter, Brie, not receiving the undistracted attention that Buffy was lavishing on her own daughter, abandoned her self-absorbed mother to play with Jill. Shortly after, recoiling her pointer finger several times, Elli beckoned Dani to sit beside her.

"What's up?" Dani asked, sliding down the bench seat.

"You told us last night that we were going to take the girls to the beach today," Elli whispered.

"We are."

"You didn't say anything about farmer John or the senior citizens tagging along. And what is Georges' wife doing with Kansas' real life version of the scarecrow? Although, he could just as easily be confused with the rusty tin man or cowardly lion I suppose."

"I didn't mention it because I thought you wouldn't join us if I did, and we so wouldn't want to be without your charming company."

"Very funny. And you're right, I would have said no. I just don't get it. The hot bartender I understand. It's not like you can just bang him on the ship. Not unless he snuck you into his cabin or a lifeboat or some dark place on deck where no one could tell he was an employee. But here Buffy and I can run interference with the kids while you two find some secluded spot to play red snapper finds sea cucumber or whatever."

"Nice. Very crass. No wonder your ex upgraded to a librarian."

Elli huffed. "I bet underneath her reading glasses and fully buttoned blouses, she's just as kinky as a Bangkok flight attendant."

"And who cares if she is? He paid you off; you should be happy."

Gazing at Rita, Elli said, "I'll be happy when I land George. He's worth real money—millions."

"Pretty sure of yourself?"

"We made a connection."

"I bet you did."

"Did you guys ask yourselves what's going to happen if George comes to the beach and sees Rita and John together? He's still pissed about John accusing him of banging a hooker in Cozumel. He knows John told you, you told me, and I told him."

"Nobody is worried about that possibility."

"Why's that?"

"Well," Dani stood up, "because we invited him."

Dani enjoyed the dumbfounded expression on Elli's face for a moment before she joined Will and the Clawsons on the opposite side. Elli relied on multiple glasses of wine to keep her company for the remainder of the trip while the others talked and laughed amongst themselves. Even Brie paid her mother little attention. Sitting side-saddle, arm resting on the window ledge, and gulping Chardonnay, Elli blankly stared at the passing landscape. She was wondering why Dani, or anyone for that matter, would have invited George.

The ride down the winding mountain seemed slower than the trip up. Gravity forced Dave to pump hard on the heavy trolley's brakes. Everyone held their breath when audacious locals sped around and ducked in front just before the next blind turn. Glimpses of powder blue water flashed through breaks in the trees, until the trolley descended over a thousand feet to near sea level. Entering a white sand parking lot speckled with mature palms, Dave paid the per-head admission fee out of the sum Will had given him.

"Welcome to Magens Bay!" Will announced. "Bring your drink and don't worry about the back-ups. Dave has promised to keep the reserves iced down until we need them again." Will walked to the front and leaned over Dave and said, "You good on sitting here? It might be four or five hours."

"Ain't but a thing," Dave said propping his feet on the wheel. An ex-Floridian from the Orlando area, Dave, like many other menial laborers, moved to the island five years earlier to escape. He found life in St Thomas to be a more pleasing lifestyle than the paternity suit and minor drug charges he left on the mainland. Below the aristocrats with Hollywood-style homes and a large population of poor natives, there was a revolving crop of misfits anxious to move to paradise. They were willing to clean houses, serve meals, and crew boats in exchange for the relaxed island lifestyle. St. Thomas was American, running almost as professionally as any state side beach community and feeling more like Fort Lauderdale than a third-world, shanty-home Caribbean island. Still, it was an island. Dave figured if anyone wanted him they'd have to brave the moat of the Caribbean to get him. "You paid for the day. Chilling here with some brews sounds like a good way to pay the rent to me."

"Just make sure you're straight to get us back."

"No worries, bra! I'm going to burn one and take a nap. Here when you need me."

Will turned back to the busy group sorting through their beach gear. "Follow me," he said. "I want to show you guys something." Finding Garrett, Will said, "You take your sister. I'm going to talk to your mom for a minute."

"Got it!" Garrett said.

Will escorted Dani off the trolley ahead of everyone else. "Did you tell Buffy what to do?"

"Yeah, but we'll probably have to remind her. You want to tell me yet what you really have planned?"

"Shortly," Will grinned. He took her bag and her hand. "Too bad Garth had to pull a shift today. He would have enjoyed this. It should be worth the price of admission. Just follow my lead."

Dani turned with smitten eyes. "Honey, I'll definitely let you lead."

Waiting for the others to catch up, Will kissed Dani, then asked, "You remember what to say?"

Clenching her jaw, Dani said, "It's not like I had to memorize a script."

Through the rustling palms the parking area opened up to one of the world's most beautiful beaches, heart-shaped, like two abutting crescents at the bottom of the horseshoe bay. The deep water sand bottom and northwest exposure meant only swimming pool lapping waves—ideal for children.

"Beautiful," Mary said. "It's amazing what God can build."

"It's more amazing that human beings haven't screwed it up," Richard said. "I don't see one piece of trash anywhere. I expect that in the Keys, but this beach sees hundreds of people every day."

"You've been here before, haven't you, Richard?" Will asked.

"Yes. A few times."

"We aren't crazy about how crowded it gets, though," Mary said.

"I'll see what I can do about that," Will said. "I like this place, but I had something else in mind." Will continued before anyone could ask. "As Richard and Mary probably already know, most of this place was a gift to the municipality of St. Thomas in 1943 to be used as a public park."

"By Arthur Fairchild," Rita added. Everyone turned with impressed looks. "I'm naturally a product of the Caribbean, you know. You should see Cuba. It's splendid."

"Very good," Richard said. "She's correct. I believe the same family donated the remainder of the west side ten years ago or so?"

"Give that man a cigar!" Will said.

"The sand is so soft," John said, digging in with his feet. "It's softer than Cotton's hair."

"I think you mean softer than cotton," Elli said. "Cotton is made of fiber, not hair." Her smug tone caused everyone to silently stare.

"Cotton is the name of my friend's dog in Jamaica," Will defended.

"Oh," Elli said, mildly embarrassed.

"Anyway, let's walk down to the far east side," Will said.

After a hundred yard march the group reached the beach's main building, housing a bar, souvenir shop, and snack concession.

Trying not to sound rehearsed, Dani halted and asked, "Maybe the kids would like a snack?"

Being one of only two people not to have been briefed, John said, "I could use a snack!"

Thrown for a loop, Will said, "Ah…I have food planned for everyone, but it wouldn't hurt if the kids want something now. You can wait, *can't you, John?*"

"Sure," John said, taking the hint.

"Maybe some…*ice cream?*" Dani asked, kneeling down to the three girls who all jumped, giggled, and screamed *yeah*. "Why don't you take the girls for some ice cream, Buffy, and then catch up?"

"That's a good idea," Will said.

"Now?" Buffy whispered, even though everyone could hear her.

"Yes, sweetie, *now*," Dani scowled.

Anxious to continue the wine buzz she'd been working on so diligently, Elli said, "I wanna drink. I'll go with you."

Forgetting her role, Buffy said, "Okay!"

Rita, the Clawsons, and Garrett anxiously watched to see what Will was going to say next.

"Ah...it looks pretty busy," Will said. "There's no reason for you both to wait in line when I have *special* drinks waiting for us down by the boats. Plus they're free. Can the adults wait?"

"Yeah, let Buffy take care of the kids' snack," Dani said, wrapping her arm around Elli's shoulder. "Come on! We've been too short with each other lately. Let's go get a drink together and bury the hatchet."

"There's my girl!" Elli said. "We have been a couple of bitches lately—one of us more than the other, I think," she winked. "I guess I can wait. Do you promise your drinks are better than what's here, Will?"

"Trust me, I've got just what you need!"

"Ah...am I still supposed to take the kids for ice cream?" Buffy asked.

"Yes," Dani glared and gritted. "Take-the-kids-for-ice cream."

"Okay."

Finally able to corral the adults farther down the beach, Will and Dani exchanged a wink.

Beach chair and boat concessions grew more apparent with each step. Small wind-crafts with neon sails, paddle boats, and several kayaks lay on the sand at the far east end. A spattering of skiffs and inflatable Zodiacs were anchored just off shore and a man with a ball-cap covering his face lay in one as if killing time or sleeping off a hangover. Moored in deeper water a hundred feet out, a forty foot catamaran morphed the tiny water toys.

Elli was first to notice a bald, black waiter wearing a brilliant smile and dark sunglasses, guiding an oval drink tray on top of the water. He waded towards lazy sunbathing rafters. Swaying his head from side to side in a Stevie Wonder manner he slowly, almost romantically, as if singing his sales pitch, kept repeating: *"c-o-c-k-t-a-i-l-s*, anybody need a ...*c-o-c-k-t-a-i-l?"*

"Look at that!" Elli said. "That guy brings drinks right to your raft. You don't even have to get out of the water!"

"That's Niles," Will said. "He's kind of famous around here—been working here forever—makes a lot of money. The women love him, too."

"I can see why," John said.

"Now that's what I call a real character," Richard said.

"I want him to wait on me," Elli said.

"You'll get your chance in a little bit," Will said, trying not to laugh. "Right now, we're supposed to meet up with George."

"Does he know we're all meeting him?" Elli asked.

Rita shot her best glare. "He will in a minute," she said.

"Did I *do* something to you that I should be aware of?" Elli asked.

Rita feigned confusion. "I don't know...did you?"

"I understand he's divorcing you, so you shouldn't be upset with him talking to other women, right?"

"Not at all!" Rita shrugged. "He's been *talking* to other women for years. All I'm concerned with is getting his signature on my divorce papers." She reached into her bag that was hanging from John's hand. "See! I carry them with me wherever I go—never know when the opportunity will present itself. That way I can get them to my attorney quicker. Yes, I'm quite looking forward to that signature. It's going to be better than sex!"

"Maybe that's why he's divorcing you," Elli said under her breath.

"I'm sorry, did you say something else?" Rita asked.

"Look!" Will said, not wanting to have to break up a cat-fight. "I think I see George." He pointed to a shirtless man sitting in the sand and talking on his cell phone.

Glancing to the side, George quickly recognized the people walking towards him, dismissed his caller, and stood. John felt a nervous tingle at the sight of George's bulging chest, muscular arms, and chiseled face. George stood and stared like a caged gorilla with his arms dangled slightly in front of his torso in a sort of posed, relaxed flex. John couldn't pull his eyes away from the Chinese symbols running down George's right bicep.

Fucking China, he thought.

Breaking the ice, Will said, "Morning, George! I'm glad you could make it! Sorry we're a little late—trollies don't take the mountain like a good four-by-four."

George looked a little taken aback both at seeing Elli and by Will's cheer. He frowned at John who stood next to Rita, still uneasily clinging to her bag. "What's all this?" George asked.

"It's a party, dude!" Will said, slapping George's shoulder in a good spirited manner. "Lighten up!"

"What the hell, Rita, you told me we were going to spend the afternoon together on the beach?"

Matter-of-factly, Rita said, "Here we are and here's the beach. Which part are you confused about, honey?"

Seeing the older couple and young Garrett, George tried stifling the obscenities pushing at the inside of his mouth, but the sight of John caused him to fail. "What the fuck are you doing here?" he growled. "And why are you holding my wife's bag? I thought I told you to stay away from her!"

John quaked and lifted his hands allowing Rita's pastel sack to sway back and forth. "I —"

"Whoa now!" Will said. "Take it easy there, cowboy."

"You watch your damn mouth!" Richard warned.

"I got this, Richard," Will smiled. "He's here for the same reason everyone is, because I invited him. Although I'll have to admit, you and your girlfriend I invited indirectly."

"I don't know what you're talking about," George said calmly. "But if you're feeling frisky, just jump. I'm not afraid of you."

Laughing, Will replied, "That may be the case, but I bet the thought of losing ten million dollars might send a load into your bathing suit? It's nice, by the way—Tommy Bahama?"

John's inner dragon was still napping and the voice in his head was saying to avoid confrontation. Timidly, he said, "Will, let's not start something."

"Oh, we're not here to start something," Will said, still very calmly. "George took care of that Monday when he was rude to Dani and threatened you."

"What the hell are you talking about?" George asked. "I did no such thing. What ten-million dollars?"

"Yes you did!" Dani said.

"See," Will said. "She thinks you did. And when a woman thinks something like that is true, it must be. You must remember—at the bar? My name's Will Catcher and I don't miss much, especially when I'm working."

"And that stunt you pulled at Solace Point," Mary said. "I mean, *really*…pouring liquor over John's head and threatening him just for applying suntan lotion to Rita's back! You must be insecure?"

John's inner dragon stirred at the sound of people defending him. Blindly passing the bag to Rita, he took a step forward and said, "And I'm not standing at a urinal in Mexico now."

George laughed. "The eye's starting to lose its color, John, you want me to touch it up for you, or you going to let all these people fight your battles for you?"

Clenching his fist and gritting his teeth, John used the memory of leg teif to pour a shot of gasoline down his dragon's throat. "Just me, George. Just me."

Taking a fighter's stance, George turned sideways and raised his fists to chest level. Reading John's shirt, he said, "Let's go, Mr. Not-big-but-smart?"

Still managing to sound light, almost chipper, Will interjected by stepping in front of John's right side and saying, "Easy there, Muhammad Butterfly! Like I said, we didn't start all this, but we're going to finish it. And I'd like to hurry up. I hate wasting port time." Slinging two fingers in Garrett's direction, Will said, "You're up kid!"

Everyone had aligned themselves in a semi-circle in front of the main draw. Garrett stepped forward and reached into his bathing suit pocket to retrieve his mother's iPhone. "Thanks, bull-rider!" he said.

"Why do you always have my phone?" Dani asked. "I told you not to put it in your suit pocket. What if you forget it's in there when you go swimming?"

"Mom, never mind about that. I have something to show you."

"Is this really the time and place?" Dani asked. "It's a bit…tense right now."

"Definitely the right time and place," Will chuckled. "You're going to love this," he said to George.

Walking to his mother, Garrett said, "You know I like taking pictures and since you won't get me my own iPhone, I have to use yours."

"Yeah, I know. I can't keep track of all the pictures you take. But they're all very good, honey!"

"Well, I think there are a few you should look at now," he said, turning on the phone and scrolling his fingers across the touch screen until he found what he was looking for. "Here," he said, handing over the phone and grinning smugly as his mother's eyes widened. "There's three more after that one."

"Holy s-h-i-t," she gasped. "You need to see this, Rita!"

Rita took a step and leaned in. "Oh my!" she barked with a half laugh, half shocked gasp. "You dirty boy, George!"

George had replaced his fighter grimace with a drawn expression of curiosity. "What is it?" he asked.

"And Elli!" Rita said with an escalating tone as she bashfully turned. "Looks like you have been doing more than just talking to my husband."

"What the fuck?" Ellie asked, dashing over as Rita handed over the phone. Stunned, Elli stumbled over to George with her eyes glued to the pictures. "You're not going to like these," she mumbled.

"Let me see," George said, taking the phone.

"What is it?" John asked Garrett.

"Turns out the kid is quite a good photographer!" Will announced. "He could be the next Ansel Adams, if he changes to landscapes that is. I especially liked the one where you turn her into a wheelbarrow, George. You look pretty strong but you're flexible too! That must have been a difficult move on those deck chairs?"

Mary let out an abashed laugh inside her hand and Richard howled.

George clasped his fist around the phone and stared up with piercing eyes. "So what?" he asked, looking around before stopping at Rita. "So the brat took some pictures of us screwing. You don't want to be with me anyway. I thought if we took this trip I might be able to convince you to stay, but you've made it abundantly clear the entire trip that you weren't going to give me another chance. What's the difference?"

"That's right," Rita said. "You used up all your chances long before this cruise. And what better way to say you're sorry than ten-million dollars. You do remember the prenup clause that says I get a hundred thousand if we split?"

"Of course I do."

"Then you should remember the paragraph in there that states with proof of infidelity on your part, that pittance turns into ten-million."

"Should have stuck with hookers, George, they're a lot cheaper," John said.

Infuriated, George whipped around and tossed Dani's phone into the bay. "Fuck you!" he said, scowling in outrage towards John and then Rita. "Now you got nothing, but tomorrow you'll get your divorce and the two-hundred we agreed upon. You can sink it into that flailing boutique of yours for all I care."

"Why'd you have to throw my mom's phone into the ocean?" Garrett asked. "I already emailed all the pictures to her account."

Wry chuckles sounded.

Walking over to Garrett, Rita wrapped her arms around his shoulders. "From now on you just consider me your rich aunt Rita—whatever you need!" she said. Then resting one arm on the young man's shoulder, she planted a big kiss on Garrett's cheek and turned to George and Elli. Everyone broke out into laughter; everyone except George and Elli, that is.

"Now!" Will said. "I believe you owe us one phone and one signature—really no reason to wait 'til tomorrow, is there?"

Enraged, George said, "Fuck you, bartender! I'm going to kick your ass!"

As if the words directed at his friend triggered a spring, John's inner dragon wielded a haymaker. But the swing proved too long and too slow. George tilted his head in time, enough that John's knuckles skimmed only a right ear. Being a southpaw, George returned his left fist with full might—not the jab John felt in Cozumel. Defenseless, John saw it coming but could only close his eyes. A loud thud sounded in his brain, like two coconuts had been slammed together. An instant later he was relieved to open his eyes and feel no pain. However, George was writhing in the sand holding his bloodied face.

"You picked the wrong guys," Will said. "I used to ride bulls! You ain't nothin' but an inconvenience. And I've seen Butterfly here hogtie a deranged Rastafarian like a new born calf!" Will laughed so hard he had to bend over to relieve a stomach cramp.

Elli—crouched down to aid George—stood and said, "Why couldn't you all just mind your own business! This is all your fault!" she screamed at John. "And yours—you little crippled shit!"

Nothing in Elli's lifetime had prepared her for the swiftness of a protective mother defending her child. Dani shot forward when the first syllable of *crippled* stabbed her ears. One right-cross against Elli's jaw later and she was lying beside George.

"Last strike!" Dani said.

"Wow!" Garrett shouted.

"Nice punch, hun!" Will said.

"This is my kind of day!" Richard said. "Best shore excursion ever, don't you think, Mary?" Shocked by the violence, Mary remained silent, her mouth open and her hand partially veiling her eyes.

"Do you need a pen?" John asked, watching George spit blood.

"Oh, I have one!" Rita said digging through her bag. "Here's a towel, honey. Don't get any blood on the papers—the lawyers might think I forced you to sign."

George accepted the towel while steadying himself into a seated position. "I can have your job for this."

"You can try, but I don't think you'll have much luck!" Will cheerfully declared. "We're in port, not on the ship, plus…well, let's just say, it would be useless to try."

Pressing the towel to his pancaked nose, George reluctantly signed his name in four places as Rita flipped through the divorce pages—pages she knew better than the attorney who drew them up. Elli moaned as she shuffled her bruised jaw back and forth.

"Now you can go have Niles serve you that cocktail," Dani said.

"Better than that!" Will said. "You guys can have the whole beach without us bugging you with pictures or asking for autographs and we'll call your busted nose even payment for Dani's phone. Anyway, we're going to a better beach, so you guys can keep this one. You might want to go to the bar as soon as possible for ice. It helps with the swelling, right John?"

"It sure does!" John said, mimicking Will's enthusiasm. "And if you need a touch-up, I'm afraid you'll have to antagonize someone else. As you can tell…I'm not much of a fighter."

Rita cupped John's cheeks and began kissing him the way two lovers say goodbye at the airport. "But you're a wonderful lover," she said.

George stood and helped Elli to her feet as the group parted to let them through.

"I've gotta get Brie," Elli said.

"Let's go," George said.

Waiting 'til they stumbled ten feet or so, Will said, "By the way, Elli, Dani tells me you had a good time in Jamaica—topless beach, ganja brownies? I hear you even rode a mechanical bull?"

Turning back, she said, "So what?"

"Nothing really," Will said, "just a piece of advice. The way to ride those things is exactly the opposite of how you ride a real bull."

"Come on," George said. "Let's get away from these assholes."

"See," Will continued as George walked away, "when a real bull bucks his head or flank at you, you move in the direction it's going, not at it—that's how you get smacked. A fake bull doesn't have a head and horns to smack you in the face so you move against the bucking."

"Like I care," Elli said clenching her jaw.

"I only mention it because, just like in real life, you get better results when you go with the flow, not against it. You strike me as a person who thinks life is a fake bull. Maybe I'm wrong but you sure seem like an against-the-grain gal."

Elli didn't try to respond. Maybe her jaw hurt too much or maybe somewhere deep inside there was a voice telling her: *he's right*. Sulking, she followed after George.

"You can do it whichever way you like on the fake bull!" Will continued. "Just keep in mind, in the real world, there's not usually a mat to break your fall!"

"Don't waste your breath, my boy," Richard said.

"It's our job to try," Will grinned. "Besides…I'm havin' fun!"

Richard laughed as John watched Buffy and the girls approach Elli and George. The couple paused just long enough for Elli to grab Brie's hand before continuing towards the snack building.

"Poor Brie," John said. "The kids always pay the price."

Dani jogged up the beach to meet Jill.

"Did I miss something?" Buffy asked.

"Hello, sweetie," Dani said. "Did you enjoy your ice cream?"

"Hum-huh," Jill smiled, with chocolate covered lips.

Dani used her thumb to clean Jill's face. "You missed a lot, but I'll fill you in later," she said.

"Was there a fight?" Buffy asked. "George's face was all bloody and Elli was mean to me."

"I wouldn't call it a fight, but a couple of punches were thrown. Everything's good now. But just so you know, you won't be cutting Elli's hair any more. She's no longer welcome in the shop. Any problems with that?"

"Heck no! It's your shop Dani, whatever you want. I never liked her much anyway. She's always talking about herself—never asks about me or Kayla. She tips bad, too. Why have all that money and never leave more than ten percent? I really like being your friend and working for you. You know, a lot of people look at me like I'm stupid or something, but you never have. You treat me with respect. Some people look at me like I'm a dumb blond with big boobs."

The two women took their daughters' hands and began walking back towards the boats.

Laughing, Dani said, "I love you, Buffy. You're my best friend. But…you did buy some damn big boobs!"

"You think I should change back?"

"Never!" The four joined hands to swing Jill and Kayla. "Of all the people I know, you're the most perfect of all. Don't ever change."

"Thanks, Dani!"

Rita and Mary met Dani and Buffy for a chance to act silly and fawn over the two little girls while the men made their own loose huddle.

"You guys did a good job of keeping the children away from that nonsense," Richard said.

"Thanks, Rich," Will said. "I thought John was going to screw up the program there for a minute."

Throwing up his arms, John said, "How was I supposed to know I wasn't allowed to have a snack? You guys put me on a *need to know* basis. Maybe no snacks was something I needed to know?"

The four men laughed.

"How in the world did you get those incriminating pictures?" Richard asked.

Garrett played modest. "Just by paying attention, I guess. I listened to everyone talking when we were at Carlos 'n Charlie's about Rita needing proof for her divorce. Plus, I knew John had the hots for her so I wanted to help him out."

"I don't know where you got that from," John said, playing dumb.

"Come on dude, Mom called you out on that one," Garrett said. "Plus, I saw you checking out Elli and George at the bar. I knew that asshole hit you in the bathroom. After that I figured I'd do a little recon. I got my chance the other night. Just luck I guess. I was walking around and I stopped to climb up to the little sunbathing area on top of the pool bar. It was too dark for them to see me."

"Didn't they see the camera flash?" Richard asked.

"Guess not. If you look at the pictures, they have their eyes closed. I didn't know it was them 'til he turned her around. I might not 'ave gotten their faces if he didn't do that."

"Thank the Kama Sutra for doggie-style!" Will said.

"I saw a flash," John said. "I thought it was something in the sky or maybe the couple taking pictures of themselves. Did you know I was on the other side of the ship?"

"Yip. The flash you saw was from the picture I took of you, the others I took before you got there. Mom always says, sometimes paying attention is just as important as doing or saying something. I wasn't sure what to do with them so I showed them to Will and he came up with the idea of presenting them to everyone today."

"Nice play, Will," Richard said.

"Your mother's a smart woman," John said. "I'm sure glad you asked me to play basketball." Instead of their normal fist punch, John took a step forward and offered a hand.

Shaking John's hand, Garrett smiled and said, "You got a lot more game than you did Monday."

"Thanks to you," John said. "Thanks to *all* of you."

Will laughed. "We gotta work on your boxing skills though, John. I've seen little girls make better swings. And that move in Jamaica—I don't know what fighting school teaches chewing through someone's thigh?"

"Am I that bad?"

"Not if you were swinging with a broken arm," Richard teased.

"Looked like you were throwing wet spaghetti," Garrett said.

With everyone laughing, John said, "What can I say? I'm a lover not a fighter."

"Okay lover, you ready to see a different Virgin Island?" Will asked.

"Huh?"

"St. John's or the BVI's?" Richard asked.

"If it's okay with everybody, I chartered that cat out there and thought we could go over to Jost Van Dyke for lunch," Will pointed.

"What are the BVI's?" John asked.

"The British Virgin Islands off to the northwest of us," Richard said. "They're pristine islands like our St John which is mostly national park land. They're much less populated and more laid back than St. Thomas—geared more towards the *boaties* than the land lovers. What were you thinking, Will, Foxy's?"

"I was thinking the The Soggy Dollar in White Bay. It's nicer for the kids."

"Perfect!" Richard said. "Haven't been there in years—beautiful as I recall. I doubt it's changed much."

"They finally have a road so you can get there by car now from Great Harbor, but still no dock. Other than that, no change. How about everyone grab a woman or two while I wake up our ferryman."

"You got it!" Richard said.

Will walked calf deep into the water and blew into a thumb and forefinger. He followed up the shrill whistle with, "Yo! Max! Rise and shine!"

The man in the Zodiac sat up, dunked his hat over the side, and splatted it crookedly onto his sweaty head. "How many?" he asked.

"Eight big, two small!" Will replied.

"I can take maybe five big and the two small," said Max. "You got three swimmers or you want me to make two trips?"

Will turned to find nine smiling bodies anxiously waiting behind him. "Any swimmers?" he asked. Everyone raised their arm. Turning back to Max. "Wanna race?"

LAST ADVENTURE

MAX FERRIED THE BULK OF the group to his full-time home—a forty-foot catamaran named *Don't Cat-Chup*—while Will, John, Dani, and Rita enjoyed a leisurely swim out to the stocky day-charter. Of course, there was plenty of ice cold beer and wine along with the enchanting vocalization and steady beats of Bob Marley songs to escort them out of Magens Bay. Will helped Max cut the motor and unleash the jib and main sail when they hit open water. Garrett lounged with Jill, Kayla, and Buffy on the open netting that spanned the boat's two hulls as they stared down at the rushing blue sea for any signs of fish or dolphin. Mary and Richard applied generous portions of suntan lotion to their skin while Dani sat with a grin, stealing glances from behind her glasses at John and Rita snuggling on the opposite side.

"This would be easy to get used to," Dani said.

"I have the money now," Rita said, adjusting her hat to keep her hair from blowing in John's face. "Maybe I should buy one of these and keep it in Miami for everyone here to use?"

"Don't tease us," Dani said.

"I'm serious."

"What would you name her?" Dani asked.

"How 'bout...*On George?*" Rita laughed.

"You could name it after Garrett," Will said tightening a sheet. "Maybe...*The Terminator* or *Take A Picture?*"

"That's good," Dani chuckled.

"Or after John," Will continued, seeing numerous possibilities. "You could call it *My Inner Dragon* or *Salty Butterfly?* How about after Elli? She helped! You could call her *No Elli-Phant?*"

John chimed in. "How about after you, Will? After all, in a big part, you made this happen. How about...*Bull-Rider* or *Sun-Cat-Cher!* Didn't Max say a lot of catamarans have the word *cat* in them?"

"Yeah, lot of 'em do," Will said.

"They don't have to though," Richard said, rubbing his nose. "You can name a boat whatever you want. They're like houses, expressions of who the owner is and how they view life. Even a trailer can be someone's palace."

"So what would you name her?" Rita asked.

"If it were *my* boat we're talking about?"

"Yeah," Rita said.

"*Clawing A-Bow-T,*" Richard beamed.

"Of course!" John said. "I should have known it would be something like that."

"You came up with that name pretty quickly," Dani said. "Do you have a boat?"

"Hopefully next month," Mary said, rubbing a spot her husband missed. "Too many delays."

"You're buying one?" John asked.

"Building," Richard said. "It's going to be a surprise for the family. It's often a dreadful pain in the ass for families to load up the grand-kids for a trip to see the old grandparents. Doesn't seem like much of a vacation for anyone involved—more like a chore. But if the grandparents lived on a big toy that could take everyone wherever their little hearts desired, then everyone has something to get excited about. I've spent the last year getting my captain's license and Mary's a great chef. When we're resting in the marina I can hire some deckhands to do maintenance and when we're traveling, between the five kids and all the grand-kids, we should have no problems assigning tasks—kind of an 'earn your meal' kind of deal. It'll be a good way to teach the grand-kids discipline, work-ethic, and the general common sense that is mandatory when you're on a vessel—especially out at sea. Ships aren't like houses—there are much bigger concerns than putting the toilet seat down."

"We still love to travel," Mary said. "We thought this would be best for the whole family as a way to go into retirement."

"It must be a big boat to accommodate five families plus yourselves?" John asked.

"A hundred and twenty-five feet," Richard said.

"Jesus!" Dani said.

"Sail or motor yacht?" Will asked.

"I'm too old to sail a boat that big," Richard said. "I know the purists don't believe in them, but I want to be able to turn a key and go. I'd have to hire a whole crew to sail a yacht that size. It's a huge boat, but we still can't take the entire family on long trips. We can sleep eight comfortably plus eight more in the small crew cabins."

"Basically, three of our kids and their families can come for long trips at one time," Mary said. "That's about the maximum we can get together at one time now anyways. If we stay in the marina or just travel up and down the eastern seaboard, versus going overseas, we can always get extra hotel rooms for the nights everyone's onboard."

"Must cost a boatload of cash to build a yacht that big," Will laughed, curious about the price.

"We've been very fortunate over the years," Richard said.

"And we give a lot back," Mary added.

"The kids are all doing well," Richard continued. "Once you hit eighty you start thinking more that every year might be your last. *Clawing-A-Bow-T* is going to take us on our last adventures." Richard's jovial demeanor turned slightly sentimental and romantic. He put his arm around Mary's shoulder and pulled her tight. "It's time to reflect on all the colors we've collected on our canvas and pass the memories on to the kids and grand-kids. They're all good people who we trust will continue to do good things with our money and their talents long after we fade into the sunset."

"You're lovely people," Rita said. "I hope that last sunset is a long way off."

"We don't plan on going out without a bang," Richard said. "And I mean it when I say all of you are invited to visit as often as you can stand being around a couple of old farts."

"He means it," Mary said. "We've cruised for years because we enjoy meeting people. Owning our own boat will be a trade-off. It's going to be great to have something that's all ours to tinker with however we choose, but we still want people around."

"I'm in!" Dani said.

"How's next week?" Will asked.

"I'll buy a little one so we can tailgate," Rita said. "I'll bring my mother! She's a widow and would love to have some company around her own age."

"We'd love to meet her," Mary said.

"I bet she's a looker!" Richard said.

"Isabella is very elegant," Rita said.

"I'm out of a job," John said. "Maybe I could be first mate?"

"I have plans for that position," Richard said. "Our middle son has an eighteen-year-old who is kind of the black sheep in the family."

"He's in a band and parties too much," Mary said. "Says he doesn't want to go to college."

"His father wants him to learn to be a bit more practical and focused on the future. After all, it's not easy to make it as a rockstar. We're going to offer him a less orthodox education—kind of a working year abroad on the boat. I'm sure he's going to jump at the chance, thinking it's going to be a king's life aboard a mega-yacht. His uncle Oliver, our youngest son in the Navy—"

"He's not married yet," Mary said. "He's been in over twenty years and is retiring next year, thank God. I know being in the Navy isn't as dangerous as what Carson did in the Army, but a mother still worries."

"I totally understand," John said.

"He's the only one who knows about the *Clawing A-Bow-T*," Richard continued. "He's been our free consultant throughout the boat's conception. Being a Navy guy, he really understands the language and detail stuff more than we do. He's agreed to help us with his nephew's education. We're going to put the lad to work! He's going to get to see a lot of fabulous places and have opportunities to experience things that most kids his age don't get the chance to explore, or most people for that matter, but we're going to make certain he earns those opportunities."

"I think that's a stellar idea," Dani said. "I hope he learns how lucky he is to have such caring family willing to help him."

"Oh, he'll learn," Mary said. "We're all fun-loving people, but we don't take crap—especially Oliver. He and Richard are true leaders. If Gary—that's our grandson's name—if Gary gets out of line he'll find himself swimming home!"

Everyone laughed.

Richard made his way to the cat's cooler where he grabbed a beer for Will and a bottle of wine to top-off everyone's glass. Finishing with John, he said, "You don't want that job anyways. I see bigger plans in your future." Shuffling his eyes back and forth between the couple's sunglasses, he tried to penetrate the dark tint with his squinting eyes. Richard sat back down after Rita obliged him with a tickled dimple.

"Your job today is to master the ring toss," Will said.

"What's a ring toss?" John asked.

Dani sat up in disbelief and said, "You've never played ring toss?"

"Not that I recall."

"You've missed out," Richard said. "It's almost as good as watching the bikinis go by on a lazy day at the beach."

"Damn skippy!" Will said. "It's the simplest game on the planet. You have a hook screwed into a tree and a string tied to a metal ring from a branch above. You just stand about ten feet away and swing the ring until it catches on the hook."

"Sounds easy enough," John said.

"Simple doesn't always mean easy," Dani said.

"What, no cliff diving, alligator wrestling, or maybe something with fire today?" John laughed.

"Not today, Butterfly," Will said. "Sometimes the adventure is in the little things." Will walked to Dani's side. "Wanna join the kids for some *fishies* watching?"

Dani sat up from sunning herself and held out her hand. "Love to."

RING TOSS

DON'T CAT-CHUP DRIFTED INTO WHITE Bay, stopping short of the parking lot of boats moored just offshore. A few dozen bronzed sunbathers peppered the beach and bar area; they were listening to Jimmy Buffet and sipping beers and The Soggy Dollar's signature drink, a Painkiller. Max and Will secured the sails while the children marveled at a few bait fish darting in the turquoise water.

"The sand is whiter than the other beach!" Buffy said.

Max stared shamelessly through his sunglasses at Buffy's breasts that were heaving inside their small, yellow triangle holsters. "Any whiter and it would be invisible," he said. "Everyone have a Painkiller for me! See you when I see you!"

"Don't we have to go through customs?" John asked. "This is a different country, isn't it?"

"Yip!" Will said. "Consider yourself in the British Riviera right now. And no, we aren't going through customs. We're just here for a couple of hours to grab lunch and drink some beer. Most of the smaller boats hopping over here for the day don't bother with customs. You have your passport, don't you?"

"I left it in the cabin," John said, starting to look nervous. "All I grabbed was a few hundred-dollar bills, my ship card, and my driver's license."

"You planning to drive?" Will asked.

"No, but—"

"Relax," Will laughed. "I'm sure it'll be fine. They hardly ever do checks."

"And when they do?"

"You might want to arrange a flight home, 'cause you definitely won't make it back to the ship by five." Will slapped John's back. "Don't regress now, you've come so far and I'm sure everything's going to be fine. When in doubt, offer *the-man* one of those bingo bills! That should take care of any misunderstandings. Now come on, start swimming. We'll let Richard take the kids over in the dinghy."

John noticed how far away Max stopped from the other boats that were hugging the beach. "Why didn't we pull up closer to those other boats? We're still a hundred feet from the beach?"

"Max likes to fish and it's better fishing away from all the people. Do you know why they call this The Soggy Dollar bar?"

"Because everyone's hands are wet?"

"Almost! See, there's no dock here. They just recently built a road in from town. Used to be, the only way to get here was by boat. People moor just off the beach and swim in, hence, wet money!"

"That's a pretty cool name!" John said, hushing the worry voices inside his head. "Well then, you going to show me this ring toss thing?"

"At a boy!" Will turned. "Rich! You can take the kids and whoever else wants to ride in the dinghy, okay?"

"Can do!" Richard said, making his way aft to command the small Zodiac.

The group split in half as Mary, Garrett, and the two little girls climbed in with Richard and everyone else jumped from the steps on one of the stern hulls. Rolling over for a few backstrokes, John saw Max cast a line over the cat's port side. Fumes of gas mixing with a puff of white smoke blew across the swimmers' path as Richard fired up the Zodiac's two stroke and zipped away.

"What a beautiful day," John said, switching to breast stroke. "I wish Carson was here."

Swimming slowly alongside, Rita said, "He is. And quite proud, I'm sure."

"Do you believe in an afterlife?"

"How can you not on days like these?"

"But what if it's all for nothing?"

"Then we better enjoy it while we can!" Taking a deep breath, Rita dove under to wrestle John's swimming trunks down. Releasing a shrieking laugh and succumbing to her tugs, he sank beneath the water to frolic and kiss. When they emerged, Will, Dani, and Buffy were already waist deep and walking ashore.

"Come on," Rita said. "We better catch up. I want a Painkiller."

As they weaved through the maze of boats rocking in the topaz shallows, John asked, "What's in this painkiller everyone keeps talking about?"

"It's Pusser's rum made here on Tortola, pineapple and orange juice, cream of coconut, with some grated nutmeg. The rum's name is British Royal Navy slang for purser. In the Navy, the supply officer is called a purser. He was the one who rationed the sailor's rum, but I think they abolished the ritual in the early seventies. You're going to love it, sailor!"

John's feet touched bottom. "I'm game," he said. "Race you to the bar!" Pushing his hips sharply through the water to gain a head start.

"Ouch!" Rita cried.

"What is it? Are you all right?"

"I stepped on something sharp!"

John rushed back.

"Let me see."

Rita lifted her foot out of the water and held it in front of John's face. "You see anything?" she asked.

Clamping both sides, John looked closer. "Nothing but some cute toes."

"Watch how fast they go wee, wee, wee, all the way to the bar!" Pushing hard with her right leg, John fell backward into the water while she scurried ashore.

The beach sand extended the whole way up to the bottom of the open air bar. Above the sandy floor, the bar's paneling was painted with colorful, but amateurish, Caribbean seascapes as if whimsically painted by children. On the other side, a happy go lucky West Indian bartender was serving Painkillers and sodas to the Clawson's group.

"I won!" Rita said.

"You cheated," John said.

"Poor baby," Rita pouted.

"Nice of you to join us, Butterfly," Will said.

"We'll go see if there's a line for the ring toss," Richard said.

"Buffy and I are going to take the girls into the water," Dani said. Then she kissed Garrett and Will's cheeks and skipped down to the beach holding Jill's hand.

"Three more Painkillers, Marvin," Will said.

"Where's mine?" Garrett asked.

Will looked around before turning back. "Can't do it, brother, but," leaning over to the boy's ear, "a taste is the best I can do."

Garrett grinned and nodded.

"Marvin, let me have a virgin Miami Vice and a little plastic shot cup."

"You got it, Will," Marvin returned.

"You know everybody," Rita said.

Will sat on a wood stool and rested one knee against the bar mural. "You have to remember you're here for a day, but I come here once a week. That's thirty-six times over the course of one contract. That's more than enough times to get to know people. Islands are just small towns. It's hard to hide and easy to get to know the usual suspects."

"How about the trolley driver, Dave?" John asked. "You seemed to know him."

Laughing, Will said, "Dave's a character. A bit of a screw up, but a damn nice guy. He's probably smoking a joint right now. Days when he's not driving the caboose, he waits tables at a little bistro in town. Garth and I met him one day after shopping for a fresh supply of Cruzan rum and we'd stopped for lunch. We told him we were cruise ship bartenders and he hooked us up with some free beers. We've been friends ever since."

"Here we go, Will," Marvin said setting down three Painkillers. "I'll get the boy's drink in a second. These all on you?"

"Nah, this guy's buying," Will said, thumbing towards John.

"How much?" John asked.

The bartender's upbeat island persona morphed into a queer look. "You American?"

"Ah. Yeah."

"You come over on a boat?"

"Ah. Yeah." John added, "With Will!"

"Him I know. Let me see your passport."

"Ah...I kind of forgot it on the ship." John looked to Will for help; he got a silent blank expression.

Marvin's face turned angry. "So you're just another one of these ship-clots that thinks they can come here for the day to drink, throw trash on our beautiful British sand, and pick up our women? You think you're above checking in with customs?"

John felt his face turning hot and flushed. He had learned the word *clot,* and knew that in any of its variations it was never a term of endearment. "No. I wouldn't...*this* is the only woman I want to pick-up," he said, motioning to Rita.

"Awwhhh, that's sweet!" Rita said.

"You make it a habit of traveling to foreign countries without bringing your passport?" Marvin asked, without so much as a twitch.

"Well...no, but..."

"I'm sorry, Will, but I'm going to have to call this in," Marvin said.

"Wait!" John said. "I have this!" Shakily rummaging through his suit pocket he handed over his driver's license.

Marvin barely glanced at the damp card. "What do you want to do, rent a car?"

Wiping his face, John reached back into his pocket. "How about this?" he winked, offering a limp, wet hundred-dollar bill.

Marvin seemed more agitated. "You trying to buy your way out of this?"

"Can I?" John asked timidly.

Breaking into laughter, Marvin clenched his stomach and slammed the bar with his palm. "We're just messing with you, mon!" Will and Rita cut loose with howling cackles while John stood dumbfounded, feeling his anxiety instantly blow away. But there was still a tightness in his gut.

"Very funny!" John said. To his chagrin he joined in the laughter. "When am I going to learn?"

"You should have seen your face!" Will said.

"You sure you don't want to throw some trash and pick-up other girls?" Rita asked, patting John's cheek.

"You just got punk'd!" Garrett said.

John grabbed one of the drinks and said, "Being around all you is often painful. I guess I should be grateful you brought me to a place that serves the antidote." He chugged long and hard through the neon pink straw until he'd depleted over half the sixteen ounce cup. Meanwhile, Will poured a couple ounces of his Painkiller into a plastic cup below the counter top while Marvin laughed his way back to the blender to make Garrett's drink. Garrett downed the shot, made a *yuck* face, and handed the empty back to Will.

Smiling, Will said, "Good! That expression means it's not time for you. You should enjoy not being an adult yet. There's plenty of time for that in the future, but you only get one childhood. Trust me partner, it goes by in a flash."

"That tasted like shit!" Garrett said. "I don't know how you can drink that?" It was the first taste of alcohol he'd ever had and like most firsts, the memory would last a lifetime; not so much from the taste, but because Will had shared an adult experience with him. Will knew that sharing two ounces of a first drink was the sort of male bonding a thirteen-year-old boy craved, like a father and son catching their first fish together.

"The older you get the more tolerant you get of swallowing shit," the bartender joked over his shoulder. "Even the stuff in life that tastes bad on the way down can turn out pretty good once it has time to settle."

"You remember the first time you ever had a drink with your old man?" Will asked.

"It was beer for me," Rita said. "I think I was about eleven, but I don't remember the brand. I do remember my first Cuban cigar! It was a *Cohiba*. Daddy and I were on the veranda at sunset one night. He always had some brandy and a cigar at sunset. Cuban sunsets are amazing! Really… they're different. But I digress, I always liked the way he smelled while smoking his cigars—you know one of the things that attracts women to men is familiar smells, particularly ones that remind them of their fathers. When I sat on his lap he smelled of roasted walnuts, espresso, and dark chocolate. I remember peppery notes intertwined with leather and cedar. He's dead now, but my fondest memories of him are of watching those sunsets. A little girl and her woodsy, manly smelling father with sweet hints of orange zest and currant from the brandy fumes dancing in a haze of creamy smoke. I miss him. I miss those smells." Recalling the memory put her in a trance, like a baby, half asleep.

"Wow," Will said. "That must have been one hell of a first cigar?"

Rita's head jolted from her daze. "Actually, I coughed so hard during that first puff that I didn't take another drag until I was eighteen. I shouldn't have inhaled. Dad huffed when I asked to try his cigar that first time. He said, 'Well you *are* Cuban. Your palate should be introduced to our country's most refined and famous delicacy. It's in your blood and in the soil that will bury me one day.'"

"What happened to him?" John asked.

"Heart attack when I was twenty-nine. Mom has never remarried. I don't believe she can bear the thought of lying down with another man, not unless, maybe all those same aromas came with him."

John hugged Rita.

"That blows mine out of the water," Will said. "I remember my dad reading the newspaper one night, like he always did after work. He usually drank beer and one night when I was around eight or nine, I asked if I could try a sip. He folded one ear of his paper over, looked at me for a second, and asked why. I stammered out the words 'I want to know what it tastes like.' So, after making sure Mom wasn't around, he handed over his can of Budweiser." Will looked at Garrett. "Tasted like shit!" he laughed. "I still can't drink Bud." Marvin placed the drink he made for Garrett on the bar while they were sharing stories. Will passed the Miami Vice, "Here you go, dude. Your turn, John! First drink story?"

"That's easy," John said. "I'll never forget. My parents had a BBQ for some friends one summer when I was fourteen. My mom caught me trying to pilfer a beer from this large igloo cooler on our screened-in porch. All the adults were outside by the grill or throwing horseshoes. Mom came from inside the house behind me and I got busted before I could pop the top. She was *pre-tty* mad. I still remember her fists pushing into the top of her hips and this contorted expression on her face. She grabbed me by the ear and drug me inside to the kitchen where she pulled a bottle of green Crème de Menthe from the top cabinet. She said, 'If you want to try drinking alcohol so badly then drink this!'"

"She didn't?" Rita said.

"That's just mean," Will said.

"Yip. She poured two ounces—no shit, got out a measuring cup to get it exact—then made me drink it right out of the same cup she used to measure cookie ingredients." Everyone including Garrett began laughing. "I chugged it all down not knowing what it was, just that it was dark green and smelled like a Christmas tree."

"Did you get sick?" Rita asked.

"Is Kansas flat?"

"From what I hear," Rita said.

"Mom told me to go outside and tell Dad what I'd done. The minty syrup coated my tongue like oil and took forever to drip down my throat. I started to gag and wanted to grab a soda out of the same cooler, but was afraid my mother would think I was going for another beer. I walked outside to find Dad and I got sidetracked by a plate of ready to eat hotdogs by the grill. I loved hotdogs and thought a couple of bites would wash the flavor away. And *boy* did it! I barfed all over the lawn in front of twenty people. There's nothing like regurgitated green mint hotdogs to spoil a BBQ."

"Priceless!" Rita said.

"What did your dad say?" Garrett asked.

"He came when he heard the retching sounds and asked me if I was okay. I looked up at him with green teeth and said Mom caught me trying to drink a beer."

"Did he punish you?" Will asked.

"Nope. He was really cool. I think he realized what Mom had done. So he took me around the side of the house where the hose hung and told me to rinse my mouth out but not to swallow too much. While I rinsed, he went back around the side. When he returned I was feeling a lot better and he asked me if I had learned a lesson. I told him 'Yes, I'm not allowed to drink.' He looked at me for a second, smiled, and then popped the top off a bottle of Coors Lite. He takes a swig and then hands me the bottle and says: 'Or at least don't let your mother catch you.'"

"Classic!" Will said.

"Your mom and dad obviously had different training methods," Rita said.

"Yeah," John said finishing his Painkiller. "Everything always seems clearer in hindsight. I think she always got her way and he allowed that to happen by never confronting her. Maybe he knew he would lose. Maybe he was afraid. I don't know. I just remembered a couple of nights ago the only fight I ever remember them having. The reason for their fight was because I think my dad had cheated. I've blocked that fight out of my consciousness all these years."

"From the sounds of it nobody could blame him," Rita said. "Maybe he was forced to swallow a different kind of Crème de Menthe?"

"It doesn't matter," John said. "They are still together and obviously worked through it. What's past is past."

"That's right, John," Will said. "And today is a new day!"

"Hey!" John snapped. "When did you get here? Marvin! Another round, please. And keep the change!" he said slapping another soggy one-hundred dollar bill down on the bar. "So where's this ring toss?"

"Right outside," Will laughed, proud of his older protégé. "I know it's confusing since the inside is really outside."

Will led the three about fifteen feet to a bent palm tree that looked like a trumpeting elephant's trunk. Beside the tree, Richard had found a better game, called resting in a hammock.

"It doesn't go on the hook unless you actually swing the ring," Rita said.

"I couldn't help it, this hammock was calling my name," Richard said, sipping his drink. "I figure every pretty girl on the beach has to walk by me at some time to get a drink or use the bathroom. Now that's a fun game."

"Where's Mary?" John asked.

"She and the girls are down there in the water. See the beach chairs in the water?"

"I think I'll leave you men to your games and join the girls," Rita said. "Sitting in one of those chairs and having that beautiful water lap over me looks more my speed. Do you mind, John?"

"Not at all," he said, as they exchanged a quick peck.

Will lifted the ring off the hook from the tilted palm and asked, "You playing, Rich?"

"After everyone else has made one."

"You got it!" Will said. "Let me show you boys how it's done." He walked back until the string was taunt, holding the silver ring in front of his face, he said, "Everyone does it a little differently, but I think the trick is to let the ring drop from the same starting position each time. Once I see where it misses, I adjust my feet slightly right or left to compensate, but always from the same forward position. Here we go!" As if releasing a child on a swing-set without pushing, he let go of the ring. The ring performed three slow helicopter spins, the last one turning just enough at the swing's apex to clank onto the hook as if it were magnetized.

"Ho!" everyone cried.

"You boys catch that?" Will asked self-assertively.

"Is there anything you're not good at?" John asked.

"I'm an expert at things that have little or no importance!" Will chuckled. "You're up, Garrett."

For the same reason an athlete has a natural throw or swing, Garrett immediately deviated from Will's instructions. Standing perfectly sideways, Garrett took more of an archer's stance. His release also differed from Will's, pushing the ring into its run with his forefinger and thumb. Once against the left side of the tree and back; two times hitting only dead air over the tree's right side and back; once careening against the hook's face and back, and on the ring's fifth ride; *clank*, spin, *rattle*, hooked.

"Yes!" Garrett said, raising his arms in triumph. "Five tries!"

"The kid's a born ringer, so to speak!" Will said.

"You both are," John scoffed.

"Like everything else, it's all in the attitude," Will said.

"Show 'em up, John," Richard said, connecting his fingers around the back of his head.

"I don't know, the pressure's on," John returned.

John stood at an angle, compromising between Will's and Garrett's stance. After a dozen throws which included four *clanks,* he shuffled his feet and changed hands. Being ambidextrous gave him no better results. He moved forward and backward, side to side; he tried pushing, throwing, spinning, and zig-zagging the ring without any more reward than a harsh rattling in his ears. He kept track of every try until losing count shortly after one hundred. Twenty minutes passed and Will and Garrett were becoming restless. Richard watched every throw—all but ones hindered by passing bikinis.

Growing bored, Will said, "I brought a Frisbee—you game?"

"Sure!" Garrett said.

"Ah…John? I think Garrett and I are going to throw the Frisbee for a while. You want to join us?"

"I'm not leaving 'til I get this damn ring on the hook!"

"Maybe you should take a break," Will suggested. "It's really not as easy as we made it look. Sometimes I stand there for a long time before making one too."

"More than a hundred tries?"

"Ahhh…no, but—"

"Go throw the Frisbee, Will. I'm not leaving," John snapped, sounding determined and frustrated.

"Okay," Will said. "Get us when you make one. It's a lot easier after you get your first one."

John turned and glared as Will and Garrett smiled, shrugged, and then walked down to the beach.

As if the first twenty minutes wasn't bad enough, the next twenty drove John into angry obsession. He stopped changing positions, opting for continuous catch and releases from his original stance. Richard watched almost every miss for the sake of support, and because the game had turned into a sort of comedy of defeat. Although there were moments when Richard wanted to, he didn't dare laugh, remaining silent for fear any advice or chatter might cause John to quit.

Even by 1:00 when everyone gathered back at the bar for grilled cheese, tuna melts, flying fish, and burgers, John refused to stop. Richard asked Mary and Rita to bring them a couple of orders of conch fritters and fries. He was afraid if he joined the others at a table and John made one without a witness, it wouldn't be official to John's ego—a case of the tree falling in the woods without making a sound. So, Richard chose to dangle one foot over the side to rock his hammock.

"I would think this game is impossible if I hadn't seen John Wayne and Michael Jordan over there each make one," John grumbled.

"Perseverance, John, perseverance," Richard said, ogling a green Brazilian cut.

"Why don't *you* take a turn?"

"I don't think that would be wise."

"Why's that?" *Clank.*

"'Cause if I get out of this hammock and make one, it's going to piss you off even more."

"That's true." *Clank.*

By 1:30 Mary had joined Richard in the hammock, feeding him fritters and fries but remaining silent. When John refused to take a break for lunch with Rita, she stood fast beside him, sticking fritters in his mouth after ring releases. Ten minutes later after John swallowed the last french fry, Rita copped a squat and sipped on her third Painkiller.

"Either a woman, a psychologist, a lawyer, or a politician must have invented this game," John said. "It's designed to frustrate even the most patient priest!"

"I resent that, John," Rita said, tickling his foot with her toes. "I thought about becoming a psychologist."

"I'm going to need counseling if I don't make one of these." *Clank.*

By 1:50 John's endeavor had grown into a public affair. Everyone, including strangers feeling the effects of multiple Painkillers were made aware of John Smith's quest to slay his great white buffalo. Will personally saw to it. Enlisting Garrett's help, the two walked around informing patrons about the enigma taking place at the ring toss. They recruited dozens of bare-chested, bloated men, and overly tanned, drunken women to huddle around the elephant-trunk palm tree and cheer.

Standing on top of one of the outside tables, Will started to chant. "John! John! John!" In seconds, the chant spread like a wave in a football stadium.

Dani came to John's side with some paper napkins to blot beads of perspiration from his brow between throws. "You can do it!" she whispered. "You the man."

By 1:55 Will joined Dani's side.

"We only have a few minutes 'til we have to leave," Will said. "We can't miss the ship. Do it!"

"John! John! John!" The crowd continued.

John ignored Will and continued throwing. His method had grown quicker, more mechanical, and deliberate. "I'm going to do this," he whispered. *Clank.*

Every person in White Bay made an exodus from the beach towards the ring toss; even a few stragglers tinkering with their boats swam ashore to see what the commotion was all about.

When John felt his tenacity turning to defeat, he grabbed the ring from the air upon its return from its last trip to *Clankville* and sighed. "I think I'm going to give up."

A flurry of no's and sighs bellowed from the crowd.

"He needs a boost!" a burly man cried. "Come on ladies! Give John some motivation!"

Over at the hammock, Rich's and Garrett's eyes widened as a half dozen bikini tops were untied and twirled in the air.

"Stop drooling!" Mary said playfully.

"That's what I'm talking about!" Garrett clapped.

"Yeah!" the crowd cheered. *"Yeah! Woo! John! John! John!"*

Two men and a topless fifty-something-year-old woman with pruney stretch marks on her droopy breasts came to the forefront with half-full beers.

"Woo!" the woman screamed, dancing and twirling her breasts like tassels.

"Here you go!" one of the men offered, jamming his bottle into John's mouth. As soon as John choked down the half beer, the second man followed suit.

John swallowed again, coughed, and said, "Okay, okay!" The crowd hushed. "I'll try again!"

The crowd raised their drinks and screamed as if someone had just scored the winning goal in the World Cup. The topless woman lurched forward and chained John with a full embrace, during which he thought he could feel her breasts pressing against his belly button.

Not willing to concede her man, Rita stood to pry the woman off. "That's enough," she said. "He's mine! Let me dry you off, honey." Rita grabbed her towel and wiped the beer and sweat from John's face, kissed him hard, and stepped back after a wink of support.

Taking a second to revel in the moment, never before was he so comfortable being the center of attention in a large group. If only he could earn their affection? Taking a deep breath, he reclaimed the ring that was hanging vertical and motionless from its limb.

"Come on, Butterfly!" sounded a familiar voice.

When John turned, Buffy flashed a broad smile along with a quick open and close of her right bikini triangle, above, and out of sight from Jill and Kayla playing in the sand. "Thanks, Buffy, you're perfect!" he said, before shaking his head and trying to regain focus.

"Now or never," Will said as John aimed. "Time to earn your wings!"

In a moment of clarity, all the noise and crowd images subsided and Carson's smiling face replaced the hook. John smiled back and whispered, "I love you, son. I made it," before dropping the ring. *Clank*…a second time; *clank*…a third time; *clank, rattle,* silence, *roar* from the crowd.

Standing as still as a British Royal Palace guard, John whispered to himself, "Thank you, son."

Like bees to honey, the circle of sauced Soggy Dollar Bar patrons closed in to congratulate their hero of the day. Conscious of the time, Will ran around informing *Don't Cat-Chup's* passengers that it was time to go. Richard and Mary relinquished their hammock and escorted Buffy and the girls to the dinghy while Will penetrated the mosh-pit of fans to find his swimmers.

"When did you get here?" Will asked, bumping up against Dani's shoulder.

"I was going to ask you the same thing," she giggled. "This is crazy! And all because a guy made a ring toss!" The two were forced even closer by the constricting crowd.

"People love an underdog!" Will said. "But we gotta go! You find Garrett and I'll grab Rita and the Butterfly!"

"Kiss me first!" Will did as he was told. "You know I think I—"

"Finish that thought tonight," he grinned in a self-assured southern manner. "I've got something to tell you too."

"I can't wait," kissing him again.

WHAT BASKETS?

THE VIVID MEMORY OF THE ring toss game would forever be painted on John's canvas. The group entertained themselves by reliving their own versions of the day's adventures while Jost Van Dyke drifted towards the horizon behind *Don't Cat-Chup's* wake.

Although no one said anything, running into George and Elli again was on everyone's mind when Max dropped the group back off in Magens Bay. John scanned each floating mat and periodically checked the group's rear for any possible signs of an ambush, but they made it to the trolley without seeing the bruised couple. And Dave performed soberly enough to earn a two-hundred dollar tip on completion of the twisty ride back to Havensight's harbor. They even found enough time to poke around the shops for a half hour before the ship's horn blew.

The gang agreed to share a casual last dinner in the ship's Island Grill at 8:00. Richard loved Will's idea to send the kids to a show after dinner while the grown-ups hit the casino for a night of blackjack, craps, and slots. Will had to work both shows in the theatre, but assured everyone he'd be finished early. He had another surprise for anyone feeling up to a little nonconformist's escapade.

Rita hadn't thought about her personal things until everyone boarded and began discussing their pre-dinner plans.

"I guess I'd better pack up my things," Rita said. "I certainly can't stay in my cabin tonight. Anyone up for a roommate?"

"I think I could be persuaded to make a little room," John teased.

"Problem solved!" Dani said.

"Do you think it's going to be a problem if George is in your cabin when you get your things?" Mary asked.

"Not if he knows what's good for him!" Rita scoffed. "But I should go take care of it now to get it out of the way. Hopefully he's not there."

"Where's your bunk?" Richard asked.

"We have one of the sky suites—number fourteen."

"You're right around the corner from Mary and me!"

"Well howdy, neighbors!"

"Rita, why don't you come with us," Mary said. "You can pack your things and bring them over to our cabin. Richard will pour you a nice glass of wine and you can shower before you meet John."

"That's a splendid idea," Richard said. "That way you don't have to lug everything very far. I'll call a porter to ship your bags down to John's Shangri-La."

"That sounds wonderful!" Rita clapped. "I think I'll take you both up on that offer."

"Done!" Richard said.

"That will give me time to get cleaned up and see if Sylvia left me any cash to gamble with tonight," John said.

"That's *right*," Dani said. "I guess we should have cleaned up all that money. Do you trust her?"

"I'm sure it's fine," John said. "If not, I'm no poorer than I was before bingo, if you don't count losing my job, that is."

"I have a little moola now," Rita said, rubbing her fingers together. "If you find you've been pilfered, maybe we can arrange something?" Her dimple made John melt every time she showed it to him.

"Now I hope I've been robbed," he said as everyone laughed.

"Okay," Dani said. "Buffy and I better get these kids a snack if we're not eating until eight."

"Can we get some pizza?" Garrett asked.

"If that's what you want," Dani said. "I believe you've earned it. But you have to promise me you won't ever become a photographer for Hustler magazine when you grow up!"

"Deal," Garrett said.

Rita smothered Garrett's cheek with kisses, fanned her fingers at the girls, and smacked John's lips with a loud pucker. Then she and Mary accepted one of Richard's arms and he rotated them toward the elevator. "It's good to be me!" Richard chuckled. "See you all at dinner!"

The voice inside John's head returned as he walked back to his cabin. This time it wasn't resisting change, questioning his manhood—certainly he had done his best over the course of the week to quell that doubt—or wondering about Rita's feelings towards him. No, instead, it was asking, "*Who bought my ticket?*" In an attempt to silence the voice and once and for all settle the mystery, he made a detour to the business center on the outside chance his benefactor might have sent another email.

As usual, the glass encased room was vacant. He sat and logged in with Carson's name. To his disbelief, a new message from harmony23@gmail.com appeared at the top of his inbox. He clicked the message with hopeful anticipation.

John:

I'm sure by now the question of who sent your cruise ticket and these emails is driving you crazy. I'm sorry for the mystery, but I thought it best. It's almost time for us to meet and I promise to explain everything. I'll be in the ship's main lobby at 9:00 a.m., Sunday. See you then.

P.S. Losing a job is not always a bad thing. Hope you like the following passage.

"I too had woven a kind of basket of a delicate texture, but I had not made it worth any one's while to buy them. Yet not the less, in my case, did I think it worth my while to weave them, and instead of studying how to make it worth men's while to buy my baskets, I studied rather how to avoid the necessity of selling them. The life which men praise and regard as successful is but one kind. Why should we exaggerate any one kind at the expense of the others?"

By: Henry David Thoreau

"Baskets?" John scratched. "What baskets? How does this person know I lost my job?"

TWO RARE VINTAGES

RITA WAS RELIEVED TO FIND an empty cabin when she returned to her room. Richard stood guard outside, just in case. Blood in the sink let her know that George had come and gone. Rita filled her lungs deeply and sighed in liberation.

In the Clawson's suite, a glass of 92 Bordeaux, a hot shower, and the exchange of some comforting, light-hearted conversation carried Rita miles away from her second failed marriage. By 6:30 her desire was ablaze; she couldn't deny herself any longer. She stuffed a few overnight necessities into a beach bag, thanked the Clawsons, and hastened to the elevators. Outside John's cabin door, she felt the excitement, like butterflies fluttering in her gut.

Knocking. "Miss me?" she asked as John opened the door.

"All my life," he answered, a coy smile on his lips. He inhaled the bouquet of rich fruit and flowery notes coming from her breath and freshly washed skin.

Falling into each other's arms, they kissed long and hard in the doorway.

"You taste delicious," John said, gazing into her eyes.

"Richard and Mary have excellent taste in wine," she said. "That was one of the problems with George. He preferred light young wines. Even with all his money, every November he bought enough cases of Beaujolais Nouveau to last the entire year."

"Is that bad?"

"I guess his girl-toys liked it. It tastes fine—fruity—but it's hardly aged, because there's very little tannin. Tannin's the stuff that allows wine to age, refine, and mellow. There's just no substance in those young fruity ones. They're drinkable, like beer, but you end up drinking too much and wind up with a hangover because there's just not enough in your mouth to really savor or talk about—not like a really good Cabernet Sauvignon. A mouthful of Cab can entertain and nurture for quite a long time. George hates Cabernet."

"So that's what happened—he only wanted you when you were young and fruity?"

Rita laughed.

"I think *so*. He has an excellent business sense, but he's much too shallow to understand the depths of a fine vintage Cabernet."

"And us?"

"We're Cabs, John. Life has given us both many tannins. I suspect enough to prevent our fruit from ever spoiling. Those same tannins that we found bitter when we acquired them can now protect and delight us through the greatest of celebrations and our most painful losses."

Stroking the hair above Rita's right ear, he said, "I suspect your father was full of tannin, perhaps I could learn to occasionally smoke a Cuban cigar while watching the sunset?"

Tingles coursed through Rita's spine. Softly, she placed the side of her face on John's chest and whispered, "I would enjoy that very much…I love you, John…I love you."

"And I love you," he whispered back.

Shuffling his feet backward, he pulled Rita into the cabin until the door slammed behind her.

In the dim light from the bedside table lamp, they slowly stripped each other until all their clothes lay in a heap. As if reading braille, they took the time to lightly explore each other's skin. Their arm-hairs stood like flagpoles on tiny goose-bump mounds. When their desire grew too strong, Rita cupped John's penis in her right hand and his right bicep in her left, and drawing him to the bed, she fell onto her back carrying him with her. They coupled effortlessly—slowly savoring one another. Their blissful lovemaking passed the time the way every good thing seems to never be enough. And Rita insisted at 7:50 that they go to dinner without washing away the redolence of their sex. John happily obeyed her wish.

He couldn't remember a time in the course of his own marriage when Page ever suggested or entertained the idea of something so provocative. Once married, their love-making sessions had become deliberate, purposeful, and brief. When Page gave up hope of having another child, sex between the two turned into nothing more than a rare obligation before sleep.

Dressing, John was impressed with his own stamina and wondering if all Latin women were so sexually voracious, he couldn't help letting out a little giggle.

"That's exactly how I feel," Rita giggled back, as she lifted her skirt.

"I'm starving!"

"Well, we'd better feed you then," she said, squeezing his cheeks until his lips were puckered enough to kiss. "You're going to need your strength for when we get back here tonight."

"Finally, I found a good way to get hurt."

"You ain't seen nothin' yet. Between the spa and the last hour here, it's been all foreplay so far."

"That's a scary thought."

"Come on. Let's get you fed, Butterfly."

HARMONY ANYONE?

T HE ISLAND GRILL WAS TEEMING with young families when John and Rita arrived at 8:05. It was a perfect casual alternative to the dining room and pricey themed restaurants. Parents were happy to have the all-inclusive buffet's seemingly endless spread. Their children loved helping themselves and not having to wait to be served. The room bustled like a Hawaiian luau— minus the coconut shell bikini tops and Samoan fire-eaters. Multi-colored lights, ice sculptures, and fresh flowers provided a rainbow of color and texture. Children were laughing and playing at, between, and under the tables. A hostess armed with the mandatory ship employee pleasantry, greeted the couple. She dropped faux leis around their necks and said, "Aloha!"

"Aloha!" Rita said.

"I believe I see our party over there," John pointed.

"Go right ahead," the hostess waved. "Enjoy your meals!"

Richard stood upon seeing them.

"There's the happy couple!" Richard said.

"Hi everyone!" Rita said.

"You guys save us any food?" John asked.

"Are you kidding?" Mary asked. "They put out enough food to feed the entire ship."

"Good, I'm starving!" John declared.

Richard raised a brow upon noticing the couple's disheveled hair and glowing faces. "I guess the ring toss really works up an appetite, eh, John?" he asked. "I suppose you didn't have time for a nap?"

"Sit down and eat, you old snoop," Mary said.

"Ah…nope," John said. "I went to the business center for a while, showered, and then Rita and I talked until it was time for dinner." John threw a familiar smile. Richard recognized it from bingo when he finagled the truth about John's real spa treatment.

We did talk, so not a total lie, John thought. He was feeling the change inside himself as confidence was replacing guilt.

"Was all your money still on the floor?" Garrett asked.

Happy the boy had changed the topic, John said, "Yes! It was. Not on the floor I mean, but it was all there. Sylvia neatly stacked every bill on my nightstand—even took the time to face each bill in the same direction."

"That's an honest woman," Dani said. "You were lucky."

"I'm starting to believe I'm the luckiest man alive."

Rita turned slightly and mumbled out of the corner of her mouth. "You're going to be lucky multiple times when we get back to the room."

Fidgeting nervously with his collar, John said, "Where's Buffy and the girls?"

"They're still in line," Dani said. "Grab a plate, we'll wait. Try the oysters. They're an aphrodisiac!"

"What's an aphrodisiac?" Garrett asked.

"Something you don't need to learn about until you're twenty-five," Dani said.

Rita giggled, grabbed John's hand, and scurried off.

Choices and more choices, John was no longer intimidated by the buffet's selection, although strange bathroom guy had forever turned him off of oysters. Pan fried sole, lamb curry, asparagus tips, calamari with lemon garlic dip, Indian spiced butterfish, rosemary flatbread, vegetable orzo, mashed yams, and on and on; he scooped small portions in an attempt to try everything. When John's plates—one dinner, one salad—were piled to overflowing, the couple rejoined the table.

"Hi guys!" Buffy said. "Long time no see!"

"Too long," Rita said. "Sorry we're a little late."

"You're here now!" Buffy giggled.

"Hungry, John?" Garrett asked.

"I'm taking after you. I still remember the pile you had that first breakfast when we met."

"They put it out, might as well try it all," he smiled.

"I couldn't agree more," John said.

Conversation slowed to a minimum as they all enjoyed their food and chit chat was centered around how good the spoonfuls of root vegetable soup were and how mouthwatering the buttermilk soft-shell crabs tasted.

John was just as amused with Rita's persistent knee grabs and groin pinches under the table as he was captivated with each succulent bite above the table. After his stomach bulged and he'd contained Rita's wandering hand in his own, questions about the most recent email took center stage in his mind. He silently interrogated every adult member at the table as if he were playing a game of Clue. In John's mind there were only three explanations: the ticket and emails came from someone at work who would have known he lost his job; either his or Page's parents could have also learned the news; or, someone on the ship was responsible.

"I was thinking this is as good a time as any to get everyone's contact information," John said, feeling clever. "I left my phone at home, but maybe we could just do it the old-fashioned way and write down our numbers and email addresses?"

"Good thinking," Rita said. "I've got a couple of pens and some paper in my bag."

"Do you think you'll lose your email address since it's tied to your company, John?" Mary asked.

"I suspect so. I'll write down my cell number for now and then forward my email after I set up a new account. I might even change *millions of John Smiths* to something shorter, more post-cruise appropriate."

"Something with butterfly in it!" Buffy said.

"Maybe," John said. "What's your email Buffy?"

"Buffy slayer six at gmail dot com."

"I'd like to see the other five," Richard said.

"Not in my lifetime," Mary said.

"How about you guys? Mary, any catchy address?" John asked.

"Of course! You know us. Richard and I share one account—bushel of claws at hotmail dot com."

"That's good," Dani chuckled.

"You already gave me yours, Dani," John said, mentally crossing her off the list. "What's Will's? You have it, don't you?"

"Yip. Bull catcher one at hotmail dot com."

Everyone laughed.

Quickly moving on, John asked, "How about the most important one? What's yours, Rita?"

"I don't have a clever personal account. I use my store's address for everything—rita at chic linen dot com."

John sighed as everyone finished exchanging bits of paper.

"Something wrong?" Garrett asked.

"Me? No, no. It's just…"

"You seem pretty curious about email addresses," Richard said. "What's up? I can see your hamster spinning its wheel."

"Well…I did want everyone's contact information of course, but I was hoping someone here had an email with the word *harmony* in it."

"Why's that?" Richard asked.

John managed another bite of brie and papaya quesadilla. "I haven't mentioned it to anyone, no one but Will's Jamaican friend Lloyd, but I didn't book this cruise. I was in the process. I mean I was going to. I mean, I promised Carson I would…and I would have, but I was just too depressed after he died. I was putting it off. Then one day, about three weeks ago, the ticket showed up in my mailbox with a typed note that said: *It's time.*"

"How intriguing," Rita said.

"Yeah, I thought so. That's not all. Wednesday I got an anonymous email and another one a couple of hours ago."

"What'd they say?" Garrett asked.

"The first one said that I was doing great—implying only someone onboard could know how I was doing—if in fact *doing great* was referring to my vacation. Which I believe it was. Both emails had quotes from Henry David Thoreau and the one today said that whoever it is, is going to meet me tomorrow morning in the ship's lobby. At nine a.m. it said, and all would be explained."

"Wow!" Dani said. "That's really cool."

"Unless it's been driving you crazy for three weeks," John said.

"That's why you were so interested in Thoreau?" Mary asked.

"Yes."

"And harmony?" asked Rita.

"The emails were from harmony twenty-three at gmail dot com."

"Which quotes?" Mary asked.

"Something about leaving the woods for as good a reason as I went there and something about not selling baskets."

Mary grinned.

"What is it, Mary?" Rita asked.

"'…and instead of studying how to make it worth men's while to buy my baskets, I studied rather how to avoid the necessity of selling them,'" Mary recited.

"Yes! That's it!"

Mary continued. "'I left the woods for as good a reason as I went there. Perhaps it seemed to me that I had several more lives to live, and could not spare any more time for that one.'"

"Exactly!" John pounded and pointed.

"That's wonderful, Mary," Dani said.

"The woman is a voracious reader!" Richard said. "An angel and a genius!"

"I don't get it," Buffy said, trying to keep her daughter from stealing Jill's desserts.

"I'll explain later," Garrett said.

"I love it when people are able to quote from the classics out of thin air," Rita said.

"Are you sure you didn't send my ticket?"

"No, dear, I'm afraid not," Mary laughed. "Anyone else?"

Everyone shook their heads.

"Then what do you make of the quotes?" John asked.

Richard stood to refill everyone's wine glass.

"Well, all authors' words are open to interpretation," Mary said. "What the writer tries to express is often very different than what the reader gets, and what one reader gets usually varies from reader to reader. That's the beauty of all art. We all don't buy the same paintings, but we all believe the ones we *do* buy are beautiful, or else we wouldn't waste the money."

"But I'm asking your opinion."

Mary squinted and thought for a moment. "In a way, you have just left one life behind. You no longer have the life you had with Page and Carson. You could have given up, but you haven't. You're making a transition...and very well, I might add. A person can only move forward when they realize they can't spare any more time in the past. As for the baskets, this person obviously knows you just lost your job. But there are many kinds of success—marriage, kids, work, money, philanthropy, spiritual, self-fulfillment, and so on—and many different ways to go about achieving those successes. Maybe the *baskets*, if you will, that you wove in your previous business and personal life weren't the kind intended to afford your success? Or maybe they were once, but not now? People change because they truly want to. If not, they don't. Have you changed, John?"

"Yes. I have. I am."

"In my opinion, the real question isn't what I make of the quotes. Someone cared enough to share them with you, probably because they found them relevant to the things you've been going through. You should be asking yourself what you find in the words. That's what I think, and that's as much advice as I ever give."

"Smarter than an MIT full of Dalai Lama's!" Richard said. "I must have done something right!"

"Stop kissing up," Mary said. "It's the last night of the last commercial cruise we'll probably ever take. I don't mind how many drinks or desserts you clog your heart with tonight."

"Everyone here heard *that* quote, right?" Richard asked.

Everyone laughed and nodded.

"She's right, John," Rita said.

"Yes," John said. "Very right."

"Did you ever think maybe your son had something to do with all this?" Dani asked. "He's the one that made you promise to take this cruise. He has to be involved."

"That's what I've been telling myself for weeks. But the ticket came almost six months after he died. And even if he arranged the trip before he did, that doesn't tell me who's been sending the emails. Nobody I've met here knew me prior to this trip. Whoever sent them knows what I've been doing the past week and they know I lost my job. They have to be onboard, or, if they're not…there's a mole working for someone back stateside." John panned a dubious look around the table.

"Ooooo!" said everyone sharply glancing at the next person.

"I wouldn't worry about it," Richard said, forking a hunk of citrus cheesecake. "From what you said, everything is going to be explained to you tomorrow. Grab some dessert, pour some wine, kiss the beautiful woman beside you, and get ready to increase your bingo money in the casino."

"I'm really not much of a gambler."

"Then how do you know to say exactly what a professional gambler would say?" Richard asked.

"He got you there," Rita said. "Come on. I like his dessert idea." Rita stood and held out her hand.

"I'll give both a whirl," John said, pushing back his chair. "The dessert and the gambling."

The couple took a few steps when Garrett asked, "Where was the postmark from?"

"What?" John turned.

"You said your cruise ticket was mailed to you. Where was the postmark from?"

"Afghanistan. Why?"

"No reason. Just a question."

"Mmm," Richard said, smiling wildly and mauling cheesecake. "Smart boy. Athlete, photographer, and detective."

By the time John and Rita returned with a dinner plate full of sweets, John had disregarded Garrett's question, chalking it up to youthful inquisitiveness. While the adults consumed decorative chocolates disguised as little candy gift boxes, or their last sips of Riesling and brandy, Garrett took Jill and Kayla to the youth center to see the show. *Hallucinations,* was a trio of magicians who specialized in getting the audience to participate with their bag of tricks, illusions, and funny gimmicks.

The children's departure sparked an eagerness to get to the casino, as if money truly was burning holes in their pockets. Buffy's excitement was more rooted in the idea of gambling than actually having money to blow. Her divorce hadn't garnered the large payout that Rita's, or even Dani's had. On top of that, her best friend owned a thriving business and had the insurance money from Garrett's accident. The money didn't matter; being included and having fun was enough for the delightfully simple, carefree, buxom blond, who wore her silicone breasts for the same reason she bought new clothes—they made her feel pretty.

John was feeling more than fat and happy. His libido was sitting somewhere inside—wherever libidos sit—smoking a cigarette, scratching it's ass, and singing a *Journey* ballad. If everyone thought it would be fun to jump off the ship, he was in a mood to go along. Nonetheless, a pocket full of cash or not, he knew he was way out of his league when it came to letting a dollar ride on the flip of a card or the spin of a wheel—especially after the rubber band had broken. A couple hundred in Jost Van Dyke was already a tad wasteful for a man out of work. He was prepared to throw caution to the wind, as long as it was tied to a string. Sadly, he thought, as much as he didn't want it to, money *did* create an invisible but real barrier between him and everyone else, except maybe Buffy. And he didn't want anyone treating him differently because of it. Sure, he could just watch; about as much fun as hitting a strip-club with a blindfold and mittens. He was usually an observer—no longer though—everything was different now and changing. If he opted to play versus watch there was more to lose; conversely, more to gain. Bingo, or a friendly low stakes card game was one thing, but with booze and sexual empowerment coursing through his veins, combining with the 'don't give a shit' financial attitude of a bunch of well-offs, who knew how the night would end? He could lose a year's worth of mortgage payments and part of his severance if he didn't stay alert. Then again, Carson wanted his father to be more adventurous.

The new voice in John's head was saying: *Just go with it. If your relationship with Rita doesn't work out, if you gamble away your money, if you wind up back in Kansas with nothing, you'll at least have the memories. They can't take away those experiences from you and you'll be a more colorful canvas—people like that! People don't like people who hesitate or flounder; they like people who do. You can't be anything unless you try.*

Richard, half closing a fist and shaking his hand back and forth as though he were stroking an invisible lead pipe, said, "What's missing here?"

Mary dropped her face into her hands as the three younger women laughed and choked.

"We respectfully decline to answer," Rita said with a blush.

"Dice!" Richard said. "I don't know what you gals were thinking. Let's hit the tables!"

"Let's go!" Dani said.

"Well, all right!" Rita said.

"You guys have to promise to show me what to do," Buffy said.

"Stick with me kid," Richard said. "Ready, Butterfly?"

"I wasn't born that way, but I am now. Just remember…I'm not a gambler."

"So you say," Richard scoffed. "So you say."

911

IN APPEARANCE, THE CASINO WAS modern enough to fit in anywhere on the Vegas strip; in size, it broke the rules. It was an intimate, yet open rectangle, with the bulk of slot machines on one side, gaming tables on the opposite side, and a large rectangular bar in the center. Large openings at either end made it both easy to enter and to escape. In contrast, Vegas' labyrinths were designed to keep its suckers wandering around in maze-like circles while flashing lights and cosmic sounds wore down their logic—and their wallets.

John imagined he had entered Rick's Americana Cafe in *Casablanca*. He went so far as to picture the room in black and white—even mentally changed his attire to a perfectly tailored, snug-fit, white tuxedo with black tie. With slicked back hair and a lit cigarette, he was prepared to enter the private back room, fix himself to a green felt table where he would nonchalantly whittle away the wee hours of the morning until a few thousand grew into the sum of a lifetime. In reality, he was afraid of wasting money.

"Ah," Richard sniffed. "You smell that?"

"Sanitizer?" Buffy asked.

"Money, dear!" he patted. "Smells like money. Let's see if we can't fill our pockets with that smell. Blackjack?"

"Sure," said everyone.

Rita, Dani, and Richard took three open seats at the closest blackjack table while John stood contently behind Rita to watch. After exchanging various amounts of cash for chips, all three players anted the fifty dollar maximum.

"All bets in!" barked the dealer with a British accent. "Coming around!" Six cards up and one down for the dealer spit out of his hand like water from a revolving sprinkler. Ooh's and aah's sounded from the six gamblers as he tossed the second up cards, finishing with the house's second down card, he then flipped over his first card.

"Can I have your ace?" Richard asked Dani.

"Get your own," she laughed.

Richard looked to his right where a 30-something, Brooklyn type guy was dwelling on a three and a jack.

Brooklyn signaled to be hit.

"Eight of diamonds!" chimed the dealer.

"Twenty-one!" Brooklyn cried. "See."

"Good for you man!" Richard said. "Good for you. Hit me gently!"

"Jack of hearts!"

"Dammit! I said gently. I already have a ten."

"I'm good," Dani signaled.

"Standing on eighteen!"

"Me too," Rita waved.

"Holding on twenty!"

An old woman with gray hair like an eagle's nest to Rita's left cried, "Hit me!"

"Seven of diamonds!"

"Again!" she commanded.

"Nine of clubs!"

The woman smacked the table and adjusted her thick bifocals. "Oh, kitty litter!"

"Twenty-two! Bust." Turning over a five to his ten, the dealer said, "Dealer shows fifteen! Have to play." A jack caused everyone, even the two busted players, to cheer and clap. "Twenty-five! Dealer busts. Everyone loves the dealer!"

"See," Rita said, turning for a kiss. "You're with a winner!"

"I already knew that," John kissed.

"So, you don't want to get more than twenty-one?" Buffy asked.

"That's right," Dani said. "But even a low hand can win. You could draw four aces and four two's, stand, and win with twelve if the dealer goes over."

"Wouldn't that be…" Buffy pursed her lips and looked to the ceiling to do the math. "Fifty-two?"

"Aces can be either *one* or *eleven*," Richard helped. "It's your choice."

"Do you have to say which one when the dealer guy gives you your cards?"

Everyone laughed in a non-mocking way. "No, dear," Richard said. "You can change them back and forth if you want."

"That's good!"

A half hour passed before a chair opened up. The old woman beside Rita grudgingly lost enough to retire to the quarter slots. Changing in a hundred, John took the end seat and cautiously stuck to the minimum five dollar ante for a good forty-five minutes.

"You're up at least twenty bucks, but you know it's easier to win more if you bet more," Rita said.

"It's also easier to lose more," John reminded.

"I wouldn't worry about it. Luck's on your side—this side," she smiled.

"True. I'll go ten."

"Where's that inner dragon of yours?"

"Okay, twenty!"

"Now you're playing!"

"No more bets," the dealer warned. "Coming around!"

"See there," Rita said as the dealer tossed John an ace. "What I tell you!" A second ace joined the first. "Split them, John."

"Doesn't that mean I have to double my bet?"

"Trust me," she squeezed under the table.

"Okay."

"Son of a witch!" Richard said, busting again and now down a couple thousand.

"It's not your night," Mary said. "Why don't we try some craps? I like to watch that game, it's more exciting than cards. Look at them all over there cheering and shouting."

"You go ahead," Richard said. "I'll give it a couple more hands."

"Okay, but don't make me wait." Mary leaned down closer to Richard's ear. "I'll blow on your dice."

Both chuckling, Mary kissed Richard's cheek before walking away.

"That sounds hard to pass up," Dani jested, overhearing Mary's offer.

"Indeed! Even old men like their dice blown on."

"Double blackjack!" the dealer cried.

Everyone cheered.

"Not a gambler, eh, John?" said Richard, looking down the table.

"I guess I'm getting the hang of it," John said.

"Obviously, this table is tilted toward your side," Richard said. "All the luck is rolling towards you three."

"You want to switch seats?" Dani asked.

"I wouldn't dare. I'm going to take my wife's advice and try some craps. If you guys cool off, feel free to join us."

"Good luck," Rita said.

"Go get 'em, Rich!" John said.

Richard surrendered his chair to a young couple who was patiently waiting to play. John scanned the room. It was 10:30 and the casino was filling up with stuffed dining room guests. All the game table chairs were occupied and onlookers crowded the action. The sound of rattling coin deposits and computer generated beeps and chirps spit from the slots as if the gamblers were giving the machines a good tickle.

Dani and Rita respectively, were both up a couple thousand to John's couple hundred. Beginning to feel the gambler's bug, he upped all his bets to twenty dollars, splitting and doubling down at the appropriate times like an old pro.

By 11:00, pulling and releasing a pile of chips like they were on a string, John joined the women's quadruple digit earnings. He was beginning to understand how people could piddle away home equity and college tuitions. Buffy had briefly taken a seat, but after losing four straight hands she opted for a Mai-Tai and the mindlessness of playing the slots—a game seemingly designed for her. Craving something exotic, Dani and Rita sipped rum runners while John slouched with a scotch in one hand and used the other to gesture commands to the dealer. Truly, he felt like Bogie sitting beside his Bacall.

"I really like this company!" Dani said. "They let you win back the price of the cruise."

"And your bar bill," Rita added.

"True," Dani said. "Mine might be higher than my ticket."

"Maybe we should buy another trip?" John suggested.

Rita turned. "*Maybe.*"

Intermittently, loud cries from the other tables were signaling the victories, the defeats and the long disappointed sighs of the oh, so closes.

"I wonder how Richard's doing?" Dani asked. "I can see Buffy over at the Pac-Man slot— looks like she found a game suited for her intellect. But I don't see Rich."

"He's over at that far table somewhere," John pointed.

"Somebody must be winning," Rita said. "There must be thirty people around that crap table and every couple of minutes they all scream."

Just two hands after Rita's comment, a different, but equally recognizable cry sounded from the far table. It was the sound of terror and panic. Thirty people jockeyed for position around someone on the floor.

"Oh my God!" Dani said. "Someone must have had a heart attack."

"Richard!" John leapt from his chair and darted to the scene. He could hear people yelling, "Call 911." In the past, he certainly wasn't known for being inquisitive, but during his dash to aid Richard he wondered if dialing 911 on a ship worked the same as it did on land. On a ship, maybe 911 rang the engine room, or even the pastry chef?

He tried squeezing between the bodies blocking whoever was on the ground, but the crowd was too thick. "He's not breathing!" someone cried. "Anyone know CPR?" another asked. "Get the ship's doctor!" a third shouted.

John pleaded to the roadblock of bodies in front. "Who is it?"

"It's an old man," a woman said.

"Please! Let me through! I think I know him!"

"Your father?" a man asked.

"No! Please! Step back so I can get in!"

"Where do you want us to step back to?" the woman asked. "Everyone in the casino is jamming in behind you."

Fear joined forces with the crush of bodies to wring streams of sweat from John's pores. His heart was racing and the strong stench from perfumed gamblers was burning his nostrils. Time froze, as if trapped in the tiny gaps between anxious bystanders.

A call beckoned behind John like a cry from a dream. "John! John, can you see anything?"

Wrenching his neck enough to make out Rita and Dani two deep behind, he shouted, "It's an old man, but I can't see him. I can't see if it's Richard."

Fortunately, the ship's head doctor—a spindly Swedish man with golden hair and slim glasses—arrived within minutes, armed with a defibrillator and a team of security guards. "Everyone give us some breathing room." John heard him say.

Like bouncers, the five security guards parted the congestion so the doctor could get through. Peeling two of the core's inner layers back towards the exit, security cleared a partial window, through which, John saw ten or so people still hiding a collapsed figure. The back side of one of the gathered was terrifyingly visible. He recognized the subtle pastels of Mary's cover shirt, her unmistakable pear shape, and the timeless short cut of her silver, gray hair. His worst thought dropped like a guillotine onto his swollen Adam's apple. He couldn't rush to her; security was fending off the crowd with outstretched arms. Sobbing noises poured out from the huddle along with the thump sound of electricity that was shooting through the defibrillator paddles. John found it difficult to see as the people in front kept shifting their heads in parrot-like side-to-side motion. Two more thumps sounded and then…wailing, blubbering cries.

Additional medical personnel rolled a pop-up stretcher into the casino after the worst had been realized. Security loosened their rein after the lifeless figure was loaded, covered from head to toe with a sheet, and carted away. Relaxing their morbid grip, the crowd slowly milled away enough for John to break through—Dani and Rita scrambled right behind. Fifteen feet felt like a hundred and Mary was all that was left of the near dozen closest witnesses.

John approached Mary's side delicately. "Mary?"

With head down, one hand over her mouth, and tears trickling over her knuckles, Mary said, "He's dead."

Sighing, the three each put an arm around Mary's back.

"Was it…a heart attack?" Dani asked.

"Yes."

"I'm so sorry," Rita sniffled.

"Be sorry for his entire family," Mary choked.

"That's what she means," John said, almost whispering. "We're so sorry for your whole family."

Mary looked up just as a phone rang. Embarrassed by the inappropriate pop ringtone, Dani hurried into her bag to silence the cheery song.

"Why are you sorry for my family, John?"

Dumbfounded, everyone silently froze until a chipper voice broke their stupor. "Who's the stiff?"

John turned. "Richard!"

"You're not dead!" Rita said, springing into a hug.

Dani followed Rita's lead. "We thought we'd lost you!"

Confused, but thankful for the fawning, Richard said, "Dead? Lost me? A guy sure misses a lot around here when he goes to the head. Who was on the stretcher? I saw them carting it down the hall?"

"Sherman," Mary half cried, half laughed. "He clenched his chest and dropped two minutes after you left for the bathroom."

"Sherman from our craps table?"

"Yes."

"Good for him!" Richard laughed.

Dani and Rita pulled back, horrified.

"That's terrible!" Rita said, smacking Richard's chest.

"Does that mean no more hugs?"

"Why would you say good for him?" Dani glared.

"Look, you don't understand," Richard said. "Sherman—rest in peace—was ninety-three. The folks I saw with the stretcher were his family; two children, their spouses, and three grandchildren and their spouses—right Mary, three grandchildren?"

"Yes," Mary said, blowing her nose. "They all seemed like very nice people."

"Yes," Richard said. "Turned out craps wasn't any kinder to me than blackjack, but Mary and I enjoyed talking with Sherman's family while he was rolling a small fortune—magical, I tell you, the man was on fire! Anyway, Sherman's daughter, about ten years younger than me and Mary, told me his age and that he had been a widower for several years now. How perfect is that?"

"I think I'm with the girls on this," John said. "What's perfect about any of that?"

"You pups are still too young to understand," Richard laughed. "We all have to go sometime. The older you get, naturally, the thought of one's mortality grows. When you're young and in good health the topic might come up from time to time, used as philosophic or comedic conversation during dinner parties. But when you're our age, the thought of death creeps into the day's most common routines and when you're clinging to each other in the dark of night. Thoughts of *when* and *what if* can overwhelm a morning bowl of bran flakes and loiter into the evening's last kiss. You pray that you'll be waking another day next to your life's companion. From what we learned, Sherman led a long, full life. He died in the casino while winning. And what I mean by *winning* is not only the fact that he was up big, but at ninety-three, he was definitely a man who got his money's worth. It's the last night of his cruise, not day one. And more importantly, the people he cared about most were all here to see him through the big fade-out. The man's either super lucky or a genius!"

"Now that you put it into perspective, I guess it was about as good a death as anyone could ask for," Dani said.

Rita perked up. "Sort of romantic when you think about it—like *Titanic*."

"That all might be true, but I still find it sad," Mary said.

"That's because we're approaching our time, my love. I'm sure old Sherman is now reunited somewhere with his sweetheart. They're probably dancing and…" Grinning romantically, "Gearing up for a stroll."

"I hope so," Mary grinned back.

Listening to all the talk about mortality and death, combined with the sight of watching a dead body being wheeled to the morgue caused John to miss Carson even more than he always did. Still, he found encouragement in Richard's words. "So, in due time, death can be something to look forward to—assuming we are strong and have faith?"

"I believe so," Richard said. "Well put! And you are strong enough. I should think Carson will be quite pleased when you meet again."

"I'm eager to find out."

"Don't get too eager," Richard said. "You have a lot of years left, and trust me, they go by in a flash."

"Don't worry. I can wait. I have a feeling my son wants me to do more than just take this cruise."

"And you might learn more of Carson's wishes tomorrow morning," Rita reminded, reaching around John's waist.

"I can hardly wait," John said. "It feels like Christmas Eve."

Missing Will, Dani checked her phone. "Hey guys, I got a text from Will. He says he's finished with work and wants us to meet around the corner—outside the port side lower dining room. He wrote that tonight's our chance to party like crew!"

Knowing Mary was still shaken up from watching a man die and feeling guilty about not being there to protect her, Richard said, "Sounds like an adventure for young people. I don't know of any crew in their 80s. Darling, would you care to stroll?"

"Why thank you for asking. I'd love to."

"You kids have fun," Richard said, wrapping an arm around Mary. "Thank Will for the invite. Sometimes that's just as good as the party. We'll hold our goodbye's 'til morning." When he shook John's hand, Richard noticed a firmer grip than at their first meeting. After everyone exchanged goodnight hugs, Richard said, "I can't believe you guys thought I was dead. Who dies in the crapper?"

"We didn't know you were in the restroom," Rita said.

"We thought you were at the table," Dani said.

"When I go, I intend to be dressed for the occasion," Richard said. "No self-respecting man enters the afterlife while squatting on the can. Even a massive stroke won't stop me from pulling up my pants and crawling to a more dignified spot. I don't want to meet God Almighty and all my old pals with my pants down. I'd never hear the end of it! I can't imagine being the laughing stock of heaven."

Everyone laughed as the couple said goodnight.

"Oh…let Buffy know we said goodnight," Mary said.

"We will. She's playing slots," Dani said, turning back. Over the bar counter through an open seat between two drinkers, Dani made out the back of Buffy's head. She was still seated at the same Pac-Man machine. Laughing, Dani said, "It's true what they say: ignorance really is bliss."

THE LAST YELLOW BRICK

Buffy was oblivious to Sherman's last farewell and tired of gambling—although she was happy to report winnings of thirty-eight dollars. She went to play with the girls while Dani went off to meet Will.

Despite Sherman's death, the trio was in high spirits upon leaving the casino. Richard's philosophy had gone straight to their hearts and replaced pity; still, John's inner voices were fencing with some new questions. Even though he realized that feeling sorry for Sherman was quite silly—especially if he was now really dancing with his wife through the heavens—he couldn't quite accept the idea of celebrating a person's life in their death without tangible sadness. After all, there was Sherman's family's pain to take into account—something John knew about, all too well. On the other hand, the man had gotten his money's worth out of life; why feel bad for his family? It's not like he was a teenager killed by a drunk driver or a child cheated by cancer. Sherman played the game of life as well as one could, at least as far as John knew. He went out quickly with dice in his hand and family by his side, not his pants around his ankles. His family should be celebrating a life well lived, not selfishly mourning their loss.

Richard's words and attitude towards death caused John to question his own grieving process. He rationalized that Carson died much too young, justifying John's depression and lack of motivation for a vacation. No parent on the planet could be expected to put aside the pain of losing a child they'd only known for twenty-some years and then celebrate—genuinely celebrate—the time they *did* have. But why? Society would certainly be wary of that person, thinking no one in their right mind could honestly celebrate in death. A person would have to be stricken by delusional grief, or have gone completely insane—that's why. Nearing the meeting place, John welcomed the debate going on in his head—entertaining new ideas didn't seem nearly as threatening as in his former life.

"I think this is where we're supposed to be," Dani said. "The dining room entrance is around the corner and we can't go forward any more without changing decks or going through that door."

"You mean the one that says *Employees Only No Passengers Beyond This Point?*" Rita asked.

"Knowing Will, I have a sneaking suspicion we're going through that door regardless of what's painted on it," John said.

"This is exciting!" Rita said.

"It is!" Dani said. "But what if we get caught?"

"We'll be in Miami in about five hours. What can they do?" Rita asked.

John's Cinco de Mayo experience allowed him to confidently throw in his two cents worth. "What I gathered from Will and Garth during my own little excursion down into Oz was that the employees are the ones who get into big trouble, not the wandering guest who decides to break the rules."

"I hope we don't get Will in trouble," Rita said.

"I don't think he's too worried about it," John said.

"That man could sweet talk a Manhattan cab driver into driving him to Long Island for free," Dani said.

The opening of a metal door sounded while the three laughed.

"*Pssst*—over here," Will hissed, peeking out the door with a toothy smile. "Come on!"

Leading the dash, Dani said, "Time to go!"

"Just the three of you?" Will asked, closing the door quickly.

"Buffy's with the kids," Dani said.

"And Rich and Mary are strolling," John said.

"I think the idea of two people their age *strolling* is just precious," Rita said.

"Mary was a little upset," Dani said. "She watched a man die tonight."

"I heard."

"Already?" John asked.

"Come on, Butterfly, you know by now that news travels fast among the crew. Speaking of which," Will pulled a black jacket out of a plastic bag and handed it to John, "you're all hired! Here's your uniforms." Everyone immediately recognized the mandarin collared style from the dining room. It was what all the assistant waiters wore during dinner.

"Where's ours?" Dani asked.

"Right here." Will pulled something from his pocket.

"Name tags!" Dani said. "That's all we get? How come John gets a flashy coat?"

"'Cause John's special, that's why. Some people change after their shift before they go to the crew bar, but most don't. You guys are perfect just the way you are. All you need is a name tag to fit in. Plus, I don't think you want to strip down in this staircase to change into a hot uniform. Okay? What are you waiting for, Butterfly? Do I have to dress you? Strip off that polo. I'll put it in my bag."

John did as he was told.

"Sexy!" Rita said.

"Who do you want to be?" Dani asked. "Margaret Sanchez from Chile, or Emily Ho from China?"

Frowning, Rita said, "What do *you* think?"

"Okay, you can be Sanchez, but I don't look like no Ho from China!"

Everyone laughed.

"You know what I mean," Dani said.

"Just pin the damn things on," Will said. "It's going to be dark and no one's going to read them anyways. It's just insurance. You both work in the hair salon if anyone asks. That should be easy enough for Dani since she owns a salon."

"So this is a Halloween?" John asked.

"You got it, partner. People notice you less if you're dressed like crew or at least wearing a name tag."

"Where'd you get this stuff?" Rita asked.

"Garth and me have a whole box of tags and shirts that we've bought from people in various departments—sadly, we can't seem to get a first officer or captain's shoulder boards. People just report the stuff lost or damaged and their department heads issue new ones. Ho and Sanchez don't work for the company any more, so no need to worry about running into them. Now can we get a drink?"

"Don't I get a name tag?" John asked.

"You got the coat! You don't need a name tag."

"But what if I want a fancy name too?"

"Yeah," Dani said. "Give him a name!"

"Seems only fair, Will," Rita said.

"You guys are killing me," Will snickered. "I didn't bring any men's tags. If Richard had come I was going to pass him and Mary off as exec's from our Miami office. I already gave you a moniker but if you want another one, tonight your name is Buck Wilde from Needmoreville, Louisiana. Take it or leave it!"

"I like it," Rita choked. "Very 70s porn-star."

"Perfect!" Dani said.

"Okay, I'll be Buck Wilde," John clapped.

"Good!" Will said. "Now, follow me."

Once behind enemy lines, Wilde, Sanchez, and Ho felt the nervous but intoxicating adrenaline that's released when doing something off limits, like breaking into a stranger's swimming pool for a midnight skinny dip. John was experiencing more of a 'been there done this' attitude, and so, was enjoying every corkscrew flight of stairs and every vault-like door that opened in the maze. The final door opened to a last set of descending stairs leading down into the worker bees' playground; a vast lounge extending the full beam of the ship. It was filled with club chairs and couches, video games and pool tables, even a movie rental kiosk and full Karaoke stage. Dim lighting gave the vivid carpeting, big screen TV's, and game machines a lava lamp, black light effect.

"Wow, this is nice," John said.

"Yeah, it's state of the art. Much nicer than the facilities on older ships," Will said. He paused at the bottom of the stairs to recon the glancing onlookers dressed in a plethora of uniforms. Unable to detect any red flags; aka, double-takes or suspicious officers, Will said, "Okay. Follow me outside. Just go look at the water when we get out there until I bring some drinks from the bar. And try to look like you're supposed to be there."

"You want us to put our hands in our pockets and whistle while we stare at the ceiling?" Dani asked.

"No, I think what he means is that we should introduce ourselves to everyone and ask if they know Will Catcher," John said, folding his arms.

"Maybe we could hike-up our skirts and do some toe-touches?" Rita suggested.

"Okay smart-asses, I think you know what I mean. All I'm saying is, try to blend in." The three crossed their hearts, raised a palm, and switched to somber faces. "All right, all right, let's go," Will waved.

Will chose an exit door between a bunch of dining room workers playing Golden Tee on one side and air hockey on the other. Too busy with their games and chugging Heinekens out of the three cases piled at their feet, neither side paid any attention to Will's party.

Outside gave access to an open air seating area with as much square footage as the inside lounge. Two large hot-tubs gurgled on the starboard side and there were two Ping-Pong tables situated on the port side. Dozens of white patio furniture sets filled out the space, along with a simple square bar serving beer and wine in the center. Teasing Will, Dani whistled on her way to the stern while he went to the bar.

"Rain," John said, placing his arms on the stern rail.

Rita stared out through the large windowless openings cut from the steel of *The Princess'* rear quarters. Light rain was falling into the ship's massive wake. "It's like a majestic movie being played on Mother Nature's humungous screen," she said. Wisps of breeze filtered in from the side openings before escaping through the stern, pushing the misting rain away with the trailing aquamarine wash. "This picture reminds me of all the pain I'm leaving behind on my way back to a familiar, yet new home. It's going to be different now. You know what I mean?"

John did, and said, "I feel I've cast away a few of my own poor qualities and nagging demons during the last week. But the pain of missing Carson is something I know I'll always carry." Dani turned her back and placed her elbows on the railing. The breeze fluttered her hair as she studied Will and thought of her own children. John continued, "Though I believe this trip has taught me to carry that pain in a different way. I'm learning how to rebuild my life. Instead of using blocks of pain, I'm reconstructing with fond memories, new experiences, and friends' smiles. Faith. That's really what it's all about, right? I should be allowed to celebrate my son's life, rather than destroy my own because he's not here. It's on account of my faith that he's in a better place and faith that I will meet him again one day."

"Absolutely," Rita said, caressing his back.

"What I miss?" Will asked, toting a case of beer in one hand, a bottle of white wine and three glasses in the other.

"We're talking about faith," Dani glowed.

"Good topic!" Will said. "Let's take that table over there. It's kind of away from everyone else and I can keep an eye on the room." The two couples confiscated a table in the starboard stern corner where everyone could enjoy the breeze and the sounds of the churning sea; Will kept his back to the wall to survey traffic. "Faith, huh? I wouldn't call myself religious, but I definitely believe in faith." Will uncorked the wine and two bottles of beer.

"Sure you bought enough beer?" Dani asked.

"They only sell it by the case. We take any extra soldiers back to our cabins, but everyone shares around here so there's hardly ever any extra. Beer, wine, and smokes are really cheap because they sell them to us at cost." Will filled Dani and Rita's plastic wine glasses.

"What do you attribute your faith to, Will?" Rita asked.

Pounding half of his first drink of the night in one go, Will burped inside his mouth causing his cheeks to puff out. "I look at it this way…if you have faith everything takes care of itself: friendships, work, love, mistakes, money, and death. On the ship I meet employees and passengers from every place on the planet. This place is a melting pot of conflicting beliefs, but it works. Sure, there's plenty of heated discussions around here. Usually the more people drink the more heated the discussions become. But for the most part, people are just sharing ideas without any bloodshed. It *happens*, but I find people are pretty open-minded if you talk to them right and present them with an opportunity to learn something new. Look at them," Will pointed. Everyone turned, causing their chair legs to squeal against the rubber coated deck. Countless oval tables filled with people wearing various uniforms peppered the floor. They were laughing, listening, flirting, and learning about one another over soft alcohol and burning cigarettes. "Over sixty-eight different nationalities and all getting along. That doesn't mean they're changing their core beliefs very often, but they will truly listen. And I figure vacation makes guests more tolerant and capable of trying new things, even ideas—right, Butterfly?"

"Thanks to everyone here and then some!" John toasted.

"Nah," Will said. "It was already inside you long before you met us. We just helped open a door, the same way your mysterious benefactor sent your ticket. It's just a nudge, you did the work."

"You're not telling us you believe everything simply works out because you have faith, are you?" Rita asked.

"Course not," Will said. "I mean *maybe*, but life sure as shit won't be what it could be for someone who doesn't put in the work. But if we do put in the effort, we should be content with the results, bad or good—if you have faith. Faith is the currency that buys us more chances when we fall down and the voice that tells us *I told you so* when you put in the effort and things turn out the way you wanted. I like those monk guys, nothing seems to faze them. At least that's how they're portrayed."

"You mean Buddhists?" Rita asked.

"Yeah," Will gulped. "Buddhist, Catholic, Jew, Muslim, Protestant, or *whatever*. Religion is a weird thing. When you start comparing all religions you find they really aren't that much different. They promote two common beliefs: life after death and a supreme being. The rest is semantics and bureaucratic bullshit that fanatics use to start arguments, other religions, or wars. Religious institutions aren't threatening—people are. The Koran isn't telling anybody to go blow up an embassy. I don't care what religion anyone claims, as long as it doesn't promote physical or mental violence, but the only one I need is the church of *faithfulness*. I take it everywhere and we ain't got no weird rules—just make the effort is all! Yip, I'd say my practice or denomination is the continual effort to be faithful!" Will chased his beer with a fresh bottle.

"That's good to know," Dani grinned.

Will winked. "I've found people either follow what they learned from their parents or they find their own way, but most of us are hybrids."

"What about the ones who never really had parents?" John asked.

"There's a lot of dead weight out there, John," Will said. "Jails, homeless people, cults, angry soldiers, drug addicts sleeping in abandoned buildings, and on and on. Without good parents, life is a lot steeper a climb. My faith can't fix their lives, but theirs can."

"What about you?" Dani asked. "I'd assume you're a rebel walking a different path than your proper southern parents?"

"I'm following in their exact footsteps: think outside the box, question everything, travel, work, love, and play like tomorrow's my last day—and have faith. What about you, John? You adhere to any special religion or Kansas cults?"

John leaned back still holding Rita's hand, sipped his beer, looked Will dead in the eyes, and said, "I would say I'm a born-again...born again into the church of exercising faith," he grinned.

"Feels good, don't it?" Will asked. "Faithful people can go everywhere, accomplish anything. That's what *no fear* really means."

"Faith can defeat the largest goliaths," John smiled slyly.

"Damn right!" Will raised his beer.

"I think everyone here can relate and will drink to that," Dani said.

After toasting and more refills, Will said, "I do feel I have to add a disclaimer to the denomination of *Faith*. It is possible that the life we're living now is a cake walk compared to what's waiting after our deaths. This could be the heaven and after death could be the hell. Like the movie asks, what if this is *As Good as It Gets?*"

"Boo!" Rita and Dani heckled.

"Boo!" John thumbed the top of his Heineken bottle, shook it, and sprayed beer at Will.

"I'm sorry! I'm sorry! It was just a thought! Isn't that what that purgatory stuff is all about? I have faith the disclaimer is not the case. I just thought I should warn you!" Everyone laughed. "I'm using your polo to clean my face, John."

"Go ahead, I have faith it will get washed again," John said.

Still laughing, Will said, "I can't believe it, take you to Oz and you throw beer on the wizard."

"When was the last time you watched that movie?" John asked. "When they finally meet the wizard, it turns out he's full of shit. The real wizards are inside us all, waiting to use their powers during our adventures down our very own yellow brick roads. You should know that, Will, you helped teach me."

"Here, here!" Rita said.

"You've come a long way since our first margarita together," Dani said.

Will stood with open arms as John met him. Feeling like true friends, the two traded in their man-hugs and fist punches for a brief, but strong, full embrace. "Love ya like a brother," Will said.

"Me too," clenching his wrist and squeezing hard into Will's spine. "You're one hell of a catcher."

"I just love male bonding," Rita said.

"I do too," Dani said. "I think most men are just big, sensitive, and less-furry teddy bears."

The two men released and returned to a manly activity—they drank.

"I, ah…" Will paused to wipe his nose with the back of his hand. "I wanted to let you all know, especially you Dani…" His eyes shifted over Dani's shoulder.

"Yes?" Dani wondered.

"Um, this would be a good time to get into character for your Halloween costumes," Will warned.

"Huh?" Rita squinted.

"Good evening, Mr. Catcher!" said a woman approaching the corner table.

"Hi, boss," Will casually smiled.

"I see you're enjoying some of the best beer on the planet!" said the squatty, creamy-skinned woman dressed in a white skirt and officer's top.

"No arguing that!" Will said, rising. "Oda here is from Holland. She's just about the best bar manager I've ever worked for!"

"You're full of shit, Will, but I love you for it," Oda said. "We're going to miss you around here. I still don't understand why you never wanted to be a manager. You could have been a hotel director by now."

"You heard?" Will squinted.

"Of course I did," placing her hands on her hips. "You should have told me first instead of calling Tony, but I know you guys go *way* back so I guess I can't blame you for giving your notice to him." Oda dropped her arms and offered a smile to Will's three co-workers. "Hello. I don't recognize any of you. New hires or transfers from another ship?"

Stunned, the trio smirked.

"Just got on Sunday," John spoke up.

"You liking the dining room, Mr.…."

"Wilde. Buck Wilde," John swallowed. "Yes. It's a lot of work, but yes!"

"Good," Oda smiled. "Your parents sure gave you a good strong name. I like it!"

"Thanks!"

"And…" Oda drug out, squinting and leaning down, "Margaret Sanchez and…Emily…*Ho*. What department are you ladies in?"

"We work in the salon," Rita said, as confidently as a trained actress. "You should stop in some time. I'm great with nails and Emily works magic with hair—not that yours needs any, it's gorgeous. I always wanted to be a natural blonde, but it's not a common hair color in Chile."

"Thank you, Margaret," Oda feigned embarrassment. "We Dutch girls can relate. I've always dreamed about what it would be like to have beautifully thick dark hair like yours." Shifting to Emily. "Are you as good as Margaret says?"

"I can honestly say, I am," Dani said.

"I'll have to stop in then. The Caribbean must be a big change from China? I must say, Emily, you don't look Chinese."

Dani kicked Will's calf, causing him to wince. "I was adopted from a California orphanage by my Chinese parents," she lied with a straight face. Everyone but Oda swallowed outbursts.

"Adopted?" Oda said.

"Yes! My Chinese parents were very important people. Sadly, they're dead now."

"I didn't know people from other countries could adopt an American child?"

"Like I said, they were *very* influential people. You know, politically powerful. They had a lot to do with keeping Chinese communism…*democratic looking*. The adoption agency made an exception. It made international news!"

"You're very fortunate," Oda said seriously. "It must have been interesting for an American child to be raised in…?"

"Beijing!"

"Yes, of course," Oda said crossing her arms. "Your Chinese must be very good? I love to hear it spoken—such an animated language," she said, patiently waiting for a sample.

"I-uh, actually never picked it up. My guardians assumed I would return to the US one day, so they put me through a private school where we only spoke English." Dani glanced at Will, who appeared to be taken with her lying skills. "Anyway, they died when I was eighteen, after that, I moved back to the US to attend college."

"Good for you, Emily, and I'm sorry about your parents," Oda said. "Welcome aboard—all of you. Well, I better go make the rounds. Garth is working in the disco, so who knows what's happening there. He doesn't know it yet, but the home office is giving him a shot at assistant cruise director."

"That's great news!" Will said. "Tell him we said hi!"

"I will. Goodnight everyone!" Oda waved and turned, before turning back. "And Will?"

"Yes, boss?"

"Remember you have that sanitation course in the morning."

"I'll be there! You know how much I love listening to lectures about germs."

"Yes," Oda smiled. "And if anyone else catches you with these passengers you'll be getting off in Miami a couple of weeks early." She enjoyed watching Will's normally slick expression turn to humble guilt. "I'm sad you're leaving us, Will. Your sense of humor will be greatly missed. Make sure nothing happens to them and I'll pretend like I was never here."

"Yes, ma'am," Will cowered. "Thank you."

"Really, Will…Buck Wilde, Sanchez, and Ho?" Oda laughed as she walked off.

When she was out of ear shot the group let out a collective breath, laughed like fools, and congratulated one another on stellar performances.

"So your boss's name is Oda and you call this other guy that you look up to Yoda?" John asked.

"Kind of funny, right?" Will asked. "Oda and Yoda."

"Hysterical," Rita cackled.

"She said you quit your job," Dani said, turning serious. "Why?"

"Well," Will shuffled, "that's what I was trying to tell you. I've been doing this for a long time and I'm feeling like it's time for a change—plant my feet back on real ground and wake up in a real bed. Living in the moment only gets you so far. Real men, husbands and fathers, plan for the future. I was thinking…" Sipping some beer. "I own a house in southern Maryland, just outside the D.C. beltway. And that's not that far from New Jersey—not really. I was thinking…" Will searched for any changes in expression in Dani's face or eyes.

"Yes, Will, what were you thinking?" she asked.

Rita squeezed John's hand tighter.

"I was thinking you might want to get to know each other better?"

"You know I have a business and two kids," she said without expression.

"Two wonderful kids," Will stated. "I'd also like to know them better. I always wanted to be a father. I know I'm not their father, but that doesn't mean I can't be a good father figure. And I could, you know. If that's a possibility you might be interested in exploring?" Will felt his hands turning clammy and the breeze suddenly felt hot. Dani's silence and blank face made his stomach feel like he'd swallowed glass. John and Rita watched intently for a response as Rita squeezed even harder.

After what seemed like an eternity, a single tear dropped from Dani's left eye. "Would you take us to all the museums if we came to visit?"

"Every last one," Will sighed. "I'm soon to be unemployed so I'll have lots of free time."

Dani rose, hunched over, and gently held Will's cheeks. Lovingly searching his eyes, she whispered, "I think we can talk." Will lifted her off the ground with ease as he stood. She wrapped her legs around his waist and they kissed like a young military couple, rejoined after a long deployment.

Clapping, John and Rita egged them on and cat calls and whistles sounded from the rest of the deck.

"Careful, cowboy, that bull rides back!" Rita said.

"Hey, when did you guys get here?" John asked. *They were—here, that is—*John thought. It didn't matter what they had gone through separately or how long it took to get where they were—only that they made it. John recognized the love he felt. Twice before he experienced the gift: when Page asked him to the prom and the day she brought Carson into the world. And now thanks to Rita Hernandez, John Smith had found love again for only the third time in his life. "The east coast seems like the place to be," he said, looking to Rita.

"What about the comfort of Kansas?" Rita asked.

"I think I've worn that blanket into tissue paper," John said, leaning in to kiss the dimple from Rita's half grin. "Good intentions just aren't good enough anymore. I think it's time I earned my ticket."

Drinking and laughing, the two couples whiled away the early hours sharing stories about the past week like they were all old friends, and in a way, they were. Destined hearts, true friendships, and the eternal love for one's children, don't concern themselves with time. The gaps between meetings—be they hours or years—don't diminish the bonds or the love, not when they're genuine and faithful; on the contrary, each time is as good as the first, but in both new and versed ways. Put another way, when you *get there*, you realize with hints of déjà vu, that *there* was the place you always were—but now there's a home.

DAY 8
(BACK IN MIAMI)

IT'S AN HONOR

A T SUNRISE *THE PRINCESS* TOOK her place among the other floating hotels in Miami's vast harbor. When John arrived in the main lobby at 8:45, it was abuzz with passengers finalizing their ship affairs. He prowled back and forth through the crowd, sipping coffee and carrying an herb cream cheese bagel. He examined everyone for any tell-tale signs. No one got a pass: children, the elderly, ship employees, blatant yahoo's, even a pair of smiling nuns got a good solid visual inspection. Yes, no matter how cursory, people who smiled anywhere near John's direction made themselves bigger targets for his scrutinizing stares.

Tired of having his hands full and thinking a stationary position might be better for spying his benefactor, he took a seat in the lobby's corner, placed his decaf Cappuccino on the coffee table, and began nibbling his bagel. Decaf was the right choice for a man brimming with restless anticipation. Between drinking in the crew bar until almost 2:00 in the morning, Rita's insatiable sexual appetite, and the suspense of finally meeting whoever sent his ticket; he didn't get much sleep. But caffeine wasn't needed to start his motor. John was wide awake, not groggy in the slightest.

Ten minutes of knee jittering later, too nervous to eat, John rested the half-eaten bagel beside his coffee. Scanning the room as if he was trying to identify a suspect in a police lineup, a man's profile caught his attention. Talking to someone out of John's sight, against the wall of the far corridor opening, the profile definitely belonged to Richard. John leaned to the edge of his seat, lurching over the coffee table. When Richard noticed John, he flagged a wave and made his way through the lobby.

"Good morning, my boy," in his usual jolly tone.

Standing, John shook Richard's hand. "Rich! Good morning. What are you doing here?"

"Oh, just taking care of a room service discrepancy."

"Where's Mary?"

"We had breakfast together and now she's packing. I squared my stuff last night. I don't know why women can't pack the night before. Speaking of which, did Rita get her bag? We left it in our foyer before we met you for dinner last night."

"I believe so. I mean, we had a late one last night in the crew bar—a lot of fun by the way."

"I'm sure!"

"When we got back to the cabin, I realized I should have left a light burning. The two of us were a little tipsy and…distracted," John laughed shyly. "I think her bag was what we tripped over. I didn't look for it this morning, so she probably moved it under the desk or somewhere. But I'm sure it's there."

"Good! I know how disorienting those distractions can be," Richard said, elbowing John's chest. "Would you find it nosy of me to sit and read my paper while you wait for your ghost?"

"Not at all, Rich. A friend's support would be good. I don't know how I'm going to react."

"Closure is always a good thing. You'll be fine." The two sat. "Where's Rita?"

"Asleep when I left the cabin. I couldn't sleep and left at six to…" John caught himself and grinned. "Let's just say I took care of a few things in the business center."

"I see—business? I have some business myself this morning."

John looked pensively at Richard. "Tell me the truth, Rich. Are you here because you and Mary sent my ticket?"

"We already told you, son, it wasn't us." Opening his freshly pressed *Wall Street Journal,* "No, I have another meeting with our yacht builder, about detail stuff."

"Oh." Not wanting to interrupt Richard's reading, John went back to visually interrogating passengers. At the same place he'd spotted Richard, two men, both in white officer uniforms, were chatting in a familiar way as if they were more than co-workers. "Is one of those guys over there the Captain?"

Lowering his newspaper, Richard said, "Yes, the one on the left. That's Bill. The other one is a real naval officer."

"How can you tell?"

"See those medals? They don't give those out to cruise ship officers. He's a Lieutenant Commander." As quickly as he'd recognized and explained the difference, Richard went back to reading about Johnson & Johnson's latest earnings report.

John watched the two men as they continued conversing. Richard was right about the difference in uniform. Despite numerous gold stripes on the shoulder epaulets, the Captain's seemed almost fake, like a rental costume, compared to the other man's crisp and polished outfit. The Lieutenant Commander's shoes gleamed like white diamonds and his colorful ribbon medals were much showier than the two pens sticking out of the Captain's left breast pocket. Studying the men's attire made John think about Carson and how happy he'd been when he was issued his first Army fatigues and weapon. He finally had the BB gun, so to speak, that he so desired all his life. He'd called home first chance he got to share his jubilation.

John's head drooped toward the coffee table with his Carson flashback. But instead of feeling depressed, he smiled fondly. When he looked up, he was shocked to see the Lieutenant Commander standing before him.

Towering above John to what looked like all of 6'5", with a formidable build and steely, but kind blue eyes, the man said, "Hello John," in a soft voice.

John heard Richard folding his paper away, but didn't look. "I'm sorry, do I know you?"

"I believe my father's mentioned me. I'm sorry, may I sit?"

"Certainly," John said, extending his hand to a third chair. "Who's your father?" As the words left his mouth, John's eyes fell to the uniform's name tag: O. Clawson.

"I'm Oliver, Oliver Clawson."

"Oh! It's an honor to meet you, sir!" John said, exuberantly shaking Oliver's hand. "I guess you are here to meet with your dad and the yacht builder?"

"I am," Oliver said, looking dramatically poised. "But that's not really why I'm here. You see…the *honor* is all mine, sir."

Glancing at Richard and back, John said, "I don't follow."

"John," Oliver said cautiously, leaning closer, hands folded. "John, I sent your ticket. I sent the anonymous emails."

Looking confused and relieved at the same time, John said, "You sent the ticket? But why? You don't even know me."

"Not directly, no. But I had the pleasure of meeting your son, Carson."

"You know, I mean knew him? But how?"

"Did Carson tell you much about what he did for the Army or where he was doing it?"

"No. His mother and I never really knew. Just that he spent a lot of time in the Middle East. We did know he was involved with intelligence and communications. He started out at Fort Meade. From what we understand, that's the Army's training center for intelligence. Everything he did was considered confidential."

"Yes," Oliver nodded. "That makes sense. I can tell you this: Carson was exceptional at what he did. Not only that, he was well liked for who he was as a person, not just as a soldier. You and his mother have great reason to be proud and miss him."

"Thank you, and I agree."

"I hope you don't mind that I invited my father? He hasn't heard any of this either."

"Not at all." John glanced kindly at Richard, who was sitting like a king on a throne. "I'm glad you did." Usually very talkative, Richard sat patiently listening.

"Good. I actually had the privilege of working with your son for a few months—six to be exact. Initially, that time began when he and his squad leader were asked to serve as part of a mixed security detail on my aircraft carrier. Carson acted as a liaison between the ship and Central Command. We worked well together and hit it off right away. Very gung-ho, your son," Oliver chuckled.

"Always! He knew from a young age he wanted to join the military."

"He loved his work, I can tell you that. I'm the only one of my brother and sisters who has never married. It takes a woman with thick skin to be involved with a husband who spends so much time overseas. Your son and I agreed about that. He thought we were both destined to marry women who were also in the military. Carson played cupid by introducing me to Rebecca Harmon—*Sergeant* Rebecca Harmon, his squad leader." Laughing. "It's common for enlisted people to have nicknames. Hers was Booty. Did he ever mention her?"

Looking like a light bulb just turned on above John's head, he said, "Yes! He often mentioned in his letters how his good buddy *Booty* always had his back. I never knew he was a girl…woman, you know what I mean. I just assumed they called her Booty because he, *she*, liked to steal stuff. You know, innocent war plundering, souvenirs and such."

"No," Oliver said, pausing as he and Richard laughed. "Let's just say she…was well blessed in the hind quarters."

"Ooohh, nothing wrong with that!"

"Sounds like an asset," Richard said, still laughing.

"Well…Becca and I slowly formed a relationship. It started with sharing meals together and progressed from there. Carson was right, Becca was an extraordinary woman. She and I used to joke that between her last name and Carson's match making abilities, it was an *eHarmony* connection."

"You're lucky he didn't try to keep her for himself," Richard said.

"Yes, Carson and Rebecca were very close, but in the same way any two male soldiers might be. There was a bond, a trust, the kind you must have when people are shooting at you. Besides that, she was ten years older than Carson. From what I learned from her, he thought of Becca as a friend and mother figure. That's to say she provided almost motherly protection, but in ways that made her come across as a man. That trait can be very endearing to a soldier. Forgive me for saying, but I suspect Carson found qualities in Becca that his own mother lacked."

"No offense taken," John shrugged. "That makes perfect sense to me. I'm sure he wished his father was better rounded as well."

"I wouldn't put it that way, John," Oliver said. "He loved you both very much. It's natural for people to be attracted to other people with both similar and opposite qualities than the ones we've learned from our parents. Life would be boring if everyone were the same. In many ways Becca was very different from my own mother."

"You keep saying *was*," John said.

"Yes, I'm getting to that," Oliver sighed. "After a few months together on the ship, we were all reassigned to the US embassy in Afghanistan to work on the Ambassador's staff. One scorching afternoon—I'll never forget how hot it got—we get spoiled on the ship. Anyway, on this one especially hot afternoon, Carson and I had just entered the first perimeter gate. We were coming back from touring an Afghan school and we stopped to talk instead of hustling inside the next two gates. Carson, God bless him, noticed a suspicious man approaching from outside—instinct, I guess. He grabbed my arm with one hand and used his other to force my back towards the next gate. We both fell, with Carson covering me, just seconds before the explosion went off. The suicide bomber took out part of the first wall, himself, and a guard, while we remained unharmed. John, I owe my life to your son, and for that, I can only say with the deepest sympathy for your loss, *thank you*."

Fighting the onset of tears, John wiped his eyes. Leaning forward, Richard placed a hand on John's back.

"Bravery isn't taught, it's passed down," Richard said humbly.

"Go on," John said, composing himself.

"A couple months later, Carson and Rebecca went back to their unit. I believe their CO briefed you on the ambush during their routine patrol?"

"Yes, but I had to beg for the exact details."

"Well, you probably know as much as I do then. What you might not know is that Sergeant Rebecca *Booty* Harmon was also in your son's truck. All four soldiers in that vehicle were killed."

"I'm so sorry, son," Richard said, looking dejected. "We didn't know."

"It's okay, pop, I've learned to accept it. I was waiting to bring her home for introductions, but it turned out I waited too long."

"It's such a waste," John said.

"The time Becca and I shared was worth the pain of losing her and certainly better than having never met her at all. I'm richer for having known her and that's how I look at and cope with it."

"I agree, Oliver," John said. "I'm learning to also see that my time with Carson was a gift."

"He loved you so much, John. Two weeks before their convoy was attacked, I received a letter from Carson. I have it with me. May I?"

"Please."

"Dear Lieutenant Commander Clawson,

"Sergeant Carson Smith here. Hope you're staying safe at the palace without me around? I sure do miss embassy meals! They were like home cooking compared to MRE's. I do like being back in the sandbox though. It might seem strange, but it's kind of like being home. Becca and

I talk about you all the time. She misses you a lot. I told you the two of you would make a good couple! I hope I get to meet your parents someday. They sound like such interesting people. Maybe we can all go somewhere exotic on that yacht they're building? It would be good for my dad to meet people like them. Which, by the way, is the reason for this letter.

"You told me if I ever needed a favor to let you know. I'm not one for calling in markers, but I'm making an exception. I told you I was worried about my dad. I'm afraid he's just not dealing with the divorce too well. I wrote him a letter asking him to come out of his shell and do more things for himself and I made him promise to take a cruise, but he still hasn't gone.

"If anything should happen to me before I can convince him to go, it would sure mean a lot to me if you could give him a push. If I die, knock on wood, I'm afraid not only will he never take a cruise, but he may fall into a deeper depression, or worse. Life's short. When I go, I want everyone who knew me to throw a big party, and instead of shedding tears, I want them to celebrate the time we shared. Maybe they could all take a cruise together!?

"Thanks Oliver,

"Your friend always, Sergeant Carson Smith.

"P.S. I'm enclosing his address, email, and a photograph."

"God, I miss that kid," John laughed, while no longer able to hold back his tears.

"I wish I could sail that boy around the world," Richard said, restraining his own emotion.

"Regretfully, I told myself that I was too busy to respond promptly, plus I wanted some time to think about Carson's wishes," Oliver said. "I responded three days before he died. Carson's CO found my letter. Seeing it was from a naval officer, he returned it to me with a letter explaining what had happened instead of forwarding it to you with the rest of his personal items. I was crushed, John. But I'm in charge of a lot of people doing important things. Mourning was something I had to keep to myself. I knew you were hurting, but it took a long time to process everything that had happened. I thought about sending you a condolence letter, but when I sat down to compose it, I remembered Carson's letter. I waited six months so you had time to grieve. I figured there was no way you were going to take a cruise during that time, if you hadn't already done so when he was alive."

"But what about your parents? How did they know who I was?"

"We didn't," Richard said. "Not unless being given a photograph of someone is the same as knowing them."

"We have been dealing with the yacht builder for a long time. Yachts don't get built like a Ford off of an assembly line. I told Dad I wanted to send them on their next cruise. And that he should arrange to have a meeting with Gary, the CEO at Harding Ship Builders to talk about any concerns or design details. What better place to discuss them than on a cruise ship, I thought. He agreed and I made the arrangements. A couple days before your cruise, I told Mom and Dad that I knew someone who had suffered a great loss who would be on the same voyage. I told them I didn't want you to know that I'd mentioned anything about you or that they mention any affiliation between you and me. I gave them your picture and told them that if they ran into you, to keep an eye out and email me of any contact the three of you might have. I didn't tell them about Carson's death. I figured that was up to you to share or not share with whomever you wanted. I sent the ticket anonymously to entice you, but also so you could make up your mind whether you wanted to go or not. That's what Carson wanted you to learn to do: make decisions, take risks, embrace change, become more adventurous, and celebrate life. You didn't need to know about me until now. This trip was so you could learn about—*you*. I just thought you needed some encouragement. And I thought it would be a good idea to have somebody looking out for you. I think everyone knows you're not exactly a world traveler." The three men laughed. "I think you can agree, Richard and Mary make good company?"

"The best," John said purposely. "But how did I meet them so quickly? There are thousands of people on board and I met them before we even left Miami."

"Dad says you skipped a bridge tour?"

"Yes."

"If you'd gone, you would have met Bill. I believe you saw us talking together a few minutes ago."

"Yes, the Captain? Your dad said you served together."

"That's correct. He's a great guy. Loves his vino, eh, Dad?"

"The man knows more about grapes than *Welch's*."

Everyone chuckled.

"Well, all I had to do was call Bill up and explain the situation. And all he had to do was switch out your life vest to the same section as my parents."

"Son of a gun," Richard said. "Your mother and I were wondering about that too. We thought we'd have to comb the ship to meet you, John. My boy's pretty slick!"

"Like oil," John said. "And what about the quotes?"

"Mom loves the classics and I guess I inherited that love. Thoreau was one of the first books that really touched me. I thought the passages I emailed you were appropriate for the occasion. Thoreau left the city to go to the woods and then back again. It struck me that you were leaving the woods, so to speak, to go to the city and…I guess we don't know yet? It doesn't matter which way you do it, the point is the same. Everything runs its course, even if we stay in one place. Change occurs and life doesn't wait on us, but it is there for the taking for those brave enough to grab hold. And when I heard you lost your job—which I am very sorry about, by the way. Fucking Chinese, not much you can do."

"Fucking China," Richard said.

"Fucking China," John felt compelled to agree, although he didn't know anything about China.

"Yeah. So when I heard you lost your job I remembered the second quote. Maybe working in a rubber band factory wasn't really your life's calling? Carson didn't think so. He told me that. Whatever basket you decide to weave or not weave, make sure you're doing something that makes you happy, that's all. That's all your son wanted for you. The military, along with my parents, taught me to live deliberately and purposefully. That's what Thoreau learned and passed on from his time at Walden. You did that for Carson, John. By working day in and day out and doing all the unselfish things you did over the years for him and your family. You sacrificed for others. The shortcomings and mistakes don't matter, just the end result. Carson was a hell of a fine man and now he wants you to live deliberately and purposefully for yourself."

"Thank you, Oliver. And I'm learning to. They are wise words, just like everything that comes out of your family's mouths."

"Oh, don't say that!" Oliver said. "Especially not with him sitting here!"

"You should come to Christmas and meet Oliver's siblings," Richard said. "You'll hear plenty of unwise BS from everyone, except me, of course!"

"Of course!" John said.

"Yeah, right!" Oliver said. "Like building a catapult on *Clawing-A-Bow-T's* stern?"

"I thought it was a good idea," Richard said. "We can use it to chuck beers to you all when you're in the water."

"Right, Dad! That's all we need, to be pelted with beer bottles while we're swimming in some cove miles away from the nearest hospital. Fantastic idea!"

In the midst of laughter, John stared away from the Clawsons.

"I'll be right back," he said, standing up.

"Where you going, John?" Richard asked, spotting what John was looking at. "Maybe we've prodded that dog enough?"

"Is there a problem?" Oliver asked.

"Maybe," Richard said.

"George!" John said, stepping away from the table.

"What the fuck do you want?" George asked, stepping to meet John. His face was much more bruised than John's.

"I'm glad I saw you, George. I wanted to tell you something."

Richard and Oliver stayed seated, but kept a close watch.

"Yeah, what's that?" George flexed. "Maybe you'd like to talk outside?"

Laughing, John said, "You know, George, you can't be all bad, although I wouldn't know it from this trip. But Rita saw something in you once—enough to marry you. And it wasn't for your money."

"You sure about that?"

"Yes. I know she'd be just as happy without your money. I'm not the smartest guy, but I know when people are genuine. I think somewhere along the line, something made you into a man who thinks life is all about you. Maybe you feel insecure because you can't have children?"

"That's it! I'm going to fuck you up!"

Oliver sprang to his feet while Richard took a few seconds longer. Before George could cock his fist, the two men were on either side of John.

"You always need bodyguards to protect you, don't you, John?" George asked, having to bend his neck back quite a bit to look into Oliver's steely eyes.

"No, these aren't bodyguards, they're friends, real friends," John said, fearlessly. "I would have talked to you regardless of whether they were here or not. I'm not afraid of you, George. I'm afraid of being afraid. That fear is causing me to confront the things I used to be afraid of."

"You're not making any sense," George said.

"See if this makes sense," John said, reaching into his pocket. "I want you to have this."

"Why are you giving me two hundred dollars?"

"It's for the other half of your tattoo."

"What?"

"You remember what you told me at the hammock about the strong surviving? Well, maybe the Asian artist who did your work never read the rest of that proverb. The strong may be the only ones who survive, but it's the meek that shall inherit the earth. Let me put it another way, I'm sure a well-educated man like yourself has seen *The Good, The Bad and The Ugly* at some point in your life." Waiting, but no response. "Well, this is the end of the story and I'm leaving you with half the gold. Metaphorically of course, I don't have any gold bars. I don't even have a job."

"Get to the fucking point," George said.

"You can keep your memories, but I'm taking Rita," he said, gritting his teeth and squeezing his fists.

George huffed and said, "Keep her." Starting to turn, he asked, "What are you going to do when your friends aren't around?"

"Not let people like you intimidate me, no matter what the outcome."

"And he has thousands of friends," Oliver grinned. "All over the world."

"I've got a business to run," George said, walking off towards the gate.

"Well done, my boy!" Richard said, squeezing John's shoulder.

"I guess it's been some vacation?" Oliver asked.

"I think I could use another one," John laughed, wiping sweat from his forehead. "I better go check on Rita and set our bags outside for the stewards."

"We're headed for lunch at eleven-thirty if you'd both care to join us?" Richard asked. "Oliver's coming and Mary called Dani, the girls are coming. Maybe we can set Oliver up with Buffy?"

"Buffy?" Oliver said, looking skeptical.

"She looks like cotton candy and is as sweet as apple pie," John said.

"Intriguing," Oliver said.

"Sounds great, Rich," John said. "Just let me run it past Rita. Where we going?"

"Where else?" Richard asked. "Joe's Stone Crabs. I'm sure Rita knows the place. It's just over the causeway and hang a right."

"Perfect!" John said. "I can't thank you enough, or tell you how much everything you've done for me means, Oliver. You're a great man."

"It takes one to know one," Oliver said. "I'll share more Carson stories at lunch, or better yet, when you join us on the yacht."

"That sounds like heaven," John said. He thought pensively for a second.

"What is it, John?" Richard asked.

"All this time I thought Carson sent my ticket."

"He did, John," Oliver said. *He did.*

DID U HAVE FUN?

JOHN THOUGHT HE WAS LOOKING at a ghost when he arrived back at his cabin. Rita had packed their two large suitcases and placed them outside for pick-up. Beside John's stood a very old, vintage leather suitcase. Timeless in style, like a suit from a Bogart movie, the bag was showing signs of wear and tear, but it had obviously been oiled and well preserved. Bending down, he read the inscription on its silver badge: A Bagly Bag. Smiling, he unlocked the door with one quick swipe.

"Good morning!" he cried.

"I'm in the bathroom, honey!" Rita said. "Tell me, tell me, tell me! Who sent your ticket?"

Flushing, then Rita yanked the door open.

"It was Richard and Mary's youngest son. The one that's in the Navy—Oliver."

"Wow! How? Why?" Wrapping her arms around him, Rita kissed a dozen kisses.

"I'll tell you all about it at lunch. I mean, will you have lunch with me, us? The Clawsons want to meet at Joe's for stone crabs. Dani and Buffy are coming too."

"Sounds delicious!" More kissing.

"Rita, where did you get that bag?"

"What?"

"Your suitcase! The one outside."

"Oh, that's Mom's. I told you about her trip across the United States?"

"Yeah."

"Well…" Rita laughed. "She says she carried a map the whole time and studied all the names of dots that sounded interesting in each state. When she got to Kansas, she saw a town named Cuba."

"Yes, I know it. There's only about a hundred and fifty people that live there."

"That's what she said! But she didn't know that before she got there and wasn't about to *not* visit a town named after her own country. I don't think she stayed long. When she left, she stopped in another nearby town and discovered this quaint luggage store. I told you she was carrying all her stuff in a laundry bag?"

"Yes."

"Okay. So, she goes into this boutique and falls in love with this beautiful hand-made bag. The owner is there and tries to sell it to her, but she explains that she has just enough money for the rest of the trip. The owner—I remember she said he looked like Santa Claus."

"I'm sure he did," John laughed.

"What?"

"Nothing. Tell you later."

"Anyway, he treated her like Santa Claus! I think he was smitten by Mom's beauty!"

"I'm sure he was, based on yours."

"Kiss for that!" she said, using the muscle between her nose and top lip to smutch John. "So

Santa Claus tells her a woman with such courage and passion needs to have a proper suitcase. He insists on giving it to her! She of course refuses, saying it's not good business to just give things away. After much debate, she accepts, giving her name and address and taking the shop's business card. She promises to repay the total amount, which I think was negotiated to an extreme discount. This man was such a saint! I guess he couldn't stand the idea of this poor woman, now with this big suitcase, schlepping her way across country. Apparently, he made some phone calls, because Mom had no more problems finding rides. Every time she caught a ride and got dropped off, another car was right there to take her on the next leg. I think she caught on when one of the drivers said something about working for a luggage shop. Can you believe it? This guy had people drive her to California and back to New York on his own dime, just so she was safe!"

"I believe it. Good old Fred Senior."

"What? Fred Senior?"

"Did she pay him back?"

"When she got home she worked at a cigar factory where she met my father. She mailed four dollars a month until the bag was paid for."

"Your mother has integrity. Rita...I don't mean to change the subject, but I have something else to ask you."

"Yes?"

"Well I...I didn't sleep much last night."

"I know! Me neither."

"That's not what I mean. I left the room at six to use the business center."

"I know. I woke up to discuss some business of my own and you weren't here."

"Yes, well...I don't want to be presumptuous, but..."

"Yes, Butterfly? What don't you wish to presume?"

"I know we don't really know each other all that well."

"I beg to differ, but," flashing a crooked dimple, "that gives us plenty to talk about."

"I agree. I-uh...booked another cruise...together...the both of us—together."

Rita's smile died into a blank face.

"For when?"

"Ah...tomorrow."

Sighing and rolling her head, Rita said, "Well...you better come over for dinner."

"I'm sorry?"

"We're Catholic, John! I'm not even divorced yet! Mom's going to want to meet the man I'm headed back out to sea with! What am I supposed to tell her?"

Grinning, John said, "You tell her: Everyone's got to go somewhere, sometime. When they do, they're going to need a good bag, and our two antiques are already packed."

"All things become fashionable again—even when they're a bit beaten up?"

"*Especially* when they're a bit beaten up."

"I love you, John."

"Then maybe we should discuss logistics?"

"After lunch," Rita said cutely. "There's a package for you on the bed."

John walked to the site of their recent love-making and picked up an unwrapped box—no card, no ribbon. Opening the top, he laughed and pulled out a t-shirt by the shoulders. *U GOT TO HAVE U SOME FUN* was written across the chest.

"I'm guessing it's from Will?"

"It was outside the door this morning, but I think that's a safe bet."

Thinking for a moment, John looked quizzically and asked, "Rita, what do you find more beautiful…a caterpillar or a butterfly?"

"Well both, of course, they're one in the same! Beauty transcends what our eyes see. Everything that matters is on the inside. Sylvia told us you loved her towel swans?"

"I do. She did?"

"You don't feel for those swans because of what they look like, you feel for them because you're a caring, passionate, nurturing man, who doesn't want to see harm done to any living creature—even if it's an inanimate object. And I love you even more for that quality."

"Do you like dogs?"

"Why? Do you have one?"

"Not any more, but I was thinking I might like another one."

Pulling her checkbook from her purse, Rita said, "We have plenty of good pet stores around here, or perhaps you would prefer a shelter?"

"A shelter, definitely. What are you doing?"

"I'm writing a check for Will's tip from the both of us. That's what these envelopes are for—tipping any of the staff you want, like Sylvia. Will is the only one I have left."

Picking up one of the envelopes laying on his desk, John pulled out five one-hundred dollar bills. He slipped the bills inside, sealed the envelope and wrote: "Sylvia, Thanks For All The Swans, John."

"You sure I can't chip in for Will's tip? We should leave him a big one. He deserves it."

"I think this should cover it," she said, holding up the check.

"Ten-thousand-dollars! Yeah, I think he'll be pleased with that."

"Come on, we'll leave this with the purser to give to Will, then we have enough time before lunch to run over to Chic Linen. I can check on the shop and you can talk with Mom about luggage!"

"I look forward to that discussion," John grinned.

Five pursers typed feverishly to settle the accounts and complaints from the lines of passengers waiting to check-out. When it was John and Rita's turn, John noticed a familiar face behind the counter. She was helping the guest beside him.

"Hi, Regina!" he said.

"Good Morning! *Mr. Smith*, right?"

"Yes! Excellent memory."

"Well, did you have fun? I hope!"

Recalling Regina's declaration when he first boarded, John flashed a wide smile and replied, "I can honestly say your brochures didn't do it justice. I've had the time of my life, Regina. The time of my life!"

THE END

THANK YOU!

I hope you enjoyed your adventure with John Smith on his maiden voyage aboard *The Princess of the Seas*. Following this short note, you will find information about the author and a very important acknowledgements page thanking the contributors who helped make this book possible.

This page, dear reader, is just for you.

Thank you.

Truly, heart felt, thank you for investing your precious time in the pages of this labor of love.

I sincerely hope you were entertained!

You've come this far and I do hope you won't mind taking just a few more minutes to let me and other readers know what you thought of the book.

Please leave a review and star rating at Amazon.com.

I can't tell you how much it would mean to me to hear from you!

Let's connect on social media!
https://www.facebook.com/andrewharkless43/
https://twitter.com/andrewharkless
https://www.goodreads.com/author/show/9300981.Andrew_Harkless
https://andrewharkless.com/

ACKNOWLEDGEMENTS

I would like to express my deepest gratitude to my beta-readers: Maripat Wright, Kathy Hammond, Carol Norris, Dave Nelson, Lynne Eisel, Walt Bagley, Jackie Robertson, and to Megan Robinson. And, to Megan, who also provided solid input and advice during the first draft—thank you for taking the time to compose motivational feedback and unbiased critiques, both of which challenged and propelled me forward.

My heart and prayers go out to Karen and her entire family. Thank you for taking the time to read while coping with the onset of extreme adversity and during a family vacation at that. I hope you found some strength and comfort within my story. I think often of you.

Many times in life we need a slight push and appropriate time in order to accept opportunity and achieve our goals. Siobhan Budine provided my slight push and Thad Huston, my cherished friend, unselfishly furnished the logistical tools I needed to get started. Without both of you, through your own unique ways and consciously or not, the road to this project's completion surely would have been bumpier and more prolonged. I wish the best for both of you and your families.

I would like to extend the deepest reciprocated warmth and friendship toward the Ransone and Small families, whom I trusted to give honest comments after reading the early draft of my manuscript. Thank you Amy, Diane, and Gerald for all your kind words and support. My hope is that you all might find some solace through this story when and how we remember those we have lost, like your son and brother. My apologies to Gerald for some of my characters using too many four letter words. I don't know why characters, like real people in real life, feel the need to color their sentences with cheap curses—but we do. And to my beloved friend Brad Small: Thank you for sharing your family, time, and continued friendship with me. You are a rock star for expeditiously reading my manuscript in just three evenings (probably because you had to listen to me talk about this project for twenty years) while juggling so many child, family, and work responsibilities. I cherish our twenty eight year friendship.

This is my debut novel and each one that follows will be a new and unique story, as I have no interest in writing a version of the same story over and over like the publishing world seems to enjoy (as long as they are all successful). With that said, in a way, I will be saying goodbye to this book and its characters upon publication—a cathartic necessity in order to move forward to find the next story and characters. So, here is where I must thank all the passengers and crew I had the joy, and sometimes horror, to meet during my more than sixty cruises working as a bartender. Like college, in the end, we are lucky if we wind up with one lifelong love or friendship. Phil Hatcher is that one good friend from all my cruises. Thank you, Phil…oh, we had some fun. Working for the cruise lines was the most wonderful job I never want to do again. My vocation… has always been for writing.

I am extremely grateful to Mary C. Simmons of Indie Author Publishing Services for both her cover design and interior formatting. Mary's timely, self-sacrificing contributions helped move this project forward when it needed a good push. Also, thank you to Emily Brock, an award winning artist, for delivering the beautiful water color rendition used for the cover on *U Got to Have U Some Fun*. I hope the reader has fun recognizing the details and subtle reflections surrounding Everyman John Smith and the characters who will help this caterpillar become a butterfly on the cruise vacation that will forever change his life.

Lastly, for the purpose of emphasis, I wish to thank my tirelessly devoted, immeasurably patient, and cutting-edge capable editor, Debra L Hartmann. Her unyielding dedication and belief polished my dream into a tangible reality. If you ever find yourself in the presence of someone willing to do that…hold dear and respect them for life. I have, often reluctantly, learned more from you than any teacher (outside my own parents) I've ever studied under. Finally, thank you for choosing my manuscript to both showcase and launch Welcome Home Press. My hope is for us to work together for many years to come. Thank you, my friend!

LIFE'S TOO SHORT…U GOT TO HAVE U SOME FUN!

ABOUT THE AUTHOR

Andrew Harkless was born in Orange, California in 1970, but raised in central Pennsylvania. He currently resides in coastal North Carolina.

Many typical luxuries were put on hold in exchange for devoting unbridled time to writing with the ultimate goal of becoming a successful literary author along the caliber of his idol, John Irving—inarguably one of the greatest contemporary American storytellers.

Andrew writes coming-of-age stories (regardless of the age) about Everyman characters who reach extraordinary crossroads where change is the only path. No matter how average a person may seem at first glance, everyone holds a remarkable story inside. His goal is to write stories for the Everyman, about the Everyman.

Writing is an outlet for his innate passion—aka "inner dragon"—a love, and like any love, frustration accompanies. But, even love agitated by frustration seeks an audience....

"I wish to work for you in a way that you might discover how extraordinary you are in ways previously unrecognizable. And I want to write for you, to entertain you. Really think about it: the Everyman isn't inside the magazine at the grocery store check-out. Many of the people we idolize inside those magazines (in my opinion) would gladly exchange their fame for, at the very least, anonymity, and, if honest, a chance at the life of an Everyman."

Please share your opinion of the book by writing a review.